THE
SIDE OF THE
ANGELS

THE
SIDE OF THE
ANGELS

Leona Blair

BANTAM BOOKS
NEW YORK   TORONTO   LONDON   SYDNEY   AUCKLAND

THE SIDE OF THE ANGELS

A Bantam Book/July 1992

Library of Congress Cataloging-in-Publication Data
Blair, Leona.
The side of the angels / Leona Blair.
p.   cm.
ISBN 0-553-08924-2
I. Title.
PS3552.L3463S57   1992
813'.54—dc20   91-45510
                                        CIP

Published simultaneously in the United States and Canada

PRINTED IN THE UNITED STATES OF AMERICA

BVG   0 9 8 7 6 5 4 3 2 1

For the
Dune Dames,
to whom I owe some of the
most enlightening, encouraging and hilarious
hours of my life.
And for Kristina Marit
with love.

Is man an ape or an angel?
I, my lord, I am on the side
of the angels.

—Disraeli

BOOK I

I

———◦•◦———

1961

Catherine Earnshaw, may you not rest as long as I am living! You said I killed you—haunt me then! . . . Oh, God! It is unutterable! I cannot live without my life! I cannot live without my soul!

Bitch!"

It was her father's voice. It shot up like a missile through the air shaft from the bedroom below and exploded in the attic, wrenching Kate from her book. She dashed away her tears and sat up on the old divan, clutching the worn copy of *Wuthering Heights* to her heart.

"WHORE!"

The book slipped from Kate's hands. Her father never raised his voice, and he never used words like that!

"Spare me your outrage," her mother said, anger obscuring her soft Carolina drawl.

"What the hell do you think you're doing?" Tyler demanded.

"Packing," Sydney retorted. "That must be obvious even to you, Professor. I'm leaving you."

"For your lover?"

Kate covered her ears with her hands.

"If he'll have me."

"You'd better hope he will, because I'll never take you back!"

"I'll never come back. I can't stand the sight of you. My flesh crawls when you touch me. But with him . . ."

"I don't want to hear it!"

Kate shook her head, trying to empty it of the ugly picture in her mind. She felt sick. Her mother was describing a malignant love, the kind people whispered about, the kind Kate had been too ignorant to imagine. Shame erupted like bile from deep within her, where it had lurked unsuspected throughout the twelve placid years of her life.

3

Her mother doing *that* with a strange man!

They were ominously quiet down there. She got off the divan and, silent in her sneakers, crossed the wooden floor of the attic. She went swiftly down the stairs and along the corridor, stopping short of the open door to her parents' bedroom. She could see neither of them from where she stood, only an open suitcase on the blue bedspread and her mother's hands, fair and graceful, putting things into it, the delicate, sheer underthings Sydney loved, the elegant skirts and cashmere sweaters. Blue was Sydney's favorite color, the same bright blue as her eyes.

"Who is he?" Tyler demanded hoarsely.

"Royal Benedict," Sydney said.

"Your cousin? My God, that's incest!"

"If that's incest, I've been committing it since I was fifteen."

"I don't believe you!" Tyler's voice shook.

"We made love on the day I married you," Sydney said, her voice soft and insinuating. "While Mother was pretending she accepted you, we were in the boat house together, naked."

Kate's hands covered her ears again, but the words came through.

"God in heaven!" Tyler gasped. "Why?"

"Because I hadn't seen him in two years and I adore him. I always have. He and I are made of the same stuff. He's the only man I've ever loved."

"There were others?"

"Of course there were others." Sydney paused, and when she spoke again her voice was cool, dry. "You're not the world's most exciting lover, Tyler."

"You knew damned well what kind of lover I was before the wedding. Why did you marry me?"

"Royal's not the marrying kind. I was sick of school and damned if I'd go home to my mother." Sydney snorted delicately. "Perfect Polly, model of female rectitude."

There was another taut silence.

"Katherine!" Tyler said tightly. "Whose child is Katherine?"

Katherine tried to dissolve into the cold, hard wall.

"She's yours, Tyler," Sydney said. "All you have to do is look at her to know that."

"But I loved you," Tyler said with pathetic irrelevance. "I loved you."

"The more fool you," Sydney said. "But I can bear fools. It's boredom I can't tolerate. I did my best to be a faculty wife in a college town, but I've given my last tea for your adoring students. I've baked my last goddamn cupcake."

"I won't let you have Katherine."

"I know that." Sydney stopped speaking for a moment and her voice was husky when she resumed. "I don't want to leave her, but she'll be better off with you anyway. She's sweet, my little Miss Sobersides, but she's like you. Two peas in a pod. No passion except for history. But I live in the present."

Kate moved to the doorway. She could see them now. Even in anger and haste, Sydney Ballard was a gorgeous woman. To Kate she was the most beautiful creature God ever made, with the willowy, blond magnificence of a classic American beauty and a fairy-princess radiance that Kate, dark-haired like her father, too tall for a girl and growing more gawky every day, knew she would never have.

Tyler Ballard was handsome, with his thick shock of black hair and the strong, clean lines of his face, but now he was ash pale, his hands clenched in fury.

Pity for him flooded Kate—and then rage for letting this happen, for letting her go.

"You're an unnatural woman," Tyler said bitterly. "A Lilith."

Sydney shrugged. "I'd be the last to deny *that*. Poor Tyler. You marry the fair Elaine and end up with Morgana la Fay. You'll be glad to see the back of me."

"Don't go!" Kate shrieked suddenly from the doorway. Her parents whirled to face her, and she braced her arms hard against the jamb to hold herself up. "Don't leave me, Mother, please don't! Take me with you!"

Sydney's face collapsed, the sardonic smile fading into shock. She was as pale as Tyler. "Baby, I didn't know you were home!"

"You'd have left me without saying good-bye?" Kate whispered, incredulous.

"Kate—honey, I just couldn't face saying good-bye to you."

"Then stay!"

"I can't."

"Why?" Kate looked at her father.

"I can't explain. You're too young." Sydney's voice shook, like her hands. "But it'll all work out, you'll see." She turned back to her suitcase, her hands moving aimlessly.

"Katherine," her father said. "You don't understand . . ."

"Oh yes I do! I heard everything you said—about that man—about everything. Why can't you forgive her, Daddy? Why can't you let her stay?"

"Oh, God!" her mother said softly. "Kate . . ."

"She doesn't want to be forgiven," her father cut in. "She wants to leave us, both of us."

Kate's dark eyes returned to her mother's face. She waited for a denial, her tears checked by the paralyzing suspense. The seconds plodded by and still she waited until she knew there was no hope.

"I hate you!" Kate said, strangely calm. "Both of you! I'll hate you till I die!"

"Katherine!" Her father was appalled. "I am not to blame. If you heard everything, you must know that."

"Something," Kate said. "We must have done something."

She fled then, hurtling down the stairs, out the front door, and into the long shadows of a New England evening in early spring.

She stood near the hedge that separated their property from their neighbors' and watched the lawn become a black pool as dark descended. After a while a taxi stopped at the curb and her mother came out of the house with her suitcase and got into it. Kate watched the taxi pull away. In the small entry hall, her father watched, too, until the taxi lights faded.

He turned to look at Kate for a long moment before he stepped back and deliberately slammed the door between them, punishing her treachery more clearly than words could have done.

Kate found the small space in the hedge that she and Rebecca used to go back and forth when they were little. She wedged herself in and huddled there, the tiny leaves trembling with her while she waited for Rebecca to come.

"I won't think about it," Kate whispered. "I'll think about Rebecca."

Rebecca was all she had left.

2

|

Rebecca Salter was Kate's alter ego. They had been born on the same day and had lived in each other's pockets all their lives, separated only by the hedge between Professor Salter's property and Dr. Ballard's. The houses were not identical. Kate's was a white clapboard with green shutters and a screened-in veranda; Rebecca's was gray with white shutters and dormer windows on the second floor. Neatly clipped shrubs bordered both houses, and their lawns would be smooth and plush in the summer.

The girls were both A students. Becca got straight A's because it was easy for her, "but I don't plan to waste all of my youth studying," she had announced recently. "I like school, but not as much as you do." They both adored John Fitzgerald Kennedy and his beautiful wife, but Rebecca wanted to be a ballerina and Kate wanted to join the Peace Corps.

People said it was the academic atmosphere in both homes that had made the girls precocious as well as bright. It had distanced them somewhat from other children, had drawn them even closer to each other. They thought of themselves as sisters.

"Only better, because we don't have to fight over sharing a bedroom or a bathroom or the same parents," Rebecca assured Kate after she read a book on sibling rivalry.

But they had shared everything else—including the conviction that neither of them was quite acceptable: Becca was too chubby and Kate too tall.

Half of that equation had changed. Becca had slimmed down drastically over the past year.

"But I'm stuck with my height and still growing," Kate moaned to

the hedge with the hopeless misery of those who are young and different.

It wasn't only height. Rebecca had study dates now, while Katherine, who loomed like a redwood over all but a few inarticulate boys
on the basketball team, spent even more time with her books.

Becca felt bad about that, but "What can I do?" she often asked
Kate. "Cut you down to size like Procrustes in the myth?"

Rebecca had tried to make Kate abandon her braids and "those
frumpy jumpers and ghillie shoes—with flaps, no less!" But Kate,
who had a will of iron, insisted she was indifferent to fashion. Even
Kate's mother hadn't prevailed.

Kate could hear Sydney's soft, low voice as clearly as if they were
back in the Ballards' kitchen, with Rebecca hanging on every word.

"Honey, you don't have to wear Harris tweeds and brogues just
because your father does," Sydney had protested, her southern drawl
very pronounced that day. "You're not a schoolmarm yet!"

"How would I look in a frilly blouse?"

"Like a Christmas tree, I agree, but you could wear brighter colors
—or a blouse with a bow! You look like a little *professorin.* I keep
expecting you to smoke a pipe."

"I thought about it, but I'm afraid it would stunt my growth," Kate
answered.

Sydney had burst into laughter and put an arm around her daughter. "You have wit, baby, and they say a witty woman outlasts a pretty
one. Wear what you like. You will anyway."

"Well," Rebecca had sighed when they were on their way to school,
"she tried."

"She wants me to look like her, but I never will, so why pretend?"
Maybe she wouldn't have gone if I looked like her, if I were pretty.

But she mustn't think of her mother now! Kate forced her mind
back to Rebecca.

Disappointed but loyal, Becca had continued to follow Kate's lead
in everything, including clothes, for a while longer. But now that
she was almost as thin as Kate, Becca wore vivid colors like acid
green and chrome yellow and the tightest sweaters her mother would
allow. She wore her almost-platinum hair in a ballerina's knot or a
ponytail.

What's going to happen to me? Kate wondered. *What am I going to do
without my mother?*

But she could see Rebecca now, a small figure dancing along Elm
Terrace as more lights winked on in the neat houses. Rebecca was
spinning and leaping with more audacity than talent, but she was so
pretty that no one really minded if she didn't dance like Margot
Fonteyn—provided, as her mother told her twenty times a day,

Rebecca stayed on her diet. Rebecca did. She wanted a figure to match her face.

"And when I really want something," Becca had assured Kate more than once, "nothing gets in my way."

Kate would be valedictorian of their grade school graduating class, but Rebecca was the prima ballerina of Miss Bisbee's School of the Dance—intermediate level.

"Rebecca!" Kate sprang out of the hedge, sobbing with anguish, and streaked along Elm Terrace, while Rebecca executed three pirouettes. She didn't hear Kate calling her until the last one.

II

The girls sat on the Salters' back steps, slumped in misery. "But it was a perfect marriage!" Rebecca said.

"No. It only looked that way." Kate's voice sank. "And she wouldn't take me with her."

"Lovers don't want a kid around!"

Kate winced but made no reply, and Rebecca went on.

"What a story! *He* marries one of *the* Benedicts right out of his History One class at Wakefield college, and thirteen years later *she* runs away with her Benedict cousin!"

"I'll die if anyone finds out he's her cousin!" Kate quavered.

"But the newspapers are bound to print it."

"Then I won't go to school or graduate or give the valedictory address!" Kate's voice still sounded wobbly and her cheeks were wet. Kate rarely cried, except over books and movies. Rebecca didn't either, because neither of them had found anything much to cry about —until now.

The kitchen door opened. "What are you girls doing out there?" Marjorie Salter asked. "It's getting chilly. Come inside at once." She paused when she saw Kate's expression. "Katherine, what's wrong? Are you sick? Why are your legs all scratched?"

"Her mother left home," Rebecca said, her arm around Kate's shoulders. "Just walked out. And her father slammed the door on her so she went and hid in the hedge. And there'll be gossip and Kate says she won't go to school or graduate or be valedictorian."

"Come inside," Marjorie said after a momentary pause to absorb all that. "Come along, Katherine, you're shivering. I'll make you something hot to drink while you tell me what happened." She put antiseptic on the scratches and made Kate wash her face and drink a glass of water. She listened closely while she took out milk and cocoa and marshmallows. She was a small, slender woman who wore sober colors and very little makeup. She had very definite ideas about clothes and behavior, not in the least like the permissive Sydney. Kate had often wondered why they were friends.

"Now, see here, Katherine," Mrs. Salter said, smoothing Kate's dark hair when the brief story was told. "There *will* be gossip and it *will* be hard, but eventually it will pass. Your father can't stop teaching his classes. He must go on and so must you."

"I don't know if I can." Kate shook her head, wondering why Marjorie wasn't more surprised by the news.

"Well, I do," Marjorie said firmly. "You have character, Katherine. Just like your father."

Kate looked up at the plain woman she had known all her life. Sydney had often ridiculed her, but tonight Kate would have traded glamorous Sydney for Marjorie Salter in a minute. "Have I?" she asked, the balm of praise falling sweet upon her bruises.

Marjorie nodded. "Yes, you have, and it will see you through this. Now, girls, take your cocoa upstairs. I'm going to call your father and tell him I'll bring you home after you've had some supper here with us. I'll call you when it's ready." She waited until they were halfway up the stairs before she picked up the telephone.

"As if we couldn't guess what they're saying!" Becca remarked.

"It was nice of her to tell me that," Kate said.

"It's nothing new to me! I've been hearing about your character for years," Rebecca sniffed. She didn't add that her mother always compared Kate's character to Sydney's lack of it, or that Marjorie had predicted Sydney would do something awful someday. "But if you come to school tomorrow," Rebecca said, "I'll really believe you have it."

III

Rebecca's room had maple furniture and blue-checked gingham draperies and upholstery. One wall was covered with pictures of Rebecca and of Kate and Rebecca from the time they were infants. The opposite wall had framed prints of Degas paintings—ballerinas standing, resting, tying their pale satin shoes.

Under three of the dormers ran a window seat that boasted a menagerie of stuffed animals. Rebecca's favorite of the moment, a marmalade kitten, was on the bed. Kate grabbed a black puppy and flopped down on the bed next to Rebecca.

"It was such a fabulous love story," Rebecca said. "I thought true lovers were faithful unto death."

"I'm sorry if this has crushed your illusions," Kate snapped.

"I didn't mean it like that." But Rebecca did. Her plan was to make herself beautiful, like Sydney, and to fall madly in love with a handsome man who worshipped her, just as Dr. Ballard worshipped his wife. Of course, Rebecca's husband would be a lot richer and he wouldn't be a college professor. And he would never, never leave her. "I only meant that this makes love seem a lot more dangerous," she explained.

"Did you think married people always stayed married?"

"Most of them. You have to admit that nice women don't usually run off with their cousins!"

"No," Kate agreed glumly. "They don't."

"I wonder," Rebecca said suddenly, "if my parents still love each other. They're not at all romantic."

"People don't have to be romantic to love each other."

For once that was a comfort to Rebecca. Paul Salter was a tenured professor of history; Marjorie was a faculty wife, far from glamorous, who seemed resigned to being a small frog in a small puddle.

"Sometimes my mother says her life is over," Rebecca confided, "but she wants mine to be perfect."

"That's how mothers are," Kate said in a small voice. "Real mothers."

"You can share mine," Rebecca said.

"I want my own," Kate said, crying again.

"After what she did?" Rebecca passed her a box of tissues.

"I hate her for what she did!"

Rebecca put an arm around her friend. "Come on, Katie, stop crying. I hate Sydney, too, and I'll stand by you every minute, if that's any help."

Kate nodded and the two girls sat in silence until Mrs. Salter called them down to supper.

IV

Kate made breakfast for her father the next morning. That was not unusual; Sydney never got up for breakfast. Last night, when Marjorie brought her home, Kate had rushed past her father and up to her room, but this morning they talked about his book and her valedictory address as if nothing had happened.

Dr. Ballard didn't say "I'm sorry for shutting you out last night," and Kate didn't say "I'm sorry I begged to leave you and go with her."

In fact, he never commented on the void left by his wife of thirteen years. Years later Kate realized she and Tyler had been involved in a conspiracy from the start. It was as if Sydney had died, and death was not a subject one dwelled upon.

After breakfast Kate waved Tyler on his way to his office in Campbell Hall on the Harmony College campus, where he was head of the history department. His colleagues called him an authority on political history. He had won a Pulitzer Prize for *Troy* and was working on a study of Pompeii. He let Kate help him with his research, even though some of it—about the prostitutes and the bordellos in Pompeii that advertised with huge erect penises outside the doors—made her blush.

Kate was very proud of her father. She loved him, too, of course, but she was proud of his accomplishments, his brilliance. One of her greatest treats when she was little had been to sit, quiet as a mouse, at the back of his classroom and watch him teach. He held his students spellbound and not only because he was so handsome, although they all had stupid crushes on him.

Now her heart ached for his sadness and his shame and she couldn't stop herself from crying. She loved him all the more for his courage in not speaking of their disaster. Neither would she.

Watching her father's tall figure diminish into the distance, she took off the heart-shaped locket she wore around her neck, a gift from her parents on her twelfth birthday. She removed the tiny photograph of them, crushed it, and threw it into the trash. She would wear only her father's likeness.

But who—Kate covered her face with her hands—who would read with her on rainy afternoons? Or tell her personal things about being a woman in a way that made it all less frightening? Or take her to New York at Christmas to see the tree in Rockefeller Center and stay with Sydney's cousin Eugenia in her elegant triplex on Park Avenue?

"No!" Kate admonished herself, pressing her lips hard to make them stop trembling. "I don't love you any more than you love me. I'm Daddy's daughter now, not yours."

Her mother had said Kate was just like her father. Well, why wouldn't she want to be just like him? He was brilliant, loyal, and kind. *He* would never leave her.

After Tyler turned the corner and was out of sight, Kate dried her eyes on a tea towel, did the dishes, and changed the sheets of the double bed in what was now her father's room.

Then she got some large boxes from the pantry and collected what remained of Sydney's things from the bureau and dressing table drawers, tossing them into the boxes, hoping they would break.

The closets were the hardest, but Kate made herself gather an armful of dresses and dump them into a carton—when suddenly she swept them up again and sank to the floor, hugging them to her as if they were Sydney herself, breathing deeply of their Sydney scent.

"Mommy," she pleaded. "Oh, Mommy, what did I do? Please, just tell me what I did and I promise I'll never do it again."

For a long moment she sat there, yearning over the clothes. Then she mastered herself again and carried everything down to a dark corner of the basement.

She found a smaller carton and went into the parlor to gather all the pictures of Sydney—with Tyler, with Kate, and by her deceptively lovely self. Without the slightest impulse to cry now, Kate looked longest at the largest one. It was her parents' wedding photograph, taken at Kel Regis, the Benedict estate in South Carolina that Kate had never seen.

The photograph had always dazzled her, but now she was aware of a boat house somewhere out of camera range and of what had happened there not long after the picture was taken.

"How could you?" Kate whispered, appalled. "How could you when you were already going to have me? And then go on a honeymoon with Daddy? What kind of woman are you?"

Her father had said it: a Lilith. A temptress with no purpose but her own pleasure.

She dropped the photograph into the carton and carried everything up to a cupboard in the attic. Then she bathed her eyes again and gathered her schoolbooks to go next door and call for Rebecca.

"You did it!" Rebecca said, beaming. "I guess you do have character after all! How does it feel? Where do you keep it? Does it ever itch?"

"Oh, Becca, don't carry on!"

"How's your dad?"

"He's the best father in the world! He didn't say a word about her or about me—begging to go with her, I mean."

"He didn't?" Rebecca was astounded.

"I'm going to take good care of him," Kate vowed. "He doesn't need her. I'll keep house and cook for him, and every night I'll do my homework in his study while he works."

"We were going skating on Friday night."

"Maybe another time, but he needs me now. Come on, we'll be late."

Kate wondered, as they walked to school, if anyone else knew yet.

V

When the story finally appeared—not only in the newspaper gossip columns, but in those cheap magazines at the supermarket—Kate, trembling inside, behaved as if Sydney were someone else's mother. She ignored the little groups of girls who whispered and giggled when she walked by. She hated Sydney more with every snicker, but no one knew that. She didn't allow herself to go home on the stroke of three o'clock either, but stayed to attend the History Club and work on the yearbook.

It was a monumental effort. Even Rebecca didn't know how hard it was.

On the other hand, Kate could not keep from riding her bike to the outskirts of Harmony to buy all the tabloids, gossip sheets, and glossy magazines in a neighborhood where no one knew her. Stony-faced, she pored over them in the attic, where once she had wept over make-believe lovers and believed that passion endures forever.

Sydney had loved those books too. Sydney used to curl up with Kate on the couch in the attic and talk about Heathcliff and Maxim de Winter as if they were real, as if they'd walk through the door the next minute. Sydney loved romantic stories as much as Kate did.

There were times now when Kate's whole body ached for her mother, for her light step and her musical laugh, for her southern drawl and her soft skin, for the sound of her voice reading *Little Women*.

"I'll never read another romantic novel," Kate told Rebecca. "Love is bullshit."

"What'll you read?" wondered the practical Becca.

"History. At least you know what's going to happen."

As if to shock romantic fantasy out of her system with gross reality, Kate began, with Rebecca's help, to make scrapbooks of all the photographs and salacious articles published about her mother.

"She's *so* beautiful!" Rebecca said, poring over a *Vogue* portrait Kate had just cut out of Sydney in a Givenchy gown. They were in the attic on the couch.

"No," Kate said, stabbing another page with her scissors. "She *looks* beautiful."

"Her cousin Royal's gorgeous too."

Kate's voice was sharp. "He's beneath contempt."

"You'd think God would smite her with the pox or something."

"I'm sure God has better things to do than smite Sydney Ballard."

"Can you believe she calls herself Sydney Benedict now?"

"I don't care what she calls herself," Kate said.

"But—all these fabulous places!" Becca said, pasting the *Vogue* photograph into place. "Paris and Biarritz, Venice, Madrid." She paused. "You still haven't heard from your grandparents?"

"I didn't expect to."

Rebecca shook her head. "I thought you'd surely hear after what happened. After all, you've got only one set, and they were angry at your mother, not you."

Kate, grown suddenly still, took a deep breath. "They didn't approve of my father either. Why would I want to see them?"

"Out of curiosity, to find out what they're like."

"I'd rather not know."

"Don't you miss her at all?" Rebecca ventured softly.

Kate, absorbed in cutting out another photograph, took a minute to answer. "Would you, if she were your mother?"

Neither of them spoke for a moment.

"But it wasn't your fault," Rebecca said adamantly. "You have to believe that."

"Of course I believe it."

But a part of Kate didn't. If her own mother didn't want her, there had to be something wrong with her, something she did that drove Sydney away—or something she hadn't done to keep her from going —or something she was or, worse, was not.

Out of consideration for Rebecca, Kate never admitted her guilt in the matter. She never let Rebecca see her hug those scrapbooks in moments of shameful weakness. She had to show fortitude so that Rebecca would admire her. Without Rebecca she would never have made it through the last weeks of grade school.

The girls were getting to be an odd match in personality as well as appearance. Conservative Kate, five feet seven inches tall when they graduated from elementary school, was a reedy, developing brunette, unsure of how to manage her arms and legs except on the tennis courts, where she was as sought after as Rebecca was at parties. Kate knew her looks had always been a disappointment to her mother, but even Sydney had admired her wit and Kate honed it into a defensive weapon.

"You can cut people down better than the queen in *Snow White*," Rebecca told her. "I hope you never do it to me."

"Why should I? You're not a fool and the others are."

But it was true that Kate could use words like blades to cut people down to size. Even when there was no need to defend herself, she let her intellect shine brightly so that no one noticed she was too tall and not pretty enough.

Kate loved Rebecca even though Rebecca was beautiful and the right height and had a graceful manner as eye-catching as her hair. Her wide-set, sparkling blue eyes made her seem far more angelic than she really was, but she had an air of expectation about her that attracted boys like chocolate bars.

It was something they had never discussed, but Kate was very much aware of it all the same, this basic difference between them that became more apparent as they matured: Rebecca had the urgency of most female creatures to attract and to please males. Boys were the measure by which they rated themselves. It was a standard imposed by the outside world, so it was the outside world Kate resented, not Rebecca. As for Kate, she did not intend to please any man but her father.

VI

Étampes, Anne de Pisseleu,
duchesse d', 1508–1580?,
official mistress of Francis I of
France from 1526.
Intelligent as well as beautiful . . .

Kate printed neatly on an index card. She had always loved the tranquility of her father's study, where the smell of books and journals, furniture polish and leather armchairs, mingled with the mellow richness of his pipe tobacco. She loved the steady tick of the clock on the mantelpiece and the brassy little chime that rang the hours. She loved the scratch of her father's pen as he wrote; she looked up frequently from the encyclopedia for the assurance of his tall body bending over the mahogany desk and his beautiful profile with its high forehead and Roman nose silhouetted against the lamp.

Like Heathcliff, she thought.

With a pang she saw there were a few streaks of gray in his hair she had never noticed before. She wanted to put her arms around him. She wanted to talk to him, to someone. Rebecca was at their class graduation party escorted by two boys. No one had asked Kate, and she would not go alone.

She wanted to tell her father how miserable she was about that, but she had learned never to interrupt him when he was working and so she held her peace, swallowing hard to keep her longing down and her sadness and her hurt.

In a moment or two, she returned to the Duchesse d'Étampes.

3

I

Who is that stunning man?" Rebecca demanded as the small boat approached the dock.

"Make fast the lines, Ishmael!" Kate ordered, reefing the sail. "For Pete's sake!"

"Aye, aye, Captain Ahab!" Rebecca clambered onto the dock.

When the Sunfish was tied up, the two girls gathered their picnic basket and blanket and left the dock, their suntanned legs lithe and shapely as they walked.

In two years Kate had grown two inches taller and rounder in the bosom. Her hair was in a ponytail today and she wore cut-off jeans and a bright red jersey. Rebecca, still petite but perfectly proportioned in a scanty swimsuit and one of her father's overlarge shirts, seemed the elder of the two. It sprang from a circumstance of vital significance to nubile girls: Rebecca was popular with the boys and Kate was not.

"They're all afraid of you!" Rebecca harangued her. "You still act like Lady Macbeth with a bloody secret—and by now everyone's forgotten what Sydney did. They worry a lot more about their pimples. How are they supposed to know you're really very funny and terrific to be with?"

Kate had succumbed to the praise and promised she would try, but she was glad of summer's reprieve.

"Who is that man?" Becca repeated now.

"His name is Theodore Barrows and he's a lawyer and a political consultant."

"Ah, one of those people who knows how to get other people elected."

"Yes. He's come to talk politics with Tyler."

"I hope he's staying for supper."

"He is. Are you happy now?"

"Delirious."

Kate shook her head.

Rebecca shook hers back. "Don't be a prig, Katie."

"Becca, he's a grown man, not one of your high school jocks. What possible romantic interest could you have in him?"

"Who says it's romantic? I just like to be around handsome, successful men, especially if they're not college professors. Can I have the shower first?"

"Sure, but clean up when you've finished!"

"Yes, Mrs. Danvers."

Rebecca was already halfway up the path to the Ballard cottage on Cape Cod, where she was very much at home. This was the third summer she had spent all of her vacation there with Kate and Tyler, and she looked forward as much as Kate did to opening up the house each June, stripping dust sheets off the well-worn but divinely comfortable furniture, and raising all the windows to let the sea air in. The cottage was larger than it looked. It had a sitting room, a full dining room, a big kitchen tiled in red and white, a pantry with glass-paned doors on the storage cabinets, four bedrooms, and three bathrooms, two up, one down.

The beach was only a short walk away, and they could hear the breakers at night when they fell asleep. Each of the girls had a room to herself, furnished with narrow beds and robust, if somewhat battered, night tables and chests of drawers; but most of the time they talked themselves to sleep in the same room.

Rebecca felt she had a responsibility to make Kate more popular. She knew she could do it: Kate listened to Becca now more than Becca listened to Kate.

Somewhere along the line, the girls had changed places. It was as if Kate, deprived of beautiful, imperious Sydney, now gave her devotion to beautiful, imperious Rebecca.

Rebecca gloried in it. Those whom Rebecca loved she loved excessively, and she was jealous of anything that took Kate away from her —even a book. She had to put up with Kate's worship of Dr. Ballard and Kate's secret obsession with Sydney, but Sydney was gone and the professor totally engrossed in his work. Kate was hers.

Rebecca ran upstairs to take her shower.

II

Kate stayed on the path a minute or two, looking at the back of the cottage. A large screened porch ran its length, wonderful for sleeping out on or watching the sunsets. At the corner there was an open deck furnished with lounges, parasols, and tables. The cottage had been bought with Sydney's money, a discovery Kate had made a year earlier when she put some research notes on Tyler's desk and found the deeds to both the cottage and the house in Harmony.

She knew her mother's family was very, very rich and that Sydney had a trust fund of her own that was turned over to her when she married. That was why Dr. Ballard's house in Harmony was furnished more elegantly than other faculty houses and why Sydney's tweeds and cashmeres came from New York and London. But Sydney had never once spoken of her family, and it was obvious from their silence that the Benedicts cared nothing for her, or the man she had married, or the daughter she had borne.

But they don't even know me! Kate found herself thinking. *How can they dislike someone they don't even know?*

Shaking off her resentment, she went to tell her father they were back and was introduced to Tyler's guest, a very tall man with a deep tan and prematurely white hair. She liked Theodore Barrows. Rebecca, she knew, would be in raptures over him, although Kate found his face interesting rather than handsome.

"Katherine's very knowledgeable about politics," Tyler said proudly.

"Political history," Kate amended.

"She'll be helping me with the research on *Medieval Majesty*," Tyler added. "She's my little amanuensis."

Kate could hardly be called a "little" anything, but she loved it when her father praised her. He never did it directly, only through other people, as he was doing now. It was part and parcel of the restraint she so admired in him and strove to emulate. Dignity was more reliable than naked emotion.

"I'm sure the book will be as well received as *Pompeii*," Barrows was saying.

"*Pompeii* will win another Pulitzer!" Kate said with quiet assurance.

III

When she smiled, a warm, sweet smile, Theo abandoned his first impression of her: she was not plain, she was lovely. Her features were fine and sensitive, like a Modigliani model's or a twelfth-century Madonna's. She was very tall for her age—as Theo had been—and he knew that made a girl feel awkward.

"Dinner will be at seven, if that's okay, Tyler," Kate said. "We're having steamers, salad, and corn."

"Marvelous!" Barrows said. "I'll help."

But he didn't. He stayed on the deck talking to Dr. Ballard about what Tyler called the decline of the West and, what was more important for Theo's purposes, about patterns in American political history.

"Of course, wars aren't the only events that interrupt cycles," Tyler said. "In my view, John Kennedy's image may save the youth of this country from the decay of the twentieth century—and keep the Democrats in the White House for quite a time to come."

Theo listened attentively, but he wasn't sure he could buy that. Still, to be on the safe side, he made a mental note to add more Democrats to his client list.

They finished a second drink, then Theo went to see how much longer supper would be.

IV

Becca and Kate were busy in the kitchen, Becca with her tanned midriff showing between a skimpy top of hot pink and a pair of abbreviated yellow shorts. Kate wore a cotton skirt and one of her father's faded blue shirts under a huge apron.

"There, I've finished shucking the corn," Rebecca said, picking the silk from her hands. "You know, I've been thinking."

"Oh, God," Kate said with mock consternation.

"If I've learned anything important in high school," Rebecca went on, "it's that I need to know a lot more about boys."

"Why?"

"To get what I want from them."

"Is that their purpose in life?"

"From a girl's point of view, can you think of any other reason for them?"

Kate thought a minute. "No. And they're certainly single-minded about what they want from girls."

"Yes, they're beasts," said Rebecca, hugging herself. "Isn't it delicious? Maybe that's the reason for them."

Rebecca spent a lot of time petting in the backseats of cars, but she knew that Sydney's romantic exploits—read *affairs*, Rebecca corrected herself—had made Kate negative about sex and boys and marriage.

Kate would be revolted if she knew how Rebecca touched boys and let them touch her. Kate was getting to be more of a grind every day, mooning over her father as if he were a wounded hero home from the wars.

"I think the men need more ice, don't you?" Rebecca said.

"They have plenty. I think you want to parade around in your teeny-weeny outfit."

"Now that my hair's dry, I'd like to meet him. He *is* nifty, isn't he?"

"Very nifty," Kate agreed.

Rebecca boosted herself up to a seat on the counter and helped Kate tear lettuce into small pieces. "Think how exciting it is to be a king maker and live in Washington!"

"Most politicians aren't the least bit regal."

"You can be blasé because your grandfather's a governor and your grandmother's the Benedict queen bee and they founded Wakefield College."

"Pretty hard to be blasé over people I've never met."

"Well, it's their loss and I say to hell with them!"

V

Theo Barrows heard the murmur of their voices before he made out their words. He stopped where he was, on the path under the kitchen windows, reluctant to go in when he heard his name mentioned.

He smiled when Rebecca called him a king maker. It was a title he was working hard to earn. He was a very successful lawyer, but it was political consultancy that fascinated him, and he had never regretted his decision to try his hand at it. Very soon now he would devote himself to it altogether. He had helped to seat a senator and two congressmen already, and his reputation as a canny fund-raiser was growing. Someday he *would* be a king maker. Someday he would put a president in the White House.

For the moment, his fee was $15,000 per month plus expenses and a ten percent override on media buys. It made for a very respectable income.

Theo had had many women, but he had never pretended to any of them that he wanted a wife. His work was the most intriguing mistress he could imagine, and the getting of power excited him more than the conquest of women, beyond the regular boff that a vigorous body demanded.

He had never had much to do with children, but he was intrigued by Kate. From what Theo had seen tonight, she was not only clever but mature for her age. He had yet to meet her friend.

"Most politicians aren't the least bit regal."

He recognized Kate's slightly husky voice and smiled. She was right on the mark there.

"You can be blasé because your grandfather's a governor and your grandmother's the Benedict queen bee and they founded Wakefield College."

"Pretty hard to be blasé over people I've never met."

"Well, it's their loss and I say to hell with them!"

Theo's smile faded. It startled him, there on the walk, to discover that the Ballards were not even on speaking terms with Governor Benedict and his formidable wife. Theo had intended to use this meeting as a stepping-stone to the governor. He wanted to be the man who got Oliver Benedict elected to the United States Senate. The word in Washington was that the governor's wife, who managed his life and a big chunk of the Benedict fortune, was in favor of the change.

Polly Benedict's reputation was pure gold, as her daughter Sydney's was not. If that was the reason for their estrangement—and everyone said it was—why did Polly still avoid contact with the Ballards when her daughter was no longer around?

Even so, Theo did not consider his time here wasted. He admired Dr. Ballard's scholarship and would put to good use the professor's insight into modern politics. The girls were an unexpected diversion. He had been touched by wistful, brilliant Kate and now was taken by her friend's fierce protectiveness.

"Hello in there," he called during the pause in their conversation. "When's supper? We're starving."

A girl appeared at the screen door. Young as she was, her lovely face had nothing of the child in it.

"Hello," she said. "I'm Rebecca. And you're Mr. Barrows. There, we're introduced. If you'll help, supper will be ready in half an hour."

"Done." Theo came into the kitchen. He received instructions from Kate, filled and hoisted two big steamers to the top of the old-fashioned range, and, when Kate took the salad out to the deck, stayed behind to talk to Rebecca, enchanted by her freshness, her blossoming beauty, her intelligence. Odd, he thought during the meal and the game of Scrabble that followed, how small, exquisite Rebecca dominated tall, serious Katherine.

"They're a remarkable pair," Theo said to Tyler that night after the girls had gone to bed. "Not women yet but not children either. You and Kate must be lonely."

He was immediately aware, from Dr. Ballard's posture and expression, that the subject was not to be discussed.

Theo went on. "They're both very sophisticated, aren't they? I wonder how they'll turn out."

"You must come by often and see."

It was precisely what Theo had hoped his host would say. One way or another, a connection with the Ballards had to put him a step closer to the Benedicts.

He soon stopped phoning ahead for an appointment before he dropped in. He was always made welcome. Sometimes he took them all out to dinner and played Scrabble with the girls afterward, even though he always lost. They were more than bright, although Rebecca shielded her intelligence and Kate let hers show.

Long before the cottage was closed and school had started again in

Harmony, Theo was Tyler's friend and an unofficial uncle to Kate and Becca. He came to Harmony several times in the year that followed.

"You're the closest thing I have to a family," he told them, and was surprised when Kate, who was not demonstrative, hugged him.

VI

The first snow of the winter was almost an inch deep and still falling on Harmony when Kate came up the walk carrying her books and her flute case. Kate loved the flute; the pure sound of it soothed her. Her music lesson had ended early today because her teacher had a ferocious cold.

She put the kettle on and got out of her boots and into the fleece-lined slippers she always left near the door. She made cinnamon tea and drank it while she peeled some potatoes for dinner and covered them with cold water. Then, taking her books, she went into the study to do her homework until Rebecca got home from dance class.

One of the wing chairs had been relegated to the attic to make room for a larger desk for Kate, but today, for no reason she could fathom, the familiar room looked suddenly strange and the single wing chair incongruous without its mate.

The mate had been her mother's chair. She could almost see Sydney sitting there, making granny squares or doing needlepoint, the only domestic arts her mother enjoyed. She could almost hear her, calling Kate her little *professorin*, insisting that they put on their boots and make the first footprints in the fresh snow.

How they used to laugh when Kate was little, rolling around in the beautiful, soft snow.

A wave of desolation overcame Kate, a fierce longing to see her mother mingling with rage at Sydney's departure, and she sank down in the window seat, shivering, and pulled up the afghan she had made after she gave her mother's to the Salvation Army. In some way she had never sought to understand, it gave her comfort to do for her father what her mother had done, to keep his house and cook his dinner, to sit in her mother's chair and crochet as Sydney once did while he worked.

By now it should have become second nature to be always cheerful and serene for her father's sake, but sometimes she wanted to wail like a baby. Sometimes, up in the attic with Sydney's photographs, she did—and felt as if she dishonored her father with every tear she shed.

"Do you ever regret what you did?" she murmured now to the place where the chair once stood. "Do you ever miss me?"

But Kate knew the answer to that. There had never been so much as a card from Sydney, not one single solitary word. And there never would be.

She was relieved when the telephone rang. "Theo!" she said. "You couldn't have called at a better time."

"Anything wrong?"

"No. Well, yes. I was feeling blue."

"For a reason?"

She almost told him. He made it easy to tell him things, and she knew he would never break a confidence. "Does there have to be a reason?" she asked.

"No, but it makes it easier to get rid of the blues. Are you going to be home this weekend?"

"Oh, yes! Are you coming?"

"If himself can spare the time."

"If he can't, I can. I'll get your room ready."

"Thanks, honey. I'm driving. Be there after lunch on Saturday."

VII

"Where are you?" Rebecca called a few minutes later.

"Up here, fixing up the guest room for Theo."

Rebecca bounded up the stairs. "Wonderful! When?"

"Saturday afternoon."

Rebecca studied her carefully. "Hey, who's got the crush on Theo, you or me?"

"You do. I just like him very much."

"Enough to polish all the furniture?"

"Rebecca!"

"Okay. I have news, too, even if it's not nearly so exciting. Donald Reed has asked me to the movies Friday evening."

"You're not going?"

"Of course I am. He's cute."

"He's silly. They're all silly."

Rebecca flung herself into a chair. "Maybe he'll improve with age. I'll bet Theo Barrows was silly when he was fifteen, and look how well he turned out. If you don't stop being so picky, Kate, you'll end up an old maid."

"I'd rather be an old maid than waste my time on stupid boys."

"Well, I want to know what sex is about, how it feels."

"Read a book," Kate advised. "Read *Ideal Marriage* or *Lady Chatterley's Lover*."

"I already have. I want to see how it feels for *myself*," Rebecca insisted, "like those girls in *The Group*."

"Oh, Becca," Kate said sadly. "You're not going to be another Tillie Beckwith, are you?"

Tillie Beckwith, the class strumpet, had taken on the whole basketball team in the boy's loo during a senior prom. "You don't really see me like that, do you?" Rebecca glanced at her friend and suddenly understood. *It's her damned mother again!* she thought. *Now Kate thinks any woman who likes sex is as bad as Sydney.*

"Anyway," she lied, "I'm not going to the movies alone with him. You're coming with us. It's *Lawrence of Arabia.*"

"Oh," Kate said, clasping her hands. "I've been dying to see it. But Donald won't want me tagging along."

"It was his idea!" Rebecca said. *I'll touch his whosis,* she decided. *I can get him to do anything for that.*

"Then I will," Kate said. "I don't know what I'd do without you, Becca."

"Well, you won't ever have to find out," Rebecca said. "Now, what have you got in the fridge that I can eat? If I *look* at another carrot, I'll turn orange!"

4

---·••·---

I

Governor Oliver Benedict stepped out of the shower and contemplated his glistening body in the bathroom mirror. He was sixty-three, but he had been blessed with a strong constitution, a lanky frame, and, since middle age, too little flesh rather than too much. His skin, pulled tightly over his bones, had easily accommodated the years without sagging, and his complexion was rosy enough to camouflage the age spots that were fighting to displace his freckles. He stood almost six feet tall under a head of hair that, apart from some tufts of gray, was a paler shade of his youthful red.

"If you're going to run for the Senate," his wife had told him, "you'll have to tone down that gray."

"Be damned if I will. Only poofs dye their hair."

"Land sakes, Oliver, you can't run looking like a pied horse."

"Rather a pied horse than a fairy."

She had given him the look that said she would have her way. She always did. As a young husband he had let her have it to ease his conscience, but even then he had sometimes wished he'd married a sweet, dumb little girl who'd have worshipped him and let him run on a long lead. How could anyone have known little Polly Ardmore'd turn out to be such a firecracker?

And a born politician too! With her shrewdness and the Benedict money, she had made herself a force in politics, a back-room boy without the smoke and the stogies. She could help him get that Senate seat.

She had always put him through his political paces like a circus horse, and over the years her ambition had rubbed off on him. Now he wanted that United States Senate seat as much as she did.

"But I'll have to do it her way," he grumbled.

What troubled him most was that she could ruin him anytime she wanted. It wasn't so much what he'd done: hell, all men had other women. It was what *she* had done that could make him a laughing-stock from one end of South Carolina to the other if it ever got out. And Polly was the only one who could let it get out.

He shook his head as if to chase the thought away, and, once more studying himself in the mirror, he decided he was not so old, taken all in all.

Then his eyes dropped to his groin and he sighed. From this font a long line of sons had sprung, fair as the morning, replete with promise —but not one had wanted to follow in his political footsteps!

The Benedicts had been preeminent in government ever since the Carolinas were one colony. They had been congressmen, senators, governors, and judges. They had founded and endowed Wakefield College for Women—named for their ancestors' estate in England— and it remained one of the most prestigious in the South, hell, in the country, come to that. They had been Southern gentlemen before the War Between the States, planters and breeders unwilling to soil their hands in commerce. When the South was left in ruins, they buried their disdain for trade and branched out into shipping and oil and pharmaceuticals and, later, plastics, while they kept their place in society and politics. The Benedicts had always been admired and respected for keeping up antebellum standards.

Not so Oliver's sons, who flatly refused to live in the past and preferred the meretricious company of businessmen, nouveau riche or otherwise.

"Money grubbing is for Yankees," Oliver had fumed at them only last week. "Not for Benedicts."

"You and Mother don't mind pouring our grubbings into Kel Regis," Kendall said.

"Kel Regis is a national treasure. There isn't a plantation house like it in all of Dixie."

"Don't say 'Dixie,' " Polly had warned him mechanically.

"Or into Wakefield College," Brett reminded him, keeping up the filial assault.

"You boys are breaking a tradition of public service that goes back before the Constitution," Oliver shouted. "One of you has got to get involved in politics!"

"Now, Dad," Mercer said. "Don't get yourself all worked up."

But Oliver couldn't help it. His firstborn twin sons, Oliver, Jr., and Orrin, who would have turned out real Benedicts, had been taken by the Second World War; Hilliard's death two years ago, while a shock, had not been so great a blow. Oliver had never expected Hilliard to amount to much, even if he was the apple of his mother's eye.

No, the real shock was Hilliard's tombstone.

Oliver had thanked God ever since that he and his wife were alone in the Benedict family plot at Kel Regis when he saw that marker for the first time.

II

```
HILLIARD ARDMORE BENEDICT

1928–1961

BELOVED SON OF

PENELOPE ARDMORE BENEDICT

GOOD NIGHT, SWEET PRINCE
```

"They've made a mistake," he had exclaimed, pointing to it.

"No mistake. I ordered it that way."

"Jesus, Polly! He was my son too."

"No, he wasn't."

He had turned to her, aghast. "Honey, you're beside yourself. I know you loved him more than all the others put together, but you can't mark his grave like that. People will talk."

She shrugged off the arm he put around her. Derision blazed from her swollen eyes and her whispered words had been heavy with contempt.

"I've put up with a lot of talk about you over the years, Oliver, you and your women."

"For God's sake!" he exclaimed, looking around furtively, as if the trees could hear and tell tales. He was flabbergasted. She had never alluded to his infidelities, not once in thirty-nine years of marriage, but he knew there was no denying it now.

"Maybe I was unfaithful with my body," he pleaded, "but never with my heart. Those women . . ."

"Don't tell me those women didn't mean anything to you! I know that. It's what they meant to *me* that matters!" She had pounded her chest with a closed fist. "You never thought about that, did you? You never once thought about the humiliation and the whispers I endured because everyone knew and I had to pretend I didn't."

"God almighty," he said softly. "You hate me. You've hated me all these years, even when we made love."

She didn't answer that. She went on talking in that unholy whisper, like a madwoman. "The Lord only knows how many bastards your trollops spawned for you—but Hilliard isn't yours. He belongs to me and I won't sully his memory with your name."

Oliver had managed to choke it out. "Who was his father?"

"I won't tell you—unless I decide to tell the whole world."

He was dazed. "Why would you do that?"

"To watch *you* deal with whispers and ridicule for a change! Governor Benedict!" She said it with utter scorn. "I made your career, Oliver. You didn't have the brains *or* the drive to do it yourself. And I can break it with one word about Hilliard, whose he was and how he died."

"And shame us all? Yourself included?"

"I'm accustomed to shame. You saw to that."

"But you won't," he had told her harshly. "You want my career as much as I do."

They stood by the tombstone, glaring at each other.

When Polly spoke again, the anger seemed drowned in grief. "Now that Hilliard's gone, I don't want anything. I don't care about anything, least of all you."

III

Oliver sighed.

Of course she had not ruined him. Lately her interest in politics, dormant for two years, had revived, and she was determined to get Oliver elected to the Senate. Her involvement in Wakefield College's board of trustees was increasing too, along with concern for the school's drop in enrollment. People said she was her old self, but Oliver knew she wasn't and, in fact, had never been her old self. She had been a very good actress. It was unsettling to discover that he knew so little about the woman he'd lived with most of his life.

He had almost come to believe that it wasn't true about Hilliard, that in her grief she had turned on him and made it up. But he couldn't be sure.

And so they had gone on together. The difference was that now he was playacting too. They seemed like the same united couple in public. Even in private they clung to small habits of affection in that asexual fashion of long-married couples. And the talk about the tombstone had stopped: people had put it down to Polly's extravagant grief, to her wild preference for her youngest son, by comparison with her matter-of-fact treatment of the others and her total rejection of her only daughter.

Oliver's other sons thought judges and politicians mere commodities to be bought and sold by industrialists. The final straw was that they were pressing their own sons, Oliver's grandchildren, to stay out of the political arena too. So far not even Polly had been able to make them consider seriously a future in government.

If she could have her way, one of the grandsons would be president.

"She never thought I could," Oliver mused aloud, with a mixture of resentment and relief. He had always suspected that her opinion of his talents as a legislator wasn't very high, but she had never expressed it outright until that day at Hilliard's grave. Oliver knew he wasn't presidential material, but he was well liked in his role of a hearty, rubicund southern planter who smelled of bay rum and bourbon. He sometimes overdid the part, but it made him the candidate of choice for the professional politicians who were the real power in government but never ran for office.

He sighed and returned to the contemplation of his once-glorious member. He was sorely troubled that lately it was apt to grovel supine between his legs rather than rise to the attack. Sometimes it took a really talented whore to make it stand up and take notice. For a man who had been a champion cocksman since he was twelve, this was devastating.

"You'll make no more sons for me," he murmured sadly. "You'll soon be fit to do nothing but pee, as if I were a puling infant again."

His wife's voice, reaching him from the salon, interrupted his colloquy.

"Well, I'll be damned!" she said.

"What about?"

"Come in here and I'll tell you," she said.

He pulled on fresh underwear, slacks, shirt, and blazer—they were dining alone tonight—smoothed his hair and patted his cheeks with eau de cologne. Then, as he would have donned a cloak, he wrapped pretense around him and went to join his wife where she sat in the private parlor of the South Carolina governor's mansion at Columbia.

IV

Penelope Ardmore Benedict—Polly to most people—was not as lean as her husband. Neither was she fat. She was round, as she had always been, and she still filled her healthy pink skin as firmly as a sausage. She was of average height and, with her halo of curls, deceptively benign in appearance for a woman whose word was law—well, almost law—to a large and far-flung family.

It was to Polly they turned—not so much her sons as her sons' children and a host of third cousins, great-nieces and -nephews, and in-laws from both sides of the family—when they needed money or advice or help getting out of a scrape. With the sole exception of the infamous Sydney, Polly had always managed to save the day, using money and connections, yes, and blackmail, too, if she had to, to avoid besmirching the family name.

She knew Oliver would have been grateful for that even if he hadn't loved her when he married her.

Seventeen she had been then, "a ripe, luscious Carolina peach," Oliver had called her, smacking his lips over his plump, pretty Polly. Even way back then he had complained that "women aren't succulent anymore, they're hard and tough and stringy, not like my Peach." Oliver had never had any use for skinny women.

Now he bent to kiss her cheek, careful of her white curls: Polly had turned white when Hilliard died and some of the light had gone out of her forever, but she still dressed like a cross between Gypsy Rose Lee and the English Queen Mother and wore jewels suitable to her rank. Whatever happened, Polly carried the family banner high.

Tonight she wore a fawn velvet dinner gown flounced with lace and her pearls, flawless, matched Orientals set in diamonds.

"You must have a date with a sailor," he teased, but it was self-conscious now. "Tricked out like that."

"Look at this," she replied, waving the paper. "Tyler Ballard has won a second Pulitzer Prize! He's been invited to the White House."

"Not bad!" Oliver exclaimed.

"The man's worthy," Polly announced. "There's no denying it anymore. It's time I did something about that child."

"What?" Oliver didn't want her digging around in the past. "Why?"

"If he's worthy, maybe she is. And if she is, I want to know it. Tyler's had the grace to keep his distance and never ask for favors. Maybe there's more to him than I thought. As for Katherine, the child didn't choose her parents." She glanced at him briefly, reminding him that she had chosen some other parent for her favorite son. "Sydney is her cross to bear as well as mine."

Oliver scrutinized her carefully. This was a turnabout of major proportions! Sydney and her daughter had always been anathema to Polly. But he would welcome anything that would take her mind off Hilliard. Maybe the girl was just what the doctor ordered.

"Well, sweetheart, you go on and see her," he said. "If she's a true Benedict, we'll take her up and make something out of her."

She gave him an enigmatic smile. Once he would have thought it fond. Now it said she didn't require his permission to do anything.

A week later she was aboard one of the last private railway cars in America, bound for Harmony.

As was typical of Polly, she had sent word of her coming at the last minute, when it was too late for Tyler to reply and put her off. She knew he would be in Harmony; it was the middle of the winter term.

Polly liked trains. The dusty smell of them, the sound of their wheels on the tracks, the wail of their whistles—all of it had a soothing effect on her. There was a pile of books and magazines on the coffee table in the car's rather rococo salon, but she spent most of her time gazing out the windows, half hypnotized by the vistas that seemed to be moving past the train.

Gradually, imperceptibly, she gave over thinking about Katherine, her secretly observed but still unknown granddaughter, and surrendered to thinking about herself. It was something she avoided because it usually led her right to Hilliard, but this time she let the movement rock her more deeply into the past.

"Come here and lie down by me, you lovely little thing," she heard Oliver say, and Polly was on another train, a seventeen-year-old bride on her honeymoon.

V

The muscular, redheaded husband chosen for her seemed nice enough, and it had been a sumptuous wedding with Polly the center of attention for the first time in her life: she had been the one girl among many brothers, and her features, although comely, were not so arranged as to make her a great beauty.

Once in the railway car, her maid helped her undress and put on a lace-frothed nightdress and matching peignoir before the girl fled, giggling, and left Polly to her fate.

Oliver was already in the double bed when she entered the bedroom, and she had stayed at the mirror brushing her hair, feeling self-conscious and awkward and apprehensive.

When he asked her—or was he telling her?—to come and lie down alongside him, her mother's faltering instructions, communicated in a pained whisper, came to mind.

"Just let him do whatever he wants and it'll soon be over."

Polly had only a vague idea of what "it" was, but she put down her hairbrush and went to him obediently, sliding beneath the covers Oliver held up for her.

He leaned on one elbow, looking down at her. He had a craggy, freckled face under that red hair, a nice face. "You've been my wife for six hours and I only got to kiss you once," he said. He bent and kissed her, gently at first, then more insistently until she was kissing him back, lost in a small romantic rapture when he took her in his arms.

She was startled when he pushed her gown up, but he hushed her and went back to kissing until she let him stroke her breasts. She demurred again when his hand went between her thighs but, "Let me," he said, and she remembered her mother's instructions and let him. He touched her in a way that first made her breath come faster and then made her dissolve into a strange and unexpected bliss. She was beyond stopping him, whatever he wanted to do.

"Here, Polly honey," he whispered, pulling the pillow from beneath her head. "Put this under you. It won't hurt so much."

It had hardly hurt at all, so eager was she to have more of him.

Later on she realized, from guarded conversations with other young married women, that Oliver had been the most considerate of bridegrooms, taking her step by step from one erotic technique to another. By the time they returned from their honeymoon in Europe, Polly was an accomplished voluptuary and supposed, in her innocence, that all marriages were as uninhibitedly erotic as hers.

On the night they returned to Kel Regis, she was six months pregnant and enormous, embarrassed by her bulk and resigned to being sexually frustrated for months to come.

"Why?" Oliver asked when she refused him for the first time.

"I'm too big. And it might hurt the baby."

"The baby'll love it—and there's one thing you're not too big for. Just you lie back there and I'll prove it to you." And he had, calling her his ripe, luscious peach, and she had reciprocated, and they had gone happily to sleep in each other's arms.

He wasn't there when she woke on her first morning at Kel Regis. Oliver was studying law with his uncle Maynard Benedict and had warned her he had to make up for the time lost on their honeymoon.

"Lost?" Polly had protested. "Well, I declare, Oliver! It wasn't lost."

"No, sugar," Oliver agreed. "It sure enough wasn't."

But all the same, life suddenly became very serious. For a while, Polly's time was taken up with the mansion and the novelty of her twin sons, Oliver Junior and Orrin, who were soon followed by Kendall and then Brett. By the time Brett arrived, Oliver was practicing law and Polly was bored with breeding and spent most of her time finding out how badly Kel Regis was being run.

"The truth of it is," she told Oliver after the uneventful delivery of Brett, "I'm bored."

"Bored?" Oliver stood over his wife and newborn son and laughed aloud. "Soon as you're mended I'll see you're not bored!"

"I'm not bored with you, Oliver. I'm bored all day without you, and canoodling can't cure that. There are more nursemaids and nannies on Kel Regis than there are babies."

"We'll soon fix that," Oliver promised.

"Now, you stop it, hear? I'm deadly serious, Oliver. Your practice is growing, so you have no time for Kel Regis, and the place is being run into the ground. You know I love it, that I can't abide flower clubs and garden parties and bridge afternoons. I want you to fire that fool manager of yours and let me run it!''

At first, scandalized at the thought of letting a woman run his estate, he stubbornly refused. Eventually he gave in because he was feeling guilty about the high yaller gal he'd been visiting in Steadboro. Not that Polly wasn't a prime bedmate, but one woman had never been enough for Oliver.

Anyway, Polly would soon tire of being a plantation chatelaine. And he loved her. It was hard to say no to a wife if a man loved her the way he loved his Peach. And after all, Oliver was head of the family now that his father was dead, and he didn't have to answer to anyone.

Finally, it wasn't as if Polly were taking a job in a shop or a mill! Womenfolk had been running southern plantations since Colonial times.

Baby Brett was a landmark for Polly. Not only did she take over Kel Regis after he was born, she discovered that Oliver had been unfaithful to her for years.

VI

"That lowlife snake!" she raged to her mother.

"There are worse things," her mother said.

Polly was appalled. "I can't think of any!"

"Penelope, take my advice and don't let on you know. It only complicates things. You're not the only woman whose husband cheats on her. All men are like that, my dear, especially Benedict men."

"You might have told me that before you married me off to him."

"Are you sorry we did?"

Polly had to admit she wasn't in the least sorry. Apart from his deceit and a certain lack of ambition that was indigenous to southerners—but had never afflicted Polly—she had loved him mightily. She still did.

For a while she was too furious and too devastated to think clearly. She ordered her maid to pack and unpack her bags half a dozen times. And then she realized that many women were not a threat. Unlike a steady mistress, they were anonymous body parts. She was sure Oliver wouldn't remember their names if she confronted him.

In the end she said nothing, not even when she was sure everyone knew—and had known for a long time. She swallowed her rage like a big balloon and said nothing. Instead, she set about turning Kel Regis into a profitable enterprise, abandoning a lot of little crops for beans, corn, and peaches in quantity. On the advice of one of her brothers—the Ardmores were bankers—she began to invest the profits in oil fields and companies that used oil by-products. She had always loved horses and she began breeding racers. And she managed to put Oliver's infidelities at the back of her mind. Oliver was a simple man and in his simple way he adored her. She had come to realize that it was all any woman could expect.

She gave birth to the twins Maynard and Mercer a year later, and then she went to New York, to a gynecologist whose address she had been given by a woman of like mind, and came back with a pessary to protect her from any more pregnancies. Six sons in five years had earned her a rest.

She was proud of her robust children, and when she was not too busy she showed it by trying to inculcate in them her own rigid standards, with what indifferent success she was not to discover until much later.

Often, in the years that followed, she rode out to inspect her domain with one of the boys perched on the saddle in front of her, careless of the jealousy she had provoked in those she left behind. For the most part, though, she cultivated her fields, watched over her investments, and left her sons to a raft of maids, nannies, and governesses, carefully monitored by the family's numerous maiden aunts and widows, who traveled from house to house making themselves useful.

"Who's the one who came today?" Oliver asked as they dressed for dinner one evening when Maynard and Mercer had turned seven.

"Lucia," Polly said, pronouncing it *Loosha.* "My brother Stuart's girl. She isn't all that old, and if you ask me, she's no maiden, but she's mighty unhappy over an unfortunate love affair with a Yankee."

"They can't say that about our love affair, can they, sweetheart?"

"I don't know, Oliver. Can they?"

"Hell, no! Strikes me we won't be needing maiden ladies much now that the O's are at school and Kendall is getting ready to go." Oliver always referred to the older twins as the O's and the younger set as the M's. "Unless, of course, we start having babies again."

"We'll cross that bridge if we come to it. I'd have thought six boys were enough progeny for any man."

It abruptly dawned upon Oliver, who had just wangled his way onto a judge's bench, that his wife of seven years was no longer a girl bride. He was not thinking about her age but about *her.* Polly had turned into a woman with more authority than wives twice her age. She ran Kel Regis like a well-oiled machine, crops and children, land and horses, house and husband.

He didn't mind that she ran him, but he wasn't going to let on he knew she was doing it.

VII

Polly had known it for some time. Somewhere along the way she had accepted the fact that she was a sight smarter than her husband. She had never been content to gossip with other women about children, sex, or soybeans; she was interested in a multitude of other things. She had always enjoyed school and now she began to read omnivorously, ordering books from Charleston and Boston and New York and tearing down a wall to expand the library.

But with Oliver's reading limited to legal briefs, lewd books, and dirty magazines, she had no one to talk to about what she read. She began inviting the prep school and college generation to stay at Kel Regis during their term breaks.

"Another raft of scholars?" Oliver exclaimed every time a group descended.

"They're our kin and they're bright young people," Polly told him. "I like talking to them."

"Clutter up the house," Oliver muttered. "Take up all your time." But, being Oliver, he hung upon their coming and made them welcome. The house resounded with his deep laugh. He bought trinkets for the girls and gave the boys pocket money. They adored him.

Polly reminded herself that a man beloved by children couldn't be all bad. She still loved him. She regarded him, for the most part, with indulgent contempt; he needed guidance, like one of the children, if he was to get anywhere in state politics.

At least three of her boys—Oliver Junior, Orrin, and Brett—had the brains and the drive to go further in politics than their father ever would, and she decided that he must pave the way for them. He was climbing the judicial ladder by getting along and going along, but she wanted him to go a lot further than that.

"Oliver," she told him, "it's time you got off the bench and into the State House."

"Not on your life! I'm happy right where I am."

"Honey, it's nowhere near what you deserve." *A man,* she thought, *will believe anything a woman tells him if she flatters him first and scratches his belly.*

"You really think so?"

"I do. You've been a first-rate judge, but you're also a good ol' boy with powerful connections and a name that means something in this state. Why stay in the court system? With a little push and some

Benedict Industries money spread around in the right places, you'll be a state senator before you can say damn Yankee. A few terms in Columbia and you'll be a shoo-in for Washington." She paused for effect. "United States Senator Oliver Benedict! Won't that be wonderful, honey?"

And Oliver, tempted by the fabled naughtiness of Washington, the whorehouses that pandered to exotic foreign tastes, agreed.

Polly had thrown herself into his new career with the same spirit she had put into her marriage and Kel Regis. She worked tirelessly behind the scenes, acquiring a reputation among the local pols for shrewdness and guile that they put down to "women's intuition," when, in fact, she was simply smarter than the lot of them. Two years later, Oliver was State Senator Benedict and Polly, who had been The Judge's Wife became The Senator's Wife and a kind of parlor politician.

"But it nags at me," she told her cousin, Dodie Phelps, "that as sure as God made little green apples, I'd have been a better state senator than any of those muzzy-headed fools sitting up there in Columbia."

Dodie Phelps Ardmore Westerby was a widow newly liberated from an unhappy marriage which ended, mercifully, in its first year. She had come to Kel Regis "to recover," she told Polly, "from the excessive joy of my bereavement." Polly, delighted to find a woman who had a sharp mind and spoke it freely, had persuaded her to make Kel Regis her home.

"Don't you dare say such things to a paragon of southern manhood like Oliver!" Dodie Phelps advised Polly. "He'll lock you in the cellar!"

"They're still true!"

"When did that ever change anything? Where are you sending Oliver next?"

"I've decided he needs the experience of the governor's mansion in his home state first. He's nowhere near ready to deal with those big-time brigands in Washington."

"Polly Benedict, you're thinking of yourself as First Lady!"

But Polly knew Oliver would never get that far. Sometimes, when she went to the State House to hear him deliver the speech she had written for him, she wanted to thrust him aside and take the floor herself. He was good, but she'd have been better.

For the most part, though, she resigned herself to her life. She had the same affectionate disdain for Oliver that she had for her sons. She liked hearing him sing when he shaved in the morning. She liked the clean smell of him—the odors of other women were always washed away before he came to her—and the shape of him when he was in her arms and in her body. If the thought obtruded of other female bodies he had penetrated, she pushed it away and gave herself over to sensation.

And to exorcise the demon inside her that hungered for something more, she began a full-scale renovation of Kel Regis, inside and out.

All things considered, she had been a happy woman . . .

VIII

There was a knock on the door of the parlor car and Polly roused herself.

"Come in."

"Good evening, madam," the steward said. "What would you like for dinner?"

"Something light," Polly said. That was a lie. She didn't want something light at all. Polly's appetite was as healthy as she was, but she had to take off five pounds before her next visit to the doctor or he would lecture her. She longed for the good old days when a woman nearing sixty was entitled to some padding.

Polly decided on consomme, grilled sole, asparagus, and green salad with gelatin for dessert.

"In an hour," Polly said, peckish already but in no hurry for such bland fare.

The steward left and Polly lit a cigarillo and curled back into memory like a cat under a couch.

IX

. . . until she met the man she should have married. If only she had known! But how could she have known, when she was seventeen, what woman she would become? How could she have known she was far more than Oliver needed or comprehended or even wanted in a wife, and he far less than she needed as a husband? She was frustrated because of all the thoughts and feelings she couldn't share with him, stifled by all the rage she had swallowed.

And then one day she stood by her husband's side to welcome a visitor to Kel Regis. A slim man emerged from the big Packard they'd sent to the station to fetch him. He was Charles Travis, a breeder from Kentucky, and he had come to look at the Benedict Stud, among others in the area.

"Welcome, Mr. Travis, it's good to see you," Oliver boomed. "Honey, this is Charlie Travis. Mr. Travis, meet my wife."

Maybe it was the admiration in his eyes when he looked at her or his smile when he shook her hand. Whatever it was, she was not so eager to get to the point of his visit. Instead of taking him to the stables, she ordered drinks to be brought to the garden. It was one of those halcyon South Carolina days, air as soft as silk and the scent of honeysuckle sweet on the breeze, and Polly felt bathed in sensuality.

The conversation touched briefly on horses, then turned to books. Oliver, out of his depth, fidgeted and soon took his leave for Columbia on business that would keep him in the capital for a day or two.

"But it's my wife who runs the Benedict Stud," he told Travis. "She'll take good care of you." He extended his hand. "I hope we'll see each other again."

"Oliver," Polly said, yielding to impulse for the first time in her life. "Why doesn't Mr. Travis make Kel Regis his home while he's in South Carolina?"

"Fine idea!" Oliver said heartily, eager to be away. "Travis?"

"Senator, that's an honor I can't resist."

Oliver kissed his wife's cheek and hurried off. Alone, they regarded each other, smiling.

This is ridiculous, Polly told herself. *Schoolgirls feel this way, not grown women with a raft of children.*

"It was very kind of you to invite me, Mrs. Benedict."

"Please call me Polly—and it wasn't kindness. I'm perishing for someone to talk books to." Actually, she and Dodie Phelps talked books all the time, but a man's point of view was different—particularly this man's. "If you've finished your drink, I'll show you my library."

In the lofty room, its temperature carefully regulated against heat and humidity, he whistled softly as he walked slowly from section to section. At length he turned and looked at her with that smile that made her heart leap as it had not done for many a year. "I never expected to find a library like this at Kel Regis—or someone like you."

"Most people don't know much about me or my library."

"Most people are fools."

Polly nodded, gazing at him, the pull between them almost irresistible. Then, collecting herself, she suggested they both change and walk down to the stables. She showed him to his room, where his bags had already been unpacked, and went down the hall to change. In her bedroom she examined her face in the mirror.

"You're out of your mind, Polly Benedict," she told her glowing reflection. "You know too much to feel like this." But she laughed, threw her arms up over her head, and whirled her way to the closet for her skirted riding habit. They talked horseflesh until the light faded, then had a drink on the terrace before they went to bathe and change for dinner. They dined with Dodie Phelps, talking easily, but Polly felt a sense of anticipation that was as exciting as the touch of his hand on her body would have been.

Polly lay in bed that night, naked and adrift in fantasy. He was leaving his room, walking along the corridor, opening her door. He was leaning over her, kissing her, and her arms were around him, pulling him down to her, the heat from her body rising to enclose them in a cloud of passion.

X

There was nothing heroic about Charlie Travis, nothing you could put your finger on, but everyone liked him as he made his rounds of the local breeders. He was a widower, soft-spoken, slender, and mysteriously endearing. When he traveled too far afield to return to Kel Regis for the night, the house seemed cavernous and empty. When Oliver came down from Columbia, he became an intruder in their wordless tryst.

When Charlie had been there two weeks, Polly gave a party for him.

"He's the most delightful man, isn't he?" said Dodie Phelps, standing with Polly on the first floor gallery of the atrium to watch the dancing.

"I wonder why he hasn't remarried?" Polly asked as casually as she could.

"Well, it has to be one of two things. Either the man had a perfect marriage or he had a rotten one. I'd say the latter."

"Pity," Polly said.

"If you plan on giving him comfort, Polly, learn to control your face."

"When I need your advice, Dodie Phelps, I'll ask for it."

"You need it."

The next day Polly and Charlie went riding. For once, they did not talk at full spate. It was quiet under the trees, with wide fans of sunlight dappling the pines. They walked the horses deeper into the woods until, finally, they stopped and looked at each other.

He took her hand.

Polly caught her breath, then nodded and dismounted. The next moment she was in his arms and he was kissing her. He unbuttoned her jacket and her shirt, undid the brassiere enclosing her bountiful breasts, and put his lips to the cleft between them. A shudder ran through her at his touch, and another when, both of them naked, they lay down together on her spread skirt and made love.

She felt she had never made love before—as indeed she had not, not with a man who wanted her mind as much as he wanted her body. Charlie knew the Polly he held in his arms. He had come to know her profoundly before he even touched her.

"Are you happy with him?" he asked when their cries of pleasure had died away.

"I was once, before I knew fulfillment had to be more than physical."

"I'm sorry for that."

"I'm not! I'll never be sorry for anything, now that I've known you." She kissed him tenderly. "Were you happy with your wife?"

"No. She hated being touched. We were married for ten years and I don't feel as if I made love to her more than twenty times. And she had a narrow little mind. She wasn't like you. No one's like you. Where did you find time to study, married so young, with a baby every year and this place to run?"

"Oliver is away a lot. I had the evenings to myself."

"Is that idiot unfaithful to you?"

"Yes. Flagrantly."

"Oh, Polly." He rocked her in his arms. "How could he be?"

"I minded when I found out about it. Then it passed. He loves me —and he needs me, a lot more than I need him."

"Neediness can be a kind of tyranny too."

She laughed. "Oliver, a tyrant? No, my darling."

"Say that again."

"My darling," she whispered. "My darling."

He was a man who nourished every facet of her. He would never have put her on a pedestal or in a gilded cage, as Oliver had done, and she was as eager for the talks that came after love as for the loving itself. She loved him in ways she had never dreamed existed.

XI

He left her when she refused to desert Oliver and her sons to go away with him. No matter how much she loved him, no matter how far she had already fallen from grace, desertion was a shame she could not bring upon the family.

When he left she felt as if half of her had been carved away, as if she could not go on pretending she was the same person. But she had to and she did, even if it took every ounce of will she possessed.

She knew she was pregnant by him before he left, but she didn't tell him; it would have changed nothing. She had Charlie's son baptized Hilliard Ardmore Benedict in the Benedict County Episcopal Church and raised him with the others, most of them rugged and red-haired like their father, who was overjoyed to welcome the new arrival.

"Time we had another cub around the place," Oliver said.

"Now, who does this child take after?" Lila Ardmore wondered, rocking the slender, brown-haired baby.

"My granddaddy Hilliard Ardmore," Polly told her sister-in-law languidly, pretending not to have seen a sharp little movement from Dodie Phelps. "That's who I named him for."

There were so many children at Kel Regis that no one paid much attention to Hilliard's unusual coloring and his slight build. No one except Polly, who loved, with an intensity that overwhelmed her, this child of her essential self and the only man who would ever know her, heart and soul.

Charles Travis had sent a champion chestnut colt to Kel Regis to thank the Benedicts for their hospitality. His name, according to the papers that accompanied him, was Charlie's Darling. Polly rode him herself. She never considered selling him and she bred him carefully to make sure there would always be one of his get in the original colt's stall. When the original Charlie's Darling died, his grandson was rechristened with his name.

Hilliard was Polly's last son. Sydney, born a year later, was her last child and her only daughter. Sydney had been carelessly conceived after Polly's interest in Oliver was limited to his political potential. She was too young for celibacy and she still made love with her husband, but it was Charlie's voice she heard and Charlie's touch she felt.

It hadn't taken Polly long to declare that her daughter was a changeling: why else did she find it impossible to love her? The pregnancy had been a burden and the delivery difficult.

Early on, it became apparent to her that Sydney's sexual gears had been stripped in the womb, so it had come as no surprise to Polly that Sydney had got herself pregnant at eighteen by a mere assistant professor at Wakefield College—nor when she deserted husband and child for fornication with her cousin Royal. Polly had always known her daughter would come to no good.

Polly herself had put duty before the one great love of her life, but Sydney, scoffing at duty, mocking Polly's sacrifice without even knowing it had been made, ruthlessly followed her bliss.

XII

"And now," Polly said resolutely, crushing out the cigarillo, "I must deal with her child."

To be fair about it, Tyler Ballard had turned out to be far less self-serving than Polly expected. After he married Sydney, Oliver had used his connections to obtain a full professorship for him at Harmony—under the circumstances, it was unthinkable that he stay on at Wakefield—but beyond that he had asked no further favors of them and had, slowly but surely, made a name for himself that commanded respect first in academic circles and now beyond.

Two Pulitzer Prizes in a row were no mean feat.

Dr. Ballard also had a growing reputation as a political sage. That was because Tyler had an uncanny knack for using the past to predict the future. By the time a startling number of his predictions had come true, the public, which ridiculed scholarship more often than not, was fond of the handsome historian in his rumpled jackets and Mark Twain string ties. He was proof positive that America produced intellectuals as well as rock singers, tennis pros, and obnoxious tourists.

Tyler had been helping to steady a nation nervous and despondent after the Kennedy assassination. History, he had said on television and in the press, was filled with murdered leaders, but the acid test of a country's affection was how it behaved after its chief had fallen. If the public's mourning for its slaughtered president were real, it would fulfill the promise he represented.

Polly, who was usually put off by sentiment, knew a good thing when she saw it. Perhaps he could be useful to Polly's political plans for Oliver, who had yet to be tapped by his party as a candidate for the United States Senate.

The truth was that Polly wanted to meet the child. She didn't understand why she was impelled to seek her out after avoiding her for so long. It was certainly not the "worthiness" of Katherine's father. Oliver had swallowed that nonsense, but Polly never lied to herself.

"What do I want with her?" she asked aloud.

She had no reply.

She went to sleep hoping that the girl was deadly dull and that, having done her duty, Polly could leave her where she was.

5

I

Polly stopped first at Campbell Hall to see Tyler, having specified in her letter that if she and Katherine met at all, they must meet alone.

He was still a good-looking man, Polly noticed at once when she entered his office, and had considerably more presence than he had possessed when he was besotted enough to marry Sydney, but even at forty-three the telltale signs of the dedicated scholar were creeping over him like ivy on a wall.

His thick swatch of dark hair was streaked with gray and he peered like an owl over the glasses perched low on his resplendent nose. To complete the picture, there was a trace of ash on his lapel. He still dressed in leather-patched tweeds, reverse-calf ankle boots, and string ties, but he had always had a certain charm and it was with him still. He was positively Byronic.

He had that otherworldly look about him typical of people who are more at home in the past than the present, and particularly prevalent among academics. As a trustee of Wakefield College, Polly had studied the breed at close range and Tyler had all the qualifications. He seemed part of the dull ecru walls with brown woodwork, the books stuffed willy-nilly into shelves, the old desk piled with dusty papers.

"What does she think of my coming?" Polly asked after they had exchanged platitudes: it was difficult for them to share a memory that did not include Sydney, and Polly's instinct told her not to mention Tyler's ex-wife.

"Kate has agreed to meet you," Tyler said, and added with barely concealed satisfaction, "but she is not amused."

"No, I suppose not. Still, I must see her."

"You never felt the compulsion before."

"I do now."

44

"Katherine is not the sort to wait indefinitely upon someone's pleasure and then greet her with open arms."

"What sort is she?"

He smiled. "The consensus is that my daughter is bright—no, brilliant—as well as witty, generous, loyal, and somewhat introverted."

"I see. In short, her father's child."

"Entirely," Tyler said in a way that reaffirmed Polly's decision to avoid any reference to Katherine's mother.

"But she won't be a child much longer, Tyler. That's why I've come. She needs a woman's touch. And soon she'll want the things I can give her and you can't."

Tyler bristled. "Such as?"

"Kel Regis. A whole new way of life. A whole family she's never met, a heritage she knows nothing about. She can't go to the St. Cecilia Ball because of her mother, but I could bring her out with a ball at Kel Regis."

"Katherine doesn't care much for that kind of thing."

"All girls care for that kind of thing in their secret hearts. That's a perfect example of what a man wouldn't know."

"Why this sudden interest in her? Why now?"

"I wish I knew, Tyler. Suddenly it's something I have to do." She shrugged. "Call it conscience or atonement or a house without children."

She shook herself slightly, brushing off her ghosts. "Tell me, do you suppose you and I could set aside our differences if Katherine were willing?"

"I would abide by her decision," he said confidently.

It got Polly's back up, his certainty that Katherine would say no. He even indulged her by discussing a possible Christmas visit to Kel Regis.

Polly exchanged civil good-byes with him and left, her offering laid upon the altar, her gesture made. If Katherine proved to be Tyler's spiritual child, Polly wouldn't want her any more—Tyler had all but said it—than the girl wanted Polly.

Not that Tyler was a bad sort, Polly reflected as the car made its way past rambling New England frame houses and snow-covered lawns bordered by box hedges, past hibernating elms and copper beeches. It was simply that the man, however significant a scholar, had no spark, no passion.

"No fire for anything but his work," Polly muttered, and without that fire no creature—man, woman, child, or beast—compelled her interest. Tyler's child probably lacked it too.

Nonetheless, she was leaning forward in anticipation as the car turned into Elm Terrace with its row of neat houses behind tidy shrubbery that had none of the warmth and opulence of Kel Regis.

II

There were two girls on the lawn, and Polly thought fleetingly that the blond beauty might have been Sydney's child, even as she darted away to the house next door, leaving the very tall, dark-haired youngster waiting, aloof, on the snow-cleared crazy paving of the walk.

"I don't know what to call you," Katherine said, seizing the offensive as soon as Polly was out of the car. She had a husky voice Polly liked.

"Something will occur to you when we know each other better," she said.

A sardonic smile briefly disordered Katherine's impassive expression.

I have no intention of knowing you, it said.

She's no mollycoddle, Polly decided, her interest aroused by the challenge. But she knew how to deal with arrogant children.

Katherine led the way into the house, took Polly's coat, and installed her in an overstuffed chair in the parlor while she went to fetch the tea. The parlor was comfortable, even well decorated. Polly thought she saw Sydney's hand in the upholstery and the Limoges lamps, the few genuine antique pieces, the ivory draperies at the windows. The room did not seem much lived in. It was cold.

Katherine returned with a Georgian silver tea service. When she placed it on the tea table, Polly recognized it as one of Sydney's wedding gifts. The cloth and napkins were freshly laundered, the cups and saucers shining, the sandwiches and cookies obviously homemade. It was formal and proper, and it had none of the comfortable ease of family.

She's keeping me at a distance, Polly reflected, the girl's subtlety not lost on her. She watched her granddaughter pouring tea with the poise of a house mother. If it could be said of a fourteen-year-old girl, Katherine was imposing, even if she did dress like a nun. None of those frightful denim rigups for her!

Katherine wore a gray flannel skirt and a navy cardigan over a white blouse with an Eton collar. Her shiny, dark hair was tied back with a crisp navy grosgrain ribbon. She wore navy knee socks and fashionably run-down loafers. Polly, in red wool, mink, and a few everyday rubies, felt overdressed.

Banalities were exchanged—the weather, Katherine's subjects at school, Polly's train trip—while they took each other's measure, but by the time the stillborn conversation died, Polly was determined to reach this over-tall, self-possessed girl so adept at hiding the tempest any woman would have sensed within her.

At first glance, she was Tyler's, but she had all the passion Tyler lacked. She had Sydney's grace, Sydney's magnetism, and a hint of Sydney's sensuality around her mouth. There was no trace of Sydney's sluttishness, but it was something that had to be watched. Right now, having taken up a crochet hook and a granny square, Kate looked like a spinster.

Odd, Polly mused, *that she's taken up Sydney's interest in handicrafts.*

"Your mother—" Polly began.

"I will not discuss my mother," Katherine interrupted.

Ah, Polly thought. *Now I know how to breach your defenses!* "You ought to know what you've come from," she said.

"I know all I need to know. I had twelve years with my mother before she left. I know how she lives now and with whom—all of them. I know what she did to Tyler and me, but I have never known why and you can't tell me, can you?"

Polly shook her head, startled by this stingingly accurate condensation of a calamity. Katherine was laying down the ground rules of their relationship.

"So there is no reason for me to discuss my mother with you or with anyone else," the child finished.

"As you wish," Polly conceded. She recognized mettle when she saw it, and she abandoned her authoritarian manner. That was not the way to Katherine, and Polly already knew she wanted to find the way.

"Katherine, is there any way we might be friends?"

"I don't think so. I don't even know why you've come."

"As I just told your father, I don't know myself. Maybe I've come to a turning point in my life; maybe I want to put some things right and you are where I have to start because you're the one I've wronged the most. I came to offer my apologies and to ask you to let us know each other so that you can learn to forgive me and share all I have to offer you."

"Offer me?"

"Kel Regis is one of the most beautiful places in the world," Polly explained, her voice taking on the warmth of her love for it. "I had a lot to do with that and I'm very proud of what I did. There are Thoroughbred horses to ride over acres of meadow and piney woods and a river that runs beside a grove of willows. If beauty speaks to you, you'll never be lonely at Kel Regis."

Polly leaned back in her chair, looking far less like a dowager than when she walked in.

"My library," she went on, "is the equal of any private collection in the world. And then there are cousins and aunts and uncles who want to meet you and a heritage you know nothing about. Aside from all that, I'd like to buy you dresses and shoes and ball gowns that your father can't afford and you probably never considered wearing." Polly sat up. "And I'd like you to have fun. I don't think you've had much. You might even come out at Kel Regis—just for the fun of it." Polly leaned forward. "Tyler's a fine man, although it's taken me too long to acknowledge it, but maybe he's not the best person to guide a girl to womanhood."

"I could say the same about you!" Katherine said quickly.

"Touché," Polly replied. "But don't be impertinent."

"I didn't intend to be."

They regarded each other in silence.

"What have you got to lose?" Polly asked.

"You can't seriously believe I'm going to leave my father and my best friend and my school to live in South Carolina with you!"

It was exactly what Polly intended.

"No, of course not," she said. "But you and Tyler might come for Christmas. All our kin spend Christmas at Kel Regis. It would be a perfect opportunity for you to meet everyone." Polly waited, cautiously hopeful when Katherine did not refuse outright.

"What did Tyler say about Christmas?"

"He said it was up to you."

Polly sipped her tea to conceal her determination to take this young creature under her wing. Katherine was that rarity, someone of value.

Like me, Polly exulted. *She's like the best of me.* Having Katherine to shape and to mold would be almost like having a second youth in a more liberal age. She could make of Katherine what she had always wanted to be herself.

But you mustn't let her know that! she warned herself.

"Talk it over with your father," Polly said gently, pulling on her gloves. "You don't have to decide until the last minute. You'll be welcome whenever you come."

They walked to the door.

"You've come a long way," Kate said.

"It was worth the trip."

"I didn't mean the trip."

Polly touched her cheek, oddly moved. "I don't know how it's possible to miss someone I've never met, but I have missed you."

Katherine, coloring, held the door open for her and followed her down the walk to the car. She was still standing on the walk, apparently inured to the cold, when Polly's car pulled out of sight.

"You damn fool," Polly fumed in the backseat of the car. "Look what you almost lost!"

III

"What will you do?" Rebecca asked when Kate had told her everything.

"I'm not sure. What do you think I should do?"

"Travel faster than a speeding bullet to Kel Regis! Why not?"

Kate shook her head. "It annoys me that she just sails in after all those years and expects me to fall at her feet."

"That's not what you said! According to you, she was almost abject once or twice. Come on, Kate, it isn't easy for a grande dame like your grandmother to apologize, especially to a kid."

"I just have the feeling she wants more of me than a Christmas at Kel Regis."

"She wants to give you scads of clothes and a coming-out ball! She sounds like the wicked witch of the South, all right. A debut *is* durance vile." Rebecca waited. "Ah, at last! A smile doth o'erspread her countenance."

"Well, you always spend Christmas with your family in Ohio," Kate said. "So I guess I'll spend Christmas with mine." Kate loved the sound of that.

IV

"I never dreamed it was anything like this," Kate said.

The car had bowled smoothly up a drive lined with majestic oaks until it crested a small rise and, at Tyler's request, stopped so that Kate could see the mansion itself. She had seen pictures of Kel Regis in magazines, but the reality of it, sparkling in the sunlight, was breathtaking.

Eight two-story-high pillars fronted a wide veranda that continued along the wings of the gleaming white brick house. The palladian windows, rising from floor to ceiling, were shuttered in black, and Kel Regis sat serene amid the trees and flowers that fringed its vast and perfect lawn of emerald green.

"Oh, Father." Kate breathed in the almost balmy air. "What a wonderful house it is!"

He nodded.

"Does the name have a meaning?"

"Kel is derived from the Germanic for 'hall' and regis comes from the Latin for 'regal' or 'king.' Charles I, for whom Carolina was named, asserted England's claim to the territory as early as 1629. Charles II granted land to eight of his principal supporters in 1663. Charles Town was named for him. When the first Benedict built here, he called the place Kel Regis—the king's hall."

"But this house is new."

"Not all of it. The center section was the original house; it was rebuilt after Sherman's troops burned down most of South Carolina," Tyler said, signaling the driver to go on. "That was to punish the state for being the first to secede from the Union. It always had beautiful lines, but Polly's responsible for adding the wings and making it the showplace it is."

Polly was waiting for them with Oliver at her side and the family—about thirty of them—gathered behind her on the veranda. Kate was at a loss to know exactly how she was related to each of these debonair men and their slender, soft-spoken, well-dressed women. She couldn't remember any of the names that came at her in such swift profusion—except for the redheaded twins, Ambrose and Arabella Ardmore, Polly's fourteen-year-old great-nephew and great-niece who were called Brosie and Belle and appeared to be as inseparable as they were beautiful. They called Polly "Gran."

They followed Kate inside the wide entrance hall. Its three-story-high atrium made her feel like a bird in flight. There was a magnificent curved mahogany staircase rising to the upper floors; behind hand-carved railings and carpeted galleries, double doors to the master suites ringed the atrium. The twins took Kate to a large square room on the third floor that they said was hers. It had polished plank flooring, brightly colored shag rugs, and wonderfully crafted cherrywood furniture she longed to study more closely—but didn't because the twins would think her a real country mouse.

They lounged on her bed, a four-poster with sheer white muslin hangings and a hand-crocheted bedspread, while Kate unpacked, a chore she declined to let the maid perform.

"I don't know whether we're fourth cousins or first cousins three times removed from Kate," Brosie said.

"Who cares?" Belle scoffed, rapping her brother on his head with the antique lorgnette she wore on a long chain around her neck. Both of them wore gray flannel slacks and blue blazers. Each was the exquisite image of the other.

A new kind of Southern belle, Kate thought. *What would Becca have to say about her?*

"We're just so pleased to see y'all," Belle went on so warmly that Kate felt chastened. "Everyone else is so dreary, it's heaven to have two new faces here."

"They don't look dreary to me," Kate said.

"That's because you don't know them yet."

"What's wrong with them?"

The twins looked at each other. "The usual thing," Brosie said. "The men go whoring and the women drink."

Kate had to laugh. "What's usual about that?"

"This is the Southland, honey," Belle drawled. "There's ten skeletons in every closet."

"I'd just as soon they stayed there," Kate said more sharply than she intended.

Another exchange of looks between the two convinced Kate they had been warned not to mention Sydney and were chafing at the restriction. But the subject was swiftly changed to horses and shooting.

"I ride," Kate said, "but I've never even seen a gun. I don't think I want to. What do you shoot at?"

"We'll start you off on paint cans," Brosie said. "Gran's always having the place painted, so there are plenty around. When you get the hang of it, you can try quail."

"No, thank you," Kate said. "I'm not going to kill any helpless birds."

"Stars above," Belle breathed. "I never thought Yankees were so tender-hearted."

Yankees? Kate echoed silently. *They're still fighting the Civil War!*

She finished putting away her sweaters, socks, and underwear and crossed to the closet to hang up a dress. There were four dresses already there with appropriate shoes and matching coats and even hats. She was startled at the array: a navy sheer wool with a pleated skirt, a beige cashmere suit with a silk shirt, a white crepe afternoon dress, and a long deep blue velvet gown.

"I hope you like them," Belle said, coming to stand next to Kate, who topped her by five inches. "Gran came to Charleston and I helped her pick them out for you." She waited for Kate's reaction.

"They're beautiful," Kate said with mixed feelings. Her own things looked shabby as she hung them up.

Why has she done this? Kate thought.

"Lucky for you Belle went along," Brosie drawled, "or Gran would've done you up like a pincushion in a fancy house."

"Well, so much for unpacking," Kate said. "Will you show me the house?"

Brosie and Belle were eager to show her over the three-story mansion the size of a small hotel, where every room was a gem.

"Except for this one," Brosie said, pushing open a door. "Gran doesn't put anything valuable in here but what you see."

It was a nursery suite. A dozen round-eyed children ranging in age from a few months to a few years, and guarded by four black women, looked up expectantly. The women smiled. Three of the babies cried, and the rest either stared or went back to their play.

"Whose are they?" Kate asked.

"They're ours!" Belle said, blinking at the question.

"Of course, but which is whose?"

Brosie reeled off a list of uncles and aunts and Kate shrugged help-lessly, but she was touched that Belle had included her in ownership of the babies.

Ours, Belle had said. *Mine too,* Kate realized, wrapped in a warm glow because "family" was suddenly more than just Tyler and Kate.

All through the holidays Kate spent hours wandering with the twins over the vast property. They made up hilarious word games so she could remember the names of her relatives. "Felicity flutters and Jane is plain." She was unable to sort out the M's, as her grandfather referred to Maynard and Mercer, the second set of identical twins. The O's, his firstborn twins, had perished during the war, she learned; there were pictures of them all over the house. Pictures of Sydney were notable by their absence.

"Maynard's the one who cracks his knuckles whenever Gran and Grandpa are around," Brosie told her. "Mercer's the one who plays with that rabbit's foot on his watch fob."

The M's ran Benedict Oil & Plastics. Kendall was Benedict Shipping and Brett was Benedict Pharmaceuticals. No one, not even Brosie and Belle, talked about Hilliard, the one who had died two years earlier, and Kate saw no pictures of him either.

All of her new relatives were gracious and genuinely hospitable, and Christmas Eve in the large drawing room, with its sumptuous brocade couches and velvet side chairs in different tones of peach, apricot, coral, honey, and amber, was the occasion for a marvelous party. Outside of the movies, Kate had never seen such a collection of elegantly dressed people in so vast and gorgeous a room, with lovely things to see everywhere she looked. A Greek statue of a glorious young man, naked except for a fig leaf, watched them all with empty eyes. The magnificently framed paintings were from the Impressionist school for the most part, but Polly liked Gainsborough and Picasso's Blue Period as well.

"Notice that there are no ancestors," Brosie pointed out. "Gran put them in the upstairs corridors because she thinks the early Benedicts were an unattractive lot." He grinned. "As you see, the beauty comes from the Ardmores."

"Where does that leave me?" Kate demanded. "I'm a Benedict."

"You're a Ballard too," Belle said, "with a mighty handsome daddy."

Much as Kate liked the twins, she was glad everyone would be leaving before she and Tyler did. It would give her one day to explore Kel Regis on her own. She had fallen in love with it. She wanted to know every stick and stone of the place.

V

She had breakfast alone with her father on that last full day. The house was blissfully quiet with everyone gone, and instead of twenty settings on the flower-decked table in the small dining room there were only two. Polly breakfasted in her room and The Governor, as Kate had come to think of him, had been called back to the capital at Columbia.

On the sideboard were orange juice, bowls of fresh fruit, silver serving dishes whose covers revealed scrambled eggs, bacon, grits, cereal, and breads of every description. It was a prodigal display, typical of the South, Kate thought: in New England people were more frugal; she ran her father's house on a strict budget.

Kate took melon, eggs and bacon, corn bread, and Kel Regis peach preserves and sat down across from Tyler.

"Have you enjoyed your holiday, Father?"

"Very much, Katherine, as I see you have—on the rare occasions when we meet."

She heard the reproof but pretended not to.

"I'm going riding today," she said brightly. "I've been wanting to go out on my own since we came. What will you do?"

"Work," he said as if she should have known that. "I've found some excellent sources I can use for *Medieval Majesty*, and I thought you might take some notes for me today."

That was the last thing she wanted to do! It was a glorious day and Charlie's Darling—Polly's favorite three-year-old—was saddled and waiting, with Kate's lunch of chicken sandwiches and pecan pie and lemonade packed in his saddlebags.

She gathered her forces.

"It can wait until this evening. I promise to do it then."

His disapproval, although silent, was palpable.

"But, Tyler, we're leaving tomorrow," Kate said, and steeled herself for the reproach she knew was coming.

"If a horse is more important to you than I am, the notes will indeed have to wait."

Kate got up to go before her conscience could get the better of her. It would have sent her straight into the shadowy confines of the library.

An unaccustomed resentment—or had it only been unacknowledged?—spurred her escape. Tyler always expected her to subordinate her plans to his, and she always did, reluctant to displease him in any way as, she was still persuaded, she had displeased her mother— or why else had Sydney deserted her?

She had never refused him before. She knew that if they'd stayed at home, she would have worked right through the Christmas holidays without thinking twice about it.

"But we're not home," she told Charlie's Darling as they left the stable yard at a walk. "We're here in this heavenly place and I want to do what I want to do!"

Resolutely, she determined to enjoy the day. She was soon lost in the expanse of tranquil nature, in bird calls and the fragrance of the loblolly pines. She picnicked under a weeping willow while Charlie's Darling nibbled at the grass and drank noisily from the stream. She was alone, but beauty *did* speak to Kate and she knew she would never be lonely here.

She dozed in the shade of the willow tree, sunlight filtering through its lacy leaves to caress her skin, and tried to decide how far she could give in. Polly had apparently forgotten that on Kate's part, this visit was an experiment. Polly had been busy with her family, on some occasions as preoccupied as the woman who lived in a shoe, on others a serenely gracious Lady Bountiful, but never too busy for a smile and a pat and a word with Katherine. Polly made it seem as if they had always known each other, as if she were Kate's "Gran" as she was Brosie's and Belle's.

But however charming she was, Polly had done a terrible thing. For the fourteen years Kate had been alive, Polly had never acknowledged her. She had been totally unforgiving, not only toward Sydney, who turned out to have deserved it, but toward Sydney's husband and daughter as well. Now, for some mysterious reason, she wanted to wipe the slate clean as if those years of rejection had never been.

And she expected instant forgiveness.

"Aye, there's the rub," Kate said, making Charlie's Darling prick up his ears. "I can't give her that. Even if I wanted to, Tyler would disown me for it."

But she could leave the connection intact and see what developed.

Her decision made, she spent the day peacefully, searching out her favorite spots, drinking in the magic of Kel Regis. She was back by four, did the notes for Tyler, and enjoyed listening to Polly and Tyler argue about the reasons for the popularity of *Gunsmoke, Bonanza,* and *Mr. Ed.* And then the holiday was over.

VI

"I'm very glad I came," she told Polly the next morning. "Thank you for inviting me."

They sat in the morning room, a cozy place with French doors that opened onto the veranda where Brumby rockers were ranged like old soldiers. Beyond them lay Polly's gardens and the back lawn sloping down to the river. The room itself had comfortable chairs, side tables piled with books and newspapers, and well-placed reading lamps.

"Now that you know the way," Polly said, "you're to come anytime you like. Your room will always be ready."

"But I can't . . . just barge in."

"Of course you can. You belong at Kel Regis. This is my private telephone number. It rings here and in Columbia. You call anytime you want to come and I'll make the travel arrangements for you."

Taking the card, Kate regarded her grandmother quizzically. Despite everything, she was beginning to like Polly. More than that, it was hard to resist anyone who wanted her that much. Her mother hadn't, and Tyler, although she knew he loved her, was not given to saying so. It was overwhelming to be openly wanted. Kel Regis was irresistible. Having all those aunts and uncles and cousins was a revelation.

"You're trying to buy me," Kate said, struggling against an impulse to surrender completely. "With your beautiful house and your gardens and Charlie's Darling, with clothes and cousins and southern charm—and everything."

"Yes, I am. Is it so wrong to try every way I can think of to get something I want so much? Is this such a terrible place to be?"

"You know it's paradise, but you must believe me when I say I'm not coming to live here. I know that's what you want, but I'll never leave my father."

"I never supposed you would come here to live," Polly lied briskly. "But I hope you'll visit often. Someday, though, you'll marry and leave your father."

"No." Kate was adamant. "I will never marry. I want to teach."

"Those are big decisions for a woman to be making so early on. Why not wait and see?"

"Did you? You were married when you were *seventeen*!"

"I had no choice in the matter, my girl. As it happens, I fell in love with my husband on my honeymoon, so it worked out well."

"But so young! That's almost *medieval*!"

Polly smiled. "You like working on *Medieval Majesty* for Tyler, don't you?"

"Oh, yes. But a lot of what I learn makes me angry. Married off at nine, some of the girls were, even though they didn't consummate until menstruation. Imagine being deflowered at eleven years old!"

This is about history, not sex, so don't you dare bat an eye! Polly warned herself, taken aback, not by what this snip of a girl was saying but by the matter-of-fact way she said it. What kind of environment had Sydney created?

"And then," Kate went on, eyes bright with indignation, "if their husbands stayed home, they had babies every ten months until they died. If the men went on crusade, they were clapped into chastity belts, some of them made of *iron!*"

"I think chastity belts were the exception, not the rule," Polly said, relieved that none of the maiden aunts, without benefit of Kate's unusually liberal education, was within earshot. Polly was not priggish, but the times still were despite rebellion from the young. "In any case, you *do* have a choice, so keep your options open."

"I haven't thanked you properly for my Christmas gift," Kate said after a moment, looking at the ring on her finger. It was a small circlet of diamond chips around a pavé *K*. Kate had never owned a ring, much less an heirloom, as this one obviously was.

"It belonged to your many times great-aunt Katherine on your grandfather's side," Polly said. In fact, she had ordered it in Charleston the day she returned from Harmony. "I think there's a portrait of her somewhere around. I'll find it for you and put it in your room."

Kate looked at her skeptically.

"More seduction," Polly confessed with a smile.

"Like the clothes."

"You didn't wear them."

"No. I couldn't embarrass my father. It would have meant he couldn't afford to dress me properly."

"I don't think he'd have noticed," Polly said. "Tyler hasn't much interest in women's clothes, wouldn't you agree? But never mind, I'll keep them for you. Have you decided what to call me?"

"Polly, if that's all right."

"Polly's fine. I shall call you Kate. Katherine's too austere for such a young person."

When Kate and Tyler left, Polly waved them off. She was not totally dwarfed, even by the soaring pillars. "Safe journey," she called. "And both of you come back for Easter, hear?"

"You're incorrigible," said Dodie Phelps when Polly went back inside.

"I'll do anything," Polly said. "I must have that girl living here with me. It'll do her a world of good."

"Oh, Polly, you aren't fooling anyone! You want it for yourself, not for her."

"Why couldn't it be for both of us?" Polly demanded.

"Polly Benedict, what are you up to?"

"You'd be surprised" was all Polly would say.

6

I

Kate stood up on the pedals and pumped harder to get up the hill. She turned her head to see the view from the road: the white sand reached out to the water, the wind riffled the dune grass, and the gulls swooped, shrieking with joy. But Kate was in too much of a hurry to stop and drink it in as she usually did. The lobsters in her bicycle basket wriggled in their paper sack, and she wanted to get to the cottage to put them in the old aquarium that served as a lobster tank.

The summer was half over. Summer on the Cape was her favorite season, but this year Kate was impatient for it to end and college to begin. She was going to Wakefield. It was what she wanted and it would have been foolish not to go just because Polly wanted it too. She had reached a modus vivendi with her grandmother: as long as Polly didn't try to direct her life—Kate was determined that no one would ever do that—Kate would accept her largesse graciously.

Besides, Kate could hardly refuse an opportunity to spend weekends at Kel Regis. The house had thoroughly seduced her. It had made their home in Harmony seem tacky, however comfortable it was, and the cottage here on the Cape downright shabby.

Her relationship with Polly was bizarre: an affection—reluctant on Kate's side—had grown between them, but Kate was still wary of her grandmother's motives.

II

"She wants something," Kate had told Rebecca just before their high school graduation. "And I can't figure out what it is."

"Well, you want something too."

Kate was indignant. "I don't! I've never asked her for a thing."

57

"You don't have to. She showers you with gifts whether you ask or not: clothes, a horse, and a riding habit with English boots to write a sonnet about, a private sitting room and bedroom done over for you at Kel Regis, pearls! And you're as crazy about the old plantation as she is, no matter how much you downplay it for my benefit."

"I've always wanted to invite you, you know that!"

Rebecca shrugged. "Polly doesn't share your enthusiasm for me," she said sourly.

"That's what I mean!" Kate said. "That's part of it. Why doesn't she want you there? Why doesn't she like you? She doesn't even know you!"

"Jealous, I guess. She wants you to herself."

"But why?"

"She loves you," Rebecca said with a dubious grin. "Years after you were born she had a change of spots."

"Polly's never done anything for love in all her life. She always has other reasons. Sometimes I can hear her wheels turning. And look how she's wound Tyler around her little finger!"

"Everybody knows Tyler only pretended to be a scholarly recluse so he wouldn't have to face people after Sydney left." Rebecca glanced at Kate, but there was no reaction. She went on. "The truth is that he loves being the sage of Harmony College, the pastoral elder statesman. When Polly invites people to Kel Regis to worship at his shrine, it polishes his ego. No one else but you has ever done that for him."

"No one but you has ever done it for me," Kate said, throwing her arms around Rebecca.

Once, loyalty—or was it need?—would have kept her home to go to Harmony with Rebecca, but Rebecca was wrapped up in getting Theo to propose to her and Kate was determined to teach and to write and to win her own Pulitzer Prizes. *That* would make Sydney sit up and take notice!

So Kate wanted Wakefield. Tyler, vindicated by his welcome at Kel Regis, wanted it too. Theo agreed.

"Among women's colleges there's the Ivy League and *then* there are the Rolls Royces: Wakefield and Brooke Parrish."

He told her that while they danced together at her senior prom.

III

She had not expected to go, and she wanted to, Lord, how she *wanted* to! But it was hopeless: boys were more uncomfortable with her than she was with them. Girls, too, although there was something about Kate, apart from her protector, Rebecca, that kept them from being really nasty. Some of them even confided in her about their crushes because everyone knew that Kate never broke a confidence.

But what good was it to be everybody's confidante when her only possible escort to the senior prom was her father? Much as she loved him, she could not bring herself to walk into the midst of all those young couples on Tyler's arm. It would be a confession to the world that she was not attractive to boys, the worst kind of failure a girl could suffer. No one ever said it, but every female on the planet knew it by the time she was two years old and started flirting with Daddy.

"Have you got your dress for the prom?" Theo had asked her one night when they were doing dishes in the kitchen. Tyler, reading his paper in the study, had no idea that such an event was approaching, much less what misery it caused Kate. She hid it well. Theo knew only because Rebecca had told him.

"I'm not going," Kate said, scrubbing a pot vigorously. "I have a lot to do before I leave for Kel Regis."

Theo put his arm around her, and the checked dishtowel he was holding trailed damply against her back. "Kate," he said softly, "it's no crime to be tall, but it sure as hell can be heartbreaking at your age."

She nodded, dashing her tears away.

"It isn't so bad for boys," he went on, "but I still felt like a left shoe. Brilliance, however, is another matter." He hugged her. "Male or female, brilliance like yours makes ordinary people feel inferior and they resent you for that. If you're a woman, they make you think something's wrong with you. If you're different, they try to exclude you." He turned her face up to his and mopped it with the clammy towel. "Kate, you're too intelligent to let your life be ruined by foolish, worthless people who reject what they don't understand—and that includes your mother. You're not responsible for what Sydney is."

She looked up at him and nodded again, knowing he was right and overcome that he knew so much about her hidden self. Then she realized that Rebecca had told him. Ordinarily, Kate would have been furious, but this was no stranger. This was Theo, the closest Kate had to an uncle.

"I'd like to take you to your prom," he said with such a winning smile that she smiled back even as she hesitated.

"Your idea or Becca's?"

"Mine. It just popped into my head. Come on, Kate. Think what a learning experience it will be for those gawky boys to share a dance floor with the likes of us." They had danced well together on the few occasions they had tried it. Theo was a good teacher.

"I'll tell you tomorrow."

He shook his head. "You don't need Rebecca's permission."

"No," she agreed after a moment's consideration. "I don't. Yes, Theo, I'll go with you, and thank you for asking."

She had hurried him upstairs to her room to show him the dress she had bought with savings from her housekeeping money and hidden. The bodice was white jersey and the skirt layers of white chiffon, all of it polyester except the effect. A splash of sequins spilled down the side from waist to floor.

"Smashing," he said, touched by her excitement as she showed him the shoes and gloves and evening bag, things she hadn't even shown Rebecca, things she might never have worn but kept hidden at the back of her closet like her longing and her hurt.

Dammit all, Tyler, Theo protested silently, *are you blind? Maybe Sydney had good reason to leave you!*

But it was not Theo's place to teach fathering to a man who hadn't the least notion of that art—and heaven help anyone who mentioned his ex-wife!

Rebecca was delighted by the news—until she saw Kate and Theo dancing together. It was the first time in her life that Rebecca wished she were tall, like Kate.

IV

Wakefield was all Kate thought about after graduation.

"A collegiate nunnery," Rebecca had mocked only the night before as the girls were getting ready for bed. "The custodian of southern virginity."

Kate wondered why Rebecca had been so testy since graduation. It wasn't envy of Kate's Benedict connection: not even Kel Regis could have diverted Rebecca from making a career out of marriage to Theo Barrows.

And it wasn't resentment because Becca's family couldn't afford to send her anywhere but Harmony. Harmony was exactly where Becca wanted to be because she would see Theo every time he came to visit Dr. Ballard.

"And I must see him or I'll die!" Rebecca had groaned, hugging her pillow. "I'm insane about him."

"You've been insane about something or other since you were born," Kate said.

"This is different! And I *will* marry him, see if I don't! I knew it the first time I saw him."

"But does Theo know it?"

"He will soon." Rebecca was sullenly insistent.

"Oh, Becca," Kate said softly, anxious about what Rebecca would do if Theo didn't agree. "How can you be so sure?"

"I'll get him to take me to bed. He wants to, I can tell. Then he'll have to marry me. He's that kind of man."

"Do you want to trick him into marriage?"

"I want Theo any way I can get him. Besides, sex is the first thing men want of women, there's no point denying it. And Theo loves me. He just doesn't know how much."

"You're obsessed," Kate said.

"I'm in love." Rebecca had fired the pillow at Kate and sat up, her lovely face flushed, the urgency in her voice turning suddenly to anger. "I could kill you for letting Theo take you to the senior prom."

"You're not serious!"

"I sure as hell am! How do you think I felt, standing there with my stupid date and watching you dance with the only man I'll ever love."

"You should have told me how you felt when he asked me!" Kate protested.

"You should have known."

"He asked only because no one else wanted to take me, not even my father. I was so grateful I almost cried. I like Theo a lot, but just because you're in love with him doesn't mean I am. You're the one he can't stop looking at. Why are you behaving like a brat?"

Kate's anger, rare as it was, always brought Becca down from her high horse. Chastened, she had hugged Kate and apologized. "I'll be my normal, adorable self for the rest of the summer," she promised.

V

"So all of us are happy now," Kate mused as the cottage came into view, "even Tyler."

Over the past three years Tyler had grown accustomed to the luxury of Kel Regis, a place Theo called "the hottest political watering hole in the country." People in government, industry, and academia vied for invitations to the house Rebecca had called "Polly's Folly."

Its political importance was due in no small measure to Theo and the superb campaign he had run for Oliver's election to the United States Senate—"which makes Theo the hottest political consultant in Washington," Rebecca said proudly.

Theo had recruited Tyler with his two Pulitzer Prizes to keep that campaign on an exalted plane, and the whole production had made Kel Regis a mecca for image-conscious politicians from out of state and abroad. Senator Benedict was enthusiastic about Theo and The Senator's Wife was pleased with him.

"If there'd been a Theo Barrows twenty years ago," Polly declared, "Oliver would be president."

"Oh, Polly, please," Kate objected. "The Senator never wanted to be president."

"If women let men do only what men want to do, we'd be in a rare mess."

Kate and Polly went through many variations of that theme on the telephone. It was Polly's conviction that women were made to govern and had always done so but, alas, from behind the scenes, sitting on their men's laps, as it were. Women's place in politics alternated with another of Polly's grievances.

"You should have spent the summer here," Polly lamented in her daily telephone calls. "Especially now. If you arrive a week before term starts, there won't be time enough for proper fittings."

"How much fitting can a pleated skirt require?" Kate replied.

"If you're making your debut at Christmas, you'll need a lot more than pleated skirts. And the parties will start long before then."

"Polly, I won't leave Rebecca before I absolutely must, not when we're about to be separated for the first time in our lives."

"I don't know what you see in that girl," Polly grumbled.

"Brains, beauty, and the best friend anyone ever had. I love her very much."

Rebecca had always been her rock, the one person who always had time to listen, to commiserate, to argue, to laugh. Sometimes Kate dreaded facing the world without Rebecca at her side.

Kate braked to a stop and put her bike in the rack. She put the palpitating sack on the table, filled the aquarium with water, and had just dumped the lobsters into it when she heard Rebecca laugh. Wanting to join the fun, she followed the sound upstairs to a storeroom at the back of the cottage.

VI

Rebecca had been in the tiny room for some time, letting one of the boys from Princeton take great liberties. Her T-shirt was up around her neck and her bra was pushed up over her breasts, but if she didn't count his exposed penis, they had been fully clothed until a minute ago, when he reached under her miniskirt and pulled off her panties.

His fingers played with her pubic hair and then slipped inside her, exploring the wet folds. It felt nice enough, but she wished he knew where the right place was. Most boys didn't. Still, she was not there for her own pleasure. She was there to learn more about ministering to his.

She clasped his penis with a milking motion and he groaned with pleasure.

"Let me go inside, Becca, please," he pleaded.

"And get me pregnant?" Rebecca laughed. It was the laugh that had pealed down the staircase and into the kitchen, where Kate and the lobsters were.

"I've got a rubber."

"Then put it on."

He did that quickly, and she opened her knees wide to let him get inside her. He had just climbed on top of her when Kate opened the door, saw them, gasped, and plunged back along the corridor and down the stairs. Rebecca heard the door to the kitchen slam shut.

"Jesus H. Christ, I thought you said there was nobody here!" the boy sputtered, stuffing himself, condom and all, inside his zipper and his T-shirt inside his jeans. "We're going to catch holy hell for this."

"No, we aren't," Becca said calmly, pulling on her panties. "Kate won't tell."

"What makes you so sure?"

"Because I won't let her."

VII

The boy left hastily and Becca smoothed her hair and went down to the kitchen. Kate sat at the table, head down on her crossed arms, shoulders shaking. Rebecca sat down next to her.

"Come on, Kate. It wasn't as bad as all that."

Kate looked up and Becca was astonished to see that she was laughing, even though her eyes were mirthless.

"It was ridiculous, you lying there like a chicken about to be stuffed and that fool climbing all over you with his stick shift out! Is that what sex is about?"

"There's more to it than that," Rebecca said.

"I'm from Missouri," Kate scoffed. "But even if there is more, dammit, Rebecca, do it somewhere else!"

"And have someone else walk in on us instead of you?"

"I wouldn't have walked in if I'd known! How was I supposed to know?"

"I'm not blaming you. I thought you'd be longer buying the lobsters than you were. He was supposed to be gone by the time you got back."

They sat in silence for a moment.

"You're not going to tell, are you?" Rebecca asked.

"Tell? Who? My father? Your mother? No, I'm not going to tell. Just find some other place, that's all."

"Okay, okay. But sex is normal, Kate. It doesn't have to be a disease the way it is with Sydney. Lots of women make love and not all of them are trollops."

Kate moved so quickly that Rebecca couldn't ward off the stinging slap on her cheek. They stared at each other.

"God, I'm sorry," Rebecca said with all the contrition she could muster. "I'll never say it again."

After a moment, Kate looked at her. "How can you do it with someone else if you're in love with Theo?"

"I'm doing it *for* Theo, don't you see? I want to make him happy. I'll be so good in bed, he'll never look at another woman."

"Your logic leaves a lot to be desired," Kate said.

They lapsed into silence until Kate asked, "Did you really do it?"

"Almost," Rebecca said, which was true enough today. Actually she had been doing it for over a year, but Kate would never understand that those boys were guinea pigs. "I thought this was my big moment."

"Until I blundered in to save you from a fate worse than death!" Kate laughed shakily, on the verge of tears now, and Rebecca laughed, too, until they were staggering around the kitchen, clutching their aching stomachs, laughing and crying at the same time.

"If you're a virgin for the rest of your life," Kate gasped, "it'll be my fault."

"If *you* are, it won't be mine. If it's the last thing I do, I'm going to get you devirginized before the summer's over. Seventeen is too old to be lingering on the vine."

"Don't waste your time." Kate reached for the paper napkins, passed one to Rebecca, and mopped her face. "I'm not interested."

It took Rebecca an hour to remind Kate that the world had changed. It was 1967! Women had as much right to sex as men did; waiting around for marriage was horribly square. She persuaded Kate that at the very least, she should get the first time over with and wrung from Kate a promise that she would be nice to a few of the summer boys, no matter how insipid she thought they were.

Kate dreaded the idea, although she still wept over *Wuthering Heights* and *Brief Encounter*, wept for what they told her of passion beyond anyone's power to deny it and of love that was as sublime as it was physical.

It was not only romantic longing that troubled her. She had more love to give than anyone wanted, and there were times when the force of it swelled in Kate's breast until she thought it would break its barriers and drown her. It was not the kind of love she could spend on her father because it demanded as much as it offered and Tyler was too immersed in his work, as Rebecca was in Theo. It was the sort of love that demanded trust, and Kate did not totally trust Polly.

Kate could no longer avoid it: it was the love between men and women that obsessed and menaced her. To judge from her parents' experience, sex was at once the ultimate expression of love and the greatest threat to it. Once satisfied, the craving turned to another object.

"Choose the one you like the most and I'll set it up," Rebecca said.

At length Kate chose Wade Stevens, a Yalie sophomore six inches taller than she was who was bound to make the varsity basketball team. She even developed a crush on him because he was blond and sweet and good-looking, Kate's one-time vision of a romantic hero.

"That innocent!" Becca teased when Kate finally announced her choice. "How much can he know about sex?"

"Maybe that's why I like him."

"Katherine Ballard, you're a hopeless romantic."

There *was* no denying it. A corner of Kate's soul yearned for romance, try as she did to insulate herself against the impulse that had debased her mother.

Sex was an enormous threat to Kate and it was growing. She could feel it in her tingling breasts, in her curiosity about the actual sensation of coupling, in the frightening cravings of her body that were sometimes stronger than all the discipline she could summon. It made her helpless to resist her own touch, the one thing she did that Rebecca knew nothing about.

Afterward she always searched the dark room, expecting to find Sydney there, laughing at her because, for all Kate's strivings to be different, the apple hadn't rolled far from the tree.

Still, Rebecca was right. Sex was built into every living creature on earth and if Kate were not to be ruled by it, logic insisted that her best hope was to confront it and, in so doing, reduce it to absurdity.

VIII

It was very dark in the Stevenses' boat house, and the sofa groaned faintly under them. Wade was on top of Kate, his mouth pressed down on hers, forcing the inside of her lip against her teeth until she opened her mouth and let his tongue slip inside. For a week they had spent their evenings necking and each night she had let him do a little more, led on as much by her own purpose, she liked to think, as by his appetite. Lately, though, her own appetite was rising.

Right now his hand was under her T-shirt and inside her bra, stroking one breast. It felt lovely, definitely not absurd. He smelled pleasantly of soap and toothpaste and the gin they had been drinking, and his body was hard and smooth and warm, like hers, from a fresh kiss of the sun that afternoon.

Wade deftly opened her bra and pulled it down. His head moved down to take a nipple in his mouth and suck it. She felt an answering throb between her legs.

It was going to happen, she knew that. She wanted it to. But suddenly she wanted it to be sweet, not merely physical. She wanted to love him and she wanted him to love her with such fierce longing that hot tears sprang up behind her lids. She kissed him lingeringly and let herself slide into the other time and other place of her imagination.

It was wartime and the gift of herself to the officer who loved her was a lucky charm that would bring him safely home.

"You've got beautiful boobs," Wade said, teasing her nipple with the tip of his tongue.

She didn't listen to him.

She was a nurse and her body was all she had to give to a lover dying of a rare disease.

"You're a good kisser," Wade said, his mouth against hers and his hand on her belly.

She was Héloise and he was Abélard and they thought the world and heaven well lost for love.

He opened the fly of his jeans and guided her hand down to his groin. She had touched it before, that alien, silken, turgid flesh, and she squeezed it because she knew he liked her to.

"Oh, wow," he groaned, and for the first time his hand reached under her skirt and inside her panties. "Let's do it, Kate," he muttered, sliding his fingers back and forth inside the cleft between her legs.

Her imagination was no match for that sudden invasion, or for the broad finger that now snaked inside her and squirmed within her very core. The crassness of it wrenched her back to the lumpy sofa and the stark realization that this was not about love or even passion but rather the heavy-handed fumblings of a lusty boy in a boat house just like the one Sydney went to on her wedding day. Sydney had rutted like this when she was already pregnant with Kate, a Sydney not pure and lovely as she was in the bridal photo, but wanton, hiding in a dark place to do her dirty little business with a man named Royal, to do what Kate was doing now.

"No!" she cried, pushing Wade so suddenly that he fell off the couch.

"What the hell? What's going on?"

"I've changed my mind," she said, hooking her bra, putting herself in order. "I'm going home. I'm sorry, I really am, but I . . . just . . . can't." And she fled before he could get to his feet.

"Bitch!" he shouted after her. "Frigid *cunt*!" And then he hurled the ultimate insult: *"EGGHEAD!"*

She ran home as fast as she could, slowing only to enter the cottage without disturbing Tyler, then speeding up the stairs, dropping her clothes on her way to the shower. She cried as she stood under the warm water, soaping herself.

"I will *not* be like you, you miserable bitch!" she wept. "I'd rather die than be like you."

She heard Rebecca in their bedroom. A moment later she opened the door to the bathroom, talking in a stage whisper over the sound of the water.

"What happened?"

"Nothing! But I hated it! I don't give a damn what you say, I hated it!" Kate turned off the water, grabbed a towel, and got out of the shower, her eyes red with weeping and her expression frantic. "I know you like it and my mother is driven by it and the whole damn world revolves around it and people write books and poems and give all they have for it but I *don't like it* and that's the way it is so get off my back about it and leave me alone!"

"All right," Rebecca said soothingly. "All right. But someday you'll fall in love."

"I'll never fall enough in love for that."

"Famous last words," Rebecca muttered under her breath.

IX

"I hope you'll like it," Polly said, standing in the doorway while Kate surveyed her new suite on the second floor of Kel Regis. The furniture in the sitting room was fruitwood, the upholstery was English glazed chintz in a narrow stripe of apricot and blue and the curtains on the floor-to-ceiling windows were pale, sheer apricot under matching watered-silk draperies.

"I never considered you a pink person," Polly remarked, watching Kate's delighted expression. "Apricot is far more sophisticated, don't you agree?"

There were two apricot velvet love seats, a large desk partnered by a serious-looking chair, and a comfortable wing chair flanked by a standing lamp and an early American workbasket for the crocheting Kate liked to do.

"I asked myself," Polly went on, "what kind of room a tall, quiet person who loves books would want." She gestured to the shelves that covered one wall, half filled but with plenty of space left open for Kate's personal choices. "And there's a stereo," Polly said, opening a console.

"There's everything!" Kate said, going into a bedroom decorated in apricot and white. "It's perfect. I'll never be able to thank you."

"Oh, you'll find a way. I ordered some plainer stuff to do up your rooms at Wakefield, and in here"—she beckoned Kate to a dressing room—"are dresses for you to choose from so you can start your fittings tomorrow morning."

Kate surveyed the long racks filled with sportswear, day dresses, cocktail clothes, and ball gowns.

"Tell me, Polly, just what does this debut business involve?"

"Luncheons, tea dances, cocktail parties, dinners, cotillions, balls."

"What a waste of time and energy! What about studying?"

Polly busied herself opening drawers and straightening neat piles of gloves, stockings, underthings, sweaters. "You'll have plenty of time for that during the week and in your second semester. You'll spend weekends here, and then there's the Thanksgiving weekend for your tea dance and the Christmas holiday for the rest. Your ball will be on New Year's Eve." Polly smiled. "No one will ever forget it."

Kate nodded. "I'll bet they won't. But what's it all in aid of?"

"In life," Polly said, folding her hands and looking very regal in one of her Queen Mother dresses with a dog collar of pearls, "it isn't only who you know, it's who knows you. Whatever you decide to be, you need to know the right people."

"And I'll meet the right people by going to debutante parties until I drop?"

Polly nodded. "It's the opening salvo of the campaign."

"And which campaign is that?" Kate demanded, hoping that this time she would discover what Polly had in mind for her.

"Whatever you choose. Maybe marriage to one of the debutante's brothers and a life of domestic tranquility."

Kate shook her head. "I have no intention of marrying."

"Fine! Marriage should be a woman's last choice. A career, then."

"You know I want to teach."

"Yes. Well, I'm only here to help."

"Pure poppycock, Grandmother. You want something. What is it?"

"To make sure you get what you go after."

"Provided it's what you want me to go after."

"Only if you want it too."

"What is it, then, Polly, that you want me to want so much?"

"All in the fullness of time, Kate."

Kate paused before she said it, knowing she was about to cross a line. "You're trying to make it up to Sydney, aren't you? I mean all those years of excommunication."

Polly's face froze. "I have nothing to make up to Sydney," she said sternly. "I've spent more time and money than you can imagine cleaning up after that girl's messes. I have nothing at all to make up. You once refused to discuss your mother. Let's keep to that bargain."

Kate nodded.

"I wish you would just relax and enjoy life, Kate," Polly went on, lapsing into her usual mode of expression—cool, bantering, occasionally blunt. "I'm sure I don't know where you get your suspicious nature."

"From you, no doubt."

Polly laughed. "Time you changed for dinner. We're formal tonight, but no bare shoulders. Among others, we have the French ambassador and our party chairman with his unfortunate wife—you know, the one with the giggle. And the governor. Oh, yes, Brosie and Belle are here. She wanted to room with you at Wakefield, but I told her you preferred to room alone."

"The twins will be miserable apart," Kate said, thinking of herself and Rebecca. Brosie was going to Duke.

"Nonsense!" Polly was annoyed. "They've been allowed to carry on far too long as it is. It's unhealthy for a brother and sister to be that close. High time they were separated. Shall I send Belle up to keep you company while you change?"

"No. I adore her, but I need a little time to absorb all of this magnificence. I won't be long. And thank you, Polly, thank you sincerely for everything."

Polly waved a hand and sailed away and Kate walked through the rooms again, feeling not quite so tall under the high ceilings but aware that in her gray skirt and black sweater she struck a monastic note in such sybaritic surroundings.

On impulse she went to the telephone and called Rebecca, describing everything and wondering, finally, how she was going to get through all of those parties. "There isn't anything less like a southern belle," she finished, "than Sister Kate."

"There comes a time," Rebecca said, "when you draw a deep breath and just let life take you. You're a Benedict. Their traditions are part of your life, and the time to let life take you is now."

"I wish you were here, Becca."

"I don't. Theo will be here tomorrow."

"Will you let life take you?"

"Oh, yes. Yes, yes, yes, yes, yes!"

"I wish you love, Rebecca. I miss you."

"You're a good old girl, Kate. I miss you too."

Kate put the receiver back in its cradle, her eyes misty at this parting of the ways. It was more than distance that separated them now; it was the vast difference between two natures.

Then she gave herself a little shake and changed quickly to one of her new dinner gowns, a white crepe embroidered in crystal beads.

She went out to the first floor gallery and started down the superb staircase, relieved that life would take her in her way and not Rebecca's. If it was not as exciting, it was far more secure.

And if something in her longed for more, she let the longing go, like some gorgeous, unattainable butterfly fluttering about the lofty atrium of Kel Regis.

BOOK II

7

1976

I

Kate put her collar up and her head down against the March wind whistling past Oxford's stately stone buildings, which always seemed to her like castles in their keeps—cold, damp castles, not very much more comfortable than her little flat. She had a microscopic bedroom, a sitting room largely occupied by her desk, a kitchenette hidden behind a screen, and a bathroom where four inches of hot water seemed to be all she could get.

The flat had been home for five years and sometimes, wearing gloves while she worked because the electric fire didn't help much, she thought of Kel Regis with longing—even of Harmony and the Cape. People scoffed at Americans for a lot of reasons, but one thing Yankees did well was comfort.

Another blast of frigid wind pushed her along the street, but she was too deep in thought to notice. She was trying to decide whether her doctoral thesis should begin with the fourteenth-century surge of legalized bordellos, built on the belief that these "nature's work-shops" would save virtuous wives from rape, or with the earlier clois-tering of women because their weak natures could not resist worldly temptations.

Her topic was "A medieval view of female sexuality and its effect on women's status." It was not a feminist diatribe, but no matter how clinically Kate presented it, some of the material was both appalling and lurid.

"I haven't colored it," Kate had pointed out to her supervisor, a pale gentleman in his fifties with a long, thin face and bushy salt-and-pepper hair, who was poring over the section on chastity belts.

"I should think not indeed! If these are the facts, they're shocking enough." He had glanced at her over his glasses, waiting.

She knew he was questioning her objectivity, as if her judgment had been compromised by her outrage over those devices of leather and iron clapped between women's legs and padlocked to prevent adultery while their husbands fought the infidels for Jerusalem.

Kate had leaned forward in her chair, exasperated but not showing it. She spoke softly in her husky voice.

"Actually, the chastity belts weren't as cruel as some things still being done today. Do you know that in parts of Sudan little girls are routinely mutilated and sewn up to protect their virginity? In Egypt removal of part or all of the clitoris—sometimes with a razor—is commonplace among girls of good family and has been for centuries. Sometimes a lot more than that is removed. Some of them bleed to death."

"Good Lord!" His fair skin had turned blotchy; it made Kate wonder briefly if he were homosexual and repelled by female anatomy in the first place.

"No one has ever explained," she had continued implacably, "why the deity provided both sexes with erotic potential if only one is meant to fulfill it. The theory has usually been that women are by nature too morally frail to deal with pleasurable sex. They would rush out to cuckold their husbands and then honor would demand that they be banished or, in some places, stoned to death. Woman as the embodiment of erotic temptation is not a new idea, nor are the cruel and unusual punishments used to repay her power to drive men to folly. Chastity belts are benign by comparison to some of them."

He had not questioned her objectivity again.

More than four years of research had taken her to dusty archives in the Sorbonne and the University of Heidelberg, as well as to the library here at Oxford and the British Museum in London. She had completed the greater part of her research the previous year and started to write her thesis in her small flat. She loved the long, quiet hours alone, steeped in the mind-set of long ago. The world of scholarship was familiar to her. It was safe. It was where she belonged.

Now Kate shivered and quickened her step. The air was foggy with that mist that is a boon to English complexions and the bane of English bones. Maybe it was the climate that accounted for British reserve—how could you be expansive when you were cold and damp? —but it was that very reserve that made Kate feel more comfortable among them than she would have been at home, where the sexual revolution was in full spate and people, she was told, went on television to tell the world their most intimate secrets.

Home! She had missed Kel Regis painfully over the last four years —she had gone back only once, for Belle's wedding—but she missed it most in summer, when the house was crowded with Benedicts and

Ardmores, with her pale, chic aunts and her tall, tanned uncles and their children and grandchildren, with Arabella and her husband and baby, and Ambrose, "a rogue male still unattached," Arabella wrote, "despite Gran's orders that he take unto himself a wife."

II

Kate and Belle had gone to Wakefield together. They had come out together at Kel Regis. "A tribal embarrassment," Kate called it at the time.

"I'm too tall to wear white organza and carry a bouquet," she had complained. "Debs should be dainty little things like Arabella."

"You look perfect," Polly had insisted. "If you tried, you might even have a good time."

While they were at Wakefield, Ambrose brought Kate date after date from Duke, everything from bespectacled philosophy majors to pre-med students to football players.

"But what a bizarre quartet we make," he teased afterward. "Reluctant Kate and the silent boy of the evening."

"And Belle and Brosie, identical and inseparable and snickering over my discomfiture," Kate countered.

"Don't let Gran know we double-date," Brosie often reminded Kate. "She'd have a stroke. She wants to separate us."

"You'd think we'd been up to something evil," Belle scoffed, tossing her red mane.

"Don't talk rot! We're trying to see that Cousin Kate has the social life Gran wants her to have."

But Cousin Kate had little interest in dating. She had earned her bachelor's degree in three years instead of four by working through the summers. It provoked Polly to amused comment.

"What is this unmaidenly compulsion to keep your head buried in a book?"

"You know I love to study! Especially history."

"That's Tyler's fell influence."

"It's no worse than yours. You want me to come down to Democratic headquarters and stuff envelopes, or ring doorbells, or go to bridal showers and engagement parties and catch the bouquets you bribe the brides to fling at me."

"Socializing is part of the human condition. For a woman it's essential."

"Maybe, but I feel a lot safer in the past than in the present."

That was never more true than at the end of her freshman year, when she went to Harmony for Rebecca's wedding, arriving the day before.

III

The weather forecast was for a perfect day.

"It can't rain." Rebecca smiled, uncharacteristically serene while Kate drank coffee at the kitchen table and Marjorie Salter filled meringue shells with whipped cream. "We can't possibly stuff everyone into the house, so the reception has to be in our garden spilling over into yours."

Rebecca looked lovelier than ever, younger, too, with her translucent skin and bright blue eyes. She seemed to float in her own patch of sunlight.

That's what happens, Kate reminded herself, *when your dreams come true.*

But Kate had doubts about this marriage, doubts she couldn't hide from Theo during the rehearsal that evening. They sat in a pew at the back of the church and watched Rebecca and her father make a practice walk down the aisle behind the bridesmaids.

"Incredible, isn't she?" Theo's voice was as suffused with love as his face. When Kate didn't answer, he turned to her. "Kate? Is anything wrong?"

The words came tumbling out, propelled by her anxiety for Rebecca and her affection for him. "I know why Becca's marrying you. She's been dreaming of nothing else for years! But why are you marrying her?"

"I love her."

"You know love isn't enough!"

Theo frowned. "You think I'm too old for her, don't you?"

"No! It's marriage that's too old for her. In a lot of ways she's barely out of the egg. We don't know what she'll be like in ten years."

"I don't know what *I'll* be like in ten years! Or you, either, for that matter." He shook his head. "I was concerned about that once, but not anymore. God knows she's the most beautiful thing I ever saw, but she's so much more. You know that better than anyone, Kate."

"I know she's witty and loving and loyal and brilliant. I know that she should have finished college."

"She flatly refused, whether or not we married. She wants to start living, right now! She says she'll charm the legislators right out of their seats and be the best hostess in Washington—and she will too. She may not be as sophisticated yet as she pretends, but we're the only ones who know that." Theo took her hand. "You're thinking about what happens when an older man is besotted by a young girl."

Kate nodded. "Or the other way around. Rebecca can be overwhelming. What happens if you feel smothered by her love?"

He smiled. "I haven't been smothered by it yet. Kate, you mustn't worry about her."

She worried equally about him. He was the kindest man she knew and the best listener. He usually heard a great deal more than she said, just as Rebecca did. She had not realized how much she depended on him, how left out she felt.

The next day Kate watched a door in her life closing as Rebecca, radiant in silk-embroidered organza with a short, bouffant veil of tulle, became Mrs. Theodore Barrows. By the time Kate was back at Wakefield for her summer courses, her misgivings about the marriage had diminished somewhat, but she knew that her friendship with Rebecca—and with Theo as well—would never be the same. That was even more painful than she had anticipated.

Polly decided she was moping and prescribed a good dose of sulphur and molasses or a round of parties, but Kate still resisted Polly's attempts to make her "socialize."

IV

Had Polly known, the long-term goal Kate had set herself would prohibit any "socializing" or activism until she had earned a doctorate in history at Oxford University. Her father supported her plan and helped her to apply, and Kate had left for England, over Polly's objections, the minute she had her B.A.

Visitors from home were frequent. Her grandparents, en route to political weekends in London, Paris, or Bonn, came several times, but Polly had failed to winkle Kate out of her studious shell.

Brosie, on what would have been called his grand tour fifty years before, had no better luck, and Belle, on an extended honeymoon, was too starry-eyed to try. It seemed she was not content unless she was touching Ross. Her overpowering lust for him was embarrassing to watch.

"Making love," she whispered to Kate in the drawl that made the statement so unexpected, "is the most intoxicating pastime ever devised."

But Polly disapproved of Oxford. "It's utter nonsense!" she often declared. "Making an expatriate of yourself."

"It's the only way I can meet my deadline," Kate insisted. "If I stayed home, you'd do everything you could to distract me. Let's not discuss it."

But Polly, challenged by one of the few personalities she could not dominate, had discussed it at length. She was clever enough to be playful about it at the start, but lately the telephoned discussions sounded more like arguments.

Kate's curious relationship with her grandmother had changed very little. On Polly's side, indulgence and pride alternated with attempts to draw Kate more deeply into the family circle and under Polly's wing with the rest of them.

On Kate's side, the old wariness was softened by the wonder of belonging to this enormous clan, so closely knit that once inside it, Kate was in a special enclave, a world apart.

A faithful "auntie" to the children as they came along, Kate kept a gift list at Harrods and wrote a dozen postcards a month, "all of them different," Belle wrote back in deep admiration even as she hovered over her firstborn. "Just like babies."

So while Kate gloried in the fellowship of family and was grateful to Polly for the gift of it, she still walked a fine line between respect for her grandmother's wishes and refusal to let Polly—or anyone—direct her life.

Of overt displays of affection between Kate and her grandmother there were none. They kissed the air in the general vicinity of each other's earlobes when they met after a prolonged separation, but that was all.

"Sometimes I think she almost loves me," Kate told Rebecca.

"Sometimes I think you almost love *her!*" Rebecca replied tartly. Rebecca had become very sure of her opinions since she married Theo. Her confidence had grown with the birth of each of her three children, Teddy, Kate, and Marian.

Kate didn't tell her how much she would have welcomed Polly's love. She knew Rebecca still nursed resentment that she had never been invited to Kel Regis. Kate finally concluded that what she herself felt for Polly was not love but awe for the dimensions of her grandmother's character.

"Kate, wait up!" a familiar voice called.

V

Kate turned toward the caller and waited in the driving wind. It was Tabitha Berling, a plump, impetuous girl from Kansas who had the flat next door to Kate's and whose passion was the theater.

Kate empathized with her drive and her ambition and liked her candor and her common sense. When they first met, Tabitha had been quick to announce that she had "worked like a peon," in order to go on studying English literature at Oxford because the Oxford Playhouse was where so many wonderful actors had got their starts. She hung around the playhouse, making herself useful, learning all she could about set decoration.

"What luck to find you!" Tabitha said now, bustling up. "I'm on my way to the Playhouse for a dress rehearsal of *Taming of the Shrew*. I worked on the sets and you must come."

"Sorry, Tabby, I have work to do at the library."

"Katherine Ballard, are you mad? It's Win Talley."

"What is a Win Talley?"

"Another Olivier, that's what, another Burton! But born in the U.S.A.! He's already been through Yale's graduate school of drama, but he's reading English lit and directing off and on at the playhouse. He's the Petruchio and you can't miss it."

Kate let Tabitha hurry her along the high street. For years Kate had been working without a stop. A little Shakespeare in the afternoon would not come amiss.

"What *are* you muttering about?" Tabitha demanded as they pushed against the wind.

"Listing my past devotion to duty, so I won't feel guilty about goofing off."

"You? People call you patron saint of grinds!"

"Is that what they call me?"

"Actually, you're called Supergrind!" But Tabitha put a placating hand on Kate's arm. "I shouldn't have told you. It's a bad joke. They're jealous, that's all. But you do work flat out, Katherine."

"So do you."

"I have to."

"And I don't?"

Tabitha shrugged. "It can't be that hard for a genius. And you don't have to worry about money. Or fame, for that matter. How many doctoral students get a mention in the People section of *Time*?"

"It isn't my fame, Tabitha, and it isn't my money. All of that belongs to my grandparents or my father or a lot of dear, departed Benedicts I never even knew."

"What about *Time* then?"

"They pretended to be scholarly, but they wrote about me only because they thought my dissertation was sexy. I don't know how they got hold of a draft. Besides, a mention in *Time* doesn't constitute fame."

Tabitha was openly skeptical and Kate didn't argue the point, letting Tabitha talk on. Kate was working to earn her own fame as fast as she could, convinced that as she had been mocked for her scholarship as a girl, she would be vindicated by it as a woman.

And as a daughter! Fame, even of the academic variety, was something Sydney understood, as she had never understood love or loyalty. Fame would make Sydney notice.

So Kate had raced through Wakefield and come immediately to

England to begin the research for her thesis. She went out as infrequently here as she had at home and almost always in groups. She had never thought about that until Tabitha told her that men were intimidated by a female brain trust.

"So were all the boys I ever met," Kate had replied with a shrug, hearing Wade Stevens shout *Egghead!* once again. "I seem to betray myself as soon as I open my mouth. I never could figure out any solution but silence."

Tabitha, an ardent supporter of women's rights, dismissed that solution vehemently, but had no other to offer; and Kate, absorbed in ideas, in proving herself in an arena where she knew she could shine, had long since decided she didn't care. She had stuck to her plan and she was reaping her reward.

VI

"On the basis of my preliminary draft," she had told Polly on the phone a month ago, "I've been offered an assistant professorship at Brooke Parrish as soon as I have my D.Phil.!"

"Judging from what I read in *Time*," Polly said frostily, "you should be teaching in a school for delinquent females."

"I've told you I had nothing to do with that. The last thing I wanted was that kind of attention—or to be pursued by radical feminists. Anyway, I'll be teaching in Parrish's new Women's Studies Department."

Polly was not impressed. "What kind of life do you suppose you'll have as a teacher?" she demanded flatly.

"The kind I want. The same kind Tyler has. An ivory-tower life."

"You're a young woman, not Mrs. Chips. There are better things you can do if you set your mind to it."

"I've set my mind and this is what I want to do."

"And at Brooke Parrish, of all places! If you must get teaching out of your system, teach at your own college."

"My own college turned down my application."

Polly had been uncharacteristically silent and Kate had suddenly grasped the significance of it.

"That was your doing, wasn't it? You blocked me at Wakefield!"

"Why shouldn't I want you to use your exceptional talents to better advantage than a schoolroom? You worry about the historical plight of women when you ought to get into politics and help them!"

"Politics? You must be mad! I'd swoon away like Scarlett's Aunt Pittypat if I had to make a speech!"

"You'd have to do that as a teacher."

"That's different. I'll be teaching history, not trying to sell myself to the public with political poppycock."

"Poppycock is a necessary part of the game. You'll learn to deal with it in time."

"There's no need for me to learn." There had been a silence while, in Kate's mind, the last pieces fell into place. "Polly, is this what you've had up your sleeve all these years? A political career for me?"

"It was always my dream. I want it to be yours."

There was a lump in Kate's throat. "So that's what it was all about. All the gifts and the attention, the pride and the support. Not for me and my dream, but for yours. It was your future you were investing in, not mine."

"Don't be maudlin." Polly's distaste for sentiment had been apparent in her voice. "Of course it was you! You're the only one in this family who's anything like me." Polly had paused briefly before she surrendered. "And if teaching's what you think you want, I'll see that our committee accepts your application."

"Don't bother!" Kate's anger had burst its bounds. "I wouldn't teach at Wakefield now if you gave it to me on an Ardmore silver tray with Kel Regis thrown in."

"You simply cannot teach at our rival college!"

"Just watch me!"

"Katherine Ballard, you're just like your mother, a monster of ingratitude!"

"Spoken like a true hypocrite! And leave my mother out of this!"

Kate had slammed down the telephone, shaking with indignation. It was *her* life, but of the influential people in it, only her father was not critical of the way she chose to live it. Rebecca accused Kate regularly of using her mind to deny the demands of her body. Sydney had always been less concerned with Kate's grades than with her looks, disappointingly plain as Kate believed they were. Even Polly, who was enormously proud of Kate's prodigious scholarship, had not been content with it but had urged Kate to concentrate on social contacts.

"Social contacts, my eye!" Kate had fumed bitterly after that telephone call. "She was counting votes!"

Polly wanted altogether too much in exchange for her favors; Kate would accept no more of them, not now that the game between the two had suddenly turned serious.

But the next day it was Kate who picked up the telephone and called Polly back. She could not risk all that Polly represented of blood relations and family ties. After making a name for herself, Kate most wanted to be part of those huge family gatherings at Kel Regis again, to pore over the old diaries and family Bibles Polly preserved so carefully, and the journals and letters and picture albums of

Benedicts long dead and newly born. She had been to Devon to visit the site of Wakefield, but it was a shopping mall now; even so, standing where Benedicts had once lived had moved her, had made her connection to them more important than ever. But Kate needed Polly for more than that. Her grandmother occupied a unique place in Kate's life. If Polly's affection for her was heavily colored by self-interest, it was what motivated everyone. Kate had come to believe that no other kind of love existed.

Now Kate missed the almost daily telephone calls, even the sparring matches. She and Polly still spoke occasionally, but the climate between them had changed. They had smoothed over an explosion, but it had left its mark, like a weak patch on a balloon.

The balloon would have exploded had Polly known about the letters from Sydney.

VII

"Here we are," Tabitha said. "Prepare yourself for an out-of-body experience."

"I can't wait," Kate laughed, following her into the Oxford Playhouse. They found places in the third row and Tabitha sighed in eager anticipation.

"Are you in love with this Win Talley?" Kate asked.

Tabitha shrugged. "Sure, along with every other woman who comes within ten miles of him."

"He must have a colossal ego."

"He's an actor. He has to."

"About women, I mean."

"That's one ego I'd love to feed," Tabitha said with a leer.

"Why do women fawn on men who treat them like lamb chops?"

Tabitha gave a short hoot, then covered her mouth as the houselights dimmed. Kate settled down expectantly, but her thoughts wandered during the opening scenes.

VIII

The letters from Sydney, postmarked from the most popular adult playgrounds of Europe, had started coming almost three years earlier, not long after Royal Benedict killed himself in his Ferrari, somewhere in Germany.

"A merciful providence to all the Benedicts, I'm sure," Rebecca had commented.

Kate, her hands shaking, had tossed the first letter into the rubbish bin unread and struggled with herself for an hour before she retrieved it and put it away unopened. When she had collected four letters, she read them.

All of them said more or less the same thing: that Sydney was overcome by grief at her loss, there had been no honorable—*honorable!*—alternative for her but to do what she did, that she had never stopped loving Kate, that Kate was old enough now to understand the things Sydney longed to tell her.

The words, like the handwriting, were curiously childlike, more the importunings of an innocent than those of a woman whose exploits had once filled the tabloids. Even more naive was the assumption behind them: if Sydney could explain, all would be understood and forgiven.

Why was she driven to seek forgiveness now? Was it because Royal was dead? Or was Sydney sick? Dying?

"I don't know what to think!" Kate had told Rebecca on one of her regular calls to Washington.

"Neither do I! But I'm glad you finally read them. Will you answer?"

"No. I don't want anything to do with her."

"Lord, don't you want to know what she has to say?"

"No!"

"Kate, don't be priggish."

"You always say that! Just remember that I'm the one she left and you hated her for it just as much as I do—did."

"We were kids. Everyone said she was sinful and wicked and dumped you and Tyler to dive between the sheets with her cousin whosis. Wouldn't you like to find out why?"

"Royal was why. Sex was why."

"Do you really believe any man can be that colossal in bed?"

"I'm no authority on the subject."

"Alas, my darling Kate, I know full well you're not. Save the letters for me to read."

"All right." Kate had been somewhat miffed by Becca's crass curiosity. "Now tell me about you."

"I'm trying to get pregnant!"

"With Marian not a year old!"

"So what? We're all healthy."

"Hoping for a second son next time?"

"I don't care what it is. All I want is to keep Theo inside me for as long as I can. Think of it, Kate! When I'm pregnant he's in there, taking over more of me every day."

Sometimes Rebecca's ardor filled Kate with envy and despair that she was incapable of love like that. More often Rebecca's passion frightened her. It was as if Rebecca had fused herself to a host creature without whom she could not survive. What would happen to her if something happened to Theo? After all, he was fifteen years older than Becca.

What an old Cassandra I am, Kate scolded herself, *always croaking on the battlements.* Rebecca was sublimely happy and hoping for a fourth child.

As for Sydney, Kate had no intention of acknowledging those letters, no matter how many of them arrived.

IX

She was suddenly aware of the play.

It was his voice that caught her attention, a voice as rich as cream and as sensual, even though he captured the rakish Petruchio to the life. When Petruchio met the shrewish Katherina, Winslow Talley's voice, with an accent that was almost English, came across the footlights straight to Kate, and she might have been the woman he was wooing as "plain Kate" and "bonny Kate" and "the prettiest Kate in Christendom."

He was very tall, with a physique most actors attained only with padding, and he moved with the grace of a dancer and the precision of an athlete. He projected enormous energy, a combination of intellect and temperament. But it was his face that really captured her: the etched features, the high cheekbones, and the keen, light eyes that sometimes looked a dazzling blue, sometimes a vivid green.

The act ended and Tabitha regarded Kate with a satisfied smirk.

"Far be it from me to say I told you so," she said.

"He's really good," Kate nodded. "Incredible-looking too."

"You bet your bippy. Don't be distressed, Katherina mia. He has that effect on all women. Men, too, I shouldn't wonder." Tabitha sighed. "You have to be born with magnetism like that; it can't be learned." She sighed. "That's why I'll be a set designer, not an actress." She glanced at Kate. "You have magnetism."

Kate shook her head. "A supergrind? Not likely."

"But true all the same. It's that intensity of yours. You're the girl most likely to succeed."

But at what? Kate wondered for the first time in her life.

They went backstage when the performance ended. Winslow Talley was surrounded by the cast, with the two girls who played Kate and Bianca clinging to him like limpets. He smiled when he caught sight of Tabitha.

"Well, Tabby, how do we look?"

"The players look marvelous, but if you ask me, the lighting needs to be fixed."

He nodded. "We'll talk about it over a beer." He glanced at Kate. "And who is this lofty beauty?"

Tabitha nodded. "This is Kate." The company laughed good-naturedly. "No, really." Tabitha said. "Her name's Katherine Ballard and she's our resident genius, soon to be *Doctor* Ballard."

Kate smiled, inwardly shrinking from that description. It sounded so dry, so dull, so sexless. At this moment, a genius was not what she wanted to be. She wanted to be gorgeous. She wanted to be sensual.

"Are you a shrew, Katherine Ballard?" Talley asked.

"No, I'm a docile, biddable creature," Kate said.

"With a voice like a cello. 'Well, there's a wench.' " He smiled wickedly, repeating one of the last lines of the play. " 'Come on and kiss me, Kate.' " He held out his arms.

Nothing could have stopped her from moving across the small space that separated them. She felt his hands on her shoulders and looked into his clear, compelling eyes. She barely heard the whistles and whoops of the company when he kissed her, but she felt the touch of his mouth on hers and something surged inside her and that was how it began.

8

|

Nature joined the conspiracy. Spring was coming, that soft, sudden, English April unlike any other in its lush greenness and its riot of bud and blossom. Kate knew what spring fever was before the first daffodil showed, and sensuality too—her own and Win Talley's—as it flowed effortlessly across the lights to her, every night.

Attending the play was the only way to see him, for he had made no attempt to contact her. Helpless to stay away, she went to every performance in the two weeks following that kiss—so brief, so casual —that had bewitched her. The cast knew she was there and glanced at her wickedly each time he said "Come on and kiss me, Kate," but she didn't care. She had learned to ignore whispers a long time ago.

When she wasn't watching him she was thinking about him. She knew she was caught up in a sexual fugue and was astonished by it, but she had neither the wish nor the will to resist it.

"Are you in love with him?" Tabitha asked her when two weeks had gone by.

"How would I know? I've never been in love before."

"You have all the outer symptoms. You haven't been working on your thesis."

"I have all the inner symptoms too. My heart goes pitter-patter and my knees are weak. I feel like an absolute ninny."

"What are you going to do?"

"Damned if I know. Tell me more about him."

"His mother's a Boston Winslow," Tabitha said. "Very high on the totem pole. She fell down in a faint when Win told her he wanted to be an actor, and his father almost had a stroke, so he compromised and got a Harvard degree in English lit, went on to do graduate work in drama at Yale, then came here. He never stops studying to get where he's going. He takes singing lessons to project his voice and give it a wider range. He takes diction lessons to obliterate what's left of his Yankee accent. You have to admire dedication like that."

"How long do you think he'll be here?" Kate had already considered staying on through the summer.

"Not long, even though he can afford to wait as long as it takes. But theatrical scouts cover university productions and Win's too good to stay undiscovered." Tabitha studied Kate carefully. "What'll happen when you go home?"

"I'll forget him."

"Like hell you will."

"I know," Kate said.

II

He saw her one day by chance. She was sitting on the floor in the library, drawing one book after another from the bottom shelf of the stacks and perusing each one attentively before replacing it or putting it aside for further study. No matter what she wore—today it was jeans and a red-checked cotton shirt—to him she looked like some kind of goddess. It wasn't only her superb body, her long, long legs, her rounded hips and full breasts. Or her face with those dark eyes that hid more than they revealed and a mouth that invited kisses.

It was the woman herself, and some quality in her he had yet to define, that captivated him even as he warned himself he had no time to waste on an affair.

She had a monumental crush on him, but that was not the only thing that had fired his interest; he was accustomed to the attentions of women. He loved women: he loved their bodies and their brains and their thought patterns that, more often than not, differed so much from a man's.

He had derived enormous benefit from his love affairs: his women had taught him how to play opposite female characters, how to make the eternal man/woman battle clear to an audience. Every new relationship was a voyage of discovery, so his love life was at the service of his career as, indeed, he wanted it to be.

But he was unduly fascinated by Kate Ballard, and that worried him even while it drove him to discover why she attracted him.

Just then Kate turned to replace a dusty book. She sat there looking at it sadly. In the subdued lighting he saw her face from a different angle. She had been immersed in what she was reading, her lips slightly parted, her attention totally caught. But now, as she reacted to it, he saw something at the core of her that spoke to the core of him. He could not name it; he only felt it, like a warm pool of sunlight on a cold day. From that moment he wanted more than her body: he wanted the essence of her.

Hold on, he warned himself. *You haven't got time for that kind of thing.* He was not quite sure what he meant by "that kind of thing."

He walked quietly toward her and said, "Hello, Kate."

She looked up at him and the light in her dark eyes made his heart turn over.

"Hello," she said, blushing.

That enchanted him all the more. They looked at each other for a long moment and he knew she felt the many currents between them as fiercely as he did. He put out his hand and she took it and stood up, slowly. It seemed a long, long journey and they were both breathless when, at last, she was standing near him, her breasts grazing his chest.

He put his arms around her with as much tenderness as lust, and she made a little sound of delight. His lips brushed her hair, her cheek, her neck.

"Come with me," he said, and she nodded and followed him out. They walked quickly and silently along the high street, through the green-scented, balmy air of spring, until he turned into a cul-de-sac lined with neat hedges and handsome houses.

III

He took her to his flat on the second floor of a converted Tudor house.

Inside, the house was dim, sunlight trickling through the leaded windows. It was quiet as they climbed a flight of stairs, but once he had closed and locked the door, he turned and took her in his arms again. Her heart was pounding when he kissed her, this time long and ardently, before he took her into the bedroom.

Anticipation flooded her while they undressed, making her face flush and her body tingle. Even fear that inexperience would make her clumsy could not have stopped her. He seemed not to expect anything of her but that she let him roam over her at will, that she become a feast for his pleasure.

She gave herself up to sensations her body knew, even if she did not, to responses she had kept in check for a very long time. She was astounded by sex, swept away by it, seduced by the act as much as by the actor in her arms until the two became inseparable. He *was* sex. She had wanted him since he kissed her on that stage, but she had never believed she was in love with him until his body entered hers and then he *was* love.

She was wild to possess him, to be possessed by him. An atavistic rhythm moved her hips, carrying her beyond herself, into him as he came into her. There was no need on this magical afternoon for fantasies of war-torn lovers or knights in armor. The man who made love to her was the man she wanted.

She lay in his arms afterward, aglow with pure bliss, utterly in thrall, intensely in love with Win and his body and how he was and how he made her feel and what a marvel it was to be a woman. She had never believed in love or in its force until this day.

He made love to her again and then she slept. He was gone when she woke at dusk. There was a note on his pillow, apologizing for a prior engagement he could not cancel and inviting her to a party the following night. "Theater people," he had written in a distinctive hand. "You've seen most of them onstage. See you at eight? You are very beautiful, Kate, in many, many ways. W."

She got out of bed and pulled on her clothes, wanting to keep the scent of him on her as she walked through the tranquil streets to home and bed, where she lay remembering every moment until she fell asleep again.

IV

The party was crowded and noisy. She had paid little attention to it yesterday, but she saw now that the flat was large and richly furnished, almost formal. Win, though, was the least formal Bostonian she had ever met.

They were together briefly a few times during the evening, but they were aware of each other constantly. It was almost impossible for her to take her eyes off him. As for herself, she knew there was a difference in the way she stood, the way she smiled, the way she looked at him. It amazed her that seduction was instinctive, that she had known exactly how to send a sexual invitation.

She sank back onto the couch, making no move to go while he said good night to his friends.

"I thought they'd never leave," Win said, closing the door.

He came to the couch and leaned over her, touching her cheek. "I'm in a champagne mood. How about you?"

She held out her arms and he bent to kiss her. "First champagne," she said against his mouth. "Then you."

He nodded and left her surrounded by the aftermath of the party, but Kate, watching the fire in the grate, was unaware of the mess. She was aware only of this man in a way she had never been of any other, real or fictional.

She took off her dress while she considered the carefully selected escorts who had squired her to balls and parties and kissed her under the mistletoe at Kel Regis. They would never be more than good ol' boys. The political bachelors Rebecca had set her up with in Washington paled utterly by comparison with Winslow Talley. The few men she had dated in Oxford were nice, but that was all she could say about them. She took off her panties and bra and stretched out on the brown velvet couch.

Win rivaled even her girlhood heroes of fiction—and he could have played any one of them: Heathcliff, Mr. Rochester, Maxim de Winter, Mr. Darcy, Count Vronsky, and either Ashley Wilkes *or* Rhett Butler.

She heard him coming back from the kitchen. Even thinking about the way he walked excited her! A hot tremor went through her when he reached the couch and saw her lying naked on it.

He set down the tray and stood looking at her for a moment with an unfathomable expression on his face before he dropped his clothes and knelt beside her. His head was pillowed first between her breasts, then on her thighs, then between them. The sensation was deeper, richer. He held her close when she shook with pleasure, reaching for him.

V

"You came to every performance of *Shrew*," he said sometime later, pouring the champagne. "Why?"

"You already know why."

He turned to look at her. "But you could have come backstage. Or called me."

"I didn't know the protocol," Kate said simply. "I never learned."

Her meaning was clear. He sipped his champagne and regarded her quizzically. "You're an enigma," he said. "A man looks at you and can't rest until he knows what's behind the Madonna's face and the Winged Victory's body."

"Lately I'm not sure I know myself."

He was still again, looking down at her, reading her as he would have read a newly opened book with uncut pages. He was no stranger to the desire of women. He had known it was sex she wanted and that she could not bring herself to ask for it. The whole world might have become permissive, but Kate had not.

Her candor moved him strangely. "How does it happen," he asked her, "that I'm the first?"

"Was I that awkward?"

"Not at all. You told me. I think it was the only thing you said to me yesterday. But tell me why."

"I hadn't met you."

He laughed. "My God, Kate, you mustn't give yourself away like that!"

"Why not?"

He took her in his arms and rocked her. "Women are supposed to have wiles. They're supposed to make men think they don't really care at all. But you hide nothing."

"I've been hiding it long enough, wouldn't you say?"

He turned her face up to his. "That's why the revelation is blinding."

"You're accustomed to bright lights."

"Not this kind."

Her heart sank. "What are you trying to tell me?"

"That I have things to do with my life that I can only do alone. That I don't want you to get hurt. That I had no idea you were so vulnerable. You seemed so self-possessed."

She looked away. He was saying that this idyll would not last. Later she would know what Browning meant by careless rapture, because in this enchanted moment she didn't care that she was vulnerable and she didn't care if it didn't last. Instinct told her he was as avid for her as she was for him, that she must hold on to the moment.

"I'm not your responsibility," she said, setting him free in order to hold him. She was dizzy with love, with desire. She would have said anything to keep him.

It was the only lie she told him and it was worth it because he believed her. After that night they were together constantly, and she slept more often in his bed than in hers. They became what Tabitha called, with touching wistfulness, "an item."

VI

"You're a *what*?" Rebecca demanded.

"An item. Oh, don't be dense, Becca. I have a beau. A lover."

"The saints be praised! What else does he do?"

"He's an actor. He's the next Burton."

"What's his name?"

"Winslow Talley."

"Never heard of him."

"Trust me, you will."

"Oh, Kate!" Rebecca's voice dripped disappointment. "You ought to know better than to fall in love with a strolling player! Half of them are gay anyway."

"Not this one."

"Well, I'm glad about that part at least! Now you know what you've been missing."

"I didn't miss anything, Becca. It had to be Win."

"Katherine Ballard! You're in heat!"

"I'm in love! What's wrong with that?"

"It worries me. You're not sensible about these things."

"I suppose you were sensible about Theo?"

"In addition to being the best, most extraordinary man in the world, Theo had position and money when I met him. After all this time, you might have made a better choice than an indigent actor."

"He isn't indigent, he's a Boston Talley. I'm told they're every bit as good as the Benedicts."

"Well, that's more like it!" Rebecca's voice became conspiratorial. "Tell me what he's like."

Kate told her.

"Then what's wrong?"

"Nothing."

"Kate! Speak to me!"

"I'm not *his* first affair, but I want to be his last."

"Marry him? You hardly know him."

"I know him well enough." Her tone convinced Rebecca to stop arguing.

"All right, then, marry him. Any woman worth her salt can bring a man to water *and* make him drink!"

"Maybe not this man."

"This man too! Some woman will get him. Why shouldn't it be you?"

"I don't think he's gettable. Win wants success the way you wanted Theo, not mediocre success but fame as big as the Victoria Falls. Nothing takes precedence over his career. I'm the same way about mine."

"Not anymore, if you're as crazy about him as you sound. Anyway, he's a man. He can have a career and a wife too. If you play your cards right . . ."

"Manipulate him, you mean. I won't do that. It would be degrading to both of us."

"Honestly, I despair! Why must you always be on the side of the angels?"

VII

Lusting for Win those first two weeks had interfered with Kate's work, but loving him revitalized her: her energy, her body, her mind. The work on her dissertation flowed, her ideas forming and pouring out like her passion for him.

Sometimes when they made love, words were inadequate to express the storm inside her, and she wept in the midst of pleasure.

"Kate," he whispered when it happened, so attuned to her that he understood it. "My incredible Kate."

"You love me," she pleaded, enfolding him, taking him deeper in. "Say you love me."

"What man wouldn't love a woman like you? You give all you have."

"Don't stop," she beseeched him.

Don't ever leave me was what she meant.

He excited her in every way, not only in those moments when she dissolved into him, but intellectually as well, and Kate's own mind had been her most exciting companion for years, often her only one. Other men had found that offputting, but Win enjoyed her intellect as much as he did her body. Win made her feel like a woman for the first time in her life.

"I want your reaction to an aspect of Hamlet," he said before the play went into rehearsal. They had bicycled into the country with a picnic and now lay on a blanket under a tree, replete with pâté sandwiches on brown bread, wine, strawberries, and the sheer pleasure of blue sky and green foliage above them.

"First tell me how it feels to play him," she said.

"Like teetering on the brink of madness."

"But is Hamlet mad? He isn't the only one to see his father's ghost."

"Tell me first, are my mother and my uncle guilty?"

"Yes, but of different things. Your uncle is a murderer. Your mother is a willing partner in lust." *As mine is,* Kate thought, but she couldn't tell him that.

"But if I'm in love with my mother, her lust for my uncle will have driven me mad. *Am* I in love with her?"

"Can you play a man in love with his mother?" She wondered what his own mother was like.

"I can play anything," he said quietly. That confidence without conceit was part of his enormous charm. "But I want you to tell me how you think it should be done. What am I trying to make the audience see?"

Kate reflected for a moment. "Don't make them see, *let* them. Play it so that the judgment is in the eye of each beholder."

"Ah, Kate!" he said, turning to lie over her. "That's exactly what I hoped you'd say." He kissed her. "How do you know so much about acting? How do you know so much about me?"

"Right now I know you want to make love," she told him, her mouth against his. "And so do I." She stood up and unbuttoned her shorts.

"Here?" He was undressing.

"Right here." She stood over him, naked. "Astound me."

He looked up at her. "My God, you're gorgeous. Do you know what you do to a man?"

"I only care what I do to this man." She lay down next to him. "How do I make *you* feel?"

"Like Antony bestriding the world."

"To hell with the world. Bestride me."

"You're so—so lavish! I never knew a woman more generous in love. What became of the Kate I met?"

"She was afraid of love. She couldn't let go."

"Let go now," he whispered, touching her.

"I will, I have."

But not of you, she entreated silently. *Don't ever ask me to let go of you.*

She loved sex: the arousal, whether it was long and slow or swift and fierce; the phallic search; the ecstatic penetration; the exquisite climax.

She did not question how an erotic appetite as strong as hers had stayed coiled and quiet inside her for so many years. She knew it was because no one but Win, at this time and in this place, could have awakened it and satisfied it. She was jubilant that she had not yielded to groping boys like Wade Stevens.

She was utterly in love with Win, with his professional skill, his generosity in sharing it with others, his daring as a performer, and the sweet touch of the poet in him. He made the simplest meal a banquet, a walk in the country an adventure.

Kate felt light-years away from the social revolution in America. She no longer tried to explain the civil rights battle to Europeans, who sometimes seemed to delight in the bloody disarray of their powerful ally. She had never understood the escalating war in Vietnam. At home those things had produced the same effect on her as on most young people: a whole generation began to question the rightness of the American way and consequently of everything their elders had taught them about the land of the free and the home of the brave.

But Kate had no desire to go home and join the battle. She preferred the enchanted country she inhabited with her lover; it was the only part of the present that was lovely. Even the militant feminist movement could not divert her from Win.

Whether he made love to her by sunlight or candlelight or in total darkness, it was with that totality of self he gave to everything he did. In that way they were alike.

"Tabby says your family didn't approve your choice of career," she said one rainy day as she watched a fire crackle in the hearth.

"My father wanted me to be an investment banker, sit on boards, and take a pale and proper Boston-cream-pie bride." He smiled at the outrageousness of such an idea.

"Why do you want to be an actor?"

"It's what I am. I've studied drama, but I didn't need to study acting. I have the gift for it. I was born with it. And on the stage I can put on any cloak I choose, be hundreds of men in one lifetime, get outside the trap of myself. I can be Caesar *and* Antony. I can move people, make them think. Does that answer it?"

"Yes, oh, yes."

"Why do you want to be a teacher?"

"At first it was to thumb my nose at my mother and please my father. He lives in the past and, in a way, so do I. The intense study of history does that to some people."

"At least there was someone you pleased. Almost everything I did appalled my family."

As what Kate was doing appalled most of hers. But she could not tell him that either. He might have wanted to know more.

"You've gone past them," she said.

"Do people ever get past their parents?"

"Maybe not entirely, but to some extent." She hoped that was true. She watched him take the poker and move one of the logs.

"You still haven't told me why you want to be a teacher," he said.

"To move women, to make them think. Each woman is a product of the entire history of her sex, not only of her own genes and her own past. Women have no idea what their history is. I want them to understand *why* they're obsessed with pleasing everyone and how much more important being competent is than being liked."

"We're a matched set," he said. "We both love what we do."

Kate went off to defend her thesis with confidence equal to Win's. Not long after that, she was entitled to call herself Dr. Ballard, which so delighted Win that he gave a party for her.

She flew to Paris for a dress. With her great height, she'd long ago given up on English clothes. She had already refurbished her entire wardrobe with the very generous allowance Polly made her, and although her style remained classic, her shirts were now silk instead of starched cotton, her sweaters cashmere, her underthings lace-trimmed satin and her dresses cut on the long, fluid lines that best became her.

"But how are the mighty fallen," she said to Tabitha after she returned from Paris. She was modeling the pale yellow chiffon she had chosen, a slip of a dress with spaghetti straps and deep handkerchief points that showed glimpses of her thighs.

"You still look mighty to me." Tabitha sat on the bed, watching.

"My father brought me up on New England thrift and I never cared much about clothes anyway. I used to turn up my nose at fashion. I never owned a dress like this."

"With that body?"

"I was too tall. When you're young that's as bad as being too fat. Or too smart, which I was as well. I felt more comfortable in a skirt and blazer, you know, a kind of regulation egghead."

"I suppose people thought you were a precocious nut."

"My mother didn't know what to make of me." Kate spun around and looked at herself in the mirror. "Do you think Win will like it?"

Tabitha tumbled over in a mock faint.

"I love it," Win said when she modeled it for him. "It's the most provocative thing I've seen you wear."

"But it's the simplest dress I could find!"

"Provocative doesn't mean Sadie Thompson in fuck-me shoes, Kate. It means you arouse a man merely by wearing it. Take it off and I'll show you what you've aroused."

It was after the party, when his affection for her had been apparent to everyone, that she decided to stay on at Oxford just a little longer, telling herself she could prepare even better, here, for the courses she would teach at Brooke Parrish in the fall.

"That's an outright lie," she challenged her reflection. "You're giving him time to ask you. Everyone thinks he will."

And then the realization that she was ready to give up all she had worked for in order to marry Win appalled her. She was doing the same thing she hated to see other women do; she was feeling the same way: there were many kinds of success—in a career, as a mother, in a profession—but there was only one *right* kind, and that required a man and a marriage.

"I would be a prize fool," she berated herself, "to throw all my work away. But I love him. I love him."

I love him, Sydney had said the day she ran off with Royal. I love him. But not like this, Kate told herself. Sydney had never loved like this.

9

|

A week later Win was packing, striding around his bedroom from closet to dresser to the suitcases on the bed. He was far too exhilarated to pack in an orderly fashion—his wardrobe was the last thing on his mind. The dream of his life was about to come true!

Suddenly he stopped his whirlwind packing. His head dropped and he bent over the valise.

"Kate," he murmured. "How can I make you understand?"

His Kate, so bright, so passionate, so unlike any other woman he had ever met. She was the second dream of his life. But a man could live only one dream at a time.

"Dammit, I can't let anything divert me from a chance like this, not even Kate!" He began taking underwear and socks from his dresser drawers and was in command of himself and packing resolutely when Kate let herself into the flat. He strode to the bedroom door, lifted her, and whirled her into the room, the words tumbling out of him.

"It's happened, Kate! I've been given an important second lead in a play called *Prelude in C-Sharp Minor*." He set her down and kissed her over and over, talking between kisses. "Rehearsals . . . begin imme-diately . . . and we open . . . in London . . . in September." He went back to folding things into his bags, beaming at her over his shoulder.

She said nothing. He knew she was waiting for him to say *Come with me,* and he knew how much he was going to miss her. He almost said it.

"I've been waiting for the role that's absolutely right for my de-but," he said instead, more to himself than to her, "and now it's fallen into my lap. It's the most incredible luck." He looked at his watch. "I'm going to London on the seven o'clock." He went to the closet and found another tie he wanted. Then, finally, he looked directly at her. "It's wonderful, isn't it, that we'll begin our careers at the same time."

She flinched at that. He realized he had just said good-bye.

"It isn't good-bye," he protested, avoiding her eyes again. "We're bound to run into each other when the play opens on Broadway. And it will, Dr. Ballard, I guarantee it!"

She stood looking at him, her face impassive. Her apparent composure rattled him.

"Kate, I can't deal with anything but my career right now," he said. He stopped what he was doing and faced her squarely, his eyes glittering like ice. "Not even you. No matter how much I care about you —and I do—I don't have time for you. I can't afford the luxury of love right now. I have to show them. I have to do what I said I'd do. I can't just build success, I have to catapult into it the first time out or they'll never believe me."

He came to put his arms around her. "I told you that at the start. I was afraid I'd hurt you and I have, but I never meant to. You must believe that."

His eyes closed briefly while he let the shape of her tall body imprint itself on his; then he stepped back and looked at her and touched her cheek.

"I'll write to you at Brooke Parrish," he said. "I'll tell you everything that's happening—and you must tell me." The watch again. "God, it's late. I'm sorry I'm in such a hurry, darling."

She nodded and turned to go.

"Kate," he pleaded, coming after her. "This isn't the end. I do love you. You must know that."

He had never said that before, not to any woman. It sounded strange to him. He put his arms around her. "Kiss me good-bye, Kate. Wish me luck."

She turned back to him and he kissed her in this room that had witnessed so much passion between them. He loved the way she felt against him. He loved the sweet, warm taste of her. Then she pulled away from him and was gone.

He went back to close his suitcases. There was a pall over his elation, but he searched for the high he had been on an hour ago, found it, and began forming the character he would play. He was on the London train before he realized she hadn't said a word to him.

11

Kate walked home mechanically, remembering what a desert her life had been before Win, apprehensive about living in that wasteland again. The door she had flung open with such joyful abandon had slammed shut.

She had been struck anew by the flawless beauty of his face and the consuming ambition behind it. There was something frightening about drive like his and something male, too, primitive and powerful and erotic. No wonder that women, for the most part denied power, fell in love with powerful men.

She ached with loss. She didn't want to be calm and reasonable, to see his side of it. She hated him for *letting* her believe they would stay together always. With that instinct that made him a superb actor and a sublime lover, he must have known she believed they would, no matter what he told her or what she said.

She felt utterly bereft and, more even than that, ashamed of her own gullibility. She was approaching her thirties now, old enough to know he had meant what he said that night after the party. She had no magic that could change his plan. She was a woman he had known, maybe loved in his fashion, but he loved his career more.

She groped through her defenses for the one that had got her through Sydney's defection. This time, thank God, she hadn't begged, and this time she hadn't cried.

I said I wasn't his responsibility, she reminded herself bitterly. *And now I'm not. I'm all mine.*

How many women had he loved in the same way he loved her? How many more would there be?

The worst of it all was that she had done what every damn fool in the world did: she had invested herself totally in someone else and, in so doing, had lost part of herself.

"Never again," she told herself sternly. "Never!"

When Kate got home, Tabitha's door was open and her two shabby suitcases stood in the hall. When she heard Kate's step she came out, wearing the pleated skirt and blazer she reserved for grand occasions.

"He told you," she said with a single look at Kate's face. "He told me a few hours ago. Do you know what he did? He got me on as assistant to the set designer."

"I'm glad for your sake, Tabby."

"Is it over?"

"It's over."

"But it was worth having, wasn't it?"

"Don't ask me now, Tabby. Ask me ten years from now. Ask me then."

|||

Kate was waiting for her taxi two days later when the intercom buzzed.

"I'll be right down," she told the porter.

"The taxi's not here yet, Dr. Ballard, but there's a lady to see the rooms," the porter said.

Conversation with the new tenant was the last thing Kate wanted. She wanted only to leave this place and the reminders of her stupid credulity lurking around every corner.

She opened the door and watched until a head appeared in the stairwell, so astonished to see her mother that she could only stare as the pale blond chignoned hair was followed by the slender neck and graceful figure Kate remembered: her mother's body, its shape and smell and texture, memorized in infancy and missed as home is missed no matter what its shortcomings.

Her mother was wearing a silk suit of navy blue over a cream-colored shirt. Amazingly expensive, Kate was sure. It took a great designer to make simplicity that elegant.

She looks absolutely prim, Kate thought, and it came to her in a flash of insight that such was precisely Sydney's intention.

Kate's impulse was to duck back inside, to spare herself a meeting she did not want, especially now, but Sydney had already reached her and Kate simply could not close the door on her mother.

"Hello, Kate," Sydney said.

Her beauty was virtually untouched. She was certainly not sick. She still looked like the fairy princess of Kate's childhood. She wore the same perfume that had clung to the boxes of her clothes when Kate finally forced herself to throw them away.

"Come in," Kate replied. "Sit down. Can I get you anything?"

"Dammit, Kate, don't be so polite!"

"That's how I am," Kate said. "And how else can I be with you? Why are you here?"

"You've had my letters. You know why."

She does look older, Kate thought. *No lines, nothing as human as that, but older in herself, not so radiant.*

"I don't want to hear about you," Kate said. "I have my own problems."

"Please," Sydney insisted, sitting down and waving Kate's problems aside as she gestured to the other chair. "Or I'll just have to try again."

Kate sat down, thinking that Sydney made the room and everything in it look tacky.

"You're young," Sydney began. "And you have your father's

nature. Now, don't get angry, I'm not criticizing either of you. It's just that you can't possibly know what passion is. It isn't in your nature to love a man the way I loved Royal. But, Kate, surely you can imagine that kind of love."

"Oh, my God," Kate said, closing her eyes.

"Well, can't you?"

"Yes," Kate said wearily. "I can imagine that kind of love."

Sydney drew a long breath. "I fell in love with Royal when I was fifteen. It was like waking up after a long time in limbo. My mother laughed when we told her. Royal wanted to marry me then, but she wouldn't allow it." Sydney shrugged. "My mother knows nothing about love. And after a few years of roaming free, neither did Royal. By then he wanted to do what he wanted to do and sometimes, if I was lucky, he wanted to do me. But he had to keep moving. I used to think he was possessed. I knew it was hopeless, but I didn't care."

Sydney opened her bag, took a slender cigarillo from a solid gold case, and lit it with a matching gold lighter. Polly had smoked the same things until she gave them up years ago.

"But what a woman knows," Sydney went on through the exhaled smoke, "can't change what a woman feels. I always loved him and I always will."

"And Tyler? Did you ever love my father?"

Sydney sighed. "I thought I did. My whole freshman year at Wakefield I was sure I did. He was so handsome and so brilliant. All the girls had crushes on him, but I was the one he wanted. And Tyler thought I was wonderful."

"The fair Elaine," Kate said.

"Yes. He was the only one who ever thought that about me. I *wanted* to be . . . you know . . . what he thought I was. I swore to myself I'd be a good wife. And I had to get away from that house."

"Kel Regis?"

Sydney nodded. "I was the only girl after a string of boys. Except for Hilliard, everyone treated me like an afterthought. Mother couldn't be bothered with me." Sydney grimaced. "And she decided I was an imp out of hell when I was only five."

"Why?" Kate was curious despite herself.

"For playing show-and-tell with the boys in the boat house." She sighed. "Hilliard used to charge them a nickel to peek under my skirt. Polly found out about it."

Kate didn't know whether to laugh or cry at the image of five-year-old Sydney, bare-bottomed, facing Polly's wrath.

"It was child's play, but Mother locked me in my room for a week. She didn't punish Hilliard, only me, but I didn't mind. I loved Hilliard. He was the best of the bunch. Mother still hadn't forgiven me ten years later, when Royal and I fell in love. By the time I got to college, I'd been unchurched by my reverend mother and cut off from Royal. Before the year was out, I was adored by Tyler and pregnant with you. I couldn't go home, so I went where I was wanted. I married your father. Mother didn't approve of him either.''

"Did you? You slept with Royal on your wedding day."

Sydney studied one of her exquisite hands. "I hadn't seen him in years. I'd have slept with Royal anytime he wanted me. I loved him."

"I love *him!*" Kate said vehemently. "I love *her*! I can't live without *this*! Or *that*! Why is love supposed to be the perfect excuse for rotten behavior?"

"Well, isn't it?"

"No, it's not half good enough," Kate said, on the brink of telling Sydney how she knew that. But she would be confiding in a stranger. She reined herself in and her voice returned to its customary evenness. "It doesn't explain how you could go to Harmony with Tyler as if nothing had happened."

"But I thought I'd never see Royal again! And I expected to spend a lifetime making it up to your father."

Kate gazed at her, dumbfounded by her skewed logic.

"I was the perfect faculty wife for ten years," Sydney protested, "and a better mother to you than I ever had. I never understood you, but I loved you! Then Royal came back. He was like one of those exotic fevers: once you get it, you always have it. Anyway, I didn't want to be cured. And for the first time in his life Royal needed me. I stuck it out in Harmony as long as I could and then I couldn't stand the hypocrisy of it anymore, not even for your sake."

She waited expectantly, but Kate said nothing and Sydney's body tensed. "It's time you knew that your father was never man enough for me," she said harshly. "I was thirty and time was flying by and I was damned if I was going to be frustrated for the rest of my life. So I ran away with Royal. He's the only man I ever knew who satisfied me."

Kate's cheeks burned at the revelation. "I don't want to hear about that! And you didn't run *with* him, you ran *after* him—and any other man who took your fancy. You did what *you* wanted to do and to hell with everyone else. How do you think I felt, reading all that filth about you and your affairs?" With another great effort Kate calmed herself. "A fine pair, you and Royal," she said evenly. "You deserved each other."

"Oh, yes," Sydney said softly. "We belonged together. I'd give ten years of my life just to hold him once more." She said it with such aching nostalgia that Kate, herself aching, was moved.

She contemplated the woman sitting opposite. What an appalling waste of a life, not really lived but given over to the quest for someone else to live it for her! And what irony, that Sydney had come now! If she had arrived a few months earlier, Kate could have been righteous and indignant.

But that was impossible now: Kate had actually contemplated following in her mother's footsteps.

It made no difference that one man was a fine actor on the brink of a great career and the other a worthless philanderer. The female impulse was the same: a surrender of self. But it was the last time that impulse would drive Kate.

"Is that all you wanted to tell me?" she asked.

Sydney nodded, opening and closing the clasp of her handbag. In profile, she seemed even younger. She was in her mid-forties, but she looked many years less even when she turned back to Kate, utterly dejected.

"I suppose I knew it wouldn't make any difference, but I needed to see you."

"Jesus! I needed to see you, too, Mother! For years after you left I needed you. I hated you, but I needed you. Now you want me to say it's all right, that I understand. All right. I do. But I'm nearly twenty-seven. Katherine-who-was-twelve will never understand."

"I know," Sydney said, flinching. "But it's this Kate I've come to see."

The buzzer sounded.

"That's my cab," Kate said, springing up. "I have to catch a plane."

"I have a car. Let me drive you to the airport. It'll give us more time together."

"After fifteen years, we've had all the time together I can take."

Kate asked the porter to come up for the bags and did an unnecessary check of the two small rooms until he arrived.

Sydney stood. "I'm getting married, Kate. He's an Austrian, Baron von Rayner."

"Congratulations," Kate said. "I hope he can satisfy you too."

Sydney ignored that. "Will you come to the wedding? You're the only family I can ask."

So that was why she had come! Dear Lord, what a child she was! Only a child would have the audacity to appear out of the blue and invite a deserted daughter to her wedding. But something in her attitude told Kate she expected to be turned down and Kate, turned down herself, could not do that to this foolish, forlorn woman, not today.

"I don't know," Kate temporized.

"Just think about it," Sydney said. "I'll write to you in Harmony."

"No!" What if Tyler saw that familiar handwriting? "I'll be teaching at Brooke Parrish. You can write to me there."

"At Brooke Parrish!" Sydney's smile was bright with malice. "That'll really put her nose out of joint!"

They followed the porter down the stairs and parted like two ladies after a tea party, and then Kate got into her cab and slumped against the seat, feeling battered. She felt battered during the flight to Washington and even after she had walked into Rebecca's waiting arms.

1 O

———◆———

I

Kate ate a large lunch while Rebecca nibbled on a salad. They were in the sunny breakfast room of the Barrowses' red brick Federal house in Georgetown. It had already been photographed for *Town & Country*, with a full-page portrait of "the Capitol's beautiful young hostess, Rebecca (Mrs. Theodore) Barrows, wife of the political consultant," and a rapturous article about the couple and their children.

The interior was decorated in beige, white, and tones of sepia, not the bright colors Rebecca had always preferred, "because color isn't in anymore," she told Kate. Rebecca dressed in soft colors and fabrics, pregnant or not. Her blond hair framed a face that had none of the puffiness of pregnancy. She was fashionable without being trendy and in her fourth month she looked lovelier than ever.

She had always been assertive, but now she was almost imperial as she directed her well-ordered domain, giving instructions to the cook and the maid, the nanny and the chauffeur.

While they ate, she listened like a cat at a mouse hole to everything Kate told her about Win.

"A first-class bastard," she said when Kate had finished.

"Why? He told me right off the bat that his career came first."

"Career? He's an amateur with dreams of glory! Why must you always see everyone's side but your own?" Rebecca shook her head.

"It isn't that," Kate said sharply. "But I *did* walk right into it, cautious, skeptical me. *I'm* the fool. Did you know that *passion* originally meant 'suffering'?"

"No, but it's no surprise that it does for you. I was lucky. I never loved anyone but Theo and I married him." She put both hands on her belly, as if, Kate thought, to communicate with him through his child. "So, what will you do now?"

"I'll teach, of course. I've always wanted to and Parrish is the best place to start."

"Too bad it's a girls' school. You ought to meet men. It's like falling off a horse: the best thing to do is get right back on."

"I'll leap onto any horse that wanders by, but no men, thank you very much."

"Maybe not this minute, but eventually you'll want a man."

"You're talking about my glands, not me."

"I know you're the most brilliant thing that ever came down the pike, but from what I've just heard, Sister Kate has learned to shimmy." Rebecca pushed herself out of her chair. "We can't talk when you're jet lagged. Have a bath and a nap and put on something pretty tonight. We're having guests for dinner."

"I'll have a tray in my room."

"No, you won't," Rebecca said over her shoulder as she led Katherine up the stairs. "You're not going into a decline over that narcissistic son of a bitch, no matter how good he was in bed."

II

It was the kind of dinner party that was the norm in Washington. The men were obsessed with power and the women with helping their men acquire more of it. Hostesses vied for the most star-studded guest list and parties were an opportunity to extend the workday and talk shop. To an outsider, much of what they said was mystifying and Kate, after so long in England, felt like an alien as well.

She had earned an approving nod from Rebecca and Theo when she appeared wearing the yellow chiffon.

"You look stunning," Theo said.

"It's about time!" Rebecca added and, in a whisper to Kate, "At least your actor made you buy some decent clothes!"

Over cocktails, Kate pretended to listen raptly to an exchange between a presidential aide and the French trade attaché—both of whom came to her shoulder and made bad jokes about it—before dinner was announced. There were twenty settings at a table sparkling with crystal and silver, and Kate found her place card at the center, between a congressman from Indiana and a member of the National Security Council.

"I've been told you're Polly Benedict's granddaughter," Congressman Clement Kilbourne Case said as soon as their napkins were unfolded. "How did I miss that when Theo introduced us?"

"Theo introduced me by my name," Kate said, "not my genealogy."

Case darted a look at her. "Oops," he said, and smiled with perfect teeth. "Tactless of me in this feminist age." He seemed genuinely contrite. He had the kind of looks, Kate decided, that belonged at a senior prom in Indiana: healthy, scrubbed, pasteurized, and bland as pabulum, the kind of looks that would irritate no one. She suspected his politics were the same.

Kate accepted his apology with a nod and returned to playing with her dinner, already regretting that she'd snapped at him. It was Rebecca she was annoyed with for seating her next to a bachelor. It was so depressingly obvious.

"Do you know Polly?" she asked, making conversation.

"In this town it's essential for a Democrat to know Polly, particularly now that we can smell victory in November. And The Senator, too, of course. Oliver's become a reigning elder of the Senate." Case nodded toward Theo at the head of the table. "Barrows has seen to that, with his wife's help. She's the shrewdest little hostess in Washington."

"Are you one of Theo's clients?"

"Not yet, but we're talking about it. Have you known him long?"

"Since I was fourteen." She turned to smile affectionately at Theo and he smiled back.

"A clever man," Case said. "Raises fortunes in loophole campaign contributions, with or without the PACs. He knows exactly which buttons to push."

Which is more than I can say for you, Kate thought, sipping her wine.

"Are you going to be a political Benedict?" Case asked her.

"No. I'm the academic variety. Didn't anyone tell you I'm Tyler Ballard's daughter?"

He shook his head. "Touché. I suppose everyone tells you this, but I've really read all your father's books. The man goes right to the heart of things." He glanced at her and cut his review short. He was clearly reminding himself of the dinner party rule that the person on one's right should be engaged in conversation for ten minutes before one turned to the person on the left.

"So you're an academic," Case remarked. "What are you studying?"

"I've finished studying for the moment. I'm going to teach." Unable to resist, Kate added "I have a Ph.D. in history."

Case put down his fork and knife and turned to face her. "Dr. Ballard, I've made a fine botch of things. What can I possibly do to redeem myself?"

"You mustn't even try," Kate said, and turned to the man on her right.

|||

"She was really wicked," Rebecca said, waiting for Theo to get into bed. He slept in the buff and she loved watching his naked body as he moved around the room. "She cut one of this town's most eligible bachelors off at the knees."

"Clem Case may be the conservatives' fair-haired boy, but he can be an ass with women. He thinks looks make up for tact. And Kate's been hurt by that Talley bastard. You've known her all your life but you still don't understand she needs to lick her wounds alone."

"Don't scold me, darling. I'm sorry if I was gauche and I will be good, I promise." She smiled. "She looks remarkable all the same."

"She always did."

"Kate's not a conventional beauty."

"She has a beauty all her own if people take the trouble to look."

"That's true. She's like one of those medieval princesses she writes about."

"Or a Modigliani."

"Too bad Modigliani isn't everyone's cup of tea," Rebecca said.

Theo got into bed and turned out the light. He put his arm around Rebecca and they settled into their preferred sleeping position, her head on his shoulder, his hand on her breast, hers on his groin.

"How do you think the evening went?" he asked.

"Very well. Especially for the first week in August, with half the town away. We had the best of what's left."

"High time we were on the Cape," he said, and lowered his hand to stroke her rounding belly. "I suppose we should have gone as soon as Congress rose last week. This weather's not good for you."

"I'm fine and you had work to do." She sighed while he stroked her. "Ummm. That feels nice."

"The baby's asleep," he said.

"I'm not." She clasped him.

"Becca! We made love this morning."

"It won't hurt the baby. I'll even lie on my side when we're ready."

"You're bigger than last time," he said.

"Am I repulsive to you?" There was genuine panic in her voice.

"You're gorgeous," he said, sliding the straps of her gown from her shoulders to bare her breasts. "You're even more luscious when you're pregnant."

"Kiss me."

He did and she moaned blissfully. "This damned gown," she said. "Why did I put it on?"

He pulled it up. "I can still get to you. I can always get to you."

"Oh, yes," Rebecca said. "Get to me. I love you, Theo. If I ever lost you, I wouldn't want to live."

"Hush," he said. "Hush."

IV

Theo had gone to his office, little Ted was at day camp, and the other children were off with the nanny when Kate came downstairs the next morning in a pair of jeans and a shirt.

"That was a long sleep," Rebecca said. She looked perfectly put together in pale blue. She always dressed and put on light makeup to have breakfast with Theo.

"It cured my jet lag."

"Come and have lunch. We'll talk. And I won't nag, I promise. I'm sorry about Clem Case, but he can be very sweet."

"I suppose so," Kate said. "I'm just not in the mood for his brand of sweet."

They had lunch on the shaded terrace. A warm breeze tempered the heat and the sounds of Georgetown were muffled by the trees. The butler brought a silver tray of mail and Rebecca riffled through a pile of invitations for the fall.

"This is your dream come true," Kate said. "You always knew exactly what you wanted."

"So did you. You just forgot to factor in men."

"Speaking of which, I saw Sydney."

"What? When?" Rebecca tossed the invitations back onto the tray.

"The day I left. She came to explain that she and Royal belonged together. Only the sobbing Gypsy violins were missing."

"I wish you were really as hard as you sound!"

"I try, but she's going to marry an Austrian baron at Christmastime and she invited me because I'm the only family member she can ask."

"And you said *yes*?"

"I said I didn't know."

"Well, I'll be stuffed!"

"I almost told her about Win, that he and I belonged together too. She's so pathetic when she talks about Royal, I actually felt sorry for her. Can you believe that? Then I was angry for letting such sentimental tripe get to me. And finally I was sorry for myself because I don't have the kind of mother I can confide in."

"My mother would drop dead if she knew half what you know about me. Girls shouldn't confide in their mothers. That's what friends are for."

They leaned toward each other and touched hands briefly.

"Aside from that," Kate went on, "I had the feeling she wasn't telling me everything. She made Polly sound like a monster." Kate repeated Sydney's story. "Polly's no saint, but she's not as bad as that."

"Don't expect *me* to be Polly's champion," Rebecca said. "We see them fairly often because The Senator's mad about Theo, but Polly still treats me like a scullery maid and she's never invited Theo to Kel Regis because I'd have to come along. If you ask me," Rebecca said shrewdly, "she's jealous of your friendship with me and always was."

"You may be right. But Polly gets bees in her bonnet. Can you believe she wanted me to go into politics? It's what she's been planning to do with me all these years."

"Better politics than teaching women's studies to a bunch of giggling girls who'll marry the men their daddies tell them to."

"You sound just like Polly!"

The English nanny, pushing Marian in her stroller and leading Katie by the hand, came out to the terrace, her starched white uniform creaking.

"Miss Katie wants to meet her auntie Katherine," she said. Kate thought she could have played a nanny in one of Win's plays.

"You're a smasher," Kate said, smiling at her tow-headed, blue-eyed goddaughter. "Do you know you look just like your mother?"

Katie stared mutely at her.

"Say yes, Katie," Rebecca prompted. Katie shook her head. "Everyone says she's the image of me," her mother went on, "except that she's quiet, of course. She can talk but she won't. All right, Nanny, you can take them for their walk now."

"I want to talk to Katie," Kate said. "And I have something upstairs for each of them."

"You can give them their gifts later. Talk to Katie, then."

Kate took her namesake on her knee and began the question and answer game that passes for conversation between adults and children. She was relieved when Katie finally responded.

"Lord, what a lovely collection," Kate said when the children had been taken off.

"You, too, can be the owner of a bouncing baby if you go back to fornication before it's too late."

"We'll see."

"Where will you go until school starts?"

"To the Cape. Tyler's already there."

"No Kel Regis?"

"I don't think so. Polly's miffed about Brooke Parrish."

"I'll bet she is," Rebecca said, and her glee at Polly's discomfiture was very like Sydney's.

II

I

It was déjà vu: Kate and Tyler sat in the parlor of the Cape Cod cottage, he working on a manuscript, she taking notes, the smell of brine blending with the smell of leather-bound books and furniture wax and logs burning in the grate.

Apart from the fact that the notes Kate was making were for her own use, not Tyler's, nothing had changed. It was familiar, it was safe; but for the first time in her life it made Kate restless. The cottage was confining, and although she found release in swimming as hard as she could in the cold, invigorating surf, the evenings were painfully long.

Her mind kept sliding to Win, to the two of them together when he was beside her, talking to her, listening to her, making love to her.

She remembered everything about him, but she couldn't conjure up his face.

That was true whether she hated him or loved him, and she did both. She wanted desperately to hold on to the hatred, but logic always reared its head, a dash of cold water over the cleansing flames of indignation. He had never promised her a future.

She wondered where he was—right now when it was two A.M. in England. She hoped he slept alone, missing her, but she knew better. She wondered how long she would sleep alone. The thought of disclosing herself to another man, of telling her story and hearing his, of showing him what she liked in bed, was inconceivable. Maybe she never would.

She looked at her father, wanting so much to talk about Win that she almost told him everything. But Tyler would be appalled by the affair. Tyler had good reason to be appalled by people who yielded to passion. And tonight she had to tell him about Sydney, and the sooner she did it the better.

But she watched him for a few minutes more. Tyler wore the same old sweater Kate had patched for him a dozen times. His silver hair glinted under the lamp as he bent to his work; he still wrote his books in longhand on legal pads. He was fifty-six and, because of his hair, looked his age but no more, a handsome man still. And he was content. It seemed a shame to break into that charmed circle of his, but Kate knew it would be better if he heard the news from her.

"Father," she said.

He looked up, somewhat perplexed. She always called him Tyler.

"There's something I must tell you before you read about it in the papers. Sydney's getting married."

He looked at her for a long moment before he put down his pen. "How do you know?" he asked reluctantly, as if he would rather not hear the answer.

"She came to see me the day I left England."

He was outraged. "Why?"

"Some notion that she could explain herself."

"And did she?" His dark eyes challenged Kate.

"Not to my satisfaction, no. She said she expected that, but she wanted to see me anyway."

He stood suddenly, pushing his chair back so violently that it fell over. "Damn the woman!" he shouted. "Will I never be free of her?"

Kate was astonished. The only other time she had heard him shout was the night Sydney left. "But, Tyler, what has it got to do with you? With us?"

"You wouldn't understand," he said angrily. "When a man's been married to a woman, lived with her for years, had a child by her . . . she's a part of him whether he wants her to be or not. What she does affects me. It always will."

So he was still in love with her! Kate was aghast at how naive she'd been to suppose that for other people love stopped just because one of the lovers said it had.

"I'm sorry," she said, "I should have realized."

He covered his face with his hands. "You don't realize what I did for that woman. She was the most beautiful thing I had ever seen. I loved her enough to risk my career, ruin my reputation." A shuddering breath, very like a sob, escaped him, and his next words made Kate's eyes fill with tears. "I wasn't always a dried-up stick of a scholar. She had no monopoly on passion then. My God, my God, all these years . . ."

His voice trailed away and Kate sat immobile, her heart breaking for him and for the hunger he had buried for so long.

Tyler shook himself and ran his fingers through his hair. "When the press gets hold of it, they'll rake up the old story. Only it'll be worse this time: I have my own reputation now, not just the leavings of hers. I'll look like a fool again while she . . . No one in Europe gives a damn about a superannuated debutante, but here they love to throw mud and they love reminding everyone that a woman like your mother rolled in it. I'm the innocent party, but they don't care how much I suffer."

"It's a wedding, not an affair," she said, trying now to comfort herself as well as him. A warmed-over scandal was not the best recommendation for a teacher. She had been preoccupied by Win, but she realized now that her students would lap up the old story as eagerly as her classmates had.

She got up to set his chair on its legs. "It won't last long. In any case, there's nothing we can do about it."

"There never is," Tyler said savagely. "Not with your mother. You shouldn't have seen her. She's a bad influence." He turned suddenly. "Who's the groom?"

"I forget the name," Kate lied judiciously. "He's an Austrian baron."

"Austrian? How old?"

"I don't know. Why?"

"A lot of them were Nazis, and in my opinion the sons still are." He snorted. "Or the grandsons. He may be very young. Your mother likes them young these days."

"There's not much we can do about that either."

Tyler did not reply, but after a moment he seemed to pull himself together. She watched him smooth his hair, knock the ash out of his pipe, refill it, light it, then search for a book among the many on the shelves and sit down with it at his desk without another word. The exchange ended as abruptly as it had begun.

Neither of them spoke of it again. It was the same conspiracy of silence they had shared so long ago. Not strange, when Kate considered that they were the same people with the same weaknesses. Time and experience seemed not to change a personality, only to teach it how best to camouflage its weaknesses.

It was not pleasant to realize that she would never be free of the monkeys on her back, merely better able to hide them from the world.

||

Polly arrived unannounced.

"But very welcome," Tyler said when she descended from a limousine that looked entirely out of place in front of the weathered cottage. So did Polly, in a navy blue silk dress, a white straw hat with small blue plumes curving over the brim, and immaculate white kid gloves.

"Come in, come in!" he said. "You should have let me know. Katherine will get a room ready for you as soon as she comes back."

"I won't be staying here," Polly said, casting a jaundiced eye around the parlor. "*You* may love it, but it's a bit primitive for me, with that ocean raging like some wild animal only yards from the door. I'll stay at the inn. Where's Kate?"

"Swimming."

"In that heavy surf?"

"She's a strong swimmer."

Polly sat in Tyler's chair and fanned herself with a lace handkerchief, refusing his offer of iced tea. "Kate's not planning to come to Kel Regis before term starts, is she?"

"I don't know," Tyler said, taking the window seat. "She hasn't said."

"For God's sake, Tyler! Don't you two *talk* to each other?"

Tyler bristled. "Katherine and I are very close. But we don't discuss details."

"*Details?* Don't you care that your daughter is going to teach at Wakefield's only rival?"

"If I did, I doubt anything could stop her. She signed a contract and I raised Katherine to believe her word is her bond." Tyler gave Polly a sidelong glance, then turned to gaze out of the window. "I thought you'd come about Sydney."

Polly looked at him scornfully while she removed her gloves.

"She's getting married," Tyler said. "There'll be talk."

"Tyler Ballard, you're an old woman. I know she's getting married. I don't care that"—Polly snapped her fingers—"for what she does or how the lumpen proletariat gossip about it among themselves. And neither should you. I came to this godforsaken place to talk about Kate's future, nothing else."

"Her life is going according to plan. Katherine doesn't change."

Polly leaned forward. "You don't know Kate at all or you'd have noticed the change in her."

"What change?"

Polly shook her head impatiently. "She's just had a wild affair with a Boston Talley who left her for a career on the stage. I'm sure she'd have gone off with him if he'd been willing, she was that besotted."

Tyler covered his face. "Oh, no, not my Katherine!" He was silent a few seconds, then lowered his hands. "Did she tell you all this?"

"No, but do you suppose I'd have let her go so far for so long and not keep an eye on her? It's true, all right."

"You had her watched?"

"Well, of course I did! Oh, for mercy's sake, you don't have to look as if the sky had fallen. She's a grown woman and we live in parlous times. The point is that she mustn't go on making these mistakes, and now that she's tried sex, she'll surely want more." Polly frowned, impervious to Tyler's recoil. "She might even run off with someone totally unsuitable, heaven help us! It's in her blood, don't forget that."

Tyler looked shaken at that. "What do you have in mind?"

"Kate's not cut out to be a professor." Polly wagged a finger at her son-in-law. "That was your doing. But she has everything it takes to climb to the top of the political ladder."

Polly ticked her list off on bejeweled fingers. "Brains. Beauty of a kind that pleases men and won't offend the women voters. The good sense to keep her mouth shut until she knows exactly what to say. Presence: she'll be perfect on television. A pair of family names that are famous. And me." Polly held up six fingers and gave a brisk nod. "I could get her elected to Congress from our district as sure as God made little green apples. There's no limit to how far she can go from there."

"And the other thing?" Tyler asked, still at the window.

"What other thing?" Polly paused briefly, peering at him. "Oh, you mean sex. I'll see she meets a few really marriageable men. But first I have to get her to Kel Regis. If she must teach until she's bored with it, she can teach at Wakefield."

"Don't count on it," Tyler said. "Katherine's got a mind of her own."

"And a hole in her heart, don't forget that! She needs someone to care about her."

"I care!" Tyler protested. "She knows I do."

"You're a good father," Polly soothed him glibly. "But sometimes a girl needs a mother and I'm all the real mother Kate's ever had."

Tyler sighed. "She's coming up from the beach now."

Polly went to the window to watch. "I think her legs got even longer. I wish she wouldn't get that color though. She looks like Pocahontas."

"She's a handsome woman," Tyler said as if he had just discovered it.

"And I thought she was going to be plain," Polly said. "Leave us alone, will you, Tyler? I'm not good at pretending to eat crow before an audience. Go make some iced tea—from scratch."

|||

"Polly!" Kate said, standing on the worn hooked rug in the hall. "Why didn't you let us know?"

"I was afraid you'd take flight."

Kate pulled the towel around her. "I'm still a little damp. I ought to change."

"Only if you're cold." Polly sounded positively maternal. "What I've come to say won't take long."

"Okay, let's have it." Kate came into the parlor wrapped in her towel. Her hair hung in damp tendrils around her face.

"I've come to apologize. I've been a rare fool, haven't I?"

"We settled that on the telephone months ago," Kate said.

"Obviously not, since you're here instead of at Kel Regis."

"It's not where I am that upsets you, it's where I'm going. I'm not about to argue the point."

There was a warning in those dark eyes. *I could lose her*, Polly thought, shocked by the profound pain that prospect caused her, something far more serious than disappointment or anger. Lose Kate? It was a risk she would not take.

I love this girl, she admitted to herself for the first time in so many words. *I love her honesty and her brains and her spirit because they're like mine. I love what she is and what she will become.*

"It's you I miss. Kate!" It burst from Polly while she sat smoothing the fabric on the arm of the chair. "I wasn't raised to trumpet my feelings. I wrap them up in euphemisms. I say that what you do is important to me. I say I have other hopes for you. I say if you teach at all, let it be at Wakefield. All of it means I care deeply about you, more than you know." She looked up at Kate. "I was a very unhappy woman before you came into my life, and if I sometimes clutch at you, that's the only way I have to let you know I need you."

It stunned Kate to hear such a declaration from such a woman. It was like finding Win, finding a love she had been wanting a long time without being conscious of its lack. But, unlike Win, Polly would never leave her, and the certainty flowed over Kate like balm, healing and irresistible. Tears stung her eyes and she almost gave in utterly: Wakefield, Kel Regis, everything.

But she was not to be seduced by love, not again.

"Do you still think I've got something up my sleeve?" Polly asked.

"Not this time," Kate said, needing to believe it.

"Well, thank heaven for that," Polly said softly. Then she stood and gathered her gloves and handbag.

"You're not leaving?"

"I've said what I came to say." Polly looked around the sitting room again, the plumes on her hat swaying.

"At least have dinner with us," Kate said, correctly interpreting Polly's opinion of the cottage. "You can sleep at the inn."

Polly nodded her agreement. "I still wish you'd come to Kel Regis. Charlie's Darling misses you."

"How is the rogue?"

"The best we have, like his daddy was and his granddaddy before him. And Arabella's baby is due anytime now. She'd love to see you."

They stood looking at each other. Then Kate shook her head. "I may come to Kel Regis for a while, Polly, but I'm not breaking my contract with Brooke Parrish."

"I didn't suppose you would," Polly said, keeping her face impassive.

If I can get her to Kel Regis, she thought jubilantly, *I'll have another chance!*

IV

But Polly's assurance deserted her as soon as she was back at Kel Regis, having Kate's rooms turned out again, adding a priceless bibelot here, a first edition there, a new saddle and a big, fluffy terry-cloth robe made to Kate's measure.

She shared her misgivings with Dodie Phelps as the two women sat in the gazebo rocking their Brumbys and drinking mint juleps. The house was air-conditioned, but both of them preferred the garden, which was wonderful to contemplate. Polly had done it all in white this year; her roses were the stars of the garden, but she had added candytuft, white tobacco plant, goatsbeard, and summer hyacinth.

"I felt as if someone had kicked me with a pair of steel-toed boots," Polly said. "I've only ever cared for two other people in my life as much as I care for that girl."

"Why don't you come right out and say you love her?"

"She's changed," Polly said, wielding a palmetto fan as big as a tennis racquet. "She was always strong-minded, and that Talley character has made her more wary than ever, especially of me. You'd think *I* was the one who seduced and deserted her."

"Neither of us knows how it feels to be left. Widowhood was a merciful deliverance to me, and you were the one who said no."

"Humph!" Polly said. She rarely referred to her long-ago love affair. "Anyway, she outflanked me and I lost the battle."

"You deserved to."

"But only because I overplayed my hand. I'll win the war yet, see if I don't. At any rate, Kate's coming. If Arabella would bestir herself and start her labor, Kate would come sooner and stay longer. I don't know what ails Belle. She's ten days overdue."

"Stars above! Do all the girls in this family labor and bring forth to suit you?"

"If they want more shares in Benedict Industries, they do."

"Kate didn't tell you about Sydney?"

"No. I didn't expect she would."

"Or about her actor?"

Polly shook her head, looking uncomfortable. "Not a word. She will when she's ready. Unless she thinks I know nothing about that kind of thing."

"You old fool," Dodie Phelps said tenderly. "You're thinking about him, aren't you?"

"Oh, yes," Polly said with a rare sweetness in her expression. "I think about him every day."

V

Arabella delivered two days later, and Kate and Tyler closed up the cottage and came south. Tyler went directly to Kel Regis and Kate to Charleston to see the new arrival, Arabella's second. The floor nurse showed her the baby in the nursery—a miniature of Belle—and gave her the number of Arabella Champion's room.

". . . the rotten son of a bitch," she heard Ambrose saying as she reached the door.

Inside the room Ambrose Ardmore was seated at his sister's bedside, holding her hand. The twins were more alike than ever, from their coloring to their gestures to their voices. Kate thought she had never seen two such breathtaking people.

"Who's a rotten s.o.b.?"

"Kate!" Belle said, holding out her arms. "Oh, Kate, it's been so long."

Kate leaned over the bed and hugged her cousin. "Well, I'll be around from now on. I've seen the baby. She's lovely. What will you call her?"

"Katherine, after her godmother."

"That's lovely, Belle, thank you. I'm very touched. Now, who's the s.o.b.?" Kate demanded.

"Her husband."

"Oh, Brosie, don't," Belle pleaded.

"I can't help it," Ambrose said. "He was out carousing with one of his tarts while she was here going through hell."

"I had no idea he was like that," Kate said angrily. "You never wrote a word. Why do you stay with him?"

"Where can I go?" Belle said plaintively, tears rolling down her cheeks.

"You can live with me," her brother said.

"Or at Kel Regis," Kate suggested.

Ambrose laughed unpleasantly.

"Gran would cut us both off if I did either of those things," Belle explained.

"Polly?" Kate was dubious. "Surely not."

"Yes, Polly," Ambrose said fiercely. "She arranged the damned marriage in the first place. Dragged Belle to the altar, pushed her into it just to separate us."

"She didn't! I was in love with him."

Ambrose said nothing and his sister flushed. She took his hand. "It'll be all right, honey," she calmed him. "He's not so bad."

The twins looked at each other for a long moment. Ambrose nodded, and there was a tenderness in the way he touched his sister's cheek that struck Kate as more than fraternal.

Maybe, she thought, *you have to have felt love to recognize it.*

Or was she seeing sensuality everywhere now?

I must be dreaming, she decided.

"Let me tell Polly," Kate said. "She'll deal with Ross."

"She already knows," Ambrose said. "Polly knows everything that goes on in this family. Thanks, Kate, but I'll deal with Ross myself."

"Polly doesn't have any patience with women who fuss about roving husbands," Arabella said. "After all, she's put up with The Senator all her life."

Kate, although well aware of her grandfather's reputation, had supposed it started late, the result of a midlife crisis. Midlife crises, like love, were supposed to excuse almost anything.

But a lifetime of infidelity was a hard burden for a woman as proud as Polly. Kate said as much to her cousins.

"She had no choice," Ambrose said. "Not in those days."

"Gran knows how to accept what can't be helped,"

"She had to accept Hilliard's suicide," Ambrose said.

Arabella darted a warning look at her brother.

"Suicide?" Kate was startled.

"Didn't anyone ever tell you?"

"My God," Kate said. "There are more skeletons in this family's closets than I ever dreamed."

"There's nothing this lot hasn't done," Ambrose agreed.

"I'm sick and tired of talking about family," Belle interrupted him. "I want Kate to tell us about Oxford."

Kate complied, but she was thinking that she must rearrange her assessment of her grandmother. A libertine husband and a son dead by his own hand! And Sydney, too, bringing disgrace and notoriety on Polly's beloved family.

Oh, Polly, Polly, Kate sympathized silently when she was on the road to Kel Regis, *how all of it must have hurt you!*

Polly and Dodie Phelps were on the veranda when Kate, in her new

Austin Mini, crunched to a stop on the gravel drive. She got out of the car and seized Polly in a bear hug, planting two loud kisses on her grandmother's cheeks.

"I'm so glad to see you!" Kate said.

"Me, too, honey," Polly said, smiling triumphantly at Dodie Phelps over Kate's shoulder.

"Has Tyler arrived?"

"Two days ago. He's scratching away in the library like something out of Dickens."

"Dodie Phelps." Kate turned to kiss the diminutive woman. "You look absolutely scrumptious." She put an arm around each woman. "Let's go in. I can't wait to see what Polly's changed while I was away."

VI

It was a tranquil week. Kate, knowing Polly would not discuss personal tragedies, never mentioned them. She spent her time as she always did at Kel Regis: walking, reading, riding one of the Charlie's Darling descendants, and poking around in the family archives.

In a set of albums stored apart from the others, she finally found pictures of Hilliard, often with his beautiful little sister Sydney in tow. Sydney had been incredibly lovely even then. Hilliard's pictures showed the usual scenes from a privileged southern boy's life. His birth and death were recorded in the family Bible, but no mention was made of a suicide.

His headstone, in the well-populated family graveyard, showed he had been thirty-two when he died, in the same year Sydney left Harmony to chase Royal.

HILLIARD ARDMORE BENEDICT

1928–1961

BELOVED SON OF

PENELOPE ARDMORE BENEDICT

GOOD NIGHT, SWEET PRINCE

Not of Penelope and Oliver, as on the headstones of the twins, Oliver and Orrin, killed in the South Pacific in World War II. Knowing Polly, the inscription might have been a punishment for her errant husband. And yet the couple had a close relationship despite Polly's having the brains and Oliver's knowing it.

Kate was very fond of her grandfather, even if he was almost a caricature of a Southern gentleman. In his seventy-sixth year, he was still a vital man, who tramped around the mansion—"like a herd of elephant," Polly said—always stopping in his tracks to hug whichever of his progeny were around. He was a wily manipulator on the floor of the Senate but an old lion whose claws had been drawn at home.

How must Oliver have felt, losing yet another son, not to war but to suicide?

But it seemed, Kate concluded, that her grandparents had managed to come to terms with it. Maybe time did heal everything. She hoped so, for her own sake. Tyler, it appeared, had come to terms with Sydney's remarriage as well; he never spoke of the impending announcement, nor did anyone else, but they were all apprehensive about the gossip it would precipitate and Tyler found comfort in numbers.

Polly did not mention Brooke Parrish either, although Kate was reproached in the slow drawl of her aunts Felicity, who fluttered, and Jane, who was plain.

"It was Polly's fault," insisted Maynard's wife, Felicity. "Our faculty committee wanted Kate, but Polly made them turn her down." Felicity regarded Kate closely. "I hear your dissertation is hotter than a tin roof in August."

"It isn't sexy, if that's what you mean, Aunt Fel."

"But it's about sex," Jane, who was Kendall's wife, said disapprovingly.

"Isn't everything?" And Kate had gone off to the stables with her aunt Felicity's high-pitched laughter following in her wake.

"Home for Thanksgiving," Polly said at the end of the week when Kate got into her square, squat little car to leave for preterm faculty meetings.

"Nothing could keep me away."

Polly and Dodie Phelps watched the car dwindle into the distance on the oak-lined drive.

"Still think I've lost the war?" Polly asked.

"You sly old vixen," Dodie Phelps replied. "I wouldn't put anything past you."

1 2

———◆•◆•◆———

I

William Neville, President of Brooke Parrish College for the past fifteen years, rose from behind his desk. He was a small, wiry man in his sixties whom Kate had met at the faculty party the night before. She had thought him a cold man then. His narrow mustache was a match for his iron-gray center-parted hair, and his hand, extended to shake hers briefly, was as cool as his manner.

"Dr. Ballard," he said with a thin smile. "I'm glad we found time for a private chat before the term begins."

"So am I, Dr. Neville," Kate said, impatient to get past the formalities and come to the point: the publicity about Sydney. The engagement had been announced right after Kate left Kel Regis, and had quickly found its way into the press. Big city papers consigned it to the society pages. Tabloids, gossip sheets, and the smalltown southern press dug up the old stories and trumpeted them on front pages.

Parrish Station was a small town. This morning's edition of *The Clarion*, lying in clear view on Neville's desk, announced:

FORMER BENEDICT DEB
TO WED AGAIN

And below that:

Spurned Daughter Teaches at Brooke Parrish

The story included details about Kate's academic career and her new post at Brooke Parrish.

"Unfortunate," Neville said, following Kate's glance at the paper.

"Irrelevant," Kate replied.

He indicated a chair for her and sat down himself. "To your abilities, certainly. But this kind of notoriety is never irrelevant."

"It isn't my notoriety."

"You've enjoyed considerable attention since the subject of your thesis was made public."

"I had nothing to do with the press coverage."

He took another tack, once more looking at the newspaper. "The parents are concerned about the effect this might have on tender young minds, and so, I must tell you, are we."

"And the students?"

He matched the fingertips of his left hand very carefully to those of his right. "That's precisely the point. We have been deluged with requests for transfer to your courses, and we can't attribute all of this interest to scholarship."

Kate's internal pressure gauge moved to the red zone. "Gossip is not what I intend to teach, as I shall make abundantly clear to the girls. When they see the reading lists for my courses, I'm sure many of them will transfer out."

"Young girls can be very difficult, Dr. Ballard. Once they take the scent of such a sensational story, they hang on like a pack of hounds at a hunt. They can make you very uncomfortable."

"I doubt that." She waited for a moment, and when he did not speak, she did.

"Are you asking for my resignation?"

"It would grieve me to do that, but you must know what effect scandal can have on any college—and on this one in particular."

"Dr. Neville, I agree that the circumstance is embarrassing, but our contract requires only that my behavior meet certain standards; it says nothing at all about that of my relatives. In this particular instance, one of my relatives is getting married, clearly not an offense against public morals. So if you *are* suggesting that I resign, the answer is no. If you discharge me, I'll sue Brooke Parrish for breach of contract."

Neville darted a murderous look at her before he conceded. "My dear Dr. Ballard, you misunderstood. I meant it as a possibility, not a request. You are free to do as you choose. I merely wanted to point out what you should expect."

"I know exactly what to expect. If that's all, Dr. Neville?"

He stood. "Except to welcome you to Brooke Parrish and wish you well in your new career." He did not offer his hand.

She was absolutely composed, even gracious, as she thanked him for his good wishes, but once in the corridor she walked very swiftly out of the president's mansion and across the wide, tree-shaded lawns of the almost deserted campus.

"Calm down," she commanded herself, then muttered, "Damn Sydney! Damn her, damn her, *DAMN her!*"

Her mother's legacy had once more fallen upon her like an avalanche, opening deep emotional fissures Kate had worked hard to close.

"Calm down," she repeated. She *was* free of Sydney and she could handle this latest invasion of her life. The students would arrive tomorrow and classes would begin the day after. There would almost certainly be some hurdles: a snicker here, a double entendre there. But eventually—probably when classes resumed after the Christmas recess—she could be a teacher.

II

Kate soon realized she had walked clear across the huge campus and had reached the terrace of Mugg's Coffee House. She sat down and ordered tea, the picture of serenity while she alternately cursed Neville and her mother.

It's no use. I'll never be free of her, Kate fumed, staring into the cup before her.

"Good morning, Dr. Ballard," a woman's voice said, and Kate looked up. It was her department head. The woman smiled, apparently out of breath. "I'm Carol Hunter," she said. "We met briefly at the faculty party last night. I saw you leave the mansion, but I couldn't catch you—and you didn't hear me call."

"I'm sorry, Dr. Hunter. I was distracted about something." They shook hands. "My name's Kate. Will you join me?"

"With pleasure. Call me Carol." Carol sat down. She talked easily, a warm, friendly, unpretentious woman who might have been anywhere from forty to fifty years old. She had a doctorate in psychology and she was amusing, not venomous, as she described the cliques and jealousies among the faculty. Her brown eyes danced with fun.

"As for the girls," Carol said, "they're delicately nurtured and very naughty and most of them are southern. They're sent to Brooke Parrish more to preserve their virginity than to improve their minds, but we manage to educate them anyway." Carol paused to put more sugar in her coffee, then went on. "They're so thoroughly spoiled that they can be unkind."

"So Neville just finished telling me. He predicted hard times ahead."

"Oh?" Carol looked at Kate steadily, hesitated, then decided to chance it. "Because of your mother?"

Kate nodded, relieved to talk to someone whose sincerity had become more apparent with every word she spoke. "He suggested—oh, very obliquely, of course—that I resign."

"What brass! I hope you told him where to go."

"I told him—not at all obliquely—that I'd take him to court if he tried to discharge me."

"Good for you! He's a terrible prig. But so is everyone on the board of trustees. There was a big fight over hiring you in the first place because of the sexual material in your dissertation."

"Strike two," Kate said. "I told him I had nothing to do with making the thing public. What made the trustees take a chance?"

"BP is losing students to Wakefield and both are losing to the coed colleges. Suddenly we're living in a different world. With all this liberation, girls want to take the bit between their legs, as it were. They don't want to be locked away from males for four years. It's unnatural in our society. They're staunch feminists—until they marry, of course—and they don't want to be taught by fossils with old-fashioned ideas. So the least BP could do was to start a department of women's studies and hire you—at my suggestion, I'm pleased to say. When your appointment was announced, we were inundated by requests for coverage from almost every women's group in the country. That makes you a bona fide feminist and, to the girls, that's as good as a bra burning. You're proof that BP has finally moved into the twentieth century."

"And then they almost backed down because of a scandal that's ancient history. And you said this was a new world!"

"Talk, Kate, all talk. After all the noise, not much is going to change for women. That's my prediction. And if it does, we'll have another challenge: men's resentment."

"I'd like to hear more about that."

They paid the check and walked back across the campus, past the immaculately kept white-columned buildings that housed classrooms and administrative offices and the dormitories that provided a bedroom, sitting room, and bath for each of its pampered students.

"Where are you living?" Carol asked.

"In a garret apartment on Libby Avenue. I can stand straight only in the center of each room, but it's charming and very private. And you?"

"In Nell Tiller Hall. I'm the house mother." The way she said it made Kate laugh. "Go on, mock me," Carol said amiably. "You got away with it because you're new and you're young, but if you stay here long enough, you'll have twenty or thirty belles whose clappers are in your charge."

Kate laughed again. "I've been told I'll have one hundred and ten belles at my first lecture. They've moved me from a classroom in Squires to Dinsmore Lecture Hall."

"I heard," Carol said. "Congratulations."

III

The wedding invitation was in the morning mail Kate picked up on her way to her first class. Sitting in her car, she examined it tentatively, as if it were a rare insect. The address was written in black ink in a copperplate hand on cream-colored vellum so heavy it creaked when Kate opened it.

Madame Sydney Benedict

requests the pleasure of your company

on the occasion of her marriage to

Hans Erik Gunther, Baron Rayner

on the sixth day of February nineteen hundred and seventy-eight

at seven o'clock

at 24, Heldenstrasse, Vienna.

A Reception and Ball will follow

Decorations will be worn   *RSVP*

Kate locked it away in the glove compartment.

"Not today, dear mother," she said sternly as she turned the key in the ignition. "Not now."

IV

Two hundred and twenty eyes were riveted on Kate as she entered Dinsmore Lecture Hall III from a side door at the front, climbed the podium, put several books on the lectern, then looked up to face her students.

"I'm Dr. Ballard," she said, "and this class is part of the new women's studies program, which we intend to make one of the best in the country. I especially wanted to teach here because of the interest Brooke Parrish students have shown in learning about women in the past so that they can make things better for women in the present.

"The past is vital: George Santayana said that those who do not learn from it are condemned to relive it. Millennia of abuse, ranging from slavery to state-sponsored cruelty, have left their mark on how women think about themselves, how they think they must behave. We're here to understand and to change the way women see themselves and, eventually, the way men see women."

She was not in the least nervous. She knew the material thoroughly and, over the microphone, she pitched her husky voice low, to fix attention, as Tyler used to do. She had dressed in a black skirt, white shirt, and low-heeled shoes. Her hair was pulled back into a knot at the nape of her neck and she wore dark-rimmed glasses for effect; there was nothing wrong with her eyes.

"The first thing about becoming the part," Win had often told her, "is looking the part."

She would be teaching them some shocking sexual facts. She didn't want to look provocative.

"I've called this particular course Domestic History," Kate said, finishing her opening remarks, "because it looks closely at what women were doing while men were making history—or, more appropriately, what was being done to women and what women had to do to survive, including prostitution. Fanny Hill to the contrary, most of the great courtesans of the past did not go into the profession for the joy of it." She paused. "Any questions before we begin?"

A hand was lifted and waved above the second row. Kate nodded and a slim, fair-haired girl stood up. There was a murmur in the audience.

Ah, Kate thought. *The ringleader.* She felt like Bette Davis in *All This and Heaven Too.*

"Dr. Ballard, will we be studying great prostitutes of recent history as well?"

A wave of laughter rippled through the front part of the hall and cries of "What did she say?" came from the back.

"The question," Kate said calmly, "is whether or not we'll be studying great whores of recent history." She turned back to the girl. "Did you have any particular whores in mind?"

Laughter again, louder this time, then silence as Kate and the girl confronted each other, their gazes locked. After several tense moments, the girl shook her head and sat down.

"If the subject fascinates enough of you," Kate said, "I'll request permission to teach a seminar on it." She pulled a sheet of paper from her notebook and wrote something on it, then held it up. "Great whores," she said, pointing to the heading. "Please list your names here before you leave today." She looked out over the auditorium. "Any other questions?"

There were no questions.

"Then we'll begin with marriage rites and requirements in the fifth century B.C." There was a stir as notebooks were opened. "According to Herodotus, in Baalbek, Syria, where a host of gods and goddesses had to be placated, virgins were required to copulate with a stranger at the temple of Astarte.

"In Babylon, prostitution to a stranger was required once in a woman's lifetime, before marriage, whether she came of a noble family or worked as a barmaid. Many of the women crowned themselves with garlands and sat in the sanctuary of the Temple of Venus to accomplish their sacred duty by surrendering their virginity. We must assume that most of them were ready and willing to observe the religious rites of their society, but we can also infer from our instinctive reaction that some of them were not.

"Once seated, a woman could not return home until chosen by a stranger, who made his selection by throwing a piece of silver in her lap. The couple would then lie together at a remove from the temple. When it was over, the man would say, 'I beseech the goddess to favor thee.' "

Kate paused, but their attention did not waver.

"I remind you again that this was not considered degrading. It was an honorable offering to propitiate the goddess—which was not, however, required of men. The money was contributed to the temple and the girl, having fulfilled her obligation to the state by offering her maidenhead and the silver to the goddess, was free to return home and to be married."

There was a breathless silence in the hall.

"The prettier girls spent a night or two waiting to be chosen. The plain ones sometimes waited for months. This implies that the act was not a purely religious ritual, not for the men, in any case. It was based upon attraction and desire, and the girl had no choice in the outcome."

Kate watched the young faces as they registered outrage. It was the reaction she wanted. She went on to discuss the required reading for the course.

When the session came to an end, there were no names listed under "Great Whores," and that afternoon the administrative office received thirty new requests for transfer to the course. There were no requests to transfer out. Sydney was not referred to again.

"They're too involved in the material to bother about Sydney," Kate called to tell Carol Hunter at the end of her second week. "Why don't you come on over and we'll celebrate? I'll fix you a New England boiled dinner."

"Sounds terrible," Carol said. "You come here and I'll have Cook make us something good."

V

Nell Tiller Hall looked like a smaller version of Mount Vernon, and Carol's suite had a spacious bedroom and bath and an enormous salon. "For demitasse with seniors," she explained. "It's to cultivate the art of social conversation—for social, read insipid."

"It's all very grand," Kate said when they had finished a dinner of squab and wild rice and green salad and were having coffee.

"Yes. I wish Joyce could see it." Joyce was Carol's daughter. She was married to a petroleum engineer and living in Saudi Arabia, and her mother missed her constantly.

"Sometimes," Carol confided, "I wish the good old days were back, even though it was tough going for us after Harold died. But my little girl and I had a lot of fun together."

It was the tender way she said it that stirred an old yearning in Kate for that unique bond between a mother and daughter.

"I've had an invitation to my mother's wedding," Kate said suddenly.

"Oh, Kate," Carol said, understanding at once. "What are you going to do?"

"I thought I couldn't possibly go. I've always hated her for leaving me. But she came to see me before I left England and she wasn't Medusa or Circe. She was . . . I don't know . . . not lonely, exactly, but bereft. She wants someone of her own at her wedding and she picked the only Benedict sentimental enough to give in and go. She can still get to me, make me want to please her. Isn't that a laugh?"

"Kate! You're not sentimental to want something so vital as a relationship with your mother."

"I never had one. Trying to get it back is like crying for the moon."

"It's true you can't get back what you never had, but there's something bizarre about living in the same world with your mother and having no connection with her. Maybe you can have *something.* Maybe it's worth a try."

Back in her garret with the invitation on her desk, Kate wasn't sure it was even worth the trip. But something made her write a formal acceptance and mail it the next morning.

VI

Prelude in C-Sharp Minor was a hit. On the night it opened in London, Tabitha rang Kate as soon as the reviews came in.

"They raved about our sets," she said excitedly.

"That's what I wanted to hear—even at this hour of the morning."

"They raved about Win too."

"I expected that."

"How's teaching?"

"Fine. It comes naturally to me."

Silence.

"I'm all right, Tabby," Kate said. "I really am. Tell me more about the opening."

Kate listened as Tabitha talked on. The play was a smash, no doubt about it. When Win was onstage, no one looked at anyone else. "The character he plays is maddening: you want to hate him but you can't. We'll get to Broadway—there's a lot of interest—but not for a while. We've signed for a long run here. I'll keep you posted."

Kate hung up and lay back on her pillow. She closed her eyes. She could visualize Win in every setting they had shared, hear his voice in the theater and in bed, even touch him, but she still could not see his face.

She began to collect clippings of him as she had of Sydney, feeling foolish, feeling guilty, sure that Rebecca would be scornful if she knew; but Kate was helpless to stop herself. After the first flurry of excitement in the English papers about "a stunning new talent" and "the next Richard Burton," the news crossed quickly to Boston, where the Winslows and the Talleys were besieged in their fortresses on Beacon Hill. Win was soon picked up by the Sunday supplements, *Esquire,* and *Cosmopolitan,* which did an interview with him about his admiration for brainy women and advised its readers not to hide their intellectual lights under a bushel. Tabby wrote:

> *Unless it's that bushel unique to females. Women still can't keep away from him and he's very generous with his favors. But it's all a game to him and you can't really resent him for it.*

Rebecca called after *60 Minutes* did a piece on the London theater and highlighted Win.

"I told you you'd hear about him," Kate said.

"It's still for the best," Rebecca insisted. "What kind of life would you have with him, running from theater to theater to watch him prance around in the spotlight, fighting off hordes of women? I can tell by looking at him he'd be unfaithful. The man's sexy as the devil, but it's plain to see he has an ego as big as the Ritz!"

"You must be the size of the Ritz yourself by now!" Kate said, changing the subject.

"Ready to pop. My belly's up to my neck already and I can barely breathe. But I feel fine. Now listen to me, Kate. Don't let the bastard grind you down. He isn't worth it, no matter how good an actor he is."

"Becca, what would I do without you?"

"God knows. Come to Washington and spend Thanksgiving with us."

"I've already promised Polly."

"Polly? Polly? What did she ever do for you?"

VII

"Today," Kate told her last class before the Thanksgiving break, "we'll address the cloistering of women in the Middle Ages and its parallel in modern times."

Her bags were already in her car when, with a sigh of relief, she turned the Austin in the direction of Kel Regis. She felt stupid for having accepted Sydney's invitation in a moment of weakness. She felt hypocritical for hiding Sydney's visit to Oxford from Polly. And she felt like a fool for still wanting a man who said plainly that he had no time for her.

Her body missed him and her mind missed him, and she knew she had been many times an idiot to let herself go so completely. Win had been the same Win with her that he was with all women. It was Kate who had changed and expected that abracadabra, he would change too.

She began to spin a fantasy as she drove. She was arriving at Kel Regis, not alone but with Win. She was taking him up the broad steps and past the columns, introducing him to her family. "Wait till you see him!" she had told them—and when they saw him they knew what she meant.

Then she shook her head to clear it of such drivel, turned up the radio, and sang along, the better not to think.

Most of the family had already gathered by the time Kate arrived. It was bliss to be welcomed by so many loving arms, to hug her cousins and hold their babies, to hear the aunts tell her how well she looked. She needed to hear that, and she had left her hair loose and her windowpane glasses in the car.

Arabella followed her upstairs to her bedroom. "How's it going?"

"Very well. There were some sticky spots when I first started, but it's pretty smooth sailing now. And you?"

Arabella shifted in her chair. "I told Ross to stop fooling around. I suppose he has."

"Don't you care?"

"Not much. Not anymore." She shrugged. "It isn't as if he's the only one; most men do it. Brosie is more upset about it than I am."

"But, honey," Kate said. "You deserve better."

"So do you. How many women do you know who get what they deserve?"

Not many, Kate had to admit to herself. Sydney hadn't. Belle hadn't, Polly hadn't, Carol had had it taken away from her. Rebecca got what she wanted, and Rebecca believed any woman could if she played her cards right; but every woman didn't have Rebecca's persistence and Rebecca's beauty and Rebecca's brains. She was quite a package, all in all, imperious though she was, and Kate was sorry Polly still put off inviting her to Kel Regis.

"I'm too busy, sugar," Polly insisted when Kate brought it up again. "There's a Georgia Democrat in the White House. I have to see he doesn't mess up."

"I'm sure you don't have to do it all alone."

"Then there's The Senator. You know how he has to be watched. The other day he said what this country needs is another Depression, to teach youngsters the value of money! I have no time for house parties. Little Becky Barrows gets on mighty well without me, I can tell you. They call her the best hostess in Washington and I see enough of her there."

"You see her, but you never talk to her."

But Polly had bustled off.

The holiday raced to its high point, the huge Thanksgiving feast served in two dining rooms: the "state" dining room, that seated forty people, and the family dining room that accommodated children under twelve with their attendant maids and nannies.

"You'd think no one had a care in the world," Ambrose said to Kate from his place next to hers. "But of course Gran won't allow sour faces on Thanksgiving."

"Who has the worst cares?"

"Two of the aunts—Felicity and Rose Ellen—are thinking of divorce, although thinking's as far as they'll get. Then one of the Ardmore girls got herself pregnant by a redneck who doesn't want to be paid off: he has notions of grandeur. And the Benedict uncles are fighting like cats and dogs with Gran and The Senator about making Wakefield coed."

"Never!"

"On the contrary, it's very likely," Ambrose countered. "Not next week, but soon."

Kate was aghast. Women did not get the same attention at coed schools as they did at single-sex colleges.

"But why?"

"Money. The uncles say Wakefield must go coed or go under, and Gran and The Senator say over their dead bodies. Maybe that's how it'll be. It's ironic: Wakefield tries to educate women to be independent, right? Well, women are getting so independent they want what men want."

"And that is?"

"Equal opportunity for sex, for one thing."

"What a shallow, sexist thing to say!"

He shrugged. "Maybe it's not so once they're grown, but they want it when they're young, same as the boys do. Belle doesn't stay with that fool husband of hers because she loves him. She stays because he's good in bed."

"Oh, for heaven's sake, Brosie! How can you know that?"

"I know. I know her better than she knows herself." He looked at her, the pain in his eyes stronger even than the love.

"I'm so sorry, Brosie," she said, meaning far more than the words.

He did not reply to that, but went on speaking. "All those little gals you teach are mesmerized by sex, obsessed by it. They want to be near men, even if some of them won't surrender the family jewel without a license. Your mother was obsessed just like them, but she was more generous."

"How would you know?"

"Lord, Kate, the aunts still talk about her, how gorgeous she was, how wild. And how Gran treated her."

"How did she treat her?"

"Like the town whore, from the time she was yea high."

Someone called him and he turned away. Kate sat stock-still, remembering what Sydney had told her. She remembered what a problem sex had been when she and Becca were growing up, remembered Wade Stevens and the musty couch and the pressure on young girls to arouse male desire, coupled with the restriction against yielding to it. Maybe the sexual revolution *was* a better way, even if it was taking all the romance out of life, all the rapture out of sex.

Her aunt Felicity spoke to her from across the table, bright and charming despite the fact that she was miserable enough to want a divorce, and Kate was bright and charming back despite the fact that she was miserable with wanting Win. As Sydney had wanted Royal. As Tyler still wanted Sydney. And what on earth had Sydney done to make Polly so unforgiving?

She put the question to her grandmother an hour before she left to return to Brooke Parrish.

VIII

I knew it, Polly told herself, feeling her face settle into the implacable wrath that was her reaction to Sydney. *I knew she'd ask me someday, but why does it have to be now, when we were getting on so well?*

"She's wicked," Polly said. "There are people like that. They're just plain bad, born that way, nothing to be done. In the old days they'd have called her a bad seed. In Salem they'd have burned her for a witch. I suppose I should have taken her to a psychiatrist, but neurosis was as scandalous then as having babies out of wedlock or cancer, and there was Oliver's career to consider."

"But what did she *do*, for God's sake? She told me about pulling up her skirt in the boat house."

"She was five then and it got worse. She slept with every boy in the family, made a slut of herself. Girls have sex now like falling off a log —and they get about as much out of it—but back then they didn't."

"Weren't the boys as much at fault?"

"No!" Polly insisted. "A young boy didn't have a chance when Miss Sydney set her cap for him. She was beautiful, more beautiful by half than your Rebecca, and she knew it. But she had no pride."

"Polly, pride isn't something you're born with. It's something you're given until you can earn it for yourself. Maybe she needed more attention than you had time to give her. Some girls think they can get it with sex."

"I don't want to hear any more armchair psychology," Polly said past the lump in her throat. "I've told you all there is, so let's drop the subject."

"I can't," Kate said. "Not until I tell you I'm going to her wedding."

Polly started to speak, then pressed her lips together, apprehensive of what she might say. It was unbearable that after all these years Sydney was coming between her and the extraordinary young woman who could be everything Polly longed to be. This was not the first time Sydney had come between Polly and the one she loved.

Kate was talking about the meeting in Oxford. "I wanted to tell you but I didn't know how. Even now her pride seems to depend upon other people, someone being at her wedding. It's the least I can do for her."

"After what she did to you? Do you blame me for that too?"

"Polly, that isn't what I said." But it was what Kate thought. Polly's antagonism didn't fit Sydney's crime.

Kate moved to the arm of Polly's chair and put her arm around her grandmother. "Polly dear, don't make me choose between you. That's impossible anyway, because you're not the same."

If I say anything now, Polly warned herself, *I'll say too much.* She held her tongue. She had Kate's gratitude in return, but it was not a fair replacement for what she wanted.

13

────── ◆ ──────

I

Sydney Benedict put down the telephone and sat staring into the fire. There was a chill in the air, and it had penetrated to the pit of her stomach when Kate called to announce her arrival time. It was meant to be a happy conversation, but Kate's voice had betrayed her reluctance to be with Sydney a day longer than necessary.

Ordinarily Sydney made fast work of disapproval: she was accustomed to it. But when she turned forty-five she had been seized by a compulsion to reclaim a relationship with her only child. At first she wanted Kate to understand her. After their meeting in Oxford she knew she would not rest until her child loved her again.

Her child: this tall, stunning woman with a grave demeanor and an anguish that had not been part of her nature in childhood. Sydney wondered if it had anything to do with men. Maybe, despite Tyler's influence, Kate wasn't unmoved by sex; after all, she was Sydney's daughter too! Why else had she chosen to write her thesis about it?

Sydney moved restlessly on her rose satin Recamier sofa, reached for one of the slim cigars she smoked, lit it, and went on with her musings.

Kate had always been aloof. As a child, she had rarely cried except over novels and films. She had been her father's daughter from the day she was born, but Kate had always had a forgiving heart and a romantic nature. Not lusty, but romantic. Life, of course, was not romantic, not for very long. Perhaps Kate had already discovered that.

Always weeping over those soppy stories. Sydney shook her head. *You'd think she'd want to stay in a castle in Bavaria, but she sounded as if it were a dungeon and I its evil queen.*

Sydney looked despondently around her boudoir here in Vienna, all rose and gilt, with thick, sculptured Chinese carpets, Lalique vases, and Rosenthal lamps. Her *petit salon* at the *Schloss* was even more sumptuous.

Sydney pulled a silken quilt up to her chin. She needed the extra warmth. Her telephone conversation with her formidable daughter had not gone at all as she had planned.

"It's my bitch mother's doing," Sydney said suddenly. "Why doesn't she just die?" Furious, she picked up a crystal ashtray and hurled it at the fireplace.

There was a light tap on the door.

"Go away!" she shouted, annoyed at the interruption.

The door opened.

"I take it I haven't awakened you," Hans Erik said, coming into the room. He looked at the splintered crystal and his mouth curled.

"I wasn't napping," Sydney said. "I was thinking."

"Destructive thoughts, I see. But, my dear, must you draw the curtains to think?" He crossed to the windows and began pulling the draperies open. Outside, Vienna was quiet. It was early afternoon and the Viennese took their meals and siestas as seriously as the French. Hans Erik, born in Germany forty-four years ago, had lived long enough in Vienna to adopt its customs.

Her anger dissipated somewhat as she watched him, admiring his compact body, broad at the shoulder and chest, narrow at the waist. He had a distinctly military bearing, although he had been a soldier only once, as a boy during the fall of Berlin in 1945, and then only for five days. He reminded her of the actor Conrad Veidt, but she never said so because it would have dated her.

He came back to her side. Beneath the ascetic veneer, he was both passionate and potent—Sydney would never have considered marriage with a man who wasn't—but he was not devastatingly handsome, as Tyler had been when she was foolish enough to marry him. Tyler was an adonis, every young girl's fantasy of the romantic lover. Hans Erik von Rayner's looks were stern, autocratic—and voluptuously menacing. She never knew what he would do to her in bed, and that excited her as tenderness could not and never had.

"Well?" he asked her now. "When will she arrive?"

"The day before the wedding. She almost changed her mind when she heard we had planned to be married at the *Schloss* all along—she obviously doesn't have our experience with those maggots from the press. But I could tell she didn't like having to spend an extra day with me."

He shrugged. "Still, she *is* coming."

"It's my mother's doing," Sydney said. "Kate and I could be friends if Polly would stop working on her."

"Calm yourself, *Liebchen*. She is coming and that makes a start. Did you ask her how her father is?"

"Yes, but I shouldn't have; she knew right away it was out of character. She said he's just begun work on a new book, a study of tyrants. Hitler's only one of them."

"Ah," he said, frowning. "This explains why he sends researchers here to dig up the 1938 *Anschluss* yet again. Most unfortunate. Still," he said, sitting in an armchair next to her sofa, "if he shows signs of going too far, you can always persuade him not to."

"I? What could I do?"

"Be a mother. Convince him that hurting us would hurt Katherine."

"As if he'd listen to me! The man despises me."

"You underestimate your powers of persuasion." He smiled, leaning toward her. "You're upset. You need to be relaxed."

"I'm not in the mood," Sydney said, recognizing the look on his face.

Ignoring her words, he pushed her negligee apart and exposed a body with a patina like marble, the breasts and belly firm and tinged with pink, the legs long and sleek. "*Schön*," he said. "*Das ewig weibliche*." He cupped one breast, pinching the nipple.

"For heaven's sake," she protested faintly. "Not now."

"Yes, now," he said.

His hand touched her hip. She moved away, still angered by the suggestion that she seduce Tyler, but his fingers closed on her thigh with an iron grip.

"You're hurting me," she whispered, excitement rising despite herself.

"Am I?" He bent down and kissed her roughly, his tongue exploring her mouth, his teeth nipping at her lips. Then he drew back and watched her while his hand roamed over her. He watched her eyes close and her face flush as he touched the delicate flesh between her legs, kneading, pressing, stroking until she breathed deeply and began to whimper. Her hips moved, then rose. In full climax, she arched her back.

"Oh, God," she moaned, her body quivering as the sensation died away.

He pulled her toward him, his penis straining.

She shook her head.

He gripped her hair and slapped her hard enough to redden her cheek without bruising it. She nodded and leaned toward him, her mouth avid.

When it was over he offered her his handkerchief.

"Why can't we ever have normal sex?" she asked after a moment. "Half the time it's like this, and the other half it's with your contraptions."

"You enjoy them, my love, you know it is true. Anyway, that wasn't sex, it was an appetizer."

"The last part isn't all that appetizing to me."

"So you pretend, until you get down to it." He smiled. "You're very talented at it."

She shrugged, her rancor somewhat dissipated by the aftermath of passion.

"Come." He drew her up and pulled the negligee from her shoulders. He turned her toward the bedroom, slapping her sharply on her rump as he followed her across the room and through the bedroom door.

Kate had completely vanished from Sydney's mind even before she was sprawled naked on peach satin sheets while he tied her to the bed with lengths of black velvet cord. From a drawer in the nightstand he took a wide leather strap.

"Now," he said, "we'll see what happens to naughty little girls."

||

Kate was met in Munich by the baron's secretary and escorted to the baron's Learjet for the short flight to the castle. They were joined ten minutes later by Elihu Brown, a wedding guest who arrived on another flight. He was a society columnist whom Kate had met at the house in Alexandria that her grandparents occupied when Congress was in session.

"All he knows about is scandal," Polly had warned her, "but you'd think he was about to emit a papal bull every time he opens his mouth."

Brown, ignoring the baron's secretary, talked incessantly during the trip, his instinct for the jugular sharp and true.

"What a surprise to see you, dear child. I thought you and Sydney didn't get on, but a wedding brings out the best in people, doesn't it? And of course she absolutely adores you."

"I'd rather you didn't advertise my presence."

"I shall oblige, of course, but it's bound to get out sooner or later. I must say, I like Sydney, no matter what frightful things people say about her. And how is our precious Polly?"

"In her element with a Democratic administration."

"She deserves a lot of credit for putting him there."

"Not that much, surely."

"Katherine, is it possible you don't know what a force your grandmother is in politics?"

"Of course, I know. It's her life."

"Polly knows absolutely *everyone* who counts. I wouldn't be surprised if she knew Ralph Nader! And she's got the Benedict millions to back up any candidate she chooses. An invitation to Kel Regis is a plum for any pol, high or low and no matter from what party. It's the place to meet everyone who's anyone in politics. No, no, one mustn't underestimate Polly."

He took a breath and peered out the window. "And here we are at the *Schloss*! How clever of Sydney, announcing a Vienna wedding to put off the paparazzi! I'm the only member of the press attending, you know. What a coup!"

The *Schloss*, originally built by "mad" King Ludwig of Bavaria, had the towers and turrets of a fairy-tale castle. It sat on the banks of a river so pellucid that the castle's reflection barely wavered as the Lear approached the landing field over trees about to bud. A dark burgundy Mercedes waited on the tarmac to whisk them through snow-covered fields to the *Schloss*.

Sydney, a striking figure in black silk hostess pajamas under a black fox cloak, was waiting for them with the baron, elegant and austere, at her side.

"Elihu, you old gossip," Sydney said, kissing his cheek. "I'm so glad you could come. Did you take good care of my Kate? Do follow the footman, he'll show you to your room."

She was nervous when she turned to Kate, uncertain how to greet her. Kate held out her hands.

"Hello, darling!" Sydney said, taking them. "You're more beautiful every time I see you. Did the dress come in time for alterations?"

"Barely. It's lovely, but you shouldn't have."

"But of course I should! A bride and her maid of honor have to match. This is my fiancé, Hans Erik. I call him Hansi."

The baron smiled and bent over Kate's hand with a click of his heels that amused her. Lacking only the monocle, he could have stepped out of one of the old movies Kate loved to watch.

"Charmed," he said.

"Delighted," Kate replied, thinking, *What the hell, why not play it to the hilt?*

"Come along now," Sydney said, repossessing Kate's hand. "I'll take you up myself."

Kate found the entire exchange too bright, too forced, and too preposterous after all that had happened, but that was Sydney. Her mother lived on the surface.

Sydney led her to a large, lavish bedroom, fidgeted for a moment, then left abruptly—"to do a million things," she said. Kate knew it was because too many dark shadows lay between them for idle chat.

Kate took a bath, changed, and went downstairs. She found the library and from it watched the preparations for a jet-set wedding. Servants bustled in and out of vast rooms paneled and tapestried and furnished in magnificent baroque. Guests arrived, the women crowing over one another's clothes and hair and jewelry, the men filling the air with cigar smoke and boisterous laughter. Telephones rang incessantly.

Kate was brought an elegant tea tray by a smiling maid and was enjoying it when the baron appeared. His stark, diabolically handsome face was intimidating: the high forehead, the hawklike eyes, the narrow nose, and the sensual mouth.

There was a covert brutality about him that was inconsistent with the polish of his style and demeanor. He was predatory. He made Kate feel absolutely naked, even ravished, as if he had already put hands on her. He was at once repugnant and fascinating, like a sorcerer, like a snake.

"I hope you know how glad I am to have you here," he said in near-accentless English; it was the formality of his speech that was Teutonic. "Your beautiful mother, of course, cannot contain herself."

"I hope you'll both be very happy."

"Do you?" He studied her. "If that is so, you are a generous and forgiving woman as well as a striking one. I trust that means we'll see a lot more of you. It's the only thing that will make your mother happy."

"My mother's happiness has never been my responsibility," Kate said. "And now it has become yours."

He put a hand over his heart. "I shall do my humble best to be a dear friend to you both."

"I must change for dinner," Kate said, impatient to get away from him.

"If there's anything you want . . ."

She fled up the broad stone staircase to her room.

III

At dinner—for the wedding party and close friends, all dressed to the nines—Kate was flanked by the baron's nephew, Freddi von Rayner, and Britt, his Swedish third wife, a former model.

"Britt will point out the oddities for you, Katherine," Freddi said. "The conventional types are cousins or business associates, so she won't bore you with them."

Britt smiled mischievously as she began. "Well, the woman in gold lamé with the headband and chandelier earrings is married to the gorgeous man on Sydney's right. They are the Hauptmans, Liselotte and Gunther, the reigning couple of the Austrian theater, a terrible pair right out of *Les Liaisons Dangereuses*. Behind the first bowl of flowers is a French pharmaceutical prince and next to him is his opera-diva mistress. His wife refuses to be seen with him in public but will not give him a divorce, while the diva refuses to be separated from him except when she sings. Next to the diva is Elihu Brown, whom you know, then comes the fifteen-year-old nymphet princess bride of the man on her left, a German chemical industrialist. They've been married for two months, and in this case it's the industrialist who refuses to leave his wife's side."

"Touching," Kate said.

"The distinguished-looking gentleman next to the bride is Axminster, the U.S. Undersecretary of State for something or other. His sexpot wife is on the baron's right."

"Yes, I recognized those two from Kel Regis." The collection of people was exactly what she would have expected of Sydney and von Rayner. Even the number of chemical magnates was not surprising: Hans Erik's family had founded Rayner Chemie, of which he had long been president and chairman of the board, at the turn of the century.

"Your escort," Freddi explained apologetically, "broke his leg skiing and will not attend."

"I am utterly crushed," Kate said.

"Oh, but you'd have liked him," Britt assured her. "He's Fabrizio Alessandri, the Italian communications giant."

It was a long dinner and a long wedding rehearsal and Kate was glad to get back to her preposterously luxurious room and into bed.

"What on earth am I doing in this zoo?" she wondered. "Why did I come?"

IV

She had her answer the next afternoon. It was the look on Sydney's face when, after the ceremony, she turned to Kate. Sydney was more exquisite than usual in a gown of blush rose chiffon and a small, veiled pillbox hat, but in that moment she had a childlike radiance as well, something Kate had not imagined she would ever see again.

Sydney hesitated, decided that Kate did not want to be hugged, and touched her daughter's cheek with her graceful fingers.

"Thank you for coming," she said softly. "I know I don't deserve it —or you."

Then she was herself again, chic and poised and impervious to anyone's opinion but her own. Kate stood beside her to receive the horde of guests, flanked by the baron's roster of cousins, nieces, and nephews. He had no immediate family; many had died during the war.

When the receiving line broke up, Elihu Brown bore down on her again.

"My dear Kate, a refreshing face among all these jaded rascals," he said. "And you, Madame Freddi. Isn't Sydney devastating? The woman never ages, but I always say, a little of what you fancy does you good."

"How like you to say that," Kate said.

"Now, Kate, I've made you angry! You looked just like Polly for a moment there. But I only meant love, Miss Katherine, the thing we've all gathered here to celebrate. I shall write a paean to the blushing bride."

"What a detestable man you are, Elihu," Britt von Rayner said.

"But I mean every word of it sincerely, I promise you. I adore Sydney and admire Miss Katherine. Who else has been clever enough to write pornography and pass it off as scholarship? Scandalous stuff!"

"Elihu! Was it you who got hold of my thesis?"

"Well, of course, darling. I've been feeding the press snippets about you for years. I knew it would please Polly. Ah, here are our thespians, Liselotte and Gunther. They'll be doing the German version of *Prelude in C-Sharp Minor*, which everyone here has surely seen."

"I haven't seen it," Kate said, greeting the couple. They were very glossy, both of them the better—or worse—for several facelifts. .

"But you must!" Liselotte crowed. "It's superb. And this Winslow Talley is delicious!" She rolled her eyes. "Broadway is bound to ruin the production. You must see it in London, my dear, on your way home."

It was precisely what Kate intended to do. She had changed her flights and booked a seat for the evening performance two days from then. She had told no one about it, not even Tabitha, nor did she plan to. It was the sort of thing Rebecca would have done. What Rebecca wanted, she went after. It was time Kate tried it. She had nothing to lose. There was even a possibility that Win Revisited was not nearly as irresistible as Win Remembered.

The party went on for hours, but Kate was up early the next morning, her body still unaccustomed to the time change. She had breakfast in bed, then went down to reexplore the rooms on the ground floor of the castle. Splendid as it was, she decided it was too formal, without the warmth and grace of Kel Regis.

She found an English copy of *The Magic Mountain* in the library and curled up in an enormous chair near the window. She had just dozed off when she was awakened by women's voices.

V

"Well, what can you expect from an old Nazi?"

It was the industrialist's fifteen-year-old nymphet bride.

"What nonsense! Ax wouldn't hobnob with a Nazi!" That was the American undersecretary's sexpot wife. "And Hans Erik was only a boy when the war ended."

"He could have been brainwashed by the Hitler Youth."

Katherine almost got up to tell them she was there, but she was fixed in her chair by Susan Axminster's next remark.

"Well, Sydney seems happy with him."

"Delirious! Old Hansi likes to smack his women around, and Fritz says that's what gets Sydney off."

"And how would Fritz know?"

"In the usual way. Sydney went to bed with half the men in Europe before she met Hans Erik, and she wasn't interested in their politics or his."

"Bugger politics! What does he do to Sydney?"

There was the sound of a lighter flaring before the princess replied.

"What he does to all his women, I expect. Spanks her bottom, ties her up, makes her do you-know to him all the time, slaps her about— things like that. Nothing serious, you see. Just enough to fill her sails. She likes it. Fritz says she demands it."

"But she's so beautiful!"

"Yes, looks like an angel, doesn't she? Most men just want to lay her down and fuck her, not tie her up and smack her. That's why she ran after that roughhouse, Royal Benedict—he was famous for it— until the poor sod killed himself on the autobahn." The bride paused. "It might be exciting, you know, just a little, nothing serious. After one's been married a few weeks, the thrill rather fades, doesn't it? And one's got to go on pretending to be excited over a husband at least until one's produced the heir and the spare."

"I must say, her daughter improves with age. I saw her several times at Kel Regis and she always made a point of looking plain. What do you think of her?"

The princess was noncommittal. "I never know what to make of female intellectuals. Fancy wanting to be a professor! With her looks, she could have been a model."

"Well, at least Sydney's out of circulation, and that's a relief," Susan

Axminster said. "No man was safe with her. But Hans Erik would kill any man who touched her now."

"But for how long? Marital bliss is such a bore, they'll both find other playmates before you know it. What else have they got to do? Come on, let's go wake Fritz. You must see him without his hairpiece. He's an absolute scream."

Katherine sank deeper into the chair, overcome by sadness for her mother. It was not because Sydney's sexuality was deviant—Kate knew that lust was a powerful charioteer and galloped in many directions—but because what Sydney wanted was degrading.

It staggered her that a woman like Sydney—lovely, graceful, charming, and far from stupid—had to be debased to find release. She wondered what Carol Hunter would say about that. She wondered— and did not want to know—if Polly's contempt for her only daughter had anything to do with it. Was it a case of once belittled, always needing to be?

Kate rested her head on her hands and thought about the spoiled, sensual woman who was her mother, a child seeking punishment for sins real and imagined. What a tragic mismatch Tyler had been for her! Tyler could no more slap a woman than pull the wings off flies. Sydney had been beset by erotic demons, apparently since she was very young. She had no pride because none had been instilled in her.

Kate had read somewhere that there are "three worst things":

> *To lie in bed and sleep not.*
> *To wait for one who comes not.*
> *To try to please and please not.*

She and Sydney had in common that both had tried to please, but Sydney had never succeeded. Of the three worst things, the last was the hardest to bear.

Kate was not sorry she had come to Sydney's wedding, but she was glad she was leaving that afternoon. Sighing heavily, she put the book back on the shelf and went upstairs to pack.

VI

Sydney came in when Kate had closed her cases.

"Must you really leave today?" she asked.

"You knew that before I came."

Sydney nodded, sitting down on a chaise longue. She looked tired and, much as Kate tried not to, she could not help speculating about Sydney's wedding night. But she and von Rayner had been together for a long time. They might very well have gone right to sleep.

"I'm exhausted," Sydney said, shattering Kate's comforting scenario. Sydney closed her eyes and put a languid hand over them. "What will you tell your grandmother?"

"Nothing. She won't ask. But there's something I'd like to ask you. Tell me about Hilliard."

Sydney dropped her hand and opened her eyes, her fatigue now changed to sadness. "My brother was the only one in that house who cared a damn about me. We were only a year apart and we were very close." Sydney searched in her pockets for a cigarette case and lighter of onyx initialed in pavé diamonds. "Mother adored him and hated the sight of me, but I loved him all the same. He stood up for me."

"Why did he kill himself?"

Sydney looked up sharply. "Who told you that?"

"Not Polly. It was Brosie and Belle, the Ardmore twins. Why would he have done such a terrible thing?"

"How the hell would I know?" Sydney protested. "*I* wasn't there. *I* had nothing to do with it."

"I never implied that you did," Kate said.

"Everyone else will. They blame me for everything. Just ask and you'll see."

"I have no intention of asking."

Sydney regarded her intently. "Sometimes I wonder if you're as benevolent as you seem."

"I'm not very good at pretense."

"Oh, all right, I'm sorry. Don't let's part on a sour note."

Kate felt nothing but relief when they parted. She hadn't let herself think of Win, not in the baron's house, but she thought of him all the way to London.

VII

When the curtain came down, it was clear that Tabitha's description had been precise. Win's character was a rotter, plain and simple, but he was irresistible for all that, a chameleon who was all things to all people. The role was a perfect vehicle for an actor with multiple talents. No wonder he had leapt at the chance to play it.

Kate left the theater and walked around the Haymarket for a few minutes before she went back to the stage entrance. She asked the porter to tell Win she was waiting.

"Mustn't stand outside in the cold, luv," the man said. "Come inside while I tell himself."

Win appeared moments later. "It's really you!" he said, regarding her from the corridor. "Oh, Kate, how I've missed you." He held out his arms and she went to him. He held her close, murmuring her name.

"Where have you dropped from?" he asked finally, still holding her.

"Bavaria," Kate said. "I've been to a wedding."

"Not yours?" He stepped back to look at her.

She shook her head, drinking him in, unable to tell if he really cared whether or not she was married.

"How long will you be in London?"

"Only tonight. I wanted to see the play, but I have to get back."

He pulled her close again, whispering, "I can't let you go. I want some time alone with you. There's so much I have to tell you. Take a cab to your hotel and I'll meet you there in fifteen minutes. Where are you? The Connaught?"

She nodded.

"Order something up for supper and we'll talk." He kissed her briefly. It had the same effect on her as that first kiss on the day they met. "Go now, darling Kate. I won't be long."

She was in a fever of anticipation all the way to her hotel suite. Her hands shook and she felt breathless ordering supper and a bottle of Château Mouton. She sat waiting for another half hour until she heard his knock.

They stood in silence after she let him in, and then he held her close and kissed her. She gave a little sigh of delight, of erotic anticipation, as they walked to the bedroom to make love, as famished as ever for each other.

"I love you, Kate," he said. "I wish there were a better way to say it."

"I love you too, darling."

"But I didn't know how much, that's what amazes me! I've never loved any woman this way."

"Does it make you so unhappy?" she asked, looking down at him.

"Not now," he said. "I don't want to talk about it now. I just want you, as much of you as I can get."

VIII

"I'm starved," he said an hour later.

"You should be. The sandwiches will be soggy but the wine's just the right temperature."

"So are you," he said, watching her nude body as she walked to the table and filled two glasses.

"To us," she said, bringing them back to the bed.

They touched glasses. Her heart turned over when she looked at him. She could read him in moments like these. She could see the man behind the actor, and the man loved her, and it was the man she loved.

He put down the glass and so did she, stretching out beside him, where she belonged.

"Kate," he said, "why didn't you write?"

"What can a woman write to a man who doesn't have time for her?"

"You have no mercy."

"Neither had you. It could have worked, Win, the two of us together."

"No," he said. "You don't know how I was when I got to London. You'd have hated me."

"I did hate you."

"I know and I'm sorry. You'll never know how sorry." He turned to her.

"Apology accepted."

"Kate, there's something I must tell you. I don't want to, but I must."

The warmth inside her diminished. "I'm listening," she said, forcing herself to lie still.

"I've done a very stupid thing. I've gone and got married."

She looked at him as if he were speaking in some exotic language she did not comprehend.

"A week ago," he said, shaking his head in disbelief. "No one knows about it yet. And I had no idea what an incredible mistake it was until I saw you at the theater tonight."

"Why didn't you tell me?"

"I wanted this. I wanted you. I still do. I love you."

She sat up and reached for a robe to cover her nakedness. "That isn't good enough, Win. And you don't have the right to say it to me." With an enormous effort she spoke quietly. "I want you to get out of here. I want you to leave."

"Kate, try to understand . . ." he began.

"I understand that you're an unmitigated bastard with no idea how rotten it feels to be me right this minute, in this room, on this bed. Your famous instinct ought to tell you how much I despise you for this. Maybe I'd have gone to bed with you anyway—hell, it's what I came for, isn't it?—but I had a right to know you were married before I dropped all my veils. You made me believe in love again and I loathe you for that. Now get out of here. I can't stand the sight of you."

She vaulted out of bed, slammed into the bathroom, and locked the door behind her, too furious to care that she was crying. She cried while she ran a hot bath and while she soaked in it, beating the rim of the tub softly with her fist, humiliated beyond bearing, until the water cooled and she shook her head, stopped crying, and reached for a towel.

She walked into the empty bedroom. The rumpled bed was repugnant to her, and she took the bottle of wine to the living room and drank herself to sleep on the couch.

Twelve hours after she had awakened and dressed she was back in the garret on Libby Avenue, swearing never to risk her lunatic heart again.

IX

Rebecca was on the telephone early the next morning.

"How was it?"

"A fiasco," Kate said before she realized Rebecca meant the wedding. "For me, I mean. Sydney's happy."

"What's he like?"

"Dr. Strangelove? Polly would say an unsavory character, but Sydney likes them kinky."

"Apparently so, ever since she emerged from the womb."

"She knows more about Hilliard's suicide than she pretends."

"That woman probably knows more about everything! Think of all the fumbling I'd have been saved if she'd given me a course on sex."

"What a wicked girl you were."

"That was a long time ago. Well, I'm glad you went, but I'm glad it's over. When will I see you? I want to hear more about Dr. Strangelove."

They arranged a weekend and hung up. Wearily, Kate lay back in bed. She had been tempted to tell Rebecca everything—about Sydney, about Win—because she had always told Rebecca everything, even when she knew Rebecca would criticize her. But that too was long ago.

In the end, Kate decided to leave Sydney to heaven and Win to his wife.

14

———●■●●———

I

Roman women," Kate told her class, "were not permitted to mingle in the Forum until Hannibal's armies butchered so many of the men. But there was still a law forbidding women to own more than a half ounce of gold, or to wear dresses with purple trim or to ride in carriages within a mile of the Capitol."

She glanced at the clock and closed her notebook. "That was the Oppian Law. Your term papers, due after the Easter holiday, should address two points. First, the reasons for the law, what changed it and how; and, second, a comparison between its restrictions and those imposed on women up to the present day. For example, some Arab women are still forbidden to drive cars or even to ride in one unattended."

The bell rang and the room emptied quickly with only two students lingering to ask for additional source materials. Kate's students were responsive and she was gratified, as always, by that.

But academic gratification was not enough to fill her life.

It was a fact that nagged at her even more following Win's highly publicized annulment soon after that night in London. He had rid himself of his bride of one month, an aspiring actress who claimed blood ties to the royal family. The gossip columns predicted that he would soon marry the American actress playing opposite him in *Prelude,* now a smash hit on Broadway. New York was no distance at all. Kate wanted to be farther away from him; each time the telephone rang she started.

So she was still not free of him—and she worried over what that told her about herself. Worst of all was the possibility that came unbidden to disturb her: had she been too quick to judge him? Win was self-involved, even egocentric, but he was not a man to deliberately humiliate a woman or to stay married to one woman if he loved someone else.

Kate was packing her briefcase when a woman appeared in the doorway of the lecture hall and started down the aisle. She was a natural blond. She wore red-rimmed glasses, a glen plaid suit and a white silk turtleneck. It was obvious that she exercised regularly.

"Dr. Ballard? The office said I'd catch you here. I'm a lobbyist for women's groups in Washington and I'd like a few minutes of your time. My name is Stan Wells."

"Stan?"

The woman smiled. "Stanton, really. Named for Elizabeth Cady Stanton. My mother was a feminist too." They shook hands.

"I'm on my way to my office," Kate said. "We can have coffee and talk there."

Stanton Wells came to the point while they walked: she wanted Kate to lecture to women's groups in the South. "I want them to hear the things you've been telling your students. I think women ought to know the mind-set they've come from, how some of their responses have been conditioned for centuries."

"I have a pretty heavy schedule," Kate said, intrigued.

"No problem. Our schedule will be tailored to yours."

"Why me?"

"Oh, we've had our eye on you since *Time* said your thesis was about women." She smiled. "It just took us a while to get around to you."

"Again, why me?"

"You know what you're talking about. You've got a name that'll draw. And you sure as hell don't look like a male chauvinist's idea of a women's advocate."

"Neither do you."

"That's why they sent me down to Dixie. Even up north, if a feminist doesn't look like Gloria Steinem, they say she's a frustrated hag and what she needs is a good lay to shut her up. Southern ideas about women are even more antiquated. But you must know that. You teach the flower of Southern womanhood."

Kate smiled. "I'm related to flowers very like them."

"So, what do you think?"

Kate knew this work would get her out of the apartment, away from memories that pursued her like the Furies. Even her new project —research for a book—didn't help. Win was always there. Her anger was there, too, and her infatuation despite the anger, making her restless, unable to concentrate.

"I'll do it," she told Stan Wells.

"Great! Can you do one this weekend?"

||

Kate was amazed at how much she enjoyed the lecture circuit. "The once-solitary Dr. Ballard," she told Carol before she left to speak in Charleston, "would rather go out than stay in."

"A promising sign," Carol said. "Go get 'em, Katie."

Much as Kate liked lecturing, she enjoyed the free-wheeling discussions after the lectures even more; women who had been through God's slow-grinding mills were more stimulating than students who had little idea of the rocky road ahead for some of them.

One woman in particular stuck in Kate's mind. She came to a meeting in a Georgia schoolhouse, in an area where most livings were scratched out of farming. Her hair was a dun color and she wore a plain cotton dress and no makeup. There was a dignity about her that transcended appearance and touched Kate deeply.

She held up her hand like a well-brought-up child, her expression reflecting how hard it was for her to speak to a large group. Her voice wobbled slightly, but she said what she had to say.

"I don't want no more equality," she said. "I worked equal alongside my husband for years and he knocked me around, even when I was carryin'. I left him and I'm raisin' five kids by myself, as equal as any man jack, and I'll tell you it's hard bein' equal when you got kids. And I don't want no sexual revolution either with women layin' down like spaniels, just like the men do. What I want is respect, and that ain't no way for women to get it." She braked her unaccustomed torrent of words and made a helpless gesture with her large, chapped hand. "What I want," she said softly while the women hung on every word, "is a man who'll come home every night and be sweet with me and take care of me and my kids."

The women murmured their agreement, too moved to applaud.

"It's what most women want," Kate said. "But suppose you're not lucky enough to get it? Or your husband dies and it's taken away? We need better laws to protect women in those situations."

"You'll never get better laws, not while it's mostly men who make them," another woman said.

"Then we have to elect more women," Kate heard herself saying resolutely. "It's the only logical solution."

Later, having coffee with Stan, she said, "I've just discovered something. I can't be sure what I think until I hear what I say. That woman got to me. I want to go out and do something for her."

"There are millions like her," Stan said. "If more women voted, we'd be a force to reckon with."

"So much potential power," Kate said, shaking her head. "And they don't even know they have it."

"They need someone to tell them," Stan suggested. "You can do that."

It was a compelling idea. Soon Kate's speaking schedule was so full that she abandoned work on her book. She was approached several times by women's groups who wanted her to run for office.

"Ah-ha! Then I'm not crazy!" Polly said, her cheeks aglow with vindication. "High time you started living in the present. The quick are a lot more exciting than the dead. Just save some time for Kel Regis."

"I know you're getting involved in it because you're lonely," Rebecca conceded. "But talking to a lot of women isn't going to change that for you. Come to Washington for a weekend. I promise I'll have someone better than Clem Case."

"Spend some time with us this summer," Sydney pleaded in each of her frequent telephone calls. "The Riviera is crawling with gorgeous men."

"I'm too busy," Kate told all of them until summer came and her speaking schedule dwindled. She went to Kel Regis but Tyler stayed in Harmony, researching his new book with a zeal surprising even for him.

III

"It'll probably win Tyler another Pulitzer," Kate said one morning over breakfast with her grandfather.

"What's this one about?" Oliver asked, attacking his eggs and sausage with the appetite he still brought to everything he did.

"Tyrants—and which of their ideas lived on after they died. He's called it *Aftermaths*."

"Is Hitler one of them?"

Kate nodded.

The senator shook his head. "That could embarrass West Germany, which happens to be our ally."

"*Embarrass* them? After what they did to the world? I can't say I'd be deeply disturbed by their embarrassment."

"With the Soviets able to pounce on us, we need Germany as a buffer. For our own good, it's time to put the Nazi era behind us. I'll have a word or two with Tyler."

"I doubt it'll do much good. Tyler's not a politician, he's an historian. He wouldn't put Pol Pot behind us, or Stalin or Ivan the Terrible. I'm proud of Tyler. He tells the truth."

"Now, Kate," her grandfather said. "You've got no call to sass me just because people fuss over you for stirring up the women."

"Why, Gramps darling, I never meant to sass you—and no one's fussing over me."

But they were—and she liked it. She liked the fact that the press covered her for what *she* was doing, not because of what her mother or her grandparents or her father did.

She was less preoccupied with Win too, and that was a blessing.

"Maybe even a cure," Rebecca said. "Any new suitors?"

"Depends what you mean by suitors. There's a Virginia banker named Jarett Lawrence who's nice."

"Nice is boring."

"Not in this case."

"Marvelous! Anything doing?"

"Give me time, Rebecca! He's only been here for two weekends."

But in the same way she would have taken medicine, Kate started taking the pill.

IV

Jarett, handpicked by Polly, was as tall as Kate, with dark hair and eyes and a swooping mustache. "Dashing as a pirate," Dodie Phelps said.

"He's perfectly suitable," Polly replied.

"Let's hope Kate thinks so."

"She needs someone," Polly said. "When she isn't busy as a bird dog, she's pining for that scoundrel, sure as I stand here, comparing every man she meets to him."

"It takes time," Dodie Phelps said. "She'll get over him."

"If you think that, you don't know Kate! She doesn't get over an outrage to her principles. She isn't over all those years I wouldn't see her. I still have to walk on eggs."

"A tricky business for you," Dodie Phelps sympathized.

"Well, at least she wasn't fooled by Sydney, and that's a mercy."

"She was fooled by Stanton Wells."

"Dodie Phelps, if you ever tell Kate I put Stanton onto her, I'll skin you alive."

"No fear," the slight, gray-haired woman said placidly to her plump companion. "Just thank the Lord Sydney's married and the fuss has died down."

"The Lord had nothing to do with it," Polly said. "It cost me a fortune to muzzle those scandal sheets."

"Well, there's nothing else for them to write about, is there? Anyway, it looks like Sydney's met her match in the baron."

"Only if he has horns and a forked tail!"

To keep Kel Regis lively, Polly invited Stanton Wells and her beau for a weekend, along with Belle and her husband—"So of course Brosie will follow," Polly grumbled, "like Mary's little lamb"—and several clever and attractive men in addition to Jarett Lawrence. In a burst of benevolence, she even invited Theo and Rebecca.

"And I can't come!" Rebecca wailed over the telephone. "I've caught Teddy's chicken pox! I'll bet the little wretch gave it to me on purpose!"

"Why didn't you have chicken pox when I did?"

"It was Christmas and we were away. At the time I thought I was lucky!"

"Shall I come and keep you company?" Kate offered.

"No, I don't want anyone to see me like this, especially not Theo. He'll be there on his own. Take care of him for me."

V

"I've been instructed to take care of you," Kate told Theo as they walked in the garden after dinner. It was rare for them to be alone together, and she had always enjoyed his company.

"And vice versa. How are you, Kate?" Theo turned to look at her with an expression of affectionate concern.

"I'm fine now. Don't tell Polly, but even before Stan Wells came along I was beginning to think I'd chosen the wrong profession."

"Maybe you did."

"After all the years it took to qualify?"

"Kate, you're capable of more than one career. I don't think you know how much attention you've attracted in only a few months."

"Meaning?"

"Meaning that some powerful women's groups in this country are interested in you and that you might be interested in them if you gave yourself half a chance. You can always go back to teaching."

Kate stopped abruptly. "You sound remarkably like Polly."

He smiled. "Everyone knows Polly and I were bitten by the political bug in our cradles. But I've been talking about you for a long time, with Rebecca as well as Polly. We want you to be happy."

Kate gave a hollow laugh. "Will politics make me happy?"

"That remains to be seen. Right now, only Win Talley would make you happy."

Confronted with the truth, Kate had no reason to reply.

"Consider the improbability of your getting over him at all until you fill your life with something really exciting. Maybe teaching isn't the answer. I don't think Jarett Lawrence is either."

God, she thought, *I miss love. I don't think I'll find it with Jarett. But I miss sex, too, and he can give me that.*

"What would a political campaign involve?" she asked Theo.

"To begin with, more lectures. I'll arrange some television appearances and interviews with the women's magazines and eventually the national weeklies—all the while denying you have any political ambition."

If she did it full-time, Theo assured her, she could easily win a seat in the state legislature, even in the state senate. She was already a South Carolina resident with a name people knew. If she moved to Kel Regis, she'd be living at the epicenter of South Carolina's Democratic politics.

"Politics dismays me," Kate said. "I have no ambitions in that direction. I do want to help some of the women I've met." She shrugged. "But I'm not sure this is how I want to do it, even if it's what Polly wants."

Theo looked troubled. "Don't turn it down just because Polly's in favor of it."

"I hope I'd never be that foolish."

"You might be that human."

Kate smiled at him. "What a comfort you are, Theo! All right, I'll think about it—but I'm making no promises. If you breathe a word to Polly, all bets are off."

"Word of honor," Theo said, and hugged her, unaware that Polly was watching them from the window.

"I think he's done it!" Polly murmured exultantly to herself. "First Stanton, then Theo. I knew that combination couldn't fail!"

But when the fall term started at Brooke Parrish, Kate had only agreed to step up her speaking schedule. She was not ready to commit herself to a new life.

VI

" 'I can't give you anything but love, baby,' " Jarett sang while they danced. He had come to Brooke Parrish for the weekend, and they went dancing at a private club that specialized in nostalgia.

"You mean you won't," Kate said.

He smiled raffishly. "I mean I won't," he agreed.

"Not very gallant of you."

"I make no claim to gallantry," he said. "My intentions are purely carnal. I want to take your clothes off, bit by bit. I want to kiss those gorgeous breasts. I want to get my hands on you, all over you. I want to lie between your thighs—after I do a lot of other things there."

"That doesn't sound like love," Kate said, excited by what he was saying, by the brush of his mustache against her ear. "It sounds like sex."

"Sex is a glorious alternative to love. Uncomplicated. No tears, except in joy; no sobs, except in passion." She felt his lips curve into a smile. "So how about it?"

She looked at him speculatively. Sex sounded safer than love. Her mouth felt dry, but the rest of her tingled. Yet she hesitated, hard-learned caution overruling desire. Maybe Jarett knew the difference between sex and love, but she didn't.

She smiled back and shook her head. "If it's all a game, I prefer chess to heigh-ho, another day, another diddle."

"That's a bit stark."

"It *is* stark. We take off our clothes, we lie down, you do things to me, I do things back, you get hard, I get soft, we engage—*et voilà*, climax ensues. *Ça, c'est l'amour?* No, *ça, c'est* an exercise in loneliness!"

"And if there is love?"

"Ah," she said softly, "then we would be incandescent, there would be—I don't know—a kind of joy, not just a mean little spasm."

He was silent for a moment, then he looked down at her. "Okay," he said.

She was almost disappointed. "May I take it that you're convinced?"

He leaned down and kissed her lightly. "No," he said, his dark eyes hugely close to hers and full of laughter. "You may take it that I'm patient."

His patience was not in vain. She accepted an invitation to a house party at his home in Virginia and she went to bed with him that night. He was an experienced lover and she responded to him, greedy for release, ardent when it came. From the attitudes of the other house guests, Kate knew there was a lot of sex going on and that she was an "item" again. It cast a slight pall on things, but when he came into her room the second night she was glad to see him. Their second coupling was, if anything, more frenzied than their first.

"I . . . knew . . . it," he said in full thrust. "You . . . love . . . it."

"Don't talk," Kate gasped. "Just do it."

They set a date for another meeting, but when Kate was back on Libby Avenue she knew she would break it. There had been no incandescence, only the heat of sex, and she felt more alone than ever.

To add to her gloom, Tyler decided to sell the house in Harmony and divide his time between Kel Regis and an apartment in Boulder, where the dry weather would be kinder to bronchitis that was turning chronic. Kate spent a weekend on Elm Terrace helping him to pack what he wanted to keep.

"Lord, there's nothing sadder than moving house," she sighed when they sat down to have a cup of tea. "Everything that was home looks so worn and shabby."

Her father nodded, looking around the study with its faded patches of wallpaper where his framed book jackets had been. "There are memories everywhere you look."

She wished she had not opened the subject. "A lot of happy ones," she ventured in a lighter tone.

He nodded agreement, and they drank the tea in silence while Sydney hovered over them.

15

|

Win could tell by the healthy roar of applause that this should be his last solo curtain call of the evening.

"Always leave them wanting more," he said to Darcy Barrington, his leading lady, when he came off the stage and took her hand to lead her back.

"In bed as on the boards," she whispered to him as they bowed. She smiled at the audience and, hardly moving her lips, asked if he was coming by tonight.

He patted her on the rump when they were off. "Alas, I have a meeting with my agent."

"It won't take all night, will it?"

"He's got a new script for me to read."

"My offer is good until dawn."

He kissed her cheek and went to his dressing room to take off his makeup, at the same time creaming away the several personalities he had just portrayed. It was a trick he played on himself, since Darcy convinced him she never knew which persona she was in bed with.

"Win Talley only emerges after a few hours. Remind me never to play opposite you if the piece calls for you to murder the female lead. Remember that old Ronald Colman film?"

"*A Double Life*, yes. But I'm not like that."

"Dear boy, but you are exactly like that. You don't play a part, you enter into it as if it were a state of grace."

Win, eventually deciding that she was right, had taken steps to master the situation, as it was his nature to do. Moreover, he wanted to reserve his acting for the theater. Squandering it offstage might diminish its intensity on.

Now, mopping his face with tissues, he thought of Kate again. He winced, remembering how she had looked when she told him to leave. That was not the girl he had too casually loved at Oxford. He had taken for granted the depth of her feeling for him. He had been wrong.

He had not come across a woman remotely like her. It upset him when he realized that he was looking for one. His marriage had been a press agent's dream that Win was too embarrassed to make public. "But not to worry," Darcy Barrington had comforted him. "The annulment got you just as much press, and if she wins her suit, you'll have the added appeal of having banged a blue blood."

Win had felt most like a fool when he told Kate about the absurd marriage. Her contempt had mortified him and the tears on her proud face had broken his heart. She was a child-woman with the vulnerability of the one and the fascination of the other. In that moment when he lost her, he knew how much he loved her.

As she had loved him. But he had ruined that for all time. It could never be like that again. He had been a bloody fool to leave her in the first place.

"But I had to," he reminded himself under the shower, not for the first time. Somehow, lately, it didn't ring true. Yet his hunger for success had always dominated his life. It still did. He could not trust himself to succeed if he divided his energies.

This was only the beginning for him; he would have an astonishing career. He had always known it and he had delighted in forcing it down the throats of the Winslows and the Talleys, all the people who had doubted him or scorned his chosen profession. But success required single-mindedness, commitment. That and women like Darcy were enough to fill a man's life.

Then why this loneliness that never left him? Why these memories of Kate?

Unwilling to deal with the obvious, he dressed and took a cab to his agent's apartment to read the new script.

||

The play gripped him. It was about a love that had been hiding in plain sight through the vigorous, striving years of a man's life, perceived only when he is mature enough to know what he has lost—and man enough to let it go. It was about the perpetual difference between what a person is and what he thinks he is, between what people want and what will make them happy.

"It's stunning," Win said, feeling the role already.

"It's sensational!" Andy Farrell exclaimed. "There won't be a dry eye in the house. It'll give you a different image too. You don't want to play one young bastard after another."

"I must do this one, Andy. Make whatever deal you can."

"We can pretty well call the shots now," Andy promised.

It was two in the morning when he left Andy's apartment, but Win was too excited to sleep. He let himself into Darcy's a half hour later, bursting with energy and eager for sex.

"Darling," she said drowsily from her nest of pillows.

"Just lie there," Win said, shedding his clothes. "I'll do everything." He got into bed and kissed her until she was breathless, while his hands moved expertly over her. "Don't move," he reminded her when he parted her thighs.

But she couldn't stop herself. Her hips heaved frantically until she whimpered with pleasure and urged him into her. He teased her with long, slow strokes until the sensation got the better of him and he let himself go.

He had never understood why orgasm was called "the little death." It made him feel almost as much alive as the theater did.

"More?" he asked after a while.

"Give me time to recover," she said. "I know what just got into me, but what's got into you?"

"A fantastic part."

"Anything in it for me?"

"Only if you can keep your lustiness down to a simmer. This woman isn't obvious. She has the kind of sensuality that glows rather than burns. She has to trust a man with her soul before she'll let him have more than her body."

"Sounds like you know this woman very well already," Darcy said. "Have you got the script with you?"

"I just happened to bring it along."

"Why don't you take a little nap while I read it?"

"I thought you wanted more," Win said.

"Winslow, darling, the part comes first. If it's that good, I don't mind coming second."

He woke the next morning to the sound of her voice on the telephone. "I don't care what you have to do, Herman," she was saying to her agent. "Or what I have to do either. I'll sleep with a Hare Krishna. Or with all the backers, if that's what it takes. Just get me that part."

She hung up the telephone and turned to smile at Win. She was wearing a towel wrapped turban style around her head and nothing else. Her skin glowed. She looked like Christmas morning.

"You were right," she said. "We're going to kill them, Winslow. We'll be to die for." Darcy lay down beside him, her sleek little body still damp from the shower. "Let's do it," she said. "Let's come like Chinese firecrackers."

III

"For the first time in my life, I'm not sure what I want," Kate said to Carol Hunter. "I don't expect you to tell me what to do, but I'd like your opinion."

Carol tapped her fingers on the arm of her chair. "A change of career can be a positive move, provided you're making the change for the right reasons."

"Maybe I can make more of a difference in politics."

"Kate, you know better! A teacher makes just as much impact—more. We get them before life does. I'm not knocking politicians. I just hope you're not abandoning the reflective life because you can't live with your memories."

Kate smiled faintly. "You're so perceptive, it's frightening."

"Only about other people's lives, not my own. You're very young and you've probably had enough of the single life—celibacy punctuated by casual sex. You feel you can burn off your excess energy a lot faster in politics than you can in a library. Hell, you might even meet a man you like better than Jarett."

"I wondered when you'd get to him. He's not what I want."

Carol shrugged. "I assume you've already found the one you really want, that there's some obstacle and that it's too soon to try again."

Kate nodded. "I'm still besotted."

"But that's not a good reason to abandon a career you've spent years planning and working for. Why not give it more time? Politics will wait."

Kate was no nearer a decision as the end of the school year approached and spring overwhelmed her.

IV

"Marry me," Darcy suggested to Win one Monday morning. The theater was dark on Mondays and they had the day to themselves.

"Why, for God's sake?"

"Spoken like a true swain! Because we're a super team, onstage and off, that's why! And it'd be great publicity for *Second Sight*."

"Not the best reasons to leap into matrimony."

"Did you have better ones the first time?"

"No, and it taught me a lesson. Anyway, it wouldn't be fair to you. I'm crazy about you, Darcy, but I'm not in love with you."

Darcy groaned. "Crazy is good enough! This is real life, Winslow. You don't have to be as noble as your new character."

"Get off your soapbox, Darcy. Or change the subject."

Darcy flung herself out of bed and went to get ready for a fitting. Win dressed and took a walk in Central Park, where new leaf trembled on the trees and he felt on the brink of something. He walked for a long time before he stretched out under a tree and closed his eyes and felt Kate lying next to him on a sunny day at Oxford.

How do I make you feel?

Like Antony bestriding the world.

Only one other thing—acclaim—made him feel like that. He was about to play the part of a man who, like Win himself, couldn't see the forest for the trees, but Darcy's suggestion of marriage had somehow made him see.

He looked at his watch. It was only eleven o'clock. He walked quickly to Fifth Avenue and took a cab to his apartment in the Essex House. He left a message with his agent and one with Darcy's service —no point in infuriating a leading lady—while he packed a carry-on bag. He made LaGuardia Airport in forty minutes, bought a ticket to Charleston, arranged for a rental car to be waiting when he got there, and arrived at the Brooke Parrish administration building shortly after four o'clock.

"I'm looking for Dr. Ballard," he told the woman at the information desk. "It's urgent."

"You're that actor! Win Talley!" she said, and turned a bright peony red.

"Yes, I am." He summoned his best smile. "And I implore you to tell me where I can find Dr. Ballard."

"Oh, my," the woman breathed, staring at him. Then she gathered her forces. "I can't give that information out to strangers."

"But I'm not a stranger." Win's voice dropped to the intimate range. He was a little boy lost. "Not to Kate. I swear I wouldn't be here if it weren't a matter of love and death."

Flabbergasted, she told him where Kate lived and how to get there. He kissed her hand gallantly, waved, and strode rapidly out of the building. He found Libby Avenue with no trouble.

Why the devil does she live in an attic? he wondered as he ran up the stairs. Then he stopped outside her door, suddenly aware of what he was doing, afraid she would say no, afraid she would say yes.

V

Kate had just put the cozy over the teapot when she heard the knock.

"It's open," she called. Then she turned and saw him.

"Don't send me away, Kate," he pleaded. "Please don't. I have something to tell you."

Her dark eyes measured him. "You're just in time for tea."

"I need a drink," he said, still standing in the doorway.

She was wearing jeans and a Brooke Parrish T-shirt. She looked utterly beautiful. Later, he would reflect that another woman might have spilled the tea or dropped the pot or thrown it at him, but Kate was Kate and all she did was gesture toward a knotty pine cabinet and say, "In there. Ice in the fridge."

He had to lower his head to avoid the slanted ceiling. He felt ridiculous and drank the whiskey neat. Then he moved to a part of the room where he could stand upright.

"Why have you come?" she asked, still standing with her hand on the cozy.

"Because I don't want to live another minute without you."

"You've managed very well for quite some time."

"Yes, all right! I can get along without you if I have to, I can even be the best actor in the world, but it won't be the same. I've made a hash of everything since the day I met you, and I know it. But I love you, Kate. I want to marry you. I want you to live with me and be my love."

She gazed at him without speaking, her face impassive.

"No," he said, aware of her skepticism. "I'm not acting."

"What's in it for me?" she asked him.

"Us!" He came closer. "We belong together. And we'll have a fabulous life, just on our own. Or we'll meet people almost as brilliant as you are, go places, do things. I want to live with that true-blue dazzling mind of yours."

"I was thinking about going into politics."

That startled him. "Give up teaching? But why? When you love it so!"

"I'd have to give it up to marry you."

"Not unless you want to. You can teach during the long runs. Any college in New York or London would be eager to have you." He was close enough to touch her. "I love you, Kate. Say you will. Say it."

She leaned toward him, then "No!" she said suddenly. "I'm not going to play Butterfly to your Pinkerton. You live in another dimension, a place where mere mortals with their petty little needs can't survive."

"You're no mere mortal. And we inhabited the same dimension at Oxford."

"But you'll have a new love in every playhouse! I couldn't live with that."

"Kate, for God's sake! What do you take me for?"

"For a man who was in bed with someone else last night and asked me to marry him today."

"Yes, I was, with Darcy Barrington. It was just a friendly fuck, but she said something that made me realize that sex wasn't enough, that I wanted you."

"What was it she said?"

"That she and I were a good team and it would be great publicity for the new play if we got married."

"And what did you say?"

"I said no. Then I got on a plane and came here."

She put her arms around him, surprised and touched when she felt him tremble. He wasn't acting. She knew him well enough to realize that. She wanted him in too many ways to count, wanted to make him happy, wanted to live with the exhilaration he brought to everything he did.

And more, he was the first person who had ever loved her for the joy he found in her and for no other reason. He was the only man she knew who wasn't threatened by her intellect.

This was like turbulence on an airplane, that sudden sinking sensation, that breathless moment that might be fatal—except that here and now, she could still control the outcome.

But she wanted him. Politics was no substitute for life.

"You're going to make me believe in love again," she said.

He kissed her. "Marry me, Kate."

"Yes," she said.

They stood with their arms around each other for a little while, then they sat down and had tea and made plans, the moment too charged for lovemaking. It was seven when Kate called Kel Regis.

"I'm driving over," she told Polly. "I have something to tell you."

"Wonderful!" Polly said. "I'll wait dinner."

"I should have told her to set two places," Kate said when they were in the Austin. But she was anxious. She knew this was not the news Polly was expecting.

"I had a fantasy once, on this road, in this car. I was taking you to Kel Regis to meet my family."

"Did they like me?"

"I don't know. I realized how ridiculous I was being and stopped fantasizing."

"Now I'm the one who's worried about it," he said, surprised that he was nervous.

It was too dark for Win to see the estate, but Kate described it to him, the love in her voice unmistakable. He felt a pang of jealousy that she could love a mere place as much as she loved him.

VI

Polly was waiting, flanked by Oliver and Dodie Phelps and, to Kate's surprise, Stanton Wells, when Kate and Win got out of the car.

"I've brought someone I want you to meet," Kate said.

Polly peered through the twilight until Win was at the bottom of the steps. "You!" she said, astonished.

"This is Win Talley," Kate said with a radiant smile.

"He needs no introduction," Dodie Phelps said warmly. Stan Wells nodded.

Polly still stood immobile, a small but imposing figure under the great columns. She did not offer Win her hand.

"What have you come to tell me?" she demanded of Kate, ignoring the others.

"Hold your horses, Peach," Oliver said. "Let them get inside the house."

"Tell me, Kate," Polly insisted implacably.

"We're going to be married and we'd like to do it here at Kel Regis." Kate looked from one to the other, but she was drawn back to Polly.

"You can't be serious!" Polly said.

"But she is," Win said. "I can hardly believe it myself."

"Katherine Ballard, do you mean to stand there and tell me you'd throw away a brilliant future to live in the shadow of a man like that? He'll break your heart again. He's already done it once."

Win stepped forward, but the pressure of Kate's hand kept him still and silent.

"How did you know that, Polly?"

Her grandmother, glaring at Kate, jutted her chin in reply.

"You've been spying on me!" Kate said softly.

"I've been watching over you," Polly corrected her granddaughter.

"I see." Kate's eyes went to Stanton Wells, whose expression confirmed Kate's suspicion. "And you sent people to lead me in the way I should go."

"Now, Kate honey," Oliver said, glancing anxiously from his wife to his granddaughter. "That's what family's for."

"No, Senator. Family's for letting you find your own way and supporting you when you do." Kate turned back to Polly. "You should have known I had to find my own way, Polly."

"I should have known a lot of things. You're your mother's daughter."

"You're my mother's mother! Did you spy on her? Did you drive her away too?"

"For mercy's sake!" Dodie Phelps pleaded. "You mustn't say such things to each other."

"Let's go, Kate," Win said, taking her arm. "This is pointless."

Polly ignored him. "If you do this thing, you'll do it alone," she told Kate.

"Meaning?"

"If you marry that man, you won't be welcome at Kel Regis, Katherine, not for your wedding or after it."

"Polly!" Dodie Phelps exclaimed. "Think what you're saying!"

Oliver put his hand on Polly's shoulder. "Peach, you don't mean that."

"Yes, I do," Polly said. Her eyes had never left Kate's face. "If you marry him, I wash my hands of you."

"It won't be the first time you did that," Kate said. "I survived it then and I'll survive it now. Come on, Win, we have a lot to do."

They got into the car, the protests of the senator and Dodie Phelps lost in the sound of the motor and the whine of the wheels spinning on the gravel drive.

"Kate darling, I'm sorry," Win said when they reached the road, stroking her arm, feeling the tense muscle under her smooth skin. "I know how much you love this place, but don't let her ruin this for us."

"Not on your life," Kate said, dry-eyed and stony-faced.

VII

Kate called Washington while she packed a few things. Her conversation with Rebecca was brisk; Kate told her what had happened but would tolerate no discussion of her decision.

Rebecca, warned off by the flinty tone in Kate's voice, kept her counsel and asked what she could do.

"Can Theo get us a special license and a judge for tomorrow?"

"Yes, Kate. And I'll do the rest."

"What rest?"

"Just a few flowers and some champagne."

"In a judge's chambers?"

"Kate, I won't let you get married in some musty old chambers! We'll have the ceremony here in my living room."

"Early afternoon," Kate said. "Win's got an eight o'clock curtain and I'm only taking a two-day leave."

"What's the rush?"

"Rebecca!"

"All right, all right! Tomorrow at two. Take an early plane and bring a pair of white shoes." And Rebecca hung up.

"All set?" Win asked.

Kate nodded. "We'll have to take an early flight. After you call your agent, we'd better think about getting some sleep."

It was clear, from the way she said it, that sleep was all she wanted. They lay in twin beds, separate, abstinent, anxious, until they slept.

VIII

They were married at two o'clock the next afternoon in the Barrowses' flower-decked living room. Kate wore a long sheath of white crepe—Rebecca had found it that morning in one of her little boutiques—and Rebecca's own short wedding veil attached to a Juliet cap. Win wore a dark blue suit hastily bought off the rack an hour before the ceremony.

"He's even more stunning in person," Rebecca said, helping Kate pin on her cap.

"I don't know what he thought of that scene at Kel Regis last night."

"He's used to dramatics."

"It was *not* a play, Rebecca."

"Sorry, darling. I just hope he's as good as he looks."

"If he weren't, that wouldn't stop me any more than it would have stopped you."

"Theo likes him. That's a good sign." Rebecca leaned down and put her cheek close to Kate's. "Be happy, Sister Kate," she told their reflections in the mirror. "Come on now, your father's waiting to take you down."

Theo had chartered a private jet to bring Tyler from Harmony; Belle and Brosie had flown up from Charleston in the Benedict Industries 727, bringing Carol Hunter, Aunt Felicity, and Dodie Phelps with them. Felicity and Dodie Phelps cried during the short ceremony.

"Thanks to all of you, it felt like a real wedding," Kate told them. "But she'll never forgive you."

"She didn't ask where we were going and we didn't say," Dodie Phelps assured Kate. "Don't worry about us on a day like this."

"I hear you really told her," Felicity said.

"I lost my temper."

"Time someone did."

"Time I changed," Kate said, and went upstairs with Rebecca. "Old shoes, new dress, borrowed veil, blue cornflowers in my bouquet—you thought of everything."

"Don't cry, dear old pal of mine. Just be happy and forget about that horrible woman."

Kate dried her eyes "God, Becca, I never knew anyone so unyielding. What must it have been like for my mother?"

"Not a piece of cake, but I always told you that. Hurry now, your groom is impatient. A fine way to spend a wedding night, watching a play! And then you go back to your classes in the morning!"

"Only for two weeks. We'll have a honeymoon as soon as *Second Sight* closes."

"Poor innocent! With him in the lead, it'll probably run for ten years."

IX

Kate watched him that night from the fifth row, as mesmerized as she had been that first time she saw him at Oxford. Whatever his character's faults, Win made him irresistible.

Don't think about Polly, Kate warned herself. *Think about your husband.*

My husband. The words were like a talisman.

She went backstage after the performance, and when Win introduced her there was a warm welcome from the cast—except for Darcy Barrington. Sharp and sexy and superior, she extended very cool congratulations to Kate.

"You're a big surprise," she said, pointedly looking Kate up and down when the two women found themselves alone for a moment.

"You're not," Kate said. "You're as good as everyone says you are."

"They say a lot of other things about me." Darcy looked across the room at Win. "How long has this been going on?"

"For several years, on and off."

"Between his women, as it were."

"As it was. I'm his only woman now," Kate said with calm assurance.

"Well, I'll tell you right now, Mrs. Talley, his first marriage didn't make a bit of difference to his love life." Darcy smiled radiantly at the approaching Win. "Darling," she said, "your little bride's too sweet for words."

"Kate, little? Kate, sweet?" Win laughed delightedly. "My Kate is larger than life and marvelous beyond words, but she is not sweet." He led Kate away to meet someone else and Darcy, watching them go, gave a faint, chilly smile and arched an eyebrow.

Later, in Win's apartment, Kate stood under the shower with him, letting their anticipation grow until they tumbled into bed and melted into each other.

"I know what love is," Kate said.

"Tell me."

"It's when delight doesn't end with enjoyment."

"Then I love you, wife," Win said. "I'll always love you."

X

The garret looked smaller when Kate opened the door the following night, and she smiled when she realized why. Life with Win was extraordinary. Everything was diminished by comparison.

"Except me," she exulted. "I feel sensational."

She was at Dinsmore Hall the next morning for her ten o'clock class, surrounded by the press and a crowd of students who behaved more like groupies than Brooke Parrish women. Some of them were so excited by their teacher's marriage to a matinee idol that they shed tears of ecstasy.

"What are you doing here, Mrs. Talley?" a large, rumpled female reporter demanded, almost nose to nose with Kate. "You just married a man any woman in America would die for."

"I have a contract to teach until the end of term. It's only a few weeks away."

"And your husband?"

"He has a contract too. I'll join him in New York on weekends."

"Are you planning a family?" The reporter backed up to appraise Kate's belly.

"We haven't discussed it yet."

"What does your grandmother think?"

"I'm sure she'd rather tell you herself."

The bell rang and Kate broke away, shepherding her students into the building and closing the doors with the help of campus security guards.

"Some of the girls," she told Carol that evening, "thought I was a traitor to feminism for abandoning my career."

"That's a bit much."

"I told them Brooke Parrish isn't the only place I can teach."

"You'll never get tenure, moving around."

Kate smiled. "Tenure has its attractions, but so has marriage to Win."

"I could see that." Carol smiled.

Kate studied her friend. "You think I've been a damned fool, don't you, rushing into it."

"No. I think you did what you've been wanting to do for a long time, and that's good. There aren't any guarantees, Kate."

"I know. It's already cost me Kel Regis. Polly cares for me, I know she does! How can she be so careless of my happiness?"

"There's something she wants more than your happiness."

"She wants her way! God help anyone who won't give it to her." Suddenly Kate was talking about Sydney, the "bad seed" Polly had washed her hands of when she was five, and the sort of woman who had flowered from that seed.

"I'm so sorry, honey," Carol said. "Hearing that about your mother was hard for you. But from what you say, she's happy with her husband."

"I don't think my mother has ever been happy."

"Don't let it stop you from being."

"Nothing could, not anymore. I just realized that for years I was miserable when school ended, but now I can't wait."

When the school year ended, Win came down to get her and they drove back to New York. It was a glorious summer. She and Win explored the city together, sometimes walking for miles. When the soggy heat of August descended, the theater was dark on Sundays too, and they spent two days each week on the beach at Amagansett, far out on Long Island.

They sat one day, he intent on the waves and Kate watching his perfect profile against the bright blue sky. Marriage to Win had made a spectacular change in her life. She spent very little time alone, where once solitude had been her habit.

Theater people turned every occasion into a party. Win's friends were interesting and their conversation was usually clever or hilarious, and often both. She enjoyed shopping for gorgeous clothes because he went with her. It was a kick to wear them, to be photographed with him, to read the most ridiculous speculations about their marriage in the columns. It was a thrill just to touch him. She understood now why Belle had fluttered around Ross like a honeybee when they got married, but Kate, no matter how much she wanted to, could not flutter.

It was no wonder she was not eager to return to academia, to stay home grading papers and reviewing lecture notes instead of going to new restaurants, jazz clubs, previews, and parties. Hers was a profession she could easily drop for a year and resume whenever she was ready. She had already decided to do that.

"I love the ocean," Win said, breaking into her thoughts. "It lets me think."

"About anything in particular?"

"About you. And how uncanny it is that I'm so much better when you're in the theater—whether I'm acting *Prelude* or rehearsing *Second Sight*."

"Darling! What a lovely thing to say."

"Maybe you won't think so when you hear what else I have to say.

I want to know if you'd consider putting teaching on hold until I've got the new play down pat."

She laughed, warmed by how close they were, even in thought. "I've been thinking about doing exactly that."

"Then you will?" he asked, as excited as a boy over a new bicycle.

"Yes, I will."

His hands framed her face. "Lord, I'm glad you're mine," he said. "There's no one like you anywhere. I love you, Kate. I'm always 'on' with everyone else. With you I can be myself. I can even let the doubts show." He smiled ruefully at her expression. "Oh, yes, Kate, I have them now. They seem to come with success. I really need you. Timing's everything in an acting career, and the new play has to be brilliant or they'll call me a flash in the pan. You've always had an unerring instinct for how I should play a part."

She kissed him, touched by his admission, moved by his belief in her, his need. "My instinct tells me that *Second Sight* will be a smash. Now stop worrying and come for a run."

It was bliss to be able to do something wonderful for him. It was bliss to have someone all her own to do things for. It seemed to her, in those first months together, to be the reason she was born.

BOOK III

16

1982

Mrs. Winslow Talley was another kind of Kate. She had always lived behind a protective wall, but the fact of having been chosen by such a man gave her the confidence to come out and be herself. Win encouraged her. She knew it shouldn't have been that way, that the confidence should have come from her alone, but "alone" was no longer an attractive state of being. Win adored her. He was proud of her. She loved being loved.

"What's become of our old, conservative, New England Kate?" Rebecca teased.

"Discarded," Win said, "with her household budget book and her windowpane specs."

This Kate liked being wrapped in fine fabrics. She liked the high life they began to lead in New York and London after Win won his first Tony and was perceived by wealthy backers to be a money-maker.

Kate would never be flamboyant, but she had the height and figure for high style, and by the time Win had his second Broadway triumph, she was wearing her distinctively elegant clothes to opening nights and galas, to the opera and the ballet. When plans for a new production of *Hamlet* were announced, critics began to speculate on the handsome actor's talent for Shakespeare, which only increased the anticipation and the attention he stirred.

Now the Talleys were invited to parties and country weekends and spur-of-the-moment trips to Cannes and Gstaad and Barbados and the Costa Smeralda, most of which they had to decline as soon as the financing was complete—producers were wary of Shakespeare—and rehearsals got under way.

Famous people were charmed by Win, and Kate had become accustomed to the occasional photograph of herself in newspapers, most often with him, once in a while on her own as an activist for women's rights, sometimes with her father or grandfather. Whenever Oliver made a provocative speech on the Senate floor or before the television cameras, the media came to Kate for comment: she was sexier than Oliver, one artless reporter had explained, and they were also hoping for a glimpse of Win.

Columnists called her, as well, when there was a mammoth reception at Kel Regis—Kate always had a good excuse ready when reporters asked why she was not attending—or when Tyler testified before a Senate committee or published a new book. Kate no longer resented that it was still reflected fame, based on her connections. But lately she had become more adept and very witty at fielding questions about both her husband and her family, about Mrs. Winslow Talley's opinions, wardrobe, and recipes.

"Of course," she told Win, "what they really want to know is what it's like to go to bed with an up-market sex symbol like you."

"What did you tell them?"

"That words fail me."

At first she had resented the intrusion. It was Tabitha who insisted that she accept it. "Celebrity is the first gauge of success, and these days it even counts for more than talent. Look what it's done for you! In place of our dowdy, reclusive prodigy stands a clotheshorse who commands attention."

"That's Win's doing," Kate said.

"Let's not overstate the case. He had excellent material to work with. So take the publicity and be glad you've got it."

Tabitha, who was making a name for herself as a set designer, spoke with the authority of experience and common sense. She was one of the few unpretentious people in the theater, and Kate valued her friendship and her advice.

Some of the people Kate met now were ordinary, some were fabulous, and some pathetic, yearning for fame or unable to deal with it. But they were a new experience and Kate's whirlwind life was all the more fun because Mrs. Winslow Talley had the kind of celebrity that Kate Ballard could use to good effect in the battle for women's rights.

"Dr. Ballard," a reporter had asked her a year ago, "you attended Wakefield and taught at Brooke Parrish. How do you feel about their going coed?"

"Not happy, although it was inevitable."

"So it's not a good thing?"

"I think it's a great loss. Women need equal attention to get the full benefit of education. In a coed school they always take second place. They're called on less in class. They get into fewer honors programs. It's a way of telling them there's no point in bothering their pretty little heads over education because they have to get married anyway."

The remark had provoked a small outcry in academic circles. Even Carol was miffed.

"It's true," she wrote, "but you shouldn't have said it."

Kate didn't know what Polly thought about her remarks, but Polly had fought hard against coeducation at Wakefield, finally surrendering to dwindling enrollments at the college. Wakefield College even had a football team now. Kate's tart observations on what that contributed to female education created another stir.

"It's getting to be a bit much!" Rebecca had said with a tinge of envy. "Every time you hold forth these days, someone prints what you say as if you were the Sibyl of Cumae."

"You really *could* run for office," Theo joked.

"You're being quoted more than I am," Win remarked, not at all amused.

"Only because women's issues are a hot topic."

"I'm a hotter one. I'm an actor. One of my fraternity reigns in the White House."

"I wouldn't harp on that if I were you."

Win's star had kept on rising. After *Hamlet*, Kate was certain, it would shine even more brightly. It was the most challenging role he had undertaken, and for the first time since she met him he was nervous about a part.

II

Kate sat in the aisle seat, fourth row center. The crochet needle flashed in her hands, although she had not turned on the tiny book lamp rigged to fit over the seat in front of her. Her fingers moved as if automatically, her eyes fixed on the stage.

Darcy Barrington watched from the other side of the theater. The two women were a study in contrasts: tall, dark-haired Kate wore a lipstick-red cashmere dress, the matching cape lined in black fox. Delicate, blond Darcy wore a wool suit and felt hat of cornflower blue, the color of her eyes.

They paid no attention to each other, both of them engrossed in what was happening on the stage.

After Win had mistakenly spitted the garrulous Polonius through the arras, Kate stopped working and sat transfixed as the actress Grace Halsey became Queen Gertrude and spoke to her son, Hamlet, in horror:

O what a rash and bloody deed is this!

Only to hear her son reply:

A bloody deed, almost as bad, good mother,
As kill a king, and marry with his brother.

Kate had been watching Win onstage since her wedding night four years before and he had never failed to entice her out of the present, to draw her into another reality, that of the play and the character he was playing.

Kate felt Hamlet's rage at his mother for being less than he wanted her to be. She rode the wave of his anguish, wishing she could release anger as he did. She had never really raged at Sydney.

Then Win stopped and Kate was wrenched abruptly out of the catharsis of his wrath.

"It's not right!" he exclaimed to the director, Hugh Sands.

"It *is* right!" Sands raised his eyes to heaven. "We settled that yesterday."

Darcy was still watching intently when Kate put her crocheting into the tapestry workbag that went with her from home or hotel to dressing room to theater. Everyone had heard this argument a half-dozen times already, and it was too late to settle it today. Win would storm back to the dressing room in another ten minutes, roaring for a drink. He would spend the rest of the evening brooding about the scene. But Kate had done some brooding of her own and she was sure she had the answer.

She headed backstage. The argument was still audible when she went into Win's dressing room. She stopped short, surprised to see a woman there. She was doubly surprised when she realized who the woman was.

III

Stanton Wells got to her feet. "I said I was your cousin—you have so many. Please, Kate, don't start hollering until I explain," she said.

"Agreed. I'll holler after the explanation."

Stan looked relieved as she studied Kate's appearance. "I like your hair like that. And that outfit! Paris?"

"London, while we were doing *Second Sight.* I caught the clothes bug from theater folk." Actually she had caught it from Darcy Barrington, who always looked glossy, whether she wore trousers or a ball gown or, Kate was certain, nothing at all. Everyone knew Darcy lightened her pubic hair; probably brushed and conditioned it too, Kate had decided.

"Would you like a drink?" she asked Stanton, putting the tapestry bag aside.

"Yes, it's about that time, isn't it? And is that woman's work I see? Knitting tiny garments, are you?"

"I'm not pregnant, Stan," Kate said simply. She didn't suppose she ever would be. Neither of them pined to be parents. She thought, as she mixed a shaker of martinis, that the life they lived wouldn't accommodate a baby.

She handed Stan a frosted glass and sat down on the couch beside her. Stanton hadn't changed much. Her hair was longer and she used more makeup, but she dressed in the same tailored style and had about her the same singleness of purpose.

Stan immediately apologized for her complicity in the plot. Yes, she had been sought out by Polly to help lure Kate out from behind her ivied walls without letting Kate suspect who was behind it. But Kate's swift acceptance, as well as her enthusiasm for the job, had convinced Stan that Polly was right, that a change was what Kate really wanted and a little push in the right direction would make everyone happy.

"You can't deny it was working, Kate," she said earnestly.

"That's not the point. Even supposing it was the road for me, I didn't need anyone directing traffic."

"But you were thinking of running for office and you'd have won in a walk—if Mr. Talley hadn't happened by."

"I'm sure Polly hopes I regret that."

"I haven't a clue," Stan said. "I haven't seen her since the night she gave you the ax. But I've followed you in the press, and from what you say, Mrs. Win Talley is still an ardent defender of women's rights."

"Are you going to tell me where all this is leading?"

"Okay, okay, but hear me out before you say anything. I want you for a segment on a late night talk show—I'm working for the producer. You'd be up against a guy named Clyde Tillinghast, a media tycoon whose forte is producing TV movies about rape and other 'hot' topics."

"I've heard of him," Kate said.

"The man gets the ratings because, as we all know, rape sells. Tillinghast defends himself nobly: he says the subject's been kept under wraps too long. Well, everyone claims to be against rape, but they sure love to watch it. You ask me, it's every *man's* fantasy—chest beating, primitive domination, and fuck the foreplay—and every *woman's* fear. Whatever, it sells diapers and laxatives and deodorant crotch powder, so there's going to be more of it. Yesterday I told my producer I knew a woman who could take the wind out of Tillinghast's sails, someone with a name who can be lethal with words and is stunning to boot. My producer jumped when he heard it was you, so here I am. You'd only have to go around the block to state our case. That's it."

But Stan was still leaning forward, ready to fight on.

"No holds barred?" Kate asked.

"None. You say what you like."

"I'll do it," Kate said.

"You mean it?" Stanton was wreathed in smiles.

"Yes."

"How come?"

The door flew open and Win stormed in. He restrained himself when he saw Stan. Kate introduced them, it was obvious that he didn't recall their prior meeting.

"Stan wants me to go on a talk show and I've said I would," Kate said.

"Fine," Win said, pouring his drink from the shaker. "What's the issue?"

"Rape," Stan said, and explained who Tillinghast was.

"My lady wife will tear him to shreds," Win said. Then he furrowed his brow in a signal to Kate. She deftly arranged to call Stan the next day to set things up and walked with her to the stage door.

"Wow!" Stan said, rolling her eyes.

"I know," Kate agreed, and hoped silently that nothing would ever change.

He was pacing the floor when she returned to the dressing room.

"Come on, darling," she said. "Let's go out to dinner."

"I'm not hungry."

"I am! Anyway, I think I know how to fix the trouble."

"You do?" He turned to her eagerly. "Tell me."

"No. I'll tell you when we've had another drink and a Caesar salad and a thick porterhouse steak."

IV

They went to a steak house in the East Fifties frequented mainly by celebrities who scrutinized their peers minutely as they entered, then left one another in peace. Win had two requests for autographs from tourists, on the way in, and then they were alone in their usual booth, sipping dry martinis and watching the headwaiter dress the Caesar salad and toss it thoroughly. Win was still on edge but trying to hide it.

"You must toss a salad once for each day of the month," Kate said, to make conversation.

"Who told you that?"

"The French chef at Kel Regis."

Win studied her. "Do you know that's the first time you've mentioned the place since the night we left it?"

"Probably because Stanton turned up. But I think about it."

He took her hand. "Maybe the old girl's ready to make it up."

"I'm not. Here's the salad and it looks scrumptious."

Still, it hadn't been a total break, Kate reflected, eating her salad with appetite. Kate corresponded regularly with Dodie Phelps, Brosie and Belle, Aunt Felicity, and of course Tyler, who wouldn't jeopardize his role as the political sage of Kel Regis by telling Polly she was wrong about Win. And to mollify Oliver, he had put *Aftermaths* aside for a monumental study of the Holy Roman Empire.

"You've compromised! You never did that before!" Kate had exclaimed, astounded, when she heard about it.

"I have not compromised!" had been Tyler's lofty reply. "*Aftermaths* needs more research before I can write it or publish it. The people in it are still living."

"You're after von Rayner, aren't you?"

"He's only one among many."

"Why can't you just let it go?" Kate had ventured.

"I haven't the faintest idea what you mean."

Kate left it at that—it was impossible to argue with Tyler when he got on his high horse—but she was troubled. Her father had his faults, but lack of integrity had never been one of them.

Rebecca was more cynical. "He's buttering his bread on both sides," she had said scornfully. "If he jostled Oliver's forgive-and-forget policy toward West Germany in the Senate, Polly wouldn't let him come to Kel Regis."

None of Kate's correspondents directly mentioned Polly when they wrote, but they let Kate know that Polly never alluded to her. On the other hand, The Senator talked about Kate all the time, Dodie Phelps wrote. "He does it to be naughty and he gets more rambunctious every day."

Both her grandparents were in good health but had been suffering from monumental pique since Reagan's election.

"That was no election," Polly had snapped to reporters. "That was a seduction. It seems all a man needs to be president these days is to be a little better-looking than the devil."

"Will The Senator run again?" they had asked her, because Oliver was getting on, even if he looked a lot younger than he was.

"Absolutely. The country needs every Democrat it can get."

Win's silence suddenly intruded on her musings. Kate looked up to see him toying with his salad.

"All right," she said. "I'll tell you what I think. Then maybe you'll stop playing the dying swan and eat some dinner." Kate looked off into the distance, a way she had when she was organizing her thoughts. Then she looked at Win. "Okay. Sands wants you to take hold of your mother when you say 'the rank sweat of an enseamed bed.' What a line that is! You can almost smell them at it."

He nodded agreement. "But Sands wants me to do more than take hold. He wants me to push her down on the bed and straddle her while I tell her what she's done."

"How about this? You're supposed to kiss her when you say good night. What if you don't release her but walk with her to the bed and sit down beside her. Say 'Go not to my uncle's bed tonight. Assume a virtue if you have it not' and the rest of that speech. Then, instead of merely describing how your uncle might seduce her, the things he might do to her, *show* her as you say the words. And leave it to the audience to decide whether you're showing her as a protective son or a hopeful lover."

He thought a moment, seeing the action in his mind's eye. Then he nodded. "You're right." A second later he smiled broadly. "By God, it's exactly right!" He sprang up, came around to her side of the booth, and pulled her up into an embrace, causing heads to turn all over the restaurant.

"Kate," he said in the voice that carried to the last row. "Great Kate, my love, my wife, my darling! What would I do without you?"

He kissed her passionately. The spectators applauded and he smiled and bowed, handed her into her seat with a flourish, and sat down. He ate the salad and an enormous steak and devoured Kate with his eyes.

They played the scene when they were going to bed that night. He was gentle at first, as he would be when he first kissed the queen, but when he showed her how his uncle would seduce her, passion overtook him, and it was a woman he was holding and touching, not a mother, not a wife, but a woman.

He had never made love to her in quite this way. It was voluptuous, elemental, almost primitive. It was like having sex with two men, one whom she knew, and another man, behind the first, strange but not alien.

She wondered, watching him as he slept the next morning, how many more sides there were to this man she loved so much.

At rehearsal that day, Win did it Kate's way, and the effect was electric. Sands admitted as much and changed his stage directions immediately.

When the scene ended, Grace Halsey asked Win, "Do you or do you not lust after your mother?"

"That's in the eye of the beholder," Win said.

Darcy, in her usual place at the other end of the aisle from Kate, shivered and hugged herself. "The man's a genius," she said to Kate. "Everyone between puberty and death will be titillated. It's as Freudian as Win is, don't you think?"

Kate only nodded. She said as little as possible to Darcy, who now lost no opportunity to refer to her former intimacy with Win. But onstage Darcy projected utter innocence.

"Have you ever seen a dewier, more virginal Ophelia?" Tabitha said sarcastically while they watched Darcy rehearse a scene with Win. "Who would suspect she's a barracuda who's ten years older than she looks?"

Win was faithful, Kate had no doubt about that. But Darcy was always there, always trying.

"She's been hot after him during two long runs, now to be three," Tabitha said the next time Kate erupted about Darcy's constant efforts at seduction.

"Are you trying to tell me something?"

"Katie darling, if I have anything to tell you, I'll say it straight out. Now tell me about this talk show."

V

Stan Wells came to call for Kate on the night of the telecast. It had been decided that Win's presence would deflect too much attention from the subject at hand. "So I'll watch it here at home," he told Stan.

"But Tabitha's coming with," Kate said. "She'll watch from off-stage, with you, Stan, if that's all right."

"Sure." Stanton admired Kate's red silk suit. "Perfect choice," she said.

"Win chose it," Kate said, smiling at him.

"Time to get going," Stan urged. A waiting car took the three women to the studio and Kate met Richard Trayner, the host of *Talkabout*. He had a reputation for doing his homework and asking searching questions.

The set was simplicity itself: three comfortable armchairs, each accompanied by a small table holding a carafe and glass, all of it on a raised platform. The flat behind was painted a vibrant peacock blue.

Trayner introduced Kate to Clyde Tillinghast, who rose to greet her and quickly resumed his seat. Then Trayner introduced both of them to a studio audience of about five hundred people, who applauded enthusiastically. While the crew fastened lapel microphones, Kate took a closer look at Tillinghast.

He was shorter than average with a baby face, pink cheeks, and the kind of nervous energy that kept his hands in constant motion and his body shifting in his chair. He was envied but not liked. That was because he'd made too much money too soon and enjoyed throwing it around.

A bantam cock, Kate reflected, and questioned the real motivation of men who are driven to build the tallest buildings, own the longest yachts, straddle the widest empires. Did it make up for a deficiency in the groin? Had Napoleon been prodigious in bed, or was he better on a horse?

She suspected, with Stan, that the flood of rape dramas so favored by television producers—most of whom were male—might be a way for men to act out their sex-and-power fantasies by proxy. And she worried because it was still men who wrote most of the scripts and even the soap operas, with power not only to influence opinion but to form it. Men were responsible for the outrageous theory that rape was every woman's fantasy! No woman had ever advised a rape victim to relax and enjoy it! No one ever made that suggestion to male prisoners sodomized by inmates.

Kate gave herself a mental shake. She was getting angrier by the minute and the situation required a cool head.

"Ten seconds," the producer called. Kate smiled at Stan and Tabitha, sitting in two molded plastic chairs in the wings, while she waited for the red light on the center camera to flash on.

VI

"Good evening and welcome," Trayner said when it did. "Tonight let's talk about television's growing tendency to use rape as a theme. For example: I counted three two-hour dramas about rape in prime time on one Monday night! Not to mention a rash of programs about date rape, acquaintance rape, marital rape, pregnancy by rape, the children of rape." There were a few nervous titters from the audience. Trayner then introduced both of his guests and turned first to Tillinghast.

"I wonder, Mr. Tillinghast, why this theme turns up with such frequency. Could profit have more to do with it than art?"

There was strong applause. Tillinghast rolled a pen in his fingers, returned it to his breast pocket, creased his lapel, and shifted the knot of his tie while he waited for silence.

"Well, Richard," he said equably, "profitability is the essence of capitalism. Any product as costly to produce as a television program has to make a profit. Apart from that, we have an obligation to the viewers. Rape is a subject that must be addressed."

"To the point of exploitation?"

"That isn't so," Tillinghast protested mildly, too shrewd to take the bait. "The public lets us know if we're exploiting a subject. So far we've had no substantial objections."

Trayner gave Kate the floor.

"So you've concluded that you're giving the public what it wants?" she asked Tillinghast.

"Absolutely."

"Responding to their deep and primal need for the sensational, the savage, and the 'R' rating?"

Laughter and a few cat calls prompted a shrug from Tillinghast.

"I'm thinking about a very successful miniseries called *Spring Canyon*," Kate said. "A young woman is abducted to a mining camp and repeatedly used by the miners throughout the winter. Aside from a mild punchup when the hero arrives to rescue her in the spring, no one is punished." Kate paused. "Is that how the public wants to deal with this crime of violence?"

Tillinghast studied his manicured nails. "*Spring Canyon* wasn't nearly as violent as the front page of our daily papers. And what went on during that long, cold winter was—" He hesitated, searching. "Gentlemanly rape," he concluded.

There was a collective gasp in the theater, then an ominous murmur.

Tillinghast grinned and turned his palms up in an I-call-it-as-I-see-it gesture as the murmur swelled, then died away to an expectant silence. "The woman in *Spring Canyon*," Tillinghast said, "was a person of light morals who, once she arrived in the camp, offered no resistance."

"She couldn't! She was a lone female in a camp with twenty-five hard-drinking mountain men who hadn't seen a woman in a year. Was that a gentlemanly request for sex?"

Another rumble of reaction swept the theater.

"It was a manner of speaking," Tillinghast explained to Kate with patronizing patience.

"Yes, it was," she replied crisply. "It's called doublespeak. 'Gentlemanly rape' is a contradiction in terms, an impossible act."

"That's only your judgment, Mrs. Talley," he snapped.

Katherine checked the reply on the tip of her tongue, feeling the tension build. Stan was making frantic gestures to Kate to speak. Tabitha raised a clenched fist, urging her on. Kate looked out at the waiting audience, over half of them women.

Why the hell shouldn't I? she decided.

"Then let's test your judgment, Mr. Tillinghast, right here, right now. Rape *me* in a gentlemanly way."

The spectators gasped again, then exploded into cheers. "Give 'im hell," a woman shouted while Trayner preened himself, obviously enjoying the tumult.

Kate and Tillinghast glared at each other, immobile and silent in the midst of the commotion. Tillinghast, his hand hidden behind his chair, stiffened his middle finger in a clear threat of comeuppance.

VII

The rest of the segment was dominated by Kate. Tillinghast disappeared as soon as it was over, but Kate stayed to talk to members of the audience.

"You were a smash," Stan said in the taxi going home. "The program will get a lot of free publicity and I'll probably get a raise."

"I'm glad you squashed that roach," Tabitha said.

"I'll call you both tomorrow," Kate told them, and walked into her apartment house.

Win had the door open when Kate stepped off the elevator at the penthouse. Behind him the telephone was ringing. "Wife," he said, "you looked gorgeous. If I'd been Tillinghast, I'd have taken you up on it."

"It wasn't a joke, Win! I was making a point."

"I'll say you were. Come on in and deal with all these telephone calls."

This time the small flurry that usually followed one of Kate's candid remarks did not die down. First the TV five o'clocks and then the weekly newsmagazines picked up the lively exchange. The gossip weeklies and the women's glossies followed. After the telephone calls stopped, sacks of mail arrived from women all over the country, along with requests from women's groups for appearances, from magazines for articles, from radio and TV reporters for interviews.

Kate accepted quite a few of them and earned a reputation for straight speaking—although Rebecca called it belligerence.

"There are some topics that require belligerence," Kate told Win. "I'd forgotten how much I love arguing a cause."

"Are you planning to desert me entirely?" he demanded.

The question seemed to have nothing to do with what she was saying. "Don't be ridiculous," she said.

"But you don't come to rehearsal every day."

"The play's near perfect. You're just practicing now."

"It's no less important to me to have you there."

Kate surrendered, up to a point. The tapestry bag now carried notebooks instead of crocheting. Under the light of the tiny book lamp she scribbled her articles in longhand as soon as the rehearsal was well under way and Win immersed in it. If he wondered where she found the time to write, he never asked her. She was there. That was what he wanted. It was what she wanted him to want.

It never occurred to her that her presence, in and of itself, was not enough for him.

17

───────•◦•───────

1

Rebecca snapped at a celery stalk while Kate lavished butter on a roll. They were lunching at La Côte Basque, "back here with the tourists," Rebecca grumbled, for they were not seated in the narrow forward section where the great and famous went to see and be seen.

"Still," Rebecca went on, "it isn't exactly Outer Mongolia." She called Kate's attention to a few very well-known faces at tables near them, which amused Kate since Rebecca was a minor celebrity herself in Washington social circles. For once Rebecca was not wearing maternity clothes. She had given birth to her fifth child a few months before, at about the time of Kate's debate with Clyde Tillinghast. There was a magnificent sapphire set in diamonds on her right hand, Theo's gift at the birth of his third son. It matched her blue silk jersey dress. Kate wore a ruby bracelet that picked up the colors of her Chanel suit.

"Very nice," Rebecca said, glancing at the bracelet.

"For *Hamlet*."

"I have babies and he has plays. What do you have?" Rebecca asked.

"A fantastic life with an exciting man." It was the kind of thing, Kate realized, she'd heard other women say.

Rebecca tossed her head. "Why doesn't Win chain you to that seat on the aisle and have done with it?"

"Why doesn't Theo chain you to the bedpost?"

"Not the same! I want these pregnancies even more than he does."

"And I want to be a part of Win's triumph. He insists his success in *Hamlet* wouldn't have been possible without me."

"Oh, Kate, Win's too good an actor to need a prop. He's just jealous —as jealous as your grandmother—of anyone or anything that diverts you from him. He's even jealous of me."

Kate did not argue with that. At the start she had welcomed Win's tendency to monopolize her; now it was becoming excessive.

"But he does rely on me," she said to Rebecca. "Everyone raves about the scene with Gertrude, and it was my idea!"

"For which he gave you no credit at all."

Rebecca was right, yet Kate had never questioned the omission. "I didn't expect any," she said uncertainly.

"Why the hell not?"

Kate had no answer because there wasn't any answer good enough. The two women observed each other, suddenly aware of the restaurant sounds: the susurrant women fearful of being overheard, the *ting* of silver on china, the murmur of solicitous waiters.

Their waiter appeared with the appetizers: chilled asparagus for Rebecca, caviar for Kate.

Rebecca watched with envy. "Lord, it infuriates me, the way you can eat and eat and never put on an ounce."

"My reward for being a devoted wife."

Again, they looked at each other.

"It was that talk show," Kate said suddenly with quiet vehemence. "I was content until then, but I've been restless ever since. Being Win's loyal retainer suddenly isn't enough to do." Kate put down the triangle of toast piled with caviar, chopped egg, and onion and gazed at Rebecca in consternation. "But I didn't realize how much I resented it."

"Well, I did. It accounts for your writing articles on the sly. It's a form of rebellion."

"You make me sound like a teenybopper."

"You're behaving like a teenybopper."

There was more to the rebellion than Rebecca knew. Kate was thinking seriously again of resuming the work she had barely begun at Brooke Parrish: expanding her thesis into a book.

". . . Kel Regis and your dragon grandmother," Rebecca was saying. "What also puzzles me is why you're so friendly with Sydney."

"One visit a year is not exactly friendship, and she wants it so desperately I don't have the heart to refuse. Now, *there's* a child in a woman's body. Anyway, Win enjoys our visits, in a removed, superior sort of way, although he's such a good actor, Sydney's crowd never guesses what he really thinks of them. He says it's like walking into the middle of the second act of an Oscar Wilde play. Nothing makes sense if you've missed the beginning."

"How much does he know about Sydney?"

"All the old gossip." Which was really all Rebecca knew, Kate reminded herself. Kate had never told anyone about Sydney's secret sex life, not even Win. He knew only the effect Sydney's promiscuity had

had on Kate, how painful it had been for her. "But Win's not nearly as fascinated by real people as by characters in a play," she went on.

"But he married an utterly real person, didn't he?"

The maître d' approached carrying a small silver tray with a card on it. "For you, Mrs. Talley."

"A secret admirer!" Rebecca cooed, while Kate looked at the card.

MALLORY BOOKS

John Mallory, Publisher

There was a handwritten message on the other side. "May I have the pleasure of a word with you? J.M."

||

Kate went to see him at his Fifth Avenue office. John Mallory was as attractive as she remembered him at La Côte Basque—"a dish," Rebecca had said of the aesthetic-looking blond man after he left their table. "I don't think he's gay, but can you trust a man who wears aviator glasses?"

Kate liked the glasses and the conservative way he dressed, in gray flannels, blue blazer, blue Oxford button-down, and a striped blue and burgundy tie. She guessed he was about forty-five, and his accent suggested that he had been educated abroad before joining his father's firm some years ago. Mallory Books was a comparatively small house, but a very successful one, and John was its driving force now.

His office reminded Kate of Tyler's study. Piles of manuscript were all over the floor and covered most of the surface of his large desk. A collection of hanging plants served as window decoration, and every inch of wall space was lined with shelves crammed full of books.

Kate, Mallory was saying, had an audience that combined her own fans, her husband's, her father's, and her grandparents'. Add all that to a hot topic, and it had to come out "blockbuster." He had unearthed a copy of her thesis and thought it was amazingly readable for a scholarly work but much narrower in scope and with a different approach from the one he had in mind. Broadly speaking, he wanted her to trace a woman's place through the ages.

"That's a lot of material to put between covers," Kate said.

Mallory shook his head. "You'd cover only a short period from each important era: classical antiquity, the Middle Ages, the Renaissance, the seventeenth, eighteenth, and nineteenth centuries." He tapped the desktop with a yellow pencil. "From what I understand, that was more or less how you taught the subject at Brooke Parrish."

"But you don't want an academic approach."

"Hell, no," he said, smiling. It lit up his face, a square, intelligent face with sparkling hazel eyes behind the aviators. "I want the kind of book any woman will understand, even if she's had only a modest education. I don't want broad concepts. I want to know how those women ran their homes, did their laundry, bore and raised their children, treated their sick, mourned their dead. I want to know how they lived and loved."

"Especially how they loved," Kate said.

He smiled again and nodded. "But I'm not suggesting prurience or pornography," he pointed out, wagging the pencil at her. "Just the facts, ma'am, just the facts."

"Because the facts, as you'll have gathered from my thesis, are shocking enough."

"Precisely," he said. "But that's no reason not to publish them, especially since you believe we all incorporate our histories as a gender and women have never understood theirs."

He offered her a sizable advance and a standard royalty scale. "It's a good offer," he said, "but have your agent go over it."

Kate had no agent, but she was sure Henry Parmenter, who represented her father, would take her on at a ten percent commission for a presold property.

"May I assume that you'll do it?" Mallory said.

"I'm leaning very strongly in that direction, but I want a little time to think it over."

His eyes narrowed slightly. "I'll better any other offers you've had."

"I've had no other offers. I'll let you know in a day or two."

He nodded and dropped the pencil, which was apparently a negotiating tool. "I'm eager to read your father's next book. They say he had started work on something else but put it aside to write this one."

"You never know where the muse will descend," she said. She would not be drawn into a discussion of *Aftermaths*—or "Tyler's Revenge," as she thought of it. John Mallory was sharp. He might detect the conflict she felt over her father's apparent surrender to pressure from Oliver.

Another illusion crushed, Kate thought.

"A brilliant man, your father," Mallory said, "as your husband is an actor. I still can't get over his Hamlet. Makes me wonder about the prince's real motives—and in certain ways about my own."

"That was the intention." Kate got up to go. "I'll pass along the compliment—and thank you for the offer."

"My pleasure." He shook her hand. "I really look forward to our working together." The exuberant smile flashed again. "I'm going to be your editor, of course."

III

Kate walked home, rapt in thought. The money was important to her. It would be the first she had earned since teaching at Brooke Parrish. Before that, her school fees had been paid by her father and everything else by Polly. For the past four years she had been Win's responsibility. To be an independent adult was as tempting to her as writing the book.

And getting back to work again was as important as the money. She loved the theater, but she was only a bystander—in that world, not of it. It was the written word that delighted her, the magical transfer of what she wanted to say to words on paper. She had never considered speaking into a tape recorder; sound would have interfered with the process, would have broken the link between her idea and the page.

She had timed the appointment with Mallory so she could go home to change afterward and be at the theater by seven. The apartment was quiet when she let herself in, the housekeeper having left for the day.

Whenever she came home to Fifth Avenue, Kate always crossed to the great wall of glass that seemed to float her out over Central Park. The very large living room reflected in it was all white except for a few touches of eighteenth-century French: the lamps, the moldings, the gilt-framed mirrors. The chairs and couches, scattered with silk cushions in brilliant colors, were arranged in groups because theater people liked to congregate in small numbers. There was a concert grand piano because theater people loved to play and sing. Some of the greatest talents of the contemporary stage had been in this room.

Kate came back to the hall and went to her dressing room. She looked through her dresses and chose a plain black silk she would wear with pearls, took out shoes, pantyhose, and a handbag. She undressed quickly and took a shower, contemplating the resentment Rebecca had brought to the surface a few days before at La Côte Basque. She knew Rebecca was as possessive of her as she had accused Win and Polly of being, but the resentment was all Kate's.

"I've been an observer too long," she told her reflection firmly as she applied her makeup. "If I don't do something, my brain will ossify."

She dressed quickly and took a taxi to the theater. When she arrived, Win was already wearing black tights and a velvet tunic, his hair lightened almost to platinum for the role. His face was like chiseled marble above the white collar. He wore the heavy gold chain and insignia she had bought him at Tiffany's for opening night.

Bought him with his money, she reminded herself.

He hugged her, but she could tell he was already well into that transformation he underwent before each performance. He was the Prince of Denmark now, not Winslow Talley. Grace was his mother, Darcy his doomed love. He had no wife; Kate was left in a kind of temporary limbo.

They rarely talked at this time. Win preferred to listen to music. He had a favorite composer for each of the plays he had done: Rossini for *Prelude;* Brahms for *Second Sight;* Mahler for *Hamlet.* Tonight it was the Adagietto from the Fifth Symphony, that brooding, melancholy music, so beautiful and so *triste,* very like Hamlet himself.

This was hardly the time to tell him her news, and the time was still not right while they had supper and Win slowly shook off the character. She waited until they were in bed.

"A book?" he said, turning to look at her. "No, Kate! I'd never see you."

"Nonsense. I'll just be making a narrative of my course notes. I can do that while you read scripts."

"But I need you to read them too, to help me decide which play to do next."

"You have plenty of time to do that. *Hamlet* will be a long run. But I'll read the ones you think have merit. Really, Win, a book will take far less time than teaching would have done."

"I had no idea you still wanted to teach. I thought you were happy!"

"Of course I'm happy! But you have your work and I need to have mine, as we planned. It was your suggestion that I teach during your long runs, remember?"

He didn't answer that. Instead, he reached out to stroke her neck. "Darling," he said indulgently, "who would want to read a book about the domestic affairs of long-dead women?"

"The same people who will watch a play about a legendary Danish prince."

He cupped her breast and kissed it, and an erotic ripple went through her. "That's different," he said. "Primal emotions are universal."

"So is the impact of history. Win, I really want to do it."

He rolled over to lie above her, brushing her nipples with the tangle of hair on his chest. Another wave of arousal traveled downward from her breasts.

"All right, Professor," he whispered, "provided you leave plenty of time for me."

"Win," she began, eager to talk about the book with him, but he kissed her into silence and she gave herself up to him and to the urgency of passion.

IV

Tyler came out of the library at Kel Regis at ten o'clock the next morning, carrying a copy of *Publishers Weekly*. It was a break in his routine: he usually sat down at his desk at eight o'clock and worked through until luncheon at one. *The Holy Roman Empire* was taking twice the time of his earlier books and he was impatient to get back to *Aftermaths*. Oliver would retire from the Senate sooner rather than later. Until then, it would have been folly to deny himself a welcome at Kel Regis, even if it meant a delay in putting Sydney's fair ass in a sling.

And he had the means to do exactly that! Tyler had evidence that the old baron, Hans Erik's father, had been an ardent National Socialist from the inception of that infernal idea. What he needed now was compelling proof that Sydney's husband, although a boy during the war, was a neo-Nazi. The case against von Rayner had to be watertight and Tyler kept his second team of researchers busy in the Nazi archives in Berlin while they were supposedly working on the Holy Roman Empire.

He sighed. All his research assistants put together couldn't equal Kate. He remembered with regret the old days, before she entered Wakefield. They had always been together then, Tyler and his reliable, brilliant, devoted daughter. He hated the fact that Kate saw her mother once in a while, but he never spoke of it. That was to spare his own feelings, not Kate's.

He went on looking for Polly. Finding the morning room empty, he continued out to the terrace. He saw her at the bottom of the garden, looking out over the river as she often did, half in sunlight, half in shade from the weeping willows.

Stubborn old beldame, Tyler thought affectionately. *She's pining for Kate and too proud to make the first overture.*

A real camaraderie had blossomed between Tyler and Polly; ever since he sold the house in Harmony and bought a small flat in Boulder, he had been staying at Kel Regis for weeks at a time, sometimes when Polly and Oliver were in Washington. He and Polly had their love for Kate in common, even if Polly refused to talk about her granddaughter. And they had their contempt for Sydney in common. Neither Polly nor Tyler acknowledged Kate's trips to visit her. They bore that iniquity in silence.

But Sydney would have her comeuppance when *Aftermaths* was published and the truth about von Rayner came out. Tyler would never admit that aspect of the book, but he didn't think Polly would mind watching Sydney share the stigma of Nazism with her odious spouse.

Tyler set off down the path, thinking as he approached Polly that longevity ran in this family. Well into her seventies, Polly was in extremely fine fettle and rode one of the Charlie's Darlings every day —Tyler could never keep track of equine genealogy. His forte was kings.

Oliver, while still hale, sometimes behaved like a schoolboy. The brain required daily exercise to stay vigorous, and Oliver used his brains only to play Wise Old Southern Colonel on the floor of the Senate. He did it well, in his rich voice, "full of honor and wisdom," Polly had once said, "signifying nothing." Oliver still left the planning of his political strategy to Polly.

And to Theo, for many years now. Tyler had the greatest affection for Theodore Barrows. Theo was the shrewdest political consultant in the business, for one thing. He could wring money from stones as well as from political action committees. And he was a loving husband to Rebecca and a devoted father to their children—how many were there now, four or five?

Theo often flew his own jet down to Kel Regis for emergency consultations, but Polly still had a grudge against Rebecca, and Theo would not stay the night without her. Heaven knew why Polly so disliked little Becca, but then, Polly's grudges were often as inexplicable as they were enduring.

As long as she doesn't have one against me, Tyler comforted himself, for he dearly loved living at this place with a houseful of servants at his beck and call and a magnificent library at his disposal.

"Good morning, Polly," Tyler called.

"Tyler, you old bookworm, why are you out in the sun at this hour?"

"I have some news about Kate."

Polly remained silent but did not turn away.

Thus encouraged, Tyler read the item from *Publishers Weekly*. "Naturally, Kate would focus on women," he said when he had finished reading. "And they say she got a healthy advance too!" He lowered the periodical and looked at Polly. "Why don't you call and congratulate her?"

"Don't meddle, Tyler."

"But it's such a waste! You're not getting any younger."

"She knew that when she lied to me."

"Lied to you? Kate?"

"As good as! She never confided in me, never shared any of her feelings. She led me to believe she was going into politics. Then, without a by-your-leave, she announces she's dropping everything to marry a man who's already made her miserable—and is bound to do it again. If there's any calling to be done, she's the one to call me!"

"But you sent her away!"

Polly sighed. "Yes, I sent her away."

"Why make both of you unhappy?"

"Happiness is a fleeting thing. It is not the business of a lifetime," Polly said with asperity now, two spots of red appearing in her cheeks. "I wanted her to fulfill her destiny and she isn't doing that. She's known as Mrs. *Him* now—except for that talk show. She's let herself be subsumed by a man. My Kate! In this day and age! No fame, no fortune, no *accomplishment* of her own."

Tyler brandished the trade magazine. "She'll have all that now!"

"She has to write that book first and she might have more interference from him than she anticipates. He doesn't love *her*. He loves the fact that a woman of Kate's caliber loves *him*. But he won't put up with any rivals, take my word for it. Now, get along back to your scribbling."

"I just wanted to help," said Tyler, stricken by her intensity of feeling, so foreign to him.

"Yes, well, you can't teach your mother-in-law to suck eggs. Now, go along. You'll be grumbling tonight that you're behind your schedule."

He took her hand briefly, patted it, then went back up the path. Polly watched him go. He was years her junior, but Tyler had been born old. It was hard to remember that he had been young once and so besotted with passion that he had abandoned his strict moral code and jeopardized his career to couple with a girl like Sydney. Still, he was a brilliant writer and a scholar non pareil. And he was old-fashioned and conservative, traits Polly could deal with. She liked having him around. It amused her to let him play lord of the manor when she was in Washington riding herd on Oliver.

She turned from the river and, her back straight despite the discomfort in her joints, went briskly through the garden and up to where Dodie Phelps rocked in the arbor, nursing her arthritis over a cup of tea. The woman was no longer thin; she was frail. Polly stood for a moment, watching her cousin, and an immense sadness fell upon her.

Don't you dare go first and leave me, Polly prayed fervently. *Don't you dare!*

Then she gave herself a little shake and continued on her way.

"Lord, what a lot of old crocks we are," Polly said, sinking into another rocker. "We look like we've been stuffed and set around the place to provide realism for tourists."

"My, but you're gloomy this morning. What's wrong?"

"Kate's writing a book."

Dodie Phelps was too astonished to reply immediately. It was four years since Kate's name had passed Polly's lips and now, just like that, she plunked herself down and announced that Kate was writing a book!

"What's it about?" Dodie Phelps finally ventured.

"Same thing she taught. But what does it *mean*?"

"What do you mean, what does it mean? It means Kate's working again."

"But why? Something's changed in that marriage, or my name's not Polly Benedict."

"If you weren't such a fool, you'd know."

"Little Becky Barrows would know," Polly murmured.

"What good is that? You won't talk to her either."

Polly smiled bleakly. "Oh, yes, I will. I'd talk to the devil himself to find out what I want to know."

V

Rebecca whirled around their large room at Kel Regis like a dancer, beaming at Theo. "It's every bit as gorgeous as Kate described it. I feel I know every room in it. Even cabbage-rose chintz can't ruin something like this!"

Theo smiled at his wife. "I love to see you happy."

"My darling, I've been deliriously happy since the night you asked me to marry you. Now, what shall I wear to dinner?"

"Short, I'd say. We're the only company. Everyone else is family."

"If you're wearing black tie, I'm wearing long. I'm going to take a bath." She disappeared into her bathroom.

Like a child at a birthday party! Theo smiled again as he went off to his own shower. But to be honest, Rebecca had never really been as carefree as a child. She had always had an adult intensity. The first time he met her he had been taken by her beauty and amazed by her maturity. And the first time he made love to her it was no shy maiden he held in his arms, but a woman so hot there was no resisting her.

Moreover, it was she who had proposed to him, something not every man could boast about.

She had stolen into Tyler's house in Harmony late that night, after everyone on Elm Terrace was asleep. She was wearing a raincoat when she slipped into Theo's room, where he was reading in bed.

"Rebecca! What are you doing here? Is anything wrong?"

"Yes."

"Can I help?"

"You're the only one who can. Come upstairs to Kate's attic. We'll wake Tyler if we talk here."

"What is it?" he asked presently while she was lighting a candle in Kate's old retreat.

"I love you."

"Rebecca . . ."

"And you love me. I know you do!"

"I've been trying not to."

"Don't try. Just marry me, marry me, marry *me*!"

"Rebecca, I'm fifteen years older than you are! That doesn't seem important now, but it will later."

"Never. It's irrelevant. Oh, Theo, kiss me and I'll prove it to you."

She opened her raincoat and he was entranced by her naked body, so smooth, so sweet, so perfect. His arms went around her. She sucked his lip tenderly while her hand reached inside his pajamas and grasped his erection. When she slid down his body and he felt her mouth on it, desire overcame caution. He picked her up and carried her to the couch and sat down, holding her on his lap.

She turned swiftly to face him and straddled his thighs, sighing as she sank slowly down to enclose him in that soft, wet heat, her hips circling, pumping until he erupted inside her. He knew then he had to have her always, that he would marry her.

He had never regretted it, not for a moment.

She was the perfect wife in every way but one: Rebecca was not a caring mother. He knew it was the pregnancies she cherished, not the children, although she supervised the care of the Barrows brood with the same devotion she gave to Theo's career. But once Rebecca delivered a baby, she turned it over to a nurse and a nanny.

A paradox, he thought now, as he toweled himself dry, in a woman with so ardent a nature as hers. But he had always believed that the sexes were fundamentally incomprehensible to each other, except, on occasion, in bed.

His memories had aroused him. He went back to the bedroom, where Rebecca sat at the dressing table. She turned to him, her beautiful face enchanting. She smiled radiantly, reading his expression immediately. Getting up, she went to the bed, removed her peignoir, and lay down, her arms held out to him. Her thighs smelled of perfumed bath oil when he kissed them.

When they went downstairs to dinner, both of them were glowing.

VI

The conversation at Polly's gorgeous dinner table, with Polly's famous roses in six low sterling-silver bowls along its length, was invariably political. Tonight, with a Republican entrenching himself in the White House, the focus was on ways to get him out. Small talk would get no quarter here. Polly, Tyler, and Theo were experts on politics. The fragile Dodie Phelps was an intelligent observer and Rebecca extremely well informed about her husband's work.

The only people obviously bored by the subject were Brosie and Belle, Kate's twin cousins, whom Rebecca had just met. They were startlingly beautiful and so much alike that it was eerie to look at them.

Fancy having a second self, Rebecca mused. *It must be like Narcissus and his reflection in the pool.*

Polly, apparently, was displeased that Belle was here without her husband and that Brosie was here at all, but the twins did not appear to be troubled by her. Their pleasure in each other's company was obvious, childlike. Together they defied their grandmother by talking about Kate and Win.

Despite the roses, the Baccarat crystal, and the succulent food—Kel Regis quail stuffed with truffled Kel Regis rice—there was an underlying tension in the air. Kate was its cause and, Rebecca realized, Kate was the reason Polly had finally invited her.

But I'm damned if I'll make it easy for her! Rebecca fumed.

"When does Kate think her book will be finished?" Brosie asked Rebecca, darting a look at Polly under his long lashes.

"She's not sure," Rebecca said, thinking what a delicious-looking man he was. "But she's halfway through."

"No author knows exactly how long it will take to write a book," Tyler said.

"It'll knock everyone's socks off," Belle said, her eyes sparkling.

"It will shock them," Rebecca agreed, unable to take her eyes off Belle's exquisite face. "Kate uses history to make a lot of points and raise a lot of questions. Why women marry, for one. It's an explosive subject." Belle's face changed, but she said nothing.

"For you, apparently," Polly remarked acerbically to Rebecca, "it's to have children."

"Partly," Rebecca returned with a charming smile. "But I still have three to go to match your production."

"Tell me about Washington," Dodie Phelps said with a warning glance at Polly, and the conversation shifted back to politics.

It wasn't until after dinner that Rebecca and Polly had a private exchange. They had moved away across the terrace and the others left them to it, as if by prearrangement. They faced each other like two adversaries.

Now I've got you, Rebecca exulted silently, resolved not to utter an unsolicited syllable about Kate.

"How is she?"

"Who?"

"Don't toy with me," Polly said. "My granddaughter. Kate."

"In fine fettle. She's mad about Win and her book is going well."

Polly's brow arched. "How does he feel about the book?"

Rebecca shrugged. "He wants her all to himself. But so do you."

"*And* you," Polly snapped. "What's more, I don't believe you really love her."

"What a cruel thing to say!" Rebecca was unable to keep her composure. "Kate's been my other half since the day we were born. She's essential to me, and I treasure her."

"Only if you can control her."

"Don't confuse me with yourself, Mrs. Benedict."

They fell silent for what seemed a long moment, watching each other guardedly. Polly wanted more, Rebecca could sense that, but she was not going to get it.

"What is there about her," Polly mused, as if she knew the answer, "that everyone wants? You, I, her actor, her wretched mother, her cousins. Is it her strength?"

"She's not that strong. She was when we were little, but she fell apart when Sydney left."

Polly snorted. "And you took over."

"I *did* take over. She had no one else. Tyler lives in the past—and she wasn't all that taken with you when you finally decided to acknowledge her existence."

"Don't delude yourself," Polly said. "She's a lot stronger than you'll ever be. And she has integrity."

Rebecca lost control entirely. "If that's what you want to call it! It's brought her nothing but grief. She's Win's handmaiden. Sydney can still wheedle her into spending time with her and Dr. Strangelove. As for you, Kate almost went into politics to please you. She thought you wanted a granddaughter when all you wanted was someone to live out your own fantasies."

Polly regarded her frostily. "That will do, young woman. You're shrewd, but I can see right through you. I never understood what Kate saw in you and I still don't, or Theo either. The Lord knows he deserves a lot better."

Polly turned and started back across the terrace to join the others. Rebecca, utterly rebuked about Theo, where she needed assurance most, followed before the distance between them became awkward.

Both women were practiced enough in deception to hide their anger, so the rest of the weekend went smoothly except for a muffled shouting match between Polly and Brosie—she said he must marry and he said he'd sooner die—of which the whole house was aware, but which everyone pretended hadn't happened.

Rebecca was relieved when she and Theo were on their way home.

"Well, that was quite a weekend," Theo said after they took off for Washington in Theo's new plane. "Now that the ice is broken, I hope we'll be invited again."

"You will. I won't."

"Why not?"

"That woman's always been jealous of Kate and me, how close we are."

"Is that what you two were talking about?"

"In part. She was sounding me out about Kate. Let's forget about that now, darling, I have a million things to do in Washington, the first of which is that cocktail party for Clem Case."

"God, I'd almost managed to forget him. The man's a colossal bore."

"So are most politicians, but he's got pots of money. I need your approval on the guest list."

"If it's your list, it's certain to be perfect."

"Theo, do you love me?"

He set the automatic pilot and turned to look at her, not really surprised. She asked that question often. "Dammit, woman, you *know* I love you!"

"Sometimes I think you deserve better."

"Darling, there's no one better. I couldn't get along without you, you know that. I wouldn't want to."

He went on talking until she was reassured. He knew he would make love to her again that night. For Rebecca, desire was the only real proof of love.

VII

"Kel Regis is glorious," Rebecca told Kate on the telephone. "Everything you said about it is true. I never saw a more beautifully appointed house."

"And Polly?"

"She only invited me to hear about you."

"Did she ask?"

"No, and I didn't tell her the merest scrap."

Kate's silence was not difficult to interpret, but Rebecca was damned if she would act as a messenger for that insulting old harridan.

"Kate, even if she were pining for you, she'd never let anyone know it, least of all me."

"That's true. I suppose things are better left as they are."

"I'll say," Rebecca agreed. "I liked your twin cousins."

"They're lovely, aren't they?"

"They're ravishing! And no more to be parted than Pavorotti and his handkerchief. Polly was raving at him to get himself married."

"That's an old story," Kate said—rather abruptly, Rebecca thought. "How's the book?" she asked brightly.

"Coming along. And I've chosen a title: *Consort.*"

"Oh, I like that," Rebecca said.

"John likes it too."

"I think John has a thing for you."

"John's thing is for any female he can stick it to."

Rebecca laughed. "Has he made a pass?"

"Made a pass! So delightfully archaic! No, not that I've noticed."

In fact, Kate had noticed but chose to pretend she hadn't. She was not in the least attracted to John Mallory as a lover; she was married to the best lover in the western world. What made John so good to be with was his enthusiasm for her work.

VIII

"Maybe I shouldn't assume that women don't know all about this," Kate said, sitting down in Mallory's office and crossing her legs.

"About what?"

"At this point, about giving birth before the nineteenth century."

"How would they, unless they'd studied it like you?"

"Maybe they'd rather not hear," Kate said ruefully. "Maybe I'm beating a dead horse, trying to convince them that what's happening now is only a continuation of what happened then."

He shook his head and held out his hand and she gave him the pages she had brought in and watched while he read them.

Sexual intercourse for the majority of people was rough and entirely at the husband's whim—as it still is in many countries. A woman did not have the right to refuse her husband, no matter what her condition or the risk to her life. Pregnancies were frequent and a woman worked—hauling water or milking cattle in the country, washing, cleaning, and cooking in the towns—up to the last minute.

At the first contraction, the midwife was sent for. It is assumed by most modern women that nature was permitted to take its course. Not so. There was gross interference.

The midwife often punctured the amniotic sac, usually with a filthy fingernail grown long and filed sharp for the purpose, before the waters could break naturally. It was a necessary precaution, she assured the quaking mother: the infant was now head down (heaven help the mother if it were not!) and would otherwise drown in the fluid.

The urban birthing was a social event, and soon the room was crowded with the midwife, assistants, neighbors, and relatives, who laughed and talked, drank home-brewed ale, and took turns telling horror tales of other deliveries to divert the mother, while the midwife encouraged her to bear down far too early in the process, exhausting her unnecessarily.

But that was not the worst.

The windows were kept closed against evil "humours" while, in that fetid air, the terrified mother labored, either standing or squatting so that gravity could help the infant, it was believed, to wriggle out of the womb. This it was eager to do, conventional wisdom held, because the food supply in utero had run out and the baby was ravenously hungry.

To encourage its swifter passage, the midwife tugged at its head —sometimes ripping it off—and plunged her hands deep into the birth canal despite agony to the mother. Sometimes, to finish the process with dispatch, the midwife tugged prematurely at the placenta, causing hemorrhage or even yanking out the uterus entirely, both conditions fatal.

And that was not the worst.

Peasant women were often up feeding the livestock the same day. They were fortunate! Middle-class urban women were confined to bed for ten days' lying-in, during which interval the attendants made them sweat profusely by means of hot bricks, blankets, and possets—or bled them. Since it was forbidden to change the birth linen until the lying-in was over, the stench is unimaginable to our soaped, sprayed, douched, and deodorized selves, and infection was rampant. Sometimes infection arose from another, incredible source.

It is on record that some men demanded intercourse immediately following childbirth, regardless of the torment or the risk of fatal infection to their wives. The wife had no choice but to submit. The act could in no way have been an act of passion on her part, nor of love on his. It was forced intercourse and that is rape and that was the worst.

"My God," John Mallory said, looking up at her. "This is outrageous."

"That's what my supervisor said about my thesis."

He shook his head. "You're not beating a dead horse, Kate. You'll have women tearing down your door, some to agree that they behave as they do now because of centuries of abuse, and some ready to stone you for stirring the feminist fires. But it's history—and the questions you raise at the end of the book are valid."

"Thank you, John," Kate said, much relieved. "I'll get on with it."

"What comes next?"

"Maybe I'll do the Victorians next."

He nodded. "I'm with you, whatever you decide. I hope you know that."

It was the way he said it that bothered her.

"Don't, John," she said. "I like working with you."

"And you won't if I carry on. I can't help it if I'm in love with you."

"That's entirely your concern."

"Are you sure?"

Kate stood up.

"Forget it," he said, holding his hands up in surrender.

He looked so anxious that she relented. "Forget what?"

IX

If Win wasn't too tired to discuss the book with her, he diverted her from talking about it, often with sex. He seemed to see *Consort* as a caprice, something that would be published and forgotten. For him, it was more important that she help him choose his next play. No matter how many scripts she read, he always had another stack ready for her.

"You're not separating the wheat from the chaff," she protested. "You're giving me utterly impossible stuff."

"I can't seem to be objective. I'm counting on you to be."

Kate called Win's agent while Win was onstage that night. "Andy, you've been sending us rubbish. Have you lost your touch?"

Andy objected. It was at Win's insistence that Andy sent him everything. "Besides," he said, "Win's nervous about the next play. It has to be absolutely perfect, 'cause when you're up as high as he is, the only way to go is down."

"That's Win talking and it's absolute rot, Andy! You mustn't agree with him when he gets that way. Go ahead and send all those scripts if he insists, but tell me which ones you think I should read—and let's keep this conversation strictly between ourselves."

In the end there were only three plays she liked. Kate reread them carefully before she made her final choice, a play about a writer who compromises his talent for fame and almost loses everything.

"It's right up your street," she told Win. "It has power, passion, and a message."

"It's a downer," Win insisted.

"No, because he does save himself. Of course, he loses her, but that's what makes it moving."

The part of the woman was tailor-made for Darcy Barrington, but Kate was accustomed to her endless presence and to the ongoing gossip that Win's leading lady was his secret mistress and his wife didn't seem to mind. "It's the tripe that sells magazines," Win had brushed it off, "the kind you wouldn't read."

But Win chose a Victorian period piece called *Rapture*, about a wife's passion for her repressed husband that leads, in the end, to murder. Kate thought it was melodramatic, but Win didn't care.

"A melodrama is just what I need right now," he insisted. "It draws bigger audiences. Backers are nervous about Shakespeare."

"You know you're good enough to make Shakespeare popular!"

But Win was adamant. Before *Hamlet* closed, rehearsals began on *Rapture*—with Darcy as the volcanic wife—and Kate went back to her aisle seat and her book lamp and the second half of *Consort*. She didn't tell Win she was working on the Victorians too.

18

I

The telephone rang at seven in the morning.

"Dr. Ballard, you've done it!" John Mallory said when Kate answered it.

"Done what? What time is it?" Kate asked drowsily.

"It's seven. I just got hold of my mole at *The New York Times* and you'll be on the best seller list next Sunday!"

"Who the hell is that?" Win demanded.

Kate sat bolt upright. "Say that again!" she told Mallory.

"*Consort* is on the hardcover nonfiction list!"

"But the book has only been out a week! How can it be on the list?"

"With the publicity you and Win get? I'm surprised it didn't get on before you finished writing it! Listen, I want to set up some interviews for you. Let's meet Sunday night."

Kate glanced at Win and shook her head. "Sorry. We're leaving for the Cape after the Sunday matinee." She almost said they desperately needed two days alone.

"Kate! This is no time for a holiday!"

Win was feigning sleep next to her. "Not a chance, John. The hype can wait until Tuesday." She hung up the telephone and lay back, wide awake.

"I know you're not asleep," she said to Win. "Don't you want to hear why John called at such an ungodly hour?"

"I'm going to hear whether I want to or not."

He was startled when she told him, then quiet, then a little too jolly as he planned a party for her.

"No," she said. "No parties. Let Mallory handle that. We can celebrate at the Cape, just the two of us." She turned to put her head on his shoulder. "Why aren't you as happy as I am?"

"I *am* happy for you! You must know that!"

"But . . . ?"

"Things are going to change. I liked them as they were."

"I'm not going to change!"

"Not you. Us. You and I."

"Never! Wait and see."

On the way to the Cape and for the first two days they were there, they said nothing more about her success. It made Kate feel as though an intruder were in their midst, a threat to their charmed circle of two.

They opened a bottle of champagne on Sunday night, sitting in front of the fire in Tyler's study. They had stayed at the cottage before, but this time, somehow, was different.

"I feel as if I were a child again," Kate said.

"That's lovely."

"No, it wasn't. Why do people always talk so wistfully of childhood when it's full of hobgoblins and complexes, confusion and misery? I never felt sure of myself as a child. I was always anxious, looking over my shoulder for disaster."

"After Sydney?"

Kate nodded.

"Poor, pretty Sydney," Win said.

"Poor, rejected Kate!"

"That too. But you built your defenses and got yourself together. From the little time I've spent in her company, she didn't and never will. She's not a woman of valor like you."

"I've never thought of myself as particularly valorous."

"You are though." He watched the fire. "Sometimes it's intimidating."

"Sometimes you are too."

He turned and took her into his arms. "Then let's intimidate each other. Neither of us wants to threaten anyone else."

She put her arms around him. "Lord, I love you," she said. "You understand so many things. Please, Win, try to understand this. It isn't as if we had children to absorb my time while you're onstage."

"Do you want a child?"

She shook her head. "Not enough to have one. Do you?"

"No. I'm happy as we are."

For those few days they were blissfully happy, but Kate returned to a whirl of book signings, print interviews, television appearances, speeches to women's groups, "and flash cameras," Win said. "You're photographed more than I am."

"Only because I'm married to you," Kate assured him, uneasy that she had to say it, resenting him for needing to hear it.

‖

"Darling!" Sydney said from Vienna. "I just got my copy of *Consort*! I'll start it tonight. Everyone says it's sensational. Oh, Kate, I'm so terribly proud of you. We both are."

What right has von Rayner to take pride in me? Kate fumed inwardly. *Or Sydney either?*

But Kate said the right things. Sydney had finally abandoned her huff at not having been invited to Kate's wedding. "I invited you to mine" had been her invariable wail for the past several years and "You could have put it off for a day or two" her reply when Kate told her the wedding came twenty-four hours after the engagement.

"Your father must be pleased," Sydney was saying rather unexpectedly.

"Yes, of course." Kate's success was no threat to her father; it only confirmed that scholarship was her genetic inheritance from him.

"Will you see him soon?" Sydney asked, as if by the way.

"All right, Sydney," Kate said impatiently, "tell me what you really want."

Sydney's languid air deserted her. "It's that wretched book he's researching! He's been digging up things better left dead and buried."

"Who told you that?"

"Hansi." Sydney's pet name for her husband would have sounded ridiculous from anyone but her. "Tyler's been researching friends of ours who are very high in government circles."

"And were when Hitler was in power?"

"They were *not* Nazis! Anyway, all that was half a century ago!" Sydney said with her talent for expunging outrage with time.

"Then there's nothing to worry about," Kate said tightly.

"It could still be very embarrassing for Hansi. And for me. And, I might add, for you."

"I can't see how. In any case, I've been embarrassed by you before, Mother."

There was a silence on the other end. Then her mother said, "Can't you see he's only doing it to torment me?"

"Tyler doesn't let personal matters take precedence over his work, and you know it." But Kate knew Sydney was right.

"I *should* know it! It's why I left him. But this is different. This is a personal vendetta disguised as history. He'll never stop punishing me. Can't you talk to him?"

"Not about this, I can't. Not about anything to do with you."

"It isn't fair! He's just like Polly, on and on about something that happened years ago! They think they're God. They carry grudges to their graves."

The silence hummed between them, heavy with Polly's grudges against both of them.

"All right, I'll try," Kate said, capitulating to her own sense of injustice. "But no promises."

After a moment Sydney resumed briskly. "That's not the only reason I called, darling. I'm having one of my weekends in August, a kind of *fête champêtre* at the *Schloss*. Everyone who is anyone will be there, and you and Win simply *must* come."

"I don't see how. I've got appearances scheduled and Win will be in the middle of rehearsing his new play." But Win liked the *Schloss*. He could talk shop with Sydney's theater friends. Maybe they could get away.

"Nonsense, Kate. Even you two need an occasional rest. And I promised Hansi. The poor pet would be disappointed."

"I'm sure you'll find a way to comfort him—but I'll ask Win if he'll be ready for a break by then."

"That's my girl," Sydney said.

It was what she always said at the end of a telephone conversation. And it always made Kate wince.

III

The hullabaloo over *Consort* began to overshadow the approaching opening of *Rapture*, and Kate felt guilty because of it.

"Guilty?" Rebecca exclaimed when she came to New York for a shopping spree. "But of course! I'd forgotten. You eat a mea culpa cupcake for breakfast every morning!"

"Oh, Becca, stop!"

"Kate, look at yourself! Look at this place!" Rebecca's gesture encompassed the spacious living room and its stunning view of Central Park. "You're famous, you're brilliant, and you're going to be making pots of your own money, not your father's or your grandmother's or Win's. But do you enjoy it? No, you worry about trespassing on Win's media space!"

"But he needs the spotlight, Becca, and I don't! You don't know how much of himself he puts into each performance. Adulation is what he must have to replace fragments of himself, to fill himself up again."

"I despair!" Rebecca wailed. "You've had people standing on your back to reach their own objectives for years: Sydney, Tyler, Polly, Win. Now the whole world's crazy about you, and you think your husband's ego will suffer because of it! Well, let me tell you, Sister Kate, Winslow Talley's ego is big enough to cope with your success, and the sooner you accept that the better off you'll be!"

IV

Not long after, Kate accepted an invitation to speak at Columbia University. It came about a month after *Rapture* was scheduled to open, and it would keep her from attending an evening performance. She decided not to tell Win until they were closer to the event; she was already attending far fewer rehearsals than ever before.

"When you're hot, you're hot!" John Mallory reminded her whenever she balked at making evening appearances. "We must gather our rosebuds while we may. Incidentally, have you considered wearing contact lenses?"

"What on earth for?" asked Kate, whose windowpanes had recently been replaced by real prescription lenses.

"I think you look smashing in specs, but TV audiences like their idols glamorous."

"You mean the glasses make me look like an egghead?"

"Exactly."

"Great! I want to look like the most flagrant egghead who ever lived." Kate made a megaphone of her hands. "Wade Stevens, are you watching?"

John rolled his eyes in mock concern for her sanity. "Who's Wade Stevens?"

"It's a long story. But, no, I will not wear contact lenses for purely cosmetic purposes."

"Even though you dress like a fashion plate and your makeup is always perfect?"

"I do that because *I* like it," Kate said. "For me!" But she did it partly because Darcy did it and Win liked it.

Every technique Kate used to hold an audience she had learned from watching Win and Darcy rehearse. From the voice coach she had learned projection and she pitched her distinctive, husky voice low, as Tyler used to do, so that people were forced to listen attentively. She took on an air of authority before she started speaking, the way Win took on an entire character. And she sometimes said shocking things in a matter-of-fact way that made people gasp.

"You're a great performer," Win told her after he had watched her on television.

"I should be. I live with the best actor in the world."

"I've created a monster," he said ruefully.

But in the role of Gabriel in *Rapture*, Win was creating another legend of his own.

V

The reviews, when they were read at the opening night party, were unanimous: Win had transformed a good play into superlative theater. His portrayal of suppressed lust as he struggled to resist Darcy's ravenous sexuality electrified the first-night audience and the critics alike.

One critic wrote:

> *As played by the incomparable Winslow Talley, this play is about much more than repressed sexuality. It is about our species' frightening will to power. When his wife, brilliantly played by Darcy Barrington, strips away Gabriel's defenses by exposing a truth he cannot live with, he is destroyed as thoroughly as if she had used a gun.*

"I told you this one was a winner!" Win shouted to Kate across Darcy's living room, crowded with noisy celebrants and now littered with newspapers.

"You're the winner," Kate shouted back. She pushed through the crowd to his side and they hugged each other.

"Let's go home," Win said softly. "I want to make love to you."

He turned and waved to catch everyone's attention. "I'm going home to tame my shrew," he said, grinning at Kate. "I thank each and all of you for making this success possible. Good night, Darcy, my delight. Good night, everyone. I'll see you all at the theater tomorrow —eleven sharp—to iron out a few wrinkles."

It was only after they made love that Kate realized she was more relieved about the play's success than anything else. She had been fearful of the effect on Win—and on her—if the play had managed no more than a modest success.

VI

"It's amazing," Darcy said to Win several months later. They were having a drink in his dressing room one night after the performance and she was thumbing through a copy of *Consort*. "Who'd have thought that ancient history would stick to the best seller list like a cocklebur?"

"Kate thought it would be a nine-day wonder."

"And you hoped she was right, didn't you?"

Win said nothing.

"Don't give *me* your little-boy-lost look, Winslow," Darcy said. "This play we're in is an absolute stunner and people are pursuing us with contracts in their hot little fists. What more do you need?"

"Would it sound petty to say I don't want to share the limelight with my own wife?"

"You don't mind sharing it with me."

"I'm not married to you."

"More's the pity." She smiled seductively, mocking her wiles even as she plied them. "If it's comfort you want, I can do everything a wife would and then some."

Win smiled and shook his head. "No, Darcy. Kate would divorce me on the spot."

He watched her, perched on the arm of the overstuffed chair Kate had moved into each of his dressing rooms. Darcy was tempting, but sex would solve nothing. What he wanted was not only the lion's share of fame. Lately, he had admitted to himself that he also wanted that total monopoly of Kate he had enjoyed for so long. Knowing that made him feel petty, and he was beginning to resent her for it.

"Better luck next time," Darcy said, refusing to accept defeat. She stretched and tossed *Consort* aside. "It's only a book! If it didn't say so much about sex, no one would read it."

"Everyone's reading it and not only for the sex. Kate's a fine writer and she has provocative theories. Only a real idiot would resent that. Sometimes I feel like one of the brutes she writes about."

Darcy came to sit on his lap. "Why? You haven't kept her barefoot and pregnant! I forbid you to talk like that. We theater folk need the roar of the crowd. It's a blood transfusion to us. It's what an actor lives on, especially one like you." She stroked his hair. "Remember when I said I'd never play opposite you if you had to murder me?"

He nodded.

"I have to tell you, Winslow, that I almost pee in my pants from fright every night and twice on Wednesdays and Saturdays when you kill me for stripping you bare and revealing your carnal lusts. You're that true to Gabriel, that good."

"Thanks for the kind words, Darcy."

Darcy tilted his head up and kissed his lips lightly. "Just don't get carried away and really do me in. I wouldn't mind if you really screwed me—everyone's sure you sock it to me eight times a week anyway—but I'm not into death." She gave him a languorous look, stood up, and glanced at her watch. "Where's Kate? It's getting late."

"She's speaking somewhere."

"I forgot!" Darcy smoothed her dress over her lissome hips and extended a hand to Win. "I won't let you sit here and brood. Let's go somewhere for a light supper and then I'll drop you off."

VII

The quality of sound from the lecture hall told Kate that it was full before she was introduced by the president of the Women's Action Coalition. Walking out, she was received with applause, as always, but there was a segment of the public that considered her theories outlandish and her conclusions a threat to women, not a solution to their problems.

"Never mind," Mallory had assured her. "The more controversy you generate, the more sales we rack up."

"But will the book make a difference for women?"

"Ask me fifty years from now."

She acknowledged the applause and began to speak about the historical periods highlighted in her book, but toward the end of the speech the thrust of her remarks was that women inherited more than genes and a different biological blueprint from that of men.

"We inherit all the fears intrinsic to having been the weaker sex for centuries, as indeed we still are. Men are bigger, stronger, rougher. Some of them could flatten a woman with one blow. Some of them do. Why don't all of them? Partly because of a triumph of environment over heredity, but also because technological skill has edged out brute force, even in war. Biology is no longer the decisive factor. Power is and a lot of it is brain power. In the end, the world will belong to the scientists.

"That means we women have a standard other than brute force by which to measure ourselves. We can abandon the illogical conclusion that we aren't as able because we aren't as strong. In fact, the world will be an infinitely safer place in our hands.

"To sum up: I hold these truths to be self-evident," Kate said, stirring the audience with the familiar words. "That all men are created equal, that they were, of necessity, endowed by nature with a constant input of testosterone to render them aggressive and combative in the wild so they could defend their caves and bring home the mammoth meat.

"Testosterone is still there and males are still aggressive and combative, but with precious little wild to roam in. Now they hunt for money, power, and fame, even if that means war and pollution and the abuse of women and children.

"Very simply put, the state to which they have brought the planet demands that we give the other sex a shot."

There was a momentary hush, then a loud explosion of applause mixed with hoots of derision. A hot debate followed before John whisked her away.

"So you think men are beasts who befoul the planet and batter their wives," John Mallory asked when they were driving downtown in the limo.

"When I consider history and the daily papers, yes, for the most part."

"Win too?"

She shook her head. "Win is unique. He charms me. I always hoped someone would. And he isn't violent."

"He is onstage."

"That's his art. He makes people see only the character and forget the actor entirely. And Win loves women."

"He's difficult, isn't he?"

"Yes, but brilliant people often are. It only makes them more fascinating."

"I've noticed," Mallory said.

VIII

Dodie Phelps and Polly sat in the lounge chairs of one of the smaller Benedict jets, each of them reading the same article in separate copies of *Newsweek*.

"They're calling it her 'testosterone' speech," Dodie Phelps said, finishing the article and closing the magazine. She studied Kate's picture on the cover. "What a lovely face," she said. "There's as much intelligence in it as there is heart."

"I wish she were on that cover because she's smart, not because she has sex appeal."

"I'm told sex is a factor in everything."

"You're no judge," Polly returned. "You hated your husband and you never had any sex worth mentioning."

"That's why I never mention it," the small woman retorted, bristling.

"Weren't you ever curious enough to try with someone else?" Polly asked in a much gentler tone.

"I left that to stronger stomachs than mine. But I have no regrets. Except for not having a child. I'd have liked a daughter."

As if by mutual accord, they stopped talking, put their heads back, and dozed until the steward knocked and came into the cabin. "Fifteen minutes, Mrs. Benedict."

"You take the bathroom first," Polly said. "You have a bladder the size of a grape."

When the plane landed, a Benedict limousine was waiting on the tarmac. Dodie Phelps walked the distance leaning on her cane, while

Polly slowed her stride to her companion's pace, waiting until Dodie Phelps was settled on the backseat before she got in herself and arranged several cushions to make her cousin comfortable.

The long car left the tarmac, swung slowly into traffic, and headed for New York. It was a clear day and at length the magnificent New York skyline came into view, limned with golden light.

"Stunning," Dodie Phelps said.

"Yes," Polly agreed. "But jagged, severe, hard. It looks like the kind of town it is. If you fall down, it'll walk right over you."

"Yes, that's so. We'd rather be among trees than skyscrapers. I expect that isn't only because we're old."

"No. It's because the southland has all that's left of civilized behavior in America."

They did not speak again until the car stopped in front of a theater on Forty-fifth Street west of Broadway, and the two women descended and went inside. They sat in the fourth row, on the aisle. Polly had Kate's seat, having determined that Kate was speaking in Boston and would not be there.

They were absorbed in their programs until the lights dimmed.

"Now," Polly murmured, "we'll see what all the fuss is about."

When the curtain came down on the first act, they turned to each other.

"That," said Dodie Phelps, "is what is meant by sexual magnetism."

Polly nodded. "An extremely attractive man."

" 'Attractive' doesn't begin to describe him. He stirs feelings I never knew I had."

"What do you think of her?"

"A toothsome morsel."

"A Delilah," Polly said. "I wonder why Kate lets her stay around."

"She's a good actress." Dodie Phelps knew better than to remark that Darcy's blond beauty was reminiscent of the young Sydney's; Darcy had incurred Polly's wrath as a matter of course.

"She was born to produce erections," Polly said. "And *he* shakes with lust when he looks at her."

"He's a fine actor. Kate says he becomes every part he plays."

"I hope he confines the transformation to the stage."

When the final curtain fell, they sat in silence, still lost in the drama of eroticism and humiliation and rage, then exploded into applause with the rest of the audience. Win and the resurrected Darcy took their curtain calls. After the house had emptied, the two women made their way to the street and the waiting car.

"It wasn't only about sex," Dodie Phelps said suddenly when they were halfway to the airport. "His weakness could have been any number of things. She destroyed him by showing him something in himself that he couldn't live with."

Did I do that unpardonable thing? Polly asked herself, her heart lurching suddenly as she remembered Hilliard.

"Kate will never leave that man," Dodie Phelps went on. "No woman in her right mind would."

"He'll leave *her*," Polly snapped. "He has before and he will again."

"Oh, Polly, I can't believe you want that to happen. She'd be so terribly hurt!"

"No, I don't want it to happen. I want her to be happy. I just don't think it's possible with him. That's what I tried to tell her."

"Then for mercy's sake, call her and apologize for the way you said it!"

But Polly did not reply and the cousins said very little more during the return flight. By ten that evening they were back at Kel Regis, too tired to do more than wish each other a restful night.

Polly did not look at her messages until her breakfast tray arrived the following morning. She read the one marked "urgent" and called Theo in Washington.

IX

"What's Oliver done now?" she asked him.

"Went skinny-dipping in the Capitol fountain," Theo said.

"Alone?"

"With a young woman."

"He was trying to do more than skinny-dip, wasn't he?"

"You know Oliver."

"Yes, I know Oliver. Can you keep it quiet?"

"I think I have, but it wouldn't hurt to have you here."

"I'm on my way."

Polly arrived in Washington in the late afternoon. She was met by Herbie Fisher, one of Theo's advance men. His raspy voice with its thick New York accent issued from a tubby little body dressed in blue jeans and an oversnug jacket of predominantly hot-pink plaid. Polly's lips twitched with suppressed amusement whenever she looked at him, but he was a street-smart pol, and she admired that.

Herbie filled her in. "The police have kept their lip buttoned. There were only three cops involved: the arresting officers and the desk sergeant. Lucky it happened at three in the morning, when half the cops at the station were snoring at their desks."

"Was he booked?"

"No. They recognized him, dried him off, dressed him in prison fatigues, then called Theo to come for him. Theo took him back to Georgetown and put him to bed."

Polly nodded and sat back in her seat until the car pulled into Theo's drive. Herbie helped her out and they went into the living room, where Theo and Rebecca were waiting. The mirrored bar was open and there was a silver coffee service on a low marble table. Polly noticed, irrelevantly, that the color scheme had been changed since the last cocktail party she had attended at the Barrowses'.

"Welcome," Rebecca said, elegant in a silk sheath that matched the pale pink scatter cushions. "I'm sorry about the occasion for the visit." It was impossible to tell whether or not she was sorry in the least. Her manner was as smooth as her dress; she was just beginning to show with her sixth pregnancy.

"I daresay we'll survive," Polly said, sitting down and accepting a cognac. She wore a lavender dress and coat, a matching pillbox with a veil, and a choker made of four rows of splendid pearls with diamond and amethyst bars. Her shoes and handbag were black patent, her kid gloves white. "Where is the old fool?" she asked.

"Upstairs, sleeping it off. He had a head like a balloon this morning."

"Anyone else would be too worried to sleep," Polly said, and was prevented from saying more by the arrival of three men from the Democratic National Committee. Two of them were well tailored, barbered, and manicured; the third was slightly scruffy, better suited to the business at hand but out of place in Rebecca Barrows's exquisite living room.

"A tempest in a teapot, dear lady," one of them assured Polly.

"I want it confined to the teapot," Polly said. "What will it take?"

"Everyone likes him, so I think a thirty-thousand-dollar contribution to the police association would be adequate," one of them said.

"Adequate only if there's a way to divide another thirty thousand among the three policemen involved," Polly said.

"That's a bit risky," one of the men said nervously.

"Would the risk be worth it if I made very robust contributions to a number of war chests? And Oliver did a campaign swing for the midterm elections?" Polly paused to look at the circle of faces. "I thought so. Then Theo will see to it." She was as gracious as if they were discussing tickets to a charity ball. "What about the woman?"

"Already on a plane to Memphis with enough money to open a house of her own," Theo said.

"Well, that should take care of it," Polly said, rising. "I'll go wake Oliver and take him home."

"He's on the daybed in the back nursery," Theo said.

"The nursery's right where he belongs." Polly started out, but Rebecca's voice stopped her.

"What about the person who reported them?"

Polly swung around. "I assumed the patrolmen found them," she said to Theo.

"So did I! But we'd better make certain." He looked lovingly at his wife. "Thanks, darling, you may have saved us a lot of trouble."

"I hope so," Rebecca said, smiling sweetly at Polly. "I especially want to spare Kate any bad publicity."

Bitch, Polly growled to herself, going up the stairs more slowly than she liked. *Smart and bitchy as they come.*

X

Polly went upstairs and walked to the nursery at the rear of the house. The door was ajar and she pushed it all the way open. Oliver was stretched out on the daybed, his shirt unbuttoned, his hair rumpled. He looked very pleased with himself.

She knew he was dead the moment she reached the bed.

For a moment she was annoyed, as if he had committed yet another folly. "You great ninny," she said softly. Then she touched him. He was still warm, as if he had waited to die until she was in the house, if not the room. He had always had such nice, smooth skin. "Pink as a peeled shrimp," she said.

And then a great sob rose from her vitals to lodge in her throat, making it ache with unexpected tears. For years they had lived at sword's point, hiding their mutual animosity—hers for his many betrayals, his for her one great sin. Yet at this moment she could remember nothing of the hurt or bitterness or disillusion of this marriage, only the sweetness of their first years together, when she had been so trusting and both of them so much in love.

She had been Oliver's "Peach" for all but seventeen years of a long life and, much as she would have scoffed at the idea ten minutes ago, love was among the echoes of their life together, and it was love she felt and love that broke her heart.

She stroked his thin hair for a moment, then put her head down on his chest and cried softly.

"Good-bye, Oliver," she said at length. "You were a child all your life. I'm glad you had a bang-up party before you died."

Then she went to call Theo.

19

I

I don't know what to do," Kate told Rebecca on the telephone. "If I go to the funeral and she doesn't speak to me, there'll be the most awful stink in front of swarms of people. Neither of us needs that right now."

"She *won't* speak to you," Rebecca insisted, glancing across at Theo as he listened quizzically from his wing chair. He wore a burgundy smoking jacket; Rebecca's hostess pajamas were ivory satin.

God, what a beautiful couple we are, she thought, and went on speaking to Kate.

"You know Polly well enough to realize she won't say a word to you. She never even mentions your name." Rebecca had completely reconstructed the conversation on the terrace at Kel Regis to suit herself.

She knew Theo was listening, but Rebecca went on urging Kate not to go. She turned to Theo when she hung up. "Polly doesn't deserve to have Kate back," she said ambiguously.

"That's not for you to judge, darling." *And she is* my *darling,* Theo thought, *however reckless she is with her emotions.* "You told me Polly tried to sound you out about Kate."

"In her peculiarly nasty way. And it *is* for me to judge. Kate's the person I love most in the world with you—and the children, of course," she added quickly. "Kate is mine and I'm hers. There isn't anything either of us wouldn't do for the other."

"Do you love her enough to let her go her own way?"

"Darling, that's unfair! I give advice only when she asks for it, as she just did. The trouble with Kate is that she's determined to see both sides of every argument. It's all very noble, but she gets hurt every time."

219

"She's managed to be happy without Polly," Theo said.

"Only because she had Win. If you ask me, she won't have him for long."

"For God's sake, Rebecca! They love each other!"

"He loves himself! So much that only a woman as extraordinary as Kate is good enough to be Mrs. Winslow Talley—*provided* she doesn't overshadow him."

"That's a narrow line to walk," Theo agreed after a moment's reflection.

"Yes, and Kate's beginning to realize that in this marriage she's the one who has to walk it."

II

In the end Kate, wearing a hat with an opaque black veil, attended both the church service and the interment at Kel Regis, careful to arrive late for both ceremonies and to stay at the outer circle of an enormous crowd of family and famous mourners, including the vice president, sixteen senators, seven governors, and dignitaries from every level of the state government and judiciary.

From where she was, Kate could see Rebecca and Theo, most of her aunts and uncles and her father, but her eyes lingered longest on Brosie and Belle, who had loved Oliver dearly. Both Polly and Dodie Phelps were seated, hidden from Kate's view.

I should be there with them, she thought, longing for the family she had come to love despite its eccentricities and peculiarities. She was back where she had always been, until she married Win: on the outside.

She left the graveside before the coffin containing her flamboyant grandfather was lowered into the grave, Oliver's booming voice forever stilled, and walked quickly toward her waiting car. She was newly bewitched by the beauty of Kel Regis. She ached to stay, to be part of it again, to be with the family when they gathered for Thanksgiving and Christmas. She had fallen in love with family as completely as she had with Win, but Polly had made it impossible for her to have both.

And there was no hope of reconciliation. A woman who had cut a child out of her life, who had refused to acknowledge her own granddaughter for fourteen years, who had spied and plotted to make Kate's life conform to Polly's dream—such a woman would never make the first move.

"And she must," Kate whispered, hurrying down the path. "Because I won't."

Kate was startled when someone called her. She turned.

III

"Aunt Fel," she said, relieved. "I was afraid you were a reporter."

Felicity was one of Kate's favorite aunts, a spirited woman with the courage to demand a divorce from Polly's son, Maynard. She had been flatly refused, but if it had broken Felicity's heart, it had not broken her spirit.

"Come back to the house, Kate honey, for your own sake. *We* all want you, even if *she* doesn't. And who knows? Funerals are when most people reconcile."

"I've thought of that, but ours was no ordinary break and Polly's not most people."

"That's the God's truth. All right, Kate, I won't harp on it. But I'll make sure she knows you were here." Felicity took Kate's arm and walked with her toward the parked limousines.

"How is she?"

"As you'd expect. Playing the plucky widow who refuses to succumb to public grief. We all know she's glad to be quit of him. It's all been an act since Hilliard killed himself, maybe longer than that. Personally, I couldn't care less how she is. If it weren't for her, I wouldn't still be tied to her son when I've been in love with someone else for years. Not a penny would I have, she said, and my lover's not rich."

"You can't live on love, no matter what the poets say. Gramps always said when poverty flies in the door, love flies out the window."

"Oh, Oliver was full of platitudes. But at least he had a long life and a merry one. I can't really weep for him."

"No, somehow I have to smile whenever I think of him. I suppose that's the best way to be remembered. How are Brosie and Belle?"

"The hottentots are still inseparable," Felicity said, but her eyes were guarded.

She's not sure I know, Kate thought, and wondered at Felicity's loyalty to a family that was hers only by virtue of a marriage she wanted to dissolve.

"People are beginning to leave," Kate said. "I must escape. I'll come to Charleston and visit soon."

"Yes, do. We see so little of you since you married the prince of Denmark. You always cheer me up."

IV

But it was Kate who needed cheering. She had a difficult choice to make: she had been offered her own prime time talk show on one of the independent television stations. She could accept it—or she could put her marriage back on track. She couldn't do both.

She had known for some time that part of the light had gone out of her marriage. Was it that she and Win loved each other less? Or that a no-man's-land had appeared between them, a disputed area where neither cared to tread? The focus of his life was still his career; that Kate could not make it hers as well, that she was eager to work at her own profession in her own field, was a subject they had only recently begun to discuss.

No. To argue about.

She had to ask herself whether Win's insistence on monopolizing her was motivated by love—or something that only looked like it. For almost five years she had been content with that strong resemblance. Now she was beginning to feel the same sense of suffocation that Tyler's and Polly's attempts to control her had produced.

The need to make a decision about the television program nagged at her during the flight and the helicopter ride to New York City.

V

It was Clyde Tillinghast who had made the offer ten days earlier over lunch at Lucretia, where society women dressed by the most famous designers in the world gathered to pick at the extraordinary food and gossip without mercy. There was a little buzz of comment when Kate and Tillinghast entered.

"They'll probably decide we're having an affair," Tillinghast had said, rather smugly, Kate thought. She laughed heartily, as if the idea were ludicrous—as it was—and devoted her attention to the menu. She could feel his eyes on her and sense his brittle hostility.

"Now I'd like to know what this is about," she said when the waiter had departed. "I know you hated me after the Richard Trayner show."

"I did," he replied, apparently disarmed by her candor, "but then was then. At the moment you're a hot personality. I can't afford to hate you." Now his grin had a diabolic charm.

Kate had been hesitant. "I like doing television, but I don't think of myself as a personality."

"You are, though, like it or not. You're a natural in a medium that has no mercy. It exposes you, warts and all." He grinned again. "You have no warts."

"You'd be surprised," Kate said. "What would the format be?"

"You, discussing a specific theme each week, with guests on both sides of the feminist fence to debate it."

"Celebrities?"

"Not exclusively. Housewives relate best to other housewives. We'd have a mix. The producer's your old friend, Stan Wells. She knows what sparks you."

"Yes, she does. And I'm interested, but I can't give you an immediate answer."

"Think it over. Take two weeks. Fair enough?"

VI

Win was against it.

"I don't want you tied to any program," he had told her flatly.

"You're tied to a play. And I don't think that's your real objection." She had stepped into no-man's-land and she knew it. The tension between them had been palpable while she waited for him to respond to that.

"You want me to say it?" he demanded at last. "I'll say it! I don't like living with a star."

"I live with a star."

"You knew that going in. You used to like it. It was enough for you. Hell, *I* was enough for you. Now you'll do anything to grab the spotlight, including a talk show that's bound to be successful if you're part of it."

"Win, don't you think I've spent enough hours of my life sitting in the theater, in the dressing room, at home while you do what you love? Why can't you understand that I want to do what *I* love? Anyway, I'd give only one performance a week, at an hour a shot, not eight!"

"It'll take more than an hour and you know it. There's all that goes with it—the press and the hype and the interviews. You'll be out of town half the time."

"What you really mean is that my publicity is a threat to yours!" She had never said that before. *Fools rush in*, she thought, *where angels fear to tread*.

"Call it what you like. I don't want a part-time wife. I want you with me all the time. I need your judgment. I especially need it now."

"Why now?"

"They want me to make a film of *Rapture*."

It was a total surprise to her. "But that's wonderful, Win! Think of the millions of people you'll reach!"

"Do you really think it's the right move?" he had asked, watching her intently as she nodded. "But it's Hollywood," he reminded her. He had paced around their living room, charged with that contagious energy of his, tall and stunning and *hers*.

"One mistake," he had told her. "That's all it takes in the movie business to turn 'wonderful' into 'disaster.' Wrong script, wrong co-star, wrong director, wrong makeup. Anything. It's crucial, Kate. I need your fine critical eye. And I want you with me. Kate, I love you."

Am I crazy? Kate had thought, gazing at him. He was the most fascinating man she had ever met, and the brightest and most loving and the most generous—and all he asked was that she stay at his side because he loved her!

Wasn't that worth more than a talk show?

Oliver's death had intervened before she could answer that question. There were only a few more days left before she had to tell Tillinghast her decision and now, as Kate unlocked the door to their apartment overlooking Central Park, she knew what she would say.

VII

"Win?" she called from the circular foyer.

"Coming." He came to the foyer to take her coat and her handbag. He lifted the black-veiled hat from her head, tossed everything onto a chair, and put his arms around her. "Was it awful?" he asked, rocking her.

"Sad," she replied, clinging to him. "Frightening, too, that someone who's been around so long suddenly isn't. No one saw me but Aunt Felicity. It's lucky you didn't come; you'd have been mobbed. There was an enormous crowd."

"I know. I saw it on the news, but I couldn't see you. I made some sandwiches. Want tea or a drink?" He released her and took her hand.

"In a minute. I want to tell you something first. I've made up my mind about the show."

"Yes?" he said, his whole body intent.

"I'm going with you. I'll put Tillinghast off until the picture's rolling."

He gave a deep sigh and enveloped her again. "God, Kate, I don't know what I'd have done in that jungle without you."

"But I want to do the show once you're off and running. With Stan's help I'm sure I can get Tillinghast to tape in L.A."

He held her at arm's length, as if to judge how firm that decision was. She could almost hear him thinking that the important thing was to get her to Hollywood. Once there, she would be too involved in his work to think of hers.

"Fair enough." He pulled her close again. " 'Well, there's a wench,' " he said softly. " 'Come on and kiss me, Kate.' "

He enfolded her, taking her in from the cold.

VIII

She told Clyde Tillinghast the next morning that Win was moving to the West Coast.

"So?"

"I'm going with him."

"Does he need a nursemaid?"

"Mr. Tillinghast, happily married people like to live together."

"Not always possible if they're both entertainers."

"Not always necessary if the show were produced in L.A."

There was a momentary silence before he said, "I'll have to think about that. When you're settled on the coast, let my office know where to reach you."

IX

The house they rented in Bel Air was small as Bel Air houses went and furnished in Swedish modern throughout. Kate felt as if they were living in a very expensive furniture store. It had six bedrooms, a vast living room, a dining room that seated twenty, a screening room, a pool and a pool house, a sauna, a hot tub, two tennis courts, and three garages.

They were met by Andy Farrell's coagent in Hollywood, a woman named Harriet Kahn.

"In England she'd be called 'horsey,' " Win told Kate when Harriet had left them to unpack and settle in.

"I like her," Kate said. "She has the killer instinct."

"Is that likable?"

"For a woman in her business, in this place? I'd say it was essential."

Harriet had hazel eyes, freckled white skin, a flat chest, wide hips, and a habit of curling and uncurling one lock of her coarse red hair around her left index finger. There wasn't a person of influence in the movie community she didn't know. She trusted none of them.

"Sharks," she said the next day when the three of them were en route to a party at the producer's house. "They'll tear you to bits and spit out the bones. Just let me do the talking when it comes to business."

They already knew it would come to nothing *but* business. In that way, Kate reflected, Hollywood was very like Washington, and that was not the only similarity. These people were totally image-conscious too, no matter which end of the camera they worked.

The politicians counted ballots, and the movie industry counted box office receipts. If one movie was a smash, they made a second, then a third, sometimes as many as five on the same theme with the same actors—very like incumbents who repeated successful election slogans ad nauseum. Oliver had built a career on his southern-squire act and he had never changed it.

"But you're a special case," Harriet was assuring Win. "Like Olivier was when he first came out here, and Burton. The money is good; in fact, they gave away the store to get you. But I wish you had approval on the other stuff: cast, costumes, final cut, and publicity."

"It's my costar I'm most worried about."

"You want Darcy?"

"Who the hell else? We've been doing it together for over a year! We know each other inside out."

Harriet flashed a look at Kate, then went back to twisting her hair. "She wants equal billing. She doesn't want to be below the title."

"Put her above the goddamn title," Win said easily. "She's earned it."

Harriet turned to Kate. "What manner of star is this?"

"A very generous one," Kate said. *Except with my time.*

"What a lovely thing to say, darling." Win kissed Kate's hand before he turned back to Harriet. "What are the chances of getting approval of the other stuff?"

"They say nil. I say we've got a shot. Here we are at Chateau d'If." Harriet named things: her car was Boanerges, she called her house Manderley and referred to her ex-husband as Genghis Kahn.

X

They pulled up to a house famed as the most palatial residence in Bel Air; the tour bus was required to keep a safe distance from its perimeter. California sunshine poured down on clipped hedges, fruit trees, and grass and flowers so perfect they looked artificial.

The house was English Tudor, beamed and gabled; it stretched on and on once they passed the deceptively modest entrance. To Kate, the people inside, like the flowers, looked as if they were made of wax.

"I'm not going to introduce you around," Harriet hissed as they entered. "You're both too famous and this lot will introduce themselves."

They soon did, approaching Win in groups of two or three. They were cordial, welcoming, and nearly all stunning. They were more circumspect with Kate; apparently authors were creatures from another world, and Kate's height and dress didn't help.

"Small" was the theme here, Kate had already noticed. Five feet six was as tall as a woman was permitted to grow. Their very clothes were Lilliputian: they wore tiny little camisoles over their fulsome breasts—their nipples were in a permanently turgid state—and skimpy little skirts, shorts, or pants over their tight little, tiny little bottoms.

Their clothes were embroidered, sequined, or studded. Kate, in her beige silk shirt and calf-length skirt, standing six feet tall in high-heeled sandals, stood out like a Greek statue at Disneyland.

She soon found herself next to a gorgeous streaked blonde named Kimmy, who resembled every other young woman in the room. She and Kate smiled tentatively at each other.

"We're in awe of writers," Kimmy finally said, gesturing at the people hovering just out of talking distance. "It's words that start the wheels turning out here. I mean, like, where would all of us be without a script?"

"I wouldn't know how to write a script," Kate said.

Kimmy looked at her with eyes of contact-lens green, a color not seen in nature. "Why should you? Dr. Ballard, I read your book and I think you're absolutely right. Women have this cockamamie idea of themselves, all scrambled up by what's been happening to them since Eden. Do this, be that, don't be the other, and it's all over when you're thirty. It's like the Middle Ages out here. Just look at this collection, me included. We're all this year's model—designed by the men. We're like interchangeable parts! If one of us gets old or sick, they get another. I even had my lips done to make them puffier, can you believe? Hurt like hell and it won't even last."

"Still, everyone looks so healthy," Kate said. "I have visions of blenders full of soy milk and wheat grass juice."

"Ha! You know how long it takes to put makeup on so it looks like it's natural? That healthy glow comes out of bottles, not blenders." She turned her extraordinary eyes on Kate and took a breath as if she were about to make a confession. "This place is like Babylon in your book. Women are still sucking up to the men." She snorted. "Literally, I mean." She scanned the room. "You know where your host is? He's getting blown in his gazebo by some bimbo from Schenectady who wants to make it big in Hollywood." Kimmy laughed bitterly. "Promises, promises."

"Sounds like a darling fellow," Kate said. "Tell me his name so I can avoid him."

"Bruno Baxter, but you can't avoid him. He's bankrolling your husband's movie. He'll try to lay you, sure as you're standing there. He'll think you keep your brains in the same place he keeps his and some of yours'll rub off on him. He'll come on to you, all right."

"Then he'll be hoist with his own petard."

"What with his what?"

"Shakespeare. It means Mr. Baxter will trip over his own penis if he raises it at me."

Kimmy laughed heartily. "God, I love the way you talk! But you'd be surprised how many women cooperate—wives too—to get better deals for their husbands. And the husbands pretend not to know. Between the girls and the pretty boys, wives are an endangered species in Hollywood."

She looked meaningfully at Kate just as Harriet bore down upon them, twisting her strand and talking to a fiercely bronzed man, attractive in a musky way. He wore a shirt opened to his waist. Three large gold medallions clanked amid the hair on his chest as he walked. He wore tight, well-worn blue jeans with a bulge at his crotch that must have been a codpiece and he smelled overpoweringly of Brut.

"Meet Bruno Baxter, Win's producer," Harriet said. "He owns this dump. This is Kate Ballard Talley."

"Hey, Harry, I know who she is! Hello."

"Delighted," Kate said to Baxter, extending her hand formally. He took it and held it.

"Hey, you got some husband," he said. "Attracts women like bees to clover."

"They fall all over themselves," Kate agreed, purposely lofty. "It's too ludicrous."

Baxter tried another tack. "Handsome bastard."

"Never saw a man to match him."

Baxter dropped her hand. "Yeah. Hey, Katie, I read your book. If it'd been a novel, I'd of made a movie out of it." He looked her up and down. "With you in it, maybe, as the high priestess of Babylon. Hey, Harriet, how's that for an idea?"

"Completely off the wall," Harriet said.

"Yeah, I guess so. Now I gotta circulate, see my guests are happy. A pleasure to meetcha." He winked at Kate. "Keep your man happy. A star with his ashes hauled regularly is a happy star."

"I'll keep a chart," Kate said.

Harriet snorted when he was out of earshot. "He can't cope with class."

"I was forewarned," Kate said with a nod toward Kimmy. "I saw some lounges around the pool. I'm going to sit down in one and drink something long and cool. Want to join me, either of you?"

"Sure," Kimmy said immediately.

"No can do," Harriet said. "I have to protect Win. But you go ahead."

Kate, approached by people from time to time, stayed on the lounge even after Kimmy, who had kept up a revealing commentary on the guests, was called away. Win and Harriet finally came to collect her. Hollywood parties, it appeared, did not drag on. People who had to be at work by five in the morning went to bed early.

"God, what a zoo," Win said in the car.

"This was mild," Harriet told him. "And you did very well."

"My face aches from smiling," Win complained.

"I got the lowdown from Kimmy," Kate said. "She knows the intimate details of everyone's sex life."

"She should," Harriet said. "She's been in every bed in Hollywood."

"So I assumed, but she's no fool. There's something very touching about her."

"Touch is the operative syllable. She wants to play the maid in *Rapture*. That's why she was being so darling."

"Am I really that naive?" Kate demanded.

"It's part of your charm, my love," Win said.

But Harriet had summed up the place neatly: as time passed, Kate learned that the only reason anyone did anything was to score, one way or another.

20

---•◆•---

I

When shooting started, Kate went to the set as she had gone to the theater, the tapestry workbag once more in evidence. But she did very little crocheting. The mechanics and technique of movie-making fascinated her: the disjointed filming, almost always out of sequence; the endless retakes; the mastery with which actors could produce emotion on demand instead of building steadily to a fever pitch.

Between takes people played cards, had their horoscopes cast or their palms read, did crossword puzzles or just gossiped. Win learned a card game called Spite and Malice and played it with Kate by the hour.

The director, Seth Cross, was intelligent and professional, and Win got along well with him. Darcy was soon embarked upon an affair with him. All, so far, was well.

"Brilliant!" everyone said when they saw the first rushes, but Win made no comment until he and Kate were driving home in the white Rolls Corniche.

"Tell me what's wrong with it, Kate."

"That camera magnifies emotion like the Mt. Palomar telescope. Maybe that's what it is."

He nodded and patted her thigh. "Kate, I knew you'd see it! The question is, how far do I lower the flame?"

The next day she went to the studio library for films made by actors Win admired, and they watched them together that night.

"What's compelling on the stage," Win decided, "looks melodramatic on film."

"They adapted," Kate said, pointing to the screen. "So will you."

"Come on," Win said, cutting off the projector.

They left the screening room and went into the den. He pulled her

down with him onto the burgundy velvet couch, kissed her passionately, then picked up the telephone and called Harriet, holding the
receiver so that both of them could hear, his free hand sliding up and
down the smooth, tanned skin of Kate's leg.

"Sorry to wake you at such an ungodly hour, Harry, but we have to
reshoot everything we've done so far."

"Why? It's great stuff!"

"Great for the stage, not for film."

"Sez who?"

"Sez me first and Kate second." He stroked Kate's thigh.

"With all due respect, Win, Kate's not a filmmaker."

"She's not a stage director either, but her instincts are infallible."
Win's hand slipped inside Kate's panties.

"I wouldn't tell anyone else you think so."

"I won't. Just tell them we're reshooting."

"They'll holler."

"Let them. I'll pay for it myself."

Kate gave a little sigh of pleasure.

"Like hell you will!" Harriet shouted. "I'll fix it."

Win hung up the phone and looked down at Kate. "How do you
know so much about acting?"

"You asked me that once before," she said breathlessly, her eyes
closed, "at a picnic at Oxford."

"I remember. Then we made love."

He undressed her slowly, lingering on what he uncovered. "I adore
you," he said. "Did you know?"

It was wildly arousing, once more as if they had never made love.
Her skin where he touched it felt electric. She shimmered with excitement. She was impatient for fulfillment, yet eager to make this rapture
last. They lay like inverted spoons on the sensuous velvet of the
couch, bathed in bliss, consuming each other.

"Don't end it that way," she whispered. "I want you deep inside
me."

He turned then and went into her. It was a mighty climax for both
of them, a long cresting so intense that it was almost painful.

"I love you," she gasped, crying for the pure joy of loving him. She
hadn't done that in a long time, and he held her tenderly, cradling
her. They sank into a half sleep.

"My God," he said when they stirred. "Where did that come
from?"

"I don't know," Kate said. "But imagine finding it in a place like
this."

"I'm glad you're here, Kate."

"So am I," she said.

"Then stay here with me. Don't leave."
She could as soon have left herself.

||

He was gone when she woke the next morning. At ten o'clock, three dozen very long-stemmed American Beauty roses were delivered, along with an unlabeled 78 rpm master record and a vintage portable 78 speed record player. Intrigued, she plugged the player in and put the record on.

It scratched and wheezed for a few seconds, and then a crystal-clear tenor voice began singing a Lehar song. It was called "Yours Is My Heart Alone" in English, but this was in German. *"Dein ist mein ganzes Herz."*

Aside from Goethe, these were the only German words Kate knew that weren't harsh and guttural. She had told that to Win long ago, in a moment of delight together, delight that did not end with pleasure.

It was like him to have stored it away until a night such as last night, like him to have gone to all kinds of trouble to find a way for her to hear it in German. It was the side of him she loved most.

She was afraid that, as another song warned, it was too dear to lose and too sweet to last.

She was living in a city that funneled all of its energy into fantasy or display, things Kate had long avoided. But then, Los Angeles was not really a city; it was a sprawling suburb of the studios.

She simply did not belong. She was an oddity to these people. It wasn't only because of how she looked or dressed or spoke. It was because she wasn't in the business and they were.

"Up to their eyeballs," she told Win after one of the endless dinner parties people used as an excuse to slander absent friends and show their favorite films to a captive audience.

"They're not so bad," he said. "Most people in the business are self-involved."

"I know *that*," Kate said almost pointedly. "But this lot is unique. They're as crazy as March hares, but they keep telling each other they're okay and you're okay and everything is cool. Their conversation is totally inane. All they talk about besides movies is food. Heaven forbid they would actually eat anything though. Fat is one of the Four Horsemen of the Apocalypse out here."

"Come on, Kate! Beauty is part of the job description. You're talking like an intellectual."

"I *am* an intellectual. So were you, once."

It evolved into an argument that continued while they parked the car, closed the garage, went upstairs, undressed, and got into bed. Then they lay rigid and silent.

At length Kate said, "We're not really arguing about those silly people, you know."

"Then what?" he asked without the cutting edge in his voice.

"We're arguing about what this place is doing to you."

"This place is earning me a fortune while I reach the biggest audience in the world!"

"Nothing is worth harming a talent like yours."

"They reshot those scenes, didn't they?"

"They won't reshoot any others."

"There's no point in anticipating what may never happen," he said, the edge back in his voice. "And if you've finished the lecture, I'd like to get some sleep."

A feeling somewhere between fear and fury kept her from saying more, but it was a long time before she fell asleep.

Just as she was reaching the boiling point again, Clyde Tillinghast called.

III

Kate always remembered that call as a turning point. Win was still against her doing the show at all, but if it was taped in Los Angeles he had no valid basis for complaint. He made up for that by being furious while Kate packed to go to New York to discuss final details and sign her contract.

"Let the son of a bitch come here," he fumed. "I need you."

"There are things to be discussed with everyone involved. I'll be gone only a few days."

"Suppose something comes up? What if you hadn't been here when we had to reshoot that garbage at the start?"

"But I *was* here. And you knew as well as I did what was wrong."

"Why is a cheap talk show more important to you than I am?"

"It will not be cheap. And it isn't more important, just different. I want the chance to reach as many people as I can, the same as you do."

"I didn't know this was a contest for the public's attention," he shouted, heading for the door.

"Don't shout at me! And it isn't, so stop trying to turn it into one."

He had not returned by the time she left for the airport. She boarded the plane with a feeling of apprehension that was chillingly familiar and had nothing to do with flying. It receded somewhat when she met Stanton Wells at JFK.

IV

"Look at you!" Stan said admiringly while the chauffeur collected Kate's baggage. "Elegantly understated as ever. Thank heaven you didn't go Hollywood."

"Not bloody likely!" Kate said. "I hate the place." They got into Tillinghast's limo. "Ah, room to stretch my legs at last."

"If you hate the place so much, why stay there?" Stan said.

"To insure domestic tranquility."

"But the picture's almost finished, isn't it? It's going to take a while for us to set things up, and by then your husband will be back in New York."

They talked about it on the drive to the Talley apartment. The telephone was ringing when they walked in, and Kate ran to pick it up.

"I'm sorry," Win said. "Deeply sorry and horribly embarrassed."

"What you are is sozzled," Kate said, smiling with relief.

"Am I forgiven?"

"Of course." But Kate said it more because he was tight than because the issue was settled.

"Come home soon, Kate."

"New York is home for us, Win. Remember?"

"Remember you."

"Go to bed, darling. Sleep it off." Kate hung up and looked at Stan, who was admiring the apartment.

"What?" Stan said when she saw Kate's face.

"He's drunk and he never gets drunk. I wonder what it is he doesn't want to tell me."

V

The next morning she and Stan discussed details of the show with the rest of the production team, everyone growing more enthusiastic by the minute. It was decided that the show would be taped in Los Angeles temporarily but move back to New York as soon as Kate did.

Kate frowned over a list of prospective guests. "Stan, these women all agree with me. I want people who don't. Like Dora Suponik."

Dora Suponik's Congress of American Wives never stopped calling attention to the mess liberation had made of women's place in the social order. Now stupid young women gave away freely what they used to exchange for marriage, a home, a promise of fidelity. From being sex objects, CAW said, women had become sex machines.

"Dora will tear you to shreds," Stan said.

"A lot of people will tune in to watch her try."

Stan bent her head and scribbled in her notebook. "You're right.

Dora and her ilk it will be." Stan smiled. "We'll have the contracts ready for you to sign tomorrow. Now let's talk about publicity."

Win was sober when Kate spoke to him that night. She did not tell him they had scheduled pre-air appearances to publicize the show's premiere, but she felt more exhilarated than she had in months.

"There's no city like New York City," she exulted. "It's a shot in the arm."

"Umm. I'll pick you up at the airport day after tomorrow."

"Win, what's wrong?"

"Not a thing."

"If you have something to tell me, tell me now."

He sighed. "They asked me to do a remake of *A Double Life.*"

"You refused, of course."

"Not exactly."

"Win!"

"You're going to tape out here anyway," he said almost accusingly.

"Only temporarily! Tillinghast won't shoot out there permanently."

"Damn Tillinghast! Do you think I'd let him determine our future?"

"Win, you know I don't want to live in California."

"Well, come on back and we'll talk it over."

VI

For a while, when she was back in Bel Air, they were careful with each other, deliberately avoiding confrontation. *A Double Life* was still under discussion as a possible vehicle, but there had been no firm commitment yet.

"Just tell them you won't do it," Kate urged him.

"I can't refuse an offer that hasn't been made yet!"

"Once you wouldn't even have considered it."

"How do you know?"

"You had a higher opinion of yourself."

"So did you!"

They began to argue in earnest when the pre-premiere appearances took Kate out of town. Win was withdrawn each time she left and tipsy when she returned.

"It's so damned childish," Kate complained to Rebecca on the telephone.

"You're the one who's been a child all these years. All Win had to do was say he needed you, and you rolled over."

"Don't knock being needed, Rebecca. You thrive on it."

"I'm not you! We've always wanted different things. Kate, that man is a great actor and he knows it. He doesn't need you as a drama coach or a play doctor. He needs you to wear like a medal. Some dopey female made of brass isn't good enough for him. He wants pure gold, like you. He wants someone superior who's still willing to walk two paces behind him."

"Where's it all going?"

"You don't really want to know."

"Divorce?" Kate whispered. "No."

"Fine. Then abandon this show of yours and surrender."

"I don't want to talk about divorce, Becca."

Rebecca sighed. "All right, Kate. I'll be here, whatever you want to talk about."

VII

After what seemed an eternity, they were shooting the final scenes of the movie.

"But for some reason," Win said one evening while they ate supper on trays, "Seth is unhappy about your being on the set."

"Why? He and I have never had a harsh word."

He got up to stir the fire; California evenings were delightfully cool. "He thinks you inhibit me with Darcy."

"That's a hoot! I was in the theater every time you two were on-stage together and I didn't inhibit either of you. You made it look as if you stormed her Bastille at every performance."

"It has to look even more like that on the screen," he said, poking at a log.

"Why?"

"The camera gets a lot closer than a theater audience can."

Kate raised her brows. "Are you telling me they want you to screw Darcy for real?"

He laughed, turning to look at her. "It's been suggested."

"God, they're decadent! And so are you, for all I know. If that's what you're planning, Seth is right. I'd do more than inhibit you."

"Not to worry. I couldn't screw anyone with that crowd watching, not even you, and I am mightily eager to screw you." He kissed her before he sat down again and resumed eating his supper. "Do it for me, darling," he cajoled.

"So you can do it to Darcy?"

"No, so that we'll finish sooner."

"Why do I feel like a child being offered a lollipop?" Kate asked. "Or does Darcy get your lollipop? Is this my booby prize?"

"Darcy doesn't get anything she's not entitled to. Anyway, you're out of town a lot these days."

Kate did not press either subject. Both were far too sensitive.

VIII

In retrospect, it all seemed fated. Kate's first program was scheduled to air two weeks after *Rapture* premiered and it was Kate who appeared on page one of *Variety* while Win's first film was reviewed inside—glowingly, to be sure, but for Win it was not enough. An advance copy of the paper had been delivered by special messenger and Win was much the worse for wine by the time Kate got home. Her calmness infuriated him.

"Be reasonable," she said, refusing to be drawn into his hostility. "It's only a paper."

"You can say that because you're on page one!" he accused her.

"You're behaving like a child. And you've had far too much to drink."

"Don't tell me how to live!" he protested.

"You always tell *me*!" she shot back.

"What a fool I've been to love you," he raged. He threw his arms wide in a gesture he would never have used on the stage. " 'A fool there was and he made his prayer to a rag and a bone and a hank of hair, the kind of woman who couldn't care!' "

"I cared," Kate shouted, her control evaporating. "No one *ever* cared more."

"But about which one of us? About me or the demigod on the stage?"

"Oh, get off the stage for once, will you? I'm not an audience. I'm not in awe of you."

"A real wife would be!"

"You don't need a wife," Kate said. "You need a nanny."

"I need a divorce!"

The word went through her like a knife. Suddenly she was back in the attic in Harmony, watching her life collapse around her and break into bits, feeling as helpless now as she had been then to stop it. She stared at him, breathless with pain and incredulity.

"Do you really mean that?" she asked him, her voice shaking.

"Mean what?" He steadied himself on the back of the sofa and shot her a lowering glance.

"What you just said."

He looked at her. He knew full well what he had said. Shaking his head, he denied it.

"I'm too drunk," he said. "Ah, Kate," he went on, smiling his most winning smile, "I don't want to argue with you. I love you too much. I'm going to bed."

He was asleep and breathing heavily when she finally got into bed beside him. She had burned the offending copy of *Variety*, but she could not burn the word. *Divorce.* And it wasn't only the word, it was the state of mind that had made him use it. She was caught between anguish and anger, wondering if Rebecca had been right, that she and Win were on an unalterable path.

But I can't live like this! she protested silently. *I can't do nothing but shop and have manicures day after day after day! I'll die of boredom.*

For several days they behaved warily, with that terrible consideration people show each other when a great abyss has suddenly opened between them and only a fragile bridge remains, in need of repair or condemnation.

IX

"Congratulations!" Bruno Baxter said. He looked very small under the cathedral ceiling of his office. The office itself was furnished in Chinese antiques, authentic to the last incense burner and somehow oppressive. Baxter was bending over his intricately carved desk, sliding three newly signed contracts into a red leather folder.

"I'll bet he's had the bubbly laced with cocaine," Darcy whispered to Win when Baxter's Oriental servant entered with champagne in a cooler. She tossed Baxter a brilliant smile while she whispered again. "He keeps trying to get me into bed."

"Will you go?"

Darcy smiled as if Win had just given her a compliment. "Darling, I'd rather fuck a red-assed baboon!"

Win threw back his head and laughed heartily as Baxter began to hand out the filled glasses, offering the first one to Darcy.

"You see, Harry," he called to the agent over his shoulder, "I told you we could put it together." He beamed at Win, jerking his head in Harriet's direction. "That one is the world's worst pessimist."

"So I was wrong," Harriet said, twisting her lock. "You're a better man than I am, Gunga Din."

"This picture won't be easy," Seth Cross remarked, stepping between Win and Darcy with a proprietary air. The inside gossip was that Cross had lost his mind over Barrington, but not enough to interfere with business: he hadn't objected to Win's screwing his leading lady on a closed set.

"The original version will be a hard act to follow," he observed.

"Nah," Baxter said. "It never got good reviews, and Winnie Boy here is a better actor than Colman."

"No," Win said firmly. "Different, but not better."

Win's coagent, Andy, swelled with pride. "That's my boy," he announced. "Not an ounce of creep in him. Always generous."

"And my girl isn't?" demanded Herman Zach, putting a proud arm around Darcy.

"Don't get carried away, Herman," Darcy said, her nostrils flaring delicately as she slid out of her agent's embrace. She turned back to Win. "What's the missus going to say?" she asked.

Win grimaced. "She'll get over it."

"I suppose so, considering your talents for persuasion. But what if she doesn't?"

"She *will!*"

Darcy shook her head slowly. "Apart from their erogenous zones, you don't know much about women, do you?"

"I've been lectured enough. Don't you start, Darcy."

She held up her free hand. "Heaven forbid, darling. I'm just one big erogenous zone where you're concerned. I never cared what you did, as long as you were doing it to me."

But he was not listening to her. He was hearing what Kate would say when she heard that he had signed a contract for two more films.

When he told her, Kate packed a bag, got on a plane to New York, and called Rebecca as soon as she had closed the door of the apartment behind her. She paid no attention whatever to the stunning view of Central Park.

X

Rebecca was practical, as always. "If the lease on the apartment is in Win's name, you'd better pack the things you want and move out tonight."

"Oh, Becca," Kate said. "I've had time to cool off on the plane, and I don't want a divorce."

"Come on, Sister Kate. Why did you walk out and come to New York?"

"To shake him up, to bring him to his senses."

"Then you can't sit meekly at home until he comes back and seduces you all over again. If you really want to put the fear of God into him, move out. Theo knows someone who knows someone at the Carlyle. He'll arrange an apartment for you. It's too bad we have to fly to Denver tonight, but we'll be back tomorrow or the next day, latest. Then you can come to Georgetown and we'll figure out what to do next. But you can't stay there."

Kate knew she shouldn't. Win would come sooner or later, and the sound of his voice, the touch of his hand, the sight of his face, would bewitch her back into a marriage that was valid only on his terms, subject to thrive or wither at his whim. In California, she knew, she would become an appurtenance, a giver of parties for the same papier mâché people to whose parties she and Win would go. She would become a haunter of Rodeo Drive. She would hire a private yoga instructor, a trainer, a manicurist, and a hairdresser.

Or she would retire totally from the madding crowd and write another book, thereby infuriating Win because he needed a hostess and a date, not a rival for front-page space. They would argue more than they did now.

"Which one of us did you fall in love with?" he had demanded. The question had disturbed her profoundly until she faced the answer. She *had* fallen in love first with the man on the stage. And she had expected him to be as godlike offstage as on. For a long time he had been, but she could not deny that he might have seemed that way only because of the blinding power of love. The great pity was that this blindness never lasted. Living together almost always cured it.

She wandered into the kitchen for something cold to drink and switched on the radio for company, paying no attention to it until she heard the film critic mention *Rapture*.

The talk of Hollywood is that steamy sex scene in Win Talley's first film, *Rapture*. It was shot on a closed set and someone who was there says the passion was the real thing. No simulation required. Neither Talley nor Darcy Barrington was available for comment, and Mrs. Talley seems to have dropped from sight.

"Dammit, Win!" Kate said. She switched off the radio and picked up the telephone to call the Carlyle.

XI

She gave a forwarding number to the service and, taking only her clothes and their wedding photo, moved to the Carlyle. She sat by the telephone, waiting for it to ring, growing more confused by the minute. More than once she began to gather her things and return to the apartment to have it out with him when he arrived, as surely he would.

Between crests of anger there were depths of heartache when she wondered how she could bear going back to life without him. A few times she almost rang Stan to tell her that unless Tillinghast agreed to tape permanently in L.A., the deal was off.

She felt as bleakly lonely as a child. It shocked her that it was loneliness as much as love that made her sit there and wait for Win to call. And lust too. They were perfect together.

But when at last the phone rang, it was not Win but Theo. He broke down when he heard her voice.

"Oh, God, Kate," he sobbed, unable to talk coherently.

"Theo? Theo, what is it? Is it one of the children? Try to tell me what's wrong."

It was a freak accident, he finally managed to say. His plane had hit a patch of ice and skidded on landing. It had turned over.

"I haven't got a scratch," Theo mourned. "But Rebecca. Jesus, Kate, she's badly hurt. They're not sure she'll live. And it was all my fault."

"Theo, don't believe that! Unless you put that patch of ice on the runway and made a three-point landing smack on it. Listen to me, Theo. It was *not* your fault."

"All right," he said, and began to cry again. "That's not what matters anyway. It's my baby who matters, my beautiful little girl."

"I'm coming," Kate said, dread clutching at her heart. "I'll get on the shuttle and be at your house in a few hours."

"Come to Walter Reed Hospital," Theo said.

"Okay. It'll be all right, Theo. It's going to be all right."

But what if it wasn't?

In the plane Kate clutched the arms of her seat, unaware that her knuckles were white with fear that she was about to lose the one constant in her life, the only person who had never left her.

Hang on, my Becca, she pleaded silently. *Sister Kate's coming.*

XII

When Win arrived at the hotel a few hours later, having traced Kate through their answering service, she was gone.

"Gone where?" he demanded of the receptionist who let him into Kate's suite.

"She didn't say, Mr. Talley. She left in a great hurry. She only said she would send for her things."

Her clothes were still in the closets. Their wedding picture was on the night table.

Win dismissed the receptionist and sat down in an armchair. There was only one conclusion to be drawn: the thing with Darcy had been the last straw. Kate didn't want him or their marriage and had fled rather than tell him so to his face.

Anger and remorse battled within him. Anger won.

"To hell with you," he shouted at the photograph. "If you don't want it, I don't want it either."

He picked up the telephone.

"Kate's gone," he told Darcy when she answered.

"Where?"

"She didn't say. Just ran out of here like a bat out of hell. I gather she wasn't eager to see me."

"Separating's always a messy business, Win. Maybe it's better this way."

"I'll be back on the next plane. Can you pick me up?"

"You bet, honey," Darcy said softly. "And I'll take good care of you."

BOOK IV

21

1986

|

Theo sat behind his desk, trying to concentrate. The atmosphere of the office was serene enough, although it was designed to suggest position and power. The buff walls were hung with photographs of people he had helped put in office. There were some hunting prints, a few Picasso bullfight sepias, and one exquisite Renoir. Rebecca had placed it behind Theo, opposite the client's chair, so that it would scream power at everyone who sat down to discuss business with Theo.

Rebecca, whose lovely face smiled at him from a silver frame on his desk, had done it all. The mahogany desk had been custom-made for a man of his size, as were the sofa and three side chairs upholstered in silky tobacco leather, in one of which sat Senator Clement Kilbourne Case.

Theo's mind kept wandering from the wholesome, handsome senator to Rebecca, to the upheaval in their lives since the accident six months before, to the strain it was for both of them to pretend that nothing had changed when everything had.

They would never get it back either. The doctors had told him just this morning that Rebecca had recovered as much as she was going to. The chance of her ever walking again was virtually nil.

But I can't tell her, Theo agonized. It made him feel both guilty and inadequate, but he dealt badly with illness, above all when it was that of the woman he loved.

He suddenly realized that Senator Case was smiling at him. Theo smiled back.

"Yes, of course," he said heartily, totally unaware of what Case had been saying.

A quick glance at Herbie Fisher assured Theo that his words and his smile were appropriate. They usually were with Case; the man whose bland, scrubbed blondness reminded Theo of the old Arrow shirt ads, seemed to be in perpetually high spirits.

Well, why shouldn't he be? He hasn't crippled his wife for life.

"It's never too early to start a campaign," Herbie said a little too loudly, giving Theo another cue.

"The sooner the better," Theo agreed.

"Whatever you say," the senator assured Theo. "I've relied entirely upon you since the day we first joined forces." He shook Theo's hand and turned to go. "By the way," he turned back to ask, "how's your wife?"

"Coming along," Theo said cheerfully. "It's going to take time."

"Of course," Case agreed. "These things do. Keep your chin up, old man."

Easy for you to say, you smug, glossy bastard, Theo reflected. Case was still standing there.

"Is Dr. Ballard still living with you?" he asked.

Theo nodded.

"Talley didn't behave very well," Case said. "She didn't deserve that kind of publicity. It must have upset her."

Theo shook his head and frowned. Kate was none of the senator's damned business. Theo was quite capable of defending her. "She's far above that kind of behavior. She wasn't upset for long."

But, of course, she was. She needed as much comfort as he did. They had been holding each other up.

When the door had finally closed behind Case, with Herbie following in his wake like a low-slung tugboat behind a trim cutter, Theo turned back to Rebecca's photograph.

"Why you?" he whispered. "Why us?" He had never been the sort who feared divine retribution for his good fortune, a balancing of the books, as it were. Now it seemed that he and Rebecca had been living in a fool's paradise, unaware that every joy carried a price of bitterness and pain.

Herbie came back, his pudgy face crumpled with concern. "You okay, boss?" he asked.

Theo didn't reply directly. "Make sure his account is current," he said. "The richest clients are always the last to pay." He looked at Herbie. "After what those doctors told me this morning, I'll be of no use here," he muttered. "Tell someone to cancel my appointments. I'm going over to the gym to work off some of the tension."

"You gonna tell her?" Herbie asked.

"Not yet."

"Yeah, better wait till she's a little stronger."

Theo nodded. He wondered why it was that he could confide so easily in a character like Herbie when he'd have cut out his tongue before he told one of their so-called "friends" that Rebecca was in that wheelchair for life. But he couldn't tell Herbie about the thing that worried him most. He couldn't tell Kate either; it was too intimate. And yet, Kate knew Becca better than anyone. Maybe he should talk to her.

Sweet Jesus, what would he have done without Kate?

II

"Believe it," Stanton Wells was telling Kate on the telephone. "I can't hold him off any longer. He gave you these six months, but that's all he's going to give. He's preparing to take you to court for breach of contract." She paused. "Hell, Katie, you can't live with Rebecca and Theo forever. You ought to have a life of your own."

Kate said nothing for a few moments. She paced slowly in her bedroom in Rebecca's house in Georgetown. The idea of telling Rebecca she was leaving to go back to New York dismayed her, but a lawsuit was a convincing reason. And Stan was right: it was time to leave, as much for Rebecca's sake as for her own. It was time for the Barrowses to resume their life as a couple.

"All right," she said finally. "Tell Tillinghast I'll be in your office in New York in ten days. That's a week from next Monday. I'll stay at the Carlyle until I can find an apartment."

"Great!" Stan said jubilantly. "What a relief!" Then her voice softened. "How are you doing, Kate? I mean about the divorce and all that."

"Win and I split up almost five months ago, Stan! Besides, I'm too preoccupied with Rebecca to know how I'm doing. I'll probably find out when I'm on my own again. I don't particularly look forward to that."

"Who likes to sit alone and contemplate failure?" Stan, who had been through two divorces, was sympathetic. "Kate, is Win going to marry that bitch?"

"I don't know. What difference does it make?"

"None—except to Darcy. Dammit, there's no justice! For years she sits there like a spider in a web, waiting to snare him, but it takes a tragedy of errors to make the man move in with her, bam, like that! You'd think he could have restrained himself a little longer than a day!"

"Stanton," Kate said flatly.

"Oh, shit, I'm sorry, Kate! It just makes me so mad! But not another word, I promise. Want me to pick you up on Sunday?"

Kate declined, said good-bye, and put the telephone back on the nightstand. She needed to be alone; she had not been alone since the night of the accident when she and Theo, shaken and virtually speechless, had clung together waiting to know if Rebecca would live. When at last they were told the odds had turned in her favor, they had gone home to sleep.

III

They had been like thoughtless children that night and the next few days, not daring to ask *how* Rebecca would survive, whether the damage to her spine would have consequences, how grave they would be and how long they would last.

It hadn't registered on either of them that Rebecca's accident had slipped past the press and only surfaced two days later. After that, Kate and Theo were nagged by reporters each time they went home to rest, but they were still far too weary to estimate how long they had been sitting in the hospital waiting room, or to look at the papers or to turn on the news.

On the third day Kate began to wonder why Win had not called her. She rang their house in Los Angeles several times from a phone booth in the hospital corridor, but there was never an answer. She called the studio once and was told they didn't know where he was.

It was Polly who told Kate about Win.

Kate, too tired to get out of bed on that third morning, had supposed she was dreaming when she heard her grandmother's voice in the entrance hall, but a moment later Polly was in the doorway looking at her across the shaft of sunshine that bisected the bedroom.

IV

She was still Polly, with her jewelry, her hat, and her white gloves, but the daylight was harsh to the deep carved lines around her mouth and eyes. She seemed to have aged a great deal more than she should have in the years since she and Kate stood on the steps of Kel Regis in a contest of wills.

The change in Polly was like a cold wind whipping at Kate's already ragged emotions. Polly mortal? Polly's life as much in danger from the inexorable march of time as Rebecca's from a freak accident?

Kate sat up, too drained for rancor, too stricken to be distant. "Are you all right? Why are you here?"

"I came to help, if I can."

Kate shook her head, sadness engulfing her.

"No one can help. And you've never liked her anyway."

Polly's mouth trembled. "Oh, Kate! Do you despise me that much!"

"No," Kate said. "I shouldn't have said it."

Polly hovered near the door. "I should have come long ago, to beg your pardon."

"I wish you had," Kate said wearily. "Why didn't you?"

"I wanted to, but pride is a treacherous emotion." Polly crossed to the bed. "It's got me through a lot of bad places, but it's kept me trapped in others." She stood looking down at Kate.

It was like a litany inside Kate's head. *Someday, maybe soon, she'll die.* The immensity of that eventual loss shook her.

"I don't have time for pride anymore," Polly said.

"Neither do I," Kate said, her eyes brimming. "Not when Becca's lying there all broken. I love her. She's part of my life, part of me. She's always been there. I thought she always would be." She held out her hands.

Polly sat down on the bed and took Kate into her arms. "I know, Kate honey," she said gently, stroking Kate's hair. "But Rebecca's going to make it, you'll see. She has grit, just like you. I went to see her at the hospital and she's getting better every hour." She rocked Kate, letting her cry for a good while before she gave her a fresh handkerchief and spoke again.

"There's something I have to tell you. Rebecca's not the only reason I'm here. I want you to know about Win before you hear it from those degenerate reporters."

"Where *is* Win? I've been trying to reach him."

"You're not going to like this, Kate."

A little shiver ran through Kate and she stayed in the circle of Polly's arms. "Tell me," she said.

"He's moved into Darcy Barrington's house. He's filing for divorce. It was in the papers."

"Divorce?" Kate leaned back and looked at Polly incredulously. Her emotions by now were too blunted to register more than a dull pain along with astonishment. "That's not possible. Win wouldn't do that when I need him, when Rebecca's so close to dying."

"He couldn't have known about her, honey. No one did. It wasn't on the news until late last night. Maybe it's all a misunderstanding."

Kate lay back on the bed, piecing it together. "We'd been arguing about . . . several things. I went to New York to convince him I couldn't go on living in California, not the way things were." Her reddened eyes gazed at Polly. "I guess I convinced him, didn't I?" She turned her head away and closed her eyes. "You have every right to say you told me so."

Polly shook her head. "It gives me no satisfaction to have told you so. I thought it would, once, but it doesn't. I just wanted so much for you I didn't think about what you wanted."

"Neither did he. But he must know about Rebecca by now!"

"Everyone does. I'm sure he'll call you. He'll want to explain."

"What's the point?" Kate shook her head.

"If he does call, talk to him. Maybe it isn't too late."

"He's moved in with Darcy! How can I talk to him?"

But she did.

V

"What can you possibly have to say to me?" she asked him, her voice flat with fatigue.

"You disappeared without a word!" he exclaimed across the long, long distance that stretched between Los Angeles and Georgetown, between him and Kate. "When I got to New York, I didn't know about Rebecca. There was no sign of you, nothing! I thought you'd dumped me!"

"So you dumped me back, as any thinking adult would have done."

"I was hurt, Kate. I thought it was your way of telling me you didn't want me anymore."

"Have you ever known me to be at a loss for words?"

"Kate, it was an honest mistake."

"Even so, you might have given me the benefit of the doubt." Her temper crested suddenly. "Damn you, you might have waited a few days before you jumped into Darcy's bed and held a press conference to announce it!"

"What difference does it make how we hurt each other?"

"It makes a big difference. Once it's done, you can't cross it out and do it differently the next night. We aren't characters in a play!"

"All right! All right! I know I'm the bastard in the piece. I admit it. I wish to God I'd never met Darcy. Just say the word, Kate, and I'll be on the next plane to Washington. I'll make it up to you, I swear it."

Anger enveloped her like a sheet of flame and she shouted at him. "You can't make up for this! You *know* that! You knew it when you went to Darcy, but you went anyway because you wanted to. You've been wanting to for months because I didn't want to be a concubine in never-never land where they play musical beds. You deserve each other. So stay with her and be damned to both of you!"

VI

Sydney telephoned a few days later.

"I'd have called before, but I didn't know what to say. I never know how to deal with this kind of thing."

"What kind of thing, Mother? There are several catastrophes going on."

"Yes, darling, I know. But no one can avoid a freak accident. I meant Win. Such a lovely man."

"I'm glad you still think so."

"It's hard to believe."

"It sure as hell is."

"But that woman *has* been after him for years."

"Are you implying that I should have seen this coming? That I should have kept him in a cage?"

"Well, that's what I'd have done!"

"It may have escaped your notice, Sydney, but we're not at all alike, you and I!"

"Why does everyone take things out on me?"

Kate said nothing.

"Then you'll divorce him?" Sydney persisted.

"He filed first so I suppose he'll divorce me."

"I'm damned if I'd let a man humiliate *me* like that!"

"He's already humiliated me! I don't have the time to go squat in Mexico for however long it takes. What difference does it make which one of us files?"

"Well, if you don't know . . ." Sydney began. Then, "Oh, dear," she said pathetically. "I'm no good at all in a crisis. I always say the wrong thing. Kate, let me come and help you."

"No!" Kate said more sharply than she intended. She immediately tried to cover her panic at the mere idea of Sydney's presence, but her voice grew more strident as she spoke. "I mean, there's so much confusion at the moment, I don't have time for anyone else. All Theo and I do is run back and forth to the hospital, with reporters calling us at all hours, slavering to know how badly hurt she is, how Theo feels about his crippled wife, how I feel about my adulterous husband, and did I suspect it was Darcy all along! Life is a soap opera to them! People are made of cardboard. All they want is intrigue and pathos and a blubbering woman on the six o'clock news."

Kate realized she was almost shrieking and stopped abruptly. "But thanks for offering. I'll let you know if I need you."

"It'll be a cold day in hell before you need me."

"Sydney, please."

"All right! I didn't call to make a nuisance of myself! I'll call again tomorrow to see how you all are. I'm truly sorry, Kate, about everything."

"I know. And thanks for calling."

"You don't have to thank me. I'm your mother. And you're my girl."

It was amazing, Kate reflected when, flinching at that last remark, she hung up. Sydney always moved herself to center stage, even in the midst of other people's tragedies. Now she was the mother scorned, whose help was cruelly refused by an idiot daughter who didn't know how to hold on to a husband. She was the clever woman who would have sniffed Darcy out and got rid of her before it was too late. She had too much pride to let any man divorce *her*.

Kate shook her head. The last thing she needed to ponder right now was that supreme narcissist, her mother, and that supreme egoist, Win.

Win had called several times more, but she refused to talk to him again. Theo found her a lawyer to deal with their very simple separation agreement. Neither wanted anything of the other. Win went to Mexico. Kate did not contest. It was over in two months.

VII

"All that love," Kate had told Polly during one of the daily calls that were, once more, a habit. "Where does it go?"

"It gets used up," Polly said. "Human beings cling together for safety, but they weren't designed to live peaceably with one another for any length of time. Smarter folk keep pets or houseplants and are content with an occasional visit when their carnal lusts obtrude."

Kate laughed, then turned serious again. "I thought there was too much love between Win and me for it to get used up in eight paltry years."

"Sometimes it doesn't even take that long. Why do you suppose Dodie Phelps never remarried? She was a very young and pretty widow and a merry one too."

"I never thought about it. She was always so happy at Kel Regis."

"At least I've been able to do that for her," Polly said wistfully.

"How is she?"

Polly's worry over her cousin was unmistakable. "Poorly at the moment. In a lot of pain this past week with arthritis. Not that she ever complains."

"Oh, Polly! It's torture to stand by and watch someone you love suffer so! It isn't fair!"

"I had to watch Hilliard and, no, it isn't fair. Everyone tries to warn you how unfair life is when you're young, but you don't believe it until you learn it for yourself. If you find a few moments of happiness, it's usually by sheer accident. The biggest risk of all is love." Kate suspected she was weeping silently, Polly who never wept.

Oh, God, I should be with her and Dodie Phelps, Kate thought, doubly stricken because Polly had never mentioned Hilliard before. Her grandmother was getting on. Her sorrows, rigorously hidden all her life, were coming to the surface and needed solace. But Rebecca needed Kate and so did Theo. And Kate needed to live her own life as well. She felt pulled in too many directions.

"We should listen to the bard," Polly was saying, cheerful again. " 'Violent delights have violent ends, therefore love moderately.' "

" 'Moderate love' is an oxymoron. And the bard never got cuckolded in the headlines. It makes a woman feel defective."

"The defect is his, not yours," Polly said. "Do that talk show and everyone will be convinced of it."

Everyone can go hang, Kate thought. *I'm the one who needs convincing!*

"I will never understand," she wondered aloud, "why I didn't come unstuck over the divorce. I guess I didn't have time—and I couldn't, or Rebecca might have."

"You're not the sort of person to come unstuck when you're a guest in someone else's house."

"What big hints you drop, Grandmother. You mean it's high time I had a home of my own."

"Kel Regis is your home," Polly said hopefully.

"I love Kel Regis," Kate said softly. "And I'll come down to visit soon. But it isn't mine. I've lived in Tyler's house and your house and Win's and now Rebecca's, but never in my own—except for that garret on Libby Avenue. I'll move to New York when the time comes."

"I hope it'll be soon."

VIII

Polly put down the telephone and went along the corridor to her cousin's suite, which had been moved to the ground floor to eliminate the problem of the stairs. Polly's stride was still energetic, and if she moved a little more slowly than once she had, she was remarkably vigorous for a woman her age.

Dodie Phelps was reading. The book was on a specially designed lectern attached to the arms of her chair; it spared her arthritic hands. She still managed the pages by pushing them with the side of her hand, rather than turning them with her fingertips.

She looked up and smiled when Polly appeared.

"How's Kate?"

"Asking after you."

"My sweet Kate. But she must have had more to say."

"She was wondering where love goes."

"You're the last person to ask."

Polly sat down and leaned back in the Queen Anne chair opposite. "I suppose I am. I have never let go of one single emotion in my life.

Anyway, Kate says she can't leave Rebecca quite yet, but when she can, she'll move to New York."

"You didn't really think she'd come here!"

Polly raised her eyebrows.

"Oh, Lord," Dodie Phelps intoned, gazing upward. "Spare us going through all that again!" She turned back to Polly. "What mischief are you planning now?"

"None at all—unless television doesn't turn out to be Kate's cup of tea."

"Why wouldn't it?"

"Because it's run by mercenary people who produce trash and butcher the English language. She thinks she's going to love being back in New York City, and maybe a madhouse is the right place for her to recover from that toad she mistook for a prince. But I know Kate. She's spent too much of her life in an academic environment surrounded by people with values other than money and with I.Q.'s as high as her own. Sooner or later she'll get fed up with the mediocrity that passes for talent these days."

Dodie Phelps shook her head in sheer amazement. "How can you go on like that? She'll be getting her message across! How many women have that opportunity tossed into their laps?"

"Not many, I agree, but there's more than one way for her to do that."

"Polly Benedict, what do you imagine would tempt Kate away from a career on national television?"

"Becoming president of Wakefield College!"

"My stars," Dodie Phelps breathed softly after a moment of reflection. "I do believe you're right. But the trustees might not agree."

"The trustees will do as I tell them," said Polly, who was chairman of the board. "Four of them are my sons. Two are my grandsons. Tyler'll bend over backward to please me. And I'm about to offer a place on the board to Theo Barrows. He deserves it after all he did for Oliver and it'll give him something else to think about."

"And of course he'll be on your side too," her cousin said. "You're a crafty wench, Polly. I just wish you'd stop tinkering with Kate's life."

"I'll be making her an offer, that's all!"

"An offer she can't refuse."

"Anything's better for her than television—or keeping house for Rebecca in Georgetown!"

IX

The staff ran the Barrows establishment, but Kate supervised it and tried to comfort the two children—Paul, five, and Mark, eighteen months—who weren't away at boarding school. Although Rebecca had never been an adoring mother, she was the focal point of her household. Mark withdrew and wouldn't let his nanny out of his sight except when he was with his mother. Paul clung to Theo while Rebecca was in the hospital, uncertain how to behave when, finally, his mother came home.

By then it was two months since the accident and she was greatly changed. She had been so pinched and frail at first, rarely speaking, shrouding herself in the affliction she refused to discuss.

"Is that normal?" Kate asked the nurses who cared for Rebecca.

"Each case is diffcrent" was the inevitable reply. "It takes more time for some of them to fight back."

"But they all do?"

Ominously, that question was never answered. For weeks Rebecca lay spiritless and silent. The only one who roused her was her baby son, Mark. He was brought daily to sit on Theo's side of the king-size bed and to play quietly or listen while his mother sang him songs or told him stories.

But now another four months had passed and, since the physical therapist began coming, Rebecca had been eating more. She appeared to have gained back a few badly needed pounds. Her drawn face had filled out and there was a hint of natural color in her cheeks. Best of all, she was interested in how she looked. Her hairdresser came regularly, she put on makeup every day, and she had ordered robes and hostess gowns by the score, to Theo's delight.

"She's getting better," he told Kate jubilantly. "She'll soon be herself again."

But Kate was afraid that it wasn't recovery that was motivating Rebecca now. It was her old uncertainty about Theo.

"I don't know what you mean," Rebecca snapped when Kate tackled the subject one day.

"A part of you has never really believed he loved you."

"One part of me believed it, and it's the one part he hasn't touched since the accident."

"Good Lord, Rebecca! You almost died! He's being careful and considerate and you take it as rejection. You're the same person you always were. He has no reason not to love you."

"*Look* at me!" Rebecca shouted. "Doesn't he have a reason? Doesn't he?"

"No!" Kate persisted. "Theo's a better man than that. Don't belittle him by doubting him. He adores you."

"Win adored you, didn't he? And he left you anyway."

They looked at each other in silence.

"I shouldn't have brought that up," Rebecca apologized swiftly. "But please, let's not talk about love."

"You're right," Kate had whispered.

Win was still a sore subject and their divorce a calamity Kate preferred not to replay in her head, like a recurring nightmare with an ending she dreaded but could not change. He was still living with Darcy, although he never answered questions about whether or when they would marry. Work on *A Double Life* had been delayed until a new director could be found: Seth Cross's ego had not been up to Darcy's sudden and very public change of housemates.

"She tossed me aside like a used towel to go panting after him," Seth complained to Kate when he called her. "The woman's pure bitch."

"Not too long ago you thought I was."

"Never! I only thought you might inhibit Win in a few scenes."

"Especially the one where you insisted on stark realism, otherwise known as a bona fide fuck."

"Kate! That was art. And business. The damned film will make a fortune because of that scene—and no one can tell for sure. It was a sacrifice for me to direct it. After all, I was in love with Darcy at the time. So you can't hold that against me!"

"Now that I understand the logic of it, how could I?"

He told her that Win and Darcy's next project was going to be an original screenplay, still untitled, that was rumored to be "hot."

X

"I hope it's a terrible flop," Rebecca had said with a glimmer of her old acerbic style when Kate told her at breakfast that morning.

"So do I," Kate replied with feeling. "But *Rapture* is a blockbuster. People *are* going just to see that scene, but the critics liked it too."

"So he really did screw her on the set! Kate, did you know they'd do it?"

"No, because I didn't want to know. I'd have had to deal with it. Anyway, I'd probably have let him convince me that it was just play-acting and art justifies all."

"You? My absolutely straight Kate?"

"I," Kate replied bitterly. "I've had months to think about it and I know now that I'd have capitulated eventually. Lived in California. Started wearing shoulder-duster earrings and lamé shorts that barely covered my behind. Had my lips siliconed so all the men would think I had a doctorate in fellatio and envy Win his shrewdness in marrying a mouth that could do more than talk."

"You wouldn't have done any of that," Rebecca said, laughing.

"I would." Kate raised her hands to heaven. "But why, O Lord, are women *like* that?"

"According to your theory, our need of masculine protection was once a matter of survival. To be protected we had to please—and we're still doing it."

"But there are other reasons why I'd have stuck it out, given the chance, the most compelling being the alternative need to get used to some other man. I felt the same way when Win and I broke up the first time. I only had one affair, and it made me feel rotten because we shared nothing but our bodies."

"You could share much more than that with someone else."

"You know what that means! All that tedious revelation of past history and future hopes! All those hit-or-miss encounters in bed until you find out if you like what he likes and vice versa. It's either that or celibacy, which is probably what I'll choose now. The truth is that I despise Win for what he did and how he did it, but I still love him and my body misses his. I hope it'll all go away before too long."

"Amen," Rebecca said fervently.

XI

Kate stirred. She had been sitting near the telephone, nursing her memories since her conversation with Stanton. She roused herself now and looked around the room she would shortly leave, admiring Rebecca's taste: the blue flocked wallpaper, the silk draperies, the Louis XV armoire and Bergère side chairs. The prints were original nineteenth-century fashion sketches of women with broad shoulders, wasp waists and accentuated bosoms. The candlesticks and pin trays were blue Wedgwood china. Finely bound first editions of the complete works of Jane Austen and the Brontës sat atop the dainty desk between cloisonné bookends. The room and its sitting area were perfect—and far too dainty for Kate, but at first she had been too worried and too exhausted to notice the decor. Now she was accustomed to it.

She realized now that she might have stayed in this sanctuary indefinitely had Tillinghast not forced her back into the world. She wondered how she would feel out there without Win—solitude was not as tempting as independence—but she knew better than to dwell on it. Better to hold her nose and jump into a new life.

She put on her jacket and grabbed her handbag. Rebecca was with her physical therapist and this was a golden opportunity for Kate to have an hour to herself.

She went out through the garage entrance and got into the Mercedes just as her car phone rang.

"Kate, it's Theo. I have something important to tell you."

"Me too. Can we meet?"

"How about that coffee shop in the mall in Alexandria?"

Kate looked at her watch. "I'll be there by three o'clock."

22

I

They were both grim and silent after Theo told her what the doctors had said. In Kate's mind was the ineffable memory of Rebecca pirouetting under the street lights of Elm Terrace on the night Sydney left, of naughty, comforting, loyal Rebecca, graceful and domineering and endlessly dieting, of Rebecca's slim legs tanned and healthy on Cape Cod.

"I can't tell her," Theo said, looking down at his trembling hands. "I haven't got the courage. Will you?"

"No," Kate said, blinking back tears. "You must—because you must make her believe it doesn't make her less of a woman in your eyes."

"She'll never believe that! You know how she is. She's never been completely convinced that I love her."

"You must convince her. She'll believe it if it's true! Is it?"

Oh, God, Kate pleaded with all her might, *be a man, Theo, not a child.*

His face was inscrutable until, at length, he started speaking.

"I love Rebecca with all my heart and I always will, whether or not she can walk. I've done everything I can to show her how much I love her—except the one thing that will persuade her that I do."

Kate was virtually certain of what he would say next. "Maybe you shouldn't tell me any more, Theo."

"There's no one else to tell." He looked at her sadly. "She wants me to make love to her, Kate."

Kate nodded. "That's what all the makeup and the new gowns are about."

The waitress came and they ordered coffee.

"For her, sex is the acid test, the real proof," Theo said when the woman had gone. "If a man wants a woman, he loves her. If he doesn't want her, he doesn't love her." There were tears in his eyes. "But I dread getting into bed with her each night. I dread the way she waits for me to do more than kiss her on the forehead like a brother. I lie there trying to breathe evenly so she'll think I'm asleep and fall asleep herself and stop . . . *reaching* for me in that terrible, wordless way."

It was as hard for her to listen as it was for him to speak. He began sorting the packets in the bowl on the table—white sugar, brown sugar, sugar substitute—as if his life depended upon their proper order.

"All right, then," Kate said after a moment. "Does the fact that she's crippled turn you off?"

"No, Kate, no!" He took a deep breath. "But pity makes me impotent."

"Then her condition *does* turn you off, whether you want it to or not! You must get help, Theo. There's too much at stake for both of you, all the rest of your lives. Becca pretends to be very worldly, but she could never live with infidelity."

"I have never been unfaithful to her!"

"Can you swear you never will be if this goes on?"

He made no reply.

"Theo, you've been so happy together in every way, including that one. Why should her injury change that? Is it because she can't wrap her legs around you? Are you that puny a man?"

His face was wet with tears that now poured, unheeded, from his eyes. "No," he whispered. "I'm not. I'm just afraid my body may be. Or that I'll hurt her."

"If you love her, your body will love her too." Heartsick for him, she took his hand. "And she won't break."

He took out his handkerchief and dried his face. He nodded, still holding on to Kate's hand for dear life. "Thanks," he said hoarsely. "I don't know what I'd do without you."

"You'll have to do without me soon," she said, and told him she was leaving for New York and why. "But even if Tillinghast weren't threatening to sue me, it's time for me to go," she said, "for all our sakes. It's unhealthy for me to be a perpetual boarder and you have to be a couple again. Rebecca has to run her own house and give her political dinners. She needs that as much as she needs you."

"But will she do it?"

"That depends on you." Kate's voice was low but urgent. "Theo, she isn't all that stable, you know. She never has been."

"I know," he said. "Rebecca runs on high all the time. Her emotions rule her." He squared his shoulders, as if in resolve. When he looked at Kate again, it was with true affection. "You're a real beauty, Kate. Win's a fool."

They regarded each other with the special kindliness of old friends before he spoke again.

"When should I tell her about her legs?"

"When she can take it. You'll know when that time comes better than anyone."

||

Theo took longer to shower and brush his teeth than usual, but finally there was nothing else to do. He reached for a robe before he left the bathroom. Since the accident he had covered his nakedness. He felt guilty that his body was whole and hers was not. Sometimes his guilt outweighed his pity.

It was three days since he'd sat in a coffee shop and told Kate he was impotent—and probably not only with his wife. It would have been easy enough to find out, but adultery would add insult to injury.

Last night and the night before he had resolved to make love to Rebecca and both times his resolve had failed him. He simply had no desire. He had not felt any for six months, not even the undirected, random desire any man feels when he sees a good-looking woman or even, God help him, a photograph in one of those asinine magazines.

He had even considered watching some porno tapes downstairs in his den before he came up to bed, but that would degrade Rebecca unless she watched with him, and this was a time for tenderness, for love, not for gross sex. He wondered if he and Rebecca would ever watch blue movies together again. He'd been too embarrassed to tell Kate about them.

Kate! With her dark eyes and her enormous heart, her long legs and her husky voice! She was a woman in a thousand, a woman whose passion was guarded but, he had always sensed, explosive. Kate, with a sensual mouth that belied her composure. What an unmitigated bastard Win was, what a fool! And Theo had actually liked him!

He turned out the bathroom light and went into the bedroom. Rebecca was reading in bed, propped up on pillows, as he had seen her countless times before the accident. He was suddenly aware that the covers came only to her waist, that he could see her breasts through the sheer nightdress.

She had beautiful breasts, voluptuous and firm with small pink aureoles and responsive, velvety nipples. The thought of kissing them, sucking them, aroused the first flicker of desire he had felt in many weary months.

"You're very beautiful, my darling," he said.

"Am I?"

He heard the doubt in her voice where once there had been the assurance of a seductive woman, but he ignored it. He took off his robe. Her eyes moved up and down his body with desire she made no attempt to conceal. It excited him. He felt himself begin to stir.

He got into bed and leaned over to slide the pillows out from under her until only one was left. He reached across her to turn out her bedside lamp and then he kissed her, not a chaste salute this time, but a deep, passionate embrace.

She gave a little cry and her arms went around his neck with more strength than he knew she possessed. Her mouth opened under his and he felt the flicker of her tongue inside his lips. He pushed her gown up and bent to kiss her breasts, and when she reached down and touched him he was fully erect.

He stroked her belly and then her thighs. They were slightly separated. He wondered briefly if she had told her nurse to position her legs in this way, and with the thought his passion died. He felt himself begin to slacken and panic seized him.

Not now, please, he pleaded. *Oh, God, don't let me fail her now!*

Suddenly, without willing it, he thought of Kate, of holding Kate, of touching Kate.

Kate took his hand and drew it between her legs and he was hard again, deep in his fantasy, opening Kate, touching her, feeling her pearl with desire. She began to tremble, whimpering with pleasure. Desire made him separate her legs, made him ignore the dead weight of them, made him mount her. He had to slide his hands under her and turn her up in order to penetrate her, but it didn't matter. Now it made no difference who this woman was, whether she was strange or familiar to his flesh. She was a female, she was hot, he wanted her.

He took her, unable to tell which gasp of delight was his and which hers at that exquisite glide that sealed them together, while the cadence of sex overcame him. He did not know whether she moved or not. He was surrounded, taken in, clasped by the velvet ridges within her.

"Harder," she gasped. "As hard as you can."

It excited him so much that he obeyed her, reveling in her, reaching in and up as far as he could go until he heard her small scream of pleasure and shot over the edge with her.

They lay together trembling but not speaking. It was Rebecca he held now, and instinct warned him not to ask if he had hurt her, not to ask anything, just to kiss her and hold her and stay inside her as long as he could and, after he had dwindled from her body, to lie beside her and stroke her until she crested again and then to cradle her until she was asleep. Together they fell into the most profound slumber they had known in months.

III

"So I have to go or he'll sue the hell out of me," Kate said on Monday morning at the breakfast table. The two women were alone; Theo had left early for his office, but from the change in Rebecca over the last few days, Kate knew he had convinced his wife that he loved her.

Theo seemed uncomfortable in Kate's presence. She concluded that it was because he had revealed so much in the coffee shop and she found his diffidence endearing.

"But New York is so horrid," Rebecca began, and stopped because Nanny was leading the children in. Paul had made a drawing for his mother and Rebecca discussed it with him as gravely as if it were to be exhibited at the National Gallery. Kate tried to engage little Mark, but he only gazed at her from Nanny's arms with round, wary eyes and sucked his thumb. Of all Rebecca's children, he most closely resembled Theo. When the chauffeur came to drive Paul to school, Nanny placed Mark in Rebecca's lap and he clung to her, ignoring a new toy she had for him.

"I want to hold him for a while," Rebecca told Nanny. "Come back for him in about ten minutes."

Rebecca held the child close, stroking his hair. She looked at Kate over his head. "I have more patience with him than I ever had with the others and I love him as I never did them. A mother's not supposed to love one child the most, but I'm sure they all do in their secret hearts." She kissed Mark's head. "Maybe it's because he's the last of Theo's babies."

"High time you closed up shop," Kate replied, forcing herself to speak crisply despite the lump in her throat. "Six is a fair number."

"I wish you could have put Tillinghast off a little longer," Rebecca said. "A week's not enough time for me to get used to the idea of doing without you."

"You don't need me anymore, Becca," Kate said firmly. "This is *your* domain and it's your job to run it. I'm not much good at your kind of thing anyway."

"What, exactly, is my kind of thing?"

"You know! A fabulous house, perfectly run by you and your hand-picked staff. A troop of well-mannered, spanking-clean children in freshly pressed clothes. And your dinner parties. Nobody does that better."

"No parties until I can walk again!" Rebecca said vehemently. The child looked up at her anxiously. "It's all right, darling," she soothed him.

"You're wrong to put it off," Kate said, struggling against the appalling prognosis Rebecca had yet to face. She almost told Rebecca the truth—surely friends deserved the truth from each other!—but it was not for her to tell. "Theo needs you," she finished rather lamely.

Rebecca kept her voice low and even for Mark's sake—a bizarre contrast to the heat of her words. "That do-it-for-Theo bullshit isn't going to work with me! Do you think I'm going to invite those harpies to come and stare at me as if I were a freak at a sideshow?"

"Oh, spare me the dramatics," Kate said. "You sound like you're stuck in a Bette Davis movie! Everyone's seen people in wheelchairs, you know. You're not that unusual—except that you're still the most beautiful woman in Washington."

Rebecca glared at her, face flushed, lips pressed tightly together. Kate winked and Rebecca began to laugh. Her son, delighted, laughed with her.

"That's more like it," Kate said.

"But you must come back on weekends," Rebecca said, hugging the baby. "Promise you won't desert me for Polly and Kel Regis!"

"I won't have time to go that far that often, but I *will* go. I think she needs me."

"Needs you! That woman doesn't need anyone."

"She's changed, Rebecca. And our relationship is not the same as it used to be."

"Of course not," Rebecca said. "You've lost your innocence."

"I thought I'd lost that for all time when Sydney left."

Rebecca shook her head. "You lose your innocence once for each relationship in your life. A husband's not the same as a mother. Neither is a grandmother. And I wonder if you'll ever really trust a man again."

Kate shrugged. "Probably not. Polly says that one of the few compensations of growing older is not having to deal with misplaced trust."

"For once I agree with her. Except for us, Kate. We'll always trust each other."

Kate, tempted again to tell Rebecca the truth, felt as if she were drowning in deceit. She went to kneel beside Rebecca's chair, enclosing her and Mark in an embrace. They were quiet until Nanny came to fetch her charge and Kate and Rebecca began to talk of other things.

23

I

Kate stood at a window in her living room at the Hotel Carlyle, breathing in the carbon monoxide of Madison Avenue as if it were attar of roses. It was early, but the city was always pulsing with the energy she needed.

A month had gone by, but Kate had yet to regain the habit of single blessedness she had so blithely tossed away when she married Win. She had been too preoccupied, first with Rebecca, then with her new show, to deal with her anger, but she welcomed it; anger kept the other wounds from aching. But when she thought of Win, and she thought of him often, it was not always with wrath.

There were too many moments when she missed Win and love and marriage so intensely that it was painful, when she could not believe that a man like him could have destroyed everything in a moment of petulant, childish rage. Sometimes, when she woke, she would have the impression, for a few happy seconds, that she had imagined all of it. Then she would strive again to forget the delight of being Win's wife. Delight was like an amputated limb that, eerily, seemed still to be there.

"What ails me?" she berated herself when she spoke to Rebecca. "*Why do I miss him?* How can I harbor anything but contempt for such gross, heartless, idiotic stupidity?"

"In time," Rebecca soothed her, "your feelings for him will be absolutely neutral. Trust me."

"Do you know what irks me most? That brilliant, solid, cynical me, with my head firmly on my shoulders and my feet on the ground, fell in love with a man as absurd and as immature as Win!"

"People can't be brilliant about love."

"But, Becca, if I'm not brilliant about everything, what am I?"

"What you've always been. A good soul, a loyal friend, and, despite your unflappable veneer, a hopeless romantic."

But there was nothing romantic about Kate's life now. She came back most evenings to the bland impersonality of her hotel apartment and stayed there. She had decided to put off finding and furnishing an apartment of her own until she knew whether or not the show was a success.

Tillinghast had decided it would be live, not taped.

"Tilly's right," Stanton said. "We'll have a better draw with the possibility of some feathers flying. I just hope it doesn't make you nervous."

"After all that's happened this past year, there's very little that can make me nervous," Kate said.

But one thing did. *Rebecca still didn't know the truth about her legs!* Kate had come close to arguing with Theo about it during the weekend she had just spent in Georgetown.

"Theo, she'll be furious when she knows how long we've deceived her. Just when she needs us most, she'll trust us least!"

"It's the wrong time," Theo had said firmly. "She's running the house and the children again, even redecorating the dining room! It's better to wait until she sees that her life can go on just as it always has. If I tell her before she's convinced of that, she'll withdraw again. She'll be the way she was when she came home from the hospital. Is that what you want?"

He had looked so miserable that Kate relented, put her arms around him, and murmured words of comfort. They had held each other close for a long time. Her compassion for him was boundless.

II

By the start of her second month in New York, Kate began to nurture her independence. She made friends with solitude, accepting few dinner invitations. She saw a lot of movies. Sometimes she dined alone in a small Italian restaurant nearby; more often, she had the hotel kitchen send up a light meal, watched "MacNeil-Lehrer" while she ate it, then worked on the themes around which each of her shows would be built, or read the stack of magazines that kept her current with life in this metropolis.

"I can't get over how much they know about this city," Kate marveled to Stan, nodding at the people on the production team, most of them in their twenties. "And how little they know about anything else."

"Spoken like a true schoolmarm."

"No, really. Think about it for a moment. They're wildly ambitious, of course, and talented, too, but they can't speak English! The younger set knows where all the important art exhibits are, but they say 'mischeeveeous.' They know which of the new movies are must-sees, which are the 'in' restaurants, who's appearing at which club, and where to trade their slightly used clothes for someone else's—and they say 'for Danny and I' and 'none of us are.' They're in communications but they're murdering the language in which they communicate. They know which sitcom will make it and which won't, but they've never read Faulkner or Melville or, heaven help us, Shakespeare, and 1939 is ancient history to them. I'm damned if I know why I feel I have to keep up with them."

"They won't notice if you don't."

"But *I* will! I'm almost thirty-eight!"

"You look ten years younger."

"Around them I feel ten years older."

The preliminary preparation for the show, an hour to be called *Kate & Company*, was complete. The program would air in a week: they had a name, a logo, the Brandenburg Concerto No. 6 as a theme, and a ten o'clock slot on Friday nights.

"Why so late?" Kate asked Stan.

"This program is not for the ears of innocent children! You'll open the show. We'll show sketches and photos of women in the time period you're covering on each program, but you'll be saying some racy stuff to hold the women's attention."

"Not the men's?" Kate turned to Tillinghast.

Tillinghast shrugged. "Time will tell. But you come across very sexy so we've got a shot at seducing the men."

Kate's contract was for the usual thirteen weeks with an option to renew for only thirteen more.

"Twenty-six weeks is more than enough to know if we're a hit or out on the balls of our ass," Tillinghast said. Tillinghast cocked his head to study the ruby-red wool crepe suit Kate was modeling for him. He insisted on choosing her wardrobe.

"Kate's right, Tilly," Stan said. "It may take longer to call that one. This isn't a sitcom."

"We'll see," Tillinghast repeated. "Great oaks from little acorns grow. We might want to change the format, have call-ins."

"And why Friday night?" Kate demanded. "It's one of the least-watched nights of the week!"

"Doesn't signify anymore, Dr. Ballard. They'll tape you." Tillinghast was nodding his approval of Kate's suit. "I like you in that soft stuff, you know, unstructured jacket, satin shirt, bias-cut skirts."

"You know a lot about fashion," Kate said, surprised.

He smiled. "I learn it from my daughter. Most gorgeous little thing you ever saw, apple of my eye." He whipped out his wallet and showed Kate a picture of a pretty blue-eyed brunette, about sixteen, with long legs and enough naïveté to come through on film. "That's my Melinda," he said proudly.

"She wears minis," he went on with touching affection after Kate had admired her. "But skirts up to the kazoo are not for the star of this show, even though you do have great legs." He leered purposefully at Kate. "You have to project a scholarly image so you can get away with talking dirty. We'll go with this look for now."

"This isn't meant to be a sex show, Mr. Tillinghast. And my clothes have nothing to do with the business at hand."

"Dr. Ballard, your business is to make whatever remarks you like, the more shocking, the better. How you look while you're making them is my business. Read your contract."

What a beastly little popinjay you are, Kate thought. She always addressed him formally and he had stopped calling her Katie and seizing every opportunity he could find to put his hand on her waist or her rump. She had finally told him flatly that his advances weren't welcome and since then he had kept his distance. But the rejection sometimes made him testy, particularly on evenings when John Mallory picked Kate up at the broadcasting station in the West Fifties and took her out to dinner.

III

Mallory had made no overtures yet, for which Kate was grateful.

"*Consort* will be out in paperback in time for the program," he assured Kate over dinner a week before her first telecast. "Here's our special edition." He handed Kate a copy. "You might sneak in a mention that it's in the stores. And I'm already talking to Tillinghast about publishing transcripts of your hottest programs as a collection."

"How about talking to me?"

"His production company owns the rights to the program. You can cast your pearls, but he has to approve before anyone can gather them."

"And you won't make a final decision to publish these transcripts until you're sure the program is a hit."

Mallory nodded. "Wouldn't be worth it otherwise."

"I'm sure it would be to one of the university presses," Kate said angrily.

He put down his fork. "Why are you angry at me?"

"What I have to say to women is important, whether it gets ratings or not! Money and ratings and best seller lists *do not* determine merit."

"Kate, it's not my fault that no one believes in excellence anymore!"

"Well, I do and you should!" He looked so mortified that Kate made herself calm down. "I realize that you don't make the rules," she conceded.

"No one does, not with you."

"It's infuriating that some money-grubbing fool can determine the disposition of my work!"

"Thanks for the compliment."

"I didn't mean you."

"Yes, you did. But the ideas are still yours, Kate."

Kate sighed. "What's the point of ideas no one hears?" She sipped her wine. "And of course your answer to that is 'business is business.' "

"It must be exhausting to be a woman of principle in today's world."

Kate smiled ruefully. "Is that what you think I am? An idealist with addled wits? You're a very patient man, John."

He took her hand. "Kate, I don't want to rush you, but you must know how I feel about you."

"The trouble is that I haven't the least idea how I feel about you—or anyone else right now. If you want more than a dinner companion, you're wasting your time."

"I'm willing to wait."

"That's entirely your decision."

He smiled and resumed eating his dinner. "What's your first program about?"

"Tillinghast has decreed silence until D-day on pain of dismissal."

"Surely you can trust me, Kate!" He looked genuinely grieved.

She studied him for a moment, thinking that men were children with egos as tender as their testicles. "All right," she said at last. "It's prostitution."

He smiled his approval. "And your 'company'?"

"A streetwalker and a pricey call girl."

"Sensational!" He took her hand again and kissed it. "You can't miss."

IV

The studio audience, the majority of whom were women, was silent and attentive. When Kate talked, she established a link with one or two people in the front rows and spoke directly to them, turning her head often enough to include the rest of the audience. Tonight, as she gave a brief history of prostitution—illustrated by sketches and photos of its practitioners, some of them amusing—she established contact with a well-put-together woman in her sixties who was probably widowed, and an overweight girl in her twenties who was almost certainly not popular with men.

"No matter what their status," Kate said, "streetwalker or call girl, prostitutes from here to Hong Kong will tell you that theirs is a profession like any other, a service industry with a service rendered and a fee paid; in short, a commercial transaction. They insist that the service they render benefits society, just as it did when prostitutes were priestesses of the goddess or accepted to save good women from rape. They say their profession benefits all women, including you and me.

"Prostitutes claim they provide the novelty that fades from marriage, that by keeping husbands sexually content, they reduce the divorce rate. They say they relieve reluctant wives of too frequent sexual intercourse. They remind us that many men have unusual sexual tastes and that by satisfying them they relieve wives of that burden. For that alone, they feel, they're more to be honored than scorned.

"What's it like to be a prostitute? When we come back, we'll ask two women who are, as they say, in the life."

The audience applauded, the red lights went out and Kate leaned back in her chair. She sipped some mineral water. Tillinghast and Stanton Wells bore down on her with exuberant smiles.

"Great stuff, Kate," Tillinghast said. "The camera sure loves you!"

"Why are they so quiet?"

"Maybe your new view of hookers as social workers shocked them. They didn't fidget and they hardly coughed. Anyway, you're in," Stan assured her.

"How can you know that?" Kate sat still while her makeup was retouched and two chairs were placed on a darkened dais to protect the identity of her guests. A curtain was drawn to hide them until they were safely in place.

"Because the board's been lit up like a Christmas tree since you went on the air."

"Thirty seconds!" someone said, and everyone melted away. The red light came on, the closed curtain was opened, and Kate began to interview the two women whose faces were obscured by darkness.

V

The streetwalker had a high, childlike voice. "I hope Roscoe is watchin'," she giggled. Roscoe, she then explained, was her pimp. In response to Kate's question, she said she had become a prostitute to get away from her uncle.

"I hope that louse is watchin' too," she said heatedly. "He started doin' it to me when I was ten, but I was too scared to run away right then. When I did, I had nothin' to sell except me. A lotta guys pay top dollar for girls with no bust and hardly any fuzz. I was like that until I was fourteen, so I made extra good money for a coupla years."

"Would you like to get out of the life?"

"Why should I? I'd rather lie on my back five minutes than stand behind a counter sellin' socks all day."

"What is it like to have sex with so many men in one day?"

There was utter silence in the studio while they waited for a reply.

"Whaddaya mean?"

"Do they touch you intimately?"

"Not unless they pay for it. Mostly they get in and get out."

"Does it hurt by the end of the day?"

"Sometimes. Depends on the size of the guys and how long it takes them. But my feet would hurt if I was sellin' socks, wouldn't they?"

"Do you feel humiliated?"

"Say what?"

"Do you feel as if selling your body puts you down?"

"Hell, no! It's the guys who come sniffin' after me that's lowlifes, most of 'em married with kids. But a guy with a hardon—par'n the French—is a real nerd."

"Do you ever enjoy it?"

"Are you for real? It's a job. Who likes workin'?"

"Well, then, do you enjoy sex with Roscoe?"

The piping voice assumed an unexpected dignity. "That's personal."

"I understand," Kate said. "Thank you for telling us as much as you did."

VI

Kate turned to the other girl, who had a low, well-modulated voice. She had agreed to appear, she said, because people had so many misconceptions about call girls. They weren't tarts. A number of her colleagues were housewives, mothers, students. They did it for extra money and a little fun.

"If a prostitute is someone who sells her body for money, I know some virtuous wives who qualify," she said frostily. "There are women who hate having their husbands touch them. They put up with sex in exchange for a home and security and the husband's pension when he dies. That's hypocrisy."

"What kinds of men come to you?"

"Gentlemen, mostly. I have my regulars. Some are New Yorkers, some are out-of-towners who want an evening out. All of them have money."

"How did you get into it?"

"I wanted to buy my husband a Rolex for his birthday. A friend of mine introduced me to a dating service."

It was the last reply Kate had expected, but she collected herself and went on. "Are you still married?"

"No, but my profession had nothing to do with the divorce." She paused. "He never knew and he still has the Rolex."

"Would you like to get out of the life?"

"Not at all. The risks are minimal—everyone uses condoms now—and I have a lot of fun."

"Aren't you afraid a man might be criminally dangerous?"

The girl was silent for a moment. "Most of my men are regulars. I've learned to spot a man with a flipped switch and get away before the main event."

"Do you enjoy sex, or do you do it for money?"

"Yes to both questions. The level of enjoyment depends on how well I know the man."

"Do you ever get emotionally involved with a man, and, if so, how often?"

"It happened to me once," the soft voice said. "It'll never happen again."

There was a hush in the audience, then applause when Kate thanked the women and the curtain was drawn. Another commercial began. Kate stretched her arms over her head and drank more Evian water. She looked at the woman she imagined to be a widow. The woman's face was sad and she shook her head slowly and somberly. The girl looked furious.

For the last half hour Kate took questions from the audience, who were variously compassionate, outraged, curious, or disgusted. Then Kate was saying, "Thank you and good night for *Kate and Company*," and her first show was over.

Stan and Tillinghast whisked her away to the bar of her hotel for a drink.

"Some of the women were responsive and some were just plain mad," Kate said.

"That call girl made me sad," Stan said. "I got a good look at her, and she's absolutely gorgeous. Smart too. Why does she *do* it?"

"Because she needs to punish herself."

"I'm gonna find out what for," Tillinghast said smugly.

"Tilly! You made a date with her?"

"Why not? I'm a free man."

"Did the switchboard stay busy?" Kate asked.

"You bet," Stan said, patting Kate's back. "And a good twenty percent think you must either take a moral stand on the issues you discuss or get off the air. Isn't that sensational?"

Tillinghast raised his glass to her. "The best kind of publicity is an uproar from the do-gooders. In two days, everyone in America will have been warned that *Kate and Company* is wicked. Some will believe it."

"So, of course, they'll tune in next Friday," Stan said.

And they did, in numbers big enough to put Kate on the cover of *TV Guide* several weeks later. Tillinghast had a champagne party to celebrate and gave Kate the cover, blown up to poster size and framed in silver.

She got back to the Carlyle at midnight and was amazed to find her mother waiting in her apartment.

VII

"I had to see you tonight," Sydney said, hugging Kate and releasing her very quickly, as if she expected to be pushed away. "No matter how late it was." She sat down, smoothing her houndstooth-check skirt beneath her and crossing her shapely legs in their sheer black stockings. Her blondness was enhanced by a cardinal-red cashmere sweater. She looked as dashing, elegant, and beautiful as the last time Kate had seen her, virtually unchanged at fifty-six.

"How did you get in?" Kate asked. It was something to say.

"Everyone knows I'm your mother! They let me in. But don't worry, we're not going to be roommates. Hansi and I have a suite at the Plaza Athenée."

Kate took off her coat and flung it onto a chair. She slid off her shoes and walked to the bar to pour herself a cognac. "Want one?" she asked her mother.

"No, thank you. Alcohol ages the skin. It's time you began to think about things like that. You won't stay young forever, although I must say you look marvelous—on television too, and they say that's the acid test. Hansi and I ordered a tape of the program. Of course, I'd have asked different questions."

Kate swirled the cognac in the snifter. "But why have you come? You hate the States."

"I simply had to see you."

"Sydney!" Kate shook her head.

Sydney's animation deserted her and she slumped in her chair. "It's Tyler and his bloody book."

"I should have known," Kate said. "So he's back at work on *Aftermaths*."

"And Daddy's not here to shut him up this time."

"I was certain it was The Senator who stopped him."

"Well, of course! West Germany is the richest, most stable country in Europe, for one thing, and Benedict Industries isn't the only one doing business there. So here was Daddy, praising the new Germany on the floor of the Senate, and there was his ex-son-in-law, scratching away at a book that rakes up those nasty Nazis—and accuses The Senator's present son-in-law of being one of them!"

"I had no idea you were in touch with your father," Kate said.

Sydney stood up. "I think I *will* have a drink." She poured a small cognac and added a lot of water. "Only about Tyler's book," she said. "And Daddy was a nervous wreck about it, afraid Mother would castrate him if she found out he so much as spat on me. It's pitiful to see a grown man so frightened of a woman."

"Why does she hate you so?"

Sydney gulped her drink. "I told you all I know about that years ago."

"She said she had to watch Hilliard suffer. What did she mean by that?"

"I don't know! Can you explain a madwoman? Anyway, she's not why I came. I want you to talk to your father. He'll listen to you."

"No, he won't. I've already tried. I won't try again."

"How can you refuse?" Sydney was genuinely astonished. "What sort of publicity will it be for you and your career if your own father says your mother is married to a Nazi?"

"I'm an old hand at living through headlines about you."

Sydney flushed and Kate, feeling petty, tried to dismiss her mother's fears. "Guilt by association went out with McCarthy," she said dryly. "The media don't concern me."

"Well, they concern *me*! I've never been happy before, not ever in my whole life." Tears welled up in Sydney's eyes. "Tyler will ruin everything for Hansi and me. That's exactly what he wants. He's such an unforgiving man!"

"He had a lot to forgive."

"Oh, for heaven's sake, Kate, people get divorces every day, as you well know! Do you hate Win enough to ruin him?"

"Yes," Kate flared, "sometimes I do! Calm, controlled, reasonable me! Why does everyone assume that because I don't carry on like an infant I'm not capable of anger? Anyway, it isn't just the divorce Tyler can't forgive! It's the humiliation, the things you said when you left him, the things you did while you were still legally married to him. How could anyone forgive that?"

"You always took his side!"

"I could hardly take yours, could I? You weren't there." Kate contemplated the cognac swirling in the bottom of the snifter and drank it off. "But I don't want to take either side now."

"Kate, help me, for pity's sake!" Sydney covered her face with her hands and sobbed.

Kate watched her with a feeling so close to gratification that she was appalled. Had she been waiting all these years for Sydney to get her comeuppance? Was she secretly hoping Tyler's book would do the job?

She gave in and went to sit on the arm of her mother's chair. "Come on," she said, patting Sydney's shoulder. "Stop crying. He's on a lecture tour. As soon as it's over I'll talk to him, but there's no guarantee he'll listen."

"I know he will!" Sydney said. "He respects you. He's proud of you."

As no one, Kate thought, looking at her mother, *ever was of you, except your Dr. Strangelove, who roughs you up and probably* is *a Nazi.*

Sydney repaired her face and combed her hair before she left. Both women were subdued. They did not embrace.

"I'll call you tomorrow," Sydney said. "Please have dinner with us just once while we're here."

Kate nodded and waved as the elevator doors closed. She went back inside to confront the rancor she harbored, not only against Sydney but against Win. It was very quiet, the traffic on Madison Avenue light at this time of night, but she could not concentrate on grudges. When she thought of Win, it was with an overwhelming memory of hours spent talking to him, listening to him, laughing with him, loving him.

The telephone rang.

"You miserable hypocrite," Rebecca said, panting with rage. "Why didn't you tell me the truth?"

24

———————

I

From the window of the upstairs hall in Georgetown, Rebecca watched the Rolls she would never drive again turn into the circular driveway and come to a stop. The chauffeur opened the door, but apparently Kate was reluctant to get out, to come upstairs and face her best friend even though she didn't know what Rebecca really wanted of her.

But Rebecca had no choice. She must do what she must do and Kate would never be more likely to acquiesce to the scheme than right now, when she was suffused with guilt.

Rebecca had already begun to suspect that her condition was far more serious than she had been told. Physical therapy had not produced the slightest improvement, although her nurse-companion, Alice, was diligent and reassuring. Hope had been peeling away like the layers of an onion. Hope was almost gone on the day, a week before, when Rebecca had maneuvered her motorized chair closer to the window to eavesdrop on Theo and Kate. Rebecca had her suspicions about *them* too.

They were downstairs in the garden, talking politics. Rebecca's garden in summer was a smaller version of Polly's, although Rebecca never planted and pruned as Polly did. It amazed Rebecca that Kate had reconciled with her grandmother, but at least she would never again be so thoroughly hoodwinked by the old bitch.

"I don't think we stand a chance," Theo said. "The country's been thoroughly bamboozled by Reagan and wants more of the same."

"He fooled all of the people most of the time," Kate replied.

"When the economy collapses they'll know they've been fooled."

"By then it'll be too late."

Rebecca's attention drifted away from them to the photographs of her six children, arrayed in Victorian fashion, on a round table near the window. Four sons and two daughters! She had been ready for another pregnancy. Now she would never know the bliss of carrying a child of Theo's again—even if he didn't deserve it!

That was because Rebecca had another suspicion, far stronger than the one about her legs: Theo was in love with Kate. She could tell by the way he behaved in bed. He was there but not there. She could tell by the way he looked at Kate—or avoided looking at her. His conversations with her lately were as stilted as the one going on then. Rebecca didn't give a damn about politics. It was her life she cared about, her life with Theo. She had to protect it.

There they were, the two of them, friends for so long, both of them needing comfort, needing love, needing sex. To whom would either be more likely to turn than the other?

II

"You must tell her," Kate had said, drawing Rebecca's immediate attention.

"How can I? Maybe you have the strength, Kate, but I haven't."

"Theo, she has a right to know she'll never walk again."

Rebecca's mouth opened in a silent scream. No matter how much she had feared it, it was unbearably cruel to hear it said, to know that it was true! Rebecca bit down hard on her knuckle to keep from screaming aloud, from throwing up, from fainting. She rocked back and forth in her chair.

". . . little girl, my perfectionist." Theo's voice brought her back to the two in the garden. "She's always demanded the best—and deserved it."

"And got it too, thanks to you." Kate again, being fair, damn her! Kate, whittling away at Theo's guilt.

I want you guilty! I want you to pay the price! Rebecca shrieked soundlessly out the window while she listened.

"I wish she would scream at me," Theo said uncannily. "I wish she would rave and holler and yell!"

"It wasn't your fault!"

It was! It WAS!

"I was at the controls of that plane!"

"Theo, that's irrational."

"So is the whole damned tragedy. And she's so gallant about it. It breaks my heart."

I hope your heart does break! I hope it breaks in bits!

"She has to consult other doctors."

"If I can persuade her!" Theo said. "Some of the best of them are in Europe, and she's reluctant to leave home."

I'll go! I'd go to the moon if it meant I could walk again!

Her fear of losing Theo almost strangled her. Theo had never been able to deal with illness. Theo had fled when one of the children scraped a knee or had to have a broken bone set or a wound stitched. How could he live with an infirm wife? He would certainly leave her, not now, but some day. She had always known good fortune like hers was rare, that it would never last.

III

Neither of them had said a word to her. The evening had passed like so many others and Theo had driven Kate to the airport to take the shuttle. God knew what they talked about when they were alone.

Rebecca had let a week go by, locking her emotions away as she would have locked up a rabid animal, waiting for Theo to tell her, to prove he could face it, could take her as she was. But something inside her snapped and she had forced the truth from him.

They had been at dinner, just the two of them, at the game table in the living room, when she asked him.

"What was the last prognosis the doctor gave you?"

"The same." He avoided her eyes. "It will take time."

"Liar! I know I'll never get out of this cage!" She pounded the arms of her chair.

"Who told you?" Theo whispered.

"What kind of fool do you take me for?" She glared at him.

He sprang up so suddenly that his chair overturned and came around to her. "Rebecca, I was afraid to tell you."

"Tell me what? What else are you hiding from me?"

"Nothing, *nothing!*"

"What are you going to do?"

"Help you in any way I can. What else would I do?" He looked utterly bewildered.

She didn't tell him what she suspected. She collapsed against him and let him think he was comforting her. She had not reproached him for not telling her sooner—and certainly not for causing the accident or for escaping from it unhurt. Rebecca knew she must never express resentment if she wanted to keep him. She had been forgiving, patient, and courageous while she watched him wallow in the guilt that was her insurance policy.

When Theo went downstairs to heat some milk, she had called Kate in New York.

IV

"You miserable hypocrite! Why didn't you tell me the truth?"

"Theo wouldn't let me, Becca."

"Damn Theo," Rebecca whispered. "I hate Theo! I watch him get out of bed every morning and I *hate* him for being whole and healthy. I hate *you* because *you* are! I hate my children because *they* are! But most of all, I hate him. This is his fault, all—his—fault! And he walked away without a scratch! It isn't fair! *It isn't fair!*"

"No, it isn't fair, but it isn't his fault either."

"Why are you defending him? What's going on between you two?"

"I can't believe you said that! If you say it again, I'll hang up."

"Oh, don't, Kate, please don't!" Her voice had trembled with need then, not malice. "I didn't mean it. I adore Theo. I always have, since the first day I saw him. You know that better than anyone else." Rebecca began to sob. "And you're my best friend, my only friend now. None of the others really cares."

"I'll come tomorrow morning and we'll talk," Kate said. "Now you have to sleep. You sound exhausted."

"I'm a lot worse than that," Rebecca said before she hung up.

Rebecca had sipped the milk when Theo brought it and feigned sleep, but sleep had not come. In the darkness her desperation had swelled until, finally, she knew what she had to do.

V

I've got to be calm, Rebecca told herself now, watching the Rolls parked below. *It's the only way to make her agree.*

She knew how to handle Kate. Rebecca had always dominated, Rebecca had always led. She could make Kate do anything. Kate would be loyal no matter what their friendship demanded of her.

She owes me this, Rebecca told herself. *All the more because she lied to me.*

Kate had her troubles too, but they were nothing to compare with this. Kate had never suffered overmuch. Her mother walked out? Kate got a Ph.D., married a matinee idol, and wrote a best-selling book. Her husband left her? Kate got herself on a television show that was the talk of the country.

Life had not been that easy for Rebecca. She wasn't a Benedict and her father didn't write prize-winning books and her mother didn't have lots of money from an irrevocable trust. She didn't grow up in exalted social and political circles because her grandfather wasn't a senator with an estate like Kel Regis. The Benedicts had style. Rebecca's mother had had no style. Everything Rebecca knew she had taught herself.

Kate was getting out of the car. Two long beautiful legs emerged first—the pain in Rebecca's heart sharpened at the sight of them—and the rest of her tall, lissome body followed. Rebecca switched on the motor and rolled quickly down the corridor to her bedroom and swung her chair around to the door.

She heard Kate hurrying up the stairs on her perfect legs. Rebecca sat rigid in her padded chair, facing Katherine as if she were a firing squad.

VI

"Rebecca! Why aren't you downstairs by now?" That was Kate's schoolmarm pose.

"How dare you ask me that?" Rebecca demanded, her eyes glittering. Then her face crumpled. "I'm not going to get through this, Kate."

Kate dropped her attitude and her handbag and ran to kneel at Rebecca's side. "Yes, darling, you will! It was a terrible shock, but it's better to know everything. Now we can deal with it."

"*We?* I'm the one sitting in this chair, not you! What do you know about this . . ." Her hands spread above her crippled legs, as if searching for a word. "*Degradation!*" she finally whispered.

"Oh, Rebecca, surely not that," Kate said, embracing her again.

Rebecca let Kate hold her and rock her while she wept.

"Hush, now," Kate said after a while. "We'll work something out. There are other doctors. Theo has a list of specialists in Europe. Don't give up, Becca. Theo needs you. So do the children."

"Damn the children!" Rebecca moaned, pummeling Katherine's back softly with her fists. "It's Theo I want. I only wanted them because I wanted him. Don't you understand anything?"

"You *have* him," Kate said. "You'll have him all your life! If you don't know that, you don't know him."

Rebecca drew back again and dried her face, looking steadily at Kate as she spoke, willing her to hear the agony in every word she said.

"Listen to me, Kate. I know you're trying to help, but . . . just . . . listen. Theo made love to me last night, right in there." She pointed to the huge bed custom-built to accommodate Theo's height. Her arm dropped in heavy despair as she went on.

"He's been doing it regularly, as if he had made himself a chart headed 'make love to my crippled wife twice a week' and checked it off." She looked away. "Every time he does it I can feel how nervous he is, afraid he won't get an erection or that he'll lose it. I can feel him slipping away from me and then he's all right again, but I know it's because he's thinking about some other woman. What I don't know is who she is or if he's slept with her yet." Her eyes shifted back to meet Kate's.

"I don't think he has, Rebecca. I don't believe he will."

"It's humiliating!" Rebecca went on, half covering her trembling lips with her fingers while she strained to speak the unspeakable. "I can't move, Kate, I can't move! I lie there like a felled oak. He has to separate my legs so he can push himself inside me. He pretends to be carried away by passion, but he isn't! Neither am I. It's mechanical, the way it must be when a man uses one of those inflatable rubber dolls."

"Oh, my God," Kate said, turning her head away.

"Look at me, Kate, *look at me*! How much sex appeal can a cripple have for a man like Theo? Sooner or later, if it hasn't happened already, he'll find someone who can respond to him the way I used to, who can give him the kind of sex he wants. He's far too passionate to be satisfied with half a woman for the rest of his life. Oh, he'll try to be faithful, I know that, first out of love, then out of guilt, but he'll fail eventually and feel more guilty still and end by hating me for making him feel that way."

Rebecca's face was stony, even while the tears rolled down her cheeks again.

"Then he'll leave me because she'll make him leave me, the woman, whoever she is. I can't let that happen. I can cope with anything as long as he doesn't leave me. And don't tell me it'll never happen. Be realistic, Kate. He's only human. Even I know that."

Kate was silent.

"I couldn't have said that to anyone but you. Or what I'm going to say now." Rebecca paused, gripping Kate's hands tightly. "You're the only one I can trust not to take him away from me. Kate, please, Kate! If there's going to be someone else for him, I want it to be you."

She watched while Kate's dark eyes widened in disbelief.

"Rebecca! That's preposterous."

Rebecca persisted, her face pinched and white as she spoke. "Is it? You're alone now in the same way he is. You know each other so well. It would be so much better than sleeping with a stranger. You could help each other."

"No!" Kate shook her head. "That's crazy! I could no more go to bed with your husband than fly."

"Don't you care for him?"

"I love the man! But not in that way. Even if I did, he's *your* husband. For God's sake, Rebecca!"

Rebecca began to cry again. "If he leaves me, I'll die. I will. I'll find a way to kill myself." It was her high trump, and she played it with all the desperation she felt. She knew, in the next moment, that Kate believed her.

"Don't say that!" Kate begged. "He won't leave you."

"Promise me, then. At least promise me you won't let it come to that."

"*Theo* won't let it come to that."

"Promise me. Oh, Kate, I'm so frightened. Help me!" She threw her arms around Kate's neck, clinging to her.

"I'll help, Rebecca, I will, in any way that's reasonable."

"Tell me you won't sit by if you think something's developing between him and another woman," Rebecca whispered urgently. "If I know you're watching, I can go to Europe to see those doctors but, Kate, please, if I mean anything at all to you, promise me you won't let him fall into some other woman's clutches while I'm gone."

"Yes, darling, all right, I promise."

They sat in silence for a while. The sunlight, filtering through the oak tree outside the window, made filigree patterns on their faces.

VII

Kate stayed for dinner. It was a strained affair. All three of them were emotionally spent, and Rebecca did not protest when Kate said she wanted to catch the next shuttle. Rebecca's smile was enigmatic when Theo offered to drive Kate to the airport as usual.

"Theo, she's beside herself," Kate said as soon as they were in the car. "She's certain you'll leave her for another woman sooner or later. She says she can tell you're thinking of someone else when you're making love to her." When he didn't reply, she turned to look at him. "Is that true?"

"Yes. I couldn't make it if I didn't. Her body is so pitiful—and pity is the antithesis of passion."

"But you mustn't let her know it!"

"I've tried not to," Theo said. "Obviously I failed."

He stopped the car at a red light.

"Theo, forgive me for asking this, but is there someone else?"

Theo was silent for a moment. "Yes, but not in the way you mean."

"Is it serious? Do you love her?"

"Kate, I don't know! I only know I will never leave Rebecca."

The light changed and the car moved forward.

Kate dropped her head into her hands. "I'm afraid this is affecting her mind, Theo."

"What do you mean?" he asked anxiously.

Kate hesitated before she told him. "She wants us to be lovers. She says I'm the only woman she can trust not to take you away from her."

"Oh, Jesus," Theo said.

Kate nodded. "Yes. I told her it was unconscionable and she seemed to drop it, but I know Rebecca! She wouldn't agree to go to Europe unless I promised to keep an eye on you." She looked at him. "She isn't rational."

He drove without speaking for a while, although several times it seemed he would. He finally said, "Would you be rational after what she's been through, after what she's just found out? She needs a change. She hasn't been out of the house in months. This trip will be the best thing for her. We're crossing on the *QE II* and I'll spend a week in London with her. She'll have Alice to look after her when I leave."

Kate shook her head. "I'm not sure even Alice can keep her in order when you leave her on her own."

"She'll be all right. You promised her to keep an eye on me."

"I plan to! I'll spend as much time as I can with you!"

He took her hand. "I'll look forward to that."

Kate sighed. "When do you leave for Europe?"

"In a month. I need to set up the medical appointments and Rebecca wants to order new clothes. I want to take it in easy stages, so we'll spend a night or two in New York."

"Good. Stay at the Carlyle. I'll make the arrangements when you give me the dates."

The car swung over to the passenger dropoff. Theo leaned over and kissed her. "I love you, Kate. You're a good friend."

"I love you too," Kate said, and got out of the car.

25

Dora Suponik was the kind of woman who made Kate's hackles rise. Dora was certain that the only truth was her truth, and her conviction was such that women listened and often believed when Dora glorified the good old days.

The chairwoman of the Congress of American Wives sat in the guest armchair across from Kate. She was a homely woman, but an impressive one, tall and angular, with large eyes, thin lips, and hair sprayed to rigid perfection. For her appearance on *Kate & Company* she wore a teal blue suit and a cream blouse with a Peter Pan collar fastened by a cameo pin.

At her insistence, the format of the program had been altered. She and Kate had taken questions for the first half hour and were now dueling their way to the end of the program.

"Let me tell you something, Dr. Ballard," Dora said, keeping her better profile to the camera. "A great many women in this country wish liberation had never happened. In the old days there was a place for women and a place for men. Maybe it wasn't a fair division of the spoils, but at least we all knew who we were and what we were expected to do! Men protected women and earned a living; women kept house and raised clean, decent children. I ask you, what was so terrible about that?"

"It was too risky," Kate said. "A man might lose his job or simply leave town or die. It's hard to earn enough to raise a family when the only skills you have are domestic. Moreover, men have rarely been protective of women, except in fiction. The female was a reproductive vessel who died young."

"That isn't true! Men put women on a pedestal!"

"No, they didn't. The Victorian woman, although she was honored

284

and protected and almost deified, was actually a slave. When she married, everything she owned, including her body, became her husband's absolute property to do with as he liked. If he beat her or locked her in the attic or squandered her dowry, that was his business. In this century it's clear that chivalry has expired utterly, if it ever existed at all. It's unwise to put all your faith in the benevolence of anyone, men included. That's why we need statutes."

"You'll never get that legislation through Congress," Dora snapped.

"Not as long as women like you lobby against the ERA."

"We are already protected by the Constitution. It's madness to lose any more respect from men than feminists and sexual permissiveness have already cost us."

"Feminism is not about sex, it's about gender and dependence and unequal pay for equal work."

Dora quivered with rage. "You can't blame that on our husbands."

Kate nodded. "I agree. I think the worst enemies of women have often been other women. We were brought up to believe that the men were after our virtue and the women were after our men and we have distrusted each other for centuries—but that's a topic for another program."

Kate turned swiftly to the closeup camera, forestalling Dora's reply. "Our time is up for tonight. Our thanks to Mrs. Suponik for being a guest on *Kate and Company* and to you for watching. We hope you'll join us again next week."

Dora Suponik waited for the off the air signal, then stood and smoothed her jacket. "Bitch," she said. "You cut me off."

"Yes, I did, at the knees. You're dead wrong, Dora dear, and you're too smart not to know it. My bet is that you do your number to get in the papers."

"And you don't?"

"No. I do it to show up women like you."

"I'll remember that next time we meet."

"Let's try to avoid another meeting, shall we?"

Kate went to her dressing room, relieved that the program was over. She seemed to be on a short tether lately, and Dora had pressed her to the limit.

More important, she was not content with her soapbox, although the program was a great success. It did nothing to help Kate decide how to live the rest of her life.

Stan knocked and put her head in. "Got to you, didn't she?"

Kate nodded. "The woman drives me up the wall. All that horseshit about gallant, faithful men cherishing their women until death!"

"Some do!"

"If you find one, bring him to me! Stan, can we skip supper? I'm too tired to eat. We'll talk on Monday."

Stan nodded, said good night, and left. Kate gathered her things and made for the door.

"A moment of your time, Dr. Ballard," Clyde Tillinghast said, walking with her toward the exit. "Your famous cool was almost blown tonight. What's up?"

"To tell you the truth," Kate said, "I'm frazzled. I need a rest."

"The weekend is just beginning."

"I'd like an extra day or two."

Tillinghast nodded. "Take two. We don't need you until Wednesday."

She nodded and hailed a cab. Tillinghast held the door for her and watched her get in, admiring her hips and those long, long legs.

One of these days, he promised himself.

‖

Win used the remote to turn the television off. He leaned back on Darcy's ice-blue satin couch, his long legs extended, his arms crossed behind his head.

Darcy, on the other end of the couch, sipped her champagne, trying not to look at him. His looks always made her melt, and she had a bone to pick with him tonight.

"The unflappable Kate finally flapped, didn't she?" Darcy said, darting a glance at Win.

"Almost. That Suponik woman's an old battle-ax."

"Maybe so, but Kate wasn't fair. She left Dora with her bloomers down."

"Kate will be forgiven. There's something about her."

"Last week you said it was integrity." Darcy's eyes began to shoot daggers.

"Yes, that's it. Integrity."

Darcy rose from the couch abruptly and did her Lauren Bacall slink, back and forth before the fire. "Really, Winslow, it isn't at all the thing to live with me and languish after her!"

He surveyed her, elegant in a satin hostess gown the same blue as the couch, her slender feet in silver sandals, her ears dripping with diamonds. She was a very exciting woman, but possessive, as were most women, in his experience. Except Kate. What other wife would have allowed an article like Darcy to be an integral part of their lives from day one? What other wife would have supposed he was as incapable as Kate was of being petty or unfaithful?

"I'm not languishing," he said.

"You could've fooled me! Dammit, if you want her, go get her! Life is too short for unrequited love."

Kate wouldn't let me through the door, he thought.

"Love?" he said. He held out a hand to Darcy. When she sat down beside him, he said, "Darcy, we've never pretended this was love, requited or otherwise."

"It was a figure of speech," Darcy said. "But why couldn't it be love?"

"Because love is too damned exhausting. Thank God there's only one true love in a lifetime."

"And yours is Kate?" Darcy shot to her feet again. "You didn't think so when she left you standing there like a spare prick at a wedding! I don't care what the reason was, she could've left a note, for God's sake! And that wasn't all. For weeks before that you were calling her an ungrateful brat, a selfish shrew. And when she finally buggered off, where did you turn for comfort?"

Again he pulled her down and turned her to lie across his lap. "To you, because I don't know another woman who's easier to be with. No demands. No expectations. No ideals to live up to."

"No integrity."

He was unbuttoning the bodice of her gown. "I don't have any either," he said.

Responding to his lovemaking, she didn't tell him he was still in love with Kate. She didn't want him to know.

A Double Life was going to be a winner. Fame was what he lived for. With that—and a woman to wear on his arm and make him happy in bed—he would be content.

III

"Kate fired off a few tonight," Polly said to Dodie Phelps, switching off the television.

"Kate can be deadly when she wants to be. Probably gets it from you. But I'm not sure that Suponik woman is all wrong. I'm damned if I'd want to be a young girl today! No romance at all. Meet a man and you're in bed with him without so much as a handshake! Pictures of female genitalia in those awful magazines for all the young boys to see! Being made to feel virginity is a disgrace!"

"You ought to go on Kate's program." Polly smiled.

"Maybe I will!" Dodie Phelps paused. "Kate looked a bit tired to me."

"She looked marvelous. Kate's a crowd pleaser, always was. Think what a politician she'd have made! I swear that girl could have been president." Polly sighed. "It breaks my heart when I think of what she gave up to marry that man! But in her heart of hearts she's still a teacher."

"Polly, you don't know anymore what's in Kate's heart of hearts."

"She's my flesh and blood. Of course I know."

"So is Sydney, and you never knew beans about *her*."

Polly made no reply.

"Polly honey," her cousin said gently. "Last time you meddled with Kate you were estranged for years and it took a tragedy to bring you together. You don't have time for another falling out."

Polly looked at her sharply. "Why do you say that?"

"Because it's true! At our time of life, a few years could be a life-time."

"I hate that kind of talk."

"Polly dear, you can't fight nature."

"Oh, yes, I can!" Polly said fiercely. "I refuse to let go—or to let go of you."

"I'm not planning to leave. I've decided paradise would be dull without you, so I'll stop on until you're ready."

"That'll be the day! I'm not leaving before the last trump sounds. I want to see how it all turns out!" Polly nodded her head vigorously, then settled back in her chair. "I suppose you're right about getting Kate's dander up. She's a bit edgy these days. Still, what's best for Kate isn't the only thing urging me on. Wakefield enrollment keeps falling. We need fresh blood to give us some glamour. If she were president, our enrollment would skyrocket!"

Polly's private telephone rang and she picked it up. "Kate! We were just talking about you." She listened and a great smile lit up her face. "Yes, of course! No, no one but Tyler and us. What time? I'll send the car for you. Yes, honey. Good night." She hung up and grinned at her cousin. "She's coming on the red-eye tomorrow morning."

IV

"Kel Regis never fails me," Kate said from her chaise. She and Dodie Phelps were alone on the terrace overlooking the garden. Polly was in her office with one of her bankers, cosigning a loan for her butler's son. That was typical of the many things she did for her employees but refused to discuss. Kate, in shorts and a T-shirt, was sprawled on a lounge in the sun, her eyes closed behind oversize sunglasses. "It's like the vent on a pressure cooker."

"You look winnowed out," Dodie Phelps said from her chair in the shade of the oak tree. "Working too hard, I expect."

"It isn't the show. It's Rebecca. There's virtually no hope of recovery and it's been exhausting to pretend there is."

"Maybe you should all stop pretending."

Kate nodded. "You're right, and we almost have, but not until she's seen several specialists abroad. She mustn't feel she hasn't tried everything." Kate turned on her side and looked fondly at her companion. It had always been easy to talk to this clever, loving woman. "There's something else. I'm here in part because of Sydney. She wants me to persuade Tyler to leave the baron out of his new book."

"And you agreed?"

"I know I shouldn't have, but she was so wretched, I said I'd try. She's convinced it will ruin her life, and she says she's never been happy before. I wonder if that's true."

"I think it probably is," Dodie Phelps said. "And that's strange because she had everything a young girl's supposed to need to be happy: beauty, wealth, a gorgeous home, and a famous family."

"What was she like as a girl?"

"Breathtaking, even as a baby. The first thing you noticed was her beauty, it was that striking. For most people, it was all they noticed, but I always believed how she looked got in the way of how she was, the way it did with poor little Marilyn Monroe. There was that same wistfulness about Sydney. It seems to be an aphrodisiac to men of all ages. Oliver could refuse her nothing and her brothers adored her. Hilliard loved her to distraction. Of course, Polly couldn't bear Hilliard to love anyone but her, but Hilliard couldn't help himself. It was a strange triangle, and because of it there was a tension in this house right out of Freud. Everyone knew Polly and Sydney were battling for Hilliard, but they had this unspoken agreement not to talk about it. It was uncanny!"

"What was uncanny?" Polly demanded, coming onto the terrace from the morning room.

"The way women take on over rock musicians," Dodie Phelps said smoothly. "In my day it was movie stars."

"Those women are like cats over catnip," Polly said. She sat down in the shade next to her cousin and rang the silver bell on the table between them. "Unusually warm for this time of year," she said.

"It's delicious," Kate murmured, on her back again.

"I have a secret, but you must both promise to let me tell it to Theo. He's flying down to spend a few hours tomorrow, and I'll give him the good news then."

"What's the news?"

"He's been asked to sit on Wakefield's board of trustees."

"But that's wonderful!" Kate said, lifting her glasses for a moment. "He'll be so pleased. That was kind of you, Polly."

"She didn't do it to be kind," Dodie Phelps murmured.

Polly turned to the butler, who had appeared in response to the bell. "It's such a lovely day, Curtis, I think we'll lunch out here, please. And please ask Cook to put plenty of mint in the iced tea." The butler left and Polly turned to Kate again. "You look positively limp. Are you coming down with something?"

"No. I just feel like one of those cartoon characters who runs so fast she goes off the cliff and doesn't realize there's nothing holding her up."

The two older women looked at each other.

"What are you running from?" Polly asked gently.

"My divorce."

"It wasn't only yours, dear," Dodie Phelps said.

Kate nodded. "I know. But I've been so busy since it happened that I've had no time to make a conscious transition from married to single. All of a sudden I looked down and there was nothing there!"

"Kate, maybe it hadn't been there for quite some time."

"Oh, it was there, all right," Kate said. "We were good together." She sighed. "I've been filling up the empty space with a television program, but it's a poor substitute. I'm not even sure I like what I'm doing or if I started it because Win was against it and kept on with it for something to do."

Another look passed between Polly and her cousin.

"I can't seem to get organized," Kate said. "I don't like living in a hotel, but I don't have the energy to find a place of my own."

"Better not do that until you decide where you're going to be. You don't want to get tied to a long-term lease." Polly said it idly, but her eyes sparkled and she resolutely avoided Dodie Phelps's warning looks. "Kate," Polly said blithely, "why don't you take a long ride this afternoon? It always helps you think."

"I'm too lazy. Maybe tomorrow."

"As you like. Carolina foaled early this morning. We have another little Charlie. Come and see him with me after lunch."

Dodie Phelps put a finger to her lips and pointed at the lounge. Kate had drifted off to sleep, and when luncheon was brought Polly waved Curtis back inside with it and wheeled Dodie Phelps into the morning room, where the two of them ate lunch, talking in low tones. They exchanged several significant sentences.

"She sounds like she's ready to leave New York," Dodie Phelps said.

"It's safer to wait until she's really fed up."

"Do you ever do anything spontaneously, without plotting?"

"Occasionally, but it isn't nearly as satisfying."

Curtis opened a parasol to shade Kate, and Polly spread a light cotton quilt over her. She slept until four o'clock. Tyler arrived at seven with just enough time to change for dinner.

V

Tyler Ballard walked to the stables the next morning and found his daughter playing with the foal. Tyler thought she looked very young in jeans and a plaid shirt, her hair pulled back with a bit of ribbon. Her tall, strong body curved over the foal protectively, and Tyler wondered, for the first time, why Kate had never had a child.

The mare nickered nervously and bent to nuzzle her foal when Tyler approached.

Kate spoke softly to reassure her. "There, Carolina, it's all right. Tyler's not going to hurt your baby boy." Kate hugged the colt. "Isn't he sweet?"

Tyler smiled and patted the little creature affectionately. To Kate, her father became more attractive as he aged—and more removed. He had always been a man who inhabited whatever world he happened to be writing about; maybe it was that removal from reality that kept his skin so smooth and his body so trim. His white hair gave him the look of a nineteenth-century romantic poet. She wondered suddenly if there had been other women since Sydney left him.

"I'm so glad you came down, Katherine. It's been a long time since we were at Kel Regis together."

"Will you be staying on?"

He looked pleased with himself. "Yes, my lecture tour is finished and I've cleared my calendar. I can work steadily for several months."

"On *Aftermaths*?"

"Yes. I think it's the best thing I've ever done."

"I couldn't believe it when you stopped working on it," Kate said, "until Sydney told me Oliver insisted."

Tyler colored. "That was politics. Now I'm free to write what I like."

Kate stood the wobbly colt on its overlong legs and gave her father a level look. "Free to punish Sydney, you mean."

He flushed again. "Nonsense!"

"It's true, Tyler," Kate said. "You know it is. I read a big chunk of the manuscript last night. It would be far better if you didn't use it to stab your ex-wife's husband in the back."

"I write what is true," he said coldly. "You disappoint me, Katherine. I thought you knew better than to trust your mother."

Kate set the foal under Carolina's teat and began picking straw from her jeans. "After this, I will not be drawn into any more arguments, grudge wars, or vendettas between you and Sydney, but I promised to talk to you about the book."

"I fail to see how it concerns you in the least."

A bubble of anger formed inside Kate's chest at his monumental self-absorption, and she railed at him for that, not for Sydney. "It'll concern all of us, Polly too! The press will link von Rayner to Sydney and Sydney to you and you to me and Kel Regis to all of us. I've been chewed over by enough scandal sheets, thank you. You did it for Oliver. If you don't want to do it for Sydney, do it for me. I need a rest."

Abruptly, it had become vital that he do something for her. It was an old feeling, surfacing without warning, that he come out of his shell and protect her, that he be a father.

"Are you suggesting that I compromise my principles," her father demanded pompously, "and cover up a dangerous plot to spare you publicity?"

The bubble burst. "Principles! You compromised them when you gave in to Oliver. All you want to do is punish Sydney! Couldn't you, just once, consider me?"

"I've always considered you!"

"You couldn't have. You never knew how I felt!"

"I don't know what you mean!" He looked genuinely astonished, as if she had turned into a snake-haired Medusa before his eyes.

"Why did we never talk about Sydney after she left? Why did we have to pretend she'd never even been there, never lived in the house on Elm Terrace, never slept in your bed, never been part of us?"

"It was better that way! You didn't want to talk about her either."

"I did! I did! I *hated* her, yes, but I missed her too, and I had no one to tell it to but Rebecca. I thought it was my fault Sydney ran away. If you had once talked to me, you'd have known that."

"I did my best!" Tyler protested. "What could I have said? For years I couldn't pronounce her name. I didn't know you were so . . . emotional." He held his hands wide in supplication, then dropped them. "*I'm* not, Katherine. I never was. I thought you were like me. Your mother always said you were."

"You've never even asked me how I feel about Win! I feel horrible. I loved him just as much as you loved Sydney, maybe more, because he loved me back. But you didn't want to hear that. Maybe that's why you didn't ask!"

He made no answer. He stood in the paddock and gazed at her helplessly. He looked overwhelmingly pathetic and totally out of place in his dark suit and starched white collar and black string tie, his polished black wingtips dusty with straw and soil. Was it any wonder that he lost himself in his work? It was all he had. She put her arms around him.

"I'm sorry," she said, her cheek pressed to his. She was—sorry for him and herself and everyone whose best seemed never to be good enough. "I know you did your best and I was happy in Harmony. Do as you like about the book. I don't really care."

"My little girl," he whispered. "Please don't cry. I can't bear to see you cry." He took out his handkerchief and dabbed her eyes, then at his own. "Come," he said, "let's walk in the orchard for a while. We can't let Polly see us like this."

They did not discuss *Aftermaths* again, but she knew he could not let it rest.

VI

"I'm sorry to drink and run," Theo said, setting his frosted glass of lemonade on the patio table, "but Rebecca expects me back for dinner. She doesn't know I flew down today—or why. Polly, I don't know how to thank you."

Polly smiled. "Theo, I'll find a way."

"Tyler," Theo said, turning to him, "I appreciate your confidence more than I can say."

"Not at all, my boy. I've always had confidence in you."

"Kate?" Theo turned to her. "Walk me to the plane, will you? There are a few things I need to discuss with you."

He waved at all of them and, with Kate at his side, left the terrace.

"A handsome couple," Tyler said, looking after them. "Well, I have some notes to organize before dinner, so if you ladies will excuse me until then?" He made a courtly little bow and went into the house.

"Yes, they are," Polly said.

" 'Yes, they are' what?" Dodie Phelps asked.

"A handsome couple, both of them tall as redwoods. If people were mated like horses, Theo'd have married Kate, not Rebecca, and bred a line of giants."

"Married couples are either logical pairs or terribly ill assorted, have you ever noticed?"

"Did Theo barely take his eyes off Kate the whole time he was here, or am I dreaming?" Polly asked.

"If you are, we shared the same dream," Dodie Phelps replied. "But they've been through a miserable time lately. It's only natural that they turn to each other for comfort."

"I hope comfort's all they're after. Kate's very vulnerable just now, and the last thing she needs is half a loaf."

VII

Kate, walking with Theo across the carpet of grass between the house and the field, was very conscious of her hand in his. She had been uncomfortable in Theo's company since Rebecca's wild suggestion. It had been impossible since then to look at him in the same way she had before. It was like one of those trick photographs: once the eye converts the shapes into a new pattern, it's impossible to see the picture any other way.

"It's always a treat to see you," Theo said.

"You too." Her hand tingled in his. She was intensely aware that he was male and virile, kind and familiar, a part of her life, someone she loved, someone she needed. "Are you about ready to sail?" she asked him.

"Yes." He paused. "I wish you were coming too."

She almost said she would; it was going to be lonely without them.

"I have a show to do," Kate said.

"I don't think your heart's in it anymore. I think it started as a way of asserting yourself with Win and you went on with it just to keep busy."

Kate was surprised. "How did you know that?"

"Because I know *you*. You're very important to me, Kate."

She looked for something uncompromising to say and could think of nothing at all. They had reached the plane. He put his hands on her shoulders and bent his head to kiss her lips, as he had always done. She turned her head and his mouth grazed her cheek. She realized how much she wanted to be kissed, to be held, to be loved by someone who cared about her as he did.

She moved away from him. "See you two in New York next week," she said.

He looked at her for a long moment, almost spoke, then nodded and climbed into the plane. She waited until he took off before she left to walk slowly back to the house.

Theo, aloft, knew he was in love with her. He had always loved her as a person; now he desired her. It was a puzzle to him because he still loved Rebecca. He would never have believed that a man could love two women at the same time; that kind of drivel was for romance novels. But there was no joy in a revelation that must not and could not lead anywhere. She was like a princess in a tower; he had to keep her locked inside his fantasy.

"Easier said than done," he told himself while the plane hurtled toward Washington and home and Rebecca.

VIII

Brosie and Belle were waiting when Kate got back to the house. Brosie held up a pitcher of martinis and Kate nodded.

"We just piled in the car and drove out as soon as we heard you were visiting." Belle handed her a glass. "Why didn't you tell us?"

"I was going to call you tonight. I was too wrung out to do more than sleep in the sun like a lizard when I arrived. Barely uttered a word until lunch today."

"You do look a little peaky," Brosie agreed. "I was hoping you'd pay us a visit in Charleston."

Kate smiled fondly at them. The twins were wearing their favorite gray flannels, Oxford button-downs, and V-necked sweaters the same blue as their eyes. They were Kate's age, but the radiance of youth was still upon them, and they looked like beautiful children to Kate. They grew ever more alike, as if time were superimposing each upon the other, making one of two. They finished each other's sentences and seemed to communicate without speaking. Arabella never talked about her husband, although she occasionally referred to her two daughters. Ambrose never mentioned his sister's family at all.

"I don't have the energy to drag myself to Charleston this time," Kate said. "But stay for dinner so we can visit."

"It's fixed. As soon as Gran went in to rest I told Curtis to set two more places," Belle said.

"Is Polly still badgering you two?"

Bella nodded. "She wants me to do charity work and have more babies and Brosie is an unmarried disgrace. She says we're lazy and shiftless."

"Maybe she's right. What do you do with yourselves all day?"

"The usual." Brosie smiled disarmingly. "We play tennis in the morning, have lunch at the club, swim or ride or play bridge until tea time, and then drink steadily until we fall, drunk and disorderly, into bed."

Kate shook her head. "Stop joking. I really want to know."

"Well, Belle's had about enough of teas and hospital committees and I of stockbrokering," Brosie began.

"So we're going to open an antiques shop!" Belle finished breathlessly. "But don't tell Gran! It's on Battery, in a corner room of one of those stunning old houses near the gardens. The sweetest old lady owns the house . . ."

". . . but she's outlived everyone in her family," Brosie took it up, "and she's so lonely she'd have let us sell dirty postcards if we wanted to."

"I think that's a terrific idea," Kate said. "But why not tell Polly?"

"She fusses whenever we do anything together," Belle said.

"At your age?" Kate said. "I'd think you were old enough to do whatever you want."

In the good old days, Kate thought, *they'd have lived together, spinster sister and bachelor brother, and no one would have said a word about it.*

"I keep telling Arabella we're old enough," Brosie said meaningfully.

The twins looked at each other, then at Kate.

"He's still after me to leave Ross," Belle said.

Don't tell me, Kate pleaded with them silently, her face absolutely impassive. *I don't want to know.* Other people's secrets and sorrows were weighing her down. She had enough of her own. Why couldn't everyone be simple-minded and uncomplicated and happy?

The moment passed.

"I want to hear about your show." Belle clapped her hands like a girl. "We're glued to the screen every Friday night."

"Our ratings have been pretty decent in the South," Kate said. "I don't know if it's the content or the Benedict connection."

"The content," Brosie assured her. "Genteel southern ladies are all closet feminists. If they ever come out, they'll come out swinging. Look at Aunt Felicity, kicking over the traces at her age."

Felicity had finally gone off to live on Bali with her lover.

"Is she all right?"

Brosie nodded. "She got a good divorce settlement. Maynard was glad to be rid of her, and after she made a scandal by running away with that man, there was nothing Gran could do but agree. Felicity sent us a picture. She was done up like a native, hung all over with exotic flowers."

"It sounds lovely," Kate said.

"I suppose you'll be doing your show for years," Belle said to Kate.

"I'm not sure I want to."

Two pairs of blue eyes turned on her, waiting for an explanation.

"I didn't really know I felt this way," Kate said thoughtfully, "until I'd had a few days down here to think things over. Sometimes, in New York, you run so hard just to keep up that you forget what you're running for. I don't have the least interest in pushing my ratings by talking about sex. That's what they really want, you know, sex dressed up to sound like scholarship. No politics, no economics, just sex."

"Come on, Cousin Kate, you're better than that, and you know it," Brosie said seriously.

"Yes, I do know it. That's why I've put off signing another contract.

I'm about convinced I've had enough. But don't tell Polly! If she thinks I'm free, she'll have me running for office before we know it!"

By the time Kate returned to New York, she had virtually decided to quit *Kate & Company*, but she had no idea what she would do in its place. First she had to face a dinner with her mother and von Rayner.

26

I

"You could have done better than that!" Sydney said reproachfully to Kate. She turned to her husband for support, but von Rayner went on eating his dinner.

"No promises," Kate reminded her. She had purposely chosen to discuss Tyler in a restaurant so that Sydney's inevitable scene would be brief and sotto voce.

"You didn't really try!"

"Come, my dear," von Rayner calmed her. He had buttered a bit of roll and now he tucked it into his wife's mouth tenderly, as if he were feeding a child. It seemed ludicrous to Kate, knowing what she did about their intimate relationship.

The tiny hairs on the back of Kate's neck rose each time she set eyes on the baron. It always took her several moments to compose herself and behave normally in his company. Yet the man was unfailingly polite, sartorially impeccable, and attractive. It was more what one could sense about him, Kate decided, than what one could see. He was terribly clean, almost excessively so, from his starched, high shirt collars to his buffed, manicured nails.

Von Rayner was buttering another piece of roll. "I'm sure Kate did her best." He favored Kate with a red-lipped smile before he put the bread into his mouth and chewed it neatly.

"I told him it would be a better book without it," Kate said. "Maybe that will sway him."

What am I doing here? she wondered. *Apologizing for history to a Nazi?*

More than that, by what peculiar combination of circumstance did she now find herself, crowding forty, divorced, and uninspired by her work, dining with her errant mother and her errant mother's aberrant

298

husband? The girl who hid in the hedge on Elm Terrace had not come very far if this was the best she could do.

"Really, Hansi," Sydney was saying. "Maybe it's not so serious after all. What can Tyler possibly say about a political union fifty years ago between two countries that have always been joined at the hip? If Waldheim weathered that SS storm—and the mess was his own fault, mind you, for putting himself in the limelight as he did—we can deal with this. There's nothing Tyler can do to harm the few supporters of the *Anschluss* who are still alive." She waved a deprecating hand, sparkling with jewels. "Or their sons."

"People are always ready to believe the worst," von Rayner said, favoring Kate with another meager stretch of his lips. "Alas, we can do nothing more than wait and see."

"Hansi, it's nothing to do with you," Sydney said. "You were only thirteen years old."

Kate found it very difficult to imagine him at thirteen. It aroused her curiosity. "I've never met anyone who was in Berlin in 1945," she said. "Do you remember what it was like?"

He put down his fork and knife, touched his napkin to his lips, and sighed. "I shall never forget. It was Armageddon. The end of everything. *Die Götterdämmerung.* But I didn't think so then." His voice grew nostalgic as he looked inward to his memories. "Then it was dynamic, electrifying, stimulating. Even that flattened, devastated city had a certain savage beauty, the beauty of courage, of blood and war. The roar of the guns was like cosmic thunder. It was, after all, a cosmic event, attended by the gods, the collapse of one of history's mightiest empires. I was thirteen, and at thirteen one feels not only omnipotent but immortal. At thirteen, one's heroes still live."

Sydney watched her husband raptly, lips parted, eyes aglow.

"What were you doing there?" Kate asked, unnerved by both of them.

"I was a courier. Communications had been destroyed by the bombings, so we ran messages between the *Führerbunker* and the units defending Berlin."

"Were you ever inside the bunker?"

"No, but I saw Him once." Kate could hear the upper case H. The baron still looked inward, remembering. "It was near the *Reichstag*—a field of ruins by then—and he came to talk to us."

"What was he like?" Kate wondered, fascinated.

"People say he was not the most prepossessing man at first sight, but he was greater than the sum of his parts, as genius often is. He had pale skin—the more so then because he had been in the bunker for days—and the most hypnotic eyes I have ever seen. It was when you saw his eyes that you felt his extraordinary power. He was pure in his mission and in himself." The baron smiled fondly, still gazing into the past. "He had an encouraging word for each of us. He patted my cheek." The baron's hand moved to his face and hovered, searching for that ghostly caress. "He was very fond of children and young people."

"Unless they were Jewish or Catholic or Gypsies," Kate said. "Then he gassed them."

"Kate, for heaven's sake!" Sydney protested.

"Let's not romanticize the monster," Kate said.

Von Rayner had come out of his reverie. "I discovered those things only later on," he said in his normal voice. "You may imagine, Kate, what it was like for me, a boy on the brink of manhood, to learn of such horrors, to watch my world collapse, to see my heroes destroyed or degraded by trial."

"And your father?"

"Killed in that same Battle of Berlin."

"What is Tyler likely to say about your father?"

"That he was a charter member of the Nazi party and a member of the SS. That is true. What is not true is that I have followed in his footsteps, that I belong to a group which believes that the reunification of Germany will be the first step to a Fourth Reich which will finish the business of the Third."

"That is not true?" Kate asked.

"Of course not!" Sydney said.

Von Rayner sipped his wine. "The destruction of my country left deep scars. Even though West Germany flourishes now, I never go there without remembering the massive ruin of our cities at the end of the war. That is why I prefer to live in Vienna. No," von Rayner said, shaking his head. "I would not risk such colossal destruction again."

"Unless you were sure you'd win," Kate remarked.

"May we please change the subject," Sydney said loftily.

As soon as they were alone, von Rayner told his wife, "If she cannot stop him, you must."

"What can *I* do?"

"Go to see him. It's vital that he not stir things up at this point when everything is going so well for our cause. We *must* have reunification! We will never control Europe unless we do. The man is still in love with you. If need be"—he paused significantly—"you must charm him into submission in bed."

She glared at the suggestion. "I doubt he's capable anymore."

"He is not required to make love to you. You are required to make love to him."

"But he despises me! You still don't understand how much! When

Tyler has a bee in his bonnet, he might as well be on another planet. I'm the only one who could ever . . ." Her voice trailed off.

"Quod erat demonstrandum," he said. "You don't usually underestimate your charms, Sydney. You are still a beautiful woman. Few men can resist you, and certainly not Tyler."

"If you really loved me, you wouldn't send me to bed with him!"

"Don't talk like a middle-class hausfrau," he replied. "What possible difference could it make to you to go to bed with your ex-husband? You've done it so many times before. We are threatened, Sydney. We must take desperate measures."

"All right," she agreed sullenly. "But only after we've seen the galley proofs."

"I have arranged to get one of the advance copies sent out by his publisher's foreign rights department." He pinched her cheek. "All in all, *Liebchen*, the trip has not been a failure."

II

In two days the baron and Sydney were gone. Theo and a reluctant Rebecca sailed not long after on the *QE II*. Aside from Stanton and Tillinghast, Kate knew no one in New York except John Mallory. Maybe that was why she went to bed with him.

Or maybe it was the divorcee's affliction, that need to prove she was still attractive to men. Maybe she missed the muscular feel of a man's body or succumbed to the heady wine of his desire for her. After all, did it matter which man's hands aroused her, whose mouth excited her, which body penetrated hers in pursuit of the ultimate twitch?

"What a lot of work," Kate said when they were lying side by side, "for a paroxysm that lasts only five or six seconds."

"A paroxysm? Is that all it was to you?" he asked, and her heart sank. Win's ego would not have been bruised. He would have laughed with her.

"That was a philosophical reflection," she said, "not a rating."

"Thank God for small mercies," Mallory said. He was still for a time, stroking Kate's hair. Then he said, "Kate, will you marry me?"

"No, but it's sweet of you to ask."

"Why not?"

"You're a good man, Mallory. You deserve more than what I have to offer. I don't love you."

"You must feel *something* for me, or we wouldn't be here like this."

"I feel a great deal for you, but I don't love you. I like your company, your conversation, and your technique."

"What more do you want?"

"Nothing more. I'm content. Let's leave it at that."

She was virtually certain he wouldn't be content to leave it at that indefinitely. He had never been married; maybe that was why he was so eager to try it.

III

Over the next several weeks Kate did her show, continued to see John Mallory, and arranged to spend alternate weekends at Kel Regis; she usually arrived on Saturday morning and flew back on Wednesday night. Polly's other guests were almost invariably political. Benedict money and influence were as sought after as The Senator's vote had been.

The guests and their wives or mistresses rode, hunted in season, played tennis, volleyball, croquet—and talked politics. Deals were made, feuds ended or begun, plots hatched, and plans made for the next election.

"Have you really settled on Clem Case?" Kate demanded of Polly.

"Golden Boy'll be all right. He just needs to be brought on a bit."

"Do you really believe people will vote for him because he's pretty?"

"He's more than that, although looks are an asset to a politician. Think of JFK. And Clem's wife is no fool. She's the one who winds him up every morning, the way Nancy does Ronnie. She whispers in his ear what we tell her to whisper. I've always wanted to be the power behind the power behind the throne."

Kate shook her head. "You wanted to be the throne itself."

"And you wanted to be the best academic in the world."

"Do people ever get what they want?"

"Sometimes, for a little while. Never for longer than that, unless they're one of the lucky ones with a calling." Polly paused. "What do you want now, Kate?"

"To go riding," Kate said, avoiding a question to which she had no answer. "I'll see you at tea time." She picked up her crop and her sweater and made for the stables. The groom waved when he saw her coming and went inside to saddle up one of the Charlies.

"Was the first Charlie's Darling foaled here?" she asked the boy when he led the horse out to the stable yard.

"Ask old Joe Singer." He gestured to the grizzled old man who was always to be found somewhere near the horses. "He'll know. He's been here a long time." The groom laughed. "Mama says he was here for Noah's flood."

Joe Singer, wizened, white-haired, and garrulous, remembered. "That colt was a gift to Missy from a Kentucky horse breeder name of

Mr. Charles Travis. They said no one knew more about horses than him. He stayed a long time, tradin'. Seem like he'd never leave, but one day he did and sent a present. That colt was the primest horse-flesh I ever did see, and Missy knew it too, so she bred him and his get real careful through the years." He nodded toward Carolina's stall. "That new little fella's a champeen. Spit of the first one."

"What will they call him?"

"Missy say Charlie's Pride. If he outlive his sire and granddaddy, we rename him Charlie's Darlin'."

"Well, thank you, Joe Singer. That's a nice story."

Riding through the orchard toward the woods, she wondered idly about Polly's devotion to the horse and its descendants and about the Kentucky horse breeder who had given such a magnificent creature to the Kel Regis stud so long ago when Polly was still a young woman. Sitting on Polly's bed later that night, brushing her hair, she asked about Charles Travis.

IV

"Charlie Travis was a fine man," Polly said. "Everyone liked him."

Kate was struck by the tenderness in her voice, by the flush in her cheek. Polly was very seldom sentimental.

"He was a great reader too," Polly went on with a hint of pride. "I had just finished building and stocking my library, so we had a great deal to talk about."

Kate, thinking that young Polly must certainly have had a soft spot for Charlie Travis, went on brushing her hair. "Did he ever come back?"

"No."

"Did you ever see him again?"

Polly glanced at Kate and replied in her usual brisk fashion. "No, but he sent Charlie's Darling to thank Oliver and me for our hospitality. He stayed here, you see, while he was trading all over the neighboring counties."

"Those were the days of lavish hospitality and grand gestures," Kate said.

The days of wine and roses, Polly thought. *Was I ever that young? How could I have let him go when I loved him so much?*

"It's not all gone yet," she said, "not here in the South."

"No, I suppose not."

Polly peered at Kate over her eyeglasses, and her instinct told her that this was the moment. "I have something important to tell you," she said.

Kate put down her brush. "I'm listening."

"I've been asked by the board of trustees to offer you the presidency of Wakefield College."

Kate gazed at her, speechless.

"Before you decide, you should know the facts. Wakefield's in trouble, along with a lot of other fine institutions—Brooke Parrish among them. Our enrollments are falling. You'd be surprised how many youngsters still think of us as a predominantly female academy. We must give qualified students reasons to come here instead of going elsewhere. Our football team is one."

"And you think I'm another?"

"For the parents, you combine new ideas with old values. For the students, you have the glamour of television and, regrettably, your liaison with a famous actor. I'm not the only one who thinks you'd be a draw. I happen to know you'll get a similar offer from Brooke Parrish. I took advantage of blood ties to get our bid in first."

Kate's first reaction was mixed: eagerness and suspicion.

She wants something, Kate thought, regarding her grandmother. *Polly always wants something, but what?*

She temporized. "I have no administrative experience," she said.

"We can hire that. What we need is flair."

"Flair," Kate said skeptically. "A figurehead. Is that part of the job description?"

Polly laughed. "Nowadays it is, for presidents of all kinds."

"What about President Hines?"

"Heart attack. The doctors say he'll be all right, but he'd be foolish to go on working. We need someone immediately."

"I'll go to see him," Kate said. "But first tell me how you envision the job."

"You'll set the academic tone. Inspire the students. Represent the establishment to the world. Keep the faculty in trim. Raise funds."

"I don't know the first thing about fund-raising."

"Don't have to. Theo will tell you how and when you're needed."

Kate shook her head with an admiring smile. "Is that why you made him a trustee? What a foxy lady you are!"

"Only if I can put you in the president's chair. Why don't you go and sleep on it?"

But Kate's uncertainty would not let her sleep. What was Polly's real motive? Did she think this would bring Kate under her control at last? Or did she want a president she supposed she could dominate? Was all of this personal or professional?

"But think what I could do!" she told herself softly, lying flat on her back in bed that night. "If I make it a condition that she cannot interfere with my academic decisions, just think how I could bring balance into a coed school, enlarge the curriculum, add some courses to make them think!"

Enthusiasm began to weigh more heavily than her suspicions of her grandmother. She would soon be at loose ends, and the presidency of a fine college had suddenly been offered her.

The groves of academe were home to her, the most compatible surroundings she had ever known. A scholastic environment appealed to her infinitely more than television. Even New York had lost a lot of its charm for her; it was inextricably tied to the first golden years of her marriage. And her desultory affair with Mallory had to be terminated before it became a problem.

She could think of no reason to refuse Polly's offer, and the next morning she was up early, waiting impatiently for Polly to ring the bell that announced she was awake and awaiting her breakfast tray.

Kate strode up and down the corridor outside Polly's bedroom, stopping from time to time to look at the miniatures of Benedicts and Ardmores that adorned its walls, thinking about her student years at Wakefield, remembering the broad green campus and the lofty oaks shading it, remembering the red brick, white-columned president's mansion where she would live, the bicycle lanes and the bridle paths, the neoclassical library. Maybe it was possible for her to go home again, to put herself together and be as she was before her disastrous marriage.

At last the maid appeared with Polly's breakfast tray and Kate opened the door for her and followed her into Polly's room.

Polly, propped up by a bed rest with overstuffed arms, wore a pink gauze cap to protect her hairdo and a pink shawl crocheted by one of the maiden aunts. The bed was strewn with morning papers, one of which she was reading.

"When will Clem learn to keep his mouth shut?" she demanded, rattling the paper. "He misspoke himself again!"

"I told you so," Kate said. "But never mind him. I've decided."

Polly put down the paper and gave her a piercing look. "Yes or no?"

"Yes."

Polly beamed. "Well, great day in the morning! You'll do us proud, Kate."

"There's one condition."

"I know. You want to do it your way."

"Or there's no point in my doing it at all. I don't intend to interfere with things I know nothing about, but when it comes to curriculum and learning environment, I want complete authority."

"Done," Polly said.

"I think I should have it from the board," Kate said warily. "Or are you the board?"

"Almost. And it's a joy to know just how much you trust me! But I'll arrange a formal meeting about terms and conditions."

"I can't believe it!" Kate said excitedly. "This is the best thing that's happened to me in a long time. I'm too impatient to sit still."

"Go for a gallop. Then come back and we'll talk."

But they had no time to talk when Kate came back. There was an urgent message from Theo. Rebecca had collected enough sleeping pills to very nearly kill herself.

V

"She was depressed when I left her over there," Theo said, "and in the past two months, with two negative prognoses from the specialists, she must have gone downhill. I should have known."

"How bad is she?"

"Still sleeping—or so they say. She's in a top-notch private clinic in Zurich. They assured me they got to her in time. She'll recover."

"Where was Alice, for God's sake?"

"Alice found her. It wasn't her fault. You know how clever Rebecca can be. But Alice is hysterical with guilt and won't be much moral support when Rebecca awakens. I'm flying over tomorrow. Will you come with me?"

"I can't come with you! I'd just have to turn around and fly back for my program. I'll come on Saturday." Kate thought a minute. "I'll call Sydney. She can sit with Rebecca until you get there."

"*Sydney?*"

"Yes. She's not as bad as she was. She doesn't get hysterical over anyone but herself. Anyway, Sydney's better than no one at all. And she's always fascinated Rebecca. They can talk about the good old days."

Theo was quiet for a moment. Then he said, "If she can talk at all. Kate, I don't know what's going to become of Becca and me."

"Nothing good unless you stop lying to each other."

"I must go," he said, evading an answer.

"I'll see you in Zurich."

VI

Stanton was more upset about Kate's decision to leave the show than Tillinghast was.

"My princess wants to go someplace in California," he said, "but I told her it's one big whorehouse out there. If you're at Wakefield, she'll agree to go there."

"Wakefield is coed now, and the preservation of maidenheads is not guaranteed."

"But the odds are better." He paused to survey Kate, his head tilted back. "I had an idea you'd decide to leave. You're good at this, but it isn't your thing."

"Hire Dora Suponik to replace me."

He guffawed.

"I'm serious. The woman wants to be a star. Then you can book a bunch of feminists to mop the floor with her."

He exchanged a look with Stanton, who cast her eyes heavenward.

"I'm sorry, Stan," Kate said. "I didn't plan it this way."

"It's your life. Frankly, I think you're crazy."

"No. A campus is where I belong."

All the way to Zurich, Kate felt as if she had put her life back on track. But first she had to deal with Rebecca's.

27

I

Sydney sat in an armchair in Rebecca's room in the private sanitarium near Zurich. She was reading Anaïs Nin's *Delta of Venus*, the erotica discreetly concealed by a burgundy velvet cover decorated with von Rayner's crest in gold. Every once in a while she glanced over at the sleeping woman in the bed, but Rebecca hadn't moved since Sydney's arrival.

Sydney stirred restlessly, not much entertained by the book. She hated hospitals and would not have come here for anyone in the world but Kate. Sitting up with a suicidal woman—and God alone knew what grotesques were chained up down the hall!—was not Sydney's cup of tea, but she hadn't dared refuse the first thing Kate had ever asked of her.

"I must go," she had told the baron.

"Of course you must."

"Come with me."

"You know I detest Zurich. It's provincial and boring."

Sydney knew, but she had her suspicions about Hansi and the child bride who had been at her wedding all those years ago. The child had grown into a woman notorious for the number and variety of her lovers, and Sydney was certain Hans Erik was one of them. She was not principally concerned about where he put his penis; what upset her was that he might fall in love with the younger woman. Men were so foolish at his age. For the moment, however, he was so discreet about it that all Sydney had were suspicions. Sydney knew that as long as a man was discreet, a wife was safe. Once a man went public with an affair, divorce was as inevitable as snow in winter, unless a woman had absolutely no pride at all.

But if she divorced him, what sort of replacement would she be able to find?

Sydney put her head back and closed her eyes. She felt lonely and horribly old. She needed another face-lift. It was so unfair that women didn't age as well as men. Kate said nature had planned it that way so that men would discard their withered, barren wives to mate with younger women and produce more children. It guaranteed survival of the species.

Kate tended to be infuriating about such matters. Who else would look at betrayal and blame nature for it? In Sydney's opinion, men dumped their aging wives because men were bastards and that was that.

Sydney couldn't believe she had come to be as old as she was. Nearly sixty! Where had all the years gone? She put the book down and remembered.

II

A week after her sixth birthday party, Sydney stood on a table in the boat house at Kel Regis with her panties down around her ankles and her small skirt hitched up to her middle.

"Gosh," her cousin Stuart breathed, round-eyed at the revelation. "They gone and cut Sydney's off!"

There was a loud bray of laughter from Sydney's brother, Hilliard. "You're such a dope, Stuey."

The six-year-old bristled. "Who you callin' a dope? There's the scar, plain as day."

"They didn't cut it off, dummy. She never had one. Girls don't. That's why they're so weak and puny." Hilliard turned toward the closed door of the boat house, which was situated on the river, a half mile from the mansion, and called to the boys clustered outside it. "Anyone else want to look? It's only five cents."

"How much to touch?" came a somewhat deeper voice through the door.

Hilliard, tall for a boy of seven, glanced at his little sister. She shook her head, but he grinned and called out "Two bits," precipitating a buzz of whispers from the other side of the door.

Sydney sniffed. "Mama says it's common to use slang expressions like 'two bits,'" she said, and dropped her skirt.

"Pull it up," Hilliard ordered.

"My arms are getting tired," she returned haughtily. "Anyway, there's no one here but Cousin Stuart, and he's already had his look." She smiled down at Stuart, whose face was still scarlet with dismay at his awful discovery. "I'd have let you look for free, Stu," Sydney said sweetly. "You're my cousin."

There was a tap on the door and the same voice called, "We have four to look and one to touch. We'll pay an extra nickel if the lookers can stay to watch the toucher."

"Hot damn," Hilliard whispered. "A dime," he called back.

After a moment's consultation on the other side of the door the bargain was struck, the door opened, and five boys came in. They ranged in age from six to twelve. Most of them were from neighboring houses, none of which were nearly as grand as Kel Regis; half of them were related, closely or distantly, to the Benedicts. They had all been at Sydney's birthday party the week before, dressed in short pants, knee socks, and round collars, their hair slicked down and their Buster Brown shoes polished.

Only one of them, Royal Benedict, was old enough, at twelve, to wear long pants every day. Now he swaggered in and stood at the back of the cluster of little boys, chewing on a straw, grinning at Sydney's panties lying like a crushed flower around her ankles.

With a defiant little toss of her head, she stepped out of the panties and kicked them away. They landed in the corner on a coil of rope.

Sydney, who was not making her debut in this performance, waited unruffled, more than content to be the center of attention no matter how she attained the position. Under ordinary circumstances, she never did.

Just a week ago, on the day of her very own birthday party, she had come down with a fever and been forced to watch her brothers take turns riding her new pony on the lawn beneath her window. She had not endured that outrage quietly, and her howls were silenced only by the appearance of her mother in the room, a rare event in this household of maids and aunts and nannies.

"Explain yourself, Sydney."

"They're riding *my* pony," Sydney had retorted from the window seat, sobbing less noisily.

"What of it?"

"I missed *my own* party!" Sydney wailed again. "And the pony's *mine*. No one's supposed to ride *my* pony before I do."

"Be still, Sydney! You're not that important."

"Yes, I am! I'm beautiful! Daddy says so!"

"That doesn't make you important. Now get back into bed. If I hear you caterwauling again, I'll lock you in the closet."

So there it was, from the fount of all wisdom: Sydney wasn't important. But she wanted to be. The only girl in a houseful of brothers, she needed to be.

When she stood on the table in the boat house, she was.

|||

The boys crowded around the table while Hilliard collected his fee.

"How do I know she'll let me touch her?" Royal demanded, reluctant to part with his money.

Oh, I will, I will, Sydney thought. He was as beautiful as she was.

Hilliard shrugged. "She does what I tell her to do."

From her lofty height, Sydney gave the two boys a bored glance, then looked off at a patch of sky visible through the high window.

"Lookers line up first," Hilliard commanded. "Toucher is last. All right, Sydney. Curtain up."

There was a mixed reaction to the plump, bifurcated mound Sydney displayed. The smaller boys gazed at the spectacle, two in stony silence, two in horror. One of the innocents repeated Stuart's remark, to outbursts of laughter from the others.

"If that's so, how does she pee?" the second startled child asked.

"From somewhere inside," he was told.

"I want to see her pee."

"That'd cost you more money than you'll ever have. Next."

When the lookers had finished, it was Royal Benedict's turn.

The boat house fell suddenly silent as the tall boy stood looking at his prize. Royal was one of the "dark Benedicts," an impecunious branch of the family favored with curly brown hair, olive skin, and dazzling white teeth in place of money. Some people whispered about the origins of that skin and those teeth, but the Benedicts always pointed to portraits of eighteenth-century cousins by marriage who had been sugar merchants and governors of Cuba.

"A lick of the tar brush," some people whispered, "is a lick of the tar brush, no matter what lingo it speaks."

At this moment Royal's winsome smile was not in evidence. He stared at Sydney, and this time she did not look away.

"Go on," Hilliard said. "You're using up your time."

"You didn't set any time limits," Royal said. "I paid good money and I'll feel her up as long as I want."

"She's *my* sister," Hilliard said, his thin brows gathering into a scowl as he stepped between Royal and the table. "I say how long you can feel her up."

Royal stepped around him and, still watching Sydney, thrust his right forefinger into his mouth. A gasp sounded from the watching boys as they pressed closer to see, but Sydney was oblivious to them.

Mesmerized, she watched him withdraw his finger from his mouth, slip it inside her, and slide it back and forth. It was what she did to herself, alone in bed at night, but this felt even better. The pleasing digit was removed, remoistened, and replaced, and this time it curled upward and snaked a little way inside her. She closed her eyes, basking in the sensation. In and out it went with a lovely silky feeling.

"You, Royal! You stop that now, you hear?" she heard Hilliard say in a funny voice. "That's enough. You'll break her cherry and there'll be hell to pay."

"I'm not hurting her," Royal said. "Look at her. She loves it."

"Hello, down there!" a flutey female voice called from the road. "What are you children doing shut up in the boat house on such a lovely day?"

There was a hasty scramble. Sydney was lifted down from the table and her skirt smoothed. In absolute silence the table itself was moved to its habitual place in the corner.

Hilliard glanced quickly around. "Jesus Christ," he said, pointing at Royal's crotch. "You got a hardon!"

"So do you," Royal retorted.

"Children?" The high female voice had come closer.

"Here," Hilliard pleaded, extending a piece of canvas to Royal. "Put that in your lap." He sat down quickly himself and drew his knees up to his chest.

"We're just tellin' ghost stories, Auntie Lucia," Hilliard called. Among themselves the children called her Auntie Lush.

He glared at the boys, two of them rolling on the floor in an attempt to muffle their mirth. "Y'all shut up or I'll whip you," he whispered fiercely. "You, Sydney, you get over here by me."

Reluctantly, Sydney left Royal's side and was sitting meekly with her brother when Hilliard noticed the panties lying on a coil of rope. His face went white as the door opened.

"What's this?" Lucia demanded, looking around the circle. "Sydney, what are you doing here? You know you're forbidden to play with the boys. They're a sight too rough for a little thing like you."

"They weren't rough, Auntie," Sydney said, smiling at Royal. "They were real sweet."

"We weren't playing games, Auntie," Hilliard said. "We were just telling ghost stories."

"That's no better. The little ones will be having nightmares for a week. Come along, Sydney honey." She stretched out her hand and bent to peer more closely at her charge. "Are you all right, sugar?" she asked solicitously.

Sydney could smell the wine on her breath and the faintly stale perspiration preserved in her well-worn silk dress.

"I'm fine, Auntie Loosha," Sydney said. "I'm just fine."

She looked at Royal and then, with a wicked little glance at her panties, she took her aunt's hand and trotted dutifully out of the boat house. She was led up to the mansion by her aunt, who lectured her all the way about playing with those rough boys. Sydney's mother, who always seemed to be everywhere, saw them coming.

Lucia told her story. "Only the good Lord knows what might have happened if I hadn't seen their bicycles, if I weren't here to keep an eye on Sydney," she finished, justifying her position in the household.

Sydney's mother was studying her daughter's flushed face, when a puff of wind from the river lifted Sydney's small skirt.

"Holy Jesus!" Lucia screamed. "She's buck naked."

"I have eyes," Mother said curtly. "Sydney, explain yourself."

Sydney said nothing.

"What were you doing in the boat house without your underwear?"

"They just wanted to look," Sydney said.

"Lord preserve us!" Lucia breathed.

"And you obliged them? What kind of devil are you?"

"I don't know," Sydney said, beginning to cry.

"You're not normal," her mother said. "I swear I don't think you're mine. You're some kind of changeling."

"I *am too* normal," Sydney wept.

She was locked in her room and fed only bread and milk for a week —supplemented by all the goodies Hilliard smuggled in to her. He kept her entertained by climbing the big tree outside her bedroom window and reading her stories. She didn't tattle on Hilliard's part in the boat-house affair. She loved him too dearly and he loved her back. She knew that surely. The one she was never sure of was Royal.

IV

Mumbled words from the hospital bed roused Sydney. She went quickly to the bedside. Rebecca looked very small and not much older than the last time Sydney had seen her. She had been an exquisite child and she was a beautiful woman.

But what good is beauty, Sydney reflected, *when it's chained to a wheelchair?* She wondered what kind of husband Theo Barrows was and whether the couple still made love.

Suffused with pity, Sydney took her hand. "Rebecca? Rebecca, are you awake?"

"Where's Mama?" Rebecca demanded.

Sydney was startled. Rebecca's mother had been dead for years.

"Busy in the kitchen," Sydney said. Marjorie had spent most of her time in the kitchen—and much good it did her! "But I'm right here."

"Kate stayed late at school," Rebecca mumbled.

Have those pills destroyed her mind? Sydney wondered. "Kate will be home soon," she said.

Sydney pushed the nurse's call bell. In moments, Rebecca's starched, bulky private nurse appeared, but by that time Rebecca was in a deep sleep again.

"Well, it's a good sign that she spoke," the nurse said.

"But she talked as if she were about twelve years old!" Sydney said.

"She was dreaming," the nurse said. "Talking in her sleep."

"She was wide awake!" Sydney insisted. "Is she out of her mind? What does it mean?"

"We won't know until she's fully conscious. Time enough for her to take up her burden then, poor thing. Come along to the nurse's station, Baroness, and I'll give you a cup of tea."

Sydney followed her along the corridor, accepted weak tea in a thick pottery cup and saucer, and lit a cigarette. She looked at her tiny Patek Philippe watch, annoyed that she had to squint to see what time it was. Theo would be there soon, but Sydney had promised to stay with Rebecca until Kate arrived, and she wanted to please Kate—although Kate's disposition had been a bit tart lately.

She wants her actor, Sydney decided. *She's a one-man woman, just like me.* She finished the tea, crushed out the cigarette, and went back down the hall and into Rebecca's room.

She stood by the window, looking out at the tranquil, moonlit grounds of the clinic, and a little shiver went through her. It was unnatural to be alone in the deep of night with Kate's best friend going loony behind her. Sydney had absolutely no business there. Kate had no right to ask her to come.

Why do I always have to please other people? Sydney asked herself.

V

After that day in the boat house, Sydney trailed after Royal at every family party. She was in thrall, but he brushed her off like a ladybug.

"You're a baby, Sydney," he protested when she was eleven and trying to flirt with him at a family picnic. "Come around and see me when you grow up."

Sydney had set her mind to growing up as fast as she possibly could. She was overjoyed when her period began six months later and thrilled when her breasts started to develop. By the time she turned twelve, she had wheedled money out of Oliver and ordered a garter belt and black stockings from the OOH La La boutique in New Orleans. She "borrowed" her mother's high heels and practiced walking up and down, naked and clothed, in front of her bureau mirror, admiring her body as it rounded and produced fluffs of golden hair. She smuggled a medical book out of the library and located the relevant parts.

"Have you done it yet?" she asked Hilliard when he came home from prep school for Christmas.

He shook his head, blushing scarlet. "No one to do it with."

"Do it with me! I'm dying to know what it's like, aren't you?"

"Sydney! Brothers and sisters can't do it. It's a sin!"

"We're not getting married, Hilliard! We'll only do it once! How much of a sin can that be?"

Hilliard, who had begun to sweat lightly, agreed that she was probably right.

"But where'll we go to do it?" he worried.

"There are rooms on the third floor that haven't been used in years. I cleaned one up a little. Come on, I'll show you."

"You didn't clean it up much," Hilliard said when they got there, surveying the dusty room and its ramshackle bed.

"Nobody ever died from a little dust," Sydney reassured him, dropping her clothes.

Hilliard swallowed hard at the sight of her naked body. "Gosh, Syd, you've sure grown up."

She lay down on the bed. "Come on," she said, "before someone misses us." She watched him undress. "You've grown too," she laughed, pointing at his erection. "Is it always that big?"

He made a dive for the bed, landing next to her in a puff of dust. Sydney took his hand and held it to her breast. "Look, if you do this, the nipple stands up."

"Sydney," he groaned. "I'm going to pop in another minute."

"Don't you dare pop before we do it!" she said. She giggled when he couldn't find the way into her and, taking hold of him, guided him in. It was over almost immediately.

"Holy cow!" Hilliard said, collapsing on her.

"Well," Sydney said, "I don't think much of that, do you?"

"Sure. It was great."

"You sounded like it was hurting you."

"Hell, no!"

They began to laugh again, rolling around on the bed.

That was how Polly found them. She stood, livid with rage, as the two of them scrambled into their clothes. When they were dressed she called them before her and spoke in a voice that sounded to them like Judgment Day.

"What were you doing?"

"Nothing," Sydney said quickly.

"Why did you take your clothes off?"

"We always used to when we were kids. We were just fooling around."

Polly looked from one to the other as if she could read their thoughts.

"Listen to me," she said, still in that terrifying voice. "What you have done is not only a terrible sin, it's also a crime. They arrest people for doing that with their own kin. If it weren't for your father's political position, I'd call the police in right now and slap you both in jail. I blame Sydney for this," she went on, glaring at her daughter. "Sydney has always been evil, even as a baby, exposing herself to young boys in the boat house."

"But, Ma . . ." Hilliard protested, wanting to confess his part in all of it.

"Not a word from either of you," Polly commanded. "You will both swear to me, each on the head of the other and on pain of eternal hellfire, that you will never tell anyone what you've done and that you will never do it again."

They swore, more frightened of prison than of hellfire. The next day Polly said Hilliard needed tutoring and sent him back to school before the term began. Sydney was dispatched to her boarding school for the same reason. Polly barely spoke to Sydney after that. She saw to it that Sydney's clothes were ordered on time, that she attended the right dancing class and the right birthday parties, but mother and daughter were enemies from that day forward.

"I don't see why she's still so angry about it," Sydney wrote to Hilliard months later. "We were just curious."

"It was wrong," Hilliard wrote back. "I know that now. It was a serious sin. I'm sorry we did it and I don't want to talk about it anymore."

It was clear that Polly had been at him. Polly doted on Hilliard and hardly ever scolded him, but she did go on about this. Sydney loved Hilliard too much to nag him. As for *it*, there were plenty of young cousins around who were eager to do it with her. She never got a "reputation." The cousins knew they had a good thing going and never told anyone outside the family that Sydney "put out."

VI

"Who's there?" Rebecca demanded, rousing Sydney from a half sleep. Sydney got up and walked, somewhat stiffly, to the bed.

"Sydney. Kate's mother."

"I know who Sydney is." Rebecca spoke softly but with authority. "What are you doing here?"

"Sitting with you until your husband gets here. Kate asked me to come."

"I suppose she's coming too?"

Sydney nodded.

Rebecca sighed. "She'll lecture me."

"You deserve it."

"You're hardly the one to moralize, are you?"

"What I did was my fault and mine alone," Sydney said. "Suicide is everyone's fault. People think you wouldn't have if only they'd done better by you." She had always felt she could have saved Hilliard if she'd been there.

"Well, they have nothing to worry about now," Rebecca said bitterly. "Obviously I'm no good at it."

"I can't say I blame you for trying it," Sydney said. "In your place, I'd have wanted to do the same thing, but I wouldn't have had the courage."

"At last, someone who isn't perpetually cheerful, who doesn't treat paralyzed legs like heat rash!" Rebecca's voice was stronger.

"I never cared much for pretense," Sydney said.

Rebecca nodded. "Whatever else you are, Sydney, you're honest. On reflection, I'd have to say you always were."

"You're worried about your marriage, aren't you?"

Rebecca covered her face with her hands and nodded. "Oh, God," she moaned. "If he leaves me I'll die. I won't need pills, I'll just fade away and die. What am I going to do?"

"Get through it or try again."

Rebecca's hands came down. "You don't mince words, do you?"

"I thought you were all for honesty."

"So did I. Turn on the light so I can see you."

When Sydney obliged, Rebecca looked at her carefully. "Not bad," she said admiringly. Her eyes dropped from Sydney's face to inspect her figure and her jewelry. "You always looked so out of place in the kitchen on Elm Terrace with Kate worshipping at your shrine."

"Did she?" Sydney sounded genuinely pleased.

"Oh, yes. You really messed her up when you left."

Sydney said nothing.

"It can be a great burden to be adored by Kate," Rebecca went on. "You have to live up to her expectations of you." Rebecca began to cry. "Kate and Theo. I love them both, but they'll be so disappointed in me."

"Everyone I know is disappointed in *me*, but I survived and so will you. Now, stop crying. It stretches the skin around your eyes."

Rebecca's tears stopped abruptly. Then she gave a bark of hysterical laughter that went on and on, bringing the nurse on the run. The doctor was called and administered a sedative.

"This is ridiculous!" Sydney protested. "We've been waiting for her to wake up and when she does you put her back to sleep!"

"Baroness," the nurse said sharply. "This will calm her, not put her to sleep. Please be so good as to sit quietly or I shall have to ask you to leave."

Sydney sat down in the lumpy chair.

VII

Sydney was presented at the National Debutante Cotillion and Thanksgiving Ball in Washington, where Polly's ambition for Oliver was now directed, but her real coming-out party was in June. It was a lavish debut, held on the lush green lawns of Kel Regis with three dance floors under three marquees of pink and white silk and cascades of pink and white roses everywhere. Sydney's dress was white peau de soie, the fitted bodice embroidered in pink silk. Her father said she looked like a Gainsborough painting. Her brothers told her she was the prettiest girl in South Carolina—all but Hilliard, who partnered her first dance and was not pleased. He talked to her in low, desperate tones as they danced, his sensitive face reflecting his distress.

"Sydney, you've got to stop it."

"Stop what, honey?"

"Sleeping with every male relative we've got." He blushed. He was slim and dark-haired, not in the least like her other brothers.

"Who told you that?"

"It doesn't matter. I know you do. It's dirty and it's all my fault. If I hadn't done what I did, you wouldn't be like this. You'd be normal."

"You've been listening to Mama," Sydney said, giving him a dazzling smile to hide her anger from anyone who might be watching. "I *am* normal and it's not your fault and it's none of your business either."

He shook his head. "I haven't talked to Mama about it in years. *I'm* the one who's responsible for you. Sydney, please, you have to be good."

"I'll be whatever I want! And I don't need you preaching at me!" She broke away from him and walked, smiling and nodding, through the dancers. It was then that she saw Royal watching her from the line of young men who ringed the dance floor. Much as she loved Hilliard, Sydney didn't care two pins what he thought about her, once she set eyes on Royal Benedict.

VIII

Royal's education had been financed by the family, and after graduation he had been sent to Atlanta to work at Benedict Pharmaceuticals. He had stopped coming to family gatherings.

"My daddy says he hardly ever shows up at his office either," her cousin Stuart told Sydney. "He found out he could make more money on Atlanta society women than by working for the company."

"What does he do for the women?"

"Humps them, dummy! He's become a gigolo, and from what I hear, he's real talented at his trade."

"I'll bet it's the women who run after *him*."

"You're right about that. He's a handsome bastard."

He certainly was! She smiled radiantly now as he walked across the dance floor toward her, the most beautiful young man she had ever seen.

"I've been waiting for you," she told him. She had been, for years.

"Well, look at you, Sydney! You're unbelievable!" he said, his gorgeous dark eyes admiring her face and her pale gold hair and her breasts under the fabulous dress. "You've finally grown up."

"Am I old enough to dance with?"

He held out his arms, and she felt as if her dress would melt away when her body pressed against his. It was the way he held her, the way his hips moved against hers. She could feel him getting hard.

"Remember," he whispered, "that afternoon in the boat house?"

She nodded.

"I wish I were doing that to you right now."

Her face was hot. "So do I."

"Then let's go there and do it."

He danced her to the edge of the floor, then whisked her out of sight behind the marquee. Neither of them said a word until they were in the boat house, and then all he said was "take off your dress." He put it aside carefully and then took the rest of her clothes off himself.

He was a man who loved women's bodies, and he did things to her she had read about and blushed over, things the cousins had never had the nerve to attempt. He kissed her until she was dizzy and then he pushed her thighs apart and kissed her there until she almost fainted. He did it with such heat and passion that she wanted to do it to him. She had never wanted to do it before and she had never done it, but somehow she knew exactly how.

Royal made her body burn with desire and then he put the fire out. None of the cousins had ever done that either. She had never felt such utter bliss before, and it was more than sexual.

He gave her a handkerchief to stuff in her panties, helped her do up her dress, and lent her a comb to untangle her hair. "You're one helluva girl, Sydney," he said.

"I love you," she whispered. "I've loved you for years."

His arms went around her and he kissed her. The taste of her still lingered on his lips. "I think maybe I love you too," he said.

They were back at the party, dancing decorously, before they were missed, but from the day of her debut Royal was all Sydney dreamed of and thought about and waited for. The cousins lost their easy source of sex. She wanted only Royal, who came secretly to see her whenever he could. They met in a pine grove in the woods, and their appetite for each other did not diminish with time.

"I'm going to marry him," she told Hilliard.

"They'll never let you marry him, and you'd be crazy if you did. He's a lowlife and everyone knows it. Anyway, he won't ever ask you."

But Royal did ask, the Christmas of her freshman year at Wakefield, and Sydney said yes. They went hand in hand, like two innocents, to announce their engagement to Polly and Oliver.

Polly laughed before she said no. It was Polly who offered to make Royal a rich man provided he stayed far away from Sydney, and it was Royal who agreed to the bargain, looking somewhat relieved.

"I'll have the money from my trust the day I marry," Sydney protested. "They can't keep it from me, no matter what. I'll give you that."

"I'm sorry, honey," he told the clinging, weeping Sydney before he left her. "I can't turn down a fortune of my own. All I ever wanted was to be rich enough to do as I please. Anyway, I'd've been a lousy husband."

"I hate you!" Sydney screamed at her mother when he had gone.

"The feeling is mutual," Polly said. "You'll stay at college until you graduate. After that you'll marry the man I choose for you."

IX

But Sydney was damned if she'd let Polly choose anything else for her ever again, and above all not a husband. She so artfully seduced her history professor, Tyler Ballard, during the spring term that he considered himself the guilty party and was as much overcome with remorse as love. She was pregnant when her parents, seeing no alternative, announced her engagement.

It was certainly not the brilliant match everyone expected for Sydney Benedict, but Polly and Oliver, as Benedicts were raised to do, hid their dismay and told everyone the couple had their blessing. Oliver used his influence to have Tyler made head of the history department at Harmony College in New England since it was unthinkable that he stay on at Wakefield.

"And the less I see of that girl," Polly said more than once, "the better."

The wedding was even more sumptuous than her debut had been but, for Sydney the day was memorable because Royal was there. He had a note smuggled to her, saying he was waiting in the woods. She tried not to go to him, not after what he had done. And she really wanted to be Tyler's lily maid of Astolat, the pure angel he believed her to be. No one but Tyler had ever believed she was wonderful.

But resisting Royal was futile. She went to him, hating him, loving him, full of rage and passion and guilt, swathed in white satin and orange blossoms.

"Why did you do it?" he asked her after they made love.

"You don't want me. He does."

"Of course I want you! You're mine. You'll always be mine."

"Then take me with you!"

"No. I won't marry you—or any other woman. I can't live the way people are expected to, Sydney! Not even for you. I wish to God I could." He said it with such sadness that she flung her arms around him.

"Hush," she said. "Never mind. We're together now."

"I do love you, Sydney, in my own mixed-up way. You're the only woman I'll ever love."

That half hour in the woods was the most rapturous interlude she was to know until ten years later, when Royal came back into her life again. By then Sydney was thoroughly bored with being a faculty wife and mother, with living up to Tyler's idealized perception of her whenever he emerged from his work long enough to notice she was there.

Her trips to New York, ostensibly to see her cousin Eugenia, became more frequent when Royal was in town. How could she keep away? In bed, Tyler was gentle and dull; Royal was wild and exciting. Often he was rough. Sometimes he hurt her, but that only made the pleasure keener when it came. She still dreamed and hoped and waited to see him while she went through the motions in Harmony. She managed to do that for two years before she ran away with him.

It was an obsession that Sydney believed was love. But Royal loved no one for longer than a moment, and Sydney was hard put, when he would not be faithful to her, to love anyone but herself.

X

"Sydney?" A hand shook her gently and Sydney stirred and looked up at the tall man bending over her. "I'm Theo Barrows," he said. "Rebecca's husband."

She came awake with the grief and glory of her memories still upon her and a great void within her.

"I can't thank you enough for what you did," Theo said.

"I didn't do much," Sydney said. "Has she awakened?"

"Not completely. I have a car waiting downstairs to take you to your hotel. I'll stay with her now."

"I promised to stay until Kate got here."

"There's no need, really." He helped her up. Almost automatically, she smoothed her hair. He was a marvelous-looking man; that white hair was stunning. How in the name of God was Rebecca going to hold on to him? No wonder she was suicidal!

Theo helped her into her coat and would have accompanied her down to the car, but she told him to stay. "She needs to see you when she wakes up," she told him.

She went out, her melancholy over Rebecca's catastrophe mingling with that old, visceral grief for her own lost love.

28

Theo watched Sydney walk down the corridor to the elevator, her sable coat rippling around her. The once-notorious baroness intrigued him. Her legendary beauty was still there, even if it was long past first blush, and so was the sleek aura of a cosmopolitan woman of fashion. She had not lost her fabled sensuality either. Some women never did.

Theo closed the door and stood in the silent, dimly lit room. Sydney and Kate were a strange match as mother and daughter. There was something vaguely corrupt about Sydney while Kate . . . He sighed. He thought about her far too much, and his sexual fantasies about Kate had become an obsession. He manufactured ways to be with her. He called her several times a week. He could hardly contain himself when she accepted the presidency of Wakefield; it meant they would see each other far more often than before, might even spend weekends at Kel Regis together, grow closer, come to terms with the feelings they had for each other. He was certain they were mutual; she was as bereft and as bruised as he. It was her love for Rebecca that kept them apart.

Theo crossed to the bed and stood looking down at his wife, so lovely, so helpless. His heart lurched. He loved her deeply! He depended on her. The idea of life without her was agonizing. He sat down beside the bed and studied her. How vulnerable she was, how young, the small traces of the years smoothed away by sleep.

Tears filled his eyes. He was racked with guilt for the accident that had ruined her life—a moment's inattention on his part or a lack of skill?—and his desire for Kate only compounded the felony with disloyalty. He didn't want to feel that desire, but fighting it was like swimming against a current, making no progress, beginning to tire, longing to give in and let the whirlpool take him.

Rebecca stirred and opened her eyes. They looked at each other.

"Water," Rebecca whispered.

He helped her to sip some cool water and knew, when she winced, that her throat was sore from the tube they had used to pump her stomach.

"Darling," he began, taking her hand when she had finished.

"Don't scold me, Theo," she pleaded so softly he had to put his ear close to her lips to hear her. "I can't bear it."

He wanted to rage at her for planning to abandon him, but he said gently, "All right, little girl, I won't scold you."

He sat looking at her, his love for her written clearly on his face. She reached up to touch his cheek.

"Don't cry, Theo. It'll be all right."

He wanted to tell her that it would never really be all right again, that it would get worse unless he could tell her the truth about how he felt, but he hadn't the heart to berate her now.

They sat in silence, gazing at each other, both of them utterly miserable. When she closed her eyes and slept again, he rang for her private nurse and went to his hotel for a shower and a few hours of rest.

He was back at the clinic when Kate arrived. It made him feel better just to look at her, his tall, strong, sedate Kate, who hugged him as tenderly as a lover. He wanted her desperately, sweetly. He wanted to hold on to her, to lose himself inside her and rest.

"Maybe it's better for me to see her alone," Kate said.

Theo nodded. "I'll be in the waiting room."

II

Kate stood with her back against the door while the two women looked at each other.

"I never dreamed we'd come to this," Kate said.

"To what?"

"I don't know what to say to you! Help me, Rebecca! What would you say to me if I'd tried to kill myself?"

"I wouldn't say anything." Rebecca's voice shook. "I'd put my arms around you."

Kate went quickly to the bed, gathered Rebecca into her arms, and held her close. "Forgive me, dear old pal of mine," she whispered, "for whatever I didn't do to help you. I love you so."

Kate eased Rebecca back against her pillows and sat next to her on the bed.

"Tell me why, Becca."

"Kate, you haven't the faintest idea what it's like to be me, do you?"

"I know it's bad. I didn't think it was bad enough to die for."

"I thought so when I swallowed those pills."

"And do you still think so?"

Rebecca shook her head. "I can't answer that yet."

They sat in silence. *I wish I could read your mind*, Kate mourned. *I wish I could help you.*

Rebecca broke the silence. "I had it all worked out," she said. "I thought that after a decent interval you'd marry Theo and raise my children." Rebecca's blue eyes questioned her and Kate shook her head.

"No," she said. "Absolutely not. Not now, not ever. You can't blackmail me into it, not even this way, so you might as well live."

"Don't lecture me!"

"Someone has to."

"You know something, Kate, Sydney's a lot more sensitive than you are! She understood it perfectly."

"What did she understand? Your suicide attempt or your mad plan for Theo and me?" Kate seized Rebecca's shoulders and shook her. "Did sensitive Sydney tell you that you might have spent the rest of your life as a vegetable? Or, worse, that you might have retained just enough of your faculties to peer out from inside your pumpkin shell and be unable to scream for help?"

Rebecca began to cry.

Kate's anger evaporated as suddenly as it had come, and she clasped Rebecca tightly again. "My darling, you have to make the best of a rotten deal. What else is there for you to do?"

Rebecca wept silently and Kate stroked her hair. "I'll help you all I can—but don't try to arrange my life. You're as bad as Polly."

"Polly's an amateur. She never tried this."

They looked at each other and began to laugh, then to cry, then to laugh again.

"Do you remember?" Kate gasped, still holding Rebecca. "We had one of these jags the day I caught you in the storeroom with that boy —what was his name?"

"I forget," Rebecca said breathlessly. "He went to Princeton, but he was no tiger."

"At least I saved your virtue." Kate offered her the box of tissues from the nightstand.

"No, you didn't. My virtue had been lost for some time before that day."

"Rebecca!"

"Kate!"

"And you did it all for Theo?"

"Yes, I did."

"Have you ever told him?"

"No! You know how men are."

"I seem to know very little about men—and you look too done in to teach me right now," Kate said, smoothing the covers and tucking them in. "This is no time to discuss your murky past. Go to sleep now. I'll see you in the morning."

She kissed Rebecca's forehead, stroked her hair for a few moments, then turned out the lights and left the room.

III

"She'll never be happy," Kate told Theo in the waiting room, "but I don't think she'll try this again."

"Lord, I hope you're right," Theo said. He got to his feet. "I'll just look in on her, then I'll take you back to the hotel. Sydney's waiting to have dinner with us."

"When can Rebecca travel?" Kate asked him in the car.

"The doctor said anytime after tomorrow. I thought we might go home by ship if she likes the idea."

"It would do you both a world of good."

"Won't you come with us?"

"I haven't got the time, Theo. I owe Tillinghast several shows before my contract's up and I have to get organized for the move to Wakefield."

"You'll be happy there."

"Yes, I really think I will."

Sydney was waiting for them in the lobby of the Baur au Lac, and while Theo went to check for messages, she clucked over Kate. "You look very tired, darling. People weren't meant to hurtle through the air, not even on the Concorde. It scrambles your cells. You must go straight to bed after dinner."

"Sydney, don't mother me," Kate said. "You're not good at it." She sounded testy, even to herself.

"Rebecca seems to think I am," Sydney said, stung.

"I don't know why I'm being so bitchy," Kate apologized, trying not to scream.

"You're on edge," Sydney said. "We all are."

They went into the dining room and ordered drinks and dinner.

"She's so terribly sad," Theo said, breaking the silence that had descended upon them.

"Because she can't stand all of you being perpetually cheerful," Sydney said. "She told me so. It kills her when you pretend nothing has changed, that this is just a minor incident and it'll go away if you ignore it." She turned to Theo. "She's afraid of losing you. I think that's why she did it more than anything else."

Theo turned pale and took a long pull at his whiskey.

"Theo doesn't deserve that," Kate said.

Sydney shrugged. "I didn't say he did. I just told him what she thinks."

"You were right to tell me," Theo said, recovering. He glanced at Kate, grateful to her for defending him.

"You must make sure she doesn't try it again," Sydney said. "I think of the girls as a pair. They were always inseparable."

"They were inseparable until college, when I stole Rebecca away."

"She was eager to be stolen," Kate said. "Did you know she was jealous, Theo, when you took me to our high school prom?"

The two smiled at each other, and Sydney's eyes narrowed slightly, watching them. She watched them all through dinner and followed Kate upstairs and into her room afterward.

"What's going on between you and Theo?"

"Oh, for God's sake, Sydney," Kate sighed, hanging her dress in the armoire and putting on a robe. "It's called friendship."

"There's no such thing as friendship between a man and a woman," Sydney said briskly. "Sex always gets into it eventually. I think that man is smitten with you."

"You're wrong and I'm tired. If you really want to be a good mother, go away."

Sydney turned abruptly and started for the door. She stopped when Kate said, "Sydney, wait! I'm sorry. Thank you very much for coming to Zurich to keep watch until Theo could get here. It was a great favor."

Sydney's tense expression relaxed. She nodded and went out.

I should be nicer to her, Kate thought just before she fell asleep.

IV

"Odd," Kate said to Theo in the visitors' waiting room the next day, "that Becca and Sydney get on so well." Sydney was with Rebecca, saying good-bye.

He studied her. "Does it disturb you?"

"It surprises me. And yes, it disturbs me. Sydney's the wicked witch. No one's supposed to like her much, especially not my dearest friend. You're all supposed to admire me for my forbearance in her regard."

Theo took her hand. "I admire you for all sorts of things."

Kate smiled and disengaged her hand, reaching for her handbag as if she needed something in it. "Thanks for that. Now tell me how the Wakefield board of trustees operates."

There had been no time for the meeting Polly had promised. Kate and the board had accepted each other on faith.

"Polly runs the show," Theo said, "with the sure support of your father and a few old-timers. Among your uncles, Kendall couldn't care less, Brett always fights her, Maynard sometimes does, and Mercer follows his twin, but they're all practical businessmen. If they hadn't made Wakefield coed, it would have closed. Polly obviously put me on the board to direct the kind of upscale fund-raising that classy colleges do—nothing vulgar, you know, just elegant pressure to swell the endowment fund. And there's the trustee who manages the endowment fund: Gabriel Tennant of Clovis, Cadwallader, and Tennant in Charleston."

"Gabriel?"

"Do you know him?"

"No, but it's an unusual name. It was Win's character in *Rapture*."

He looked at her. "Do you still miss him, Kate?"

She nodded. "I miss the things he knows about me that other men don't. You know, the kind of secret language that evolves between married people."

Theo nodded.

"I miss his humor and his intelligence," Kate went on. "And his talent for making everyday things romantic and extraordinary."

"Kate, you're still in love with him!"

"Not I. The woman I used to be is and will always be, but not the woman I am now."

"How are you different?"

"I expect less now. I don't expect people to invest as much in me as I may be willing to invest in them. I don't expect them to reciprocate my feelings on equal terms. I respect their limitations."

"But there's no one else?"

"No one who matters."

Theo turned and stared raptly at an insipid watercolor hanging on the opposite wall. "Kate, there's something I want to tell you."

"Go ahead."

"You remember our discussion in the coffee shop that day?"

"Yes. And very soon after that it was clear that the difficulty between you and Becca had been resolved."

"That's only because when I make love to her I pretend it's you."

Kate moved imperceptibly away from him. "I don't want to hear this, Theo."

"It was a fantasy, Kate, to get me past the pity! But now what I feel for you is more than fantasy. Why deny it?" He spoke softly, quickly.

"You and I are in the same fix. Each of us loves someone we can't have in the way we once did; each of us needs the comfort of someone who doesn't inspire us with guilt or anger. Dammit, Kate! Why shouldn't we comfort each other?"

"Why does that have to be in bed?"

"It's what Rebecca wants! You told me so yourself."

"I shouldn't have. And what Rebecca wants is no reason for anything! She also wanted to kill herself! And it's not what *I* want." She turned to him. "Theo, we're all a little crazy. You'd never have said this to me otherwise."

They were silent for several long moments.

"I feel like a fool," Theo said. "I can't understand how I could have been so mistaken. I thought you needed someone as much as I do."

"I need someone—and I need you, but not in the same package. I want you to be the same friend I've had since I was a girl, a man I can rely on, confide in, and trust absolutely."

"You were a child then, Kate. The boundaries expand. The rules change."

"People change, Theo, not the rules."

"Do you have any idea how stuffy you sound?"

"I don't care how I sound. I care what I do."

Sydney appeared in the doorway, stunning in a dress of clear red that matched the lining of her leopard jacket. She wore a leopard fedora with that dash that was as uniquely Sydney's as was her smile when she greeted them. "She seems in much better spirits and we've promised to write. I'm going back to the hotel to pack. Will you be there in time to see me off?"

"We'll have lunch with you," Kate said.

There was a heavy silence when Sydney had gone, then Kate and Theo went down the hall together, both of them somber until they crossed the threshold of Rebecca's room. As if on cue, they smiled brightly. Rebecca, watching them, thought they looked as if they had something to hide.

V

Once back in her Carlyle apartment, Kate packed, reflecting that in forty years she had accumulated very little beyond her clothes, her books, about thirty videotapes of romantic movies from the Thirties, Forties, and Fifties, some cherished photographs, and the recording of "Dein ist mein ganzes Herz." The furnishings from the apartment she'd shared with Win were still in storage. Win had made no claim on them, and she neither wanted them nor made any attempt to get rid of them.

Now Kate was going to live in the president's residence at Wakefield. It was large and handsomely furnished, but not one stick of it was or ever would be hers. Since Tyler sold the house in Harmony, home was anywhere she hung her hat.

The telephone rang and she picked it up.

"Hi," Stanton said. "Want to have dinner?"

"Yes! Packing depresses me. I'll be glad of a break."

They arranged to meet in an hour. Kate had barely hung up when the telephone rang again. "Stan? Did you forget something?"

"Hello, Kate," Win's voice said.

"Oh! I thought . . ."

"You thought I was someone called Stan. No such luck. How are you?"

"In the middle of packing, and that's something I hate to do."

"You're packing for the move to Wakefield, right? That's why I called, to congratulate you, Madam President."

"Thank you. And where are you?"

"At the Plaza Athenée."

"In New York?" Kate was unsettled.

"No, in Paris."

She was steady again. "On vacation?"

"Yes, before I start rehearsing a new play."

"Tell me about it."

It was a political drama called *The Fencers*, about a clash of wills between two fast friends who now find themselves on opposite sides of the political fence—and in love with the same woman, to be played by Darcy, of course. It was left to the audience to decide whether the men were motivated by principle or passion.

"Sounds good to me," Kate said. "Right up your street."

"I miss you, Kate."

She was not prepared for that. She said nothing.

"Does that astonish you?" he asked.

"It's not the sort of thing one ex says to the other during their first post-divorce conversation."

"We're not like other exes any more than we were like other spouses. Don't you miss me, even a little?"

"I miss you," she said. "Is that what you called for?"

"I called to congratulate you. It's what you worked so hard for, an office you'll fill superlatively. I wish you well, Kate. I always will."

"And I you."

"You were great on television too."

"I had a good drama coach. You were great in *A Double Life.*"

"Better than Colman was?"

"No one's better than Colman."

Win laughed. "I agree! May I call you from time to time inside your ivied walls?"

"Yes, of course."

"Good luck, then. Good-bye, Kate."

"You too. Good-bye."

She put the telephone in its cradle and stood looking at it while she took stock of her reactions. Just the sound of his voice after two years was enough to confound Kate, who prided herself upon keeping a cool head under any circumstances. She wondered what she would have done if he had called from New York, not Paris, from a mere dozen blocks away. Would she have gone to meet him if he'd asked her to?

Yes—and that annoyed her. She wished she hadn't been so charming, so hail-fellow-well-met. Win had behaved like a brat, and no amount of water under the bridge would wash that away. She wished she had told him so, told him not to call again, that she was no longer his Kate and had no desire to be his chum, that the core of their liaison no longer existed and any other relationship would be a travesty.

One thing she couldn't deny: she still wanted to go to bed with him. It was a difficult admission, that she wanted to make love to a man who had publicly rejected her, a man whose behavior had been reprehensible.

"I ought to listen to my own lectures," she said, throwing things into the suitcase.

VI

"Is it ever finished?" she asked Stan over dinner.

"You have to separate the loves in your life," Stan advised, eating her lasagna with relish. "You have to put them into airtight compartments. Each one is valid for the time and place it happened, but you must never cross-pollinate."

"Your metaphors are very mixed." Kate had ordered ravioli but had little appetite for it. She munched on a bread stick.

Stanton nodded. "No more so than your feelings. You just have to go with them."

"Go with your feelings! There's a piece of pop-culture advice for you! If everyone did that, the crime rate would double overnight! Civilization depends upon *managed* feelings. That's been the trouble with this country since the Sixties. People just slop around, feeling any way they want to and not caring who knows it."

"Blah, blah, blah," Stan said. "The guy still makes you crazy and that's all there is to that."

"That doesn't say much for female intelligence."

"The craziness is not in your head."

Kate nodded. "Agreed. How long will this craziness go on?"

"Some say it stops the minute another guy makes you crazy. Some say time does the trick. Some say it's all in the mind, curable by therapy. And some say you never get over it."

"Well, *I* will."

Stanton nodded. "Probably. You're a strong-minded woman."

"You make me sound like Elsie Dinsmore."

"When was she ever strong-minded?"

"She wouldn't profane the Sabbath by playing the piano, not even when her beloved papa finally noticed her enough to tell her to. She sat on that piano bench until she fainted—heroines, of course, never have to pee. Now, *that's* strong minded."

"I guess it is. And my guess is that you *will* get over Win long before he gets over you."

Kate didn't argue the point. It was gratifying to suppose that Win wasn't over her. Vengeance, apparently, was not the Lord's. Vengeance belonged to discarded women.

VII

"Why did you choose to write historical romances?" Kate asked the guest on her farewell program, one Adora May, née Dorothea Mae Fesselmeyer, who fluttered like the ruffles on her pink dress. She wore an enormous diamond, the fruits of what Kate privately called "hysterical fiction," wherein all the men had hour-long erections and the women's breasts were big enough to burst out of their bodices but never sagged.

"Because women need romance," Adora replied, smiling with heavily glossed pink lips. "Most of them get precious little of it. My books fill an empty place in their lives. They love tales of strong heroes and lovely maidens having exotic adventures."

"But wouldn't it help those women more to read about things as they are?"

"They already know how things are!" May said with a sly glance at Kate. "Reality is washing dishes and making ends meet. Women are entitled to some escape from that. They're cooped up with chores and children all day. If they have any free time, they want to lose themselves in fantasies like mine. What else can they do?"

"Take a course in budget management."

"Ah, Dr. Ballard—" May dimpled. "Not all of us are as brilliant as you. Or as embittered by love."

There was dead silence in the studio. Not once, in all the weeks the program had aired, had anyone on the show referred to Kate's divorce.

Kate smiled. "Let's talk about fictional heroines," she suggested. "Do you have a favorite?"

"Anna Karenina. She gave all for love: morality, social status, even her son."

"But she believed herself a sinner and paid for her sins by throwing herself under a train, a particularly ghastly death. Count Vronsky was equally guilty of their adultery, but he was never punished. Women are almost always punished in fiction—even fiction written by women —because they're temptresses. That's the rock. The hard place is that they're supposed to have higher moral standards than men and, above all, to abide by them."

"Another favorite of mine," said May, clearly exasperated, "is Scarlett O'Hara. She was a strong woman who competed with men and won. Scarlett got everything she wanted."

Kate shook her head. "Melanie got everything Scarlett wanted: Ashley, the respect of the community, and Rhett's admiration. There's a very strong message in *Gone With the Wind* about how a woman should behave to get what she wants: be like Melanie—pliable, submissive and trusting—and someone will take care of you, in this case Scarlett, in most cases a man."

Adora May scowled, ready to explode, and in the wings Stan made motions as of pulling a stake from her chest. Kate relented. "Tell us about your latest book, *Purple Shadows*."

May tossed Kate a triumphant smile as she launched into a description of her book.

When the program ended, there was more applause than usual and Kate went down to say good-bye to the regulars in her studio audience.

"They were very flattering," Kate told Stanton when it was over.

"I hope you're having some regrets," Stanton said.

"A few."

"There's a woman waiting to see you in the green room," Stanton said. "I'll come by in the morning before you leave."

"Come for breakfast," Kate said. She went through the set doors and into the green room. The slim, stylish young woman waiting for her was Tabitha Berling.

VIII

"One of those liquid diets," Tabby explained, sipping Perrier in the Russian Tea Room and watching as Kate ate blinis covered with sour cream. "And a personal shopper at Saks."

"You look sensational!"

"So do you."

"What's happening?"

Tabby smiled. "I'm doing the sets for Win's new play, *The Fencers*. Win insisted on it."

"Congratulations, Tabby! It's high time you were captain instead of the crew." Tabitha had worked steadily in the London theater while Win was in Hollywood, but always as an assistant.

"With you off to Wakefield, it looks like we've all got our wishes," Tabby said reflectively. "When do you leave?"

"Tomorrow."

"Think of it! A college president! Will you talk to me?"

"Come down and visit. There are twelve bedrooms in my mansion."

"What about Win?"

Kate looked at her in surprise. "What do you mean?"

"Is it really over?"

"We're divorced. I think that qualifies as over."

Tabby looked uncomfortable. "Just checking."

"For whom? Darcy?"

"Hell, no! For me, if you must know. I know no one ever thinks of me in that way, but I do. Theda Bara has always lurked beneath the blubber." She blushed painfully. "I've always been mad about Win, so I wanted to be sure you weren't, in case . . . well . . . anything happens."

"Tabby, you're such an honorable soul! There aren't ten other women in the world who'd ask the ex-wife for permission. But feel free, as free as he is to love whom he likes."

Kate took a cab to the Carlyle, wondering if she would have been so noble if there were the slightest chance of an affair between Win and Tabitha Berling. She still felt proprietary, but then, marriage gave rise to possessiveness; that was what it was for.

"Oh, to hell with all that," Kate told her suitcases when she reached her apartment. "I have a college to run."

BOOK V

29

I

Kate checked herself carefully in the dressing room mirror to see if she had achieved the desired effect. She wore a simple long-sleeved black crepe dinner dress cut low enough to offset the severity of her hair, which was pulled back into a chignon. Her black silk sandals made her an even six feet tall. Her diamond earrings and the diamond brooch that partially obscured her cleavage had been gifts from Win.

"The spoils of war," she said.

Her vision shifted to the reflection of a Great Dane lying across the threshold, head on paws, eyes rolling to watch every move she made. He, too, was a gift from Win, delivered on the day Kate took up residence in this house.

The enormous puppy—white with black spots—had worn a red bow with "I am a housewarming gift" printed on it when he arrived, along with a very large doghouse—perfectly designed in Southern Colonial style—and an assortment of puppy essentials.

"Clever bastard," Polly had snorted. "Wants to make sure you think of him a dozen times a day."

"I suppose so," Kate agreed.

"Are you going to keep him?" Dodie Phelps asked.

"He's adorable—all legs and those gorgeous eyes! How could I send him back?"

"But if he reminds you of Win . . ."

Kate bent to hug the diminutive woman. "They don't resemble each other in the slightest," she said, and they laughed together.

"What will you call him? Spot?"

"This magnificent brute? I'll call him Harald after the Danish kings."

"But just look at his paws! He'll grow bigger than any Danish king!"

"Polly, he suits me. I'd look silly with a little dog."

Looking at the Dane now, Kate reflected that he had grown great indeed. To judge from the quantities of beef he consumed every day, he might grow even larger. He already measured thirty-three inches from floor to shoulder. Taken all in all, he was stunning.

"Well, Harald," Kate said, turning to face him. "What do you think?"

Harald lifted his powerful head with its erect triangular ears and regarded her for a moment, then replaced his head on his paws.

Kate nodded, pleased with his response, and stepped over him to get to her bedroom. Harald rose, reversed his position so that he could see her, and plopped down again.

The president's mansion was one of the few houses apart from Kel Regis with proportions big enough and high enough for Kate. The great antebellum four-poster, covered and canopied in green and white striped silk, sat on a hand-hooked rug from the same period. The fruitwood chairs were upholstered in gros point, all of it restored. Kate went to her dressing table, picked up a crystal atomizer, sprayed Joy into the air and walked through the perfumed mist. Then she selected a pair of eyeglasses, put them on, regarded herself, shook her head, and chose another pair with black frames.

"Ah, Dr. Ballard," she said to her image. "There you are."

Followed by Harald, Kate went through to her private sitting room, where her collection of photographs sat on the mantel of a fireplace flanked by two overstuffed chairs. Their persimmon velvet upholstery would soon be slip-covered in chintz for the spring, along with the couch. The carpet was Turkish, the lamps French, the desk and book-cases English. There were even some carefully preserved Duncan Phyfe chairs.

"It's a hodgepodge," she remembered Polly saying on the day Kate moved in. "But it works."

Kate remembered, too, that she had been dismayed by the way Polly looked that day; it was hard to ignore the ever-encroaching signs of age in her grandmother. At eighty-five, Polly rode several times a week and directed the affairs of the family, the university, and the Benedict Stud with her customary élan, but it took her longer to get out of a chair and she no longer walked at her former brisk trot. Their relationship was both stimulating and comforting to Kate. She did not like to think what life would be like without it.

The grandfather clock in the hall and the French *pendule sous verre* on the mantel were striking seven. Kate, with Harald loping along at her side, went out to the hall and started down the elegant curved staircase, her hand on its burnished balustrade. She had been in this house many times during her college years, but it looked entirely different from her new point of view. She had been living here for eight months, having finished up the former president's term. She had divided her summer vacation between this house, Kel Regis, and the Cape, where the Barrowses owned a cottage too, and where she timed her visits to coincide with Theo's absences.

There was always tension in the air when she was in Theo's company. Kate blamed it on that unfortunate conversation in the waiting room in Zurich—a clear result of emotional stress. And yet, Rebecca, who knew nothing about it, was different when Theo was with them. She became more rigid, more distant.

"But this is not the moment," Kate told Harald, "to think about that."

Kate had officially started at Wakefield soon after her return from Zurich and had opened the new school year four months before. She thoroughly enjoyed being president of Wakefield College and the chatelaine of this house. She felt at home in it. She wanted to live here for a long, long time.

She reached the bottom of the stairs, where a wide entrance hall opened onto a vast drawing room on the right and a formal dining room on the left. Kate went into the dining room first to check the table, pleased by the settings, the Sèvres china, the silver candelabra, the floral centerpieces from the mansion's greenhouse. She walked around the table, checking the place cards.

"Tonight," she told Harald, "we're having young people to a black tie dinner—which is why we've got ourselves up so severely. They think we're over the hill, but in our hearts we're only nineteen and we can't let them guess that or they won't take us seriously."

II

Crossing the hall, she went into the drawing room. When its four sets of sliding doors were open, it ran the full depth of the house and was large enough to accommodate well over three hundred people. At Kate's instruction, the first set of doors had been closed to make the room a suitable size for the small group expected tonight. The furniture, some of it nineteenth-century, was formal but comfortable. The room, done in cream and mushroom, bespoke serenity and tradition.

"That's for me," Kate murmured, and laughed from the sheer pleasure of being at one with her surroundings. She had never been so content in her life. She was where she wanted to be, doing a job she wanted to do. Among the people she loved, Rebecca was brittle but determined; her parties were as perfect as they had been before the accident. Theo, a frequent visitor to Wakefield as a trustee and to Kel Regis for political powwows with Polly and the Democratic Party people, behaved with an awkwardness that Kate hoped was apparent only to her.

For the rest, Sydney had stopped nagging Kate about Tyler's book and Kate had promised herself that come what might, she would stay out of her parents' feud.

Polly had not yet interfered with how Kate directed the college; perhaps she never would. She came to Wakefield often but not to talk about university business; she reserved that for the trustees' meetings. She often brought Dodie Phelps, whom she cherished like fragile heirloom lace. They never stayed the night.

"At our age," Polly explained, "we need to pack all of our pills and potions, along with our pillows and hot water bottles and other gear, just to turn and toss on strange mattresses."

The first months had been hectic for Kate, settling in, meeting her faculty, staff, and colleagues, giving interviews to the press to milk the most publicity from her appointment. But since the turn of the year she had concentrated on running Wakefield, putting some of her ideas in motion—not to everyone's unalloyed delight, she knew. That was one of the reasons she gave frequent dinners for different groups of faculty: adults tended to be less guarded around a dining table.

Except for Natalie Marsh, the academic dean. Natalie felt that she would have been a far better administrator than Kate and was, in any case, more deserving of the top slot after having spent thirty years at Wakefield. She was too clever to be obvious about it, but Kate was very much aware that Natalie coveted her position.

But that night there would be no faculty. Kate had invited, with or without dates, the presidents and vice presidents of each of the four undergraduate classes, the officers of the student organization, the editor of *The Wakefield College Sentinel*, and Pritchard Keating, captain of the football and basketball teams and campus heartthrob. Kate had invited him not only because he was rich and handsome and a good student, but because he was far too influential on campus to be ignored. His date was Melinda Tillinghast.

"An odd couple," Kate told her old friend Carol Hunter, who now held the Corliss Chair in Psychology at Brooke Parrish. "What's a senior jock doing with a lowly freshman?"

"Is she pretty?"

"A gorgeous little thing."

"That's what he's doing with her."

"I don't know about that. Her mother died when she was seven and her father's overprotected her ever since. She's not at all sophisticated."

"Maybe more than you think," Carol suggested.

"From long experience of the condition, I can tell a virgin when I see one. Melinda's the 'nice' girl one takes home to Mother. She's a brunette version of Sandra Dee. Pert and pretty and pure."

"A daunting combination," Carol had agreed. "Let's hope that virtue will triumph over their glands."

III

Kate poured a martini into a frosted glass and was relishing the crisp, cold tartness of it when the doorbell rang. Harald sprang to his feet and stood at her side, sniffing the air, ready for battle. Kate scratched soothingly between his ears.

From where Kate was, she could see Lillian, her housekeeper, open the door. The caller was Gabriel Tennant—not one of the guests she was expecting. He was carrying an attaché case, which was not surprising: Gabriel was devoted to business.

He was divorced and a few years younger than Kate. By now she knew that he was very shrewd at what he did, but he still had a kind of boyish charm that both amused and attracted her. He had an engaging half grin and a dazzling smile and a thatch of blond hair worn brushed to the side.

Gabriel seemed always to have emerged from a tricky meeting and to be en route to another. His suits were conservative works of art, his shirts came from Turnbull & Asser, and his ties from Brooks Brothers. He drove a bright red Porsche. He was an ardent reader and he played polo and tennis very well. He was clever and amusing and he was very, very good with money, in particular with the Wakefield funds entrusted to his management.

"Evening, Kate," he said as Lillian showed him in. He shook hands with Kate, regarding Harald with caution. "He ought to know me by now."

"That's how he behaves with people he knows."

Gabriel smiled. "Ready to tear them apart." He looked admiringly at Kate's dress. "Dazzling," he said. "I'm sorry, Kate, I didn't mean to crash a dinner party. I'll only be a minute."

"There's no need to rush away," Kate said. "Have a drink."

"A short scotch on the rocks, please," he said, opening his case. "Theo sent this list of speaking engagements at the prep school level."

Kate looked over the list. "Isn't it a little late to lure preppies to Wakefield? Most of them have already applied to other colleges."

He nodded and sipped the drink she had handed him. "It's still worth a try," he said. "Enrollments are not what they could be. We'll have to borrow to cover our shortfall."

"I'm willing," Kate said, "provided the schedule fits with mine. I have a job to do here."

"Of course, although this place can chug along by itself for a little longer while we do what we have to do." He raised his glass. "You were really a superlative choice for president."

"How can you be sure in so short a time?"

His eyes were on a level with hers. "Just a feeling. In my field, instinct is an important factor."

"Then I'm a good investment."

"Among many other very attractive things."

She was gratified by the compliment. Her job was a lot more difficult than Polly's description of it, and Gabriel's opinion of Kate's performance was important to her. They had been out to dinner a time or two, but he was as battened down as a ship in a gale. She wondered, if he ever let go, what kind of lover he was. She wondered how long it would take him to acknowledge the attraction between them and suggest they do something about it.

She had decided on the day she met him that she wouldn't mind going to bed with him—but he had yet to suggest it! Kate, who still stood aside and watched herself, laughed about that, but she was glad that she actively desired him in a way she had never desired John Mallory. It meant she was over Win.

Kate made some suggestions about the schools on the list as they bent over a table.

"You're wearing Joy," he said when he was gathering the papers and returning them to his case. "The name suits you as well as the scent."

"What a lovely compliment! I've never been thought of as a particularly joyous person."

"I think of you that way."

They looked at each other, on the brink of something more. Then the doorbell rang and they smiled like conspirators and shook hands again. Gabriel left, greeting the first arrivals on his way out.

IV

It's strange, Kate reflected, watching Melinda Tillinghast surrender her coat and walk into the drawing room on Pritchard Keating's arm, *that she reminds me of Rebecca when they're not in the least alike.*

Melinda's dress would have been a simple sheath but for the way the fabric clung to her supple young body. Its color deepened the blue of her eyes, a striking contrast to her dark, glossy hair. She wore it loose, hooked behind her ears, and her long crystal earrings flashed in the light. She was as naturally seductive as her father was not.

Keating was a dark-haired, splendidly constructed young man, clearly an athlete, who was at ease in evening clothes and obviously accustomed to escorting the most gorgeous young women available. Melinda certainly filled the bill.

"Dr. Ballard," Keating said, "I believe you know Melly Tillinghast."

"Of course. I'm delighted to see both of you," Kate said. She turned to Keating. "And congratulations on a great game last Saturday."

He smiled with a modesty that had to be affected. The world must have been making a fuss over Pritchard Keating since the day he emerged from the womb sucking on his silver pacifier. He was no Wade Stevens, awkwardly fumbling between a girl's legs; he had the self-assurance of the rogue male.

"I owe it all to Melly's cheerleading," he said, glancing at her in a proprietary way.

Melinda smiled up at him with an air of ambiguous expectation.

That's the resemblance! Kate realized. Rebecca had projected that same expectant aura. Some women did as naturally as they breathed. The difference was that Rebecca knew it and this young woman did not. It drove young men crazy because at this age some of them weren't sure how far they could go: a squeeze here, a feel there, a consummation?

Someone ought to write a guide for them! Kate thought.

But Pritchard Keating needed no instructions.

"Please," Kate said to them before she turned to greet her next guest, "help yourselves to something to drink." Not alcoholic, of course. Wakefield frowned on that.

Holly Groehler, a sophomore and president of her class, had arrived alone. She was neither plain nor pretty, and she was unremarkably dressed in a long black skirt and a white silk blouse. Holly was studious, intelligent, and more popular with young men as a pal than a prom queen, yet she had become close to Melinda, who was the prettiest, most popular freshman on campus and certain to be next year's homecoming queen. Kate wondered what the two girls saw in each other. But their classmates had wondered the same thing about Kate and Becca.

"Dr. Ballard, we really want you to teach a course in women's studies this term, especially the seniors. It's the only chance they'll have to study with you." Holly was flushed with enthusiasm.

"It's a little late. Term's almost over. Maybe a spring lecture series."

Holly grew even more intense. "Great! You said on your TV show that you wanted to take a close look at women in nineteenth-century America."

Kate smiled. "All right, Holly, I'll see about it right away."

"I knew you'd say yes! Thanks, Dr. Ballard." She scanned the room. "Oh, there's Melly—with that conceited ape. I wish he'd leave her alone." She frowned and hurried off, a mother hen rushing to protect her chick. Kate wondered, as the girl moved off, if she had been that earnest at Holly's age. She could almost hear Rebecca saying, "You were too cynical to be earnest."

The next arrivals were another odd couple: Prince Mustafa Khan and Mary Margaret Hennessy, respectively president and vice president of the senior class. The prince was brilliant, charming, naughty, and unbelievably rich. Mary Margaret, an Oklahoma oil baron's daughter, was half as rich but far more devout, and a militant virgin from all reports. She had flaming red hair and a milk-white complexion, in exotic contrast to the dark-skinned prince. His evening clothes had been made in Jermyn Street, London, while Mary Margaret wore a pale blue gown from Neiman-Marcus and an overlarge crucifix, almost certainly to protect herself from this mischievous heathen who appeared to be smitten with her.

Tom Lewis, the owlish editor of Wakefield's student newspaper, came alone and began scanning the room to find Holly. Kate thanked him for supporting a campaign to reinforce the honor system at Wakefield.

"I think it's the right thing to do," he said. "You have to give kids responsibility or they'll never learn what it means."

"You're going to be a good journalist," Kate said. "I hope it will always be possible for you to follow your conscience."

"I don't expect it to be easy." He looked at her through his steel-rimmed glasses. *A martyr in the making?* Kate wondered. *Or just an honest man?*

"Holly's over there," Kate said.

The other class presidents and student council officers along with their dates completed the party, and the evening turned out to be a merry affair that lasted well past midnight.

V

In Washington that evening, Rebecca had been bathed and dressed for her own dinner party, cursing her condition throughout the process while Alice nodded and chirped and commiserated with her.

She has to blow off steam, Alice told herself. *But those pills are bad for her, and that I swear before God and all the saints.*

"Still and all," Alice said, "you're doing marvelous. Three dinner parties this week—and you've been to all them gatherings this season."

"It's part of being Theo's wife—and that's all I ever wanted to be."

Alice clucked sympathetically. "But Kate says you're obsessive about it."

"Kate's brilliant, but she doesn't know everything," Rebecca bristled. "Anyway, I've always been obsessive about things, from dieting to ballet lessons to Theo, most of all Theo. From the day I met him I knew I must have him or die. I got him when I was eighteen and I intend to hold on to him."

"That's easy enough. The poor man's crazy in love with you."

"Do you think so, Alice? Do you really think so?"

"Everyone who sees you two together thinks so."

It was an exchange they had repeated hundreds of times. Alice didn't mind. It seemed to comfort Rebecca, and the poor woman deserved all the comfort she could get.

It took Alice a while to get Rebecca into her gown of silver *tissu*, then to do her hair while Rebecca applied her makeup and selected her jewels, but when the two women were finished with their labors, Alice clasped her hands and smiled proudly at Rebecca in the mirror.

"You've never been so beautiful," she said.

Rebecca smiled back. She turned on her chair's power switch, swung it around, and rolled out to the waiting elevator. As it traveled downward, Rebecca gathered her forces. More than anything else, she hated greeting her guests from a wheelchair with no way to escape the pity in their eyes.

The elevator stopped and the door opened. Theo was waiting and bent to kiss her cheek.

"Darling," he said. "You look absolutely beautiful."

She looked up at him searchingly. "Thank you," she said formally, and watched the light go out of his eyes and hated herself for making that happen and wondered, as she wondered every single time she responded coldly to his warmth, if the light would be there the next time he looked at her. She knew she was alienating him, that it was dangerous to do that, but the bitterness inside her would not be denied.

It wasn't only because he was whole and she was not. Rebecca was certain Theo was sleeping with Kate, that he was in love with Kate. It was the way he looked when anyone mentioned her. It was how he sounded when *he* mentioned her. It was an intuition Rebecca had, too strong to be denied. It would have been different had Rebecca been in control of the affair, as she had originally planned to be. But this had been their own idea, these sneaky little trysts behind her back. This could get out of hand!

"Has anyone arrived yet?" she asked him, struggling to speak normally.

"No, but a car just pulled up."

He stood stiffly at her side, the two of them enclosed in a bubble of misery.

VI

"We're still in the Stone Age," Susan Axminster said as the wives took seats in Rebecca's drawing room after dinner. "When the men talk politics the women are relegated to an adjoining cave."

"Who cares?" Mrs. Deputy National Chairman said. "It's the only time we get a chance for group gossip without being overheard by the media. Have you heard about the new secretary in Senator P.'s office? They say she'll do it anytime, any how, sitting, standing, by mouth or by hand."

"Does the senator know?" Rebecca asked.

"If he doesn't, he soon will."

"Not if he's as pious as everyone says!"

"The pious ones are the worst, especially at the senator's age. He'll go after any female who can raise his flag."

The women laughed.

"Still, I feel sorry for men these days," Susan Axminster said. "Not only do they have to earn the money and run the world, they have to give us two kinds of orgasms and be able to hold an erection for as long as it takes."

"Well, I don't feel in the least sorry for them," said Mrs. National Security Council member. "They've been getting away with jiffy sex for centuries. Think of all the women who lived and died and never came! If we could harness all that unused energy we wouldn't need atomic plants."

"Speaking of history, Rebecca, how is your friend Kate Talley?"

"She calls herself Kate Ballard again," Rebecca said. "And she's fine."

"I met her at Kel Regis and at her mother's wedding," Susan Axminster said.

She fell silent as the butler brought the coffee tray and set it next to Rebecca's chair on a table made to order at the right height. Everyone stopped talking until he had gone and Rebecca was pouring the dark, steaming liquid from a Georgian silver coffeepot into demitasse cups of porcelain so fine it was translucent.

Susan Axminster, nibbling on a thin chocolate-covered mint, picked up where she had left off. "Very understated, your Kate."

"I loved watching her take those people apart on her program," the House Speaker's wife said. "She wasn't understated then."

"I'm not talking about looks," Susan said, "although she dresses very conservatively. I'm talking about demeanor, persona. Still, she must have more than brains to have landed Win Talley. He's one of the sexiest men alive."

"She's stunning," Mrs. Deputy National Chairman said. "And she has style."

"She didn't always," Rebecca said. "I remember Kate's first visit to the White House with her father when he won his second Pulitzer. Grandma Polly came to take her shopping and picked out the most awful dress for Kate, all bows and ruffles, like Blanche Dubois—except that Kate was so tall."

"Did she wear it?"

"Yes, but not until she'd cut off all the bows and ruffles. Polly was scandalized, but she could never get the better of Kate."

"Who's Kate seeing now?" Susan asked.

"I don't know that she's seeing anyone special," Rebecca said. *Except maybe Theo; he goes to Kel Regis often enough.*

She watched the other women very carefully to see if they knew what she suspected—or if any of *them* had set their caps for Theo.

Safeguarding Theo from women like these was exactly what she had asked Kate to do. The trouble was that Kate had done it far too well!

"She *must* have a lover," Susan said. "A woman who's lived with Win Talley must get in the habit of good sex."

They turned to Rebecca, ribaldly curious about Talley, and Rebecca told them about virginal Kate's desperate crush on him when they met at Oxford. She sounded fond and loyal as she gave Kate's secret heart away.

VII

"How did it go?" she asked Theo when he came into their bedroom.

"Moderately well. It seems that Polly and I see possibilities in Clem Case not apparent to everyone."

"He's popular, good-looking, and he has no skeletons in his closet," Rebecca said. "That counts for something."

"Not enough, apparently. Polly and I will have to convince them."

"Does that mean you'll be going to Kel Regis soon?"

He seemed to avoid her eyes. "Probably." He switched off the light and lay down. She knew he would not touch her tonight, but she waited anyway.

Once, Rebecca lamented, *he'd have asked me to come to Kel Regis with him, but I've refused too often.*

She simply could not help herself! Some devil possessed her, as it had tonight. She was distant when she should have been most loving to him. He was drifting away from her, drifting deeper into Kate's arms.

It isn't fair, Rebecca moaned silently. *It isn't fair!*

Kate could be hard as nails. She had refused the one favor Rebecca ever asked of her, only to seduce Theo on her own terms! After all, who stood by Kate when that bitch Sydney left her? Who comforted wallflower Kate and transformed a bluestocking into a girl clever enough to trap Win Talley? And who had arranged to move Kate out before Win announced to the whole world that he was divorcing her and moving in with another woman?

"Theo?" she said softly. "Are you asleep?"

"Not yet."

"Theo, the next time you go to Kel Regis, take me with you. Please, Theo, please!" She began to cry softly.

He turned to her, alarmed. "Yes, of course, darling. I just assumed you didn't want to go."

"Oh, Theo, I know what a bitch I've been lately, but it isn't meant for you. I love you. I love you so much."

"I know, Rebecca. I love you too."

"Don't leave me, Theo, no matter how badly I behave."

"I'll never leave you, never!"

"I want you, Theo," she whispered frantically, and Theo kissed her and closed his eyes. Slipping into fantasy, he put his arms around the two women he loved.

30

I

Kate sat at the desk in her study, working on her notes, while Harald snoozed at her feet. She had arranged to do a series of non-credit lectures and the eager response had surprised her. She was more than gratified by it, because the acceptance was for her: she had earned it on her own, without any reflected glory from family or husband.

She stopped working to savor the feeling, looking out over the park that kept the mansion removed from the campus. It was raining, a fine, soft rain that betokened spring and the riot of flowers that would come with it. The fairy tale mist, the new leaf on the trees, the gracefully weeping willows aroused an unexpected rush of nostalgia in her for another springtime shared at Oxford, but she refused to yield to the seduction of the past and she was back at work when Polly called.

Kate told her about the new lecture series. "And I'm really flying," Kate finished. "It's a great feeling."

"Multiply it by a few million and you'll have an idea of what it's like to be elected president of these United States."

It might have been you was what Polly meant, but Kate was not about to be drawn into that old argument, even after the fact. "How is bonny Clem doing? Do you think he'll be your candidate next time around?"

"Bonny Clem could win, although he must first learn how to run. Come to dinner next week and see for yourself. We're having him and the chairman of the national committee, plus the majority leader, Theo, some state party chairmen, and *all* their wives."

"You don't mean Rebecca too?"

"At her specific request, Theo said."

"That's wonderful! Polly, be nice to her!"

349

"Certainly, if she's nice to me! Will you come—with Gabriel Tennant?"

"Why Gabriel? He's not a political person."

"He's a money person," Polly said. "It all goes into the same pot. Besides, he'll even out my table."

"What about Tyler?"

"He's always paired with Dodie Phelps."

"I see. What you mean is that you don't want me to be the only beast to clamber aboard the ark without a mate."

"What I mean is, he'll even out my table!"

"You wouldn't be matchmaking, would you?"

"Matchmaking? At your age? Don't be ridiculous! I've just spoken to Gabriel and he's accepted. Now, will you come?"

"Of course I'll come! I haven't seen Rebecca in weeks."

"Seven o'clock," Polly said. "Black tie."

"With decorations!" Kate laughed and hung up. She thought a moment, then made a call.

"Gabriel," she said when his assistant had put her through. "I understand we're going over the fields to Grandma's house."

"Yes, I was about to call you. But that's a week away. How about dinner tonight?"

"Done," said Kate.

"I'll pick you up at seven."

Kate hung up and smiled out over the park, nostalgia obliterated by pleasant anticipation. How wise were the cynics who said what you needed to get over an old love was a new one! She and Gabriel had been out to dinner a few more times and she enjoyed his company. She still wondered why, after all these months, he had not made the slightest overture, because she was convinced that the attraction was mutual on all levels.

Appealing as Gabriel was, he was not the sort of man to be a grand passion, which was just as well. Kate had already had her once-in-a-lifetime love, with all of its heartache and all of its bliss. What she wanted now was someone clever and comfortable to share her interests as well as her bed.

"Maybe tonight," she told herself, and went back to her notes.

II

"You *are* matchmaking, I can tell," Dodie Phelps said as soon as Polly replaced the receiver. They were in the morning room, and although the sky was gray, this room was always cheerful and bright. The draperies were closed to keep out the damp, a fire crackled in the hearth, and a fresh pot of Earl Grey tea brewed beneath a cozy on a table next to Polly's chair.

"Kate could do a lot worse," Polly observed.

"That's beside the point."

"To tell you the truth," Polly said, "I want Gabriel here for Theo more than for Kate."

"Well, yes, of course, there's that," Dodie Phelps said, a worried frown wrinkling the delicate skin of her brow. She had always been small, but now she looked like a child in a grown-up's chair.

"There certainly is that," Polly said glumly. "A woman would have to be a fool not to see it. Little Becky Barrows is no fool."

"But she can't believe it was Kate's idea!"

"Who knows what she might believe? She's not the most stable person in the world, is she? Even supposing she thinks it's all on Theo's side, it can't make her look kindly on Kate, no matter how much she loves her."

"Poor woman. Polly, you must be kind to her."

"You people must think I'm some kind of ogre! Kate just told me the same thing. Of course I'll be kind to her!"

"You'll have to make an effort, Polly Pepperpot. The two of you never got along."

"That's true, but apparently she has more moxie than I gave her credit for."

"Most of us have more moxie than you give us credit for."

Polly nodded and removed the cozy from the teapot. "Have a cup of tea with your moxie. And help me decide what to wear to that benefit in Washington. Can't I persuade you to come along?"

"No, dear. I'm more comfortable here at home. And I know I'll get a full report from you."

Polly brought the tea and placed it on a special tray that swung out and over from the frame of the chair. She put a straw between two of her cousin's crippled fingers.

"I'll tell you everything, down to the last bit of scandal," she promised.

III

A Benedict jet flew Polly to Washington, along with her maid, Delia, and her secretary, Joan. They were met by a limousine and taken to the Benedict duplex in the capital, where the staff kept the apartment ready. Polly always stayed in Washington for presidential elections, except for the last one. "Inept," she had chided the Dukakis handlers. "He looks like a boll weevil peering out of that tank!" When no one listened, she went home declaring she had quit politics forever. No one who knew her believed *that*.

En route from the airport, Polly reflected that things were humming along nicely for her. She still thrived on a challenge and she considered herself fortunate to have so many, although there were a few she had not been able to meet with flags flying.

She hadn't been able to help Dodie Phelps, for one thing, and that was unbearable. Her treasured cousin was no better, but at least she was no worse. Polly pursued and investigated every new treatment for rheumatoid arthritis and gave huge sums for research. The benefit tonight was for such research.

The twins were another failure. She hadn't been able to bring Brosie and Belle to heel. They were still running their antiques shop in Charleston, and Ross was still running around with other women. As far as Polly knew, there had been no nasty gossip about the twins, but that was no guarantee there wouldn't be.

Then, too, Polly had lost the battle with her sons to keep Wakefield a women's college. That defeat still rankled. She had installed Kate as president to even the score.

Among her victories, she had convinced Theo Barrows—who in turn had convinced several important Democratic Party leaders—that Senator Case could win the next election, unless the present administration, by some miracle, blundered into a great triumph that made the country forget it was falling apart.

Once Case took office, Polly was determined to bring Gabriel Tennant and his financial wizardry to Washington as part of a Democratic pledge to deal with the deficit. Gabriel was ruthless about the care and conservation of money; he was not the sort to spend funds the country didn't have.

She wanted Kate to marry Gabriel. Happy as she claimed to be, Kate needed someone of her own or she would never get over Win. Gabriel was heaven sent.

He had a good pedigree and a respectable amount of money. His family owned a chunk of Alaska, but they had had the good sense not to go native and had educated their sons at Virginia Military Institute and Duke University rather than among Yankees. Gabriel had the charm of southern men and he was smart enough, tall enough, and handsome enough for Kate. He seemed to lack humor, but Kate would have to compromise on that.

"I just hope he knows his way around a woman," Polly muttered as the limousine pulled up in front of the apartment building. She didn't think Kate would compromise about sex—not after that Talley person—although a divorce sometimes gave a woman different priorities.

At the apartment, Polly had a nap and then Delia helped her to dress for the evening in white and emeralds. She was ready when Senator Case and his wife came to escort her to the gala. Ellen Case hadn't yet acquired the requisite flair for a young president's wife, but she was improving, and there was still time to polish her up. Polly had hired a stylist to dress her, and tonight she looked almost elegant in midnight-blue satin. If only her mother had done something about her overbite!

It was not until Polly was in her seat at the Kennedy Center and had opened her program that she discovered Winslow Talley was on it.

IV

Polly had never seen any point in denying the obvious. *He's a handsome bastard*, she acknowledged when he came onstage. *But he's a bastard all the same.*

She sat very erect in her chair, determined not to succumb to his charm—these days they called it charisma—as she had when she saw him in *Rapture*. Whatever they called it, he had it. This was the man who had stolen Kate from her, stolen a political career—maybe even the presidency—from Kate and then attempted to humiliate Kate, however impossible that was.

But when he began to speak, she was, despite herself, seduced by his voice, his extraordinary face, and the depth of feeling he projected. He recited Keats, Dickinson, and Dorothy Parker, and ended with a poem by Ernest Dowson that had always gone straight to Polly's heart and seemed to come straight from his.

> *Last night, ah, yesternight, betwixt her lips and mine*
> *There fell thy shadow, Cynara! . . .*
> *And I was desolate and sick of an old passion . . .*
> *I have been faithful to thee, Cynara! in my fashion . . .*
> *They are not long, the weeping and the laughter,*
> *Love, desire and hate . . .*
> *They are not long, the days of wine and roses . . .*

Win spoke for Polly. He was a kindred spirit, longing as ardently for his days of wine and roses as Polly longed for hers.

His voice rolled over her, bearing her along on a great tide of reminiscence, awakening longings Polly had believed long put to rest—painful, impossible yearnings for youth, beauty, wild infatuation, and that fire in the blood that comes only once in a lifetime. It was for that fire that Faust sold his soul to the devil. For that fire, at this moment of her life, Polly would have done the same.

She, too, was desolate and sick of an old passion: the passion betrayed—of her years with Oliver before she knew that he was not her dream; the forbidden passion of her brief time with Charles, who had been her dream from the moment she set eyes on him and would be until the day she died. Unbearable, still, that she could not have gone with him, or even let him know she had borne him a son—only to lose that son too.

But how could I have known Hilliard would do that terrible thing? she pleaded. *Should I have known? Why didn't I?*

Rebecca could tell her. Rebecca had tried suicide. If she could only get inside Rebecca's head!

There was a burst of applause, and Polly hastily pulled herself together, embarrassed by the tears on her cheeks. A glance around her made it clear that she was not the only one who had been moved to tears by the man standing in the spotlight.

Either he was good enough to project emotions he had never felt— or his remorse was as genuine as it seemed. Polly wanted to find out which. That was why she looked for him at the party following the performance.

V

He was so tall, she had no trouble finding him. He was talking to a group of people when he saw her, but excused himself immediately and came toward her, hesitant until he was sure she did not want to avoid him.

"Mrs. Benedict, I was hoping you'd be here." He towered over her, but her force of character made her his match.

"I had no idea you were on the program," Polly said. "I would not have come if I'd known. But I must tell you, putting our personal differences aside for the moment, that your performance tonight was superb."

He inclined his head. He might have been King Arthur in the fullness of his grace. He had an even tan and his hair was sun-streaked; in places it was almost gilt. Polly caught the scent of Givenchy's Monsieur and wondered why some authors supposed women were sexually aroused by grubby, sweaty men with knotty muscles and meaty hands.

"I've started to phone you many times," he said, "but I feared our 'personal differences' would get in the way."

"More than likely. I assume you wanted to talk about Kate."

He nodded. "She was very distant the last time we spoke. I have no idea whether or not she'll talk to me if I call her."

Polly shrugged. "No more do I. And don't ask me to sound her out for you, because I won't. I value my present relationship with her far too much."

He looked stricken—"his little-boy-lost look," Kate once called it—but this time, Polly was sure, it was genuine.

"Then I'll just have to follow my instinct," he said.

"Remember what happened the last time you did that," she replied.

"Nothing good, it's true. Kate's well rid of me."

They were both startled by the flash of a camera. The flash was repeated when they turned in the direction of the photographer.

"Dammit!" Win said.

"Yes, it's bound to be printed. I'll have to explain to Kate why I let down the side by talking to you."

"Kate has a forgiving nature."

"Kate has enormous pride and the fury of a woman scorned."

"She was the one who scorned me."

"After what you did, a village idiot would have scorned you." Polly shook her head. "You won't get her back. I won't fail to protect her this time."

"I just want to talk to her once in a while."

"Go ahead and try. The world is full of people who want to talk to Kate. Who wouldn't? She's superb! That's why many call her but few are chosen."

"You have no mercy," he said.

"Not a drop!" Polly scrutinized him closely. "I would like to know something."

He waited.

"Kate is your Cynara, isn't she? It's Kate's shadow that falls between you and every other woman you think you want."

"Yes," he said simply.

"That is your great misfortune. I should feel no compassion for you, but I do. Not enough, however, to tell her more about this evening than I need to. Good-bye, Mr. Talley."

"Good night, Mrs. Benedict."

VI

"When we refer to the Victorian era," Kate said to the crowded hall, "with its repressions and its egregious modesty, most of us think of England. But for the great majority of women, the rules were just as rigid in America.

"Success, if you were a woman, was based upon the spotlessness of your household and the manners of your children, the adequacy of your larder and the purity of your reputation. If your husband was a man of some means and you lived in Boston in about 1840, your house would probably be built of brick in the Gothic style, with turrets and towers. It would be overdecorated, not too comfortable, hard to keep clean, and rather gloomy. You would spend most of your time in it or at neighbors' houses very like it.

"There was no running water, except possibly in the kitchen and laundry, and no bathrooms since baths were considered both sexually arousing and unhealthy. Some sources say it was forbidden to take a bath without a doctor's prescription until about 1845. The 'necessary' was a wooden closet behind the house and called a backhouse.

"A well-to-do southern family might live in a Greek revival house graced by colonnades supporting a porch that ran the width of the house. The plumbing was no better than in Boston. Inside, the rooms were high, uncluttered, and abloom with flowers from the gardens—very like the house I live in now. There was air and light and comfort.

"But wherever home was, it was the man's castle. Children had no rights at all, and when a girl married she became a virtual slave. Her husband was literally her lord and master. Except in rare instances, she was not permitted to control her own money beyond the domestic allowance her husband doled out to her monthly. She could not own or manage property. If her husband beat her or abused her sexually, she had no recourse. She was his to do with as he liked—unless, of course, he murdered her. That was illegal. Catching a wife in adultery, however, was often a mitigating circumstance for a husband who killed.

"A woman was not expected to experience sexual pleasure, even in marriage; to invite attentions from her husband was frowned upon. Her reputation could be ruined if she so much as took the arm of a man to whom she was not related."

Kate paused. "In some Muslim countries a woman still may not touch a man other than her husband except in cases of extreme emergency. Restrictions on women are worldwide, although they vary in degree.

"Women were uneducated before the Civil War. Even those who attended the best female academies were taught to play acceptably on the pianoforte, to paint watercolors, and to write a decent hand. Their destiny was marriage—in the South that was often by the age of fifteen—and the bearing of children. Although women in the South often ran enormous plantations, they were not expected to know anything about the great world beyond their homes and gardens. They were told not to bother their pretty little heads."

Kate looked up. "Some of them still are."

The students laughed.

"All indications are that affluent women were, in general, rather insipid creatures, since they spent the greater part of their time doing nothing. Fashion required them to be pale, and since most women have ever been slaves to fashion, they drank vinegar and ate chalk to achieve the requisite pallor. The richer they were, the more idle they were, causing visitors from abroad to compare them to the wives of Turks and Arabs in their harems. They passed the time by modeling in soap or wax, painting china, hemming linen into handkerchiefs, sketching in charcoal, or reading *Godey's Lady's Book,* a far from stimulating periodical.

"Very few books were deemed suitable for women to read, lest they put dangerous ideas into those pretty little, empty little heads. Even on the library shelves the sexes were segregated, male authors on one side of the room, females on the other. A book written by a man could not be placed next to one written by a woman—unless the two authors were married. Legs—even on pianos—were called limbs; piano 'limbs' were sometimes covered by ruffled pantalettes for modesty's sake.

"Less than a hundred years ago in America, women were trussed into corsets, treated like children, and totally dominated by men. There was only one ray of light in all that darkness: a chivalrous respect for the weaker sex—provided it stayed weak. Even Europeans most critical of the New World were astounded by the attentions bestowed upon women. Women used that respect to manipulate and influence their men, who were their only conduit to power.

"This respect for women would begin to dwindle after 1848, which is when those dauntless feminists who would not conform began to catch the public's attention. When we consider the explosion of abuse and rape cases today, it seems clear that regard for women has vanished altogether. It will be one object of these lectures to ponder whether what women have gained makes up for what some feel they have lost."

The lecture hall burst into applause when Kate closed her folder and looked up. She nodded and then noticed for the first time that Gabriel Tennant was at the back of the hall. She acknowledged his presence with a smile, then went on to suggest a reading list.

She joined him when the bell rang and the lecture hall was emptying. "Will you attend all the lectures?" she asked, gently mocking.

"No, but I was in the area and wondered what you were like as a teacher."

"And?" They followed the crowd of students out of the hall and into the sunlight on the broad marble stairs.

"You're fascinating. There wasn't a sound when you were speaking."

"It's the material," Kate suggested.

"No, it's the delivery. If my mother presented the same facts, the feminist game wouldn't seem worth the candle."

"Don't you sometimes wonder if it is?"

He laughed. "What a question! Kate, you'd have had a hard time of it back then. You are definitely not what is meant by the weaker sex."

"Depends upon what you mean by weak."

"A woman of average height who wants taking care of."

"Everyone wants that. And the assumption that tall women don't need to be cherished has always amazed me."

He glanced at her but did not pursue the subject. He looked at his watch. "I have to go. I have an appointment in Charleston."

"Until tonight, then."

"Yes, I'm looking forward to it."

He got into the red Porsche, started the engine, and waved as the car pulled away. She waved back, wondering what he really thought and how she really felt about him.

Melinda Tillinghast appeared at her side. "He's stunning," she said with a conspiratorial smile.

Kate changed the subject. "How are you and Pritchard getting along?"

A painful blush spread from Melinda's face down to her neck and shoulders. "I haven't dated him since your dinner party," she finally managed to say. "Daddy thinks I should go out with boys my own age."

What happened that night is written all over her, Kate thought, regretting her blunder. She could see the two of them after her dinner party, grappling in Keating's car, the young man hot and expectant—all the girls did it—and the virgin, still hesitant, who could hear her adored father's opinion of the girls who did it ringing in her ears.

"I'm very sorry, Melinda," Kate said. "I didn't mean to pry."

"I think Mr. Tennant's great," Melinda said, dodging neatly.

"I'll tell him," Kate teased.

"I'd die if you did. But everyone thinks he's real cute and they say he's your boyfriend."

Kate laughed. "No, he's my *good* friend. How are things going, Melinda?"

"I love it here, Dr. Ballard! I'm so glad Daddy made me change— but, of course, when I knew you'd be here, I wanted to come."

"Hello, Dr. Ballard," a male voice said. It was Keating, bursting with spring and hormones, Kate thought. He glanced at Melinda. "Hi, Melly. Long time no see."

He wants me to know he dumped her, Kate thought. *The little shit is getting even with her for refusing sex.*

Melinda smiled. "But I've seen you play in every game."

She's got her father's grit, Kate reflected with satisfaction. In her tiny denim skirt and pink cotton sweater, Melinda looked as fragile as a flower.

Four of Pritchard's teammates appeared at the corner of the building and joined them. "I liked your lecture," Pritchard said.

The other boys nodded self-consciously, none of them as poised as their handsome captain.

"Thank you. Hello, everyone. Where are you off to?"

"Driving to Brooke Parrish to see some friends."

For "friends" read "girls," Kate decided.

"It's a beautiful day for it. Have a good time."

The two women watched the strapping boys walk away, muscles rippling.

Melinda looked at her watch. "I have to run. Holly's expecting me."

"Give her my regards," Kate said.

Melinda's blue eyes regarded Kate for a moment, the old quandary of young women in their depths: damned if they did, damned if they didn't. Then she said good-bye and ran off while Kate remembered how painful it was to be young with your body telling you one thing and society telling you another. Now, of course, society said "go ahead, follow your hormones and fuck," but there had always been a double standard about sex and there probably always would be.

Kate walked to the parking lot. Before she reached her car, Harald, who had been snoozing on the backseat of the convertible, erupted in a frenzy of joy. Kate told him to come out and work it off. He dashed frantically around the parking lot, stopping occasionally to lick her hand with his long, pink tongue.

"Have you got spring fever too, fella?" Kate asked him when they were driving home.

Sitting ramrod straight on the seat next to her, a safety belt across his deep chest, Harald's expression seemed undeniably romantic.

"I know just how you feel," Kate said. "We'll have to find you a lover too."

VII

Gabriel had chosen an elegant French restaurant near Charleston for a leisurely dinner and a bottle of exquisite Château Lafitte. They talked easily together, he about Alaska and its customs, she about her adventures in California. They were both reluctant to leave and lingered over liqueurs, but finally they were in the Porsche again. Kate felt relaxed, warm, happy, and triumphantly amorous. It was good to know that she could feel desire again, that she could feel more than she had for John Mallory.

Will Gabriel drive directly to his apartment? Kate wondered. She would know soon enough: they were about twenty blocks from a crossroads. The road to the left led back to Wakefield and the president's mansion, where it was foolhardy for Kate to bring a lover. The road to the right led to Charleston.

The ignition caught, the motor hummed, and the car moved forward.

Dammit, if he doesn't ask me, I'm going to ask him, Kate decided. *Settle the question once and for all. But what if he refuses? I'd be humiliated.*

She considered what would happen if she were humiliated. Her heart wouldn't attack her. She wouldn't have a seizure. If she had managed to come this far through the slings and arrows of life, could another rejection cause her grievous harm?

They were ten blocks from the crossroads when they stopped for a light. They turned to each other and smiled, and Gabriel took her hand. She felt a tiny leap of excitement at his touch. The light turned and the car rolled on. Kate waited for him to say something, but he made no sound and they were only a block away from the crossroads.

Oh, what the hell! Kate told herself. *A little humiliation never killed anyone.*

"Gabriel," she said.

"Yes?"

"I'd like to see your etchings."

VIII

The apartment was dimly lit, but he made no move to make it brighter. Instead, he put his hands on her hips and turned her to face him. She put her arms around his neck and kissed him. It was delicious to be in a man's arms again and it was a sweet, lingering kiss. When it was over, she put her cheek against his and enjoyed the warmth that was spreading downward to her thighs.

She stood within his arms until, as if he could not stop himself, he said, "Kate, I can't stop thinking about you. No other woman . . ." His mouth came down on hers, this time with passion.

He undid the zipper of her dress and she let it slide to the floor and stepped out of it. He unhooked her bra and took it off and his head bent first to her breasts, then to her thighs as he rolled her panties down and helped her to step out of them.

"Come to bed," he said, and she went where he led her. The sheets felt cool and crisp when she lay down and watched him undress.

She was surprised by him. As his hands roved over her, it was as if *his* defenses were being breached, one by one, and his control crumbling. He did not so much breathe as sigh explosively with each advance he made, as if he could fight no longer. He was at once resistant and unable to resist until she touched him, and then he capitulated to desire.

He moved up and down the length of her body, touching, stroking, until she reached for him. He moved to enter her swiftly, then for several moments he was motionless and she could feel him striving for control. When he regained it, he slid slowly in and out of her in what seemed to be an exercise in self-mastery rather than the heat of passion. She realized that she was not going to climax because his self-consciousness inhibited her. She realized, too, that he would not climax until she did.

She did what she had done several times with Mallory. She made the sounds of a woman approaching orgasm. She moved her hips in a quickened rhythm. She tightened her vaginal muscles, released them, tightened them again until he erupted. She arched her back and clasped him tightly, her long, strong legs around him, her arms holding him.

"My God," he said when his breathing had slowed. "That was incredible."

"Why didn't it happen sooner?"

He pulled himself out of her, lay on his back next to her, and slid an arm around her. "Because Talley is a hard act to follow."

In a flash Kate understood it all. "You thought I would compare you to the demon lover of stage and screen?"

He stroked her arm, waiting, and she knew what she had to say if she wanted to pursue this relationship. "I didn't, but believe me, Gabriel, you'd have nothing to worry about if I had!"

He put both arms around her. "You're quite a package all by yourself, Dr. Ballard," he said. "He just adds to the pressure."

"You thought I was keeping score? Two points for this, six points for that?"

"More or less. Some people do."

Kate shook her head. "I hope your little black book is written in code."

"I've never met a woman like you. You don't have to be recorded to be remembered." He kissed her and she kissed him back languorously, enjoying the embrace, the admiration, the tenderness.

Driving her back to Wakefield, he suggested a long weekend in Barbados.

"Sounds delightful," she said.

He wanted to see her before they went to Kel Regis, but he didn't press when she pleaded a full schedule. "It was a lovely evening," she said when he kissed her good night in the car.

"It was unforgettable. I'll call you tomorrow anyway. Maybe you'll find time for a walk on Sunday. Give me your key, I'll let you in."

"Better not. If *you* open the door, Harald might take you for an intruder."

He waited until she had let herself in. Harald hurled himself upon her, still young enough to forget his manners; up on his hind legs with his front paws on her shoulders, he was as tall as she was.

"Ah, thou noble beast," she said, hugging him. "If only I could find a man as uninhibited as you. Come on, darling, let's go to sleep."

When they were arrayed for the night, Kate in her four-poster, Harald on his rug on the floor alongside it, Kate thought about the evening. She knew that first sexual encounters were often disappointing—although hers with Win had been perfect. She told herself Win was not to blame for intimidating other men; it was to be expected when a woman had been married to a sex idol, but she resented him for it all the same.

She told herself she had been foolish to suppose there would be fireworks; the wine and the liqueurs were to blame for her great expectations. So was her celibacy for lo! these many months. She needed to get back into the swing of sex.

Gabriel was attentive and considerate as well as smart, good-looking, and clever. If the chemistry wasn't there at the first try, it would come and—she smiled—eventually so would she. She decided to give it a chance. She decided to walk with him on Sunday and to see what happened after that.

31

I

There's no doubt about it," Rebecca said gleefully. "They're lovers. I can tell about most women, and with Kate I couldn't be wrong." From her dressing table in their bedroom at Kel Regis she watched Theo covertly while she applied eye shadow and mascara.

"Come on, Becca! You saw them for only a few minutes when they arrived."

"That's all it takes, my darling."

"And do you approve of this alleged affair?"

"I think it's wonderful! She's been alone too long and he's the right kind of man for her. Neither of them cares about anything but work."

Theo finished tying his black bow tie. "Not even about each other?"

"Enough," Rebecca said. "They care enough for who they are. Kate will never feel for any man what she felt for Win. That kind of thing happens only once in a lifetime. The most any other man can ever be to her is second best. But she likes him; she told me so."

"Dammit!" Theo said. "I've put the cuff link in back to front!" He jerked at his cuff in utter frustration.

"You'll tear it! Let me help."

"No, I'll manage," he said brusquely. He reversed the cuff link and turned to her. "Ready?"

"Theo! I'm expected to wear a dress! Ring for Alice, will you?"

He realized she was still in her robe. Whenever she looked at him, her face was like a flower turned to the sun. His love for her battled with his guilt, his rage, his victimization. A great sob rose in his chest, but he suppressed it, retreating to ring for Alice. "You're so beautiful, it doesn't matter what you wear." He turned back to the mirror, picked up his comb, and ran it through his thick white hair again. "Mind if I go down and start working the room?" he asked her.

"No, you go ahead. I'll be down soon."

Theo made for the door, went through it, closed it, and leaned against it. It had taken all of his willpower to discuss Kate and Tennant without showing what he felt.

Of course they were sleeping together! When a man wants a woman as much as Theo wanted Kate, his instinct tells him if she's been to bed with someone else. There's something about a couple once they've been intimate: a different set to their bodies when they're together, a different way of speaking to each other, even about the most trivial things, and a heightened awareness of each other.

Gabriel was easier to read than Kate. When Theo attended his first trustees meeting, he had thought Gabriel starched and guarded, even priggish, concerned lest a crack appear in his armor. Now one had. Tennant hovered over Kate. He looked at her in a proprietary way that infuriated Theo. The thought of them together was sickening. But Polly was in favor of the match!

Kate mustn't marry him, Theo raged silently. *He's not good enough.*

A door at the far end of the gallery opened and Senator Case and his wife stepped out. Theo managed to pull himself together as the couple approached and the three went downstairs, Case looking handsome as ever, his wife's face wearing its tentative smile under her lacquered hair.

II

There were twenty people at Polly's sumptuous table that night. Kate had arrived just as Rebecca and Theo went upstairs to change. She managed to spend a few minutes with her father over cocktails before Theo and Rebecca reappeared and dinner was announced. As soon as everyone was seated—Kate was not surprised that she had been placed next to Gabriel—the conversation became unremittingly political.

From the crabmeat à la Russe to the Poire Belle Hélène, they discussed strategies for an election campaign that was still a few years away. Every time the Democratic Party chairmen from South Carolina and Georgia held forth in slow southern measure, Kate was reminded of Oliver and wondered if Polly was too.

"Let's hope this recession we're not supposed to be in lasts until election day," the chairman of the national committee said, spooning up chocolate syrup.

"Don't let anyone outside this room hear you say that!" the majority leader remonstrated, his heavy eyebrows furling. "We have to show concern for the average citizen."

"My sole concern is winning," the chairman said, pulling on his earlobe as he did whenever he was troubled. "My current nightmare is that something will come out of left field that puts the voters solidly behind the incumbent again."

"For example?" Theo asked.

"A war," Rebecca suggested. She was seated at Polly's left, across from the majority leader.

"Precisely," Tyler agreed.

"This country's not going to get involved in any war bigger than Panama," the majority leader said with more than his customary assurance. He was a large man with the red cheeks and nose of a heavy drinker, although no one had ever seen him even mildly high. "This is the era of international peace and democratization. No president could push a declaration of war through this Congress."

"He could if we were attacked," Rebecca said.

A silence ensued until Senator Case broke it. "But who'd be strong enough or stupid enough to attack us? The Soviets can't afford to feed themselves, much less sustain a war, hot or cold. They didn't begin playing pattycake with us out of affection, you know! And China has more than enough to cope with domestically."

"You're absolutely right, Senator," Tyler said.

The senator smiled his perfect smile, pleased with the approbation of Tyler Ballard. Polly thought Case looked particularly stunning in evening clothes and made a mental note to schedule more formal affairs when his campaign finally kicked off. Case's wife, her prominent teeth bared in delight, gazed at her spouse with total adoration.

I'll bet they're a sketch in bed, Polly sniggered to herself, exchanging a glance and a smothered smile with Dodie Phelps.

"It needn't be the Soviets or the Chinese attacking us," Rebecca said. "What if one of our allies is attacked by a lesser power? Or the Intifada turns into a real war?"

"That's the most likely scenario," the majority leader agreed.

"Rebecca, you have a keener grasp of politics than I'd thought," Polly said, raising her wineglass in a little salute.

Rebecca acknowledged the salute and looked at Kate, who arched her brows, clearly surprised by Polly's sudden benevolence toward an erstwhile enemy.

"My wife's a brilliant woman," Theo said.

Tyler beamed like a proud uncle. "She was a brilliant child as well, a delight to have about the place."

Again Rebecca glanced at Kate, this time with a triumphant little smile.

What the hell does that mean? Kate wondered.

"But pessimistic," Polly said. "I don't think even these fool Republicans would get us into a war."

"Someone has to consider the dark side," Gabriel said. "Better safe than sorry."

"I agree," Polly said. "And we'll resume our debate on the unexpected in about half an hour." Polly stood. "Ladies, shall we leave the gentlemen to profanity and port?"

"Is she serious?" Gabriel whispered to Kate. "Do the ladies retire?"

"Of course. That was the done thing when she was brought up and she's not about to change."

"Quaint," Gabriel said, smiling. "I rather like it."

"I'd pass on the port if I were you. The brandy's superb." She left the dining room, looking for Rebecca.

III

Kate caught up with the rapidly moving chair. "Becca, you're speeding! Slow down! We haven't had a chance to talk at all tonight."

Rebecca seemed frosty, but Kate, inured to her moods, persisted. "What made you decide to come?"

"Polly kept on about it. Theo thought I should."

"Come on, Becca! Tell me the real reason."

Rebecca shrugged. "Curiosity over you and the angel Gabriel."

Kate laughed. "Who told you about him?"

"Polly."

"I knew it! She's playing cupid again."

"She does it for your sake. She thinks Gabriel's perfect for you and I happen to agree with her. We were right about Win, weren't we?"

"I didn't know you and Polly were close enough to discuss me in such detail," Kate said, clearly nettled.

"We've been on the phone to each other regularly in the past few weeks."

When Rebecca came to a stop, Kate sat down in an armchair next to her. She spoke softly, but with hot resentment. "What the hell are you up to, Rebecca? First you close ranks with my mother, then with my grandmother. It's amazing how well you get on with two women you once despised for what they did to my life. Who's your next bosom buddy? Win?"

"Kate!" Rebecca smiled thinly. "You're jealous!"

"You're damned right I am! You were always in my corner when Sydney wanted to move back into my life, when Polly wanted to run it, when Tyler didn't give a damn! Why do you make a point of defending them, preening yourself because they're suddenly aware of you? Why are you so hostile toward me? Rebecca, you're the one constant in my life!"

Rebecca's expression softened and she clasped her hands tightly.

"Kate, oh, Kate, I'm sorry! I must be sweet to Polly so she'll invite me whenever Theo comes! I can't bear it when he leaves me home alone, and there aren't many places that accommodate a cripple as well as this one." Rebecca gave a laugh that was half a sob. "Dodie Phelps and I could run races in the ballroom!" Rebecca stopped the ragged laugh with a handkerchief and peered over it at Kate. Then she began to twist it as she went on. "I should have told you, but I was sure you'd know what I was up to with Polly. You always see right through me."

They looked at each other while the anger faded from Kate's eyes. At length, she said, "You're right, I was jealous. You go right ahead and cultivate anyone you choose, as long as nothing comes between us." Kate leaned back in the chair, suddenly limp. "I need you to help me nurse my grievances so I can keep all of them in the past, where they belong. I'm amazed to discover that I'm jealous of Polly's affection—and of Sydney's too, for God's sake! I don't know what got into me."

"I hope Gabriel did," Rebecca said with girlish mischief.

Kate smiled. "As a matter of fact . . ."

"Marvelous!" Rebecca said, a great smile lighting her face. She was as delighted as a child sharing secrets. "What's he like? Was it exciting? Tell me everything."

"Calm down, Becca! This is hardly the place to reveal the secrets of the bedchamber. I'll come over tomorrow."

"Promise?"

"Promise. For breakfast. About ten o'clock?"

"Make it nine. Theo's riding early, so come to my room and we won't be disturbed. I'm dying to hear all about it."

"There's not much to tell. Now I must separate some of these people from their money or Polly's wrath will be upon my head."

Rebecca nodded, feeling as if she could fly. Whatever might have happened between Kate and Theo was no longer happening. First, Kate would never have two lovers at the same time. Second, she must care for Gabriel or she wouldn't be blushing about him. Raw sex was not Kate's idea of bliss. She had dropped that fellow Jarett pretty quick, and she'd made short work of John Mallory.

The important thing was to get her married. Polly wanted it and Rebecca was equally determined to bring it about. Kate would be out of bounds to Theo when she married. She cared too much about her presidency to risk adultery.

Rebecca fairly beamed as she maneuvered her chair expertly around the satin-upholstered love seats and couches, the marquetry tables and exquisite objets d'art of Polly Benedict's drawing room. It was the most formal room in the house apart from the ballroom, and children were forbidden to set foot in either one until they were sixteen. Rebecca missed Mark, her youngest, terribly. She thought she could persuade Polly to let him visit Kel Regis.

Rebecca made her way past tables draped in damask under silver trays of petits fours, hand-dipped chocolates, an assortment of coffees and teas, and a selection of champagnes, brandy, and liqueurs. Curtis and two maids served coffee and drinks and then withdrew.

Lovely, Rebecca thought. *Everything here is so lovely!* Polly had become absolutely benevolent toward her, and Rebecca basked in the glow of her attention, not caring how much of it was due to pity and a wish to give Dodie Phelps a companion in misery. Theo admired Polly; Polly's attentions could only increase Rebecca's merit in his eyes.

Across the room, Polly stirred some sugar into a demitasse, put it on her cousin's tray, and put the special straw between her fingers.

"Did you see them?" Dodie Phelps murmured, glancing toward Kate and Rebecca. "They were having a proper dogfight, but they've fixed it."

"Gabriel fixed it," Polly whispered. "Let's hope Theo doesn't mess it up."

IV

Theo stood near the dining room window, barely listening to the conversation of the men still seated around the table. A soft breeze, smelling deliciously of freshly cut grass and buds ready to burst into bloom, wafted in, fresh, moist, sensuous. He thought of Kate with longing, of this woman he had possessed so many times and had never held in his arms.

He whispered her name, then remembered where he was and returned to the table where Gabriel was speaking to Tyler.

"Dr. Ballard, it's easy to see where Kate gets her talent for teaching," Gabriel said.

"Do you attend her lectures too?" Theo asked in a way that no one but Rebecca would have noticed.

Gabriel turned to him. "I went to the first one. It was fascinating. She's a remarkable woman. So is your wife. I can see why they're fast friends."

Theo inclined his head, accepting the compliment grudgingly.

"Well now, Tyler," said the majority leader. "We don't see much of you on the lecture circuit lately, and that means another book. What's it about?"

Tyler smiled. "It's a superstition among writers never to discuss a work in progress."

"I never knew you to be superstitious before," Theo said.

"Next he'll be telling us he's dabbling in black magic," the Georgia Democratic chairman said, his jowls jiggling as he chuckled.

"A little magic wouldn't come amiss," the national chairman said testily, tugging at his earlobe. "Maybe that's the only way to break the Republican death grip on the White House."

They returned to their favorite topic of conversation until there was a tap on the door and Curtis entered.

"Time to join the ladies," the majority leader said. The men got up and headed for the door. Once inside the drawing room, Theo looked for Rebecca, found her with Polly, and crossed to join them.

"Having a good time, darling?" he asked her.

"Oh, yes, Theo. I'm so glad I came."

"There," Polly said. "I knew she would be. She must come often, whenever she likes, with or without you, Theo." She turned to him affectionately. "It's high time your wife and I got to know each other better. Now, please excuse me. I must see to my other guests."

"What do you suppose she's after?" Rebecca wondered when Polly was out of earshot.

"Does it matter?"

"No. I rather like her making a fuss over me. Now go and charm everyone, Theo. It's bad form for married people to talk to each other at parties."

But Theo was intent upon finding Kate.

V

Theo and Kate strolled back and forth on the veranda, one of several other couples taking the air.

"Did you solve any big political problems?" Kate asked.

"I wasn't paying much attention."

"That's a first! What diverted you?"

"Gabriel Tennant."

"Why is that?"

"He's not for you, Kate!"

"He probably shares your opinion."

Theo shook his head grimly. "No, it's painfully obvious that the man is smitten. Are you?"

Kate laughed. "Theo, you old gossip!"

"I'm not joking," he said. They had reached the other end of the veranda, and instead of turning to walk back, they stopped, looking past the pool of light from the house to the blackness beyond.

"I was trying to pretend you were," Kate said. "Look, I appreciate your concern for me, but Gabriel and I . . ."

"Concern?" Theo groaned. "I'm in love with you, woman, you know that! I can't watch you throw yourself away on another man who doesn't deserve you!"

"I thought we'd settled this in Zurich," Kate said.

"Love doesn't disappear just because it should."

Kate turned and started back, Theo at her side. "I think Rebecca knows about this," Kate said.

"That's impossible!"

"No, it isn't. She knows us both inside out and she has an uncanny gift for reading people. She's never been as cold to me as she was tonight, until I told her I was . . . fond of Gabriel. Then she melted completely. It wouldn't have made that big a difference to her unless she was suspicious."

"No," Theo insisted. "I've never let anything slip, not even when we're . . . not even in bed."

"Dammit, Theo, there are some things you know without having them spelled out! It's all because of that fatal game the two of you play, pretending this is all temporary when you know she's crippled for life. You've been using me to get past the pity, but the only way you can get past it is by telling her the truth."

"It would destroy her!"

"It *is* destroying her, Theo! That's why she tried to kill herself! She's tried to pull herself out of that pit, or she wouldn't be here tonight, but you're going to pull her back."

He stopped abruptly, appalled. "I? Never! I love her."

"Then why this fiction that you love *me*! Theo, you're a threat to what I have with Rebecca, and that's much too dear to me to be surrendered without a fight. Talk to Rebecca, or I will. It's either that or find yourself another fantasy!"

She turned and left him where he stood.

VI

"Come home with me," Gabriel said when they were in the car.

"Yes, I'd like that."

He touched her cheek gently and Kate leaned back, thinking about Rebecca and Polly. It was clear enough what Rebecca wanted from this new friendship between the two women, but what did Polly expect to get from it?

"Having second thoughts?" Gabriel asked.

"Not at all. Just anticipating."

Gabriel smiled, kissed her hand, and leaned forward to turn on the stereo. The first strains of Wagner's Prelude and Liebestod rose in the night, suggestively sensual, a prologue to passion.

"It's the most gorgeous music I know," Gabriel said.

It delighted her that he found such deeply erotic music appealing. He had not struck her as that kind of man. He liked sex, certainly, but the way he made a contest of it was inhibiting. He yielded because he hadn't the will to resist. How would such a man feel about a woman who consistently breached his defenses?

"They say he wrote it as a musical description of the act of love," Kate said, wondering what he would make of that.

"I've heard the same thing, but I thought it was apocryphal."

"Apocryphal or not, that music comes very close."

Gabriel hesitated. "Have you ever made love to it?"

She turned to him, again delighted. She had supposed he was a man who didn't talk about sex.

"No, I haven't."

"Would you like to?"

She nodded.

"Then let's listen to it on the way home and figure out how to keep pace with the music."

Kate laughed delightedly. "Let's." She put her head back and listened, putting everything else aside, letting her erotic imagination meld into the richly sensuous music as it climbed slowly, ardently, to its ravishing climax.

They said absolutely nothing to each other until they were side by side in bed, holding hands, listening to the music again from its deceptively peaceful start.

He turned to her and kissed her. "I'm falling in love with you, Kate."

But it was sex she wanted, not love, not now.

He kissed her many times before his hands touched her. She was responsive, intoxicated by the music, blissfully ardent. It excited him more than it had the first time.

She was aware of the many textures of his body: the skin of his face with its incipient beard slightly rough against her cheek, the smoothness of his back and the hardness of the muscles beneath the surface, the incredible silkiness of him between her legs, almost but not quite in her while his seeking fingers opened her, excited her, preparing his way into her willing, giving body. For a second she was conscious of the music beginning its last explosive surge and then she heard nothing. When he was finally inside her her hips began to pump, her breath came in gasps that blended with his until, on a crest of pleasure so acute it was almost painful, she reached the top and heard her voice repeating his name.

It was very still in the apartment when, finally, they breathed quietly again.

"What happened to the music?" Kate asked. "Did we follow it?"

"Damned if I know. After a while I couldn't hear anything but us. Shall I put it on again?"

"Why try to improve on perfection?"

He held her closer. "Ah, Kate!" he said. "What a lovely thing to say."

She stroked his hair, happy to be with him, content. She was sure that tonight had revealed more about him, but she did not want to analyze now, only to enjoy.

"Stay the night," he said. "Sleep by my side."

"I can't. I'm expected at Kel Regis at nine for breakfast and I can't turn up in a dinner dress."

"All right, but we're going to Barbados. And soon."

VII

They went three weeks later. It was under a palm tree on the beach at the Sandy Lane Hotel that Gabriel asked her what she wanted to do with the rest of her life.

"Exactly what I'm doing. And you?"

"The same, but that doesn't exclude everything else."

She agreed, waltzing around the subject with him. "Unless it were to interfere with my work."

"I'm sure it wouldn't." He sat up, regarding the sea. "That water is pure aquamarine. Want to swim?"

"I'm too lazy. You go ahead."

She watched him walk toward the water, admiring his body and wondering why he was always so indirect. They had just been talking about marriage, but the word itself was not to be used until he had completed his research—which included an inspection by his family —and had decided she was what he wanted.

She hoped it would take him a long time to decide. However desirable Gabriel was, she had finally arranged her life to her satisfaction and she had no great desire to change it.

32

The president's mansion seemed enormous after the shared bunga-
low in Barbados, far too large for one person to rattle around in alone.
Even Harald, who had attained his full growth some time ago,
seemed to have grown along with the house—and he had changed.
He did not stretch his great length across the threshold of whatever
room she was in, but sat at attention by her side, regarding her with a
vigilant, reproachful air.

"He'll never let you out of his sight now," her housekeeper, Lillian,
told her when she brought Kate a cup of tea in her bedroom. "The
whole time you were gone he barely ate more than half a horse a day.
He just sat near the front door waiting from dawn to dawn. I put his
rug down there for him to sleep on, poor thing. I never did see such a
pitiful creature."

Kate looked up from the clothes she was unpacking. "Don't tell me
any more, Lillian. I'm laden with guilt as it is."

When Lillian went off bearing clothes to be cleaned, pressed, or
washed, Kate sank to the floor and embraced her dog, scratching between his ears, stroking his glossy coat. "For pity's sake, Harald, cheer
up, I'm back now. I couldn't take you with me, but I'm not going
anywhere for a long time."

Not until August, at any rate. She had promised Gabriel she would
go to Alaska with him then to meet his family. They would have an
enormous "potlatch" and introduce her to everyone in Anchorage.

"I can't imagine why I said I'd go," she told Harald. What had
seemed a good idea on the beach at Barbados became more unreason-
able by the minute here in her bedroom at Wakefield. True, it had been
a much-needed break and she had enjoyed being with Gabriel, but he
seemed to pale in absentia. Out of sight, he was pretty much out of

mind. She had to be *with* him to know she wanted to be with him. The house was once more the perfect size for her, exactly right, not too big at all!

And yet she did not want to live the rest of her life alone, collecting memories she could share with no one. Gabriel would not be intrusive. He was as involved with his profession as she was with hers.

But if Kate went to Alaska and passed muster with his family, it was a good bet that Gabriel would ask her to marry him. He would finally put a direct question that required a direct answer. She had no idea what it would be.

Her private telephone rang.

||

"Kate?" Win said when she answered. "Where have you been? I was worried."

It was genuine. She was surprised to hear him but not put off balance as she had been the last time he called. "Is anything wrong?" she asked him. She was somewhat reluctant to ask: his last movie had been a box office flop—deservedly so, Kate had thought when she fidgeted through it, embarrassed by the material and his obvious contempt for it. Even a brilliant career like his could collapse with the wrong material.

"The usual things," he said. "Frightened investors. Bad scripts. I can't make a silk purse out of rubbish." He sounded utterly depressed.

It was unlike him to let her read his moods after they divorced. A foolish gallantry, perhaps, but it had always touched her to see him whistling in the dark so that the world would never know he was afraid. He had once told her he could step off the stage entirely only with her. She wished he had done it more often.

"Tell me," she said now.

"I'm facing one of the most important decisions of my life."

So am I, she thought, and waited for him to go on.

"I've been offered the role of King Mark in a dramatic version of *Tristan and Isolde.* The possibilities are enormous—and I'd be back in the theater, where I belong."

At the back of her mind she saw herself making love with Gabriel to music from the opera of the same name. "What's the problem?" she said. "You'd be wonderful in the part."

"There's a loyal ex-wife!"

"I really think it's a great idea."

He hesitated. "I rather fancied myself in the role of Tristan."

"Why?"

"Kate! No one's ever heard of Mark but everyone knows Tristan because he's the young lover."

Of course, she thought. *Youth is as vital to an actor as it is to a mistress.*

"But that's all he is!" she said. "The king would have more depth, more character, more poignance than a callow youth who's randy because he drank a love potion. Love is a lot more dramatic without a potion because there's a choice."

"Not always," Win said quietly. "Sometimes, even when it's hopeless, you have no choice. You love."

She wasn't about to be led into that!

"Assuming King Mark falls in love with Isolde on sight," she said, "and knows about the potion, there won't be a dry eye in the house when he has to choose between love and pride. A lot will depend on the script."

"It's the script I'm not sure of! Do you think you could . . . ?"

"All right, send it to me. I'll find the time to read it."

"Will you, Kate? I'll be so grateful. You're the only one I can trust."

"Don't flatter me, Win. Just send it."

"I could bring it."

"You could, but you *may* not. And send it quickly, before I change my mind."

"It's on the way. How are you, Madam President? Spring puts you in a vulnerable state, as I recall. You tend to fall in love."

"That was in another country," she said, "and besides, the wench has grown up."

"A pity. The wench was irresistible in the spring." His voice stroked her, stirring up memories.

"Let's not dwell on the past, Win."

"All right, then, the present. Where were you? I've been trying your private line for days."

She had not expected jealousy from Win. She didn't know whether to be gratified or apprehensive: gratified because it was every jilted woman's dream that the man who left her would regret his mistake and beg to be taken back; apprehensive because she still cared how he felt about her and she'd supposed that was over long ago.

"In Barbados for a little R and R."

He hesitated. "Did you go alone?"

"No." She was enjoying this! "I went with a flock of ardent swains."

"Will you, at least, tell me whether you're going to the Cape for the summer?"

"Not for all of it." He waited for her to tell him where else she was going, but she would tell him nothing about Alaska or her personal life. It was childish of her, but she had to withhold it from him. She had always given Win everything, but she was damned if she would do that anymore.

"Kate?"

"Yes."

"I miss you."

There was nothing she could say to that.

"I just wanted you to know that," Win said, dropping the seventh veil. "The play was only an excuse to call you. I suppose Polly told you we met in Washington?"

"She did."

"She still doesn't like me," Win said ruefully.

"The whole damned world can't like you offstage as well as on."

"I know, but I've come to realize it's what I always wanted."

"A dangerous fancy. If you keep changing in order to be likable to everyone around, who *are* you? A few honest-to-God people who know me, warts and all, are enough for me."

He didn't comment on that. "Listen, about the play," he said. "If it's an imposition, I'll make the decision myself."

"Oh, for God's sake, Win, just send it! Now I've got to go to a meeting. I'll get back to you as soon as I can." She hung up.

" 'My own dear love,' " she recited to Harald. " 'He was all my world and I wish I'd never met him.' "

Harald put a paw on her knee.

"Harald, come up here." She embraced the huge dog and he swabbed her with his pink tongue before he arrayed himself across her. "I have a hypothetical question for you," Kate said, and he turned his majestic head to look at her attentively.

"Suppose I had a choice. Would I want to be staid and serious from this day forward, devoted entirely to my work? Or would I want a little lunacy from time to time, a little magic? Why, you ask, must I have it with him? Because his kind of lunacy suits me. What have you to say to that?"

Harald yawned.

III

Kate changed out of her traveling clothes and walked to her meeting, crossing the park to the campus, tossing a stick for Harald to fetch en route. Wakefield, in its way, was as beautiful as Barbados. The lawns were thick and lush and bordered by spring flowers and the pink, waxen blooms of magnolia trees. The great oaks swayed in the breeze, shading the park.

"This is my place," Kate said softly, contentedly. "It's my responsibility and Polly's pride and I love watching over it."

The campus was peaceful, dotted with students studying under the trees, among them Melinda Tillinghast with a boy who looked like Andy Hardy. Pritchard Keating and several members of the football team sat nearby—Kate wondered if that was deliberate—and when they signaled her, Kate responded with a wave and a smile as she went by. She ran up the broad concrete steps of the administration building and then up the oak stairs to the second floor.

Her secretary told her that everyone had already arrived, and Kate walked into her office. It was a large room with light filtering through the sheer curtains of three windows on one wall. Rows of leather-bound books filled two more walls, and the fourth displayed framed photographs of all of Wakefield's presidents, including Kate, who was the youngest.

There were four people seated in armchairs upholstered in burgundy leather. The two students sitting on the couch were Holly Groehler and Tom Lewis.

"Am I late?" Kate asked.

"Not at all." Harrison Watley, dean of men, stood and held out his hand. He had a square body and a square face under extremely arched eyebrows that made him look constantly surprised. He had dealt firmly with male undergraduates since Wakefield became coeducational. Without him, Polly often said, the transition would have been a lot more difficult.

"We were early," Elinor Gates said, shaking hands in her turn. Spare in appearance—gray hair in a bun, gray suit, white blouse, walking shoes—and possessed of a refreshing, no-nonsense manner, the dean of women had a talent for sniffing out the problems of "my girls" and a reputation for strict application of the rules, although she tempered discipline with compassion.

Academic dean Natalie Marsh was slim, imperious, and dressed in the latest fashion. Kate was well aware she considered herself presidential material and saw Kate's appointment as pure nepotism. Most of the trouble Kate had with faculty was Natalie's doing. She was like a cat among the pigeons, stirring up resentment and jealousy. Her opposite number, Alan Cook, was a small, wiry man with a nervous cough and, Polly said, "seven brains."

Kate turned next to Holly and Tom. *So deadly serious,* she thought affectionately, *the pair of them.*

"Please don't mind Harald," Kate said, sitting in her chair behind the walnut desk. The Great Dane sat beside her, still at attention, his head rising above the desktop as he watched them all with suspicion. "He has spring fever."

"I think we all do," Elinor Gates said. "How was your holiday?"

"Marvelous. I was sinfully lazy." Since she and Gabriel had taken different flights, he by way of Dallas, no one knew they had gone together. "And I still am, so let's solve our problem quickly and go out to enjoy the weather."

The problem was a small group of students agitating for coed dormitories.

"I'm flatly against it," Natalie Marsh said. "Young men are getting entirely the wrong message from the feminists." She was very cool, but she made it clear that the feminists were at fault and Kate more so than most.

Harrison agreed with her. Elinor Gates was against it too, as were Holly and Tom. Alan Cook was of two minds, not unexpected in a man with seven brains, but he was soon convinced to join the others.

"That makes it unanimous among us," Kate said. "And the students?"

"Most of the men are for," Tom said.

"And most of the women are against," Holly added.

"I think we should go straight to the trustees," Natalie said. "The issue is too important to be decided by a student vote."

"Surely we can handle it ourselves," Elinor said.

Kate thought a moment. "Let's try to do that. Holly, call a meeting of the student body. We have to give the author of this folly a chance to plead his cause before we reject it."

"Who'll reply?" Harrison asked.

Natalie leaned forward.

"I will," Kate said. "But we'll keep that to ourselves."

Holly laughed delightedly. "You'll fix his wagon, Dr. Ballard."

"I hope so."

"But can you be sure?" Natalie demanded.

"What if it goes the wrong way?" Alan asked.

"Then Natalie can back me up," Kate said cheerfully. "It's worth a try."

They talked about it a little while longer, then Holly and Tom left together and Kate walked part of the way home with Harrison and Elinor, basking in the beautiful day, the company she kept—even including lemons like Natalie—and the life she lived.

She was halfway across the park before she reminded herself that nothing in life, no matter how perfect, ever stayed the same.

IV

Wakefield's presidents traditionally held open house on alternate Sunday afternoons for students and whatever parents happened to be visiting.

The weather continued perfect, sunny but not hot. On a Sunday in

May, the French windows were open, the drawing room doors rolled back. After they had tea, students strolled on the magnificent lawns while Kate held court on the veranda.

She saw Clyde Tillinghast, much less given to nervous fidgeting these days, approaching with Melinda on his arm. Among parents, he was the most frequent visitor.

"Well, Katie, there you are in all your glory," he said. "You look every inch a president." He appraised her coral silk dress and her black-framed glasses. He wore a very conservative gray suit with a striped gray and red tie that went with the new, less abrasive personality he appeared to be cultivating. Melinda wore a pale yellow dress that hit her at mid-thigh, white hose, and black patent leather Mary Janes. Except for her breasts, she looked like a seven-year-old.

I haven't done all I should if Wakefield women still dress like little girls, Kate reproached herself. But most women followed fashion blindly, like lemmings plunging headlong into the sea.

"Thanks for the compliment," she said. "Hello, Melinda. Isn't this a perfect day?"

"Isn't this a perfect daughter?" Tillinghast hugged Melinda. "Straight A's."

"Maybe, Daddy," Melinda protested. "I never said for sure. Oh, there's Holly. I have to talk to her for a minute. Please excuse me, I'll be right back."

Tillinghast watched her go. "My princess is a real beauty," he said.

"She is. She's also a delightful young woman."

He cocked his head. "What do you make of this Keating kid she talks about so much?"

It startled Kate—and made her a little envious too—that Melinda confided in her father to such a degree. Kate would never have told Tyler anything that personal.

"I don't know Keating that well, but he seems a good sort. I thought they hadn't been dating lately."

"They haven't," Tillinghast said glumly. "You ask me, she still has a crush on him. What is he anyway, crazy? Dropping a girl like that! It's a good thing he's graduating. Whoever started this sexually equal thing wasn't the father of a girl child! I told Melinda to find herself another boyfriend. I want her to finish college. She loves Wakefield and she thinks you're the cat's pajamas." He smiled. "So do I."

"You're a real charmer, Mr. Tillinghast." His efforts at civility were making him a diamond in the rough.

"I wish to God you'd call me Clyde!"

"I'll try."

"Here's a nice fat check for the endowment fund. Maybe that'll make it easier."

"Why, Clyde," Kate said with a heavy drawl. "Your generosity just makes my poor little old head spin and my heart go flippety-flop."

"You must be coming down with something," Tillinghast said as, laughing heartily, he went to find his daughter.

V

Kate finished reading the *Tristan* script late on a Saturday afternoon and called Win at the New York City number he had written on the manuscript. The telephone was answered by a breathless female voice trying to sound like Marilyn Monroe.

"Mr. Talley, please," Kate said briskly. "Dr. Ballard calling."

She heard the girl tell Win they were going to be late if he talked more than two minutes. Win told the girl to go on ahead without him. She said she knew perfectly well who Dr. Ballard was because he'd been going on about her for weeks. Win said that was because Dr. Ballard was beautiful, brilliant, and an altogether superior woman. The girl told him to fuck himself. He told her to go to the devil. A door slammed. Then Win was on the line.

"Kate? I thought you'd never call. Don't tell me: you hated it, didn't you?"

"On the contrary, I liked it very much, but some things need to be explained if you don't want King Mark and Win Talley to come off like male chauvinist swine."

"Of course not! Swine are so unromantic! What changes?"

"Well, here we have Tristan, gone on a bride quest for his king. He escorts the ravishing Princess Isolde back home to marry King Mark. En route they drink the love potion intended to make Isolde and the king nuts about each other. Instead, Tristan and Isolde fall in love and *wham!* there goes her maidenhead. That much is in the script."

"Aside from the maidenhead, what's missing?" Win asked, puzzled.

"The implications of female virginity in *that* day and age."

"Virginity? Kate, we're acting in *this* day and age!"

"You're acting a legend and the play won't make sense without an explanation of what mattered then. Virginity was absolutely vital. It had nothing to do with love. It was a matter of property and lineage that only later became a moral issue or an ego trip for husbands. A virgin bride guaranteed a man that the heir to his property was legitimately his. It was an absolute requirement, particularly when the parties to a marriage were royal and the property was the kingdom itself, as was the case for King Mark and Isolde. It needs explaining."

"Yes, go on."

"Then, the script hasn't done enough with Isolde's lady in waiting,

Brangaene. By leaving that potion lying about for the wrong man to drink, she's responsible for the whole tragedy of Isolde, who is as hopelessly in love with Tristan as he is with her. But Isolde is bereft of her virginity. When King Mark discovers that on the wedding night, she will be put to death, her name and her family will be dishonored, their kingdom forfeit to Mark's honor.

"That's why Brangaene, drowning in guilt, agrees to replace Isolde in the marriage bed and be deflowered for her. It's a lot to ask of any woman! The scene between the two women has a lot more potential than they've given it. It's a matter of life and death and honor and just plain sex."

"And how!" Win agreed eagerly.

"And the scene in the nuptial bed will be sensational as well. In a dimly lit room, Mark takes possession of his supposed bride and encounters the expected barrier. Brangaene cries out in pain. The bloody cloth is presented to the court as proof of the bride's chastity, just the sort of primitive stuff modern audiences want."

"What about Mark?" Win asked.

"According to this version, Mark knew Tristan and Isolde were lovers the moment he clapped eyes on them. King Mark is not a feckless youth like Tristan, and he's desperately in love with Isolde, his glorious young bride. On his wedding night he knows it's not Isolde he's holding in his arms, but if he falters in acquiring proof of her virginity, Isolde will be put to death! And all because of a membrane smaller than a quarter! Does he sacrifice his bride or his pride?"

"His pride," Win said.

"There's a quandary for you! How does he treat Brangaene? What does he say to Isolde, lying at his side the morning after. How does he act, knowing he will always love her but that, because of that potion, she can never love him? It's all very dramatic!"

"Kate, you missed your profession. You should have been a playwright."

"Shall I send back this copy or just my notes?"

"Just the notes. Talk to me for a few minutes."

"You'll be late for your party."

"Damn the party! The only good party I ever attended was in my flat in Oxford after we closed *Taming of the Shrew*. Remember?"

She remembered, but she would not be caught in a web of nostalgia.

"I have to go or I'll be late to my *own* party," she said. "Good-bye, Win. I'm sure the play will be a smash."

"I'll send you a pair of tickets for opening night."

"I'd like that. Take care." She hung up and pulled her robe around her, although the evening was mild. She wasn't going anywhere, and she was furious with herself for having refused an invitation from Gabriel in order to finish both the script and, she was determined, her connection with Win. The whole man/woman charade, she decided, was not worth the trouble it took.

"I'm antsy," she said to Harald. His ears twitched and he studied her as if he could fathom her meaning.

"Let's go for a walk," she said, getting to her feet. Harald did a mighty stretch and followed her down the stairs and out the front door.

It was a glorious night, with just enough light left to empurple the sky. The air smelled like all the perfumes of Arabia. The grass was wet with dew, and Kate took off her slippers to walk barefoot in the cool green velvet. It was very still, so still that from time to time Kate could hear the shouts and laughter of a crowd of students on the campus across the park. They had built a bonfire to celebrate Founders' Day, and soon the smell of smoke would overcome the scent of grass and flowers.

Founders' Day had become a far more raucous celebration since Wakefield turned coed. In Kate's day it had been a fairly decorous occasion; now it was a minor bacchanale.

"Can't stop boys being boys," Maynard had protested, cracking his knuckles when Kate suggested stricter regulations at the last meeting of the trustees.

"Or girls being girls," Polly said.

"The kids don't do any harm," Gabriel added. "It's just high spirits at the approaching end of the school year and, for some of them, graduation day and the beginning of real life."

Kate, reminding herself that she had always been uncomfortable with noise and crowds, had dropped it. If Polly sided with the others, she had little chance of carrying the board and putting a lid on the alcoholic part of the celebration.

At least Kate had won the coed-dorms debate hands down, using a combination of common sense and humor when she took on the young people who were in favor of it. She knew the majority were with her and she persuaded them to say so. The issue never reached the board, nor were Natalie Marsh's efforts required.

It was another affirmation of Kate's popularity with people twenty years younger than herself, and that made her still more certain she was doing the right thing in the right place at the right time. She smiled now at the sounds of Wakefield's high-spirited revelers enjoying themselves.

"Come on, Harald, let's eat up all the ice cream and read a trashy novel."

33

I

Melinda was separated from her date by the crowd of whirling, dancing students while the great bonfire blazed and rock music blasted from speakers rigged on the trees. She didn't care about misplacing Bobby. She wasn't that crazy about him anyway. He was nice enough but dull. Despite the promises she'd made to herself and Holly in their long talks together, Melinda couldn't forget the heady splendor of being dated by Pritch Keating earlier in the year. It seemed like ages since she was the most envied girl at Wakefield— and then, overnight, the most pitied.

But it was for the best, she reminded herself. She wanted to be the kind of woman her father had brought her up to be, not the kind who gave herself to any boy who asked her. Not that Pritch was just any boy—every girl at Wakefield was mad about him—but Melinda didn't want to be one of many and, from the things he'd said that night after Dr. Ballard's dinner party, that's all she could be whether she had sex with him or not.

"You can go to hell," she'd told him, getting out of the car. She said what her father always said about her dates. "You're not worth my little finger."

"It's not your little finger I'm interested in." He had absolutely perfect teeth when he smiled, even when he said dirty things like that. "Get back in the car. It'd take you all night to walk home from here, and there'd be a stink."

And so she had and he'd driven her to her dormitory, barely waited until she got out of the car, then shot forward with a screech of tires as if he couldn't get away from her fast enough.

That was the last time they'd spoken and her life had been pretty dull since then. Now she studied with Bobby King, walked to and from the library with Phil Carson, and, for the rest, went out on group dates, where everyone hung out together.

Someone running by jostled her, and she almost fell backward, but she was caught and steadied.

"You okay?" Pritchard Keating's voice asked.

"Yes, fine," Melinda said, and a lovely little shiver, half embarrassment, half pleasure, went through her at the feel of his hands around her waist. She felt flustered and clumsy. He didn't know she had been watching him from afar for months, but *she* knew. So did Holly, who said she was obsessed by celebrity, along with the rest of the country.

"You all alone?" Pritch asked.

"Not really. I came with a bunch of kids, but we got separated by the crowd."

"My date stood me up," he said with a little smile.

Melinda looked up at him and raised an eyebrow, a trick her father used on people and which she had perfected with practice.

"Well, not exactly," he admitted. "She got sick at the last minute. Hey, would you like to come to a party?" he asked.

She hesitated, looked away, then back at him.

"Aw, c'mon, Melly. You can't hold that night against me all my life! I had too much to drink and came on too strong."

He had put his hand right inside her panties and touched her, and to him that was just coming on too strong!

He was searching her face with his dreamy, heavily lashed dark eyes. "I've been kicking myself for it ever since." He was abashed, as embarrassed as she was.

"Hello!" Holly said, detaching herself from the crowd. She addressed only Melinda until she realized who was with her. She glanced from one to the other incredulously. She and Melinda had spent hours talking about that night, about how some girls thought nothing of having sex and some justified it if they were in love and some, like Melinda, just weren't ready until they were ready. For that last group, the permissive society didn't permit much.

And Melinda was innocent, in a way. She knew all the facts of life but not much about men and the misery they caused. Holly knew that was because her father had protected her as if she were a porcelain doll. Melinda adored her father, and Mr. Tillinghast's views on the subject were very clear.

Don't cheapen yourself, Melly. All this stuff about sexual equality is a crock. Women can't fool around and get away with it. Men can. It's because of the way we're made. We deposit. You absorb. It's *your* honor that gets stained. It's that simple and that unfair.

"Melly?" Pritchard was saying. "The party?"

Melinda studied him, standing there looking so remorseful and so appealing. The most popular man on campus was sorry for his past behavior and had invited her to a party to make up for it.

"I'd like to very much," she said, ignoring the shock on Holly's face, "if Holly can come along."

"No, really . . ." Holly began, tempted by her first invitation to an inner-circle party.

"Sure," Pritchard cut in. "Great idea." He offered an arm to each girl with an exaggerated gallantry that made them all laugh. "Ladies, shall we go?"

II

The party was a double celebration for the six star members of the Wakefield football team: the season had been triumphant for them, and two of the six team members who rented this off-campus house were graduating in June. There was plenty to drink, plenty to smoke, and plenty to snort. The party started while the bonfire was still burning; by ten o'clock most of the guests were high, drunk, or sound asleep. There was scuffling in the dark corners that meant sex.

"I think this is awful," Holly said to Melinda in the living room of the house where they sat drinking Cokes. "It's an opium den, not a party. Let's go."

"Okay. I'll go tell Pritch."

"He's too high to care."

"I can be polite even if he isn't."

Holly hated it when Melinda put on airs, but she hid it well. What Melinda really wanted was to remind Pritch she was there. "Ask him to come with us," Holly suggested.

Melinda nodded and crossed the living room. In the downstairs bedroom, Pritchard was sprawled on one of the two double beds in a tangle with two boys from Texas, Jeremy McKittrick and Terry Otis. All three were giggling like little kids.

"Pritch," she said, shaking him. "I'm leaving."

He opened an eye and smiled crookedly at her. "Hi there, Melly. What's happening?"

"Pritch, Holly and I are leaving. Curfew's at midnight."

"No problem, Cinderella, we've got plenty of time. We'll go to The Hut and dance awhile."

"I want to go now," Melinda said in a low voice. "Everyone's high and carrying on."

"Why don't you get high and carry on too?"

"You know I don't drink or do drugs."

"Hell, I forgot! You're Miss Perfect. But I don't want you to go, honey lamb. This is a big night for us, right, fellas?"

The two others laughed raucously.

"Let's just stay here and talk a little longer," Pritch said. "Then we'll go together. Okay?"

Everyone would be at The Hut. She wanted them to see her with Pritch again. It would make up for some of the snickers she had endured when he dropped her.

"Okay," she said.

Melinda went back to the living room. "He wants me to stay a little longer, then we'll go to The Hut." She hesitated. "Come with us."

"No," Holly said, catching the hesitation. She had had enough of tagging along. If Melly was that interested in Keating, she was welcome to him.

"Will you be angry at me if I stay?" Melinda asked.

"Do you remember what happened the last time you were alone with him?"

"I won't be alone with him. This place is bulging at the seams."

"They're all dorky from pot."

"I'll take Pritch some sandwiches. Food'll bring him down. And he's really sorry about what happened."

"If that's what you want to believe . . ." Hurt, Holly got up. "See you in the morning." She stepped over a few supine bodies and went out the door, heading for her own dormitory.

She wondered what it was, exactly, that made girls like Melinda attract men in droves, and what it was that made men like Pritch Keating—so stunning, so macho, and so rich—totally indifferent to girls like Holly.

Melinda was still a real virgin, not just a technical one, so it wasn't easy sex that made her so popular! Anyway, sex wasn't hard to find these days. Maybe Pritchard pursued Melinda precisely because she wouldn't give in! That's what Holly's mother always said.

But it wasn't as simple as that. Melinda had what most men wanted, whatever it was. The only man at Wakefield who wanted what Holly had was Tom Lewis, and having secret sex with Tom—she had never told Melly about that—wasn't what Holly would call thrilling.

Holly didn't think life would ever be thrilling for her, not the way it was for girls like Melinda. She began to cry with an obscure longing that filled her with pain.

III

Melinda took two piles of paper plates, stacked the top ones with sandwiches and brownies, and went into the bedroom, ignoring the bodies, some sleeping, some having sex, that were draped around the living room. "Anybody hungry?"

"Starving," Jeremy giggled.

"Honestly," Melinda said, laughing. "You're like two-year-olds. Chicken, roast beef, salami—or a brownie?"

"One of each."

She filled a plate and passed it to him. "Terry?"

"I'm starving, but for pussy not for food."

"Don't be gross, Terry."

Terry hooted. "Hell, honey, a man needs his pussy regular."

Pritchard opened an eye. "Did I hear someone say pussy?"

"No, you heard me say I brought you some sandwiches."

"Great." He sat up and she passed him a plate. "You're a real doll, Melly."

"I'm gonna be sick," Terry said.

"Then get the hell out of here!" Pritchard yelled. He watched Terry run, then shielded his eyes. "Put out the lights, Melly."

Melinda put on a bed-table lamp and switched off the ceiling light. "Better?"

"Much." Pritchard got off the bed he was sharing with Jeremy and dropped onto the other one. "Jem, when you eat, it's like feeding time at the zoo."

"We're not all as dainty as the great Pritchard Keating," Jem said good-humoredly.

"Dainty is not what I am. Dainty is Melinda. Come and sit by me, princess."

Melinda obliged. The food was doing Pritch good. He was almost down from his high. He could be so sweet when he wanted to be. He must care a little about her to have apologized and tried to make amends.

"Hey, where is everybody?" Jeremy said. "It's real quiet out there."

"They're either sleeping or making it." Pritchard grinned.

"A few of them have gone," Melinda said.

"Well, then, we'll just have to party by ourselves." Pritchard put his arms around her, slid her down to a prone position, and kissed her. She could taste the mustard from the sandwiches he had just eaten and she didn't like having Jem for an audience. She tugged at her skirt; it had slipped up when Pritchard slid her down. It was up around her hips and her lace bikini panties showed.

"Pritch, please," she said in the tone that made other boys cease and desist. "We're not alone."

"Don't mind me," Jem said, grinning.

"It's time for you to leave," Pritchard said with a wink.

"He can stay," Melinda said. "We're going to The Hut to dance."

"Five minutes," Pritchard begged. "I just want to talk to you alone for five minutes." He jerked his head toward the door, and Jem went out.

"Five minutes," Melinda said.

He kissed her again, his tongue snaking around the inside of her mouth. His hand went under her shirt to her bra, slipped it up, and began squeezing her nipple.

"Pritch, stop it," she said.

"Why?"

"Because I don't want you to do it."

"Aw, c'mon, Melly. You *do* want me to do it. Why else did you come here?"

"You invited me to a party! I came because you were sorry about what happened the last time."

He looked down at her and she felt the first tremor of fear. It became a shudder when he took her hand and pulled it to his crotch, forcing her fingers along the length of his penis. "Feel how sorry I am." She could feel the heat of him through the denim of his jeans.

She struggled to pull her hand away, but he was much too strong for her. His erection felt bigger and harder.

"This is a cock, Melly, and you're a cockteaser."

"Don't you dare talk that way to me! I never said I'd have sex with you tonight or any other night."

"Just an old-fashioned girl, aren't you?"

"I never pretended to be anything else."

"You're a stuck-up little prig, that's what you are. You want me to beg for it."

"I want to get out of here!"

She pulled her hand away, but he seized her wrists in one hand, his fingers easily encircling both of them. One of his heavily muscled legs was lying across both of hers, pinning her down. He started to kiss her again, and his free hand went up her panties and slid into her.

"Ah," he said. "There's the pretty little pussy."

"Pritch, stop it, *please!*" she said.

"Only if you quit wiggling and cooperate."

"Stop it or I'll scream." She began to cry.

"Scream away. No one will come. Except you and me."

She struggled to get free. His hand was between her legs again, rubbing.

"No," she sobbed. "No, please, no!"

"Jesus, Melly, you're dry as a bone."

"I said *no!*" she shrieked, and he covered her mouth with his. His hand ripped her panties off. She heard the sound of a zipper and struggled wildly, but she could barely move. The sound of her screams was hollow in his mouth, even when she felt him trying to push into her. She tried to shrink away from him, to melt into the mattress, but there was no escape.

She felt him going in. He pumped, hurting her.

"Uh," he muttered. "Uh, uh, *uh!*" She felt him pulsing inside her and then he lay still, gasping.

"I hate you," she wept. "I hate you."

"C'mon, Melinda," he said. "You wanted it or you wouldn't be here. You aren't even a real virgin. I suppose you lost it horseback riding?"

"I hope you die," she sobbed. "I hope you die of AIDS."

"Well, if I do, so will you. Stop carrying on, for shit's sake. You knew the score."

"You apologized," she sobbed.

"Sure I did. If you want, I'll apologize again tomorrow."

He stuffed himself inside his jeans and went out. She found the torn panties and used them to mop up the stickiness between her legs. She lay there sobbing. In a few minutes the door opened again.

"Hey, Melly? It's me, Jem." The door closed, blotting out Jeremy's tall, broad silhouette. "How about a little loving?"

She sprang off the bed and looked around for something to hit him with. She grabbed a lamp from the second bedside table and yanked the wire out of the wall.

"Keep away from me, or I'll kill you."

He laughed. "With that fly swatter? Come on, Melly. I know Pritch made the first down." He walked toward her.

"I'll tell him!"

"Hell, Pritch sent me in here." He took the lamp out of her hand. "You're a present from our captain to his mates."

"*Liar!*" Melinda screamed.

"Hey, we're pals, teammates, and fraternity brothers. We share everything, especially snatch." He put his hands on her shoulders.

She battered him as hard as she could with her fists. At first he laughed, but when she tried to kick him in the groin he got angry. He slapped her hard and she tumbled onto the bed, wailing.

The door opened again. "What the hell's going on?" Pritchard's voice asked. "Shut her up or we'll have the police down on us."

"Pritch!" she screamed. "Get him off me."

"Snap it up, Jem," Pritchard ordered. "She's got a midnight curfew."

"Well, lend a hand, then," Jeremy said. "She's like a Mexican jumping bean."

She didn't have enough strength left to fight them off and scream too. She thought she was going to die, at the very least to faint. She tried to will herself to pass out when hands seized her thighs and pushed them apart, when someone secured her wrists and a hand clamped down over her mouth. She went limp when McKittrick straddled her. She tried to escape from her mortified body.

She had killed a beetle long ago in summer camp. The first blow hadn't finished it and it had fallen on its back with its legs thrusting feebly at the air. It had made her sick to see it. She was that beetle now, flailing weakly while she was invaded by another spear of turgid flesh.

"Oh, God," she sobbed, but the sound was muffled by the hand over her mouth.

When the shuddering and the panting ended for the second time, they both left the room. This time she did not stay where she was. She was a present from the captain to his mates, Jem had said. Another would soon walk through that door.

She ran to the window, stripping the case off a pillow as she went. She climbed out and ran as fast as she could across the sleeping streets. She took the long way home because if they came after her they would almost certainly think she'd gone the other way.

She stopped behind some bushes to get her breath and dry herself as best she could. Then she rolled up the pillowcase, stuffed it deep inside the shrubbery, and ran again, past the open gates of the campus, along the paths and over the lawns to her dormitory.

She could see the clock in the hall. It was five minutes to twelve. The door stood open. She heard voices from the loggia, but there was no one in the hall. The register was on the desk, a pencil attached to its binding with a string. She signed in, took off her shoes, and scurried up the stairs to her floor.

She dropped her clothes as she raced into the shower. She stood shivering under the pounding hot water for a long time, washing herself, slowly becoming conscious of how sore she was, of the swelling on her face where McKittrick had hit her, of the bruises on her wrists and ankles.

The soap burned her but she kept on washing between her legs, wishing she had something to flush the two of them out of her completely.

"Oh, God," she whispered over and over, "please don't let anyone find out about this, please don't let them tell." Whatever happened, she swore she would die before she let anyone else know what they'd done to her. If her father found out, she'd kill herself.

Finally she got out of the shower, wrapped a towel around her hair, put on her terry-cloth robe, and got into bed. She lay on her side, curled up, knees to her chest, shivering, dry-eyed, and nauseated, until she fell asleep.

IV

"Melinda?" It was Holly's voice. "Melinda! What happened to you?"

Melinda opened one eyelid, swollen from crying by the feel of it; the other stayed stubbornly closed. She saw purple marks on her wrists where Pritchard had held her. Then she saw Holly's face, appalled, anxious.

The sympathy on her friend's face made her cry again. Holly sat down on the bed and held her until she could talk.

"We have to call the police," Holly said when she had told it all.

"*No!* I don't want anyone to know."

"Melinda, for God's sake! You were raped. You're lucky that bedroom was on the ground floor, or the others would have raped you too!"

"It's not something I want to advertise. My dad would get sick every time he looked at me."

"You're talking as if this were twenty years ago and rape was always the woman's fault! No one's going to blame you! You're just a little thing. They're great big football heroes, the dirty rotten bastards. Look what they did to your face, your arms!"

"Holly, if you say one word—one word—to anyone, I'll deny it."

"Anyone who looks at you would know it was true!"

"They won't look at me. I have a plan. You tell Mrs. Loomis I have a bad cold. I'll stay in bed for a few days, then I'll wear makeup and sunglasses until my eye heals."

"What if it doesn't heal? What if you get pregnant? And Mrs. Loomis will come to check on you. The house mothers always do."

"I'll keep the blinds shut and hide my bad eye in the pillow."

"Melinda, please!"

"You're no help at all," Melinda said, crying again. "If you won't help me, then just go away and leave me alone!"

Holly stroked her hair. "I'm not going to leave you. I'll do whatever you want."

"Swear you won't tell anyone."

"All right, I swear! Now, is there any ice in your fridge? We'll put a pack on your eye, then I'll make some tea and get you some aspirin."

Holly did what she could and, when Melinda dozed off again, she sat in the armchair and looked out the window. There was a Sunday hush over Wakefield and its red brick white-trimmed dormitories, a serenity that went with order and discipline and civilized behavior. It was almost impossible to believe that an act of such brutality could have happened in a place like this.

She wondered where the rapists were this morning. She was appalled by Keating's treachery, his sneaky gallantry toward both girls at the bonfire when all the time he was planning a gang rape!

And I envied her last night, Holly thought. *I envied her because every man who sees her wants her.*

Holly's pity grew until her throat ached with it, and she wept softly. She looked at Melinda and wished she hadn't sworn not to tell anyone. She felt responsible too. If she hadn't left Melly alone with those brutes, it might never have happened.

But if she hadn't left, would they have raped her too?

V

"If you don't mind my saying so," Polly said to Rebecca, "you could help Theo with a lot more than dinner parties."

They were in the living room of Rebecca's house in Georgetown, where Polly had become a frequent visitor. She had been coming to Washington often lately to convince other Democratic hopefuls that they should get behind a Case candidacy for the good of the party. She never failed to call on Rebecca, or to invite her to Kel Regis.

"How could I help him?" Rebecca asked dutifully, pouring tea from the silver pot, offering milk, sugar, cookies, lemon sponge cake.

"By speaking to women voters," Polly said, obviously enjoying the cake.

Rebecca laughed, although she forced herself to be content with plain tea. "You've got me confused with Kate."

Polly shook her head. "Not likely. I never saw two women so different. But I know you a lot better now. You have sense and you can string one word after another. That's all you need."

"A pair of working legs would help," Rebecca said.

"I think you'll draw bigger crowds with the pair you've got. FDR did."

Rebecca's eyes flashed angrily. "You're utterly heartless."

"Not at all! Why ignore reality? As well pretend that I'm a maiden fair and willowy."

Rebecca had to laugh at that. She stirred her tea. "Theo ignores reality," she said softly.

"He's a man. They're not very good at facing disagreeable facts."

"Well," Rebecca conceded, "I'll give you this: you're one of only four people who'll admit I'm going to be in this chair for the rest of my life."

"Who are the other three?"

"Kate, Dodie Phelps—and Sydney," Rebecca said with obvious relish.

Polly's brows rose. "Sydney?"

"It was when I was in the hospital in Zurich. Kate asked Sydney to come and sit with me until Theo arrived. We got on very well."

"Sydney's the last person in the world to sit with an attempted suicide."

"On the contrary, she knew just why I'd done it."

Silence fell upon them again.

"Why did you do it?" Polly asked.

"You wouldn't understand. You have to know the meaning of despair."

"I do," Polly said. "My favorite child was a suicide. Think how you'd feel if Mark did away with himself one day."

Rebecca shuddered and shook her head. "I'd forgotten Hilliard killed himself. I'm sorry. No one talks about him. No one seems to know why he did it."

"I was hoping you could tell me why."

The two women stared at each other across the table, and Rebecca's blue eyes narrowed.

"Is that why you became so suddenly fond of me?"

"Yes, but now I'm fond of you for many other reasons."

"How very nice for you," Rebecca said frostily.

"Yes, it is," Polly said. "So don't get your knickers in a twist. You're very bright, Rebecca. You have courage and drive and you fight for what you want. I admire that. What difference does it make what detour I took to get to you? I know you now."

Rebecca clasped her hands under her chin, thought that over, and nodded. "Thank you, Polly. That means a great deal to me."

"If it really does, then tell me what I want to know."

"My God, Polly, there are as many reasons as there are suicides! How could I possibly know his reasons? Heartache? Anguish? Guilt?"

"The boy had nothing to be guilty for!" Polly's love for her lost child, her pride in him, her unremitting mourning for him flooded every word she spoke. It surprised Rebecca. Polly was not given to the public display of sentiment. "At least," Polly said, "tell me why *you* did it. Maybe that will help."

Rebecca sat very still, obviously concentrating. At length, she said simply, "I did it to escape what I could not bear."

"But the courage to face the unknown like that! That kind of courage should be enough to bear anything!"

"I didn't want to bear it. I wanted to get away from it. I didn't care where I went or what happened to me afterward. I just had to get away from being crippled."

Polly took that in and, after a while, nodded. She sat motionless, looking at nothing. An almost palpable grief emanated from her. Rebecca switched on the motor of her chair and moved close enough to Polly to take her hand and feel an answering pressure.

"Polly, there's nothing I can say to comfort you. There can't be anything worse than losing a child, except to lose one in that way."

"That's so," Polly agreed, her voice husky. "There is nothing worse."

They sat in silence, holding on to each other. After a while, Polly stirred.

"What was it you couldn't bear?" she asked. "It had to be more than being lame."

"It was fear of losing Theo."

Polly scrutinized her. "But Theo would never leave you."

"There are many ways for a man to leave a woman," Rebecca said. Polly nodded.

Rebecca watched her carefully. "Don't you know he's fallen in love with Kate?"

"Nonsense!" Polly said evenly. "He only thinks he has. It'll pass."

Rebecca leaned forward eagerly. "Do you honestly think so?"

"I'm sure of it," Polly said.

"And Kate?"

"She's still in thrall to her actor, but I hope she'll marry Tennant."

"So do I!" Rebecca said fervently.

"That's got nothing to do with your problem, Rebecca! If Kate wanted to have an affair with Theo, marriage wouldn't stop her."

"Then you don't know her at all! Kate's incapable of hypocrisy. Kate has integrity. Kate's wonderful. Kate's marvelous." Rebecca closed her eyes, her hands, curled into fists, pounded on the armrests of her chair. "Sometimes I hate her for her virtues, but how can you hate her when she doesn't know she has them? And she's not going to have an affair with Theo. I know because I asked her to, to keep him safe from the women who don't have her blasted integrity, and she refused."

"Saints preserve us!" Polly whispered. "You asked her to do *that*?"

Rebecca nodded. "So it's not the thought of his physical infidelity that kills me. I think he may even be faithful. It's knowing he wants her—or any woman—more than he wants me, maybe enough to leave me for her."

After a long silence Polly roused herself and said briskly, "You'll go scatty if you don't do something more challenging with your life than interpret Theo's mating calls. If you don't want to be a speaker, come to Kel Regis and help me set up the state campaign headquarters for the ninety-two election. You'll see Theo as often that way as you will waiting for him here at home while he crisscrosses the country raising money. We'll give you some kind of party title, executive something-or-other. There's a lot to do. Interesting people come and go, the conversation is often stimulating."

"Why me?"

Polly cocked her head to one side. "I told you: because you're much more than I thought you were. I even enjoy your company."

"Thank you again for the gracious compliments, but I can't leave Mark."

"Bring him. He can go to nursery school in Charleston with my great-grandchildren."

"He's only four. He'll make messes."

Polly shrugged. "Someone will clean them up."

"Then, yes, I will come."

Polly nodded with satisfaction. "Dodie Phelps will be pleased. She adores children."

"She was married once, wasn't she?"

"Not enough to matter. Nowadays a young widow would find something to do and Dodie Phelps would have done so many things well. Back then, she had two choices when she was widowed: live with her dreary in-laws or come to Kel Regis and live in my menagerie with me."

"Menagerie?"

"Maiden aunts breezing in and out with broken hearts and hidden bottles of gin. Politicians in droves, most of them dull as dishwater. And all those hulking boys tramping about in Oliver's wake."

"You miss all that commotion, don't you?" Rebecca asked.

"Yes, I do. It'll help having you and your son. I hope he makes a lot of noise."

VI

". . . so she's coming with her little boy," Polly told her cousin the next day at Kel Regis. "They'll stay as long as they're happy."

Both women wore what they still called "morning gowns" of long, loose cambric, Polly's blue, her cousin's peach. Sitting in the high-ceilinged room with its graceful furniture and lovely bibelots, they could have been characters in a nineteenth-century play.

"How lovely it'll be to have a child around the place again! I'll read Mark stories and he can walk beside my chair in the garden." Dodie

Phelps looked down at her twisted hands. "I hope he won't think I'm a witch."

"Don't be ridiculous! He'll adore you—or I'll take a hickory switch to his backside!"

Dodie Phelps laughed. "Polly, you never cared anything about charming children."

Polly said nothing.

"Forgive me, Polly. That was unkind of me."

"You didn't intend it to be." From the round table next to her, covered with lace over pale green satin, Polly picked up a photograph in a silver frame of an Ardmore relative, looked at it without seeing it, and put it down. She did the same thing with a cloisonné letter holder, a matching letter opener, and a round malachite box rimmed in gold.

"Polly dear, did Rebecca tell you what you wanted to know?"

"She said she had to escape something that couldn't be borne." Polly picked up the box again.

"Namely?"

"That because of her condition Theo would fall in love with another woman."

"Mercy on us! Does she know it's Kate?"

Polly nodded. "But I told her it would pass."

"My poor Polly! She didn't help you to understand Hilliard at all."

"No, she didn't," Polly sighed. "I loved that boy to distraction—and well he knew it! Whatever it was *he* couldn't bear, he could have told me! I'd have fixed it! I'd have done anything for him. I adored him. He was my Charlie's son, all I had left of the love of my life." She sat very still, looking now at some private picture only she could see.

"Polly darling," murmured her cousin, "you mustn't live it all over again."

Polly sat up abruptly, made some further adjustments to the bric-a-brac, then resumed her customary disposition as if she had put it on like a cloak. "I thought we might drive to town today and buy some toys for Rebecca's boy."

"Oh, I'd like that," Dodie Phelps said, watching Polly covertly. "Maybe we'll have time to drop in on the twins."

"Better ring them first. God knows what they might be up to."

"Polly! Love is expressed in many ways. Sex is only one of them, and I'm sure they haven't done that."

"You're incredibly naive, my dear!"

"I'd rather be that than a suspicious old fool."

"Enough! Go put on your hat! We're going to town."

34

I

There were no men in the hall for Kate's last afternoon lecture of the term. Once they discovered that Kate was interested in the economic, political, and social cloistering of women in nineteenth century-America—and not sexual behavior—the men had gradually melted away.

Just as well, Kate thought. *What I'm about to say is not for the faint of heart.*

Holly Groehler was in the second row, her notebook at the ready. Kate thought she was looking glum, not merely serious. Melinda was not with her, and what was even more unusual, Holly hadn't saved a seat for her bosom buddy.

They've had a squabble, Kate decided, remembering the few she'd had with Rebecca.

Mary Margaret Hennessy sat behind Holly, her fair skin slightly pink from the sun, her red-gold curls a halo around her face. What kind of upbringing had made this tiger lily so glacial? Was that what attracted Prince Mustafa Khan, the dusky libertine?

"We've seen," Kate began as a few latecomers found seats, "that women were believed to have an intellectual capacity limited to things domestic and thought to be sexually passive, while at the same time they were expected to be wise, compassionate, faithful, industrious, and virtuous. The ideal woman might be as strong as she was pure and many times smarter than she let on, but she was considered just as much in need of protection as her feather-brained sisters.

"Women were also believed to be prone to hysteria—the word comes from the Greek meaning 'uterus'—and no appraisal of a woman's lot in nineteenth-century America would be complete unless it included the outrageous medical treatments to cure this condition. Recent studies tell us there have been unnecessary hysterectomies and

C-sections. In the nineteenth century there were circumcisions. Circumcision is not limited to Africa, where it is still widespread. It was practiced in the west and doctors performed it right here in America."

Kate paused. Mary Margaret had turned beet-red and Holly was staring at Kate, her mouth slightly open in astonishment. Her pen remained poised above her notebook. There was a restless stir in the lecture hall.

"By female circumcision I mean anything from removal of all or part of the clitoris—the preferred treatment in nineteenth-century America—to pharaonic, or total, circumcision, which is practiced in parts of Africa, usually with infibulation. Infibulation is the closing of the outer parts following partial or total removal of the inner ones. This is accomplished by joining the raw edges, whether with thorns in more primitive societies, or with sutures when the procedure is performed in a hospital, so that they will grow together. Only two small openings are left, one for voiding and the other for menses and sex, hence the need for these women to be opened for childbirth.

"Imagine the shock of American doctors and nurses when they first saw these mutilations in diplomats' and businessmen's wives who came here with their husbands and turned up in obstetrical hospitals to give birth! Imagine the further shock when the women demanded to be closed up again.

"Discussion of the practice has always been taboo, but Herodotus reported female circumcision in Egypt in the fifth century. There are writings about the practice in Greece in 163 B.C. and in Egypt in 25 B.C. Slave girls were routinely infibulated to prevent pregnancies. For women of high social rank, simple clitoridectomy, partial or total, was performed, as it still is among certain groups in Egypt, Kenya, and elsewhere. The more extreme method is used in parts of Sudan. It is done among rich and poor alike, 'westernized' or not.

"It is part of those cultures, a deep-rooted tradition not easily dismissed, because the women believe their genitals are ugly and disgusting. It is, in most cases, the mothers and grandmothers who insist upon circumcision of the daughters. Sometimes pubescent girls who have escaped because of enlightened parents demand it out of fear of being different and even unmarriageable, since the practice is meant to protect virginity and to prevent adultery by calming female lusts.

"You must ask yourselves this: why have women not only permitted such butchery but joined forces in perpetuating it?"

Kate paused again. Holly's expression showed distress. Mary Margaret and others had covered their faces with their hands, as if they were at a horror movie. Some of the girls looked sick. Many appeared angry.

Good, Kate thought. *It's time women were angered by this.*

"The practice is not confined to Africa," she went on. "Excision of the clitoris was practiced extensively in America and Western Europe in the nineteenth century. It was the preferred treatment for little girls who indulged in 'excessive' masturbation, and for 'hysterical' women.

"The man who made excision the treatment of choice in nineteenth-century England was a gynecologist named Isac Baker Brown. He pronounced it a cure for women's mental disorders, all of which, he said, were caused by masturbation. Although he was expelled from the Obstetrical Society in 1867, there is some question whether his colleagues were really outraged by his mutilation of perhaps as many as several thousand women—or simply begrudged him his fame.

"At the same time Dr. Brown was busy in England, so were doctors in America. Circumcision was a cure for female afflictions including lesbianism, masturbation, epilepsy, melancholia, kleptomania, and orgasm, at that time considered an ailment in the female. Sources report that American mental hospitals performed the operation frequently up to *1935*!

"Today we still hear isolated reports of the practice in the United States, usually on the unsuspecting patients of a gynecologist, as well as in England, France, and Germany, although legislation has been introduced to make it illegal." Kate looked up. "The legislation confirms the existence of the practice. What is ominous is that every once in a while we are urged to revert to it.

"Here in our United States, not very long ago, there was a suggestion that excision and infibulation would put an end to promiscuous female sex among teenagers. Absurd? Yes, but remember that it was believed to cure 'female complaint' not too long ago."

Kate stopped and looked around the silent room.

"The mutilation or abuse of women springs from the age-old conviction that we are not only an inferior sex, but a menace to men as well. We tempt them into sin. On the other hand, they must beget heirs. Some way had to be found to preserve male pleasure and provide legitimate heirs while at the same time neutralizing the sorcery of women. Circumcision was only one of the ways they found, arguably the most painful if not the worst.

"It follows that an inferior sex, not mentally equipped to experience orgasm without going insane, was equally unfit to run companies, design buildings, or hold political office. Despite recent triumphs in equality for women, the old rationale still exists, *consciously or not*. We must cope with a past we had little, if any, voice in creating. Today, it is brain and not brawn that prevails—and we have the brain power if only we will cultivate it. That is why women come to Wakefield. If you came for any other reason, you're in the wrong place.

"Part of our heritage, as much as the color of our eyes and the curl or lack of it in our hair, is that dreadful concept of female inferiority which, in my opinion, still lingers deep in the subconscious of both sexes. There are many ways to humiliate a woman, and too many women who believe they deserve humiliation.

"I hope you will fight against the latest wave of woman bashing. Men are now doing in fantasy what it's illegal for them to do in fact. I refer to sadistic novels, magazines, and films and to the alarming rise in rape—not only by the sociopath who springs out of the bushes, but more and more by dates, friends, family members, by men we know and should be able to trust, men who sometimes don't even understand that what they've committed is rape."

Kate closed the folder containing her notes and looked at her audience. Then she smiled and wished the undergraduates a happy summer, said good-bye to the graduates, and wished them a happy and productive life.

"Whatever you do, I hope what you've learned about women in our recent past will prepare you for some of the attitudes we face. If I've motivated you to become activists on any one of those issues, I'll have done something worthwhile."

Her audience sat in silence for a few seconds, then there was applause and they stood while she crossed the platform and came down the stairs to talk to them.

II

It took some time for Kate to reach Holly, whose face was wet with tears. "Are you all right?" Kate asked.

Holly nodded, mopping her cheeks with a handkerchief. "It's just so . . . horrifying."

"Yes, it is. Where's Melinda?"

"In bed with a bad cold," Holly said.

Kate had the impression that the usually forthright Holly was hiding something.

"Oh? I'll drop in to see her."

"Better not," Holly said quickly, confirming Kate's impression. "She sleeps most of the time."

"Does she? How long has she been doing that?"

"Since Monday morning." Holly seemed on the brink of saying something else, but finished lamely, "She's almost over it."

"Dr. Ballard," interrupted Mary Margaret, who was standing at Kate's side. "I think I could have made my way through life without knowing all that."

"Undoubtedly, but we're not in the business of prolonging ignorance."

"Would you have given such a lecture if there'd been men here today?"

"Not without a warning."

"You didn't really warn *us* you were going to talk about such repulsive things!"

"You're a woman, Mary Margaret. You'll have to face repulsive things with no notice at all. Still, you have a right to object."

Mary Margaret shook her head. "I don't want to object formally. It was disgusting, but you were right to tell us." She turned and joined the others leaving the hall. Holly had already gone.

Kate stayed on to talk with the remaining students for a while, then she walked over to the administration building and up to her office, where she looked up the number of Melinda's dormitory and called Mrs. Loomis, picturing the white-haired, bosomy house mother as soon as she picked up the telephone.

"It's about Melinda Tillinghast," Kate said after they exchanged greetings. "Holly says she's sick."

"Yes, but not seriously," Mrs. Loomis said in her chirpy voice. "No fever, just a nasty cold. She ought to be up and around in a day or two."

"Well, that's a relief! Have you called Mr. Tillinghast?"

"Why, no." Mrs. Loomis was perplexed. "We're instructed not to call parents for something as minor as a cold."

"Yes, of course. I'm glad I won't have to field a call from an overprotective father."

"He does adore Melinda, but then, so does everyone. Not to worry. I've checked on her several times, but she's always asleep and that's the best medicine."

They said good-bye and Kate began to read through files on students accepted for admission the following year. Enrollment was up considerably over the past year. Gabriel will be glad to hear that when I see him tonight, she thought.

III

Gabriel had other things on his mind.

They went to the same club she had gone to with Jarett for dinner and dancing. Gabriel was a good dancer and she liked the authoritative way he held her. She was surprised that he knew the lyrics of the old songs she loved: *As Time Goes By, My Romance, These Foolish Things.*

"*Everything* reminds me of you," he said, pressing his lips to her cheek.

"I never thought of you as a romantic."

She moved closer to him. They were a good fit. She liked the feel of his body, the smell of his skin. She wanted him more than she ever had. She thought with blissful anticipation of making love to him later.

"Kate."

"Mmm?"

"Will you marry me?"

It shook her out of her sensual reverie. She had been so sure she wouldn't have to make this decision until they returned from Alaska, possibly not even then if his family proved to be less captivated by her than he was. Her esteem for him rose because he had made his own decision.

"Gabriel, I don't know what to say. You surprised me."

"I surprised myself."

She smiled. "Then I won't hold you to it."

The set ended and they returned to their table. "It was a genuine offer," he said.

"I have to get used to the idea."

"You must have expected it."

"Yes, but not so soon."

"Kate, will you give me a clue?"

"I'm leaning toward the affirmative. But it's an enormous step and there's no reason for us to rush into it."

Later on, when they were making love, she felt almost certain she would marry him. She felt warm and desired and comfortable.

"I love you, Kate," he whispered, still inside her.

She was not sure enough to say that to him. "Gabriel, could we be engaged while we're thinking it over? I've never been engaged before."

He laughed softly. "Kate, you're enchanting. Of course we'll be engaged. I'll buy you a ring tomorrow."

"No, that's too formal. Let's just keep it between ourselves."

"If that's what you want."

He had the knack of making her feel very young. She had not felt young since she was twelve years old and Sydney left—not even at Oxford with Win during the most intoxicating days of her life. Then, she had felt like the quintessence of womanhood, sensual, ripe, proud, and fearless; that had been better than green youth with all its pain and self-consciousness. She had been bursting with love, with a passion for living that was as electrifying as sex but wider in scope. She had been ready to risk everything because a real woman couldn't fail.

This was a new experience. Provided everything else stayed the same, it was sweet to be looked after by Gabriel, delightful to feel young.

When he drove her home, he unlocked the door for her. Harald knew him now and licked his hand. It was a good omen.

IV

Kate was still asleep when Harrison Watley telephoned early the next morning, asking to see her at the mansion on an urgent matter.

"Give me half an hour," she told the dean, a prickle of worry waking her completely. "We'll have breakfast."

She called Lillian and ordered breakfast for two before she showered and dressed in slacks and a shirt. Harrison was waiting when she came downstairs. He looked grave as he accepted coffee but refused anything else. Kate stopped eating soon after he began to speak.

"I was in the men's shower at the gym," he began, plunging right into it. "There's an air vent between the showers and the locker room and sound carries. I heard some fellows talking—I'd rather not say who they are at this point—about a party organized by one of them last Sunday after the bonfire. Two of them had sex with a girl at that party. They'd all been promised a go at her, but the girl got away after the second one. They were pressing the ringleader to honor his promise by finding them another woman."

Kate shivered.

"Inhuman," Harrison agreed, noticing it. "It was rape. She fought back before she ran. I heard them say so. They knocked her about a bit."

"Did they say who she was?" A weight sank in Kate, like a stone in water. Kate knew who she was.

He shook his head. "But she's a Wakefield girl."

"Harrison, has she notified the police?"

He shrugged. "No way of knowing—and we can't arouse suspicions by asking the police."

"We can't just sit here covering up a rape, particularly when another girl is going to be lured into the same trap!"

He reminded Kate that no one could be arrested for a crime not yet committed and that in any case, Wakefield had to be protected from the worst kind of publicity a college can suffer. "Especially here in the South," he added.

"Oh, for God's sake, Harrison! Rape isn't any different in Dixie. It's still a criminal invasion of a woman's body, wherever it happens." Kate sat back, controlling her temper. "If you really believe there's nothing we can do, why come to me? Why didn't you just walk away and keep it to yourself?"

He shook his head. "I don't know. I just couldn't."

"Then there's still hope for you! But I want you to tell me if one of the boys was Pritchard Keating."

It was several long moments before he nodded.

"I'm going to call the police," Kate said.

He warned her not to. There had been other cases of rape since Wakefield became a coed institution, and each time the trustees had moved heaven and earth to keep it quiet. The girl's parents hadn't wanted it known and neither had the boy's. The men were promptly expelled. It would probably be handled in the same way this time.

"If you open this can of worms without the board behind you," Harrison said, "there'll be hell to pay. I'd hate to lose you, Kate."

She took a deep breath. She didn't want to go. Then she thanked him for his advice and said she would ask for an emergency meeting of the board. When he had gone, she called her assistant to put it in motion.

"No need, Dr. Ballard," the woman said. "You've been sent a telegram about a board meeting tomorrow afternoon."

"No hint of the reason?"

"No, just that it's urgent."

"Thank you. I'll be late this morning. Not sure exactly when I'll get there."

"I'll cancel your morning appointments."

Kate changed and went to see Melinda.

V

"She's in three sixteen, Dr. Ballard," said the student on the reception desk with an arch expression. "I hear I missed a sensational lecture yesterday."

"I'd have called it infuriating," Kate said, and got into the elevator. Suite 316 was at the end of a long, carpeted corridor. Kate knocked.

The door opened a crack. It was Holly who peered out. "Dr. Ballard!" she whispered. "What are you doing here?"

"I want to see Melinda."

"She's asleep," Holly said.

"I won't wake her." Kate swept past Holly, through the sitting room and into the darkened bedroom.

"Who's there?" Melinda asked.

"It's Dr. Ballard," Holly said.

"Thank you for coming," Melinda said politely. "But you woke me up."

"Can we put on the lamp?" Kate asked.

Melinda grabbed for something on the night table, knocking over the lamp. Kate picked it up and turned it on as she replaced it. Melinda was putting on huge sunglasses, but they did not cover the angry bruise on one side of her face. Her hands shook.

"Oh, Melinda," Kate said. "I'm so sorry."

Melinda looked at Holly, who shook her head.

"It's only a cold," Melinda said.

"What happened to your face?"

Melinda's hands flew to cover her cheeks. The shirt-sleeves pulled back, disclosing the deep purple marks on her wrists.

"And your wrists?" Kate pressed.

"I fell," Melinda said.

"No, you didn't fall," Kate said with all the compassion she felt. "I wish to God you had."

"I don't know what you're talking about," Melinda whispered.

"Melinda, you can't let them get away with it!" Kate turned to Holly. "You know what I'm talking about, don't you?"

"I know only what Melly told me." The tears in Holly's eyes spilled over. "She fell."

They were all speaking in whispers.

"Melinda, if you don't go to the police, those brutes will walk away scot-free, but not before all of them do to another girl what two of them did to you. The person who overheard them talking about what happened also heard them making plans to do just that."

"If you know so much about it," Melinda said tightly, "why don't you go to the police yourself?"

"Because I wasn't raped. I can't press charges."

"Did they say it was me?"

"No."

"And I say it wasn't me. I don't want to be rude, Dr. Ballard, but I wish you'd leave me alone."

Kate shook her head sadly. "It's amazing, isn't it? All this liberation and nothing's changed. A woman is assaulted and *she* feels guilty! *They* break the law and *you* are ashamed." She got up. "Melinda, I must report what was overheard. That didn't include your name, but do you think those men will keep it secret if they're questioned?"

"Yes. Will you?"

Kate looked at her. "Absolutely—but, of course, you don't know what I'm talking about, do you?"

"I don't want anyone else to know."

"If you need me," Kate said, "call me, anytime. I'll help in every way I can."

"Melinda?" Holly pleaded.

"*No!*" Melinda said sharply. She turned off the light and slid down under the covers.

Kate followed Holly to the door. "Try to persuade her, Holly."

"I can't. She says she'll kill herself if anyone finds out what happened to her. I'm afraid she means it." Holly burst into tears.

Kate put her arms around the girl. "All right, Holly. Just look after her as well as you can. Leave the rest of it to me. I wish we had some real proof."

Holly hesitated, thinking of the pillowcase stuffed somewhere in the bushes, determined to find it, but she said nothing about it.

"You won't tell anyone!" was what she said.

"No. That's Melinda's decision. Call me if you need anything."

Kate drove back to the mansion, deep in thought, trying to find a way out.

VI

Sydney waited nervously in her suite at the Plaza Athenée in New York, wishing she had never agreed to do this, wishing Tyler had never agreed to meet with her. His agreement had been no surprise to Hans Erik, who had insisted Tyler would see her because "he's still in love with you."

"Yes," Sydney said now to her reflection, "but is my husband?" She eyed herself critically. She wore a satin and chiffon creation— something between a nightie and a hostess gown—in that soft peach color that was so kind to older women. She thought she looked particularly smashing, but her looks hadn't stopped Hans Erik from straying.

He had sworn by all his Teutonic gods that he had merely been indulging an erotic whim with "the princess bride," as people had been calling that erstwhile child wife ever since a movie with that title came out. It was meant to be sarcastic. The bride, no longer a child, had ripened into a fuckabout who provided her impotent old husband with a rubber woman and a dildo while she popped in and out of other men's beds.

"An erotic whim!" Sydney sneered at her reflection. What a scene she had walked in on! Both of them naked as jaybirds, Hans Erik on all fours, his participles dangling, and the princess bride on his back with her bubble breasts bouncing, riding him as if he were a stallion, whipping his flanks with a crop.

Sydney had stood stock-still until they noticed her. She said, "If you're training for Ascot, you haven't got a chance" before slamming out, locking her door, and refusing to eat or to admit Hans Erik for three days. She had lost five pounds—a silver lining in every cloud— and Hans Erik had wormed his way back into her good graces, as usual. She always gave in because sixty was no time of life for a woman to divorce, even if she still looked stunning.

But how many more face-lifts could she undergo? She already had that wide-eyed look that comes with repeated tucks, and she knew her mouth wore the hint of a smile even when she was in a complete snit.

There was a knock at the door. Heart pounding, she went to open it and confronted the man she hadn't seen for almost thirty years.

"Hello, Tyler," she said with convincing insouciance. "Come in, sit down. I'll get you a sherry."

Without speaking, he walked in, took a chair, and waited for the sherry. She handed him the glass. "I must say, my dear, the pictures on your book jackets don't do you justice."

It was true. He had always been prodigiously handsome, and he had an ageless face with a clear complexion and healthy pink cheeks. His body was tall and straight under the rather mediocre suit and tie he wore, but Tyler had never been interested in clothes. His white hair made him only more attractive.

Maybe I should let myself go gray, Sydney reflected, checking her eternally blond hair in the mirror. But, of course, it wasn't the same for women.

VII

Tyler sipped his sherry. He was damned if he would make it easier for her to ask him what she had to ask him.

She was a beautiful woman. Sixty was no great age these days, especially for a woman like Sydney, who probably went to every spa in Europe and took those lamb fetus injections and lived on wheat grass juice and soy milk. She had always been the most gorgeous woman he'd ever seen and she still was.

It was hard to believe that once, long ago, he had slept with her, made love to that still-tantalizing body, begotten a child on her pliant, willing flesh. He wanted her. He had not felt desire like this since she left him, but there was no tenderness in it.

"I suppose you know why I came to see you," she said.

"Haven't the least idea."

"Oh, Tyler, please don't make it difficult! I can't believe you really want to make my life miserable at this point."

"My dear, of course not," he lied blithely to keep her hopes up.

"I knew it!" Sydney said with that ravishing smile of hers. Some people's gums showed when they smiled, but Sydney didn't have small, square teeth like theirs; she had perfect rectangles, even and white, and a luscious mouth. He remembered the first time he had kissed that mouth amid the scent of roses in the conservatory at Wakefield College and the first time he had lost himself inside her hot and eager flesh.

"Then you won't write those terrible lies about Hans Erik," she was saying.

"But every word I've written about him is true."

"But your book makes it sound as if he's the only one!"

"Ah," he said with a smile of satisfaction. "So he got his hands on the manuscript! And he *is* one of a group."

Sydney tossed her head. "He has his cronies, like any other man."

"Most other men are not obsessed with restoring the Third Reich."

Sydney had a brief mental picture of Hans Erik and the princess bride. It would serve him right. "No, no. It's a Fourth Reich they want." That was all she intended to give away. She faced Tyler defiantly.

"Fascinating," he said.

"Politics bore me." She refilled his sherry glass and he caught a whiff of her signature scent, the same that once lingered on their bed sheets. "I just don't want to be hounded by those hypocrites who pretend to have hated Hitler but still get starry-eyed when they talk about the good old days. So, you see, he's only one of many who will firmly deny it." She smiled. "There's no point in publishing it."

His affable manner vanished, and he looked at her with venom. "Oh, yes, there is. You're the point!"

Her smile faded and her blue eyes misted. "My God, how you must hate me," she said.

"As I would a demon out of hell."

"But I don't hate *you*! And it was all so long ago!"

"It's not something that passes with time, Sydney! I haven't forgotten one word you said to me the night you left. I never will. I had to face all those people at Harmony while you were carrying on like the whore of Babylon. Every time I published a book, they'd drag out your sordid past and tie it to me. You even ruined the Pulitzer Prizes for me. You've never been out of my life, Sydney! You were always there, mocking me, humiliating me."

"Oh, Tyler, I'm sorry! I'm so sorry. I don't even remember what I said that night. I just wanted to make you mad enough to let me go. I never dreamed it would hurt you that much or last this long. But what will it change to ruin me through Hans Erik?"

"*Damn* Hans Erik! And damn you too. He's a Nazi and you're a trollop." He was panting slightly and his face was flushed when he pushed himself out of the chair. "You and your baron deserve everything you're going to get. I've waited and worked for years to pay you back."

"Tyler, I'd do anything to change what happened, for Kate's sake as well as yours, but I can't."

"No. *NO! I won't listen to you!* You think I have only to set eyes on you again to forget everything and do whatever you ask. But I'm not such an easy mark anymore. I'd publish that book even if it weren't true."

She put her head down on the arm of the chair and cried.

For a moment her tears elated him, but soon he could not watch that silky blond hair, that shuddering body. He turned to go and heard her come after him. She put her exquisite hands on his shoulders and he smelled her perfume and thought his heart would break with longing for a life unlived.

"But I *did* love you," she sobbed. "I did, I do. Oh, Tyler, no one but you was ever proud of me, no one in all my life! No one but you really loved me. How could I forget that?" She leaned against him and pressed her lips to his neck. "I'll always love you for it."

He spun around to look into her face, to catch her in a lie. Her eyes were rimmed with smudged mascara and her makeup was streaked, but she was not lying to him. She was pathetic. She was no longer the wanton who had first corrupted and then humiliated him. This was not the infamous Sydney Benedict who had slept her way across Europe in pursuit of her despicable cousin, Royal. Where had that woman gone while his image of her stayed unchanged, etched in acid on his memory?

She was not a woman at all, but a child, an intransigent, rebellious child who didn't know the meaning of discipline or responsibility. Taking revenge on her would reduce him to her level. He *had* waited years to pay her back, but now, in a rare moment of insight, Tyler knew he had to let it go if he wanted any peace for the rest of his life.

He put his arms around her warily and patted her back. "All right, Sydney, stop crying," he told her. "It'll be all right."

"You won't name him?"

"I'll name him but I won't single him out. I'll name the others too."

She was so relieved she almost volunteered the names of every man she had ever seen with her husband, but in the end she decided she had given Tyler enough.

35

I

Kate went to Kel Regis early to spend some time with Rebecca before the meeting. She took the service road to avoid meeting other early arrivals, and Curtis directed her to a sunny room tucked away between the morning room and the library, where she stood quietly for a moment, watching Rebecca as she worked at her desk.

The desk had been built to accommodate Rebecca's wheelchair, and she bent over some papers, the tip of her tongue emerging now and then. She had always done that when she concentrated.

Why did it have to happen to you? Kate thought with an ache in her throat.

For a moment Kate was back on Elm Terrace, swaddled in illusion and as hungry for romance as Rebecca had been for sex, both of them convinced that they knew everything. Back then they awoke every day wild with anticipation. Maybe it would snow, maybe a great movie would come to town, maybe they would fall in love!

If Satan had appeared at this very moment and offered to take Kate back to that time of emotional intensity, when they were immortal and their griefs short-lived, she would have gone, even though in retrospect the joys of youth were hardly worth its anguish. On the other hand, she was beginning to think that the common sense and moderation that were supposed to come with the years were apocryphal. Most people didn't grow wiser with age; they just stopped caring.

But not the two of us, Kate thought. *We'll always care about each other.*

Rebecca had always been lovely to look at. Today she was superb in navy blue silk piped in white. The dress was long, as were all of Rebecca's dresses, to cover her useless legs. The pink camellia on her shoulder was typical of her: delicate, lovely, fragile, and feminine. Only Kate knew about the streak of steel that was in her from infancy.

"Kate!" Rebecca looked up, smiled, and held out her hands. The two friends kissed each other. "Let me look at you! You're the only woman I know who can look glamorous in washable silk. Come and talk to Mark for a second, will you, while I finish this up? Mark darling, here's Auntie Kate."

Mark sat on the window seat, one leg tucked under him, the other swinging as he worked diligently on his coloring book. He showed it to Kate with great pride, accepted a hug but not a kiss—"too mushy" —and returned to his labors, allowing her to watch. He was a slender, handsome little boy, very like Theo except for his dark, almost black hair.

"Do you like it here at Kel Regis?" Kate asked.

He nodded.

"What do you like best?"

"The horses and Aunt Dodie Flips."

"Aunt Dodie Flips'll be glad to know that."

"I already told her."

"There!" Rebecca said, closing the ledger she had been writing in. "I'm all yours." She examined Kate again. "You're worried," she said. "You must be in love."

"Gabriel and I are engaged to be engaged."

"Congratulations! But why don't you get on with it, instead of taking baby steps?"

"Because there's no rush," Kate said. "We don't intend to announce it yet."

"Come on, Kate! What's missing?"

"Damned if I know. On paper it all adds up."

"And in bed?"

"It's fine."

"So?"

"So I'll probably marry him."

"Then where is the glow of a bride-to-be?"

"I've traveled this road before." Kate smiled at Rebecca. "I can't work myself into a frenzy about it. And I'd rather talk about you."

"I'm having a great time! I've lived politics all my married life but on the outer fringes. Now I'm right here where the money comes and the candidates are chosen and the dirty little deals are made. It's very exciting. Personally, I think there must have been a better Democratic candidate out there than Clem Case, but it doesn't matter now. He's being thrown to the lions for an election we can't possibly win, a kind of dress rehearsal for the next one."

"Politics, politics," Kate said. "You're as bad as Polly."

"You're right. Let's go get a drink, shall we? I'm parched." She turned to Mark. "Pick up your things and go up to Nanny, darling. It's time for your bath."

Mark obeyed, stopping to show his mother what he had done. He hugged her with all his strength, and they looked at each other in a moment of love that Kate could literally feel. Then Mark waved good-bye to Kate and skipped out of the room.

"I adore that child," Rebecca said.

"I guessed."

"I'm an unnatural mother: I don't miss the others at all." Rebecca sighed. "But I couldn't get along without Mark. And I think Polly pretends he's Hilliard when he was little."

"Did she tell you that?" Kate asked, astonished. Polly never mentioned Hilliard to anyone.

"No, but Hilliard had the same coloring—and it's the way she treats Mark. Gives him the run of the house, listens to his prattle as if he were the Delphic oracle, spoils him terribly. I think he's the real reason I'm still here." Rebecca smiled, switched on her chair motor, and led the way. The house, having been equipped with ramps, a lift, and other comforts for Dodie Phelps, was easy for her to get around in.

It's marvelous, Kate reflected, *how she's become guest mistress of the manor in only a week.*

Some weeks before, Kate had asked Dodie Phelps what the Rebecca-Polly alliance was all about.

"Polly needed to find out about suicide from someone who'd tried it."

"Oh, no!" Kate had groaned. "Of all people to ask!"

"Rebecca couldn't tell her much, but in some way she convinced Polly there was no answer to the Hilliard mystery. It helped Polly to stop gnawing away at it."

"But having learned all she could, why does she still go on with Becca? She's never liked her."

The woman who knew Polly best had no doubts on the matter. "She needs someone to form. I wasn't young enough. You were so strong she couldn't get a snaffle and a bit on you, much less a saddle. There isn't another girl in the family smart enough for her. Ergo, Rebecca. Polly will have her running for office, mark my words. They're becoming great friends."

And I resent that, just a little, Kate told herself now as she followed Rebecca to the morning room.

"The board is meeting on the veranda," Rebecca said, busy near the drinks tray. "I'm not allowed to attend." She smiled at Kate, handing her a glass. "I ordered iced tea for you. You'll want your wits about you for the meeting."

"Have you any idea why it was called?"

Rebecca looked surprised. "It's about you and your circumcision lecture."

"So soon?"

"Polly says the phone calls started coming in as soon as you finished lecturing. Some of the girls called home in shock because you talked about the privities."

"Incredible," Kate said just as Polly came in. Kate turned to her grandmother. "You might have told me I was the reason for this meeting."

"I called, but you were out." Polly came to embrace her. "How are you, dearie?"

"Amazed at the flap."

"Well, they seem to think that clitoral excision and infibulation are not matters for their daughters' delicate ears."

Kate sat down and crossed her long legs. "And what do you think?"

"I think it was an odd choice of subject."

"Polly, women will never be emancipated until they know how they were rendered powerless—and, what's worse, snookered into joining the conspiracy against them. If they don't know what happened, they won't recognize new attempts at more of the same, especially when they're disguised as tradition or security or tender loving care."

Polly pursed her lips. "I fail to see how emancipation will ensue from a study of the female pudenda in Sudan."

"That was background, history. How about the female pudenda in America?"

Polly's eyes widened. Rebecca said, "You're not serious!"

"Deadly serious! Circumcision was a treatment of choice for female complaints in the last century. I think it went out of style only when the medical establishment decided the seat of hysteria was in a woman's head, not her crotch, and switched to prefrontal lobotomies in the Thirties. If they couldn't mutilate us at one end, they managed to do it at the other." Kate crossed her arms and studied her grandmother. "I'm disappointed in you, Polly, going prudish over anatomy. You were the first real live feminist I ever met."

"And still am. But we have the college to consider. What will you tell parents who want to whisk their daughters out of Wakefield?"

"That we don't teach history selectively. We leave that to police states. We teach the truth to the best of our ability to uncover it, even when it isn't pretty. I'd tell them that standard applied to this series of lectures. I'd have told you if you'd taken the trouble to ask me. I am not pleased that you didn't. Did you think I'd stamp my foot and refuse to come to the meeting?''

"Yes," Polly said, "but I see I was in error. Come and talk to that lot out on the veranda. Then they can have a drink and get on home."

"Is everyone here?"

"Everyone who could make it on such short notice. Not Tyler. He's still in New York, but no one seems to know why."

"Too bad," Kate said, rising. "Tyler believes in academic freedom too. Let's go."

Polly smiled at Rebecca. "Sorry you can't attend, but you can eavesdrop at the window."

"Exactly what I planned to do! Give 'em hell, Katie!"

II

It was decided that Kate would write to the parents who had protested.

"It'll go away faster if we keep it low key," Theo said.

"What a to-do over a few witch doctors long in their graves," Maynard hooted. He was bigger and more florid than ever, very like his father at that age. He still had all his hair, "but he's lost whatever wits God hid under it," Polly often said. That was because her son had taken unto himself a voluptuous wife thirty years his junior. "The only good thing about that marriage," Dodie Phelps said, "is that he doesn't crack his knuckles anymore."

Gabriel, who was half sitting on a table near Kate's chair, wore a blazer and lightweight gray slacks and looked even better than usual. "But we have to phrase this letter carefully," he cautioned. "The parents are paying close to thirty thousand a year in fees. They have some rights." He smiled down at Kate.

Kate met his glance but did not return the smile. "Not the right to decide what we can or cannot teach."

Kendall yawned, his bald pate reflecting the setting sun. "Kate, we all know your reputation for integrity, but parents have the right to decide what information their daughters may or may not have inflicted on them."

"This was a noncredit, open lecture series," Kate reminded her uncle. "They were under no obligation to attend."

"If it had been a course," a gentle voice said, "the description would have mentioned the material to be covered."

They turned to the speaker. Maybud Chisholm Rawlins, a very wealthy widow in her sixties, was clearly a lady, from her narrow white T-strap shoes to the white-gloved hands folded in her lap. "Personally, I think it's all a tempest in a teapot," she went on, "but these things make people emotional. A description is the best way to protect ourselves."

"Good idea, Maybud," Kendall, who had squired her to dances long ago, said with a wide smile. "Will that do you, Madam President?"

"That'll do me fine," Kate said. "Mrs. Rawlins, I'd appreciate your help in composing the letter."

"Certainly, Dr. Ballard." Maybud smiled. "I'm only sorry I missed the lectures."

"Maybud, you haven't changed a bit." Kendall chuckled and slapped his thigh.

"Are we adjourned?" Maynard demanded. "Mother, where's Curtis? I need a drink."

"We're not adjourned," Kate said. "I was about to call an emergency meeting when I received notice of this one. We have another problem."

"Well, out with it!" said a gentleman as spare as Jack Sprat, a retired diplomat whose name was John Wilbur.

"There's been a rape," Kate said.

III

Rebecca, observing just inside the window, watched Gabriel with disdain. Moments ago she had had to restrain herself from telling him that he was taking the wrong tack if he wanted to ingratiate himself with Kate. But it was Theo who enraged her more. It was the way he looked at Kate, spoke to Kate, adored Kate.

You're so transparent, Rebecca rebuked her husband. *Gabriel's a fool if he doesn't see what's going on! Why doesn't he do something?*

But Rebecca herself did nothing. Better to endure Theo's behavior than to give him an ultimatum that might cost her her marriage—or Kate. Rebecca depended on Kate, even if she wasn't always easy to love.

A word interrupted Rebecca's thoughts. Rape?! Everyone was staring at Kate. So that was why she had looked so worried! It had nothing to do with Gabriel at all.

"Jesus H. Christ," Maynard groaned.

"Who was raped?" Theo asked. Rebecca could see he had stopped paying court and was now as businesslike as his suit.

"I can't tell you that. The girl denies it ever happened."

"Do you know who was responsible?"

"Pritchard Keating, for one."

"Oh, my God," Gabriel said.

Who the hell's Pritchard Keating? Rebecca wondered.

"How do you know all this?" Polly asked.

"Harrison overheard a conversation in the locker room. He recognized their voices. They didn't name the girl, but I know who she is. There was a second rapist, as yet nameless. Both of them are seniors, the others are lower classmen. Six of them planned to rape her, but she got away after the second one finished with her."

Polly made a sound of anger and disgust.

"Thank God for small mercies," Maybud said, clasping her hands more tightly.

Kate nodded. "But it's a disaster all the same."

"Not for us, if the girl denies it," Gabriel said.

"It's a disaster for *her* either way." Kate looked at Gabriel coldly. "She won't feel so helpless if I can persuade her to go to the police."

"You can't do that!" Gabriel exclaimed. "If this came out, we'd be overrun by the media. They're always looking for a crack in our armor. Don't you realize what that kind of publicity would do to Wakefield?"

"We can weather publicity." Kate said. "But not a cover-up."

"They'll be punished," Kendall assured her, "but privately. It's not going to help anyone to have it smeared all over the media, least of all the girl."

"You're right," Polly said to her son.

Rebecca, watching Kate and Polly, knew they were going to be at each other's throats again. How would that affect her own welcome at Kel Regis?

"Kate," Polly said to her hostile granddaughter. "We can't force that poor child to press charges, and unless she does, the law is powerless to punish the men. But we are not. They'll be expelled and we'll tell their parents why."

"You said they're both seniors," Gabriel said. "We can refuse to grant them degrees."

"Rape is a felony!" Kate was controlled, but her contempt for that argument was apparent. "It's punishable by a prison sentence, not secret expulsion and the withholding of a degree!"

"We've all been through this before," Polly said. "Believe me, discretion is the better part of valor."

"Discretion means letting the rapists get away with it," Kate said to her grandmother. "Again."

"Expulsion is no small punishment for a student who's spent four years working for a Wakefield degree," Maynard said.

"Be reasonable, Kate," Theo pleaded with a worried frown.

"We have no choice but to be reasonable," Maybud Rawlins said sadly.

Kate looked around the circle of familiar faces. "Does anyone agree with me that those boys should be turned over to the police?"

"I do," John Wilbur said.

The others offered only stony silence.

"I see," Kate said.

Ominous, Rebecca knew. When Kate used that tone, her mind was made up.

"Without the girl there's nothing to be done anyway," Kendall reminded her. "They'll just deny it."

"Kate, you can see what the consensus is," Theo told her almost tenderly.

You're in for a surprise, darling, Rebecca mocked him. *Kate couldn't care less what the consensus is. That's what makes her Kate.*

"If this were murder, there would be no question of informing the police. I'm forced to conclude that, Mr. Wilbur excepted, none of you considers rape a serious crime."

"Well now, that's a pretty high-handed accusation, Kate," Kendall said. "I detest rape as much as old Wilbur here does. But we're not even sure the girl didn't bring it on herself."

"Yes, we are," Kate said disgustedly. "The rapists said she tried to fight them off. They had to hold her down. I've seen the bruises."

"Kate," Gabriel said. "Brutal and unfair as it is, unless the girl brings charges, what can we do?"

There goes the engagement, Rebecca moaned silently.

Kate shook her head. "I can't just drop it."

"See here, little lady," Maynard boomed, "if you want to stay on as president of this college, dropping it is just what you'll do."

"Don't patronize me, Maynard. I'm past forty and not little by any stretch of the imagination." Kate turned back to the others. "The four who were shut out by her escape have been promised another victim by the great Captain Keating, campus hero and student idol, who can entrap any girl he chooses. We'll have another gang rape on our hands unless someone *does something!*"

"We'll move curfew back to seven o'clock until we resolve this," Polly said. "We'll say someone escaped from one of the prison farms. And you, Kate, be realistic. I know there's a difference between what's right and what's expedient, but if the girl won't do what's right, it behooves us to do what's expedient. We stand to lose too much otherwise."

"For openers, we'll lose a ten-million-dollar-contribution to the endowment fund from Keating's father," Gabriel said. "I've been working it out with his attorneys."

Everyone looked at Kate. She made no reply.

"We need another forty-eight hours," Polly said, "to investigate further before we make a final decision. Until then, we'll remain silent. All in favor?"

Except for Kate's, all hands went up. John Wilbur, with a gesture that conveyed the triumph of money over principle, looked at Kate sorrowfully as he voted with the majority.

"Kate, do we have your word to abide by the vote?"

Kate nodded. "Forty-eight hours."

"We're adjourned," Polly said, and rang for Curtis.

Theo crossed the veranda to talk to Kate. Rebecca watched the two of them, the woman she trusted implicitly and the man she didn't. She saw him take Kate's arm and move her to a corner, the better to protect her from the others, and she saw that finally Gabriel was watching them too. Rebecca's bitterness swelled inside her like an evil pregnancy, invisible to everyone but herself. Then Polly approached them and, reluctantly, Theo stepped back.

Kate and her grandmother had a brief angry exchange, then Kate whirled and left the veranda.

"It's all falling apart," Rebecca murmured. "Nothing's sure, nothing's safe, nothing lasts." She switched on the motor, rolled silently to the lift Polly had had installed behind the famous staircase of Kel Regis, and went upstairs to wait for Theo.

IV

A half hour later Theo closed the door of their suite. "What's got into Kate? I can't do a thing with her. She insulted Polly too. Called her a traitor to women. Told her that when the chips were down, Polly had the same low opinion of women as the worst male chauvinist alive because appearances are what matter to her, not convictions." He shook his head. "Kate's not going to back down."

"Does that surprise you?"

"Yes! She usually listens to me—to both of us. She's changed."

"She's the same as she always was!" Rebecca said explosively, and Theo turned, surprised, to look at her. Rebecca curbed her temper, folding her hands over her stomach as she did when she was carrying a baby. What was inside her now was kicking to get free, just like a baby. "Kate does what *she* thinks is right, come hell or high water. On occasion, it may be the same thing you've advised her to do, but that's pure coincidence. She will not compromise."

Theo loosened his tie. "But this is not a personal matter. Wakefield College is at stake—and Kate's presidency. Polly will ask for her resignation if Kate persists." He took off his blazer and hung it over the back of a chair.

Rebecca watched his body move. It was such a powerful body. It had hardly changed since the day she first saw him. She wanted him desperately. She wanted him all to herself.

"For Kate," she said, "what matters most is helping that girl and sending those pigs to prison, which is where they belong."

"Whose side are you on?"

"That's a question you've never had to ask before," she said.

"I always knew before." He smiled.

It was his confident smile that made the thing inside her slip its bonds.

"I'm on my own side," Rebecca said, her voice rising. "In case you hadn't noticed, there's room enough in this chair for only one, and I drew the lucky number. But we're not supposed to talk about this chair or what's in it, are we? We're supposed to pretend I sit here because I like it!" Rebecca switched the motor on. She turned the chair to go into the bedroom and ring for Alice to begin the complicated task of bathing and dressing her for dinner. But she found she couldn't move until she was completely delivered of her burden. She turned the chair back to him and switched the motor off.

"And there's room in our bed for only two!" she said savagely.

He had turned away when she alluded to the wheelchair, but she could see the flush creeping beneath his skin to stain his neck. "What are you talking about?" he asked hoarsely.

"Do you think I don't know Kate's in your head every time you make love to me?"

He spun around to face her. "For God's sake, Rebecca, don't!"

"Yes, I will! It's time I did. We're a sandwich in bed: you and I with Kate between us! Do you think I don't know it's Kate you touch, Kate you take, Kate you *come* with? You're in love with her! You've been in love with her since that accident we pretend never happened."

"It's not the same! I couldn't love any woman the way I love you."

"You don't love me! You pity me, and I don't want your pity!" She pulled up her dress, exposing her legs. Intensive therapy had not prevented a certain amount of atrophy. A tanning lamp gave the skin a healthy glow and she had herself waxed and pedicured regularly, but there was no life in the legs. "Look at them!" she screamed at him.

It had been a long time since he had, but now he did. They were not repulsive. They were still Rebecca's legs, however wasted and useless. He sat down heavily in a chair and covered his eyes.

"I know you blame me for it," he said, but without conviction because she had always denied it.

"Yes, I do!" she whispered, and smiled fiendishly at the shock on his face when he lowered his hand and looked at her. "I hate you for it. Each time you take a step, I pray it'll be your last." Her whisper was venomous. "But when you make love to *her* in *my* bed, on *my* body, I want to kill you. That's why there's a kitchen knife in my night table drawer. I've tried to kill you more than once. When I knew I wasn't strong enough to strike to your heart, I tried to kill myself."

"Rebecca!" His face twisted. "Please, please!"

"Please *what*?"

"Don't torture me like this."

"It's what you do to me!"

"Listen to me! I was impotent when you first came home from the hospital! It was from guilt and I had to get past that somehow."

"Why did you have to choose Kate to get you past it? My best friend and my only comfort—and you made me hate her!"

"I chose her because she was there, because she's part of our lives, because she loves us and we love her." He shook his head. "You don't have to hate her. Kate doesn't want to be any man's fantasy, least of all mine."

"I know what Kate is. It's *you* I can't be sure of. How many others have there been who didn't stop at fantasy?"

He shot to his feet. "None," he said. "Not one."

She said nothing.

"Rebecca," he pleaded, "for you, sex is the only proof of love there is. You're wrong, but I was afraid of what it would do to you if I tried and failed."

"It would have been kinder to fail with me than succeed with her." Her mouth trembled. Her blue eyes, in that beautiful face, had lost their glitter. She had wilted like the camellia on her shoulder. She looked like a lost child.

He went to her quickly and dropped to his knees beside her chair with his head on her lap and his arms around her. "Becca," he whispered, "I love you so. Why can't you believe that?"

"I don't know," she said, stroking his hair. She wanted to believe him. When she lifted her head and saw his hand caressing her insensate legs, she almost did.

V

Tom Lewis knocked at Holly's door and waited. He could hear her approach. In a voice that was little more than a whisper, she asked who it was.

"It's Tom," he said.

The door was unlocked and opened. He frowned when he saw her. "Holly, you look terrible! What's wrong?"

Holly, her face swollen from constant crying, burst into fresh tears. He moved her inside and closed the door.

"Tell me what's wrong." He shook her gently. "Holly?"

She could barely catch her breath, and he realized that she was hysterical, that he should slap her the way they did in the movies, but he was incapable of hitting her. He sat her on the couch and went to the bathroom for a glass of water. When she pushed it away, he poured the water over her head and that shocked her out of it. Little by little, the sobs died away. He got a towel and dried her off.

"Tell me," he said.

The words were mangled by her uneven breathing, but he heard "rape."

His eyes went wide behind his glasses. "Oh, Jesus, Holly! Who raped you?"

"Not me," she gasped. "I'm not the one."

He took a breath and let it out slowly. "Then who was it?"

"I can't tell you. She doesn't want anyone to know." Holly clenched her fists and pounded her thighs. "That bastard, that lousy, rotten hypocrite! Butter wouldn't melt in his mouth that night—and then he did *this*!"

"Keating," Tom said, removing his glasses and rubbing the two red spots on the bridge of his nose. "And Melinda."

She turned to him, startled. "How did you know?"

He shrugged. "I can add two and two. He's been more obnoxious than usual this week, like a rooster crowing. He thinks he owns the campus. The way he talks about women, it's no surprise to me he did this." He replaced his glasses and tried to put his arm around her, but she moved away. He ignored it. "How long have you known?"

"Since Monday morning."

"No wonder you broke down! What are you going to do?"

"What can *I* do? She wants to forget it ever happened—and I can't say I blame her. She'd never live it down. She's so pitiful, Tom. She's about ready to crack. And it's my fault. I should never have left her there." She told him about the party.

"It isn't your fault, it's Keating's." He tried again to take her in his arms. "Why are you pulling away from me, Holly? I'm not going to rape you. I'm not Keating." He moved away from her, his face flushed.

"I'm sorry," she said faintly.

"Some son of a bitch commits rape and you women look at all of us as if we're animals! Let me tell you something, Holly. I'm out to get these guys for my own sake as much as hers."

"I'm sorry," Holly said again. She moved to lean against his shoulder and took his hand. "I know you're not like him. You're worth twenty of him." She made no objection when he put his arm around her.

They sat quietly for a while, then Tom got to his feet. "I'm going to see Dr. Ballard," he said. "Come with me?"

"Okay," Holly said.

He smoothed her hair tenderly and kissed her cheek. "Better wash your face first."

"I love you, Tom," Holly said, heading for the bathroom.

She had never said that to him before, not even when they were making love. Maybe she didn't mean it; after all, she was over-wrought. But he had never in his life felt so proud nor so determined to use the *Sentinel* for a good cause.

VI

When her private telephone rang, Kate wasn't sure she would answer it. She didn't want to pursue the argument she had begun with Ga-briel. She didn't want to hear that it was time she stopped living in a dream world where the good guys always won and justice triumphed over all. She didn't want to hear any more about the virtues of com-promise.

She didn't want to argue with Polly either.

But what if it were Melinda? Kate picked up the telephone.

"Darling!" Sydney said. "You'll never guess where I am."

"I won't even try," Kate replied. She hid her impatience; Sydney's problems were puny compared with Melinda's. Kate stretched out on the sofa and tucked the telephone between her ear and her shoulder, leaving her hands free to hold the report she'd been reading. She went on reading while she listened with half an ear.

"I'm in New York," Sydney chirped.

"Any special reason?"

"Just a shopping trip."

"Sydney, you shop in Paris."

"Well, I was restless." There was a pregnant pause. "It's Hans Erik," Sydney said mournfully. "I think he's in love with someone else."

"I'm sorry to hear that," Kate said, putting down the report. "Are you sure?"

"I kept telling myself I wasn't, but I am now." Sydney told her about the princess bride, apparently without the slightest idea of how ludicrous the story sounded. "You can imagine how humiliating it was to stand there like a potted palm and watch them. I'm no prude, but there are some things a woman doesn't expect to come upon in her own guest rooms."

Kate struggled to suppress laughter and lost the battle. "I'm sorry, Sydney, I'm not laughing at you. I'm picturing the riding academy."

To Kate's surprise, Sydney laughed too. They laughed until their stomachs ached and tears ran down their cheeks. If one desisted, the other began again. Finally, amid sighs and chuckles, they stopped.

"What will you do, divorce him?" Kate asked, relieved of some of her pent-up tension. She dried her eyes.

"I might." Sydney blew her nose. "Although being single at sixty is no laughing matter."

"There are worse things."

"It isn't as if he really loved me," Sydney said wistfully. "No one ever has."

"Daddy did." Kate hadn't called Tyler Daddy in a long time.

"Yes," Sydney said softly. "He did. How is he?"

"He's in New York. I hope it's a woman."

"Mmm," Sydney said. "Do you suppose he's still interested?"

"He's not as old as Methuselah, after all."

"That's true. Would you mind if he married again?"

"Of course not! Everybody needs somebody—it's only a question of degree. I'm on the brink of getting engaged myself." She told Sydney about Gabriel, omitting only their argument after the board meeting. The rest was unedited; Sydney was comfortably immune to ladylike shock.

"Tuna fish salad," Sydney said when Kate had finished.

"I beg your pardon?"

"Once you've had caviar, tuna fish salad just won't do it for you. America's full of tuna. Win was caviar. Find someone like him."

"Easy to say," Kate replied. "And I don't have exotic tastes."

"Darling, of course you do! All those hours in the attic with your heroes gave you a taste for men just like them."

They had never talked this way before. It was as if the shared laughter had almost leveled the mountain that stood between them.

Sydney was going back to Vienna the next day to decide what to do. "He's very contrite," she admitted. He would be even more so when she told him she had more or less accomplished her mission. At least she had persuaded Tyler to soften the blow.

"Let me know what you decide," Kate said. "And now I must go. Someone's at the door. Bon voyage, Sydney."

"Good-bye, Kate. You're my girl."

For the first time, that didn't set Kate's teeth on edge.

Harald at her heels, she went to the head of the stairs just as Lillian opened the door to Holly and Tom.

36

I

Kate phoned Carol Hunter as soon as Tom and Holly left.

"Holly says she's cut her beautiful hair! Just whacked it off. Then she called the shops and had them deliver a lot of black clothes."

"A lot of rape victims do that," Carol said.

"Why?"

"Partly because they think of rape as a sex crime. They've just learned, in the most brutal way possible, that this is what happens to women if they attract men. There's a twisted logic to making themselves unattractive and inconspicuous. It's a penance too: the crime is so intimate they feel they were in some way responsible for it."

"It's the victim's guilt that makes me furious! And I don't know what to do," Kate said. "I can't betray her, but I can't let them get away with it either."

"What about her parents? Maybe they can get through to her."

"There's only her father—and he's a volatile man. He might pick up a gun and go after those boys. Or sue Wakefield into extinction. Or both."

"Then you know him." Carol paused and Kate could almost hear her running through the short list of parents Kate knew personally. "Good Lord!" Carol said. "If it's who I think it is, you must tell him. The man could ruin you."

"I know, but not on the telephone. I'll have to do it in person."

II

Kate called Tillinghast's New York office from the airport on the dot of nine the next morning to find out where he was. She was relieved to hear that he was in town and she made an appointment to see him at

424

his office at one o'clock. She paid for her ticket with cash and boarded the plane wearing jeans, Reeboks, a cotton turtleneck, and a cord jacket. Her hair was loose and she wore no makeup behind her dark glasses. The last thing she looked like was the president of Wakefield College.

Tillinghast came out of his office to greet her. "Kate, that is one helluva getup you're wearing!" he said, beaming. "You look like a kid. Come on in."

His office had been redecorated. He had abandoned high tech and primary colors for walnut paneling, cream-colored leather, and English hunting prints. He looked totally out of place in such a setting and in the very expensive hand-tailored suit he wore over a silk shirt and paisley tie. His perpetual striving to better himself touched her. He wanted to live up to his money, as so many Americans had done, but this was the wrong century for a quiet metamorphosis; everything Clyde did was on television ten minutes after he did it.

He offered her a chair, a drink, coffee, "money, diamonds, mink, sex, whatever you want, kid." She accepted the chair. "What brings you to the Big Apple?"

"Bad news, Clyde," she said.

His smile faded and he dropped into the chair behind his desk. "Melinda?"

Kate nodded.

"An accident? Is she badly hurt?"

"Not an accident. Clyde, listen to me, please, and promise me we'll decide what to do together."

"I promise. Just tell me."

"She was raped."

He bent over, clutching his middle as if he'd just been punched. "Oh, God," he said, rocking back and forth. "Oh, God." Kate could almost see his anguish give way to rage. "Who?"

Kate held up her hands to convey that she didn't know. She had broken her word to the board by going to see Clyde, but that was all she would do.

"She says it didn't happen. She won't talk to me. She won't let Holly tell me anything. She doesn't want anyone to know, especially you. She's afraid you'll be disgusted when you look at her."

"But she didn't do anything wrong!"

"She's ashamed."

"*She's* ashamed? What about the bastard who did it?"

"There were two of them."

"Sweet Jesus! My little girl." He leaned his head on his hands and began to cry. Kate went around the desk and sat on the arm of his chair. She put her arm around him and patted his shoulder. After a while he stopped and she went back to her chair and waited until he stuffed his handkerchief back into his pocket.

"What will you do, Clyde?"

"For now, whatever you tell me." He waited.

"It isn't easy to know what's best. I've spoken to someone who's an expert on rape and also a close friend of mine. It takes a very strong woman to bring charges, much less testify, to stand up to the publicity and then to live it down. On the other hand, if they get away with it, Melinda will always feel helpless, and that could ruin any future relationships for her."

"You warned me there was too much about rape on TV." His remorse was painful to see. "You said we were responsible for some of it."

"Because television trivializes everything, from the Holocaust to rape."

He nodded. "I'm going down to see her," he said.

"Don't tell her that you know! Make the visit part of a business trip and wait until she tells you."

He nodded, buzzed for his assistant, and made his arrangements in a few minutes. Then he looked up at Kate. "I thought she'd be safe with you."

"So did I. I wish she'd been with me every minute of every day."

"I meant at Wakefield, a school like that."

"It's happened before."

"I didn't know!" he said angrily.

"Neither did I," Kate said, as angry as he was. "But I should have asked. It's happening on campuses throughout the country. They call it date rape or acquaintance rape, but it's still rape."

"What kind of rotten son of a bitch would do that to a girl?"

"All kinds. They think it's manly to overpower a woman."

"Manly! Any ape with a stiff dick can do that—pardon my French. And the schools cover it up!"

"Most of the time they do. If the girls and their parents don't want to go public with it, a district attorney can't prosecute without charges."

"Maybe I don't want my girl to go public either." He waited for her reaction.

"Then they'll get away with it," she said angrily.

"No!" he said, his whole body tense. "They're not going to get away with it." He fell silent for a moment before he asked her to tell him how he should handle Melinda.

"If she tells you what happened, persuade her to bring charges and go through a trial if they don't confess. But it's your decision, yours and hers."

He looked at Kate with bloodshot eyes. "And you'll think I'm a real slime if I let those motherfuckers get away with it, won't you?"

"What I think of you doesn't count."

"It counts to me! A woman like you! Why do you think I listen whenever you open your mouth when half the time I don't like what you're saying? Your opinion counts with me. *You* count."

"You have to consider Melinda first, Clyde."

"Yeah, yeah." He picked up the telephone and punched a memory button on the console. He seemed to gather himself together, and he seemed to be under control by the time the telephone was answered.

"Sweetheart?" he said cheerfully. "It's Daddy. How are you, honey?" He listened. His eyes locked with Kate's and glistened with tears. He had to set his trembling lips tightly to keep from breaking down at the sound of her voice. At length he swallowed hard. "Listen, I'm coming down to buy a radio station. Have dinner with your old man tonight?" He listened again. "Okay, meet me at the hotel about six. Bye, baby, I love you too."

He said nothing immediately after he hung up, striving to keep control of himself. Then, "I'll kill them," he said solemnly, like a judge delivering a verdict. "I'll kill them for what they did to her." He straightened his tie, smoothed his lapels, and got up. "You must be hungry, Kate. I'll order lunch for us."

"Thanks, but I have to get back."

"I thought you'd fly down with me this afternoon!"

"Clyde, I gave my word not to talk about this to anyone. No one knows I'm here and I want to keep it that way."

"You got it." He walked to his office door with her.

"Call me tonight after you've seen her," she said. "No matter how late it is."

"I'll never forget how much you risked to help us, Kate."

"I hope that in time we'll all forget."

But during the flight back to Charleston she knew none of them would ever forget it. Her shoulder muscles were tight with tension and she longed for a soak in a hot bath before dinner. Driving home from the airport, she saw that it was too late for that, unless Lillian had prepared something cold. At least there was time for a drink.

Gabriel was waiting for her, Harald at his side.

"*Et tu, Brute?*" Kate said to her dog.

III

Gabriel opened the door of her car and helped her out. "Where were you?" he demanded, frowning. "I've been calling you all day."

"Driving around," she said. "Thinking. Want a drink?"

"The usual, thank you." He followed her into the drawing room and she fixed two drinks, handed him one, and sat down on the couch. Harald took up his post at her side and she stroked his glossy coat.

"You're angry at me," Gabriel said, one elbow on the mantelpiece.

"I'm disappointed in you," Kate conceded.

"Why? Because the good of this college is paramount to me? It should be to you as well. That's a president's function."

"My function doesn't include sweeping crime under the carpet."

"That's not what we want. We want to keep it from becoming public because that won't do any good."

"I'll tell you what your reasoning is. Men have been raping women since God took a rib from Adam's side, and they'll go on doing it no matter how the board of trustees handles this particular case. Why look a ten-million-dollar gift horse in the mouth over an historic inevitability?"

"You sound like a real man hater."

"That has nothing to do with the matter at hand—and you've had proof to the contrary that I'm not. I'm not saying every man is a rapist. I'm saying that men's approach to the crime has been questionable, to say the least: don't punish the rapist, try the victim."

He sat down beside her. "You're twisting everything I've said."

"I thought I was drawing conclusions."

"No, you're making me sound like an uncaring s.o.b. and you know I'm not. Nor am I alone in my opinion."

"That's no guarantee that it's right—but you're not uncaring, and if I implied that, I'm sorry."

He shook his head. "Kate, think what you're doing! Think what this leg of your feminist crusade will cost you personally. If you persist, the board will ask for your resignation and no other important college will hire a maverick president who doesn't put the institution above her pet hobby horse. Have you thought of that?"

"No," Kate said. "I hadn't thought of it. And this is not one leg of what you mistakenly call my feminist crusade. What has it got to do with feminism? A felony has been committed. We know the identity of at least one of the men responsible. If we say nothing to the police, we're guilty of obstructing justice. Have *you* thought of *that?*"

Lillian appeared in the doorway. "Dinner's served, Dr. Ballard. Shall I set a second place?"

"No, thank you, Lillian. Mr. Tennant is leaving soon."

He was clearly annoyed by that, but restrained himself until the sound of Lillian's steps faded away. "I hoped we could discuss this over dinner."

"I'm too tired to talk anymore, and we'll never agree."

"I don't understand you, Kate. You've said you'd marry me. Surely a husband's views count for something."

"Of course, but not for more than mine do. And I only agreed to be engaged."

"We're sleeping together! In my book, that creates a serious engagement, at the very least a responsibility. That's why I waited so long before I made love to you. I had to be certain I was ready to shoulder that responsibility."

As if I had nothing to say about it, she thought. *As if Win's reputation as a cocksman wasn't what really made you hesitate.*

But it was also true that Kate had forced the situation. And these days there weren't many men who believed sex entailed responsibility.

"Obviously I haven't appreciated you nearly enough," she said, her voice warmer. "I'll think about that over dinner too. And I'll see you after the meeting tomorrow."

"I know what Wakefield means to you, Kate. Think very hard before you throw it away." He finished his drink, put down his glass, and left. She went into the dining room and sat down to eat.

IV

She had never liked dining alone, except on a tray upstairs. Here, in the formal room, she was aware of her solitary splendor as she picked at her melon appetizer. Did she want to live in solitary splendor for the rest of her life?

If I marry him, she mused, *I'll have someone to be with. I think I miss that. Someone at breakfast and dinner, someone on vacation and in bed, someone to bring me an aspirin when I have a headache and give me a present on my birthday.*

She should have anticipated his reaction to the Keating rape, particularly when it got in the way of the Keating money. Ten million dollars was too much for Gabriel to ignore. Money was his life. He spent his days nurturing it and making it grow.

On the other hand, he called her a feminist crusader when she was actually a historian researching the reasons for women's low opinion of themselves, their obsessive need to please, quite apart from their contemporary experience. It was clear to her that women had to rescue themselves from their collective past, from myths and legends, from superstitions about that life-giving vessel, the female, sometimes adored, far more often distrusted because of her mysterious allure and reproductive power. Kate's field was, quite simply, how women had been misjudged for so long that acceptance of the error had become automatic on the part of both sexes—and how to change all that.

Gabriel saw feminism as a popular issue Kate had ridden to certain fame. He could accept her ideas in public; that was part of the game. But he expected her to drop them when it was expedient.

Still, Gabriel loved her in his way and Kate had been very fond of him before the meeting. She didn't tremble with excitement at the sight of him, but was that a reasonable expectation at this stage of her life?

"What's the matter with me?" she said suddenly to Harald. "I know better than to expect ruffles and flourishes and rapture the second time around. Why don't I just settle for the best of the rest?"

The Great Dane came to put his head in her lap. The eye she could see rolled in its socket to gaze at her soulfully, trying to understand what troubled her.

"Relax, King Harald," she told him with a hug that made him grunt. "No matter what, we'll always be together."

Lillian brought in a baked potato and a bed of mixed greens on which nestled a scoop of tuna fish salad. The housekeeper was startled when Kate began to laugh.

"But tuna fish salad is one of your favorite suppers on a warm night," Lillian said.

"It is. I'm just a little crazy, Lillian."

"And no wonder, with such nasty goings-on."

"How did you know?"

Lillian shrugged. "Things like that get around."

"Do you think they should go to prison, Lillian?"

"Where else should they go? Here, now, you naughty dog! Get your nose out of my lady's dinner!"

Lillian left the room and Kate contemplated the tuna fish and longed for caviar.

V

Tom Lewis ordered cheeseburgers with everything and took another foaming stein of beer to the table he was sharing with Jeremy McKittrick at The Rat Trap. It was a rich kids' hangout and entertaining Jem would cut a wide swathe in Tom's allowance, but the guy was hyper and, it seemed to Tom, ready to talk to the right person.

Tom was not the right person. He was an avid sports fan, but he had a low opinion of the jocks on campus and they didn't care much for him. Still, there was an outside chance the asshole would talk if he got drunk enough, and Tom was going to go for it, no matter how much it cost. He always had a mini tape recorder in his pocket. He had nothing to lose but money.

Tom believed in fate, but it was no coincidence that he had been waiting near The Rat Trap until McKittrick went in, alone and halfway tanked. This was his third beer to Tom's first, but the bastard had a good head for alcohol.

"Here we are, Jem boy," Tom said. "Burgers're on the grill." He set down Jem's drink and slid into the seat opposite. "What's the first thing you're going to do after graduation?"

"Fuck a bunch of women." He grinned. "You like women?"

"Hell, who doesn't?"

They launched into an explicit discussion of sex. Jem had the usual adolescent adventures to recount; Tom preempted material from Henry Miller's *Tropics*. It was the carrot bit in particular that made Jem explode into raucous laughter. Tom went to get him another beer and told the guy to hold the burgers for five minutes. He didn't want anything between Jem and the beer.

"Tell you something," Jem said when Tom came back, leaning across the table and lowering his voice. "Some of the guys take you for a queer. I'm gonna tell 'em they got you wrong."

"I'd appreciate that, Jem. Not being a jock, it isn't as easy for me to attract girls as it is for you guys." Tom reached into his pocket and switched on the tape recorder, just in case.

"Ah, they're mostly only holding out not to seem easy. That's when you gotta insist. Sometimes you get a wildcat. There was one the night of the bonfire. Tried to kick me in the balls. Took two of us, one to hold her down while I fucked her."

"Yeah?" Tom said, looking eager. "Who was she?"

Jem shook his head. "Not telling. No names."

"Was anyone else there?"

"We all were! My best buddy was first. I had sloppy seconds. Little cunt got away before the rest of the guys got in."

"Too bad," Tom said, wanting to punch the bastard's face to a pulp. Tom was nervous. Had he put the tape in the right way? Had he pressed Play and Record? Was the volume turned up full? "Here's to better luck next time," he said jovially.

"Shit," Jem said, suddenly distracted. "What time is it?"

"Nine. Why?"

"Gotta get back." Jem winked. "Look, maybe Pritch has something lined up for us tomorrow." He stopped a moment, as if troubled by something he had said. Then, forgetting what it was, he went on. "Maybe I can get the guys to let you take a turn."

The burgers arrived. Tom, suddenly not hungry, realized to his dismay that talking about a gang bang was both arousing and nauseating. *Jesus, what kind of man am I?* he thought. But that was what civilization was all about: bridling the passions. *It isn't only knowing that we have to die that separates us from the animals,* he thought, *it's knowing how we're supposed to live.*

He wanted to talk it over with Holly. But would she understand that talking sex could arouse a man, even if most men would never give in to brutality?

"Maybe it's still too soon for me to push in," he said, "if you'll pardon the pun." Jem was unaware of it. "Not when there's entertainment planned."

"Tell you what," Jem said, "I'll take notes and tell you all about it next time we meet."

"Who's the lucky lady? Anyone I know?"

Jem shook his head and wagged an admonitory finger. "No names, Tom, no names. Pritch'll find someone. All he has to do is turn on the charm and they spread. That's how come he always gets to go first."

Tom forced a laugh. "What will he do? Walk up to a coed and ask if she'd like to get stuffed by six guys?"

"Invite her to a party," Jem explained. "No girl's ever turned him down yet. Hey, I gotta go. The guys'll be waiting. See you around." He grinned, waved, and walked out of the restaurant, somewhat unsteadily. Tom, not daring to check his tape recorder where anyone could see him, got up, paid the hefty bill, and left. Halfway down the street he took the tiny cassette recorder out of his pocket. It was still recording. He rewound it a little way and, with enormous relief, heard his own voice saying "stuffed by six guys?"

VI

Having fed most of her meal to Harald, Kate had coffee with him in the drawing room, then went upstairs and ran a hot bath while he guarded the door. It had been a long day and she ached with fatigue. She had brought the telephone in from the bedroom while she was in the tub, but it remained mute until she was in bed rereading the rape statistics. She snatched the receiver from its cradle on the first ring as Harald sensed her urgency and sat up.

"Yes?" Kate said.

It was Clyde, sounding utterly confused. "She didn't tell me anything, Kate. Not a word! She looks terrible, like one of those old crones in *Zorba the Greek.* I don't think she's had a decent meal in days. She's wearing sunglasses as big as bagels and she's chopped off her hair, but you'd never know anything happened from the way she talks."

Kate briefly explained denial. "I should have warned you about her hair. Can you stay another day?"

"As long as it takes."

"Get some sleep, Clyde. I'll call you in the morning."

She was just drifting off when the phone rang again.

"It's Tom, Dr. Ballard. I'm sorry to call so late . . ."

"It isn't late. What happened?"

"Keating's sidekick, Jeremy McKittrick, got drunk and told me everything. He was the second guy."

"We need better proof than a drunken confession."

"I have it on tape."

"Probably inadmissible."

"In a courtroom maybe, but not at a board meeting."

Kate thought very hard. Then she said, "I'll use it."

"I'll make a copy for you," Tom said. "I'll bring it by in the morning. Also a piece of evidence that will frighten those guys blue."

He arrived at nine o'clock on his bicycle. He handed her a large freezer bag, tightly closed, and told her where the pillowslip came from and what was on it. "I don't know how long DNA lasts, but neither do they."

"I'll find out," Kate said.

In the bicycle's basket were several cassettes and a cassette player. He offered the loaded player to her.

"Wasn't sure you had one this size. If you play the tape at the board meeting this afternoon, they'll know it's impossible to bury it this time. Either they'll do what they ought to do or I will."

She knew she should have asked him what he intended, but she didn't.

"They might expel you, Tom."

"They might ask for your resignation, but that didn't stop you and it won't stop me. I'm going to prove that most men are decent, even to you feminists."

"We already know that! Feminists have always respected men like you, Tom. We just wish there were more of you."

Tom's cheeks were turning a bright pink as he took off down the drive. He was not accustomed to praise from women, particularly superior women like Holly and Dr. Ballard. Now Holly loved him and Dr. Ballard respected him! It made him feel as if he was riding that magic bicycle in *E.T.*, flying high above the campus. It gave him the courage to do what had to be done and the conviction that the time to do it was now.

VII

The second board meeting was held in the conference room on the ground floor of the administration building. There were seventeen trustees present, including Tyler, and the mood was far more serious than it had been on Polly's veranda.

"You're looking on top of the world," Kate told her father in the buzz of conversation before the meeting began. "Aside from the new clothes, what accounts for it?"

"I haven't the foggiest notion," Tyler said. "Now, what's all this about a rape?"

She told him briefly about it and the meeting two days before.

"Ten million dollars is a lot of money," he said.

Her heart sank. She had counted on his support. "Rape is a lot of trauma! Suppose it had happened to me when I was eighteen?"

"Heaven forbid!"

"Heaven didn't intervene this time."

"There's the good of the institution to consider, and your own career. If you lose the vote, you must accept defeat graciously."

"I will not," Kate said. She might have been listening to Gabriel!

"Kate, be realistic!"

"I won't compromise my principles," she said angrily, "any more than you would. If you can't back me up, stay out of it."

Startled, he had no time to reply as Polly called the meeting to order. She was wearing a dress and hat of peach silk and her corals were magnificent, but she looked ferocious as she rapped the gavel.

"We have spoken to Pritchard Keating," Polly announced. "He denies the charges and says he has witnesses to back him up. With no complainant, I don't see what more we can do."

"Is one of his witnesses Jeremy McKittrick?" Kate asked.

Polly nodded.

"I have something you should hear," Kate said. She set the cassette player on the table, adjusted the volume, and pressed the play button. When it was clear who the two speakers were, she advanced the tape to the place where Jem talked about what Keating had done, what Jem had done after him, and what they planned to do again. It was as upsetting to the men around the table as it was to the women.

When Jem refused to disclose the girl's name and called it a matter of honor, Tyler winced.

Kate switched off the player, and the room was silent.

"Revolting," Tyler said.

"What does Tom Lewis intend to do with this tape?" John Wilbur asked.

"I don't know. He left before I heard it, and we never discussed it."

"The *Sentinel* publishes with the consent of the college," Polly said. "That paper must be enjoined from making this public." She nodded at the Wakefield attorney sitting next to her and he rose and left the room. Polly went on. "We'll let Keating and McKittrick hear it and, depending upon their reaction, we'll decide what to do."

Kendall Benedict stirred in his chair. "I hope you're satisfied, Kate.

We may be in a hell of a mess. Suppose they do give the girl's name? We could be involved in invasion of privacy."

"It's Keating and McKittrick who are in a hell of a mess. They'll go to prison."

"We don't know that yet," Kendall said. "Until we do, we need your silence or your resignation."

The trustees stirred anxiously. Polly, who had been studying the glossy surface of the conference table, raised her eyes and met Kate's. They sat in silence, studying each other.

"What reason would be given for my 'resignation'?" Kate asked him, her eyes still on Polly. *If you do this to me again,* she thought, *that will be the end of us.*

"Oh, something vague," Kendall said. " 'Fundamental differences over policy' should cover it."

"You may have my resignation," Kate said, talking directly to Polly, "much as it pains me to offer it, but I will not be silent until those two are in prison. They deserve it. There will be no blot on the college's escutcheon unless you try to conceal their guilt." Kate turned briefly to Maybud. "You just heard that tape. What if the girl was your great-granddaughter? Can you be sure she isn't?"

"Kate, for God's sake!" Theo pleaded.

"Surely there's a way around this," Tyler said, clearly agitated.

"None that I can see," Polly said, when everyone turned to her.

Kate rose. "You'll have my resignation in the morning," she said. "As soon as it's formally accepted, I intend to inform the police."

The room was utterly quiet as she replaced the player and the tape in her briefcase, closed it, and left.

VIII

Kate drove without any destination. The top was down and the wind that whipped her hair chilled her flushed cheeks and cooled her temper, but nothing could heal the ache of Polly's latest betrayal.

Harald, who sat at her side, sensed her depression. He nuzzled closer to her and licked her cheek.

"My knight in spotted armor," she said to him lovingly. "You think I'm perfect no matter what I do."

She could hardly believe that Polly would renounce her—and their relationship—to conceal the most horrific crime against a woman short of murder. Or was Polly still so jealous of her own authority that her word, no matter how wrong, must be law? And there was Tyler too. Her father was too fond of his place at Kel Regis to defend Kate's principles as he expected her to defend his.

Of Gabriel, the less said, the better.

It was depressing that disillusion wore so many faces.

She realized she had reached the outskirts of Charleston and was about to drive on through the city when she decided to stop and see the twins. She drove past the beautiful old houses along East Bay Street to East Battery and stopped along Church Street.

A sign shaped like a scroll and lettered in gold proclaimed ARDMORE & ARDMORE, FINE ANTIQUES OF THE CONFEDERACY. The house itself was a typical Charleston house, square and simple, a three-story shuttered white brick with screened-in verandas upstairs and down.

The name of the enterprise was significant. Belle was still married to Ross Champion—if that could be called a marriage—but she contrived to ignore it and to make Charleston society ignore it too. The Champions were rarely invited anywhere together. Ambrose was his sister's excort.

Belle stood in the doorway, waving and smiling a welcome. From the car she still looked like a girl. That was because she dressed as she always had, tied a fresh satin ribbon around her curls every morning, and behaved like a debutante: meek, modest, and dependent. She was also the kindest, dearest, most vulnerable woman Kate had ever met, and her brother one of the most loving and devoted men.

Kate hugged Arabella, who smelled of lavender. "I should have called, but I was out for a drive and ended up on your doorstep."

Ambrose was waiting just inside. "No need to call us. How are you, Cousin Kate?"

"Mad as a wet hen."

"Polly again?" Ambrose asked.

"How did you guess? Look, it's past seven. Close up and let me take you both to dinner so I can cry on your shoulders."

"What'll you do with your pony?" Brosie asked. Harald had vaulted out of the convertible and was standing at Kate's side.

"Buy him five sirloins and leave him in the car."

She went inside the shop while they closed up. They were still a beautiful pair of people, as if time had stopped for them when they discovered they loved each other more than they should. *It must be hard not to fall in love with yourself,* Rebecca had remarked after she met the twins at Kel Regis. For people like these two, it must be impossible.

The shop was a treasure trove of antebellum objects: dolls, albums, embroideries, tea sets, graceful tables and chairs sized for women and children. There were music boxes; tasseled cushions and lesson books; small wicker doll prams and armies of lead soldiers in Confederate gray; matched sets of Dickens, Thackeray, Austen; blown glass vials and bottles in green, purple, yellow, red—souvenirs of travels abroad. All of it spoke of a different world that for the well-to-do was protected, gracious, and gentle until the War Between the States blew away all but the memory of it.

"Someone loved each one of these things dearly," Kate said. "You must have ghosts."

"We do," Brosie said. "They're welcome here."

Belle nodded. "The place is crowded with them."

Kate beamed at them. "You have no idea how much I've missed you. Why have we seen so little of one another?"

"You're a busy woman," Belle said, closing the blinds. "And there's Mr. Tennant."

The Charleston gossip mill, Kate knew, was as effective as jungle drums, and Gabriel moved in the same social circles as the Ardmores.

"Maybe not," Kate said. "Not anymore."

"Well, that would be a relief," Belle said, but they were leaving and Kate never asked her why she would be relieved if the affair with Gabriel were over.

IX

They drove to the restaurant in two cars. Harald was provided with his sirloins and told to stay where he was.

"Will he?" Brosie asked.

"Unless I scream," Kate said. After they had ordered, she told them about the rape and the board meetings.

"Damned hypocrites," Ambrose said disgustedly.

"That poor girl," Belle sighed.

"I had no choice but to resign."

Ambrose was certain they wouldn't accept her resignation, not since she'd been clever enough to tell them she'd go straight to the police. Otherwise, he had no doubt that Polly would have let Kate resign.

"She's a hard woman, Kate. Your initial distrust of her, all those years ago, was valid."

"I thought we'd found a modus vivendi, one that allowed us to respect each other."

"Polly doesn't respect anyone but herself," he said bitterly. "Look what she's put us through."

"That's all over now," Belle calmed him. "Kate, I've just filed for divorce."

Ambrose took his sister's hand. "It's time she was free of that lout." He glanced at Kate and his cheeks burned with embarrassment.

Arabella covered her face with her free hand. "You've always known how it is with us, Kate. So does Gran. Nobody else would dare to suggest it, so we'll be all right. I hope you aren't ashamed of us."

"No, I'm not," Kate said staunchly. "You're two of the best people I ever knew."

"It won't be something dirty," Arabella said softly. "It couldn't be."

"Belle dear, I know that," Kate said, astonished to realize that they had never surrendered to their passion for each other and would not before Belle was free to do so. There was something infinitely touching about that, about them. "What will you tell the girls?" Kate asked. Belle's daughters were both teenagers.

Ambrose smiled. "They've very sophisticated about divorce. More than half the girls in their boarding school have divorced parents. And at their age they're more interested in clothes and boys than they are in us." He colored again. "They know nothing about that side of it."

"And you'll keep the shop?"

"Oh, yes!" Belle said. "We have our ghosts to look after."

"We've already bought the house on condition our dear old lady may live in it until she dies."

Driving back to Wakefield, Kate hoped mightily that they would be happy at last. They had waited long enough, buffeted by forces they had tried in vain to resist.

There was a manila envelope from the *Sentinel* on the hall table when Kate let herself into the president's house. She tore it open. It was a proof of tomorrow's front page. In large bold type the headline read:

SPORT HERO RAPES COED

The subhead said:

Reporter Tapes His Story

Photographs of Keating and McKittrick took up the rest of the page.

"Well, that tears it," Kate murmured. "The police will have to investigate now."

X

Clyde Tillinghast, lying on the bed in his hotel bedroom, listened attentively to Kate's voice on the telephone a few minutes later. There was no way the board could cover it up, not after this. But the outcome was still in doubt unless Melinda told the truth.

"Over my dead body!" Clyde said. "I just hope those bastards won't tell who she is."

Kate sighed. It was hopeless. Without her father's support, Melinda would never have the courage to come forward.

"Discretion is the only thing they have going for them," she comforted him. "Their lawyers will tell them that a show of gallantry could help reduce their sentences."

"Gallantry, my ass!" Clyde was angry about that, but the alternative was unthinkable. Melinda remained uncommunicative and brittle, in no condition to face a hearing or a trial. "They ought to be stood up against a wall and shot."

"Shoot them after they've been thrown out," Kate said. "You don't want to deprive them of that experience."

"Yeah, yeah. You think I'll forget after a while, but I won't ever forget this." He cleared his throat. "Any chance you'd come over and have a drink with us? Melinda's due here any minute. Sometimes I can't find a thing to talk about."

"I'd better not, Clyde. People might put two and two together. How about a raincheck?"

"You got it. Anytime you want. Anything you want, Katie."

"I want this never to have happened to Melinda and you."

"But when I think of all you did! What can I say?"

"There's no need to say anything."

"Yes, there is."

"Then say good-bye and God bless."

"Good-bye and God bless." He put the telephone down and rubbed the aching muscles at the back of his neck. He had never found it easy to say thank you. No one had ever helped him enough to deserve it, until Kate.

He had been wishing since he was twelve years old that he had been born tall and good-looking instead of just smart, but now he wanted more. He wanted a woman like Kate—only about two feet shorter! He felt like one of the seven dwarfs whenever he was with her!

He went into the bathroom to wash his face and comb his hair, trying not to see his short, homely self in the mirror; the best tailoring and all the money in the world couldn't change what he looked like. Then he went downstairs to meet Melinda, warning himself to watch every word he said until his daughter remembered she could trust him.

37

I

The board met again at eleven the next day. It was a meeting called hastily as soon as each of them had received the *Sentinel* that morning. Some of them were furious at Tom Lewis's abuse of his authority. Most were relieved that the matter had been taken out of their hands.

"It may not be as bad as it seems," Theo said. "The media coverage will be heavy but brief. And if these two fools know what's good for them, the girl's identity will remain a secret even if they confess."

They all turned to Kate, who said nothing.

"What happens if they don't confess?" Maybud Rawlins asked.

"There'll be a trial," Maynard said. "And it'll be a media circus."

The Wakefield attorney cleared his throat. "No, sir. There's no point in a trial without a complainant. No one has accused these boys of anything and, as for this," he said, waving the *Sentinel*, "all it proves is that a youngster drank too much and passed his fantasies off as fact." He paused and looked from Polly to Kate. "Dr. Ballard has some physical evidence—a stained pillowcase with young Keating's laundry mark—but even supposing the semen stains on it came from him"—he cleared his throat again—"there's nothing to connect him to a rape no one's accused him of. Even what Harrison Watley overheard in the locker room was boyish braggadocio."

There was a noticeable slackening of tension in the room.

"Then we'll deal with them on our own," Polly said.

"In a way that won't imply they're guilty," the attorney warned.

"At least they can't accuse us of a cover-up," Kendall congratulated them.

Heads turned to Kate.

"Not with Kate on our side," Gabriel said. "Everyone knows where she stands."

440

Kate said nothing.

"Better be sure of that." Maynard's laugh was forced. "After yesterday's set-to."

"Will you deal with the press, Kate?" Kendall asked.

Kate held up an envelope. "I think we must first deal with my resignation."

Kendall hooted. "Now, Kate, you're not going to turn on your old uncles for what was said in the heat of battle?"

Kate waited for Polly.

"Your resignation was never formally requested," Polly said, "and would not have been accepted."

Gabriel gave Kate an all-is-forgiven smile.

"Will they be punished at all?"

"Of course," Maynard said. "When the dust settles, we'll decide exactly how."

"You can help settle the dust, Kate," Gabriel said seriously, "by getting the press out of here as quickly as possible."

"It seems," Kate said tartly, "that I've gone from pariah to press representative in the wink of an eye. Your confidence in me is overwhelming."

"Please refer all inquiries to Dr. Ballard," Polly cut in smoothly. "We're adjourned until further notice. Kate, I'd like a word with you."

Gabriel, on the other side of the room, held an imaginary telephone to his ear, then pointed to his watch. Kate shrugged and shook her head: anybody's guess. He nodded; he would wait.

He is definitely the best of the rest, Kate reflected.

II

Polly waited until they were alone in the high-ceilinged room. "I hope you're satisfied," she said. "Wakefield's halo is about to lose a lot of its luster."

"Yours already has," Kate replied.

"Spare me your recriminations. You challenged my authority!"

"Not your authority, your opinion! There's a difference. Anyway, what makes your opinion sacrosanct?"

"Experience."

"After all the mistakes you've made, you old tyrant? We didn't speak for years because of your colossal ego. You promised to leave Wakefield to me when I agreed to become president."

Polly pulled out a chair and sat down. "There's no point in discussing the past."

"Then let's discuss the present! Yesterday I was expendable. The only reason you refused my resignation today is that it's expedient to keep me, not because you trust my opinion. How do you think I feel about that?"

"How fervent our sedate Kate has become! I promised not to challenge your *academic* authority. This is something vastly different. Did you know what Tom Lewis was going to do with that tape?"

"No, but I received page one last night."

"And you didn't call to tell me?"

"How could I? You'd have stopped it and it was the only way out, for us as well as the college. I wouldn't have backed down and neither would you. Do I mean nothing in your life? Does anyone?"

Polly's belligerence faded. "You know you do! So why did you turn an administrative problem into a personal confrontation?"

Kate sat down facing Polly and considered that. "It was not my intention—although I suppose I was testing your feelings for me," she said at length.

Polly nodded. "I think you'll always do that."

Kate looked glum. "With everyone. I can't take emotional risks."

"After all the people who've disappointed you, why should you?"

"Polly! Are you conceding you're part of that delightful company?"

"We all have our failings. But I've never compromised unless someone tripped me up. I never expected it would be you."

"It wasn't! It was those two men. I love this place as much as you do."

Polly sighed. "But I've loved it longer—and I come from another age, you know, when people took their secrets with them to the grave and revenge was inflicted privately."

"What is there to do? She can't rape them back!"

"I was thinking of *Sweet Bird of Youth*."

"You mean castration?" Kate was astonished. She wondered if that was what Clyde Tillinghast had in mind.

"The punishment should fit the crime."

Kate shivered. "Grandmother, what cold blood you have."

"Why should the reputation of this college suffer for what those Neanderthals did? Why should that girl be ruined? And she would be."

"That's the worst of it," Kate said.

"If she came forward and won, there would always be a lingering doubt about her: why was she there in the first place, alone with a crowd of men?"

"If I have my way, you'll be able to ask her yourself." Even as she said it, Kate knew she would not have her way. She might have persuaded Melinda, but if Clyde wanted to keep it quiet, that's how it would stay. Still, she resolved to make one last try.

"I hope you won't have your way!" Polly was saying. "I know how vicious public opinion is. I've spent fortunes hiding this family's skeletons."

"Our reputation won't suffer if she changes her mind," Kate said. "Trust me."

"I do. And I beg your pardon for appearing not to." They were not words Polly uttered easily.

"Accepted," Kate said quietly.

Polly folded her gloved hands. "I've been considering why I'm so jealous of my authority. It's because authority proves I'm still alive. I'm a victim of time—we all are—but most people don't dwell on it as I do. I can't seem to stretch the days out to be as long as they used to be. I go from bedtime to bedtime in what seems minutes. I'm being rushed willy-nilly toward the eternal nap. Can you imagine a more dreadful prospect? No garden, no roses. No one to tyrannize. No one to laugh with. No one to love." She smiled faintly at Kate. "No one to argue with."

"I should have realized that," Kate said.

"You'd still have done the same thing." Polly gathered her gloves and handbag—today's ensemble was blue—and got up. "Are you going to marry Gabriel Tennant?" she asked as if they had never exchanged a cross word.

Kate wasn't ready to discuss that with her overbearing relative. "I don't know," she said. "Did Rebecca tell you about him?"

"Come, come, my girl, I still have eyes in my head! What's going on?"

"We've talked about it, but nothing's definite."

"Why not?"

Kate folded her arms and looked down at Polly. "Because I say so. Shall we argue about that too?"

"No. But I'd like you to marry again before I die."

"Why on earth? You've always said marriage was a burden to women like us."

"Maybe we're not as much alike as I thought. If you do take the plunge, I'd like the ceremony to be at Kel Regis."

It was another peace offering. Kate linked arms with her grandmother and they started walking toward the door. "I was hoping you'd ask," Kate said.

"I was hoping *you* would," Polly said.

"When Grandma Jekyll turns into Mrs. Hyde, it's difficult to ask for anything." Kate helped Polly down the administration hall's steps and into the waiting car. "A white wedding with all the trimmings?" Kate asked.

"Of course, but better make it off white."

Kate laughed. "All right. Bridesmaids and a five-tier cake?"

"The whole shebang."

"Grandmother, what a lovely smile you have!"

"Only because *I* have a favor to ask. I've received two tickets to Win's opening night. He obviously hopes to worm his way into your good graces by way of mine. Have your tickets arrived?"

Kate nodded.

"I'd like to make it a hen party: you and I and Rebecca and Dodie Phelps." Polly sighed. "It may be the last excursion she can make."

"Of course I'll come, Polly. Is she very much worse?"

"She's old. Old people don't recover. They hang on until they're taken or they get tired of waiting and go willingly." Polly took a deep breath. "I love that woman."

"I love her too," Kate said.

"Have you noticed that most of the people you love don't love you back in the same way? Or you can't have them to keep. Or things change. But since my cousin came to Kel Regis, she has never failed me, never withheld any part of herself, never betrayed a confidence. She is as unstinting in her support as she is in her criticism." Polly smiled. "No one dares rake me over the coals the way Dodie Phelps does." She leaned forward to kiss Kate. "Good-bye, honey. I must get back to my wounded birds. I'll make all the arrangements for New York. I want it to be a smashing party."

Polly rapped on the partition with her cane and the white Rolls Royce purred smoothly down the drive.

III

It was almost midnight when Polly put her book on the nightstand, got out of bed, and went downstairs, shrugging into her robe as she went. She walked through the dimly lit morning room and out to the veranda, where she sat in one of the Brumbys and rocked herself, glad of the fresh night breeze after a warm and humid day. It was very quiet, except for a basso profundo bullfrog serenading his mate and an occasional screech owl making a scene.

Long ago, she had sat here holding Hilliard in her arms, the only one of her children she had wanted to nurse herself. She had raised the others and watched over them but, like Rebecca, she had been seized with maternal passion for only one. After he died, Polly had turned her passion to Kate, who had fought her at every turn and still did.

If only Kate had been her daughter! A mother can mold a daughter's life as a grandparent cannot. Hilliard would still be alive and Kate would have been what Polly wanted her to be: the first woman in the White House. It was still one of Polly's favorite fantasies. She often got to sleep by working out campaign strategies and counting constituencies.

At least Kate was considering the right sort of man this time! It would be the safest kind of marriage, one that wouldn't absorb more than a quarter of Kate's time or energy, and therefore could never hurt her.

"Then why can't I let her do it?"

That was the question that had been keeping Polly awake, but she knew the answer very well. Even if Gabriel was just what the doctor ordered, it would be like mating a whirlwind to a zephyr. He wasn't enough for Kate, who allowed the world to see only a tenth of what raged inside her—any more than Oliver had been enough for Polly. Polly cared far too much for her rebellious granddaughter to allow such a misalliance. Never mind that Polly had done all she could to bring it about; now she had to stop it.

Follow your bliss, that fellow on television said. Yes, but first you had to believe you deserved it, and then you had to know what it was.

"But if you don't know," Polly murmured with satisfaction, "choose a grandmother who does."

Polly pushed herself out of the rocker and went to her desk in the morning room. She snapped on the lamp and riffled through the top drawer until she found the card she wanted and called the 212 number scrawled across it.

She had called this number often since the card first arrived, tucked into a lavish bouquet. "Coals to Newcastle," Dodie Phelps had observed, "with gardens like yours," but Polly never told her who had sent those flowers or the ones that came after them. It was like having a secret lover.

And at my time of life, Polly reflected, *that's nothing to sneeze at.*

They had a telephone relationship only. She loved talking to him because there was very little she couldn't discuss with him. And he liked women, as so many men did not. Sometimes Polly pretended she was talking to Charlie, except, of course, her Charlie never would have betrayed a woman as this man had betrayed Kate.

But that stupidity was a thing of the past, Polly was certain of it. He had withdrawn from the stew of café society and his solitary life had given him time to reflect, had made a man of him.

"It's Polly," she said when Win answered the telephone. "I hope I didn't wake you."

"Not at all. I thought you might call, considering what's going on down there."

What a voice he had! *Lord*, lamented Polly, *if you're so omnipotent, why the hell won't you make me a girl again, just for a night?*

"Is it on network news already?" Polly said.

"Of course, with old clips of Kate and Tillinghast doing their debate on rape. And some bits about Kate and you and Kate and me."

"Not Sydney?"

"Polly, Sydney's sins have paled to insignificance—they wouldn't even get her on *Oprah*. And Wakefield is being praised to the skies for its moral fortitude. It'll be worth millions in your treasury, so I assume you orchestrated that."

"No, it was the little rodent who edits the school paper. He went public with it and we had no choice but to follow. I wanted to keep the whole thing quiet. It can't do Wakefield any good."

"Oh?" He thought that over for a moment. Then he said, "And Kate wouldn't fall into line! You've had another argument."

"It was the Little Big Horn all over again. But we've settled it. I don't have time for long-drawn-out feuds and she's stubborn as a mule."

Win laughed. "I can't imagine where she gets it from."

"Ummm. Will your new play be a smash?"

"Damned if I know. I never can tell when we're this close to opening night. Will you and Kate be there?"

"Yes, with Rebecca and Dodie Phelps."

"The four most formidable females on the planet!"

"Two of them in wheelchairs and one tottering on the brink of the grave! You have nothing to fear. Whom do I call to take out two seats?"

"I'll see to that."

Polly took a deep breath. "Win, Kate's thinking of getting married."

There was absolute silence on the New York end.

"He has everything—brains, position, money, even looks—but she won't be happy with him." She waited. "Are you there?"

"I'm here, God help me. You're either the kindest or the cruelest woman I've ever met. Which is it?"

"Age mellows women, as it does wine and violins."

"But you're still fiddling with Kate's life."

"This time I require assistance, and our first-night expedition is a great opportunity. What are you going to do?"

"I'll have to think about it."

"You want her back, don't you?"

"You know damn well I do."

"Then don't dawdle. There isn't much time. Good luck, Win."

"Good night, Polly."

Polly turned off the lamp and went slowly up the stairs to her welcoming bed, where she fell into the deep, refreshing sleep of the just.

IV

Shock subdued the Wakefield campus for several days after the rape was reported in the *Sentinel*. Then the tide began to turn. Keating and McKittrick denied the charges flatly, both in public and before the board of trustees, where the tape was played for them and the two high-octane lawyers hurriedly dispatched from Texas to protect them. Keating never turned a hair. McKittrick said he'd made it all up to impress Tom Lewis. That was all their counsel permitted them to say.

The press descended, but no one would speak to reporters except to refer them to Dr. Ballard. From past experience, the press knew they would get very little from her about this apparently mythical rape, only startling statistics: a woman is raped or assaulted in America every six minutes; campus rape is pandemic; the best defense of a rapist is still to blame his crime on the seductive powers of his victim. Everyone saw the logic in that. Didn't Eve get us all kicked out of Eden by batting her lashes at Adam so she could play at God-knew-what with that snake?

"Have you been in touch with your ex-husband?" one of the reporters asked Kate.

"He called to congratulate this college for thoroughly investigating the possibility that a felony might have been committed." Actually, he had congratulated Kate for sticking to her guns.

"Are you seeing him again, Dr. Ballard?"

"I'll see him in his new play when it opens. Any further questions?"

The media began to trickle away when the scandal boiled down to "a big fat nothing," as Kate told Carol. "No prison term. No record. They'll get away with rape unless I can find a way to stop them."

But she could not find a way. Melinda, who had the fortitude to avoid suspicion by staying on until the end of term, withdrew into herself when Kate tried to reach the anger hidden there, when Kate tried to persuade her to name her attackers and testify against them.

Behind her dark glasses, Melinda remained blank on the subject. Her shaggy hair had been expertly shingled into a Twenties bob, and she wore dark cotton dresses unrelieved by ornament except for the dull scarves she tied loosely around her neck so that the folds obscured her breasts. She was still a lovely girl, but you had to look twice to notice that now. The sparkle was gone.

Kate's frustration was enormous. She had spent a great part of her life trying to persuade women that they had inherited a gross misconception of themselves, had believed for centuries that their intelligence was inferior to that of men, had ignored what power they would have at the polls if they would only turn out to vote with the same enthusiasm they gave to fashion. Melinda was the acid test of her success and Melinda had reverted to the silence that had always cloaked this particular crime.

The board had decided that the men's diplomas could not be withheld: to do so would be tantamount to condemning them without a trial. It would expose the college to crippling slander suits from the Keatings and McKittricks. And so they would get away with it.

Except for what Clyde would do, Kate told Rebecca.

"I hope he takes Polly's gruesome suggestion," Rebecca said.

"If he can't do that, he'll do something else. Clyde controls a large slice of communications in America and he uses it to manipulate public opinion. Eventually he'll find a way to damage those two men, even ruin them. But I'll have to wait a long time for that, and it's killing me."

"Because you've never had to compromise your lofty principles before. Now you must because there's so much at stake. Ordinary mortals make compromises every day."

"*Leave my principles out of this*," Kate shouted. "I hate it because it's *wrong!*"

"I know," Rebecca said. "But you'll have to live with it anyway."

No one could argue that point with Rebecca, not even Kate.

V

"We did what we had to do," Gabriel said when Kate finally agreed to go riding with him. "I think it's reprehensible, but without the girl we had no choice."

They were walking their horses through a clearing, under a hot sun that filled the air with the powdery, sweet scent of wildflowers and sunbaked grass.

"By next term," Gabriel went on, trying to cheer her up, "everyone will have forgotten all about it."

"No, they won't. I'm inaugurating a required course to be called Social Relationships. It will deal specifically with rape."

"And make it look like a common occurrence on this campus! Is that wise?"

"Ask the girls who are being raped at every coed college in the country."

"Kate, could we avoid the subject just for a few hours?"

"That won't make it go away."

"But it makes you angry."

"You bet it does. So do you."

He looked at her affectionately, and she knew he was indulging her. After all, she had been badgered steadily by the press for several days before the story died for lack of evidence.

She knew Gabriel didn't suspect for a moment that it was all over between them; her decision was firm. His relief that the whole rape problem had been solved made her want to hit him. He saw her point of view as part of her image, and behind the image, he was convinced, lurked a girl just like the girl who married dear old Dad. "You don't mean that" was a phrase he had repeated often lately. It made her want to set Harald on him.

Kate eased the reins forward and tapped her heels against her horse. He was one of the Charlies and she kept him in the school stables for her own use. He broke immediately into a smooth canter and crossed the clearing to a trail that led through the woods. There she gave him his head and he slid into a gallop. It was cool in the pines and the earth smelled fresh. The speed of the horse under her and the quiet of the trees soaring high around her erased some of the ugliness of the past week.

Kate heard Gabriel closing behind her and urged on her horse. "Come on, Charlie, my boy! No one can catch you if you give it all you've got."

Charlie's ears flattened and he surged ahead. They flew along the trail together, Kate lying along the horse's powerful neck as if she were part of him, sharing his joy in doing what he was made to do. She had not felt so free in a long time.

Finally, she slowed and trotted Charlie, letting Gabriel catch up.

"Were you running from me or the devil?" he asked her.

"Neither. We were just running to run. It was great!" Her cheeks were flushed and her dark eyes sparkled. Her hair had been tossed by the wind.

"You look wonderful." He leaned forward impetuously and kissed her. "You *are* wonderful."

She shook her head. "That's only my image, Gabriel. Actually I'm difficult and demanding."

"Marry me," he said, his mouth close to hers. "I'm ready to risk it."

"I'm not."

He sat back in his saddle, nonplused. "Not now or not ever?"

"Not ever."

"Kate! You don't mean that!"

She could barely hold on to her temper. "But I do mean it, Gabriel. You're a terrific man, but we weren't made for each other. You think I'm someone else."

"I don't know what you mean."

"That's just it. You'll never know what I mean."

"Does he?"

"Who? Win? Yes, he knows." She was startled by her ready reply, but it was true.

"You're still in love with him, aren't you? You never stopped."

She started to tell him that she was in her twenties when she fell in love with Win and she was past forty now, with enough heartache in the interim to change how she felt about everyone and everything in her life. But this romantic explanation would be the most acceptable to him. There was nothing for a man to be ashamed of when his suit turned upon the vagaries of a woman's heart.

Kate owed him that. She nodded.

Dusk was falling and they turned the horses and took them in without speaking. He drove her home from the stables.

"Maybe we should talk . . ." he said when she got out of the convertible.

"There's nothing to say, Gabriel. I'd always be someone else to you. I'd make you miserable. You don't deserve that."

She watched the car go down the drive, then went into the house.

VI

Two days later Kate paced back and forth in her office. Her tension communicated itself to Harald, who lay watching her, head on paws and eyeballs moving from side to side. She glanced at her watch several times before there was a knock on the door.

"Come in."

Her secretary opened the door. "Pritchard Keating to see you, Dr. Ballard."

"Thank you," Kate said, then turned her attention to the man coming through the door of her office.

In ancient Greece he would have been a bull dancer, Kate thought. It was a hot day and he wore a tight T-shirt that clung to his powerful chest and shoulders and a tighter pair of jeans. The denim at the groin, lightened by buffing with an emery board, was as effective as a dancer's codpiece in calling attention to his genitals.

His smile, though, was not tight. It was easy, even loose, as if he were saying, "Look at me. I can have any woman I want. Even you, schoolteacher."

"Sit down," Kate instructed, addressing both Keating and Harald, who had scrambled up to inspect the visitor. Both complied, Keating lowering himself into the chair as gracefully as a cobra, Harald collapsing with a thud.

Kate sat down behind her desk, studying him as if he belonged to a different species.

His smile faded and he sat up in his chair warily.

"What did you want to see me about?" he asked at length.

"I wanted to see what I missed."

"What you missed?"

"We've talked many times. I've seen you many times more. You seemed absolutely normal to me. I never suspected you were a rapist."

He bristled. "That's a lie! No one's accused me of rape."

"Jeremy McKittrick has."

"Jem's a fool."

"But *you* know you're a rapist. *I* know it. And Melinda knows it."

He chewed his lip nervously. "What did she say?"

"I'm not going to tell you that. Why don't you ask her yourself?"

"I wouldn't go anywhere near that flake. She's trouble." He glared at Kate for several seconds, then half rose. "Is that all?" he asked in a tone that made Harald lift his head and growl deep in his throat.

"Not quite. Even though I know you're that rarity, a studious athlete, I was surprised when your application for a Rhodes scholarship came across my desk. You don't need a scholarship."

He looked angry. "My father says I've had enough school. Without that scholarship I have to go into the oil business, and when he says I'll have to learn oil from the bottom up, that's just what he means. I'm not going to waste years of my life living on an oil rig with a bunch of illiterates."

Kate nodded. "But I won't endorse your application, nor will I countersign your diploma. That's what I wanted to tell you. I hope you have a miserable life. I hope you're caught the next time you get ready to rape a girl half your size. When you *are* caught, I'll be there to help convict you. You may go now."

He shot to his feet and Harald leapt up, barking. Kate called the dog to her side and gripped his collar.

"You bitch!" Keating shouted. "My father just handed this dump a lot of money. He can take it back just as fast."

"He can have it—but not before I tell him all about his son, the team's captain and chief procurer."

"Don't you call me that!" he warned her with a glance at the barking Great Dane. "Just keep your mouth shut."

"Only if you keep your fly closed."

He was stunned. "You're crazy! Go on, tell my father. Do you think he'll care?"

"Maybe not, but at least he'll know what's behind your charming exterior."

The door opened and Kate's secretary appeared with a burly college security guard behind her. "I heard Harald bark," she said. "He never barks."

"What's going on here?" the security guard demanded.

"Mr. Keating lost his temper and was abusive," Kate said. "Harald objected."

"I should think so, indeed," the secretary said in a huff.

"*She's* abusive," Keating said. "She called me . . ." He stopped abruptly.

"Maybe you ought to apologize, young man," the security guard said.

"Like hell I will!"

"What's got into you, Keating?" the guard said. Shaking his head, he escorted Keating out of the office.

"This isn't over yet, lady," Keating shouted back at Kate. "Keep out of my way if you know what's good for you."

"Threatening too," Kate said, stroking Harald to quiet him.

"I'll report it immediately. Are you all right?"

"Yes, just fine." Kate sat down at her desk and, as soon as she was alone, put her head in her hands. She was thinking of Melinda at the mercy of all that contempt and all that violence, and the thought made her shiver.

VII

Polly had ordered luncheon packed and put aboard a Benedict Learjet for her hen party. Everything was ready for them when their Bentleys pulled onto the tarmac. There were three cars: one for Rebecca and Dodie Phelps, one for their attendants and the baggage, and the third for Polly and Kate. The interior of the first car had been modified to accommodate two wheelchairs, with a movable ramp to make access easy. A chair lift got the two women aboard the plane, and champagne was served as soon as they reached cruising altitude.

"Here's to Win," Dodie Phelps said.

Polly raised her glass. "Amen."

Rebecca and Kate looked at them, then at each other. Polly's opinion of Win had not changed as far as they knew.

"Apart from his loutish behavior to Kate, my poor, benighted cousin is mad about the man," explained Polly. "Wears out videos of his movies and orders private tapings of his plays."

"What's *your* excuse?" Rebecca teased.

"I'm indulging her," Polly said.

Kate and Rebecca joined the toast.

By the time luncheon was served the cabin rang with laughter. The four women always enjoyed one another's company, but they were in an especially festive mood today.

"Are you nervous?" Polly asked Kate.

"Why should *she* be?" Rebecca objected. "It isn't her play and he's not her husband. She's not responsible for what he does."

"Once you've been married to a man, you feel responsible if he makes a fool of himself in public," said Dodie Phelps.

"Female foolishness," Polly said tartly. "I watched Oliver make a fool of himself more times than I care to say, and I didn't feel in the least responsible."

"Win's nervous," Kate said. "He's in his dressing room already, probably listening to Gregorian chants. At six o'clock he'll take a hot shower and then a cold one and put on his costume—he doesn't have a dresser unless the changes are very complicated—and then he'll start on his makeup. Sometimes his hands shake from nerves until he walks onstage. Then he's the character he's playing, he's inside the role."

"What did you do to soothe his nerves before a performance?" Dodie Phelps asked.

"Listened to chamber music. Sometimes made love before he put his makeup on."

"You sound positively nostalgic," Polly said.

"Do I? Well, an opening night is something special."

"So is the star," Dodie Phelps smiled.

"I think you've all had too much to drink," Rebecca said reprovingly. But Kate did sound nostalgic. Was there any hope that Kate and Win would get together again? Rebecca hoped ardently that they would.

Theo and Rebecca were living in a state of suspended animation, both of them emotionally exhausted by years of pretense, suspicion, and guilt followed by naked confession. They were looking for a way back. But first Theo had to give up the dream that someday a lonely Kate would turn to him. Rebecca had come to see that Gabriel, even as a husband, was not a significant obstacle, but Theo was no match for Win in Kate's heart, and he knew it.

Rebecca put her head back and closed her eyes. She would have to let Kate know without being obvious that she approved of a remarriage to Win.

The Bentleys, flown up on a cargo plane, waited for them at JFK in New York, and they were driven to the Waldorf, where Benedict Industries kept a seven-bedroom flat in the Tower. They went to their rooms to change and met again in the lobby for cocktails before they went to the theater.

Polly and Dodie Phelps wore black silk gowns, Polly's with a rose motif embroidered in crystal, her cousin's more severe, with a white ruff to conceal her surgical collar.

Rebecca wore white silk hand-painted in a riot of colors. Kate's dress was red chiffon, the clearest, brightest red she'd been able to find. It was tucked and fitted across her breasts and then fell straight to the floor. She wore the diamond earrings Win had given her.

After drinking a glass of amontillado in the bar, the women boarded the Bentleys and were driven to the theater.

VIII

"Come in," Win called.

The door to Win's dressing room opened and Darcy appeared. "I just dropped by to hold your hand," Darcy said, "unless you'd rather I held something else."

In a pale pink beaded sheath that looked as if it had been sprayed on, she picked her way across a dressing room littered with flowers in vases and baskets, with gifts—some of them stuffed animals—and with bottles of champagne and sheafs of congratulatory telegrams.

Win turned from his brightly lit dressing table and Darcy stopped. His light eyes, rimmed in black eye liner, were mesmerizing. He had let a beard and mustache grow. The short, square beard gleamed in the reflected light with the same strands of silver that had begun to appear at his temples.

He wore soft brown leather leggings and a henna-colored suede tunic. Clasped around his hips was an ornately carved, bejeweled belt in a metal that looked like gold.

"Winslow," said Darcy. "It should be illegal for a man to look the way you do. Even your thighs are stunning."

"Wait till I put on my crown." He smiled. "You'll swoon." He turned back to the mirror and went on with his work.

She plucked a stuffed toy from a chair and sat down herself, holding the black-spotted white dog on her lap. It wore a large red satin bow.

"Cute dalmatian," she said. "Big too." She held it up and inspected its underside.

"It's a Great Dane puppy," Win said.

"It's also sexless, like the angels." But Darcy's interest in canine breeds had been exhausted. "You look like someone else in that rig, someone I could get very exercised about. All of a sudden I'm dying to know what it feels like to have a beard brush against my belly."

"Alas, I'm about to do an opening night performance."

"You're not nervous?"

"No. I hope that isn't a bad omen."

"I still think I'd have made a terrific Brangaene," she said.

"So do I, but we couldn't have a maid who outsexed Isolde."

"You mean I'm too old for Isolde," she snapped.

"*I'm* too old for Isolde," he said.

She laughed, somehow managing to retain her frown. "Your ex just arrived out front," she said.

"Ah."

"She's the reason you and I split, isn't she?"

He nodded.

"It doesn't make any difference to you that I'm the original cat on a hot tin roof every time I look at you?"

"Kate is serious about fidelity."

"So what? She's not your wife."

"Not yet," he said.

"I shudder at the thought! Fortunately, she's got the dragon lady with her, so you don't stand a chance. I can't understand why on earth you want one."

He did not reply to that. Instead, his maquillage finished, he sprayed an Evian atomizer lightly over his face to set the makeup, glanced at the travel clock on the dressing table, and got up from the bench. "Time for me to gather my forces," he said.

"Okay, I'm going," she said grumpily. She went to him and made kissing sounds about an inch away from his makeup. "Break a leg," she said, and handed him the dog.

"See you at the party, Darcy."

She flashed him a brilliant stage smile and went out. He sat down in her chair, still holding the large plush puppy, closed his eyes, and began searching inside himself for the character he was about to enter.

It usually came easily, this metamorphosis, but his mind kept drifting to that afternoon and his conversation with Kate when she called to wish him well. He had congratulated her again for trying to do the right thing at Wakefield.

"I'll bet Polly gave you a hard time, didn't she?"

"At first yes, but I'm no longer petrified, so it didn't matter."

"When were you ever petrified, Kate?"

"After Sydney left, I was always afraid of losing what I had: Tyler, Polly, you. When I blew out the candles on my birthday cakes, I never wished for castles in Spain, just for things to stay exactly as they were. That's why I was so nice to you, to guarantee that they would."

"You weren't always nice, Kate! You had your moments."

"I have a lot more moments now."

He couldn't recall her ever having been afraid of anything. She was a strong, ardent woman with a sterling character, one he sometimes found it difficult to live up to—and impossible to transplant to a zoo like Hollywood. He should have realized that Kate had her own battles to fight. But even if he had realized, he had been too involved with himself to help her. Now, with his career hanging in the balance, it was Kate he thought about, Kate he wanted, Kate he loved.

That afternoon he had told her, "I always thought you had the strength of ten because your heart is pure."

She had laughed at that, that low, husky laugh of hers, and if he had ever fooled himself that his feelings for her were more in the nature of unfinished business than of love, he made no such mistake now. He loved her—more, if that were possible, than he had done that day in the library at Oxford when a glimpse of her face in the half light had made him put aside his veneer of confidence and let her special magic in. He had wasted years of his life without her, doing movies and plays that were not up to her standards or his, spending time with people who didn't measure up. He wanted her near him. He wanted her back.

"Come backstage after the curtain and tell me how I did?" he pleaded.

"I will. I'd like to see you."

Now he looked at the clock and closed his eyes again. It took all his concentration to stop thinking about Kate and get into the character, but he did. He and his character, after all, had something in common. King Mark, too, loved a woman who would never again love him with all her heart.

38

---•◆•---

|

At first Polly found it an unexpected play for this day and age. How could people relate to things that had been passé for so long: honor, conscience, loyalty, filial devotion, romantic love, as well as the chastity of women and the punishment inflicted upon them for lack of it.

She could remember a time when all of that—or, at least, lip service to it—was not in the least absurd, and it was strange to see the precepts of her youth played out in the Dark Ages. When would the pendulum swing back again, as it always did? And what excesses would be committed in the name of morality during the swing?

Then she was absorbed by the story, transported to an age when magic potions were as real as young love. In the darkened theater she could watch Win to her heart's content and covet him as if she were a young, seductive woman.

Mark was the linchpin of the drama, not the two young lovers drugged by the sight of each other even before they drank the potion. Tristan and Isolde were about the wanton cravings of youth. King Mark was about the more complex love that comes later in life, as, long ago, Charlie Travis had come to Polly.

When the king bedded his impostor bride, Polly, still as stone in her seat, was Brangaene in his bed. The house was utterly silent and the illusion was complete. In the somber shadows of the high tester bed the king turned to Brangaene and mounted her. Her cry of defloration cut through the silence.

It was not only voyeurism that held the spectators. It was suspense. The king knew this was Brangaene. What would he do about it?

His marriage falsely consummated, the king donned his robe and left the bed. He carried a bloody towel to the door of the bedchamber, gave it to someone outside, then walked downstage to a glowing lantern that illuminated his face as he fought with himself.

Polly's heart ached for him. He half turned when, in the shadows, Brangaene rose from the bed and Isolde took her place, but something held him back. Up to the last second his pride struggled with his love for Isolde, a love clouded by the knowledge that she could never return it because the power of that potion was eternal. She would always be Tristan's.

His face conveyed his misery, his love, his anger. The seconds ticked by in breathless suspense as he struggled silently. The struggle was in his body, in the movement of his hands.

At length he squared his shoulders and returned to the bed. He stood looking at his bride for a moment. "Isolde," he said with all of his passion and all of his pain. "Isolde." Then he lay down next to her to rest. The issue was decided. He was a cuckold, but he inspired admiration, not ridicule.

The applause, generous each time the curtain fell, was thunderous when Win joined the others for a cast bow. The applause went on for ten minutes, calling him back again and again. Finally, he stood under one spotlight on a darkened stage. Then the spotlight died and he was gone.

"Who is he now?" wondered Dodie Phelps.

"I'm sure he doesn't know himself," Polly replied.

"I'm going backstage," Kate said when the house had emptied and the chauffeurs came to collect them. "I'll meet you at the party."

Her three companions made no comment until they were on their way out to the Bentleys.

"What do you think?" Dodie Phelps asked.

"I have my fingers crossed," Polly said ambiguously.

Rebecca kept her own counsel.

||

The man at the stage door recognized Kate. "I don't need to ask how *you* are, Mrs. Talley," he said admiringly.

She shook his hand. "It's good to see you again, Pat. But where is everybody?" Kate had expected to fight her way through the usual first-night mob.

"Himself said he wouldn't have a crowd scene here. He said they'll see enough of him at the party. But he's expecting *you*! It's the same dressing room. Second door on your left."

She breathed the dry, dusty smell of a theater's backstage. She remembered going backstage at Oxford to meet him when he was Petruchio. She remembered throwing caution to the wind and going to the stage door to see him in London, unaware that he had just married someone else. She remembered every word he had said in the garret on Libby Avenue the night she agreed to marry him.

She had felt misgivings then because she couldn't resist him. She felt them now because she could, and she wasn't sure it was wise to revisit Eden after the fall. She could never again entrust all of herself to Win or to anyone, and that would change the nature of their relationship from what it had been.

Win had left the door ajar, and she stepped inside his dressing room. "Win?"

"Right with you."

Kate saw the Great Dane puppy she had sent him and smiled. She picked it up just as Win emerged from the bathroom wearing evening clothes, his hair still tousled from his shower. He was pressing his beard dry in a towel.

"You look gorgeous," he said.

"So do you. I had no idea the beard was real!"

"Tell me."

"You were magnificent."

"Did you cry?"

She nodded. "But I'm not sure whether I was crying for King Mark or me or for all the Isoldes who are obsessed with the wrong men."

He took a step toward her but stopped when she retreated. It was a subtle retreat—she had barely moved—but it told him she was still out of his reach in more ways than one.

"You were crying for us," he said. "I was playing to you, so maybe you were crying for me too. Someone has to cry for a man who's too much in love with himself to see beyond his nose."

"Mark wasn't."

"I've learned a lot from him."

"But you're still in love with yourself."

"Just a little, maybe, on a night like this. But most of all, I'm in love with you. Marry me, Kate. We belong together."

"We wouldn't be together. I'd be at Wakefield and you'd be somewhere doing a play or a movie."

"I'll fly in every weekend. It'll be a perpetual honeymoon."

"Be careful, Win. I'm not in control of my emotions tonight. I'm dazzled, but I don't know if it's by you or the king or your other characters."

"Marry all of us."

Kate held the stuffed dog like a buffer between them. "It's not a decision I'm prepared to make tonight. And you have a party waiting."

"But you'll think about it?"

"Yes." She had been thinking about it for some time. She tied his bow tie, he combed his hair, put on his jacket, and they left the theater and took a taxi to the elegant restaurant the producer had hired for the party.

"Just like old times," Win said.

But they both knew it wasn't.

III

Inside the restaurant, people crowded around him, microphones were thrust at him, flash cameras winked. Kate dropped back, then disappeared into the powder room.

Rebecca was there, putting on blusher. "Well?" she asked.

"Well what?"

"You needn't tell me, I can see it in your face! You'll follow where he leads, nose to the ground, pushing a peanut. You're getting involved with him again, aren't you?"

"I don't think I was ever *un*involved, any more than you could be uninvolved with Theo."

Rebecca did not pursue that. "Can you forget what he did to you?"

Kate sat down. "Everyone I know has done something to me. Can you think of one person in your life who hasn't disappointed you?"

They looked at each other in the mirror. *Even you have let me down,* the look said.

Rebecca took out her lipstick. "I should have known what would happen if you went within six feet of him." She began to apply the bright red color.

"I get a kick out of being with Win," Kate said. "There's no one like him."

"So after holding your own with Polly, you're going to dump Wakefield!"

"No! Absolutely not."

"Then you'll be there and he'll be—anywhere! Doing God knows what! What kind of marriage is that?"

"As unconventional as we are. He says it'll be a perpetual honeymoon."

"Why marry at all? Why not live together?"

Kate shook her head. "Aside from the fact that Wakefield parents and the board might object, if I want him enough to live with him, I want him enough to marry him. I like being married. It takes some of the anxiety out of life."

Rebecca smiled. "You're still in love with that man."

"Not in the way I was. My expectations are more realistic now than they were then."

"Does Win know that?"

Kate shrugged. "The important thing is that I know it. It's kind of sad, isn't it, to lose the illusions and still be lumbered with love."

Rebecca snapped her bag shut. "Yes, it is. It happens when people grow up. I never expected it to happen to me. I liked it better when I was Theo's little girl, living in a storybook." She sat studying her reflection. "There's no use my warning you away from Win. You seem to be sweet reason itself, but I know better. You're immovable once you've made up your mind. Will you elope?"

"If I marry him, there'll be a big wedding at Kel Regis. How's that for . . ."

The door to the powder room burst open and Win came in. "Kate, I've been looking all over for you! It's Polly. I think she's had a heart attack. The ambulance is taking her to New York Hospital. Dodie Phelps is with her. You go on. I'll take care of Rebecca."

Kate, with an anguished look at each of them, picked up her purse and ran out of the room.

IV

Kate and Dodie Phelps sat in a small waiting area just outside the intensive care unit. Rebecca had sent Alice over to deliver comfortable clothes and shoes and take their evening dresses back to the hotel. There was a tray with the remains of breakfast on a Formica coffee table near the Naugahyde couch where Kate sat. It was early morning and a man was polishing the waxed floor with a virtually silent buffer.

"You ought to get some rest," Kate said.

"I won't let her die behind my back." The small woman's voice shook. "I was so sure I'd go first."

"Hush," Kate said. "She isn't going yet. Dr. Prentiss says they got to her quickly enough to save her." Kate leaned forward to pat her arm. "Why does everyone call you Dodie Phelps?"

"There were four Ardmore cousins named Judith when I was a girl. They were all called Dodie, so the family had to tack on a surname to know which one's reputation they were destroying."

"Even after you were married?"

"Oh, they never acknowledged him. Not that I blame them. He was a damned Yankee if ever there was one! No style at all. My father married me off to him because I had to marry someone and he was the first one who was ready to take *me* along with my dowry."

"You had to marry someone!" Kate shook her head. "What a preposterous idea!"

"You know how it was back then. Still is for a lot of women east of Los Angeles and west of New York City. But I hated the North almost as much as I hated him, so I was delighted when he died. Polly called me a merry widow and made me hide my happiness for a decent interval. Of course he'd spent every penny of my dowry, so Polly took me in and I went to live at Kel Regis. A bank account materialized and was always replenished. We never even discussed it. In all these years she's never made me feel anything but independent."

"That's how Polly is with you. How Polly is with me is another story."

"I know. She's trying to atone for ignoring your existence the first fourteen years of your life. All she could talk about when she met you was the treasure she had almost lost, the way your career was going to vindicate her life. It was wicked, of course, but there was no changing her, so you had to resist. I do love that woman," Dodie Phelps went on. "She has a contagious energy and she never surrenders. She's like a three-ring circus, all color and movement and life."

"She's also the ringmaster," Kate said.

"I can't deny it." Dodie Phelps looked at Kate affectionately. "You know, it wasn't until you married Win that she really knew she'd met her match. There's nothing Polly relishes more than a challenge, and you give her that."

A doctor stepped into the waiting area and the two women turned to him expectantly. Dr. Prentiss was of medium height and slender build with a warm smile. He came right to the point. "She's out of the woods."

Relief made Kate momentarily mute.

"May I see her?" Dodie Phelps asked.

He started to refuse, then saw how anxious she was, how distressed. "Only for a minute. No talking."

"If Polly can't talk, she might as well be dead."

"She isn't dead, she's sedated," the doctor assured her. The wheelchair rolled quietly toward the partition. "That's a remarkable lady," he said to Kate. "Between the two of them, they have an enormous force of will."

"They've been willing each other through catastrophes for a long time."

"Your grandmother is something else," he added admiringly.

Kate smiled. "Yes, but I've never been able to figure out what. We argue a great deal." She glanced at the doctor. "Will she be around long enough for me to put things right?"

The doctor nodded. "I'm sure she will, but life is precarious at best, and at her age there are no guarantees." He paused. "Dr. Ballard, I have two daughters and I've been scared as hell to let them go off to college in a few years. I'm grateful to women like you and your grandmother for taking a stand against rape."

"You must tell her that when she's better," Kate said, unable to resist. "It's something she ought to hear."

"I will."

The wheelchair came gliding back. "She's ordered us back to the hotel to rest." Dodie Phelps looked much better.

The doctor nodded his agreement. "You're forbidden to return until this evening. I'll see you then." He turned and went wearily down the hall.

V

Kate slept until five in the afternoon and awoke still surrounded by all of the previous night's late editions and every morning paper she'd been able to find on their way back to the Waldorf. The reviews were superb. There was nothing about Polly, but there would be in the afternoon papers.

The message light on the telephone was blinking, and she picked up her calls. Clyde, Win, Tyler, Rebecca.

She rang Rebecca's room first and was told Mrs. Barrows had left for Washington a short while ago, dropping Dodie Phelps off at the hospital en route. Rebecca would call Kate tomorrow.

Kate was glad Becca had gone home. There was a lot of tension between Theo and his wife. They were not estranged, but they were tentative, unsure. They needed as much time together as possible.

Tyler, now published by John Mallory, was staying at Mallory's apartment and was at home when Kate returned his call. He looked upon Polly's illness as a personal affront.

"She always has a big party at Kel Regis when I publish. It won't be the same without that."

"Tyler, she isn't dead. She'll recover—maybe even in time for your pub date."

"I never thought anything like this would happen to Polly."

"Just how did you suppose she'd shuffle off this mortal coil?"

"I thought she'd fade away like an old soldier. A heart attack is so commonplace, so out of character."

"She was back in character last night, giving orders. We'll fly her to Kel Regis as soon as she can make the journey safely, and you can dance attendance on her there. Why are you in New York?"

Tyler cleared his throat. "I was here working on the galley proofs when the board meetings were called."

"Considering how you failed to defend me, I wish you'd stayed here."

"Kate, be reasonable. What more could I have done?"

"When have I ever been *un*reasonable?" Kate demanded. "You could have told the board what miserable, money-grubbing bastards they are. Told Kendall to take his suggestion that I resign and stick it. Told Polly she was wrong." She was almost shouting.

"I barely had time to speak before it was all over." He sounded utterly contrite.

Why am I taking it out on him? she wondered. It amazed her that she still expected more of her father than he had to give.

"No, of course you didn't, Tyler. But what are you doing in New York?"

"Still making some changes on *Aftermaths*."

"Does that mean you're not using von Rayner as a target?"

"It means he's no longer the only one I name. They're all in it up to their necks, and I decided to say so."

"I hope the baron feels there's safety in numbers. Why did you change it?"

"You convinced me that I should. When can I see Polly?"

They arranged to meet at the hospital at seven. Kate wondered briefly about the real reason for Tyler's change of heart. It certainly wasn't her opinion. Then she went on returning her calls.

VI

Clyde Tillinghast was breathing heavily when he answered his telephone. "This is not a dirty phone call," he explained, making her laugh for the first time since the night before. "I'm on the treadmill. How's your grandmother?"

"She'll recover."

"I knew she would. Only the good die young, and she is one ornery old lady." He panted a few more times. "You're in the afternoon papers, in the gossip columns. Why didn't you tell me you were coming to town?"

"It was Polly's party. Four of us flew up yesterday for the opening of *King Mark*. We'd have been home by now if Polly hadn't collapsed."

"Yeah, yeah." He took another little rest. "The papers say you're gonna remarry your ex."

"Then they know more about it than I do."

"You ought to be married. Wanna meet some guys?"

Kate laughed explosively. "Who are you now? Yenta, the matchmaker?"

"You ask me, it's him you still want."

"I didn't know it showed. How's Melinda?"

"The same. Maybe a little better. I don't think she'll ever tell me."

"Yes, she will. When you least expect it."

They made a date for lunch at Lutèce and Kate hung up, wishing people could choose whom to love, a more sensible system than being swept away. Then she called Win at the theater.

"How's Polly?" was the first thing he asked. "The hospital wouldn't let me into intensive care last night."

"She's going to recover."

"Thank God. And you, Kate?"

"I slept all day, so I'm fine. Win, the reviews were sublime and I'm glad about that, but you deserve even better. When they've had time to reflect, they'll say so too. It's the best thing you've ever done."

"Maybe, but you're the best thing that ever happened to me."

"So are you, to me. Last night at the hospital I was bowed down with remorse for all the things I've never said to Polly. That was one of the things I've never said to you."

"Kate, I love you." She thought perhaps he did. He asked her to have supper with him after the performance, but she was in no mood for a restaurant. She suggested supper in her room and he agreed.

Kate called room service for a sandwich and coffee, ate it while she dressed, and then took a taxi to the hospital.

VII

"She's had a second heart attack," Dr. Prentiss said, a worried frown on his kind face, and for the first time Polly's mortality reached inside Kate and chilled her through and through. Desolation swept over her. So many things would go with Polly.

"What are her chances?" Tyler asked.

"Fair. We'll have to keep her here longer than we thought to see what the damage is and how best to deal with it. You can go in to say hello, but don't stay more than a minute or two." He held up an admonitory finger, like a teacher instructing his class. "She doesn't know she had another attack. She thinks it was indigestion."

They went in like three children on their best behavior. When Dodie Phelps said her name, Polly opened her eyes.

"Damned fools," she whispered. "It was only indigestion. Kate, get me out of here."

"As soon as I can," Kate promised, taking her hand.

They had the inane conversation people have in sickrooms, their voices pitched slightly louder to convey confidence and in the mistaken assumption that sick people are hard of hearing, but Polly did not seem to notice.

When they left her, Tyler suggested they go out to dinner.

"I ate something before I left the hotel," Kate said. "You two go on ahead. Take the Bentley. I need the walk." They didn't try to dissuade her. They were too confounded by Polly's condition.

It was a mild night and Kate walked along York Avenue for a while, admiring the magnolias, then turned west to Park. The flowers on the famous avenue were blooming and women in sleek executive suits and clumpy running shoes walked with almost military speed, the better to fight off flab and heart disease while their lungs gulped in the toxic air of the city.

Much as she had once loved New York, it was not where Kate wanted to be. She wanted to be at Kel Regis, surrounded by silky grass and stately oaks, by the scent of flowers and the buzz of honeybees on a warm spring day. She wanted to walk in Polly's rose garden and see the Charlies in the stable. She missed Harald. She missed home. And home, for long periods of her life, had been Polly. Polly had given her a family. Polly was generous and clever, funny and unique. Like Everest, she was *there*.

She was by no means perfect; she tried to exact slavish obedience, she was scheming, stubborn, despotic, and manipulative.

"But I love her," Kate protested. When Polly was gone, she would leave an enormous hole in Kate's life.

VIII

Back at the Waldorf, Kate ordered supper sent up at eleven o'clock, took a bath, and curled up in an armchair, shivering in the capacious terry-cloth robe the hotel provided. Thinking of Polly, she felt utterly bereft already.

Win was carrying the Great Dane puppy when she let him in. "Thought he might cheer you up," he said with his famous smile. It faded abruptly. "What is it, Kate?"

She told him about Polly and he set the dog down and put his arms around her. "Polly will get well," he said with conviction. "She's too cantankerous to die yet."

"Don't let go of me," Kate said. Suddenly she wanted him. It was seeing Polly wired up like a complicated stereo that had left Kate shivering with a dread she could not shake alone. Only an affirmation of life could banish it, and sex was the most direct affirmation she knew.

He knew what she wanted—and why—because he knew her. He reached behind him to lock the door, and took off his jacket. Then he swept her into his arms and kissed her ravenously, opening her robe, slipping his arms around her naked body.

"Darling, you're shivering."

"Don't let go of me," she said again, unbuttoning his shirt.

"Never, I swear it."

He made love to her in a wildly carnal way that crowded out death and made her feel warm again inside. Enclosing him, her fear slipped away. When he surged inside her, life came pouring back. She had been desperate for someone to hang on to, and she hung on to him.

He stayed on top of her, covering her, protecting her. It was subtly different from the way they had usually made love. He was shielding her and she was grateful for it.

"Kate," he said seriously. "We belong together. Please give us another chance."

"I can't decide now," she said. "This is a bad moment for decisions."

"There'll be more bad moments. It's easier to face them together."

That was true. It wasn't as if she couldn't be happy without him. The naked truth was that she liked living with him.

"Kate?"

"I don't know. You're a risk, Winslow. You're a screwup."

"Not anymore. I'm not Tristan. I'm King Mark."

"In that case, yes."

"Oh, Kate, I was so afraid you never would." He held her close and she heard him sigh with relief.

"I have a confession to make," he said after a while. "Polly and I have been phone mates for some time now."

"Then she's scheming again. What about?"

"Your happiness." Win moved to her side and put his arms around her. "She was afraid you'd be miserable with that man you wanted to marry. She knew you'd be better off with me."

Kate felt a flash of anger at Polly's incessant meddling, then let it go. Polly's meddling would stop all too soon.

IX

A month later Tyler and John Mallory entered Central Park near 69th Street and headed for the statue of Alice in Wonderland.

"For me, the book was better when you concentrated on von Rayner," Mallory said. "That's a name that's been familiar since the Thirties. It's a name everyone loves to hate. The others just confuse the issue."

"Kate once said I'd be taken more seriously if I didn't single him out."

"Remember your reputation, for God's sake! You'll be taken seriously."

"She said the critics might call it the ravings of a jealous old cuck-old."

"She said that? And are you?"

"I was. When Sydney's bastard of a cousin died, I still hoped she would come back to me. I'd have taken her back, that's how much I loved her. But Sydney married von Rayner and I hated him for it. Now I just hate him for himself."

"What made you change?" Mallory asked curiously.

"Older and wiser, I guess," Tyler said, looking up at the trees against a clear blue sky, remembering his meeting with Sydney that somehow had made it possible for him to let go of her.

"John, I wrote *Aftermaths* to prove that there are Nazis alive and well and plotting in Germany about what they'll do now that they've got the wall down. Sooner or later, NATO will reduce its strength to near zero because we have neither need nor money to defend our-selves against a Soviet Union in too much trouble at home to attack us. Too many people don't want to hear that Germany, like history, will repeat itself. There are stories about neo-Nazis in the press all the time, but no one is troubled about it—always excepting the Israelis—any more than they were in the Thirties. If my book is written off as a grudge, too many won't take it as the warning it's meant to be."

They walked around the pond, where miniature boats were sailing on opaque green water.

"Algae," Mallory remarked.

Some of the boatmen were small children whose parents clutched their overalls to keep them from falling into the pond. The more com-plicated models were sailed by teenagers and adults.

"What a day!" Mallory said. "It's hard to believe there are Nazis on a day like this."

"It's hard to talk business, but I'd like to tie this up and get back to Kel Regis."

"I can't make you write anything you don't want to write." The publisher shrugged.

"Then you'll accept the manuscript as it is."

"Of course."

They had reached the statue of Alice surrounded by characters from Wonderland, and they stopped, charmed by it, by Alice's dress and pinafore, by her hair and the band around it. The great bronze statue was swarming with children, for it had been designed to ac-commodate small climbers. The children reminded Tyler of Kate when she was their age. Sydney had taken her to New York to see the Christmas windows and the tree at Rockefeller Center. She had come back to Harmony starry-eyed, closely clutching the wonders she had seen; it had taken her days to share her treasures with him, one at a time. How he had loved her! How he loved her still! He wished she thought better of him. He wondered what it was she wanted of him. He had done his best to be a good father.

"What's the rush to get to Kel Regis?" Mallory asked.

"Polly's mending but they're having to tie her down to keep her from overdoing. I can make myself useful by entertaining her. She likes me to read aloud to her."

Tyler didn't mention the preparations under way for the wedding, but Mallory did.

"It'll be a madhouse down there. And weddings are women's business," Mallory grumbled.

"Does Kate know what a chauvinist you are?"

Mallory didn't answer that. "Will the baroness be there?"

"I really don't know."

That was not the whole truth. What Tyler didn't know was who would win the battle now raging over inviting Sydney. Kate was for it, as were most of the younger members of the family who were dying to see the infamous baroness. The older folk were adamantly against it, and there was no point in bothering Polly until a consensus had been reached. Dodie Phelps flatly forbade Kate to mention the matter to Polly; Rebecca and Theo agreed. Did Kate want to be responsible for another heart attack?

"The whole ritual's ridiculous," Mallory grumbled again, interrupting Tyler's reflections. "Especially the second time around."

Tyler didn't tell him that Polly was still determined to make Kate's wedding the most splendid affair Kel Regis had ever seen.

39

I

Polly was waking earlier each day. She, who had once read until three and slept until ten, now stirred at first light no matter what time she went to sleep. She supposed it was nature's way of giving her as many waking hours as possible.

She spent those waking hours presiding over her beloved house and her "keepers," as she called the people who lived at Kel Regis and watched over her. She would not put into words what they meant to her—expressions of affection had always embarrassed her except with Charlie Travis—but she was grateful.

The other Benedicts and Ardmores who came on regular pilgrimages gave Kel Regis the festive, bustling air she liked. The house had been too quiet for too long.

Today, as yesterday, she was uneasy when she woke from a vaguely remembered and disquieting dream that had made her heart pound in her breast. The dream licked at the edges of her consciousness, but she could not lure it into her awareness.

It had been her habit to ring for her maid to bring her breakfast the minute she opened her eyes, but she was reluctant to disturb her staff at five in the morning. She was hungry—she had always been a woman of robust appetites—but food paled to insignificance beside her race with death and her craving for life, and these days she followed her doctor's orders: she left the table before she felt replete and tried, as Dodie Phelps put it, "not to get into a tizzy over nothing." But at her time of life, Polly had decided, there was nothing not worth at least a small tizzy. Everything mattered.

She got out of bed and went into the bathroom, where she washed her face, brushed her teeth, twisted her long white hair into a tight curl and wound it into a doughnut on top of her head. She put on her challis robe, her glasses, and a pair of battered slippers, took her gold-headed cane for balance, and went downstairs and out the pantry door, taking the path to the stables.

She breathed in the morning freshness. It would be a perfect day for a wedding, clear and not too hot. She stopped to admire the multicolored zinnias, daisies, and pansies bordering the path. She stopped again at the kitchen garden to pull up a few carrots and once more to rinse them free of soil at the garden tap.

She laughed softly, walking slowly, enjoying her escapade. Her keepers—Dodie Phelps, Rebecca, Theo, Tyler—would fuss and fume at her for coming out alone. Only Kate wouldn't scold her. She and Kate were kindred spirits, rebels both of them.

"If I have to live life vicariously," she murmured, thinking of Win and her pleasant romantic preoccupation with him, "it's through Kate I want to live it."

Polly went into the stable, calling to Charlie's Darling, but his stall was empty. She felt a momentary panic, then remembered that Kate often took him out early, with Harald running alongside.

There was a chair in the patch of sunlight just inside the stable door. Polly sat down to wait and promptly dozed off. She woke to Kate's hand smoothing her cheek, smoothing away the memory of the same disturbing dream that had troubled her earlier.

"Polly? Are you all right?"

Polly nodded, realizing that her hand had been clutching at her heart. "It was only a bad dream."

"When did you start sleeping in the stables?" Kate smiled at the carrots. "And done up to look like the earth mother too!"

"It's such a beautiful morning," Polly said. "And I wanted to see my darling." She patted Charlie's Darling, who was nuzzling her neck, and offered him a carrot. Then she turned her attention to Harald, who rested his majestic head on her knee. "How are you, you spotted giant?" She smiled at Kate. "Stunning creatures, aren't they?"

"Fine beasts, both of them," Kate agreed, hiding her relief. Seeing Polly slumped in the doorway, her hand on her heart, had been a shock.

Kate had moved into Kel Regis after the Wakefield graduation ceremonies in order to spend more time with her grandmother. Polly's heart might be fragile, but her brain was still very sharp and demanded regular exercise. And she seemed to cling to Kate, although neither of them would have embarrassed Polly by acknowledging that.

When Charlie had finished his carrots, Kate went about the business of removing saddle and bridle and returning him to his stall. He would be groomed when the men came on at six o'clock.

Win was still asleep. He had been coming down every weekend after his Sunday matinee performance to stay until Tuesday afternoon. Polly always chose what she wanted him to read to the guests and the household, assembled in the library on Monday evenings.

Rebecca and Mark had moved back from Georgetown as soon as Rebecca got the other Barrows children off to their summer camps or on trips to Europe. Theo made Kel Regis his home when he wasn't away on political business. On occasion, Senator Case and his doting wife spent a weekend to add a little stardust to his image, but no other politicians were invited so that Polly wouldn't overdo. She got around that by speaking to them on the telephone.

Tyler was also in residence. Belle and Brosie came every weekend, having yielded to Kate's invitation to them to be part of the wedding party. And cousins from around the country flocked to Kel Regis to play tennis, swim in the pool, and make a great deal of youthful noise.

On Monday evenings at eight o'clock, though, silence descended while Win read. There might be as many as fifty people in the library, including any Kel Regis staff who wanted to hear great prose and poetry read by a master. A buffet supper was served after the reading, and the young people lingered until late. Polly was in her element. The Mondays and the wedding preparations kept her busy.

"Even though it's utterly ridiculous," Kate had said to Win, "to make such a furor over two people mad enough to marry each other twice."

Win had called it a divine madness and said it would be mean-spirited to refuse Polly her party. Probably her last, was the implication Kate was never able to ignore.

Polly now rummaged in the fridge in the stable's office while Kate was seeing to Charlie. She poured two glasses of cold Evian water, added a slice of lemon to each, returned the bottle to the fridge, and sat down in one of the plump, chintz-covered armchairs, the anxiety evoked by her dream still upon her.

Kate came in and took the chair opposite. She drank half the water in her glass. "Mmm, that's good!"

"Odd thing for a bride to go riding on her wedding day," Polly observed.

"I do it most days."

"That's why it's odd. Today should be different."

"Well, it isn't. There's something farcical about this whole production anyway. How can I appear in bridal finery when I just got out of bed with Win!"

"Doesn't signify these days. And you never had a Kel Regis wedding. It's the only kind I consider official."

"Not to mention that the publicity is sure to increase our enrollments," Kate said, watching Polly's sly little grin appear. "Tell me, are you in a benevolent humor this morning?"

"Why do you ask?"

"I want a favor, but not if you're going to fly into a rage and then keel over dead. It would ruin the wedding."

"What's the favor?"

"Sydney."

Polly grimaced. "What about her?"

"I want her to come to my wedding and Tyler would like her to be there too. I guess it's a pathetic attempt to be the family we never were, even if it's just for today."

"Do you care for Sydney that much?"

Careful, now, Kate warned herself. "Enough to let her watch me marry Win again if she wants to," she said.

"Assuming I allowed it, I doubt Sydney could make it from Vienna by five o'clock, even on *her* broomstick."

"She's in Charleston with Dr. Strangelove. They're staying with Ambrose. Everyone else has flocked to see them, but they won't let Sydney cross their own thresholds for fear it might get back to you. How's that for proof of your authority?"

Polly sipped her water, thinking about Sydney. Then she suddenly remembered what her dream had been, and her face changed so drastically that Kate sprang up and leaned over her, reaching into Polly's pocket for the bottle of nitroglycerine pills she always carried.

"Polly? Are you all right? Do you need one of these?"

Polly shook her head. "I just remembered my dream," she said.

Kate put the glass on a table and rubbed her grandmother's cold hands. "It must have been a lulu. Rest for a moment, then tell me about it and you won't dream it anymore."

When Polly spoke again, it was to tell her about Charlie Travis and the son she had borne him.

II

"That's a sad story," Kate said, touched by Polly's confiding in her and by the bittersweetness of her fall from grace. She had not been the "perfect Polly" everyone thought she was. It made her less formidable.

"I loved Hilliard all the more because I had to live without his father. I heard about Charlie Travis from time to time, but I never saw him again, except in his son." Polly reached for her glass and drank more water. "You're wondering what all this has to do with Sydney."

"I know you were jealous of Hilliard's fondness for her."

"Fondness? He was in thrall to her."

"And you never got over finding him and Sydney playing doctor."

"It wasn't a game of patty fingers by a pair of innocents!" Polly said tartly. "They'd had intercourse; the room reeked of sex. Sydney was a Jezebel from the moment she was born. I felt from the first that she was an alien seed, but she was so beautiful I dismissed the feeling. Oliver fell all over himself and so did her brothers, Hilliard most of all. The two were only a year apart and they lived in each other's pockets."

"Is she Oliver's child?"

"Of course she is," Polly said indignantly. "I was not a promiscuous woman! What I did with Charlie I did for love."

The eternal justification, Kate thought. *Always was, always will be.*

But Polly might have had other motives. What about resentment over her husband's philanderings? What about boredom, always Polly's bête noire? And there was more to it than that: by then Polly had felt no love for Oliver and presumably none for his daughter, accidentally conceived, even before Sydney was born.

"I must tell you about it," Polly was saying explosively. "I want you to understand that I had to do what I did." She was agitated. She seemed about to burst, like a child with a terrible secret.

"I'm listening, Polly," Kate said. "But try to tell me quietly."

Polly settled herself, drank more water, and continued. "Hilliard was innocent and couldn't help himself, but Sydney knew exactly what she was doing. She'd known since she was six and Royal diddled her in the boat house. Sydney was a Venus's-flytrap, but Hilliard couldn't see that, not even after she got him into bed that day. He wouldn't listen to anything I said about her. I was afraid she'd keep after him, if only to defy me. Finally, I had no choice but to tell him he had corrupted his sister."

"Oh, Polly! You didn't!"

"What else could I do? The boy fawned on her and she led him on. She made him do mischievous things: carry on at the table, put frogs in our beds—boyish pranks if you didn't know what they implied. I knew by the way she'd look at me when Hilliard was punished for what she'd put him up to. I never saw a little girl smile the way she did at those moments. It was corrupt, degenerate. It said she could have him whenever she wanted him and I could go to hell. She hated me more than she loved him. They weren't always safely stowed away at separate boarding schools and I had to find a way to be sure he wouldn't let her seduce him again. That sort of thing runs in this family, as you well know."

Polly grimaced. "But I succeeded too well. Hilliard wouldn't believe she was plain rotten, not even when she began sleeping with all her cousins. He blamed himself for what she did because I'd said he was responsible. He wasn't about to believe she was born that way."

"Oh, Polly," Kate said softly, appalled by the ruin of those two young lives, a boy and a girl made to feel evil by a mother seething with hurts, jealousies, and resentments, who had not been spotless herself by the standards of the times.

"Then came Royal and after him poor Tyler," Polly went on. "Hilliard was beside himself when she told us she was pregnant by Tyler. That gentle boy actually slapped her. He shook her until her teeth rattled. 'No one is safe from you,' he shouted, 'no one!' Oliver had to pull him away from her." Polly stopped for a moment and took a few long, slow breaths. "But we got her married and they moved to Harmony. She seemed to have settled down. Hilliard didn't try to contact her. None of us did, not even when you were born. We never talked about her."

Poor Sydney, Kate mourned. *Your mother didn't want you, your favorite brother abandoned you, and all your cousins used you for sex. No wonder you expect to be humiliated by the people who are supposed to love you. How else can you tell they really mean it?*

"I thought it was over," Polly said. "Over the years Hilliard overcame his depression, even started courting a girl. She wasn't worthy of him, of course, but I'd have allowed it in order to make him happy. And then Sydney ran away with Royal." Polly looked down at her hands. "That was why Hilliard killed himself."

For a moment Kate could not speak. Then she objected violently, as if she could change what had happened. "But he had nothing to do with that!"

"No? When it was he who made her what she was?" Polly snapped, impatient at having to restate the obvious. "That's what he believed because I had told him it was so." She tapped the arm of the chair with her fist as she spoke. "He would not understand that she was born that way."

Kate sat motionless while Polly went on in a faraway voice, tears rolling down her cheeks unheeded while she appeared to grow more frail with every word.

"He hung himself from a beam in that same tawdry little room where I had surprised the two of them. I knew where to look because he spent a lot of time alone up there. I found him, my Charlie's darling son. He looked so lonely, hanging there, turning ever so slowly while the beam creaked. There was a note that said he wasn't fit to live. I burned it." Polly seemed to look inside herself. She shivered, then raised her eyes to meet Kate's. "It was all Sydney's fault. You must see that."

Kate heard the plea behind the words. For Polly, the whole tragedy had to be Sydney's fault. If not Sydney's, then it was Polly's, and Polly couldn't have faced that and gone on living, then or now.

But to understand all is not to forgive all, Kate thought angrily. *Polly's no fool! She could have found some other way, some less destructive way to keep them apart.*

But that would have been reasonable, and what chance did reason have against hate and jealousy and frustrated passion? It wasn't that Polly desired her son; it was simply that she could not bear for him to love anyone else, innocently or otherwise. She was driven to monopolize him as she did everyone she cared about.

And if I went back another ninety years, Kate thought, *I'd find the reason for that. Where does it end, the misery one generation inflicts upon the next?*

Kate took a breath, on the point of saying all that to her grandmother, but Polly looked so devastated that she could not.

The sun was high enough now to pour through the open window, the motes dancing as wildly in the rays as Kate's emotions. The two glasses, empty of cold water, were beaded with condensation, and the sun colored the beads with a rainbow of pastels. Polly had taken off her foggy spectacles and was polishing the lenses with a handkerchief, frowning.

"You must see that, Kate," she repeated, desperation barely covering her need.

"Yes, I see it all. Hush, now," Kate said softly. "You needn't talk about it or dream about it anymore."

Polly's face relaxed, and they sat in silence for quite a while. Then she said, "You may invite Sydney and her Hun to your wedding, but neither of them is to approach me or speak to me. Now let's go back. I'm famished."

III

Kate didn't stop to bathe and change out of her riding clothes. She went looking for Rebecca. It was what she had done since childhood whenever she was elated or miserable or confused, and she always returned to the patterns of her childhood in a crisis, as if all she had learned in the interim fell away and left her as helpless and vulnerable as she had been then.

She found Rebecca sitting under one of the willows near the river, reading *Treasure Island* to Mark.

"I'm sorry to interrupt," Kate said, flicking her crop against her boots. "But I must talk to you."

Rebecca, seeing Kate's face, sent her son off to fight dragons. Kate found him a branch for a sword and put him up on Harald's back, where Mark held tight to the Great Dane's collar.

"What's wrong?" Rebecca said when they were alone.

After she heard it, Rebecca agreed it was mind-boggling. "But she had to confess and you had to give her absolution. It's all ancient history anyway, and Polly's old and sick and frightened of retribution. You had no choice."

"That's *her* excuse for everything! But I did have a choice. I could have told her she was wrong, horribly, brutally, selfishly wrong! That's what she doesn't want to know."

"She knows! That's why she had to tell you about it! And selfishness isn't the whole story. She *was* protecting her son. She was protecting both of them, no matter what her reasons were or how she went about it. Suppose Sydney had conceived a child by her brother—her half brother—Lord, this is a tale out of Faulkner. I don't know what I'd do if I found two of mine in bed together."

"*Ruin them?!* Make one of them a sexual martyr and the other a suicide? Like hell you would. You never thought a roll in the hay meant anything at all except with Theo."

"This isn't about how I think, it's about how Polly thought at the time."

"What she's always thought: that she owns us all, that whatever isn't her way is the wrong way. She's a proud, possessive, jealous, overbearing, manipulative, and treacherous woman. Look what she did to my mother! Look what my mother did to me!"

"Even so, it isn't your place to judge Polly. Leave her to heaven."

Kate, suddenly exhausted, sat down on the grass and punched holes in the turf with her crop. "I once decided to do that with Sydney. It would help if I knew as much about heaven and hell as Hamlet's daddy did when he said that."

"Hell is all around you," Rebecca said. "Polly's son. Your mother. My legs."

Kate nodded. "I've avoided asking how things are between you and Theo."

"We're being honest with each other for a change," Rebecca said. "It's easier."

"It must be a whole lot easier." Kate plucked a blade of grass and chewed on it.

"I think he has someone," Rebecca said, looking across the river.

"Spare me, Rebecca! That record is worn through!"

"He's never in his office—or anywhere else I've tried—between two and four on Tuesdays and Thursdays. But I can tell he's not in love with her, so I don't mind so much," Rebecca said resignedly. "I don't mind who it is, as long as it isn't you."

"Enough!" Kate shouted, and fell flat on her back with her arms outstretched. "That was never possible, even when it was your very own sick idea. You know something? You're a lot like Polly! Both of you like to move me around like a chess piece."

"Kate, I was mad as a hatter when I suggested that, but I never doubted your loyalty, only his."

"You could've fooled me! What a rotten day this is turning out to be! I must be insane to marry Win again on a day like this. Only grief can come of it."

"You can't put it off now. Just look at all of that!"

Rebecca gestured toward the three huge silk tents on the lawn— Polly had indeed ordered everything in off white—with ostrich plumes fluttering at each tie point. Garlands of creamy roses festooned the interiors. One tent was for the ceremony and the dancing after dinner; in the other two the tables were set with Kel Regis china on ivory damask cloths.

"It'll be a far cry from your first wedding," Rebecca said.

"In more ways than one."

"You still love him, there's no point denying it."

"He's a lovable fellow," Kate agreed. "And, as Stanton once observed, he makes me crazy."

"He's famous for making women crazy. By the way, is your mother coming?"

"Yes! My request for that boon is what got Polly started on her appalling story in the first place. But there I go, blaming poor Sydney again."

"I'm glad Sydney brought her grotesque. I'm dying to get a close look at him. What on earth do you think she sees in the man?"

Kate shrugged. "I assume he has some winning little ways—he'll need them when Tyler's book is published. I'd better call Sydney and tell her to put on her party dress." Kate got up. "Why is it that talking to you makes even the most unbearable things bearable?" She took Rebecca's hands in hers. "I hope I've done that for you."

"Many times."

Kate nodded. "That's all right, then. I'd better go and shower."

"Yes, you smell like attar of horse. If you see my son, send him back to me."

Polly must have said the same thing all those years ago, before she found Hilliard swinging from a beam. Kate flinched, imagining that. She turned back to Rebecca.

"Why did she tell me? Why am I the family washing machine, recipient of everyone's dirty laundry?"

"Because she wants you to know how bad Sydney really is so you won't be too forgiving. And because you're on the side of the angels, and if you forgive her, then so will they. I've felt the same way since you started forgiving me for my sins when we were kids."

"I can match you sin for sin," Kate called back over her shoulder. "Don't make me out to be Goody Two-Shoes."

"If the shoes fit . . ." Rebecca laughed.

IV

Kate walked up the slight grade of the lawn toward the house. Polly seemed to loom over it now, not as a benevolent tyrant but like the wicked sorcerer in *Swan Lake*. She had done a terrible thing and she knew it. That was the sum and substance of it.

But on the other side of the ledger there was Polly's care of those entrusted to her: the spinster aunts of her early marriage, a houseful of children, Oliver and his career, Dodie Phelps, Tyler, Rebecca, the young Benedicts and Ardmores who confided in her, scores of servants and their families—and Kate, who had flourished on her grandmother's strength even while she fought against it. If those good deeds didn't absolve Polly from the sin of swallowing her children whole, they were a mitigating circumstance.

Kate found Mark and hugged him tight before she sent him back to his mother. Harald followed her up to the same rooms she had occupied since she came to Kel Regis to attend Wakefield and be presented to society and meet the right people and, in Polly's dreams, become president of the United States. Polly had redecorated the two rooms more times than Kate could remember. Now the sitting room was cream and turquoise, the bedroom blue.

She could hear Win singing in the shower. For a man with such a compelling speaking voice, he sang badly.

Harald growled at the sight of Kate's dress on a form near the window, set there by the dressmaker that morning while Kate was out riding.

"Easy, boy," Kate soothed him. "And don't you dare go near it with your wet nose."

It was ivory chiffon, so sheer that its sixty yards were easily compressed into a fluid column. "A Kate kind of dress," Belle called it. "Grecian. Looks simple, but is actually very complicated."

The veil, pinned to a wig stand on a table near the dress, was the same delicate lace Polly had worn at her own wedding. Once white, it was now the color of parchment.

Kate pulled off her boots, then called her mother, who answered on the first ring.

"Sydney? I'm pleased to invite you both to my wedding."

"Darling! That's wonderful! Hans Erik," she called to him, "we're going." She came back to Kate. "I'm so pleased you could arrange it."

"So am I," Kate said. "You *should* be here today." She said it as much to the young Sydney, ruthlessly turned out of paradise, crossed off, deleted, canceled out, and with a vital piece of her missing as a result.

"Oh, Kate," Sydney said tremulously. "My darling Kate."

"Be sure you both give her a wide berth." Kate mopped her eyes with a handkerchief.

"Not to worry!"

"See you later, Mother."

"At five, darling. You're my girl."

"Yes," Kate said, "I am."

V

The tap on the door was Theo's. "I came to apologize," he said when he was inside the room.

"For what?"

"For being a fool and a burden to you when you already had more than enough to carry."

"You *were* a misery, Theo, but I accept the apology."

"You're very gracious."

She smiled. "What the hell. It's my wedding day. If I smell like a stable, it's because I'm waiting for Placido to get out of the shower. How are things?"

He walked to the window and stood beside the dressmaker's form, looking out. "We're trying to find our way. The rules of the marriage have changed."

"But not the dynamics. Becca thinks you're seeing someone on Tuesdays and Thursdays."

Theo turned to Kate and laughed heartily. Win came into the sitting room with a towel around his waist and, after a few seconds, began to laugh too, and Kate caught it from him. When at last they stopped, Win wanted to know what the joke was.

"Becca thinks he's seeing a woman."

"Is that funny?"

"But I am," Theo said. "On Tuesdays and Thursdays. She's a psychotherapist."

"Why didn't you tell Rebecca?" Kate demanded. "You know how she is."

"She'd be certain it was about her, and it isn't. It's about me."

Kate took off her jacket. "I'm going to take a shower. If I were you, Theo, I'd walk down to the river and tell her about your sessions. And make sure she knows you're not consulting a psychotherapist about her." She vanished into the bedroom, closing the door behind her.

Theo and Win looked at each other. "What do you think?" Theo asked.

"Who knows Rebecca better than Kate?"

Theo nodded. "See you in church," he said.

VI

Sydney put the finishing touches to her makeup and stood, slim in her lace-trimmed white satin slip. She stepped into her dress. "Do me up," she said to her husband, who was just shrugging into a white dinner jacket.

He shot his cuffs and obliged, slipping the handmade loops over a row of covered buttons. The dress was blush pink and it matched the hat that lay ready on the dressing table. As the last button was fastened, she set the delicate straw hat on her head and anchored it with a hat pin.

Her husband looked at her in the mirror. "You are a very beautiful woman," he said, pressing his lips to her shoulder.

"There's no point in flattering me." Sydney pulled away from him.

"It's the simple truth." He shrugged.

"The simple truth," Sydney said, "is that if you're seen at Kel Regis, you'll seem less of a Nazi."

"If I seem a Nazi at all, it is thanks to that idiot ex-husband of yours! If you had done as I told you to do in the first place, this matter would no longer be our concern."

Sydney began drawing on elbow-length white kid gloves. "Don't blame me for your political affiliations. And it's not *our* concern, it's yours. I'm not the one who spends my time plotting with sons of the SS."

"Tyler has produced no proof that I do any plotting at all."

No proof perhaps, but evidence. Sydney had supplied some of that. They had held up the printing of the book to include what she had to say.

VII

She had been restless one night in Vienna and, going downstairs, was surprised to hear men's voices coming from Hansi's study. She thought he was still at one of his eternal meetings—or romping around with one of his mistresses, Sydney was never sure which—but from their conversation she was soon aware that it *had* been a business meeting and the participants had dropped in for a nightcap.

Hans Erik would be in a good mood, Sydney knew. He always was when his leadership was acknowledged, when his itch for power was scratched in one way or another.

"He wants them all to say *Heil von Rayner,*" she muttered, and went closer to the study door, being careful to stay in the shadows.

She knew all of the men there, about a dozen. She had been to bed with most of them in the old days when, it seemed, she would be young forever. They were among the bankers, lawyers, and industrialists who had rebuilt Germany from a rubble to her position of economic power and stability.

"Let in as many East Europeans as want to come," one of the bankers said. "There's trouble in Leipzig already about foreigners, and that's what we want: Germany for the Germans. The more militant the protests become, the sooner we'll define 'foreigners' more clearly and deal with them the same way we did in the Thirties."

"We want more than Germany for the Germans," Hansi said.

"Yes, von Rayner. A Fourth Reich."

"It is our destiny," Hans Erik said, "if not by force of arms, then with money. This time we will succeed. Soon we can begin to use the techniques of our beloved leader." Sydney knew his cheeks were flushed, his body at attention, as it always was when he talked about Hitler.

"What about this Ballard book?"

"We must simply ignore it. My wife's family continues to provide a protective shield, especially against the ravings of a jealous ex-husband."

"Yes, your marriage was a stroke of genius."

"And no great sacrifice," Hans Erik said. "The baroness is a most charming lady."

So he had married her mainly to hide behind her family's political reputation! And Sydney had married a man who not only worshipped a deranged dictator and plotted to resurrect his madness, but who was an adulterer into the bargain. She had contrived to ignore it; what else could she do at her age?

The next day Sydney had listed all their names and everything she had overheard through the years and sent it off to Tyler.

VIII

Sydney picked up her bag, checked its contents, and turned to face her husband. "Tyler's book will stir things up enough so that sooner or later someone will find proof," she said with a satisfied little smirk as she headed for the door. "And then I'll probably divorce you." She might too. She wasn't so deathly afraid of being alone anymore.

"You know I love you most when you are cruel to me."

"Oh, go scratch," Sydney said. She sailed out of the room and down the stairs, one hand on the gleaming banister, the other holding up her gown. "Ambrose?" she called when she reached the bottom.

"Coming." Ambrose approached from his living room and smiled. He smiled every time he saw her. He appreciated beautiful things and Sydney was exquisite to the tips of her glorious fingers. She was not at all what he had expected an aging family strumpet to be, and her hair, although chemically assisted, was not brassy, but a pale, pretty blond.

Dodie Phelps said that Sydney's plastic surgeon had kept her face fairly close to the original model; she must have been breathtaking. She dressed with quiet elegance and wore what looked like a minimum of makeup. Despite her reputation, there was an innocence in her boundless joy at being permitted to attend Kate's wedding, and it touched him. He empathized with that. As Polly's daughter, she had been as much a stranger to happiness as Ambrose and Arabella.

His smile chilled somewhat when he greeted the baron, but Ambrose was unfailingly polite to houseguests, even if they gave him goose flesh.

"The car's at the curb, all cooled off for you," he assured Sydney. She had begged him to do that, even though it was not unduly warm.

"You're such a darling, Ambrose," she said now. "Perspiration is so vulgar."

"You look seriously lovely, Sydney."

"So do you." She touched his red hair affectionately and took his arm. They went out to the car, followed by her husband. She waved the baron to the passenger seat next to Ambrose.

"I mustn't crease," she said, and, getting in, arrayed herself across the backseat like an odalisque, propped up on one elbow.

Totally off the wall, Ambrose thought. He started the car, barely able to suppress his laughter. The only sane member of this family was Cousin Kate, and sometimes he wasn't too sure about her!

For example, why was she remarrying a man who had been unfaithful, inconsiderate, and, although Ambrose liked him very much, was composed of equal parts ego and fantasy?

IX

An hour later Win asked her the same question.

He stood at the flower-banked altar waiting for Kate, Theo at his side, and his gaze wandered over the guests. It was like counting the house through the curtain peephole, except that this drama would not end with the third act.

Rebecca, in ivory organza, was the first to appear, and Win knew how much courage it had taken for her to come down the aisle in a wheelchair. If anyone knew how Kate really felt, it was Rebecca. But she looked radiantly happy. Win turned and looked questioningly at Theo. Theo nodded and glanced at his wife. So he had taken Kate's advice and told Rebecca where he was on Tuesday and Thursday afternoons.

Win's parents, sitting in the front row on the groom's side, smiled amiably upon him and he smiled back. He wondered if their emotional temperature had ever been more than tepid, even in the first flush of youth. He thought not and was sorry for them. They had never loved each other as Win loved Kate.

Six attendants—Belle and five young Benedict cousins—in gowns like Rebecca's now followed on the arms of Brosie and five ushers in pale gray cutaways. The twins looked more alike as they grew older, not less. They were an eerily beautiful couple. Win could not imagine either of them with anyone else.

Win looked for familiar faces among the five hundred guests. He found Tabitha Berling in one of her plump periods again, and her Broadway-producer husband; media mogul Clyde Tillinghast and his daughter, Melinda; Stanton Wells and her latest beau; Grace Halsey, who had played Win's mother in *Hamlet*; the priapic Hollywood producer, Bruno Baxter, and his fourth wife, the very same Kimmy whom Kate had met at her first Hollywood party; Harriet Kahn, still Win's West Coast agent and still twisting a strand of hair; Kate's long-time friend, Carol Hunter, sat next to Holly Groehler and Tom Lewis.

Lovely Sydney and her baron were at the back, Sydney blotting away her tears before they could damage her makeup, her husband impassive. There had been a nervous moment half an hour before when Sydney and Hans Erik inadvertently came face-to-face with Polly. The two women had looked at each other with shock, then with curiosity, finally with cold hostility. It was Sydney who turned away first and Win who broke custom by escorting Polly to her seat.

"Are you all right?" Win had asked her.

"Of course. Didn't I behave correctly?"

"Like a trouper."

"So much for appearances," Polly said, and her cheeks flushed. "She's still beautiful, isn't she? You'd think her life would show in her face."

"Maybe she's got a portrait in the attic, like Dorian Gray."

"No, there's nothing in the attic now," Polly said. "It'll catch up with her. It catches up with all of us."

"You might exchange a word later," Dodie Phelps suggested.

"Never," Polly said, and set her lips firmly.

Now Win smiled at Polly and her cousin, sitting on the bride's side just a few steps away. Both ladies wore pastel silk gowns, pearl dog collars, and Queen Mary toques. They beamed upon him as upon the Prodigal Son. He had been forgiven for his sins and clasped to the bosoms of these women who were at the heart of Kel Regis, and he basked in their affection for him.

There was a pause, then Kate appeared and started down the aisle on Tyler's arm. She still made him think of the Winged Victory atop the main staircase of the Louvre: tall, imposing, and strong, but she needed to be cherished. Kate was a great actress. Only a few people knew what she was really like: tender and trusting with some of the child still in her. No one—except perhaps Polly—dreamed what she was worth.

She smiled at him over the flowers she carried, and it was then that Win knew he could not ignore the change in her. He loved Kate beyond all imagining, but he was not certain in what measure Kate loved him.

She was at his side, having handed her bouquet of Polly's famous ivory roses to Rebecca.

The minister cleared his throat. "Dearly beloved," he began.

"Wait a moment, please!" Win said to him. The man nodded, perplexed.

Win took Kate's hands in his. "Why did you really agree to marry me?"

"I like marriage and I can't imagine it with anyone else."

"And I asked you at a vulnerable moment."

"That too."

The guests leaned forward, murmuring, but they could hear nothing. Only the startled expression on the minister's face as he turned from one to the other indicated the gravity of the conversation taking place at the flower-decked altar.

"But love didn't have much to do with it," Win said.

"Would I be part of this extravaganza if it didn't?"

"You might do it for Polly's sake."

"I've done enough for her sake. This is for *my* sake, not Polly's or Rebecca's or Sydney's or Tyler's or yours."

"But it isn't like the first time."

"There *is* no time like the first time, Win. We had that. You'll have to be content with this."

"Meaning I have most of you, but not all."

"You have all I can trust you with."

He looked at her intently, then kissed each of her hands and smiled his famous smile. "So be it, Kate, but I'm going to have all of you. I won't stop trying till I do."

They turned to the nervous minister, who cleared his throat again. "Are you ready?" he whispered.

"Eager," Kate said.

ACKNOWLEDGMENTS

I am most grateful to Naomi Eisenstadt and to Harvey McGregor, Q.C., for their help on certain matters British. My thanks to Gul, who found a snag, to Sheila, who saw how to fix it, and to Betty, who named names.

Special credit goes to the following books, articles, and television documentaries: *Padlocks & Girdles of Chastity*, privately published; *Prisoners of Ritual: An Odyssey into Female Genital Circumcision in Africa* by Hanny Lightfoot-klein, Harrington Park Press: New York, 1989; "Female Circumcision" by Evelyn Shaw, R.N., M.S., in *The American Journal of Nursing*, June 1985; *Everyday Life in the United States Before the Civil War* by Robert Lacour-Gayet, translated by Mary Ilford, Frederick Ungar Publishing Co, Inc.: New York, 1972; *Richard Burton—A Life* by Melvyn Bragg, Warner Books: New York, 1988; *Making Sense of the Sixties*, PBS, Channel 13, New York, 1990; "Raped on Campus," *People*, December 17, 1990; *Harlots, Whores & Hookers* by Hilary Evans, Taplinger Publishing Co.: New York, 1979; *A History of Women's Bodies* by Edward Shorter, Basic Books Inc.: New York, 1982; *Goddesses, Whores, Wives, and Slaves—Women in Classical Antiquity* by Sarah B. Pomeroy, Schocken Books: New York, 1975; *The Feminization of American Culture* by Ann Douglas, Avon Books: New York, 1978.